PL
CRICK

48th edition

EDITED BY BILL FRINDALL

All statistics by the Editor unless otherwise credited

PLAYFAIR CRICKET COMPETITION 1995

TEST CRICKET QUIZ

£1500 TO BE WON

PLUS NATWEST FINAL TICKETS AND HOSPITALITY
PLUS 25 CONSOLATION PRIZES

First Prize	£500 +	overnight accommodation (B and B) at the Regents Park Hilton Hotel (opposite Lord's) on 1 and 2 September + TWO tickets to the 1995 NatWest Trophy Final + NatWest hospitality
Second Prize	£400 +	TWO tickets to the 1995 NatWest Trophy Final
Third Prize	£300 +	TWO tickets to the 1995 NatWest Trophy Final
Fourth Prize	£200	
Fifth Prize	£100	

Consolation prizes

Senders of the next 25 correct entries will each receive a signed copy of THE WISDEN BOOK OF CRICKET RECORDS by Bill Frindall and published by Headline at £35.00.

Closing date for entries
is 12.00 noon on 25 July 1995

Winning entries will be drawn by the Man of the Match Adjudicator at one of the NatWest semi-finals on Tuesday 15 August.

PLAYFAIR CRICKET COMPETITION 1995

CARIBBEAN CRICKET QUIZ

ENTRY FORM

Please PRINT your answers in the spaces provided and answer every question.

1 Who was the first West Indian to score 8000 runs in Test cricket? ....

2 Who prior to 1994 was the only visiting captain to win a Test in Barbados? ....

3 Who first shared in two partnerships of over 500 runs in first-class matches? ....

4 Who were the first holders of the Red Stripe Cup? ....

5 Who is the only batsman to score five hundreds in successive Test innings? ....

6 Who established a world record by bowling 588 balls in a Test innings? ....

7 Who achieved the first hat-trick in Tests between England and West Indies? ....

8 On which island is first-class cricket played at Windsor Park? ....

9 Name the first bowler to take all ten wickets in a first-class match in the West Indies? ....

10 Who scored a record aggregate of 1765 first-class runs in a Caribbean season? ....

Your name and address:

....

....

....

Your daytime telephone number: ....

Post to: PLAYFAIR CRICKET COMPETITION, Special Events, National Westminster Hall, 15 Bishopsgate, London EC2P 2AP.

Entries must be received before noon on 25 July 1995. All-correct entries will go into the prize-winning draw on 15 August and an announcement detailing all prize-winners will appear in the October edition of *The Cricketer* magazine. A list of winners is available on request by writing to Mrs B.J.Quinn at the above address and enclosing a stamped addressed envelope.

Rules: All entries must be on this official form. Proof of posting is not proof of entry. The decision of the editor regarding the answers to this quiz shall be final and binding; no correspondence may be entered into.

1994 PLAYFAIR CRICKET COMPETITION

SOUTH AFRICAN TEST CRICKET QUIZ ANSWERS

1	Who was the first to score a hundred on Test debut for South Africa?	A.C. (Andrew) HUDSON
2	Which South African bowler is the only Test cricketer to climb Mount Kilimanjaro twice?	R.J. (Bob) CRISP
3	Who is the only cricketer to captain England in his only Test match?	C.A. (Aubrey) SMITH
4	Which South African Test cricketer was born at Zagazig in Egypt?	A.J. (John) TRAICOS
5	Which ground staged Johannesburg's first six post-war Tests?	ELLIS PARK
6	Who overcame the discomfort of a fractured thumb to score 208 against England?	A.D. (Dudley) NOURSE
7	Who was the first wicket-keeper to make 25 dismissals in a Test series?	J.H.B. (John) WAITE
8	Who is the only bowler to take a hat-trick in a Test at Lord's?	G.M. (Geoff) GRIFFIN
9	What was the record number of runs scored by England on the second day at Lord's in 1930?	QUESTION VOID (year should have read 1924)
10	Who set a world Test record by bowling 137 consecutive balls without conceding a run?	H.J. (Hugh) TAYFIELD

There were 355 sets of correct answers out of a total of 402 entries. The winners were drawn by David Gower (Leicestershire, Hampshire and England) at the 1994 NatWest Trophy semi-final between Surrey and Worcestershire at The Oval.

First Prize:	£500 + two nights accommodation + two tickets to include hospitality at the 1994 NatWest Trophy Final	W.J.GREEN (Hartlepool)
Second Prize:	£400 + two tickets to the 1994 NatWest Trophy Final	N.PHYSICK (Dartford)
Third Prize:	£300 + two tickets to the 1994 NatWest Trophy Final	M.BAKER (Exeter)
Fourth Prize:	£200	M.POPE (Mexborough)
Fifth Prize:	£100	S.SOMAN (India)

25 Runners-up each received a copy of *The Innings of My Life* by Jack Bannister:

M.R.Bibby (Wallasey)
A.Borrows (Belfast)
P.Butler (Chesham)
J.P.Carroll (Chippenham)
G.R.J.Coles (Telford)
M.J.Cosh (Fareham)
J.N.Crick (Barnsley)
L.R.Deldridge (Babbacombe)
M.P.Dennett (St Annes-on-Sea)
J.B.Duggan (Fernhill Heath)
M.W.Errington (Hartlepool)
W.Galton (Teignmouth)
B.R.Hunt (Bradford)
M.G.Konstant (Stapleton)
P.J.Lane (Exeter)
M.Leddy (Formby)
L.Leppington (Patrington)
Mrs V.M.Palmer (Woodstock)
T.Pearce (St Annes, Lancashire)
Elizabeth Rimmer (Belsize Park)
P.Sheppard (Rhondda)
M.Thomas (Buckhurst Hill)
P.Thorne (Burnley)
A.Whitehead (Huddersfield)
J.A.Williams (Erdington)

EDITORIAL PREFACE

Since this annual last went to press, cricket has seldom been out of the headlines, a fair few of them proclaiming the feats of those two cricketing sensations, Brian Lara and Shane Warne. Lara's record-shattering achievements for West Indies and Warwickshire, together with Warne's remarkable trail of wickets, are covered within this, the largest of the 48 editions of this annual in terms of pages.

Students of this annual's history will be aware that the first issue (1948), in a larger (near-octavo) format, had 144 pages, the first of the present format (1963) had 192, and that it has remained at 256 pages since NatWest began their sponsorship with the 1982 edition. Regrettably, the extra 32 pages in this edition has had to be offset by an additional 51p in the price.

Fourteen of those extra pages have been required to accommodate the proliferation of Test matches during the past year plus the spread of our County Register as playing staffs continue to expand. Devotees of limited-overs internationals will rejoice at the inclusion of overseas career records and Wg Cdr Hallows of Sheringham will find the diagram of fielding positions he requested (it may also help a few captains and bowlers).

Test cricket has produced more headlines, records and controversy than usual during the past year. Apart from Lara's 375, Kapil Dev's record career tally of wickets, Devon Malcolm's magnificent 9 for 57 and hat-tricks by Warne and Damien Fleming, we have also seen England avoid their lowest-ever total by the narrowest margin before becoming only the second visiting team to win a Test in Bridgetown. Controversy has reared its head in the guise of ball-tampering both blatant (gougeing) and damned silly (dirt in pocket), and, far more seriously, in allegations of bribery and highly organised corruption. It is impossible for me to comment on these accusations; all I know is that when I lived in London and India were playing at Lord's or The Oval, a Bombay bookmaker used to telephone me regularly for a pitch and weather report!

Our own Test cricket has been full of interest and drama as Michael Atherton has had to cope with a change of selectors, an astonishing succession of injuries and a most unfair scheduling of opponents. How could the administrators accept a programme of Tests which will involve ten matches apiece against West Indies and Australia within 27 months? During the last calendar year England played more Tests (13) than any of the other eight full member countries. Perhaps there is a role for the ICC here in fairly regulating the amount of Test cricket played. Certainly the growing number of limited-overs tournaments featuring three or four countries needs to be controlled. Commercial greed in this direction is leading to players breaking down and to the World Cup competition itself being devalued. Incidentally, next January *Playfair* will be publishing a guide to the 1996 World Cup.

On the domestic front, another failed Ashes mission has prompted endless discussion about the shortcomings of our county competitions as a training ground for Test cricket. Conscripted overseas players will confirm that our current format represents considerable overkill which stifles enthusiasm and enjoyment. Now that the Board has extracted serious money from television rights, the time has surely come to prune the amount of limited-overs dross and produce a reasonable balance between the first-class game and the contrived instant version. I would abolish the 55-over Cup (returning to its interminable zonal preamble this summer) and use the generous sponsorship of Benson and Hedges to fund a new regional four-day tournament on the lines of India's Duleep Trophy. It could comprise five zonal teams (West, North, East, South and London Counties) with only England-qualified players eligible and culminating in semi-finals and a final at The Oval (the best pitch in the country).

In addition, all players not qualified for England should be phased out as quickly as possible; most occupy key bowling and batting roles thus depriving our youngsters of vital experience. Bonus points, largely irrelevant to four-day cricket, should be abolished and points for a first-innings lead reinstated (as in Australia's Sheffield Shield). If the Sunday League is to be retained it should either be removed from the middle of championship matches by re-scheduling the playing days of the latter, or, preferably, involve mainly amateur club players with an ambition to play the first-class game. This might also persuade counties to prune staffs that have grown to absurd numbers.

A new Board, scheduled to succeed the TCCB in January 1996 but still in the throes of construction, will control the game in all parts of the United Kingdom. In view of this mandate, it must surely bear the title of British and not English Cricket Board. One of its first duties should be to bring under its control all 18 county groundsmen, a simple edict which would instantly remove the power of county chairmen and captains to order doctored pitches.

The saddest news this winter concerned the passing of Peter May, very much my boyhood hero and assessed by many as the finest post-war English batsman. A memorial match will be played at Arundel on 18 July featuring the late Peter May's XI (led by his nominated captain, Mike Gatting) and a Surrey President's XI skippered by John Edrich.

Darren Gough was an easy selection for our cover profile. His infectious enthusiasm and cavalier approach excited Australia's vast crowds and lifted all England's supporters. Rumours have grown during recent years concerning the jinx imposed by being portrayed on this annual and I have to confess that the arrival in Melbourne of a proof of this cover preceded by barely an hour the injury which ended his tour. Easy payments can be arranged for players not wanting to be profiled.

Once again my task has been greatly assisted by numerous benefactors, notably the county administrations, scorers and statisticians, by Tony Brown, Tim Lamb and Kate Jenkins at the TCCB, by Clive Hitchcock of the ICC, and by David Armstrong of the MCCA. Thanks are also due to Philip Bailey for compiling the first-class career records, to my wife Debbie for secretarial assistance and for allowing my two-month absence in Australia, to Christine Forrest for her meticulous proof-checking, to Chris Leggett and his typesetting team at Letterpart, and, especially, to Ian Marshall for overseeing the entire operation with his habitual efficient unflappability.

Playfair is again indebted to NatWest for its benign sponsorship and to Barbara Quinn and her Special Events team for their support and encouragement, particularly for their highly efficient administration of our competition. Their current contract ends with this edition but we fervently hope that this long association will continue. Renewal is dependent upon NatWest successfully negotiating a new contract with the TCCB for continued association with the Trophy competition.

BILL FRINDALL
Urchfont

AUSTRALIA v SOUTH AFRICA (1st Test)

At Melbourne Cricket Ground, on 26, 27‡, 28, 29, 30 December 1993.
Toss: Australia. Result: MATCH DRAWN.
Debuts: South Africa – P.S.de Villiers, G.Kirsten. (‡ no play)

AUSTRALIA	
M.A.Taylor b Symcox	170
M.J.Slater c Kirsten b Donald	32
S.K.Warne lbw b De Villiers	0
D.C.Boon b Matthews	25
M.E.Waugh lbw b Matthews	84
*A.R.Border c Richardson b Matthews	2
D.R.Martyn b Symcox	8
†I.A.Healy not out	7
P.R.Reiffel, T.B.A.May, C.J.McDermott — did not bat	
Extras (B2, LB7, NB5)	14
Total (7 wickets declared)	342

SOUTH AFRICA	
A.C.Hudson retired hurt	64
G.Kirsten c Taylor b Waugh	16
W.J.Cronje c Boon b Warne	71
D.J.Cullinan c Border b McDermott	0
J.N.Rhodes not out	35
*K.C.Wessels not out	63
†D.J.Richardson, P.L.Symcox, C.R.Matthews, P.S.de Villiers, A.A.Donald — did not bat	
Extras (LB2, NB7)	9
Total (3 wickets)	258

SOUTH AFRICA	*O*	*M*	*R*	*W*
Donald	30	4	108	1
De Villiers	32	6	83	1
Matthews	24	5	68	3
Cronje	13	4	25	0
Symcox	16.5	3	49	2
AUSTRALIA				
McDermott	23	5	60	1
Reiffel	21	4	55	0
Waugh	12	3	20	1
May	28	7	58	0
Warne	31	8	63	1

FALL OF WICKETS

Wkt	A *1st*	SA *1st*
1st	57	49
2nd	58	157
3rd	127	157
4th	296	–
5th	300	–
6th	327	–
7th	342	–
8th	–	–
9th	–	–
10th	–	–

Umpires: D.B.Hair (6) and T.A.Prue (8).
Referee: J.L.Hendriks (*West Indies*) (1). Test No. 1242/54 (A 534/SA 181)

AUSTRALIA v SOUTH AFRICA (2nd Test)

At Sydney Cricket Ground, on 2, 3, 4, 5, 6 January 1994.
Toss: South Africa. Result: SOUTH AFRICA won by 5 runs.
Debuts: None.

SOUTH AFRICA				
A.C.Hudson lbw b McGrath	0		c Healy b McDermott	1
G.Kirsten st Healy b Warne	67		b McDermott	41
W.J.Cronje c Waugh b McDermott	41		b McDermott	38
D.J.Cullinan b Warne	9	(5)	lbw b Warne	2
J.N.Rhodes lbw b Warne	4	(6)	not out	76
*K.C.Wessels c and b Warne	3	(4)	b Warne	18
†D.J.Richardson c Taylor b Warne	4		lbw b McGrath	24
P.L.Symcox b Warne	7		c Healy b McDermott	4
C.R.Matthews c Taylor b Warne	0		c Waugh b Warne	4
P.S.de Villiers c Waugh b McDermott	18		lbw b Warne	2
A.A.Donald not out	0		c Healy b Warne	10
Extras (B1, LB4, NB11)	16		(B13, LB1, NB5)	19
Total	169			239

AUSTRALIA				
M.J.Slater b Donald	92	(2)	b De Villiers	1
M.A.Taylor c Richardson b Donald	7	(1)	c Richardson b De Villiers	27
D.C.Boon b De Villiers	19		c Kirsten b De Villiers	24
M.E.Waugh lbw b Symcox	7	(5)	lbw b Donald	11
*A.R.Border c Richardson b De Villiers	49	(6)	b Donald	7
D.R.Martyn c Richardson b De Villiers	59	(7)	c Hudson b Donald	6
†I.A.Healy c Richardson b Donald	19	(8)	b De Villiers	1
S.K.Warne c Rhodes b Symcox	11	(9)	run out	1
C.J.McDermott c Cronje b De Villiers	6	(10)	not out	29
T.B.A.May not out	8	(4)	lbw b De Villiers	0
G.D.McGrath b Donald	9		c and b De Villiers	1
Extras (B1, LB2, NB3)	6		(LB3)	3
Total	292			111

AUSTRALIA	O	M	R	W		O	M	R	W
McDermott	18.1	2	42	2		28	9	62	4
McGrath	19	5	32	1		14	3	30	1
Warne	27	8	56	7	(4)	42	17	72	5
May	10	1	34	0	(3)	22	4	53	0
Border						3	1	8	0
SOUTH AFRICA									
Donald	31.2	8	83	4		17	5	34	3
De Villiers	36	12	80	4		23.3	8	43	6
Matthews	28	11	44	0		6	5	9	0
Symcox	46	11	82	2		10	3	22	0

FALL OF WICKETS

Wkt	SA 1st	A 1st	SA 2nd	A 2nd
1st	1	10	2	4
2nd	91	58	75	51
3rd	110	75	101	51
4th	133	179	107	56
5th	134	179	110	63
6th	141	229	182	72
7th	142	250	188	73
8th	142	266	197	75
9th	152	281	203	110
10th	169	292	239	111

Umpires: S.G.Randell (15) and W.P.Sheahan (2).
Referee: J.L.Hendriks (*West Indies*) (2). Test No. 1243/55 (A 535/SA 182)

AUSTRALIA v SOUTH AFRICA (3rd Test)

At Adelaide Oval, on 28, 29, 30, 31 January, 1 February 1994.
Toss: Australia. Result: AUSTRALIA won by 191 runs.
Debuts: None.

AUSTRALIA

M.A.Taylor b G.Kirsten	62	(2)	b Snell	38
M.J.Slater c Rhodes b Donald	53	(1)	lbw b Donald	7
D.C.Boon c De Villiers b Donald	50		c Hudson b McMillan	38
M.E.Waugh c Snell b McMillan	2		c Richardson b Donald	12
*A.R.Border c Richardson b McMillan	84		run out	4
S.R.Waugh c Richardson b Donald	164		c Richardson b Snell	1
†I.A.Healy c Rhodes b McMillan	0		not out	14
P.R.Reiffel not out	32		not out	2
S.K.Warne not out	4			
C.D.McDermott, T.B.A.May } did not bat				
Extras (LB9, NB9)	18		(LB7, NB1)	8
Total (7 wickets declared)	469		**(6 wickets declared)**	124

SOUTH AFRICA

A.C.Hudson lbw b S.R.Waugh	90		c S.R.Waugh b McDermott	2
G.Kirsten c May b McDermott	43		b Warne	7
*W.J.Cronje c Healy b Reiffel	0		lbw b Warne	3
P.N.Kirsten c M.E.Waugh b Warne	79		lbw b McDermott	42
J.N.Rhodes b S.R.Waugh	5	(6)	lbw b May	4
D.J.Cullinan b S.R.Waugh	10	(7)	c Healy b McDermott	5
B.M.McMillan lbw b S.R.Waugh	2	(8)	lbw b Warne	4
†D.J.Richardson lbw b McDermott	6	(9)	c Taylor b May	10
R.P.Snell c Healy b McDermott	10	(10)	c and b Warne	1
P.S.de Villiers run out	4	(5)	c Reiffel b McDermott	30
A.A.Donald not out	1		not out	0
Extras (B3, LB10, W1, NB9)	23		(B9, LB7, W2, NB3)	21
Total	273			129

SOUTH AFRICA	*O*	*M*	*R*	*W*		*O*	*M*	*R*	*W*
Donald	38	7	122	3		11	2	26	2
De Villiers	41	11	105	0					
Snell	19	6	44	0	(4)	12	3	38	2
McMillan	30	3	89	3	(2)	11	0	33	1
Cronje	9	3	21	0	(3)	6	1	20	0
G.Kirsten	23	8	62	1					
P.N.Kirsten	4	0	17	0					
AUSTRALIA									
McDermott	27	9	49	3		19	8	33	4
Reiffel	15	4	36	1		11	4	15	0
May	25	9	57	0	(4)	32	20	26	2
Warne	44.2	15	85	1	(3)	30.5	15	31	4
M.E.Waugh	3	1	7	0	(7)	3	2	3	0
S.R.Waugh	18	7	26	4	(5)	6	3	4	0
Border					(6)	4	3	1	0

FALL OF WICKETS

Wkt	A *1st*	SA *1st*	A *2nd*	SA *2nd*
1st	83	100	23	12
2nd	152	103	79	17
3rd	159	173	91	18
4th	183	179	99	100
5th	391	195	103	105
6th	391	203	109	113
7th	464	222	–	116
8th	–	243	–	128
9th	–	270	–	128
10th	–	273	–	129

Umpires: D.B.Hair (7) and T.A.Prue (9).
Referee: J.L.Hendriks (*West Indies*) (3). Test No. 1244/56 (A 536/SA 183)

AUSTRALIA v SOUTH AFRICA 1993-94

AUSTRALIA – BATTING AND FIELDING

	M	I	NO	HS	Runs	Avge	100	50	Ct/St
M.A.Taylor	3	5	–	170	304	60.80	1	1	4
M.J.Slater	3	5	–	92	185	37.00	–	2	–
C.J.McDermott	3	2	1	29*	35	35.00	–	–	–
D.C.Boon	3	5	–	50	156	31.20	–	1	1
A.R.Border	3	5	–	84	146	29.20	–	1	1
D.R.Martyn	2	3	–	59	73	24.33	–	1	–
M.E.Waugh	3	5	–	84	116	23.20	–	1	4
I.A.Healy	3	5	2	19	41	13.66	–	–	6/1
T.B.A.May	3	2	1	8*	8	8.00	–	–	1
S.K.Warne	3	4	1	11	16	5.33	–	–	2
P.R.Reiffel	2	2	2	32*	34	–	–	–	1

Played in one Test: G.D.McGrath 9, 1; S.R.Waugh 164, 1 (1ct).

AUSTRALIA – BOWLING

	O	M	R	W	Avge	Best	5wI	10wM
S.R.Waugh	24	10	30	4	7.50	4-26	–	–
S.K.Warne	175.1	62	307	18	17.05	7-56	2	1
C.J.McDermott	115.1	34	246	14	17.57	4-33	–	–

Also bowled: A.R.Border 7-4-9-0; G.D.McGrath 33-8-62-2; T.B.A.May 117-42-228-2; P.R.Reiffel 47-12-106-1; M.E.Waugh 18-6-30-1.

SOUTH AFRICA – BATTING AND FIELDING

	M	I	NO	HS	Runs	Avge	100	50	Ct/St
K.C.Wessels	2	3	1	63*	84	42.00	–	1	–
J.N.Rhodes	3	5	2	76*	124	41.33	–	1	3
A.C.Hudson	3	5	1	90	157	39.25	–	2	2
G.Kirsten	3	5	–	67	174	34.80	–	1	2
W.J.Cronje	3	5	–	71	153	30.60	–	1	1
P.S.de Villiers	3	4	–	30	54	13.50	–	–	2
D.J.Richardson	3	4	–	24	44	11.00	–	–	10
A.A.Donald	3	4	3	10	11	11.00	–	–	–
P.L.Symcox	2	2	–	7	11	5.50	–	–	–
D.J.Cullinan	3	5	–	10	26	5.20	–	–	–
C.R.Matthews	2	2	–	4	4	2.00	–	–	–

Played in one Test: P.N.Kirsten 79, 42; B.M.McMillan 2, 4; R.P.Snell 10, 1 (1ct).

SOUTH AFRICA – BOWLING

	O	M	R	W	Avge	Best	5wI	10wM
P.S.de Villiers	132.3	37	311	11	28.27	6-43	1	1
A.A.Donald	127.2	26	373	13	28.69	4-83	–	–
B.M.McMillan	41	3	122	4	30.50	3-89	–	–
P.L.Symcox	72.5	17	153	4	38.25	2-49	–	–

Also bowled: W.J.Cronje 28-8-66-0; G.Kirsten 23-8-62-1; P.N.Kirsten 4-0-17-0; C.R.Matthews 58-21-121-3; R.P.Snell 31-9-82-2.

INDIA v SRI LANKA (1st Test)

At K.D.Singh 'Babu' Stadium, Lucknow, on 18, 19, 20, 22 January 1994.
Toss: India. Result: INDIA won by an innings and 119 runs.
Debuts: India – N.R.Mongia.

INDIA

M.Prabhakar lbw b Liyanage	21
N.S.Sidhu c Kalpage b Muralitharan	124
V.G.Kambli run out	5
S.R.Tendulkar c Samaraweera b Anurasiri	142
*M.Azharuddin c Tillekeratne b Anurasiri	47
S.V.Manjrekar c and b Muralitharan	61
Kapil Dev c Wickremasinghe b Muralitharan	42
†N.R.Mongia c Samaraweera b Muralitharan	44
A.Kumble b Wickremasinghe	4
R.K.Chauhan c Tillekeratne b Muralitharan	3
S.L.V.Raju not out	5
Extras (LB3, W2, NB8)	13
Total	511

SRI LANKA

R.S.Mahanama c Mongia b Kumble	73	c Azharuddin b Kumble	45
D.P.Samaraweera lbw b Chauhan	42	lbw b Kumble	12
H.P.Tillekeratne c Mongia b Kumble	7	c Prabhakar b Kumble	47
P.A.de Silva c Azharuddin b Kumble	13	b Kumble	11
*A.Ranatunga c Chauhan b Raju	9	c Mongia b Kumble	0
R.S.Kalpage c Azharuddin b Kumble	2	c Kumble b Raju	2
†P.B.Dassanayake st Mongia b Raju	36	b Prabhakar	15
D.K.Liyanage lbw b Prabhakar	12	c Mongia b Chauhan	23
S.D.Anurasiri b Prabhakar	2	lbw b Kumble	4
G.P.Wickremasinghe lbw b Kapil Dev	6	not out	0
M.Muralitharan not out	9	b Kumble	0
Extras (LB7)	7	(B5, LB6, W4)	15
Total	218		174

SRI LANKA	*O*	*M*	*R*	*W*	*O*	*M*	*R*	*W*
Wickremasinghe	20	3	84	1				
Liyanage	17	6	55	1				
Ranatunga	3	2	1	0				
Anurasiri	58	13	147	2				
Kalpage	22	2	59	0				
Muralitharan	41.5	3	162	5				
INDIA								
Prabhakar	16.4	7	36	2	16	3	38	1
Kapil Dev	10	3	27	1	3	0	8	0
Raju	20	10	25	2	14	5	28	1
Kumble	37	10	69	4	27.3	9	59	7
Chauhan	23	7	54	1	13	2	30	1

FALL OF WICKETS

Wkt	*I 1st*	*SL 1st*	*SL 2nd*
1st	63	120	29
2nd	84	120	100
3rd	205	132	109
4th	347	149	109
5th	370	149	122
6th	446	158	122
7th	459	191	162
8th	482	197	174
9th	501	208	174
10th	511	218	174

Umpires: R.C.Sharma (1) and S.Venkataraghavan (4).
Referee: E.de C.Weekes (*West Indies*) (1). Test No. 1245/12 (I 286/SL 51)

INDIA v SRI LANKA (2nd Test)

At Chinnaswamy Stadium, Bangalore, on 26, 27, 29, 30 January 1994.
Toss: India. Result: INDIA won by an innings and 95 runs.
Debuts: None. ‡ (A.D.Jadeja)

INDIA	
M.Prabhakar c Dassanayake b Wickremasinghe	14
N.S.Sidhu lbw b Muralitharan	99
V.G.Kambli c Wickremasinghe b Muralitharan	82
S.R.Tendulkar b Anurasiri	96
*M.Azharuddin lbw b Muralitharan	108
S.V.Manjrekar c Mahanama b Muralitharan	39
Kapil Dev not out	53
†N.R.Mongia not out	18
A.Kumble, R.K.Chauhan, S.L.V.Raju } did not bat	
Extras (B6, LB6, NB20)	32
Total (6 wickets declared)	541

SRI LANKA				
R.S.Mahanama c and b Kumble	47		c Azharuddin b Raju	36
D.P.Samaraweera c Prabhakar b Kapil Dev	0		c Tendulkar b Prabhakar	4
P.A.de Silva c Chauhan b Prabhakar	17	(4)	lbw b Raju	8
*A.Ranatunga lbw b Kapil Dev	26	(5)	c Sidhu b Kumble	28
S.T.Jayasuriya c Prabhakar b Kumble	22	(6)	c sub‡ b Chauhan	1
H.P.Tillekeratne c Raju b Kumble	0	(3)	c and b Chauhan	80
R.S.Kalpage lbw b Kapil Dev	63		lbw b Kumble	18
†P.B.Dassanayake lbw b Prabhakar	16		lbw b Kumble	0
S.D.Anurasiri c Tendulkar b Prabhakar	4		c Azharuddin b Kapil Dev	7
G.P.Wickremasinghe c Mongia b Prabhakar	8		c Sidhu b Kapil Dev	1
M.Muralitharan not out	8		not out	20
Extras (LB12, NB8)	20		(B9, LB3)	12
Total	231			215

SRI LANKA	*O*	*M*	*R*	*W*	*O*	*M*	*R*	*W*
Wickremasinghe	20	0	98	1				
Jayasuriya	8	2	26	0				
Muralitharan	65	11	179	4				
Ranatunga	4	0	14	0				
Anurasiri	45	2	158	1				
Kalpage	19	1	54	0				
INDIA								
Prabhakar	20	4	82	4	3	0	18	1
Kapil Dev	21.1	5	73	3	8.3	1	41	2
Kumble	13	2	50	3	16	3	64	3
Raju	4	0	14	0	12	2	36	2
Chauhan					16	3	44	2

FALL OF WICKETS

Wkt	*I* *1st*	*SL* *1st*	*SL* *2nd*
1st	34	7	5
2nd	182	36	69
3rd	248	94	97
4th	372	116	164
5th	459	132	168
6th	468	132	176
7th	–	189	179
8th	–	196	188
9th	–	208	189
10th	–	231	215

Umpires: S.K.Bansal (2) and K.Parthasarathy (1).
Referee: E.de C.Weekes (*West Indies*) (2). Test No. 1246/13 (I 287/SL 52)

INDIA v SRI LANKA (3rd Test)

At Gujarat Stadium, Ahmedabad, on 8, 9, 10, 12 February 1994.
Toss: Sri Lanka. Result: INDIA won by an innings and 17 runs.
Debuts: None.

SRI LANKA

R.S.Mahanama	lbw b Kumble	18	lbw b Raju	63
D.P.Samaraweera	b Chauhan	16	run out	20
H.P.Tillekeratne	c Manjrekar b Kapil Dev	5	c Azharuddin b Raju	40
P.A.de Silva	lbw b Raju	7	c Azharuddin b Chauhan	14
*A.Ranatunga	c Azharuddin b Raju	15	c Sidhu b Raju	29
M.S.Atapattu	b Chauhan	0	c Mongia b Chauhan	0
R.S.Kalpage	c Azharuddin b Chauhan	2	c Azharuddin b Chauhan	9
†P.B.Dassanayake	c Kambli b Raju	10	not out	21
S.D.Anurasiri	b Raju	4	c Prabhakar b Raju	6
G.P.Wickremasinghe	st Mongia b Raju	22	c Prabhakar b Raju	0
M.Muralitharan	not out	5	c Mongia b Raju	4
Extras	(B8, LB7)	15	(B4, LB11, NB1)	16
Total		119		222

INDIA

M.Prabhakar	b Anurasiri	14
N.S.Sidhu	c Kalpage b Muralitharan	43
V.G.Kambli	c Ranatunga b Wickremasinghe	57
S.R.Tendulkar	b Wickremasinghe	6
*M.Azharuddin	b Muralitharan	152
S.V.Manjrekar	c Ranatunga b De Silva	16
Kapil Dev	lbw b De Silva	4
†N.R.Mongia	lbw b Anurasiri	14
A.Kumble	c Kalpage b De Silva	15
R.K.Chauhan	b Muralitharan	9
S.L.V.Raju	not out	1
Extras	(B17, LB5, NB5)	27
Total		358

INDIA	*O*	*M*	*R*	*W*		*O*	*M*	*R*	*W*
Prabhakar	5	0	13	0		5	2	11	0
Kapil Dev	9	4	15	1		5	1	12	0
Kumble	15	3	30	1	(4)	28	9	45	0
Raju	23.5	7	38	5	(3)	32.3	9	87	6
Chauhan	11	8	8	3		30	14	45	3
Tendulkar						4	1	7	0

SRI LANKA	*O*	*M*	*R*	*W*
Wickremasinghe	36	9	108	2
Ranatunga	8	1	15	0
Anurasiri	28	3	75	2
Muralitharan	36.3	7	79	3
Kalpage	7	2	9	0
De Silva	23	5	50	3

FALL OF WICKETS

Wkt	*SL 1st*	*I 1st*	*SL 2nd*
1st	34	27	67
2nd	39	110	98
3rd	47	123	149
4th	59	123	149
5th	59	169	153
6th	71	203	167
7th	79	249	193
8th	89	288	214
9th	108	355	214
10th	119	358	222

Umpires: A.L.Narasimhan (1) and V.K.Ramaswamy (14).
Referee: E.de C.Weekes (*West Indies*) (3). Test No. 1247/14 (I 288/SL 53)

INDIA v SRI LANKA 1993-94

INDIA – BATTING AND FIELDING

	M	*I*	*NO*	*HS*	*Runs*	*Avge*	*100*	*50*	*Ct/St*
M.Azharuddin	3	3	–	152	307	102.33	2	–	10
N.S.Sidhu	3	3	–	124	266	88.66	1	1	3
S.R.Tendulkar	3	3	–	142	244	81.33	1	1	2
Kapil Dev	3	3	1	53*	99	49.50	–	1	–
V.G.Kambli	3	3	–	82	144	48.00	–	2	1
S.V.Manjrekar	3	3	–	61	116	38.66	–	1	1
N.R.Mongia	3	3	1	44	76	38.00	–	–	7/2
M.Prabhakar	3	3	–	21	49	16.33	–	–	5
A.Kumble	3	2	–	15	19	9.50	–	–	2
R.K.Chauhan	3	2	–	9	12	6.00	–	–	3
S.L.V.Raju	3	2	2	5*	6	–	–	–	1

INDIA – BOWLING

	O	*M*	*R*	*W*	*Avge*	*Best*	*5wI*	*10wM*
S.L.V.Raju	106.2	33	228	16	14.25	6-87	2	1
A.Kumble	136.3	36	317	18	17.61	7-59	1	1
R.K.Chauhan	93	34	181	10	18.10	3- 8	–	–
M.Prabhakar	65.4	16	198	8	24.75	4-82	–	–
Kapil Dev	56.4	14	176	7	25.14	3-73	–	–

Also bowled: S.R.Tendulkar 4-1-7-0.

SRI LANKA – BATTING AND FIELDING

	M	*I*	*NO*	*HS*	*Runs*	*Avge*	*100*	*50*	*Ct/St*
R.S.Mahanama	3	6	–	73	282	47.00	–	2	1
H.P.Tillekeratne	3	6	–	80	179	29.83	–	1	2
M.Muralitharan	3	6	4	20*	46	23.00	–	–	1
P.B.Dassanayake	3	6	1	36	98	19.60	–	–	1
A.Ranatunga	3	6	–	29	107	17.83	–	–	2
R.S.Kalpage	3	6	–	63	96	16.00	–	1	3
D.P.Samaraweera	3	6	–	42	94	15.66	–	–	2
P.A.de Silva	3	6	–	17	70	11.66	–	–	–
G.P.Wickremasinghe	3	6	1	22	37	7.40	–	–	2
S.D.Anurasiri	3	6	–	7	27	4.50	–	–	–

Played in one Test: M.S.Atapattu 0, 0; S.T.Jayasuriya 22, 1; D.K.Liyanage 12, 23.

SRI LANKA – BOWLING

	O	*M*	*R*	*W*	*Avge*	*Best*	*5wI*	*10wM*
M.Muralitharan	142.3	20	420	12	35.00	5-162	1	–
G.P.Wickremasinghe	76	12	290	4	72.50	2-108	–	–
S.D.Anurasiri	131	18	380	5	76.00	2- 75	–	–

Also bowled: P.A.de Silva 23-5-50-3; S.T.Jayasuriya 8-2-26-0; R.S.Kalpage 48-5-122-0; D.K.Liyanage 17-6-55-1; A.Ranatunga 15-3-30-0.

NEW ZEALAND v PAKISTAN (1st Test)

At Eden Park, Auckland, on 10, 11, 12 February 1994.
Toss: Pakistan. Result: PAKISTAN won by five wickets.
Debuts: None.

NEW ZEALAND

B.A.Young c Rashid b Waqar	29		c Rashid b Wasim	0
B.A.Pocock c Rashid b Wasim	0		c Asif b Wasim	10
A.H.Jones c Rashid b Mushtaq	66		c Rashid b Wasim	6
*K.R.Rutherford b Waqar	14		b Waqar	18
M.J.Greatbatch c Salim b Mushtaq	48		c Inzamam b Wasim	0
S.A.Thomson c Rashid b Waqar	29		c Rashid b Waqar	0
C.L.Cairns c Salim b Mushtaq	6		c Asif b Rehman	31
†T.E.Blain c Mushtaq b Wasim	26		c Rashid b Rehman	4
S.B.Doull c and b Waqar	0		c Salim b Wasim	29
R.P.de Groen c Mushtaq b Wasim	2		not out	0
M.B.Owens not out	2		c Rashid b Wasim	0
Extras (B4, LB8, W1, NB7)	20		(B4, LB5, NB3)	12
Total	242			110

PAKISTAN

Saeed Anwar c Blain b Cairns	16		c Young b De Groen	7
Aamir Sohail c Jones b De Groen	16		c Young b Thomson	78
Asif Mujtaba c Blain b Doull	8		c and b Doull	0
Mushtaq Ahmed c Young b Doull	0			
*Salim Malik c Young b Doull	18	(4)	c Young b De Groen	11
Basit Ali c Blain b Cairns	25	(5)	c and b Doull	7
Inzamam-ul-Haq c Young b De Groen	43	(6)	not out	20
†Rashid Latif lbw b Doull	30	(7)	not out	13
Wasim Akram c Blain b De Groen	35			
Waqar Younis c Cairns b Doull	11			
Ata-ur-Rehman not out	2			
Extras (LB6, NB5)	11		(LB3, NB2)	5
Total	215		(5 wickets)	141

PAKISTAN	*O*	*M*	*R*	*W*		*O*	*M*	*R*	*W*
Wasim	22.3	9	50	3		16.1	4	43	6
Waqar	15	2	46	4		10	3	35	2
Rehman	14	3	55	0		6	1	23	2
Mushtaq	17	1	79	3					
NEW ZEALAND									
Cairns	18	2	75	2		6	1	15	0
Owens	7	1	28	0	(4)	2	0	10	0
Doull	15	2	66	5		16	0	48	2
De Groen	17.4	5	40	3	(2)	13	3	48	2
Thomson						4	1	17	1

FALL OF WICKETS

Wkt	*NZ 1st*	*P 1st*	*NZ 2nd*	*P 2nd*
1st	3	17	0	21
2nd	67	36	8	25
3rd	95	48	31	56
4th	170	50	35	73
5th	175	87	40	119
6th	185	93	44	–
7th	228	141	67	–
8th	228	176	103	–
9th	233	207	110	–
10th	242	215	110	–

Umpires: H.D.Bird (*England*) (56) and R.S.Dunne (11).
Referee: R.Subba Row (*England*) (7). Test No. 1248/34 (NZ 223/P 210)

NEW ZEALAND v PAKISTAN (2nd Test)

At Basin Reserve, Wellington, on 17, 18, 19, 20 February 1994.
Toss: New Zealand. Result: PAKISTAN won by an innings and 12 runs.
Debuts: New Zealand – M.N.Hart.

NEW ZEALAND

B.A.Young lbw b Wasim	0	(2)	b Wasim	4
B.A.Pocock b Rehman	16	(1)	b Waqar	0
A.H.Jones lbw b Rehman	43		b Wasim	76
*K.R.Rutherford c Raza b Rehman	7		c Raza b Rehman	63
M.J.Greatbatch c Rashid b Waqar	45		c Rashid b Wasim	10
S.A.Thomson b Wasim	7		c Rehman b Wasim	47
†T.E.Blain c Saeed b Waqar	8		c Basit b Wasim	78
M.N.Hart not out	12		b Wasim	7
D.K.Morrison c Rashid b Wasim	5	(10)	lbw b Waqar	42
S.B.Doull c Basit b Waqar	17	(9)	c Salim b Wasim	15
R.P.de Groen b Wasim	4		not out	1
Extras (LB7, NB4)	11		(B1, LB5, NB12)	18
Total	175			361

PAKISTAN

Saeed Anwar run out	169
Aamir Sohail lbw b Morrison	2
Akram Raza c Blain b Morrison	0
Basit Ali b Thomson	85
*Salim Malik c and b Hart	140
Inzamam-ul-Haq not out	135
Asif Mujtaba, †Rashid Latif, Wasim Akram, Waqar Younis, Ata-ur-Rehman: did not bat	
Extras (B5, LB6, NB6)	17
Total (5 wickets declared)	548

PAKISTAN	*O*	*M*	*R*	*W*		*O*	*M*	*R*	*W*
Wasim	24	10	60	4		37	7	119	7
Waqar	22	5	51	3		25.2	4	111	2
Rehman	15	4	50	3		18	1	86	1
Raza	6	4	7	0	(5)	12	4	25	0
Aamir					(4)	1	0	1	0
Salim						2	0	13	0
NEW ZEALAND									
Morrison	31	4	139	2					
De Groen	31	8	104	0					
Doull	27	6	112	0					
Hart	31.2	9	102	1					
Thomson	17	3	80	1					

FALL OF WICKETS

Wkt	*NZ 1st*	*P 1st*	*NZ 2nd*
1st	0	34	3
2nd	40	36	6
3rd	49	233	120
4th	100	290	143
5th	126	548	209
6th	128	–	216
7th	140	–	244
8th	149	–	276
9th	170	–	350
10th	175	–	361

Umpires: B.L.Aldridge (21) and H.D.Bird (*England*) (57).
Referee: R.Subba Row (*England*) (8). Test No. 1249/35 (NZ 224/P 211)

NEW ZEALAND v PAKISTAN (3rd Test)

At Lancaster Park, Christchurch, on 24, 25, 26, 27, 28 February 1994.
Toss: New Zealand. Result: NEW ZEALAND won by five wickets.
Debuts: Pakistan – Atif Rauf. ‡ (M.A.Hastings)

PAKISTAN

Saeed Anwar c Young b Doull	69		c Blain b Morrison	0
Aamir Sohail c Hartland b Doull	60		c Young b Doull	3
Atif Rauf c Greatbatch b Morrison	16		c Young b Doull	9
*Salim Malik b Hart	18	(5)	c Pringle b Morrison	23
Basit Ali c Hartland b Pringle	103	(6)	run out	67
Inzamam-ul-Haq c Greatbatch b Doull	5	(7)	c sub‡ b Morrison	20
†Rashid Latif c Hartland b Thomson	27	(8)	c and b Hart	3
Wasim Akram c Greatbatch b Morrison	5	(9)	b Hart	17
Akram Raza not out	29	(4)	st Blain b Hart	26
Waqar Younis c Doull b Morrison	2		c Blain b Morrison	10
Aamir Nazir b Morrison	0		not out	0
Extras (LB6, W1, NB3)	10		(NB1)	1
Total	344			179

NEW ZEALAND

B.R.Hartland c Basit b Waqar	3	(2)	c Inzamam b Wasim	10
B.A.Young lbw b Aamir Nazir	38	(1)	b Wasim	120
A.H.Jones run out	81		run out	26
*K.R.Rutherford c Inzamam b Waqar	7		lbw b Wasim	13
M.J.Greatbatch lbw b Wasim	1		c Inzamam b Waqar	1
S.A.Thomson c Rashid b Waqar	3		not out	120
†T.E.Blain lbw b Waqar	0		not out	11
M.N.Hart lbw b Wasim	6			
S.B.Doull lbw b Waqar	17			
D.K.Morrison not out	6			
C.Pringle b Waqar	0			
Extras (B5, LB9, NB24)	38		(LB5, NB18)	23
Total	200		(5 wickets)	324

NEW ZEALAND	*O*	*M*	*R*	*W*		*O*	*M*	*R*	*W*
Morrison	24	3	105	4		21.3	5	66	4
Doull	25	3	93	3	(3)	5	0	13	2
Pringle	33	6	83	1	(2)	17	3	41	0
Hart	9	2	37	1		18	5	47	3
Thomson	6	0	20	1		4	0	12	0
PAKISTAN									
Wasim	22	5	54	2		38	6	105	3
Waqar	19	1	78	6		27	6	84	1
Aamir Nazir	15	2	54	1		16	0	59	0
Raza						19	5	49	0
Aamir Sohail						2	1	5	0
Salim						4	1	13	0
Saeed						1	0	4	0

FALL OF WICKETS

	P	*NZ*	*P*	*NZ*
Wkt	*1st*	*1st*	*2nd*	*2nd*
1st	125	12	0	22
2nd	147	109	4	76
3rd	169	124	26	119
4th	195	139	53	133
5th	206	147	77	287
6th	254	147	133	–
7th	261	171	152	–
8th	339	186	154	–
9th	344	198	171	–
10th	344	200	179	–

Umpires: R.S.Dunne (12) and K.T.Francis (*Sri Lanka*) (12).
Referee: R.Subba Row (*England*) (9). Test No. 1250/36 (NZ 225/P 212)

NEW ZEALAND v PAKISTAN 1993-94

NEW ZEALAND – BATTING AND FIELDING

	M	*I*	*NO*	*HS*	*Runs*	*Avge*	*100*	*50*	*Ct/St*
A.H.Jones	3	6	–	81	298	49.66	–	3	1
S.A.Thomson	3	6	1	120*	206	41.20	1	–	–
B.A.Young	3	6	–	120	191	31.83	1	–	9
D.K.Morrison	2	3	1	42	53	26.50	–	–	–
T.E.Blain	3	6	1	78	127	25.40	–	1	7/1
K.R.Rutherford	3	6	–	63	122	20.33	–	1	–
M.J.Greatbatch	3	6	–	48	105	17.50	–	–	3
S.B.Doull	3	5	–	29	78	15.60	–	–	3
M.N.Hart	2	3	1	12*	25	12.50	–	–	2
B.A.Pocock	2	4	–	16	26	6.50	–	–	–
R.P.de Groen	2	4	2	4	7	3.50	–	–	–

Played in one Test: C.L.Cairns 6, 31 (1ct); B.R.Hartland 3, 10 (3ct); M.B.Owens 2*, 0; C.Pringle 0 (1ct).

NEW ZEALAND – BOWLING

	O	*M*	*R*	*W*	*Avge*	*Best*	*5wI*	*10wM*
S.B.Doull	88	11	332	12	27.66	5-66	1	–
D.K.Morrison	76.3	12	310	10	31.00	4-66	–	–
M.N.Hart	58.2	16	186	5	37.20	3-47	–	–
R.P.de Groen	61.4	16	192	5	38.40	3-40	–	–

Also bowled: C.L.Cairns 24-3-90-2; M.B.Owens 9-1-38-0; C.Pringle 50-9-124-1; S.A.Thomson 31-4-129-3.

PAKISTAN – BATTING AND FIELDING

	M	*I*	*NO*	*HS*	*Runs*	*Avge*	*100*	*50*	*Ct/St*
Inzamam-ul-Haq	3	5	2	135*	223	74.33	1	–	4
Basit Ali	3	5	–	103	287	57.40	1	2	3
Saeed Anwar	3	5	–	169	261	52.20	1	1	1
Salim Malik	3	5	–	140	210	42.00	1	–	4
Aamir Sohail	3	5	–	78	159	31.80	–	2	–
Akram Raza	2	3	1	29*	55	27.50	–	–	2
Rashid Latif	3	4	1	30	73	24.33	–	–	13
Wasim Akram	3	3	–	35	57	19.00	–	–	–
Waqar Younis	3	3	–	11	23	7.66	–	–	1
Asif Mujtaba	2	2	–	8	8	4.00	–	–	2
Ata-ur-Rehman	2	1	1	2*	2	–	–	–	1

Played in one Test: Aamir Nazir 9, 0*; Atif Rauf 16, 9; Mushtaq Ahmed 0 (2ct).

PAKISTAN – BOWLING

	O	*M*	*R*	*W*	*Avge*	*Best*	*5wI*	*10wM*
Wasim Akram	159.4	41	431	25	17.24	7-119	2	1
Waqar Younis	118.2	21	405	18	22.50	6- 78	1	–
Ata-ur-Rehman	53	9	214	6	35.66	3- 50	–	–

Also bowled: Aamir Nazir 31-2-113-1; Aamir Sohail 3-1-6-0; Akram Raza 37-13-81-0; Mushtaq Ahmed 17-1-79-3; Saeed Anwar 1-0-4-0; Salim Malik 6-1-26-0.

WEST INDIES v ENGLAND (1st Test)

At Sabina Park, Kingston, Jamaica, on 19, 20, 21, 23, 24 February 1994.
Toss: England. Result: WEST INDIES won by eight wickets.
Debuts: None. ‡ (R.A.Harper)

ENGLAND

*M.A.Atherton c Murray b K.C.G.Benjamin	55		c Adams b Walsh	28
A.J.Stewart c Murray b K.C.G.Benjamin	70		run out	19
G.P.Thorpe b K.C.G.Benjamin	16	(7)	b W.K.M.Benjamin	14
R.A.Smith b Walsh	0	(3)	c Adams b Walsh	2
G.A.Hick b Adams	23	(4)	c sub‡ b K.C.G.Benjamin	96
M.P.Maynard lbw b K.C.G.Benjamin	35	(5)	c Murray b W.K.M.Benjamin	0
†R.C.Russell lbw b K.C.G.Benjamin	0	(6)	c Adams b W.K.M.Benjamin	32
C.C.Lewis c Adams b Ambrose	8		lbw b Ambrose	21
A.R.Caddick c Adams b K.C.G.Benjamin	3		not out	29
A.P.Igglesden not out	3		c Adams b K.C.G.Benjamin	0
D.E.Malcolm run out	6		b Walsh	18
Extras (B2, LB5, W4, NB4)	15		(B1, LB3, W2, NB2)	8
Total	234			267

WEST INDIES

D.L.Haynes c Thorpe b Malcolm	4		not out	43
P.V.Simmons c Russell b Caddick	8		lbw b Igglesden	12
*R.B.Richardson c Maynard b Malcolm	5	(4)	not out	4
B.C.Lara b Hick	83	(3)	b Caddick	28
K.L.T.Arthurton c Lewis b Malcolm	126			
J.C.Adams not out	95			
†J.R.Murray lbw b Igglesden	34			
W.K.M.Benjamin b Caddick	38			
C.E.L.Ambrose b Caddick	0			
K.C.G.Benjamin b Lewis	0			
C.A.Walsh lbw b Lewis	0			
Extras (LB10, W1, NB3)	14		(B5, LB3)	8
Total	407		(2 wickets)	95

WEST INDIES	*O*	*M*	*R*	*W*		*O*	*M*	*R*	*W*
Ambrose	22	8	46	1		24	4	67	1
Walsh	23	6	41	1		24.5	6	67	3
K.C.G.Benjamin	24	7	66	6	(4)	18	2	60	2
W.K.M.Benjamin	19.1	7	43	0	(3)	20	3	56	3
Adams	10	1	31	1		2	0	9	0
Simmons						3	1	4	0
ENGLAND									
Malcolm	23	3	113	3		5	1	19	0
Caddick	29	5	94	3		6	1	19	1
Lewis	26	4	82	2		3	0	6	0
Igglesden	24	5	53	1		7	0	36	1
Hick	21	4	55	1		3	1	2	0
Stewart						2.2	0	5	0

FALL OF WICKETS

Wkt	*E* *1st*	*WI* *1st*	*E* *2nd*	*WI* *2nd*
1st	121	12	34	38
2nd	133	12	39	87
3rd	134	23	58	–
4th	172	167	63	–
5th	172	256	126	–
6th	172	319	155	–
7th	194	389	213	–
8th	209	389	226	–
9th	227	390	228	–
10th	234	407	267	–

Umpires: S.A.Bucknor (10) and I.D.Robinson (*Zimbabwe*) (4).
Referee: S.M.Gavaskar (*India*) (1). Test No. 1251/105 (WI 301/E 697)

WEST INDIES v ENGLAND (2nd Test)

At Bourda, Georgetown, Guyana, on 17, 18, 19, 20, 22 March 1994.
Toss: West Indies. Result: WEST INDIES won by an innings and 44 runs.
Debuts: West Indies – S.Chanderpaul.

ENGLAND

*M.A.Atherton c Murray b Ambrose	144		b Ambrose	0
A.J.Stewart b Walsh	0		b K.C.G.Benjamin	79
M.R.Ramprakash lbw b Walsh	2		b Ambrose	5
R.A.Smith c Lara b K.C.G.Benjamin	84		c Richardson b Ambrose	24
G.A.Hick c Richardson b Ambrose	33		b K.C.G.Benjamin	5
G.P.Thorpe b Ambrose	0		b Walsh	20
I.D.K.Salisbury lbw b W.K.M.Benjamin	8	(9)	b Walsh	19
†R.C.Russell c Richardson b Ambrose	13	(7)	c Murray b Ambrose	6
C.C.Lewis c Richardson b K.C.G.Benjamin	17	(8)	c Adams b K.C.G.Benjamin	24
A.R.C.Fraser not out	0		b K.C.G.Benjamin	0
A.P.Igglesden b K.C.G.Benjamin	0		not out	1
Extras (LB14, NB7)	21		(B2, LB2, W1, NB2)	7
Total	322			190

WEST INDIES

D.L.Haynes c Russell b Salisbury	63
*R.B.Richardson c Lewis b Fraser	35
B.C.Lara c Atherton b Lewis	167
K.L.T.Arthurton c Thorpe b Salisbury	5
J.C.Adams lbw b Igglesden	137
S.Chanderpaul b Salisbury	62
†J.R.Murray lbw b Salisbury	0
W.K.M.Benjamin b Fraser	44
C.E.L.Ambrose c Russell b Lewis	10
K.C.G.Benjamin c Russell b Lewis	1
C.A.Walsh not out	10
Extras (B2, LB6, W1, NB13)	22
Total	556

WEST INDIES	O	M	R	W		O	M	R	W
Ambrose	30	8	58	4		23	5	37	4
Walsh	26	7	69	2		25	4	71	2
K.C.G.Benjamin	23.5	5	60	3	(4)	19	6	34	4
W.K.M.Benjamin	26	9	62	1	(3)	16	4	44	0
Adams	3	1	10	0		2	2	0	0
Chanderpaul	16	2	49	0					
ENGLAND									
Lewis	28	1	110	3					
Igglesden	24.3	3	94	1					
Fraser	29	5	85	2					
Salisbury	37	4	163	4					
Hick	20	1	61	0					
Ramprakash	15	1	35	0					

FALL OF WICKETS

Wkt	E 1st	WI 1st	E 2nd
1st	0	63	0
2nd	2	177	30
3rd	173	203	91
4th	245	315	96
5th	253	441	129
6th	276	441	140
7th	281	505	150
8th	322	520	185
9th	322	532	186
10th	322	556	190

Umpires: C.R.Duncan (2) and S.Venkataraghavan (*India*) (5).
Referee: J.R.Reid (*New Zealand*) (4). Test No. 1252/106 (WI 302/E 698)

WEST INDIES v ENGLAND (3rd Test)

At Queen's Park Oval, Port-of-Spain, Trinidad, on 25, 26, 27, 29, 30 March 1994.
Toss: West Indies. Result: WEST INDIES won by 147 runs.
Debuts: None. ‡ (P.V.Simmons)

WEST INDIES

D.L.Haynes b Salisbury	38		b Lewis	19
*R.B.Richardson lbw b Salisbury	63		c and b Caddick	3
B.C.Lara lbw b Lewis	43		c Salisbury b Caddick	12
K.L.T.Arthurton lbw b Lewis	1		c Stewart b Caddick	42
J.C.Adams c Smith b Lewis	2		c Russell b Salisbury	43
S.Chanderpaul b Fraser	19		c Fraser b Caddick	50
†J.R.Murray not out	27		c Russell b Caddick	14
W.K.M.Benjamin b Fraser	10		c Fraser b Lewis	35
C.E.L.Ambrose c Thorpe b Fraser	13		b Caddick	12
K.C.G.Benjamin b Fraser	9		not out	5
C.A.Walsh lbw b Lewis	0		lbw b Lewis	1
Extras (B1, LB13, W1, NB12)	27		(B8, LB13, NB12)	33
Total	252			269

ENGLAND

*M.A.Atherton c Murray b W.K.M.Benjamin	48		lbw b Ambrose	0
A.J.Stewart b Ambrose	6		b Ambrose	18
M.R.Ramprakash c and b W.K.M.Benjamin	23		run out	1
R.A.Smith lbw b Ambrose	12		b Ambrose	0
G.A.Hick lbw b Walsh	40		c Murray b Ambrose	6
G.P.Thorpe c Lara b Ambrose	86		b Ambrose	3
†R.C.Russell b Ambrose	23	(8)	c sub‡ b Ambrose	4
C.C.Lewis b Ambrose	9	(9)	c W.K.M.Benjamin b Walsh	6
I.D.K.Salisbury c Lara b Walsh	36	(7)	c Lara b Walsh	0
A.R.Caddick c Lara b W.K.M.Benjamin	6		c Lara b Walsh	1
A.R.C.Fraser not out	8		not out	0
Extras (B10, LB9, W1, NB11)	31		(LB6, NB1)	7
Total	328			46

ENGLAND	*O*	*M*	*R*	*W*	*O*	*M*	*R*	*W*
Fraser	24	9	49	4	25	6	71	0
Caddick	19	5	43	0	26	5	65	6
Lewis	25.2	3	61	4	27.5	6	71	3
Salisbury	22	4	72	2	9	1	41	1
Ramprakash	2	1	8	0				
Hick	3	1	5	0				
WEST INDIES								
Ambrose	29	6	60	5	10	1	24	6
Walsh	27.2	3	77	2	9.1	1	16	3
K.C.G.Benjamin	20	5	70	0				
W.K.M.Benjamin	24	3	66	3				
Adams	4	0	18	0				
Chanderpaul	5	0	13	0				
Arthurton	3	0	5	0				

FALL OF WICKETS

Wkt	*WI 1st*	*E 1st*	*WI 2nd*	*E 2nd*
1st	66	16	15	0
2nd	158	82	37	1
3rd	158	87	51	5
4th	163	115	131	21
5th	164	167	143	26
6th	201	249	167	27
7th	212	273	227	37
8th	241	281	247	40
9th	251	294	267	45
10th	252	328	269	46

Umpires: S.A.Bucknor (11) and S.Venkataraghavan (*India*) (6).
Referee: J.R.Reid (*New Zealand*) (5). Test No.1253/107 (WI 303/E 699)

WEST INDIES v ENGLAND (4th Test)

At Kensington Oval, Bridgetown, Barbados, on 8, 9, 10, 12, 13 April 1994.
Toss: West Indies. Result: ENGLAND won by 208 runs.
Debuts: None. ‡ (P.V.Simmons)

ENGLAND

*M.A.Atherton c Lara b K.C.G.Benjamin	85		c Lara b Walsh	15
A.J.Stewart b W.K.M.Benjamin	118		b Walsh	143
M.R.Ramprakash c Murray b W.K.M.Benjamin	20		c Chanderpaul b Walsh	3
R.A.Smith c Murray b W.K.M.Benjamin	10		lbw b K.C.G.Benjamin	13
G.A.Hick c Murray b Ambrose	34		c Lara b Walsh	59
G.P.Thorpe c sub‡ b K.C.G.Benjamin	7		c Arthurton b Walsh	84
†R.C.Russell c Chanderpaul b Ambrose	38		not out	17
C.C.Lewis c Murray b Ambrose	0		c Walsh b Adams	10
A.R.Caddick b Ambrose	8			
A.R.C.Fraser c Chanderpaul b Walsh	3			
P.C.R.Tufnell not out	0			
Extras (LB8, NB24)	32		(B8, LB6, NB36)	50
Total	355		(7 wickets declared)	394

WEST INDIES

D.L.Haynes c Atherton b Fraser	35	(8)	c Thorpe b Tufnell	15
*R.B.Richardson c Atherton b Fraser	20	(1)	c Ramprakash b Caddick	33
B.C.Lara c sub (N.Hussain) b Lewis	26		c Tufnell b Caddick	64
K.L.T.Arthurton c Russell b Fraser	0	(5)	b Tufnell	52
J.C.Adams c Thorpe b Fraser	26	(2)	c Russell b Caddick	12
S.Chanderpaul c Ramprakash b Tufnell	77		c sub (N.Hussain) b Hick	5
†J.R.Murray c Thorpe b Fraser	0		c Thorpe b Caddick	5
W.K.M.Benjamin c Hick b Fraser	8	(9)	c Stewart b Tufnell	3
C.E.L.Ambrose c Hick b Fraser	44	(10)	b Lewis	12
K.C.G.Benjamin not out	43	(4)	c Hick b Caddick	0
C.A.Walsh c Tufnell b Fraser	13		not out	18
Extras (LB1, NB11)	12		(B1, LB7, NB10)	18
Total	304			237

WEST INDIES	*O*	*M*	*R*	*W*		*O*	*M*	*R*	*W*
Ambrose	24.2	5	86	4		22	4	75	0
Walsh	24	3	88	1		28	5	94	5
W.K.M.Benjamin	22	4	76	3		22	3	58	0
K.C.G.Benjamin	20	5	74	2		20	1	92	1
Chanderpaul	10	4	23	0		10	3	30	0
Adams						6.5	0	31	1
ENGLAND									
Fraser	28.5	7	75	8		17	7	40	0
Caddick	24	2	92	0		17	3	63	5
Lewis	17	2	60	1	(4)	8.2	1	23	1
Tufnell	32	12	76	1	(3)	36	12	100	3
Hick						4	2	3	1

FALL OF WICKETS

Wkt	*E 1st*	*WI 1st*	*E 2nd*	*WI 2nd*
1st	171	55	33	43
2nd	223	55	43	43
3rd	242	95	79	128
4th	265	126	194	150
5th	290	126	344	164
6th	307	126	382	179
7th	307	134	394	195
8th	327	205	–	199
9th	351	263	–	216
10th	355	304	–	237

Umpires: L.H.Barker (19) and D.B.Hair (*Australia*) (8).
Referee: J.R.Reid (*New Zealand*) (6). Test No. 1254/108 (WI 304/E 700)

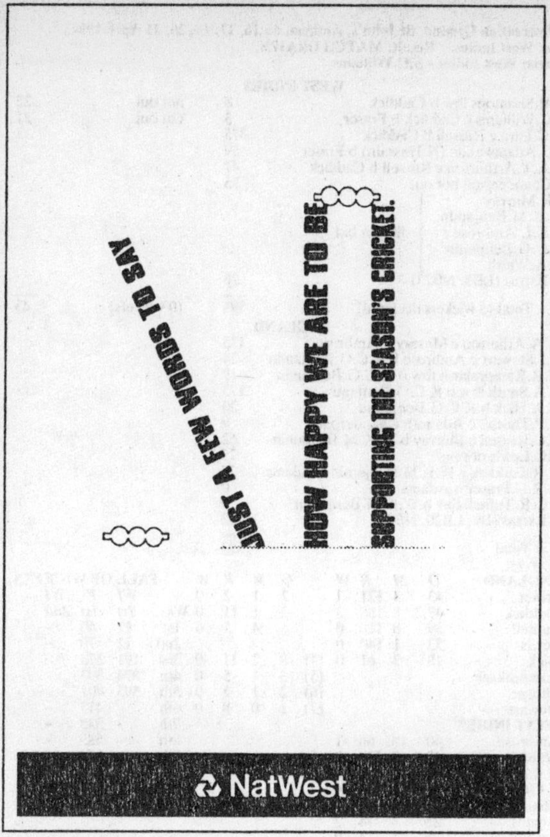
JUST A FEW WORDS TO SAY
HOW HAPPY WE ARE TO BE
SUPPORTING THE SEASON'S CRICKET.
NatWest

WEST INDIES v ENGLAND (5th Test)

At Recreation Ground, St John's, Antigua, on 16, 17, 18, 20, 21 April 1994.
Toss: West Indies. Result: MATCH DRAWN.
Debuts: West Indies – S.C.Williams.

WEST INDIES			
P.V.Simmons lbw b Caddick	8	not out	22
S.C.Williams c Caddick b Fraser	3	not out	21
B.C.Lara c Russell b Caddick	375		
J.C.Adams c sub (N.Hussain) b Fraser	59		
K.L.T.Arthurton c Russell b Caddick	47		
S.Chanderpaul not out	75		
†J.R.Murray, W.K.M.Benjamin, C.E.L.Ambrose, K.C.G.Benjamin, *C.A.Walsh — did not bat			
Extras (LB3, NB23)	26		
Total (5 wickets declared)	593	(0 wickets)	43

ENGLAND	
*M.A.Atherton c Murray b Ambrose	135
A.J.Stewart c Ambrose b K.C.G.Benjamin	24
M.R.Ramprakash lbw b K.C.G.Benjamin	19
R.A.Smith lbw b K.C.G.Benjamin	175
G.A.Hick b K.C.G.Benjamin	20
G.P.Thorpe c Adams b Chanderpaul	9
†R.C.Russell c Murray b W.K.M.Benjamin	62
C.C.Lewis not out	75
A.R.Caddick c W.K.M.Benjamin b Adams	22
A.R.C.Fraser b Adams	0
P.C.R.Tufnell lbw b W.K.M.Benjamin	0
Extras (B9, LB20, NB23)	52
Total	593

ENGLAND	O	M	R	W		O	M	R	W
Fraser	43	4	121	2		2	1	2	0
Caddick	47.2	8	158	3		2	1	11	0
Tufnell	39	8	110	0		6	4	5	0
Lewis	33	1	140	0					
Hick	18	3	61	0	(4)	8	2	11	0
Ramprakash					(5)	3	1	5	0
Thorpe					(6)	2	1	1	0
Stewart					(7)	1	0	8	0
WEST INDIES									
Ambrose	40	18	66	1					
Walsh	40	9	123	0					
W.K.M.Benjamin	41.1	15	93	2					
K.C.G.Benjamin	37	7	110	4					
Chanderpaul	24	1	94	1					
Adams	22	4	74	2					
Arthurton	2	1	4	0					

FALL OF WICKETS	WI	E	WI
Wkt	*1st*	*1st*	*2nd*
1st	11	40	–
2nd	12	70	–
3rd	191	373	–
4th	374	393	–
5th	593	401	–
6th	–	417	–
7th	–	535	–
8th	–	585	–
9th	–	589	–
10th	–	593	–

Umpires: S.A.Bucknor (12) and D.B.Hair (*Australia*) (9).
Referee: J.R.Reid (*New Zealand*) (7). Test No. 1255/109 (WI 305/E 701)

WEST INDIES v ENGLAND (FIFTH TEST)

LARA'S INNINGS PLAYED ON 16 - 18 APRIL 1994 AT RECREATION GROUND, ST JOHN'S, ANTIGUA

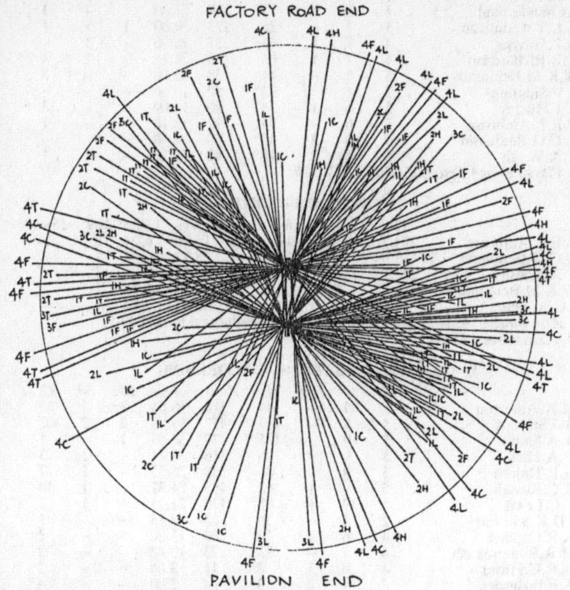

BOWLER	SYMBOL	BALLS	RUNS 1	2	3	4	TOTAL	PER 100 BALLS
FRASER	F	132	18	7	1	11	79	59.8
CADDICK	C	125	19	5	6	9	83	66.4
LEWIS	L	128	21	9	2	15	105	82.0
TUFNELL	T	100	29	6	1	6	68	68.0
HICK	H	51	12	6	-	4	40	78.4
TOTALS		536	99	33	10	45	375	69.9

BRIAN LARA'S WORLD RECORD 375

Copies of this chart, with framing mounts, are available from the compiler in a limited edition of 375.

WEST INDIES v ENGLAND 1993-94

WEST INDIES – BATTING AND FIELDING

	M	I	NO	HS	Runs	Avge	100	50	Ct/St
B.C.Lara	5	8	–	375	798	99.75	2	2	9
J.C.Adams	5	7	1	137	374	62.33	1	2	8
S.Chanderpaul	4	6	1	77	288	57.60	–	4	3
K.L.T.Arthurton	5	7	–	126	273	39.00	1	1	1
D.L.Haynes	4	7	1	63	217	36.16	–	1	–
R.B.Richardson	4	7	1	63	163	27.16	–	1	4
W.K.M.Benjamin	5	6	–	44	138	23.00	–	–	3
P.V.Simmons	2	4	1	22*	50	16.66	–	–	–
J.R.Murray	5	6	1	34	80	16.00	–	–	13
C.E.L.Ambrose	5	6	–	44	91	15.16	–	–	1
K.C.G.Benjamin	5	6	2	43*	58	14.50	–	–	–
C.A.Walsh	5	6	2	18*	42	10.50	–	–	1

Played in one Test: S.C.Williams 3, 21*.

WEST INDIES – BOWLING

	O	M	R	W	Avge	Best	5wI	10wM
C.E.L.Ambrose	224.2	59	519	26	19.96	6-24	2	1
K.C.G.Benjamin	181.5	38	566	22	25.72	6-66	1	–
C.A.Walsh	227.2	44	646	19	34.00	5-94	1	–
W.K.M.Benjamin	190.2	48	498	12	41.50	3-56	–	–
J.C.Adams	49.5	8	173	4	43.25	2-74	–	–

Also bowled: K.L.T.Arthurton 5-1-9-0; S.Chanderpaul 65-10-209-1; P.V.Simmons 3-1-4-0.

ENGLAND – BATTING AND FIELDING

	M	I	NO	HS	Runs	Avge	100	50	Ct/St
M.A.Atherton	5	9	–	144	510	56.66	2	2	3
A.J.Stewart	5	9	–	143	477	53.00	2	2	2
R.A.Smith	5	9	–	175	320	35.55	1	1	1
G.A.Hick	5	9	–	96	316	35.11	–	2	3
G.P.Thorpe	5	9	–	86	239	26.55	–	2	7
R.C.Russell	5	9	1	62	195	24.37	–	1	10
C.C.Lewis	5	9	1	75*	170	21.25	–	1	2
I.D.K.Salisbury	2	4	–	36	63	15.75	–	–	1
A.R.Caddick	4	6	1	29*	69	13.80	–	–	2
M.R.Ramprakash	4	7	–	23	73	10.42	–	–	2
A.R.C.Fraser	4	6	3	8*	11	3.66	–	–	2
A.P.Igglesden	2	4	2	3*	4	2.00	–	–	–
P.C.R.Tufnell	2	2	1	0*	0	0.00	–	–	2

Played in one Test: D.E.Malcolm 6, 18; M.P.Maynard 35, 0 (1ct).

ENGLAND – BOWLING

	O	M	R	W	Avge	Best	5wI	10wM
A.R.C.Fraser	168.5	39	443	16	27.68	8- 75	1	–
A.R.Caddick	170.2	30	545	18	30.27	6- 65	2	–
I.D.K.Salisbury	68	9	276	7	39.42	4-163	–	–
C.C.Lewis	168.3	18	553	14	39.50	4- 61	–	–
P.C.R.Tufnell	113	36	291	4	72.75	3-100	–	–

Also bowled: G.A.Hick 77-14-198-2; A.P.Igglesden 55.3-8-183-3; D.E.Malcolm 28-4-132-3; M.R.Ramprakash 20-3-48-0; A.J.Stewart 3.2-0-13-0; G.P.Thorpe 2-1-1-0.

SOUTH AFRICA v AUSTRALIA (1st Test)

At The Wanderers, Johannesburg, on 4, 5, 6, 7, 8 March 1994.
Toss: South Africa. Result: SOUTH AFRICA won by 197 runs.
Debuts: Australia – M.L.Hayden.

SOUTH AFRICA

A.C.Hudson c Healy b McDermott	17		b Warne	60
G.Kirsten b Hughes	47		c Hughes b May	35
W.J.Cronje c Border b S.R.Waugh	21		c S.R.Waugh b Hughes	122
*K.C.Wessels c Hayden b Hughes	18		c Border b Warne	50
P.N.Kirsten b May	12		c Boon b May	53
J.N.Rhodes c M.E.Waugh b McDermott	69		c Healy b S.R.Waugh	14
B.M.McMillan c Boon b May	0	(8)	b Warne	24
†D.J.Richardson lbw b Warne	31	(9)	c Border b Warne	20
C.R.Matthews c Boon b Hughes	6	(10)	not out	31
P.S.de Villiers b McDermott	16	(7)	b McDermott	4
A.A.Donald not out	0		not out	15
Extras (B1, LB10, NB3)	14		(B13, LB4, NB5)	22
Total	251		(9 wickets declared)	450

AUSTRALIA

M.J.Slater c Hudson b De Villiers	26	(2)	b De Villiers	41
M.L.Hayden c Richardson b Donald	15	(1)	b De Villiers	5
D.C.Boon c De Villiers b Donald	17		b Matthews	83
M.E.Waugh run out	42		c Richardson b Donald	28
*A.R.Border run out	34		c G.Kirsten b McMillan	14
S.R.Waugh not out	45		c Richardson b Matthews	0
†I.A.Healy b Matthews	11		c and b Donald	30
M.G.Hughes c G.Kirsten b McMillan	7		not out	26
S.K.Warne lbw b Matthews	15		lbw b McMillan	1
C.J.McDermott lbw b Donald	31		b McMillan	10
T.B.A.May lbw b De Villiers	2		c G.Kirsten b Cronje	11
Extras (B1, LB1, NB1)	3		(LB5, NB2)	7
Total	248			256

AUSTRALIA	*O*	*M*	*R*	*W*		*O*	*M*	*R*	*W*
McDermott	15.2	3	63	3		35	3	112	1
Hughes	20	6	59	3		25	5	86	1
May	22	5	62	2		39	11	107	2
S.R.Waugh	9	2	14	1		10	3	28	1
Warne	14	4	42	1	(6)	44.5	14	86	4
M.E.Waugh					(5)	6	2	14	0
SOUTH AFRICA									
Donald	19	0	86	3		23	3	71	2
De Villiers	19.3	1	74	2		30	11	70	2
McMillan	14	3	46	1		19	2	61	3
Matthews	15	4	40	2		20	6	42	2
G.Kirsten						4	0	7	0
Cronje						0.3	0	0	1

FALL OF WICKETS

Wkt	*SA 1st*	*A 1st*	*SA 2nd*	*A 2nd*
1st	21	35	76	18
2nd	70	56	123	95
3rd	103	70	258	136
4th	116	136	289	164
5th	126	142	324	164
6th	126	169	343	191
7th	194	176	366	219
8th	203	201	403	225
9th	249	245	406	235
10th	251	248	–	256

Umpires: S.B.Lambson (3) and D.R.Shepherd (*England*) (20).
Referee: D.B.Carr (*England*) (7). Test No. 1256/57 (SA 184/A 537)

SOUTH AFRICA v AUSTRALIA (2nd Test)

At Newlands, Cape Town, on 17, 18, 19, 20, 21 March 1994.
Toss: South Africa. Result: AUSTRALIA won by nine wickets.
Debuts: None.

SOUTH AFRICA			
A.C.Hudson run out	102	lbw b S.R.Waugh	49
G.Kirsten run out	29	lbw b Warne	10
W.J.Cronje b McGrath	2	c and b S.R.Waugh	19
*K.C.Wessels c M.E.Waugh b McDermott	11	run out	9
P.N.Kirsten lbw b Warne	70	c Taylor b Warne	3
J.N.Rhodes lbw b McGrath	5	c Border b S.R.Waugh	27
B.M.McMillan b Warne	74	(8) lbw b S.R.Waugh	3
†D.J.Richardson lbw b McDermott	34	(9) c Healy b McGrath	31
C.R.Matthews not out	7	(10) not out	0
P.S.de Villiers c Taylor b Warne	7	(7) lbw b Warne	0
A.A.Donald c Healy b McGrath	7	b S.R.Waugh	0
Extras (LB6, NB7)	13	(B4, LB6, NB3)	13
Total	361		164

AUSTRALIA			
M.J.Slater c P.N.Kirsten b De Villiers	26	(2) not out	43
M.A.Taylor c Richardson b De Villiers	70	(1) b Donald	14
D.C.Boon c Richardson b De Villiers	96	not out	32
M.E.Waugh c P.N.Kirsten b McMillan	7		
*A.R.Border c Richardson b Matthews	45		
S.R.Waugh b Matthews	86		
†I.A.Healy c De Villiers b Matthews	61		
M.G.Hughes lbw b Matthews	0		
S.K.Warne c McMillan b De Villiers	11		
C.J.McDermott c P.N.Kirsten b Matthews	1		
G.D.McGrath not out	1		
Extras (B6, LB17, W1, NB7)	31	(B1, NB2)	3
Total	435	(1 wicket)	92

AUSTRALIA	O	M	R	W		O	M	R	W	FALL OF WICKETS	SA	A	SA	A
McDermott	27	6	80	2		13	3	39	0	Wkt	1st	1st	2nd	2nd
Hughes	20	1	80	0		5	1	12	0					
McGrath	26.1	4	65	3	(4)	16	6	26	1	1st	71	40	33	30
S.R.Waugh	9	3	20	0	(5)	22.3	9	28	5	2nd	78	145	69	–
Warne	47	18	78	3	(3)	30	13	38	3	3rd	100	153	94	–
M.E.Waugh	10	3	23	0	(7)	3	1	11	0	4th	189	244	97	–
Border	5	2	9	0	(6)	1	1	0	0	5th	198	310	97	–
										6th	260	418	97	–
SOUTH AFRICA										7th	335	418	103	–
Donald	35	10	111	0	(3)	5	0	20	1	8th	339	430	164	–
De Villiers	44.4	11	117	4		6	0	20	0	9th	348	434	164	–
Matthews	36	12	80	5	(1)	6	1	14	0	10th	361	435	164	–
McMillan	29	8	82	1		5	0	23	0					
G.Kirsten	4	0	13	0	(6)	1.1	0	10	0					
Cronje	11	4	9	0	(5)	2	0	4	0					

Umpires: K.E.Liebenberg (3) and D.R.Shepherd (*England*) (21).
Referee: D.B.Carr (*England*) (8). Test No. 1257/58 (SA 185/A 538)

SOUTH AFRICA v AUSTRALIA (3rd Test)

At Kingsmead, Durban, on 25, 26, 27, 28, 29 March 1994.
Toss: South Africa. Result: MATCH DRAWN.
Debuts: None.

AUSTRALIA

M.J.Slater c Rhodes b Matthews	20	(2)	lbw b Donald	95
M.A.Taylor lbw b Donald	1	(1)	lbw b De Villiers	12
D.C.Boon c G.Kirsten b Donald	37		c P.N.Kirsten b Donald	12
M.E.Waugh c Richardson b Donald	43	(5)	not out	113
*A.R.Border c Rhodes b McMillan	17	(6)	not out	42
S.R.Waugh c Wessels b Matthews	64			
†I.A.Healy b Matthews	55			
P.R.Reiffel lbw b De Villiers	13			
S.K.Warne c Wessels b Matthews	2	(4)	c McMillan b Donald	12
C.J.McDermott c Donald b De Villiers	6			
G.D.McGrath not out	0			
Extras (LB1, W1, NB9)	11		(LB6, W1, NB4)	11
Total	269		(4 wickets)	297

SOUTH AFRICA

A.C.Hudson lbw b Reiffel	65
G.Kirsten c Healy b Reiffel	41
W.J.Cronje c S.R.Waugh b Warne	26
*K.C.Wessels lbw b McDermott	1
P.N.Kirsten lbw b S.R.Waugh	49
J.N.Rhodes lbw b Warne	78
B.M.McMillan c Slater b S.R.Waugh	84
†D.J.Richardson c Reiffel b Warne	59
C.R.Matthews lbw b Warne	1
P.S.de Villiers lbw b S.R.Waugh	0
A.A.Donald not out	0
Extras (B3, LB10, NB5)	18
Total	422

SOUTH AFRICA	*O*	*M*	*R*	*W*		*O*	*M*	*R*	*W*
Donald	18	1	71	3		28	7	66	3
De Villiers	24.2	5	55	2		24	5	69	1
Matthews	29	9	65	4	(4)	28	12	56	0
McMillan	19	5	56	1	(3)	22	6	53	0
Cronje	5	1	8	0		18	5	40	0
G.Kirsten	6	1	13	0		3	1	7	0
Rhodes						1	1	0	0
AUSTRALIA									
McDermott	38	11	76	1					
Reiffel	30	7	77	2					
McGrath	41	11	78	0					
Warne	55	20	92	4					
S.R.Waugh	27.2	12	40	3					
M.E.Waugh	11	3	38	0					
Border	3	1	8	0					

FALL OF WICKETS

Wkt	*A 1st*	*SA 1st*	*A 2nd*
1st	7	100	55
2nd	45	117	81
3rd	81	118	109
4th	123	155	157
5th	123	256	–
6th	215	274	–
7th	250	417	–
8th	256	422	–
9th	269	422	–
10th	269	422	–

Umpires: Mahboob Shah (*Pakistan*) (22) and C.J.Mitchley (3).
Referee: D.B.Carr (*England*) (9). Test No. 1258/59 (SA 186/A 539)

SOUTH AFRICA v AUSTRALIA 1993-94

SOUTH AFRICA – BATTING AND FIELDING

	M	I	NO	HS	Runs	Avge	100	50	Ct/St
A.C.Hudson	3	5	–	102	293	58.60	1	2	1
J.N.Rhodes	3	5	–	78	193	38.60	–	2	2
W.J.Cronje	3	5	–	122	190	38.00	1	–	–
P.N.Kirsten	3	5	–	70	187	37.40	–	2	4
B.M.McMillan	3	5	–	84	185	37.00	–	2	2
D.J.Richardson	3	5	–	59	175	35.00	–	1	7
G.Kirsten	3	5	–	47	162	32.40	–	–	4
C.R.Matthews	3	5	3	31*	45	22.50	–	–	–
K.C.Wessels	3	5	–	50	89	17.80	–	1	2
A.A.Donald	3	5	3	15*	22	11.00	–	–	2
P.S.de Villiers	3	5	–	16	27	5.40	–	–	2

SOUTH AFRICA – BOWLING

	O	M	R	W	Avge	Best	5wI	10wM
C.R.Matthews	133	44	297	13	22.84	5- 80	1	–
A.A.Donald	128	21	425	12	35.41	3- 66	–	–
P.S.de Villiers	148.3	33	405	11	36.81	4-117	–	–
B.M.McMillan	108	25	321	6	53.50	3- 61	–	–

Also bowled: W.J.Cronje 36.3-10-61-1; G.Kirsten 18.1-2-50-0; J.N.Rhodes 1-1-0-0.

AUSTRALIA – BATTING AND FIELDING

	M	I	NO	HS	Runs	Avge	100	50	Ct/St
S.R.Waugh	3	4	1	86	195	65.00	–	2	3
M.E.Waugh	3	5	1	113*	233	58.25	1	–	2
D.C.Boon	3	6	1	96	277	55.40	–	2	3
M.J.Slater	3	6	1	95	251	50.20	–	1	1
I.A.Healy	3	4	–	61	157	39.25	–	2	5
A.R.Border	3	5	1	45	152	38.00	–	–	4
M.A.Taylor	2	4	–	70	97	24.25	–	1	2
M.G.Hughes	2	3	1	26*	33	16.50	–	–	1
C.J.McDermott	3	4	–	31	48	12.00	–	–	–
S.K.Warne	3	5	–	15	41	8.20	–	–	–
G.D.McGrath	2	2	2	1*	1	–	–	–	–

Played in one Test: M.L.Hayden 15, 5 (1ct); T.B.A.May 2, 11; P.R.Reiffel 13 (1ct).

AUSTRALIA – BOWLING

	O	M	R	W	Avge	Best	5wI	10wM
S.R.Waugh	77.5	29	130	10	13.00	5-28	1	–
S.K.Warne	190.5	69	336	15	22.40	4-86	–	–
G.D.McGrath	83.1	21	169	4	42.25	3-65	–	–
T.B.A.May	61	16	169	4	42.25	2-62	–	–
C.J.McDermott	128.2	26	370	7	52.85	3-63	–	–
M.G.Hughes	70	13	237	4	59.25	3-59	–	–

Also bowled: A.R.Border 10-3-17-0; P.R.Reiffel 39-7-77-2; M.E.Waugh 30-9-86-0.

NEW ZEALAND v INDIA (Only Test)

At Trust Bank Park, Hamilton, on 19, 20, 21, 22, 23 March 1994.
Toss: New Zealand. Result: MATCH DRAWN.
Debuts: New Zealand – S.P.Fleming.

NEW ZEALAND

B.A.Hartland c Chauhan b Kapil Dev	0	(2)	c Mongia b Srinath	25
B.A.Young c Kumble b Srinath	13	(1)	c Mongia b Chauhan	85
*K.R.Rutherford b Kumble	63		b Chauhan	59
M.J.Greatbatch c Azharuddin b Srinath	12		c Manjrekar b Kumble	27
S.P.Fleming c Kambli b Srinath	16		c Kapil Dev b Chauhan	92
S.A.Thomson c Manjrekar b Raju	12		b Raju	26
†A.C.Parore c and b Chauhan	9		c Mongia b Kapil Dev	17
M.N.Hart b Chauhan	17		not out	20
D.J.Nash not out	10		not out	9
D.K.Morrison lbw b Srinath	3			
C.Pringle b Raju	18			
Extras (LB9, NB5)	14		(B2, LB1, NB5)	8
Total	187		(7 wickets declared)	368

INDIA

†N.R.Mongia run out	45		b Hart	38
N.S.Sidhu b Morrison	10		c Parore b Hart	98
V.G.Kambli c Young b Pringle	9		b Pringle	19
S.R.Tendulkar c Nash b Thomson	43		not out	11
*M.Azharuddin b Thomson	63			
S.V.Manjrekar c Young b Morrison	29	(5)	not out	8
Kapil Dev c Fleming b Nash	18			
A.Kumble c Fleming b Morrison	7			
R.K.Chauhan not out	12			
S.L.V.Raju c Young b Morrison	2			
J.Srinath c Parore b Pringle	1			
Extras (LB6, W1)	7		(LB3)	3
Total	246		(3 wickets)	177

INDIA	*O*	*M*	*R*	*W*		*O*	*M*	*R*	*W*
Srinath	31	8	60	4		33	4	104	1
Kapil Dev	9	2	29	1		16	2	43	1
Kumble	23	8	34	1	(4)	27	6	68	1
Raju	13.2	5	14	2	(3)	24	6	53	1
Chauhan	21	6	41	2		29	5	97	3
NEW ZEALAND									
Morrison	30	9	52	4		8	1	15	0
Nash	20	5	57	1		13	6	25	0
Pringle	22.3	8	52	2	(4)	12	2	29	1
Hart	19	5	33	0	(5)	15	2	66	2
Thomson	11	1	46	2	(3)	11	1	39	0

FALL OF WICKETS

	NZ	*I*	*NZ*	*I*
Wkt	*1st*	*1st*	*2nd*	*2nd*
1st	1	25	56	102
2nd	21	38	172	140
3rd	49	89	176	167
4th	100	138	220	–
5th	122	183	265	–
6th	124	216	317	–
7th	154	226	355	–
8th	155	227	–	–
9th	158	237	–	–
10th	187	246	–	–

Umpires: B.L.Aldridge (22) and Khizer Hayat (*Pakistan*) (29).
Referee: R.Subba Row (*England*) (10). Test No. 1259/32 (NZ 226/I 289)

ENGLAND v NEW ZEALAND (1st Test)

At Trent Bridge, Nottingham, on 2, 3, 4, 5, 6 June 1994.
Toss: New Zealand. Result: ENGLAND won by an innings and 90 runs.
Debuts: England – S.J.Rhodes, C.White; New Zealand – H.T.Davis, G.R.Larsen.

NEW ZEALAND				
B.A.Young c Hick b DeFreitas	15	(2)	c Rhodes b Fraser	53
B.R.Hartland c Hick b DeFreitas	6	(1)	lbw b DeFreitas	22
*K.R.Rutherford lbw b DeFreitas	25		c Atherton b Such	14
M.D.Crowe c Rhodes b White	16		lbw b DeFreitas	28
S.P.Fleming c White b DeFreitas	54		c White b Hick	11
S.A.Thomson c Hick b Fraser	14		c White b Such	6
†A.C.Parore c Rhodes b Malcolm	38		c Rhodes b DeFreitas	42
G.R.Larsen c Fraser b Such	8		c Stewart b DeFreitas	2
M.N.Hart c Hick b Fraser	36		lbw b Fraser	22
D.J.Nash c Rhodes b Malcolm	19		c Rhodes b DeFreitas	5
H.T.Davis not out	0		not out	0
Extras (LB6, NB14)	20		(LB1, NB20)	21
Total (93.4 overs; 404 minutes)	251		(106.3 overs; 428 minutes)	226

ENGLAND	
*M.A.Atherton c Parore b Larsen	101
A.J.Stewart c Larsen b Davis	8
G.A.Gooch c Crowe b Thomson	210
G.A.Hick b Nash	18
R.A.Smith run out	78
C.White c Larsen b Hart	19
†S.J.Rhodes c Thomson b Nash	49
P.A.J.DeFreitas not out	51
A.R.C.Fraser c Fleming b Larsen	8
P.M.Such, D.E.Malcolm } did not bat	
Extras (LB9, W6, NB10)	25
Total (174.4 overs; 692 minutes)	567-8 dec

ENGLAND	*O*	*M*	*R*	*W*		*O*	*M*	*R*	*W*
Malcolm	17.4	5	45	2		10	2	39	0
Fraser	21	10	40	2		23	8	53	2
DeFreitas	23	4	94	4		22.3	4	71	5
Such	19	7	28	1		34	12	50	2
White	13	3	38	1	(6)	3	3	0	0
Hick					(5)	14	6	12	1
NEW ZEALAND									
Davis	21	0	93	1					
Nash	36	5	153	2					
Larsen	44.4	11	116	2					
Hart	35	7	123	1					
Thomson	38	6	73	1					

FALL OF WICKETS	*NZ*	*E*	*NZ*
Wkt	*1st*	*1st*	*2nd*
1st	13	16	59
2nd	37	279	95
3rd	66	314	95
4th	78	375	122
5th	108	414	141
6th	168	482	141
7th	188	528	147
8th	194	567	201
9th	249	–	224
10th	251	–	226

Umpires: H.D.Bird (58) and S.A.Bucknor (*West Indies*) (13).
Referee: C.H.Lloyd (*West Indies*) (7). Test No. 1260/73 (E 702/NZ 227)

ENGLAND v NEW ZEALAND (2nd Test)

At Lord's, London, on 16, 17, 18, 19, 20 June 1994.
Toss: New Zealand. Result: MATCH DRAWN.
Debuts: None.

NEW ZEALAND				
B.A.Young lbw b Fraser	0	(2)	c Hick b Such	94
B.A.Pocock c Smith b Such	10	(1)	lbw b DeFreitas	2
*K.R.Rutherford c Stewart b DeFreitas	37		lbw b DeFreitas	0
M.D.Crowe c Smith b DeFreitas	142		b DeFreitas	9
S.P.Fleming lbw b Fraser	41		lbw b Taylor	39
S.A.Thomson run out	69		not out	38
†A.C.Parore c Rhodes b Taylor	40		not out	15
M.N.Hart b Such	25			
D.J.Nash b White	56			
C.Pringle c Hick b DeFreitas	14			
M.B.Owens not out	2			
Extras (B3, LB15, W1, NB21)	40		(LB4, NB10)	14
Total (149.1 overs; 642 minutes)	476		(68 overs; 296 minutes)	211-5d

ENGLAND			
*M.A.Atherton lbw b Hart	28	c Young b Nash	33
A.J.Stewart c Parore b Nash	45	c Crowe b Nash	119
G.A.Gooch lbw b Nash	13	lbw b Nash	0
R.A.Smith c and b Nash	6	c Parore b Nash	23
G.A.Hick c Young b Pringle	58	lbw b Pringle	37
C.White run out	51	c Thomson b Nash	9
†S.J.Rhodes not out	32	not out	24
P.A.J.DeFreitas c Parore b Thomson	11	lbw b Owens	3
A.R.C.Fraser c and b Nash	10	lbw b Hart	2
J.P.Taylor c Parore b Nash	0	not out	0
P.M.Such c Parore b Nash	4		
Extras (B4, LB12, NB7)	23	(B2, LB1, NB1)	4
Total (121 overs; 461 minutes)	281	(108 overs; 418 minutes)	254-8

ENGLAND	O	M	R	W		O	M	R	W
Fraser	36	9	102	2		15	0	50	0
DeFreitas	35	8	102	3		16	0	63	3
Taylor	20	4	64	1	(6)	6	2	18	1
Such	30	8	84	2	(3)	25	5	55	1
White	21.1	4	84	1	(4)	4	1	21	0
Gooch	5	1	13	0					
Hick	2	0	9	0	(5)	2	2	0	0
NEW ZEALAND									
Owens	7	0	34	0	(2)	10	3	35	1
Nash	25	6	76	6	(1)	29	8	93	5
Pringle	23	5	65	1	(4)	16	5	41	1
Hart	44	21	50	1	(3)	41	23	55	1
Thomson	22	8	40	1		12	4	27	0

FALL OF WICKETS

Wkt	NZ 1st	E 1st	NZ 2nd	E 2nd
1st	0	65	9	60
2nd	39	95	9	60
3rd	67	95	29	136
4th	138	101	144	210
5th	318	193	170	217
6th	350	225	–	240
7th	391	241	–	244
8th	397	265	–	250
9th	434	271	–	–
10th	476	281	–	–

Umpires: S.A.Bucknor (*West Indies*) (14) and N.T.Plews (7).
Referee: C.H.Lloyd (*West Indies*) (8). Test No. 1261/74 (E 703/NZ 228)

ENGLAND v NEW ZEALAND (3rd Test)

At Old Trafford, Manchester, on 30 June, 1, 2, 4, 5 July 1994.
Toss: England. Result: MATCH DRAWN.
Debuts: England – D.Gough.

ENGLAND

*M.A.Atherton lbw b Nash	111
A.J.Stewart c Pringle b Nash	24
G.A.Gooch c Young b Nash	0
R.A.Smith b Owens	13
G.A.Hick c Nash b Owens	20
C.White c Hart b Owens	42
†S.J.Rhodes c Parore b Nash	12
P.A.J.DeFreitas b Owens	69
D.Gough c sub (H.T.Davis) b Pringle	65
A.R.C.Fraser c Thomson b Hart	10
P.M.Such not out	5
Extras (LB8, W1, NB2)	11
Total (146.3 overs; 604 minutes)	382

NEW ZEALAND

B.A.Young c Rhodes b DeFreitas	25		lbw b DeFreitas	8
M.J.Greatbatch c Hick b Gough	0		c DeFreitas b White	21
*K.R.Rutherford c Gooch b DeFreitas	7		c Rhodes b Gough	13
S.P.Fleming c Rhodes b Gough	14		c Hick b Fraser	11
M.D.Crowe c Gooch b White	70		c Hick b DeFreitas	115
M.N.Hart c Atherton b Gough	0	(8)	not out	16
S.A.Thomson c Rhodes b DeFreitas	9	(6)	c Smith b Gough	21
†A.C.Parore c Rhodes b White	7	(7)	c Gooch b DeFreitas	71
D.J.Nash not out	8		not out	6
C.Pringle b White	0			
M.B.Owens c Stewart b Gough	4			
Extras (NB7)	7		(B8, LB13, NB5)	26
Total (57.3 overs; 260 minutes)	151		(106.2 overs; 464 minutes)	308-7

NEW ZEALAND	O	M	R	W		O	M	R	W
Nash	39	9	107	4					
Owens	34	12	99	4					
Pringle	39	12	95	1					
Hart	27.3	9	50	1					
Thomson	7	1	23	0					
ENGLAND									
Fraser	12	3	17	0	(3)	19	7	34	1
Gough	16.3	2	47	4		31.2	5	105	2
DeFreitas	17	2	61	3	(1)	30	6	60	3
Such	5	2	8	0	(5)	10	2	39	0
White	7	1	18	3	(4)	14	3	36	1
Gooch						2	0	13	0

FALL OF WICKETS

	E	NZ	NZ
Wkt	*1st*	*1st*	*2nd*
1st	37	2	8
2nd	37	12	34
3rd	68	47	48
4th	104	82	73
5th	203	93	132
6th	224	113	273
7th	235	125	287
8th	365	140	–
9th	372	140	–
10th	382	151	–

Umpires: S.B.Lambson (*South Africa*) (4) and D.R.Shepherd (22).
Referee: E.de C.Weekes (*West Indies*) (4). Test No. 1262/75 (E 704/NZ 229)

ENGLAND v NEW ZEALAND 1994

ENGLAND – BATTING AND FIELDING

	M	I	NO	HS	Runs	Avge	100	50	Ct/St
M.A.Atherton	3	4	–	111	273	68.25	2	–	2
S.J.Rhodes	3	4	2	49	117	58.50	–	–	12
G.A.Gooch	3	4	–	210	223	55.75	1	–	3
A.J.Stewart	3	4	–	119	196	49.00	1	–	3
P.A.J.DeFreitas	3	4	1	69	134	44.66	–	2	1
G.A.Hick	3	4	–	58	133	33.25	–	1	9
C.White	3	4	–	51	121	30.25	–	1	3
R.A.Smith	3	4	–	78	120	30.00	–	1	3
P.M.Such	3	2	1	5*	9	9.00	–	–	–
A.R.C.Fraser	3	4	–	10	30	7.50	–	–	1

Played in one Test: D.Gough 65; D.E.Malcolm did not bat; J.P.Taylor 0, 0*.

ENGLAND – BOWLING

	O	M	R	W	Avge	Best	5wI	10wM
P.A.J.DeFreitas	143.3	24	451	21	21.47	5-71	1	–
D.Gough	47.5	7	152	6	25.33	4-47	–	–
C.White	62.1	15	197	6	32.83	3-18	–	–
A.R.C.Fraser	126	37	296	7	42.28	2-40	–	–
P.M.Such	123	36	264	6	44.00	2-50	–	–

Also bowled: G.A.Gooch 7-1-26-0; G.A.Hick 18-8-21-1; D.E.Malcolm 27.4-7-84-2; J.P.Taylor 26-6-82-2.

NEW ZEALAND – BATTING AND FIELDING

	M	I	NO	HS	Runs	Avge	100	50	Ct/St
M.D.Crowe	3	6	–	142	380	63.33	2	1	2
A.C.Parore	3	6	1	71	213	42.60	–	1	7
B.A.Young	3	6	–	94	195	32.50	–	2	3
S.A.Thomson	3	6	1	69	157	31.40	–	1	3
D.J.Nash	3	5	2	56	94	31.33	–	1	3
S.P.Fleming	3	6	–	54	170	28.33	–	1	1
M.N.Hart	3	5	1	36	99	24.75	–	–	1
K.R.Rutherford	3	6	–	37	96	16.00	–	–	–
C.Pringle	2	2	–	14	14	7.00	–	–	1
M.B.Owens	2	2	1	4	6	6.00	–	–	–

Played in one Test: H.T.Davis 0*, 0*; M.J.Greatbatch 0, 21; B.R.Hartland 6, 22; G.R.Larsen 8, 2 (2ct); B.A.Pocock 10, 2.

NEW ZEALAND – BOWLING

	O	M	R	W	Avge	Best	5wI	10wM
D.J.Nash	129	28	429	17	25.23	6-76	2	1
M.B.Owens	51	15	168	5	33.60	4-99	–	–
M.N.Hart	147.3	60	278	4	69.50	1-50	–	–

Also bowled: H.T.Davis 21-0-93-1; G.R.Larsen 44.4-11-116-2; C.Pringle 78-22-201-3; S.A.Thomson 79-19-163-2.

ENGLAND v SOUTH AFRICA (1st Test)

At Lord's, London, on 21, 22, 23, 24 July 1994.
Toss: South Africa. Result: SOUTH AFRICA won by 356 runs.
Debuts: England – J.P.Crawley.

SOUTH AFRICA				
A.C.Hudson c Gooch b Gough	6	(2)	lbw b Fraser	3
G.Kirsten c DeFreitas b Hick	72	(1)	st Rhodes b Hick	44
W.J.Cronje c Crawley b Fraser	7		c Fraser b Gough	32
*K.C.Wessels c Rhodes b Gough	105		c Crawley b Salisbury	28
P.N.Kirsten c Rhodes b Gough	8		b Gough	42
J.N.Rhodes b White	32		b Gough	32
B.M.McMillan c Rhodes b Fraser	29		not out	39
†D.J.Richardson lbw b Gough	26		c Rhodes b Fraser	3
C.R.Matthews b White	41		b Gough	25
P.S.de Villiers c Rhodes b Fraser	8			
A.A.Donald not out	5			
Extras (LB9, NB9)	18		(B8, LB10, NB12)	30
Total (118.5 overs; 506 minutes)	357		(102.3 overs; 433 minutes)	278-8d

ENGLAND				
*M.A.Atherton c Wessels b Donald	20		c McMillan b De Villiers	8
A.J.Stewart b Donald	12		c Richardson b Matthews	27
J.P.Crawley c Hudson b De Villiers	9		c Hudson b McMillan	7
G.A.Hick c Richardson b De Villiers	38		lbw b McMillan	11
G.A.Gooch lbw b De Villiers	20		lbw b Donald	28
C.White c Richardson b Donald	10		c Wessels b Matthews	0
†S.J.Rhodes b McMillan	15		not out	14
I.D.K.Salisbury not out	6	(10)	lbw b Donald	0
P.A.J.DeFreitas c Wessels b Donald	20	(8)	c G.Kirsten b Matthews	1
D.Gough c and b Donald	12	(9)	retired hurt	0
A.R.C.Fraser run out	3		lbw b McMillan	1
Extras (B2, LB5, NB8)	15		(B1, LB1)	2
Total (61.3 overs; 279 minutes)	180		(45.5 overs; 221 minutes)	99

ENGLAND	*O*	*M*	*R*	*W*		*O*	*M*	*R*	*W*
DeFreitas	18	5	67	0	(3)	14	3	43	0
Gough	28	6	76	4		19.3	5	46	4
Salisbury	25	2	68	0	(5)	19	4	53	1
Fraser	24.5	7	72	3	(1)	23	5	62	2
Hick	10	5	22	1	(4)	24	14	38	1
White	13	2	43	2		3	0	18	0
SOUTH AFRICA									
Donald	19.3	5	74	5		12	5	29	2
De Villiers	16	5	28	3		12	4	26	1
Matthews	16	6	46	0		14	6	25	3
McMillan	10	1	25	1		6.5	2	16	3
Cronje						1	0	1	0

FALL OF WICKETS	*SA*	*E*	*SA*	*E*
Wkt	*1st*	*1st*	*2nd*	*2nd*
1st	18	19	14	16
2nd	35	41	73	29
3rd	141	68	101	45
4th	164	107	141	74
5th	239	119	208	74
6th	241	136	209	82
7th	281	141	220	85
8th	334	161	278	88
9th	348	176	–	99
10th	357	180	–	–

Umpires: H.D.Bird (59) and S.G.Randell (*Australia*) (16).
Referee: P.J.P.Burge (*Australia*) (8). Test No. 1263/103 (E 705/SA 187)

ENGLAND v SOUTH AFRICA (2nd Test)

At Headingley, Leeds, on 4, 5, 6, 7, 8 August 1994.
Toss: England. Result: MATCH DRAWN.
Debuts: None. ‡ (D.J.Cullinan)

ENGLAND

G.A.Gooch c McMillan b De Villiers	23	c Richardson b Matthews	27
*M.A.Atherton c and b McMillan	99	c sub‡ b De Villiers	17
G.A.Hick c McMillan b De Villiers	25	lbw b McMillan	110
G.P.Thorpe c Rhodes b McMillan	72	run out	73
A.J.Stewart b McMillan	89	not out	36
J.P.Crawley lbw b Matthews	38	c Cronje b McMillan	0
†S.J.Rhodes not out	65		
P.A.J.DeFreitas b Donald	15		
D.Gough run out	27		
A.R.C.Fraser c Cronje b De Villiers	6		
P.C.R.Tufnell did not bat			
Extras (B1, LB5, NB12)	18	(LB1, NB3)	4
Total (160.3 overs; 683 minutes)	477-9 dec	(78.3 overs; 341 minutes)	267-5d

SOUTH AFRICA

A.C.Hudson c Atherton b Gough	9	(2)	c and b Tufnell	12
G.Kirsten c Rhodes b DeFreitas	7	(1)	c Rhodes b DeFreitas	65
†D.J.Richardson b Fraser	48			
W.J.Cronje b DeFreitas	0	(3)	not out	13
*K.C.Wessels c Crawley b Fraser	25	(4)	b Tufnell	7
P.N.Kirsten c Stewart b DeFreitas	104	(5)	not out	8
J.N.Rhodes c Rhodes b Gough	46			
B.M.McMillan b Tufnell	78			
C.R.Matthews not out	62			
P.S.de Villiers st Rhodes b Tufnell	13			
A.A.Donald c Crawley b DeFreitas	27			
Extras (B8, LB7, NB13)	28		(B2, LB2, NB7)	11
Total (133.1 overs; 553 minutes)	447		(60 overs; 216 minutes)	116-3

SOUTH AFRICA	O	M	R	W		O	M	R	W
Donald	29	2	135	1					
De Villiers	39.3	12	108	3	(1)	25	3	98	1
Matthews	39	7	97	1		24	8	53	1
McMillan	37	12	93	3	(2)	15.3	0	66	2
Cronje	16	3	38	0		12	3	39	0
G.Kirsten					(4)	2	1	10	0
ENGLAND									
Gough	37	3	153	2	(2)	10	5	15	0
DeFreitas	29.1	6	89	4	(1)	14	3	41	1
Fraser	31	5	92	2	(4)	7	2	19	0
Tufnell	32	13	81	2	(3)	23	8	31	2
Gooch	3	0	9	0					
Hick	1	0	8	0	(5)	6	3	6	0

FALL OF WICKETS

Wkt	E 1st	SA 1st	E 2nd	SA 2nd
1st	34	13	39	43
2nd	84	31	57	93
3rd	226	31	190	104
4th	235	91	267	–
5th	350	105	267	–
6th	367	199	–	–
7th	394	314	–	–
8th	447	391	–	–
9th	477	410	–	–
10th	–	447	–	–

Umpires: R.S.Dunne (*New Zealand*) (13) and D.R.Shepherd (23).
Referee: P.J.P.Burge (*Australia*) (9). Test No. 1264/104 (E 706/SA 188)

ENGLAND v SOUTH AFRICA (3rd Test)

At Kennington Oval, London, on 18, 19, 20, 21 August 1994.
Toss: South Africa. Result: ENGLAND won by eight wickets.
Debuts: England – J.E.Benjamin. ‡ (T.G.Shaw)

SOUTH AFRICA

G.Kirsten c Rhodes b DeFreitas	2	(2)	c and b Malcolm	0
P.N.Kirsten b Malcolm	16	(1)	c DeFreitas b Malcolm	1
W.J.Cronje lbw b Benjamin	38		b Malcolm	0
*K.C.Wessels lbw b Benjamin	45		c Rhodes b Malcolm	28
D.J.Cullinan c Rhodes b DeFreitas	7		c Thorpe b Gough	94
J.N.Rhodes retired hurt	8	(9)	c Rhodes b Malcolm	10
B.M.McMillan c Hick b DeFreitas	93	(6)	c Thorpe b Malcolm	25
†D.J.Richardson c Rhodes b Benjamin	58	(7)	lbw b Malcolm	3
C.R.Matthews c Hick b Benjamin	0	(8)	c Rhodes b Malcolm	0
P.S.de Villiers c Stewart b DeFreitas	14		not out	0
A.A.Donald not out	14		b Malcolm	0
Extras (B8, LB10, W1, NB18)	37		(LB5, NB9)	14
Total (92.2 overs; 410 minutes)	332		(50.3 overs; 246 minutes)	175

ENGLAND

G.A.Gooch c Richardson b Donald	8	b Matthews	33
*M.A.Atherton lbw b De Villiers	0	c Richardson b Donald	63
G.A.Hick b Donald	39	not out	81
G.P.Thorpe b Matthews	79	not out	15
A.J.Stewart b De Villiers	62		
J.P.Crawley c Richardson b Donald	5		
†S.J.Rhodes lbw b De Villiers	11		
P.A.J.DeFreitas run out	37		
D.Gough not out	42		
J.E.Benjamin lbw b De Villiers	0		
D.E.Malcolm c sub‡ b Matthews	4		
Extras (B1, W1, NB15)	17	(LB6, NB7)	13
Total (77 overs; 373 minutes)	304	(35.3 overs; 180 minutes)	205-2

ENGLAND	O	M	R	W	O	M	R	W
DeFreitas	26.2	5	93	4	12	3	25	0
Malcolm	25	5	81	1	16.3	2	57	9
Gough	19	1	85	0	9	1	39	1
Benjamin	17	2	42	4	11	1	38	0
Hick	5	1	13	0	2	0	11	0
SOUTH AFRICA								
Donald	17	2	76	3	12	1	96	1
De Villiers	19	3	62	4	12	0	66	0
Matthews	21	4	82	2	11.3	4	37	1
McMillan	12	1	67	0				
Cronje	8	3	16	0				

FALL OF WICKETS

Wkt	SA 1st	E 1st	SA 2nd	E 2nd
1st	2	1	0	56
2nd	43	33	1	180
3rd	73	93	1	–
4th	85	145	73	–
5th	136	165	137	–
6th	260	219	143	–
7th	266	222	143	–
8th	301	292	175	–
9th	332	293	175	–
10th	–	304	175	–

Umpires: R.S.Dunne (*New Zealand*) (14) and K.E.Palmer (22).
Referee: P.J.P.Burge (*Australia*) (10). Test No. 1265/105 (E 707/SA 189)

ENGLAND v SOUTH AFRICA 1994

ENGLAND – BATTING AND FIELDING

	M	I	NO	HS	Runs	Avge	100	50	Ct/St
G.P.Thorpe	2	4	1	79	239	79.66	–	3	2
G.A.Hick	3	6	1	110	304	60.80	1	1	2
A.J.Stewart	3	5	1	89	226	56.50	–	2	2
S.J.Rhodes	3	4	2	65*	105	52.50	–	1	14/2
D.Gough	3	4	2	42*	81	40.50	–	–	–
M.A.Atherton	3	6	–	99	207	34.50	–	2	1
G.A.Gooch	3	6	–	33	139	23.16	–	–	1
P.A.J.DeFreitas	3	4	–	37	73	18.25	–	–	2
J.P.Crawley	3	5	–	38	59	11.80	–	–	4
A.R.C.Fraser	2	3	–	6	10	3.33	–	–	1

Played in one Test: J.E.Benjamin 0; D.E.Malcolm 4 (1ct); I.D.K.Salisbury 6*, 0; P.C.R.Tufnell did not bat (1ct); C.White 10, 0.

ENGLAND – BOWLING

	O	M	R	W	Avge	Best	5wI	10wM
D.E.Malcolm	41.3	7	138	10	13.80	9-57	1	1
J.E.Benjamin	28	3	80	4	20.00	4-42	–	–
P.C.R.Tufnell	55	21	112	4	28.00	2-31	–	–
A.R.C.Fraser	85.5	19	245	7	35.00	3-72	–	–
D.Gough	122.3	21	414	11	37.63	4-46	–	–
P.A.J.DeFreitas	113.3	25	358	9	39.77	4-89	–	–

Also bowled: G.A.Gooch 3-0-9-0; G.A.Hick 48-23-98-2; I.D.K.Salisbury 44-6-121-1; C.White 16-2-61-2.

SOUTH AFRICA – BATTING AND FIELDING

	M	I	NO	HS	Runs	Avge	100	50	Ct/St
B.M.McMillan	3	5	1	93	264	66.00	–	2	4
K.C.Wessels	3	6	–	105	238	39.66	1	–	3
P.N.Kirsten	3	6	1	104	179	35.80	1	–	–
J.N.Rhodes	3	5	1	46	128	32.00	–	–	1
C.R.Matthews	3	5	1	62*	128	32.00	–	1	–
G.Kirsten	3	6	–	72	190	31.66	–	2	1
D.J.Richardson	3	5	–	58	138	27.60	–	1	7
A.A.Donald	3	4	2	27	46	23.00	–	–	1
W.J.Cronje	3	6	1	38	90	18.00	–	–	2
P.S.de Villiers	3	4	1	14	35	11.66	–	–	–
A.C.Hudson	2	4	–	12	30	7.50	–	–	2

Played in one Test: D.J.Cullinan 7, 94.

SOUTH AFRICA – BOWLING

	O	M	R	W	Avge	Best	5wI	10wM
B.M.McMillan	81.2	16	267	9	29.66	3-16	–	–
P.S.de Villiers	123.3	27	388	12	32.33	4-62	–	–
A.A.Donald	89.3	15	410	12	34.16	5-74	1	–
C.R.Matthews	125.3	35	340	8	42.50	3-25	–	–

Also bowled: W.J.Cronje 37-9-94-0; G.Kirsten 2-1-10-0.

SRI LANKA v PAKISTAN (1st Test)

At P.Saravanamuttu Stadium, Colombo, on 9, 10, 11, 13 August 1994.
Toss: Pakistan. Result: PAKISTAN won by 301 runs.
Debuts: None.

PAKISTAN			
Saeed Anwar c Jayasuriya b Warnaweera	94	c Dassanayake b Warnaweera	136
Aamir Sohail b Dharmasena	41	c Jayasuriya b Dharmasena	65
Asif Mujtaba c Dassanayake b Dharmasena	44	c Dassanayake b Warnaweera	31
*Salim Malik c Tillekeratne b Dharmasena	1	not out	50
Basit Ali lbw b Warnaweera	27	b Dharmasena	11
Inzamam-ul-Haq c Tillekeratne b Dharmasena	81	not out	7
†Rashid Latif c Dassanayake b Muralitharan	0		
Wasim Akram c Jayasuriya b Dharmasena	37		
Akram Raza c Tillekeratne b Warnaweera	25		
Mushtaq Ahmed not out	5		
Waqar Younis c Gurusinha b Dharmasena	2		
Extras (B11, LB6, NB16)	33	(LB6, NB12)	18
Total	390	(4 wickets declared)	318

SRI LANKA			
R.S.Mahanama b Mushtaq	21	c sub (Zahid Fazal) b Raza	37
S.T.Jayasuriya c Aamir b Wasim	9	c Rashid b Wasim	1
A.P.Gurusinha c Rashid b Mushtaq	11	c Asif b Waqar	8
P.A.de Silva c Aamir b Raza	127	c and b Waqar	5
*A.Ranatunga c and b Mushtaq	9	(6) st Rashid b Raza	41
H.P.Tillekeratne lbw b Waqar	34	(5) c and b Raza	8
†P.B.Dassanayake c Rashid b Wasim	3	b Wasim	24
H.D.P.K.Dharmasena c Aamir b Wasim	1	lbw b Wasim	30
G.P.Wickremasinghe not out	0	b Wasim	4
M.Muralitharan c Asif b Raza	0	not out	20
K.P.J.Warnaweera c and b Raza	4	b Wasim	0
Extras (B1, LB5, NB1)	7	(LB2, NB1)	3
Total	226		181

SRI LANKA	O	M	R	W		O	M	R	W
Wickremasinghe	12	0	59	0		5	0	25	0
Gurusinha	4	1	24	0					
Dharmasena	45.3	13	99	6	(2)	31	2	84	2
Muralitharan	36	6	123	1		11	0	42	0
Warnaweera	28	5	63	3	(3)	31	1	108	2
De Silva	1	0	5	0					
Jayasuriya					(5)	13	0	53	0
PAKISTAN									
Wasim	17	4	30	3		18	4	43	5
Waqar	16	1	84	1		7	0	28	2
Mushtaq	14	2	57	3	(4)	6	1	25	0
Raza	19	7	46	3	(3)	16	3	83	3
Aamir	2	0	3	0					

FALL OF WICKETS	P	SL	P	SL
Wkt	1st	1st	2nd	2nd
1st	65	13	128	1
2nd	180	41	202	30
3rd	181	42	273	38
4th	221	60	298	52
5th	247	179	–	59
6th	260	215	–	118
7th	345	218	–	135
8th	354	222	–	160
9th	387	222	–	181
10th	390	226	–	181

Umpires: K.T.Francis (13) and I.D.Robinson (*Zimbabwe*) (5).
Referee: C.W.Smith (*West Indies*) (5). Test No. 1266/13 (SL 54/P 213)

The 2nd Test at Sinhalese Sports Club Ground, Colombo, scheduled for 18, 19, 20, 22, 23 August, was cancelled because of civil unrest following a general election.

SRI LANKA v PAKISTAN (3rd Test)

At Asgiriya Stadium, Kandy, on 26, 27, 28 August 1994.
Toss: Pakistan. Result: PAKISTAN won by an innings and 52 runs.
Debuts: Sri Lanka – K.R.Pushpakumara, S.Ranatunga, W.P.U.C.J.Vaas; Pakistan – Kabir Khan.

SRI LANKA

R.S.Mahanama c Rashid b Waqar	2	c Inzamam b Waqar	10
D.P.Samaraweera c Rashid b Wasim	6	lbw b Waqar	13
S.Ranatunga c Rashid b Waqar	5	(4) c Wasim b Waqar	4
P.A.de Silva lbw b Wasim	7	(5) c Rashid b Wasim	5
*A.Ranatunga c Saeed b Waqar	0	(6) c Rashid b Waqar	34
H.P.Tillekeratne b Waqar	9	(7) not out	83
R.S.Kalpage c Aamir b Wasim	6	(8) c sub (Ramiz Raja) b Kabir	62
†P.B.Dassanayake not out	19	(3) lbw b Waqar	1
H.D.P.K.Dharmasena lbw b Waqar	0	c sub (Zahid Fazal) b Mushtaq	3
W.P.U.C.J.Vaas c Wasim b Waqar	0	lbw b Mushtaq	4
K.R.Pushpakumara c Aamir b Wasim	6	lbw b Mushtaq	0
Extras (B1, LB4, W5, NB1)	11	(LB6, NB9)	15
Total	71		234

PAKISTAN

Saeed Anwar lbw b Pushpakumara	31
Aamir Sohail c Tillekeratne b Pushpakumara	74
Mushtaq Ahmed run out	0
Asif Mujtaba c Dassanayake b Pushpakumara	17
*Salim Malik c Dassanayake b Dharmasena	22
Basit Ali c and b Dharmasena	53
Inzamam-ul-Haq not out	100
†Rashid Latif c Samaraweera b Dharmasena	7
Wasim Akram c De Silva b Pushpakumara	12
Waqar Younis c Kalpage b Dharmasena	20
Kabir Khan did not bat	
Extras (B4, LB3, W1, NB13)	21
Total (9 wickets declared)	357

PAKISTAN	O	M	R	W	O	M	R	W
Wasim	14.2	4	32	4	26	12	70	1
Waqar	14	4	34	6	18	1	85	5
Kabir					10	1	39	1
Mushtaq					7.3	1	34	3
SRI LANKA								
Vaas	22	2	80	0				
Pushpakumara	26	3	145	4				
Dharmasena	28.5	7	75	4				
Kalpage	11	0	50	0				

FALL OF WICKETS

Wkt	SL 1st	P 1st	SL 2nd
1st	12	94	11
2nd	20	94	13
3rd	22	117	17
4th	28	158	22
5th	28	158	42
6th	43	256	78
7th	45	264	209
8th	46	297	221
9th	46	357	234
10th	71	–	234

Umpires: B.C.Cooray (4) and I.D.Robinson (*Zimbabwe*) (6).
Referee: C.W.Smith (*West Indies*) (6). Test No. 1267/14 (SL 55/P 214)

SRI LANKA v PAKISTAN 1994-95

SRI LANKA – BATTING AND FIELDING

	M	I	NO	HS	Runs	Avge	100	50	Ct/St
H.P.Tillekeratne	2	4	1	83*	134	44.66	–	1	4
P.A.de Silva	2	4	–	127	144	36.00	1	–	1
A.Ranatunga	2	4	–	41	84	21.00	–	–	–
R.S.Mahanama	2	4	–	37	70	17.50	–	–	–
P.B.Dassanayake	2	4	1	24	47	15.66	–	–	6
H.D.P.K.Dharmasena	2	4	–	30	34	8.50	–	–	1

Played in one Test: A.P.Gurusinha 11, 8 (1ct); S.T.Jayasuriya 9, 1 (3ct); R.S.Kalpage 6, 62 (1ct); M.Muralitharan 0, 20*; K.R.Pushpakumara 6, 0; S.Ranatunga 5, 4; D.P.Samaraweera 6, 13 (1ct); W.P.U.C.J.Vaas 0, 4; K.P.J.Warnaweera 4, 0; G.P.Wickremasinghe 0*, 4.

SRI LANKA – BOWLING

	O	M	R	W	Avge	Best	5wI	10wM
H.D.P.K.Dharmasena	105.2	22	258	12	21.50	6- 99	1	–
K.P.J.Warnaweera	59	6	171	5	34.20	6- 63	–	–
K.R.Pushpakumara	26	3	145	4	36.25	4-145	–	–

Also bowled: P.A.de Silva 1-0-5-0; A.P.Gurusinha 4-1-24-0; S.T.Jayasuriya 13-0-53-0; R.S.Kalpage 11-0-50-0; M.Muralitharan 47-6-165-1; G.P.Wickremasinghe 17-0-84-0; W.P.U.C.J.Vass 22-2-80-0.

PAKISTAN – BATTING AND FIELDING

	M	I	NO	HS	Runs	Avge	100	50	Ct/St
Inzamam-ul-Haq	2	3	2	100*	188	188.00	1	1	1
Saeed Anwar	2	3	–	136	261	87.00	1	1	1
Aamir Sohail	2	3	–	74	180	60.00	–	2	5
Salim Malik	2	3	1	50*	73	36.50	–	1	–
Asif Mujtaba	2	3	–	44	92	30.66	–	–	2
Basit Ali	2	3	–	53	91	30.33	–	1	–
Wasim Akram	2	2	–	37	49	24.50	–	–	2
Waqar Younis	2	2	–	20	22	11.00	–	–	1
Mushtaq Ahmed	2	2	1	5*	5	5.00	–	–	1
Rashid Latif	2	2	–	7	7	3.50	–	–	8/1

Played in one Test: Akram Raza 25 (2ct); Kabir Khan did not bat.

PAKISTAN – BOWLING

	O	M	R	W	Avge	Best	5wI	10wM
Wasim Akram	75.2	24	175	13	13.46	5-43	1	–
Waqar Younis	55	6	231	14	16.50	6-34	2	1
Mushtaq Ahmed	27.3	4	116	6	19.33	3-34	–	–
Akram Raza	35	10	129	6	21.50	3-46	–	–

Also bowled: Aamir Sohail 2-0-3-0; Kabir Khan 10-1-39-1.

PAKISTAN v AUSTRALIA (1st Test)

At National Stadium, Karachi, on 28, 29, 30 September, 1, 2 October 1994.
Toss: Australia. Result: PAKISTAN won by one wicket.
Debuts: Australia – M.G.Bevan.

AUSTRALIA

M.J.Slater lbw b Wasim	36	(2)	lbw b Mushtaq	23
*M.A.Taylor c and b Wasim	0	(1)	c Rashid b Waqar	0
D.C.Boon b Mushtaq	19		not out	114
M.E.Waugh c Zahid b Mushtaq	20		b Waqar	61
M.G.Bevan c Aamir b Mushtaq	82		b Wasim	0
S.R.Waugh b Waqar	73		lbw b Wasim	0
†I.A.Healy c Rashid b Waqar	57		c Rashid b Wasim	8
S.K.Warne c Rashid b Aamir	22		lbw b Waqar	0
J.Angel b Wasim	5		c Rashid b Wasim	8
T.B.A.May not out	1		b Wasim	1
G.D.McGrath b Waqar	0		b Waqar	1
Extras (B2, LB12, NB8)	22		(B7, LB4, NB5)	16
Total	337			232

PAKISTAN

Saeed Anwar c M.E.Waugh b May	85		c and b Angel	77
Aamir Sohail c Bevan b Warne	36		run out	34
Zahid Fazal c Boon b May	27		c Boon b Warne	3
*Salim Malik lbw b Angel	26		c Taylor b Angel	43
Basit Ali c Bevan b McGrath	0	(6)	lbw b Warne	12
Inzamam-ul-Haq c Taylor b Warne	9	(8)	not out	58
†Rashid Latif c Taylor b Warne	2	(9)	lbw b S.R.Waugh	35
Wasim Akram c Healy b Angel	39	(7)	c and b Warne	4
Akram Raza b McGrath	13	(5)	lbw b Warne	2
Waqar Younis c Healy b Angel	6		c Healy b Warne	7
Mushtaq Ahmed not out	2		not out	20
Extras (LB7, NB4)	11		(B4, LB13, NB3)	20
Total	256		(9 wickets)	315

PAKISTAN	*O*	*M*	*R*	*W*		*O*	*M*	*R*	*W*
Wasim	25	4	75	3		22	3	63	5
Waqar	19.2	2	75	3		18	2	69	4
Mushtaq	24	2	97	3		21	3	51	1
Raza	14	1	50	0		10	1	19	0
Aamir	5	0	19	1		7	0	19	0
Salim	1	0	7	0					
AUSTRALIA									
McGrath	25	6	70	2		6	2	18	0
Angel	13.1	0	54	3		28	9	92	2
May	20	5	55	2	(5)	18	4	67	0
Warne	27	10	61	3		36.1	12	89	5
S.R.Waugh	2	0	9	0	(3)	15	3	28	1
M.E.Waugh						3	1	4	0

FALL OF WICKETS

Wkt	*A 1st*	*P 1st*	*A 2nd*	*P 2nd*
1st	12	90	1	45
2nd	41	153	49	64
3rd	75	154	171	148
4th	95	157	174	157
5th	216	175	174	174
6th	281	181	213	179
7th	325	200	218	184
8th	335	234	227	236
9th	335	253	229	258
10th	337	256	232	–

Umpires: H.D.Bird (*England*) (60) and Khizer Hayat (30).
Referee: J.R.Reid (*New Zealand*) (8). Test No. 1268/35 (P 215/A 540)

PAKISTAN v AUSTRALIA (2nd Test)

At Rawalpindi Cricket Stadium on 5, 6, 7, 8, 9 October 1994.
Toss: Pakistan. Result: MATCH DRAWN.
Debuts: Australia – D.W.Fleming.

AUSTRALIA

*M.A.Taylor lbw b Mohsin	69	(2)	not out	5
M.J.Slater c Inzamam b Mohsin	110	(1)	b Waqar	1
D.C.Boon b Mushtaq	4		not out	7
M.E.Waugh c Aamir b Mohsin	68			
M.G.Bevan lbw b Waqar	70			
S.R.Waugh b Waqar	98			
†I.A.Healy c Mohsin b Aamir	58			
S.K.Warne c and b Aamir	14			
J.Angel b Wasim	7			
C.J.McDermott not out	9			
D.W.Fleming did not bat				
Extras (B3, LB3, W3, NB5)	14		(LB1)	1
Total (9 wickets declared)	521		(1 wicket)	14

PAKISTAN

Saeed Anwar c S.R.Waugh b McDermott	15	c Healy b M.E.Waugh	75
Aamir Sohail b Fleming	80	c Healy b McDermott	72
Zahid Fazal b Fleming	10	c Healy b M.E.Waugh	1
*Salim Malik b McDermott	33	c Healy b Fleming	237
Aamer Malik lbw b McDermott	11	c Bevan b Fleming	65
Inzamam-ul-Haq lbw b Warne	14	lbw b Fleming	0
†Rashid Latif c Slater b Fleming	18	c Bevan b Taylor	38
Wasim Akram not out	45	c Healy b Angel	5
Mushtaq Ahmed c Warne b McDermott	0	c S.R.Waugh b McDermott	0
Waqar Younis lbw b Fleming	13	lbw b Slater	10
Mohsin Kamal run out	2	not out	0
Extras (B10, LB7, NB2)	19	(B17, LB13, W1, NB3)	34
Total	260		537

PAKISTAN	O	M	R	W		O	M	R	W
Wasim	23.5	3	62	1					
Waqar	32	6	112	2	(1)	5	3	2	1
Mohsin	26	3	109	3					
Mushtaq	36	2	145	1		1	0	1	0
Aamir	21	3	67	2					
Aamer	5	2	16	0					
Salim	1	0	4	0					
Rashid					(2)	2	0	10	0
Saeed					(3)	2	2	0	0
AUSTRALIA									
McDermott	22	8	74	4		33	3	86	2
Fleming	22	3	75	4		26	2	86	3
Warne	21.4	8	58	1	(5)	25	6	56	0
Angel	11	2	36	0	(3)	28	1	124	1
M.E.Waugh					(4)	16	1	63	2
Bevan						4	0	27	0
S.R.Waugh						13	2	41	0
Slater						1.1	0	4	1
Boon						3	1	9	0
Taylor						3	1	11	1

FALL OF WICKETS

Wkt	A 1st	P 1st	P 2nd	A 2nd
1st	176	28	79	2
2nd	181	90	227	–
3rd	198	119	336	–
4th	323	152	469	–
5th	347	155	469	–
6th	456	189	478	–
7th	501	189	495	–
8th	511	198	496	–
9th	521	253	537	–
10th	–	260	537	–

Umpires: K.E.Liebenberg (*South Africa*) (4) and Mahboob Shah (23).
Referee: J.R.Reid (*New Zealand*) (9). Test No. 1269/36 (P 216/A 541)

PAKISTAN v AUSTRALIA (3rd Test)

At Gaddafi Stadium, Lahore, on 1, 2, 3, 4, 5 November 1994.
Toss: Pakistan. Result: MATCH DRAWN.
Debuts: Australia – P.A.Emery. ‡ (Nadeem Khan)

PAKISTAN				
Saeed Anwar b Warne	30	(2)	c Emery b McGrath	32
Aamir Sohail c Emery b McGrath	1	(7)	st Emery b Warne	105
Inzamam-ul-Haq lbw b May	66		c Emery b McDermott	3
*Salim Malik c Bevan b May	75		b Bevan	143
Ijaz Ahmed c Boon b Warne	48		lbw b McGrath	6
Basit Ali c Waugh b Warne	0	(1)	c Emery b McGrath	2
†Moin Khan not out	115	(6)	c McDermott b May	16
Akram Raza b Warne	0		lbw b Warne	32
Mushtaq Ahmed b May	14		c Emery b McGrath	27
Aqib Javed c Waugh b Warne	2		lbw b Warne	2
Mohsin Kamal lbw b Warne	4		not out	0
Extras (B5, LB7, NB6)	18		(B8, LB16, W4, NB8)	36
Total	373			404

AUSTRALIA	
M.J.Slater c Moin b Mohsin	74
*M.A.Taylor c Saeed b Mushtaq	32
D.C.Boon c Moin b Raza	5
†P.A.Emery not out	8
M.E.Waugh c Moin b Mohsin	71
M.G.Bevan c sub‡ b Mushtaq	91
J.L.Langer c Ijaz b Mohsin	69
S.K.Warne c and b Mohsin	33
C.J.McDermott c and b Mushtaq	29
T.B.A.May c Moin b Raza	10
G.D.McGrath b Mushtaq	3
Extras (B3, LB17, W2, NB8)	30
Total	455

AUSTRALIA	O	M	R	W		O	M	R	W
McDermott	24	4	87	0		19	2	81	1
McGrath	24	6	65	1		25.1	1	92	4
Warne	41.5	12	136	6		30	2	104	3
May	29	7	69	3		25	4	60	1
Waugh	2	0	4	0	(6)	6	0	22	0
Bevan					(5)	4	0	21	1
PAKISTAN									
Aqib	31	9	75	0					
Mohsin	28	3	116	4					
Mushtaq	45.1	6	121	4					
Raza	45	9	123	2					

FALL OF WICKETS	P	A	P
Wkt	1st	1st	2nd
1st	8	97	20
2nd	34	106	28
3rd	157	126	60
4th	204	248	74
5th	209	318	107
6th	294	402	303
7th	294	406	363
8th	346	443	384
9th	355	450	394
10th	373	455	404

Umpires: C.J. Mitchley (*South Africa*) (4) and Riazuddin (4).
Referee: J.R.Reid (*New Zealand*) (10). Test No. 1270/37 (P 217/A 542)

PAKISTAN v AUSTRALIA 1994-95

PAKISTAN – BATTING AND FIELDING

	M	I	NO	HS	Runs	Avge	100	50	Ct/St
Salim Malik	3	6	–	237	557	92.83	2	1	–
Aamir Sohail	3	6	–	105	328	54.66	1	2	3
Saeed Anwar	3	6	–	85	314	52.33	–	3	1
Wasim Akram	2	4	1	45*	93	31.00	–	–	1
Inzamam-ul-Haq	3	6	1	66	150	30.00	–	2	1
Rashid Latif	2	4	–	38	93	23.25	–	–	5
Mushtaq Ahmed	3	6	2	27	63	15.75	–	–	1
Akram Raza	2	4	–	32	47	11.75	–	–	–
Zahid Fazal	2	4	–	27	41	10.25	–	–	1
Waqar Younis	2	4	–	13	36	9.00	–	–	–
Basit Ali	2	4	–	12	14	3.50	–	–	–
Mohsin Kamal	2	4	2	4	6	3.00	–	–	2

Played in one Test: Aamir Malik 11, 65; Aqib Javed 2, 2; Ijaz Ahmed 48, 6 (1ct); Moin Khan 115*, 16 (4ct).

PAKISTAN – BOWLING

	O	M	R	W	Avge	Best	5wI	10wM
Wasim Akram	70.5	10	200	9	22.22	5- 63	1	–
Waqar Younis	74.2	13	258	10	25.80	4- 69	–	–
Mohsin Kamal	54	6	225	7	32.14	4-116	–	–
Mushtaq Ahmed	127.1	13	415	9	46.11	4-121	–	–

Also bowled: Aamir Malik 5-2-16-0; Aamir Sohail 33-3-105-3; Akram Raza 69-11-192-2; Aqib Javed 31-9-75-0; Rashid Latif 2-0-10-0; Saeed Anwar 2-2-0-0; Salim Malik 2-0-11-0.

AUSTRALIA – BATTING AND FIELDING

	M	I	NO	HS	Runs	Avge	100	50	Ct/St
M.G.Bevan	3	4	–	91	243	60.75	–	3	5
S.R.Waugh	2	3	–	98	171	57.00	–	2	2
M.E.Waugh	3	4	–	71	220	55.00	–	3	3
D.C.Boon	3	5	2	114*	149	49.66	1	–	3
M.J.Slater	3	5	–	110	244	48.80	1	1	1
I.A.Healy	2	3	–	58	123	41.00	–	2	8
C.J.McDermott	2	2	1	29	38	38.00	–	–	1
M.A.Taylor	3	5	1	69	106	26.50	–	1	3
S.K.Warne	3	4	–	33	69	17.25	–	–	2
J.Angel	2	3	–	8	20	6.66	–	–	1
T.B.A.May	2	3	1	10	12	6.00	–	–	–
G.D.McGrath	2	3	–	3	4	1.33	–	–	–

Played in one Test: P.A.Emery 8* (5ct, 1st); D.W.Fleming did not bat; J.L.Langer 69.

AUSTRALIA – BOWLING

	O	M	R	W	Avge	Best	5wI	10wM
D.W.Fleming	48	5	161	7	23.00	4- 75	–	–
S.K.Warne	181.4	50	504	18	28.00	6-136	2	–
G.D.McGrath	80.1	15	245	7	35.00	4- 92	–	–
T.B.A.May	92	20	251	6	41.83	3- 69	–	–
C.J.McDermott	98	17	328	7	46.85	4- 74	–	–
J.Angel	80.1	12	306	6	51.00	3- 54	–	–

Also bowled: M.G.Bevan 8-0-48-1; D.C.Boon 3-1-9-0; M.J.Slater 1.1-0-4-1; M.A.Taylor 3-1-11-1; M.E.Waugh 27-2-93-2; S.R.Waugh 30-5-78-1.

ZIMBABWE v SRI LANKA (1st Test)

At Harare Sports Club, on 11, 12, 13, 15, 16‡ October 1994.
Toss: Sri Lanka. Result: MATCH DRAWN.
Debuts: None. ‡ (no play)

SRI LANKA

R.S.Mahanama c James b Jarvis	8
A.P.Gurusinha c A.Flower b Whittall	128
S.Ranatunga c James b Whittall	118
P.A.de Silva c and b Jarvis	19
*A.Ranatunga c sub (C.B.Wishart) b Streak	62
H.P.Tillekeratne c James b Whittall	1
†P.B.Dassanayake lbw b Whittall	0
W.P.U.C.J.Vaas lbw b Streak	3
G.P.Wickremasinghe c James b Streak	15
M.Muralitharan c and b Streak	0
K.R.Pushpakumara not out	6
Extras (LB19, W1, NB3)	23
Total	383

ZIMBABWE

G.W.Flower c Dassanayake b Vaas	41
M.H.Dekker c sub (D.P.Samaraweera) b Muralitharan	40
A.D.R.Campbell c Tillekeratne b Wickremasinghe	44
D.L.Houghton c Dassanayake b Vaas	58
*A.Flower c Dassanayake b Vaas	26
G.J.Whittall c Dassanayake b Pushpakumara	4
†W.R.James c Dassanayake b Vaas	18
H.H.Streak c Gurusinha b Muralitharan	8
S.G.Peall not out	9
D.H.Brain not out	6
M.P.Jarvis did not bat	
Extras (B10, LB18, W1, NB36)	65
Total (8 wickets)	319

ZIMBABWE	*O*	*M*	*R*	*W*
Brain	5	2	9	0
Streak	42.5	14	79	4
Jarvis	41	18	76	2
Whittall	33	8	70	4
Peall	50	11	114	0
G.W.Flower	8	2	16	0
SRI LANKA				
Wickremasinghe	26	4	60	1
Vaas	37	11	74	4
Pushpakumara	20	0	68	1
De Silva	6	0	20	0
Muralitharan	32	7	60	2
A.Ranatunga	2	0	9	0

FALL OF WICKETS

Wkt	*SL 1st*	*Z 1st*
1st	28	113
2nd	245	115
3rd	281	202
4th	318	259
5th	322	264
6th	330	274
7th	361	294
8th	376	307
9th	376	–
10th	383	–

Umpires: L.H.Barker (*West Indies*) (20) and I.D.Robinson (7).
Referee: P.L.van der Merwe (*South Africa*) (2). Test No. 1271/1 (Z 8/SL 56)

ZIMBABWE v SRI LANKA (2nd Test)

At Queen's Sports Club, Bulawayo, on 20, 21, 22, 23, 24 October 1994.
Toss: Zimbabwe. Result: MATCH DRAWN.
Debuts: None.

ZIMBABWE

G.W.Flower c Dassanayake b Wickremasinghe	1
M.H.Dekker c Mahanama b Dharmasena	0
A.D.R.Campbell st Dassanayake b Muralitharan	18
D.L.Houghton lbw b Vaas	266
*A.Flower c Muralitharan b Dharmasena	50
G.J.Whittall c Tillekeratne b Wickremasinghe	12
†W.R.James c Dassanayake b Vaas	33
H.H.Streak c Dharmasena b Vaas	0
J.A.Rennie not out	19
S.G.Peall b Vaas	30
M.P.Jarvis did not bat	
Extras (B5, LB11, W2, NB15)	33
Total (9 wickets declared)	462

SRI LANKA

R.S.Mahanama c James b Streak	1		c A.Flower b Streak	4
A.P.Gurusinha c Dekker b Peall	63		c James b Jarvis	10
S.Ranatunga c James b Jarvis	4		not out	100
P.A.de Silva c James b Streak	0	(5)	b Peall	27
*A.Ranatunga c James b Jarvis	34			
H.P.Tillekeratne c Dekker b Jarvis	1		not out	15
†P.B.Dassanayake c James b Streak	8			
H.D.P.K.Dharmasena run out	54	(4)	c James b Whittall	18
W.P.U.C.J.Vaas c Dekker b Whittall	14			
G.P.Wickremasinghe b Whittall	7			
M.Muralitharan not out	15			
Extras (LB4, W1, NB12)	17		(B5, LB6, W4, NB4)	19
Total	218		(4 wickets)	193

SRI LANKA	O	M	R	W		O	M	R	W
Wickremasinghe	39	7	125	2					
Vaas	44.3	14	85	4					
Dharmasena	45	11	109	2					
Muralitharan	55	21	108	1					
De Silva	1	0	4	0					
Gurusinha	4	0	15	0					
ZIMBABWE									
Streak	28	10	68	3		14	4	28	1
Jarvis	34	22	30	3	(4)	24	14	24	1
Rennie	29	10	46	0	(2)	21	10	39	0
Peall	17	7	35	1	(5)	26	10	43	1
Whittall	17.1	6	35	2	(3)	17	7	29	1
G.Flower	1	1	0	0		5	2	13	0
Dekker						6	3	5	0
Campbell						2	1	1	0

FALL OF WICKETS

	Z	*SL*	*SL*
Wkt	*1st*	*1st*	*2nd*
1st	3	4	4
2nd	5	22	30
3rd	65	23	80
4th	186	77	164
5th	223	79	–
6th	323	91	–
7th	335	142	–
8th	419	171	–
9th	462	193	–
10th	–	218	–

Umpires: B.L.Aldridge (*New Zealand*) (23) and I.D.Robinson (8).
Referee: P.L.van der Merwe (*South Africa*) (3). Test No. 1272/2 (Z 9/SL 57)

ZIMBABWE v SRI LANKA (3rd Test)

At Harare Sports Club, on 26, 27, 28, 30, 31 October 1994.
Toss: Sri Lanka. Result: MATCH DRAWN.
Debuts: Zimbabwe – P.A.Strang.

SRI LANKA				
R.S.Mahanama c Dekker b Streak	24	(2)	lbw b Brain	0
A.P.Gurusinha c A.Flower b Brain	54	(1)	c Whittall b Brain	13
S.Ranatunga c Whittall b Strang	43		c Whittall b Streak	8
†H.P.Tillekeratne c Dekker b Strang	116			
P.A.de Silva c Dekker b Streak	25	(4)	not out	41
*A.Ranatunga c Dekker b Streak	39	(5)	not out	22
S.T.Jayasuriya c James b Streak	10			
R.S.Kalpage c James b Brain	14			
H.D.P.K.Dharmasena c A.Flower b Strang	21			
W.P.U.J.C.Vaas not out	16			
K.R.Pushpakumara c A.Flower b Jarvis	8			
Extras (B7, LB11, W4, NB10)	32		(LB2, NB3)	5
Total	402		(3 wickets)	89

ZIMBABWE	
G.W.Flower c Tillekeratne b Pushpakumara	5
M.H.Dekker lbw b Pushpakumara	14
A.D.R.Campbell c Tillekeratne b Pushpakumara	99
D.L.Houghton b Vaas	142
*A.Flower c Tillekeratne b Vaas	10
G.J.Whittall not out	61
†W.R.James c Mahanama b Pushpakumara	2
H.H.Streak c Tillekeratne b Pushpakumara	20
D.H.Brain lbw b Pushpakumara	0
P.A.Strang b Dharmasena	6
M.P.Jarvis b Pushpakumara	2
Extras (LB8, NB6)	14
Total	375

ZIMBABWE	*O*	*M*	*R*	*W*		*O*	*M*	*R*	*W*
Brain	34	4	90	2	(2)	11	1	48	2
Streak	38	8	97	4	(1)	12	4	32	1
Jarvis	37	13	58	1		1	0	7	0
Whittall	28	5	74	0					
Strang	25	6	65	3					
SRI LANKA									
Vaas	44	12	76	2					
Pushpakumara	35.4	7	116	7					
Dharmasena	35	9	71	1					
Gurusinha	13	3	39	0					
Kalpage	12	5	31	0					
Jayasuriya	2	0	12	0					
A.Ranatunga	9	1	22	0					

FALL OF WICKETS	*SL*	*Z*	*SL*
Wkt	*1st*	*1st*	*2nd*
1st	64	10	5
2nd	100	25	24
3rd	149	219	36
4th	192	235	–
5th	267	297	–
6th	280	305	–
7th	329	363	–
8th	366	363	–
9th	380	372	–
10th	402	375	–

Umpires: K.Kanjee (4) and Mahboob Shah (*Pakistan*) (24).
Referee: P.L.van der Merwe (*South Africa*) (4). Test No. 1273/3 (Z 10/SL 58)

ZIMBABWE v SRI LANKA 1994-95

ZIMBABWE – BATTING AND FIELDING

	M	I	NO	HS	Runs	Avge	100	50	Ct/St
D.L.Houghton	3	3	–	266	466	155.33	2	1	–
A.D.R.Campbell	3	3	–	99	161	53.66	–	1	–
S.G.Peall	2	2	1	30	39	39.00	–	–	–
G.J.Whittall	3	3	1	61*	77	38.50	–	1	3
A.Flower	3	3	–	50	86	28.66	–	1	5
M.H.Dekker	3	3	–	40	54	18.00	–	–	7
W.R.James	3	3	–	33	53	17.66	–	–	13
G.W.Flower	3	3	–	41	47	15.66	–	–	–
H.H.Streak	3	3	–	20	28	9.33	–	–	1
D.H.Brain	2	2	1	6*	6	6.00	–	–	–
M.P.Jarvis	3	1	–	2	2	2.00	–	–	1

Played in one Test: J.A.Rennie 19*; P.A.Strang 6.

ZIMBABWE – BOWLING

	O	M	R	W	Avge	Best	5wI	10wM
H.H.Streak	134.5	40	304	13	23.38	4-79	–	–
M.P.Jarvis	137	67	195	7	27.85	3-30	–	–
G.J.Whittall	95.1	26	208	7	29.71	4-70	–	–
D.H.Brain	50	7	147	4	36.75	2-48	–	–

Also bowled: A.D.R.Campbell 2-1-1-0; M.H.Dekker 6-3-5-0; G.W.Flower 14-5-29-0; S.G.Peall 93-18-192-2; J.A.Rennie 50-20-85-0; P.A.Strang 25-6-65-3.

SRI LANKA – BATTING AND FIELDING

	M	I	NO	HS	Runs	Avge	100	50	Ct/St
S.Ranatunga	3	5	1	118	273	68.25	2	–	–
A.P.Gurusinha	3	5	–	128	268	53.60	1	2	1
A.Ranatunga	3	4	1	62	157	52.33	–	1	–
H.P.Tillekeratne	3	4	1	116	133	44.33	1	–	6
H.D.P.K.Dharmasena	2	3	–	54	93	31.00	–	1	1
P.A.de Silva	3	5	1	41*	112	28.00	–	–	–
W.P.U.C.J.Vaas	3	3	1	16*	33	16.50	–	–	–
M.Muralitharan	2	2	1	15*	15	15.00	–	–	1
K.R.Pushpakumara	2	2	1	8	14	14.00	–	–	–
G.P.Wickremasinghe	2	2	–	15	22	11.00	–	–	–
R.S.Mahanama	3	5	–	24	37	7.40	–	–	2
P.B.Dassanayake	2	2	–	8	8	4.00	–	–	7/1

Played in one Test: S.T.Jayasuriya 10; R.S.Kalpage 14.

SRI LANKA – BOWLING

	O	M	R	W	Avge	Best	5wI	10wM
K.R.Pushpakumara	55.4	7	184	8	23.00	7-116	1	–
W.P.U.C.J.Vaas	125.3	37	235	10	23.50	4- 74	–	–

Also bowled: P.A.de Silva 7-0-24-0; H.D.P.K.Dharmasena 80-20-180-3; A.P.Gurusinha 17-3-54-0; S.T.Jayasuriya 2-0-12-0; R.S.Kalpage 12-5-31-0; M.Muralitharan 87-28-168-3; A.Ranatunga 11-1-31-0; G.P.Wickremasinghe 65-11-185-3.

INDIA v WEST INDIES (1st Test)

At Wankhede Stadium, Bombay, on 18, 19, 20, 21, 22 November 1994.
Toss: India. Result: INDIA won by 96 runs.
Debuts: West Indies – C.E.Cuffy, R.Dhanraj.

INDIA

M.Prabhakar c Adams b Walsh	0		c Hooper b Benjamin	7
N.S.Sidhu lbw b Walsh	18		lbw b Benjamin	12
V.G.Kambli c Murray b Walsh	40	(4)	c Hooper b Benjamin	0
S.R.Tendulkar lbw b Walsh	34	(5)	c Murray b Hooper	85
*M.Azharuddin c Simmons b Benjamin	0	(6)	c Arthurton b Hooper	17
S.V.Manjrekar c Lara b Dhanraj	51	(7)	c Cuffy b Walsh	66
†N.R.Mongia c Murray b Benjamin	80	(3)	c Adams b Benjamin	0
A.Kumble c Hooper b Walsh	19		c Hooper b Cuffy	42
S.L.V.Raju c Hooper b Walsh	4	(11)	not out	3
R.K.Chauhan c Williams b Benjamin	1		c Murray b Walsh	4
J.Srinath not out	0	(9)	st Murray b Dhanraj	60
Extras (B5, LB7, NB13)	25		(B12, LB14, NB11)	37
Total	272			333

WEST INDIES

P.V.Simmons c Manjrekar b Srinath	19	c Mongia b Prabhakar	0
S.C.Williams c Azharuddin b Chauhan	49	lbw b Srinath	11
B.C.Lara b Raju	14	b Prabhakar	0
C.L.Hooper c Tendulkar b Raju	28	c Mongia b Srinath	23
K.L.T.Arthurton c Tendulkar b Raju	42	c Azharuddin b Raju	20
J.C.Adams c Kambli b Raju	39	lbw b Srinath	81
†J.R.Murray lbw b Raju	23	b Chauhan	85
R.Dhanraj c Mongia b Kumble	1	c Tendulkar b Raju	4
K.C.G.Benjamin c Srinath b Kumble	0	c Azharuddin b Raju	2
*C.A.Walsh not out	2	c and b Srinath	11
C.E.Cuffy c and b Kumble	0	not out	0
Extras (B11, LB12, NB3)	26	(B13, LB10, NB6)	29
Total	243		266

WEST INDIES	*O*	*M*	*R*	*W*		*O*	*M*	*R*	*W*
Walsh	22	4	79	6		28	6	64	2
Benjamin	21.3	8	48	3		24	3	82	4
Cuffy	18	4	63	0	(5)	12	2	46	1
Hooper	9	0	23	0		24	4	69	2
Dhanraj	15	1	47	1	(3)	10	0	46	1
INDIA									
Prabhakar	4	0	18	0		3	0	17	2
Srinath	13	5	37	1		20	8	48	4
Kumble	23.5	7	48	3	(4)	12	1	39	0
Chauhan	21	7	57	1	(5)	15	3	45	1
Raju	21	7	60	5	(3)	28.4	4	85	3
Tendulkar						3	0	9	0

FALL OF WICKETS

Wkt	*I 1st*	*WI 1st*	*I 2nd*	*WI 2nd*
1st	0	34	8	1
2nd	49	82	10	2
3rd	96	120	11	26
4th	99	120	43	48
5th	99	194	88	82
6th	235	230	162	244
7th	265	241	237	246
8th	271	241	265	252
9th	272	242	309	266
10th	272	243	333	266

Umpires: S.K.Bansal (3) and H.D.Bird (*England*) (61).
Referee: R.Subba Row (*England*) (11). Test No. 1274/63 (I 290/WI 306)

INDIA v WEST INDIES (2nd Test)

At Vidarbha C.A. Ground, Nagpur, on 1, 2, 3, 4, 5 December 1994.
Toss: India. Result: MATCH DRAWN.
Debuts: None.

INDIA

M.Prabhakar c Williams b Hooper	19		c Lara b Walsh	6
N.S.Sidhu c Murray b Hooper	107		c Simmons b Hooper	76
V.G.Kambli c Williams b Hooper	0		b Walsh	6
S.R.Tendulkar c Lara b Walsh	179		c Arthurton b Benjamin	54
S.L.V.Raju c Adams b Walsh	2			
*M.Azharuddin c Simmons b Hooper	97	(5)	not out	32
S.V.Manjrekar c Simmons b Hooper	0	(6)	c Murray b Benjamin	5
†N.R.Mongia c Hooper b Cummins	44		run out	11
A.Kumble not out	52		not out	3
J.Srinath c and b Chanderpaul	6	(7)	lbw b Hooper	1
R.K.Chauhan not out	1			
Extras (B12, LB9, NB18)	39		(B3, LB5, NB6)	14
Total (9 wickets declared)	546		(7 wickets declared)	208

WEST INDIES

P.V.Simmons c Manjrekar b Kumble	50		c Sidhu b Kumble	8
S.C.Williams c Azharuddin b Chauhan	12		b Raju	8
A.C.Cummins c Manjrekar b Raju	17			
B.C.Lara c Mongia b Raju	50	(3)	c Tendulkar b Raju	3
J.C.Adams not out	125	(4)	c Tendulkar b Kumble	23
C.L.Hooper c Prabhakar b Srinath	81	(5)	c Azharuddin b Kumble	67
K.L.T.Arthurton c Azharuddin b Raju	7	(6)	not out	7
S.Chanderpaul c Azharuddin b Raju	4	(7)	not out	11
†J.R.Murray lbw b Raju	54			
K.C.G.Benjamin lbw b Kumble	0			
*C.A.Walsh b Kumble	1			
Extras (B5, LB14, NB8)	27		(B2, NB3)	5
Total	428		(5 wickets)	132

WEST INDIES	*O*	*M*	*R*	*W*		*O*	*M*	*R*	*W*
Walsh	32	7	93	2		5.5	3	2	2
Benjamin	26	4	120	0		13.4	1	69	2
Cummins	27	1	96	1	(5)	15	0	57	0
Hooper	40	8	116	5	(3)	25.1	6	62	2
Chanderpaul	20	4	63	1					
Adams	10	2	37	0	(4)	4	2	10	0
INDIA									
Prabhakar	4	1	15	0					
Srinath	14	2	39	1	(1)	7	2	12	0
Chauhan	34	9	97	1	(4)	5	3	15	0
Raju	50	11	127	5	(3)	27	4	58	2
Kumble	51	15	131	3	(2)	23	7	45	3

FALL OF WICKETS

	I	*WI*	*I*	*WI*
Wkt	*1st*	*1st*	*2nd*	*2nd*
1st	48	15	9	18
2nd	49	61	24	18
3rd	226	98	152	22
4th	230	155	157	112
5th	432	288	163	115
6th	434	306	174	–
7th	444	320	193	–
8th	537	417	–	–
9th	543	422	–	–
10th	–	428	–	–

Umpires: N.T.Plews (*England*) (8) and V.K.Ramaswamy (15).
Referee: R.Subba Row (*England*) (12). Test No. 1275/64 (I 291/WI 307)

INDIA v WEST INDIES (3rd Test)

At Punjab C.A. Stadium, Mohali, Chandigarh, on 10, 11, 12, 13, 14 December 1994.
Toss: West Indies. Result: WEST INDIES won by 243 runs.
Debuts: India – A.R.Kapoor. ‡ (S.L.Campbell)

WEST INDIES

P.V.Simmons c Mongia b Srinath	10		run out	25
S.C.Williams lbw b Kumble	34			
B.C.Lara lbw b Srinath	40	(2)	c Mongia b Raju	91
J.C.Adams not out	174		not out	78
C.L.Hooper st Manjrekar b Kapoor	43	(3)	lbw b Raju	20
K.L.T.Arthurton c Kapoor b Raju	18	(5)	not out	70
†J.R.Murray lbw b Kumble	31			
A.C.Cummins lbw b Raju	50			
*C.A.Walsh lbw b Kumble	4			
K.C.G.Benjamin lbw b Kumble	0			
C.E.Cuffy b Raju	1			
Extras (B6, LB13, W5, NB14)	38		(B10, LB4, NB3)	17
Total	443		(3 wickets declared)	301

INDIA

M.Prabhakar c Murray b Walsh	120		retired hurt	0
N.S.Sidhu b Walsh	0		lbw b Benjamin	11
S.V.Manjrekar lbw b Benjamin	40		c Murray b Walsh	17
S.R.Tendulkar c Williams b Cuffy	40		c Arthurton b Benjamin	10
*M.Azharuddin c Williams b Cummins	27		c Cummins b Benjamin	5
V.G.Kambli c Simmons b Benjamin	18		c sub‡ b Benjamin	0
A.R.Kapoor c Simmons b Cuffy	15	(8)	c Murray b Walsh	1
†N.R.Mongia hit wicket b Cummins	34	(7)	c Williams b Walsh	14
A.Kumble c Hooper b Cuffy	0		b Benjamin	1
J.Srinath not out	52		not out	17
S.L.V.Raju c Murray b Benjamin	15		c Murray b Cuffy	16
Extras (B5, LB3, W1, NB17)	26		(B1, LB13, NB8)	22
Total	387			114

INDIA	*O*	*M*	*R*	*W*		*O*	*M*	*R*	*W*
Prabhakar	18	3	65	0		9	1	34	0
Srinath	32	2	106	2		20	0	95	0
Raju	33.4	5	73	3	(4)	12.3	0	60	2
Kapoor	30	4	90	1	(5)	7	1	32	0
Kumble	29	3	90	4	(3)	7	0	56	0
Tendulkar						1	0	10	0
WEST INDIES									
Walsh	35	4	89	2		18	7	34	3
Benjamin	35.3	8	106	3		17	3	65	5
Cuffy	22	4	80	3		0.2	0	1	1
Cummins	16	2	45	2					
Hooper	17	1	50	0					
Adams	3	1	9	0					

FALL OF WICKETS

	WI	*I*	*WI*	*I*
Wkt	*1st*	*1st*	*2nd*	*2nd*
1st	36	1	85	17
2nd	93	104	135	44
3rd	103	168	156	46
4th	195	228	–	48
5th	220	262	–	66
6th	269	265	–	66
7th	368	305	–	68
8th	406	310	–	68
9th	422	323	–	114
10th	443	387	–	–

Umpires: R.S.Dunne (*New Zealand*) (15) and S.Venkataraghavan (7).
Referee: R.Subba Row (*England*) (13). Test No. 1276/65 (I 292/WI 308)

INDIA v WEST INDIES 1994-95

INDIA – BATTING AND FIELDING

	M	*I*	*NO*	*HS*	*Runs*	*Avge*	*100*	*50*	*Ct/St*
S.R.Tendulkar	3	6	–	179	402	67.00	1	2	5
J.Srinath	3	6	3	60	136	45.33	–	2	2
N.S.Sidhu	3	6	–	107	224	37.33	1	1	1
M.Azharuddin	3	6	1	97	178	35.60	–	1	7
N.R.Mongia	3	6	–	80	183	30.50	–	1	6
M.Prabhakar	3	6	1	120	152	30.40	1	–	1
S.V.Manjrekar	3	6	–	66	179	29.83	–	2	3
A.Kumble	3	6	2	52*	117	29.25	–	1	1
V.G.Kambli	3	6	–	40	64	10.66	–	–	1
S.L.V.Raju	3	5	1	16	40	10.00	–	–	–
R.K.Chauhan	2	3	1	4	6	3.00	–	–	–

Played in one Test: A.R.Kapoor 15, 1 (1ct).

INDIA – BOWLING

	O	*M*	*R*	*W*	*Avge*	*Best*	*5wI*	*10wM*
S.L.V.Raju	172.5	31	463	20	23.15	5-60	2	–
A.Kumble	145.5	33	409	13	31.46	4-90	–	–
J.Srinath	106	19	337	8	42.12	4-48	–	–

Also bowled: R.K.Chauhan 75-22-214-3; A.R.Kapoor 37-5-122-1; M.Prabhakar 38-5-149-2; S.R.Tendulkar 4-0-19-0.

WEST INDIES – BATTING AND FIELDING

	M	*I*	*NO*	*HS*	*Runs*	*Avge*	*100*	*50*	*Ct/St*
J.C.Adams	3	6	3	174*	520	173.33	2	2	3
J.R.Murray	3	4	–	85	193	48.25	–	2	11/1
C.L.Hooper	3	6	–	81	262	43.66	–	2	7
K.L.T.Arthurton	3	6	2	70*	164	41.00	–	1	3
A.C.Cummins	2	2	–	50	67	33.50	–	1	1
B.C.Lara	3	6	–	91	198	33.00	–	2	3
S.C.Williams	3	5	–	49	114	22.80	–	–	6
P.V.Simmons	3	6	–	50	112	18.66	–	1	6
C.A.Walsh	3	4	1	11	18	6.00	–	–	–
K.C.G.Benjamin	3	4	–	2	2	0.50	–	–	–
C.E.Cuffy	2	3	1	1	1	0.50	–	–	1

Played in one Test: S.Chanderpaul 4, 11* (1ct); R.Dhanraj 1, 4.

WEST INDIES – BOWLING

	O	*M*	*R*	*W*	*Avge*	*Best*	*5wI*	*10wM*
C.A.Walsh	140.5	31	361	17	21.23	6- 79	1	–
K.C.G.Benjamin	137.4	27	490	17	28.82	5- 65	1	–
C.L.Hooper	115.1	19	320	9	35.55	5-116	1	–
C.E.Cuffy	52.2	10	190	5	38.00	3- 80	–	–

Also bowled: J.C.Adams 17-5-56-0; S.Chanderpaul 20-4-63-1; A.C.Cummins 58-3-198-3; R.Dhanraj 25-1-93-2.

NO ASHES FOR ATHERTON

Ambushed by an extraordinary catalogue of illness and injury, Michael Atherton's expedition was defeated 3-1 by an Australian team which made fewer mistakes, played for each other and proved comprehensively tougher both mentally and physically. Apart from one world-class player, Shane Warne, at full strength the two sides were evenly matched. In terms of organisation and motivation they often seemed poles apart. After two heavy defeats, England fought back well and could easily have arrived at Perth all-square. There an avalanche of shelled catches buried their slim hopes and only the batting of Ramprakash earned any respect.

In addition to the varied maladies which affected practically every member of a touring party eventually so extended by replacements that few could remember the originally selected 16, England were the victims of an ill-conceived match schedule, a confused selection policy, some abysmal umpiring and a management which appeared to have little empathy with either its players or the media.

Few sides could have withstood the loss of key players such as Gough, Hick, Malcolm and Stewart for a combined tally of eight Tests. Malcolm's bout of chicken-pox proved especially catastrophic as it rendered him unfit for the first Test. Once Taylor had won a crucial toss on an underprepared pitch, his batsmen were able to feast on some of the feeblest new-ball bowling seen in any Ashes match. Gough's effervescence enlivened the three matches in which he played before fracturing a bone in his foot. He uplifted a dour team and the Australian crowds took him to their hearts. Here was a character in the Botham mould who visibly relished the big occasion and took the fight to the enemy. His injury was a tragedy for the tour.

England's original selection was based on the erroneous theory that most of Australia's Test pitches have pace and bounce. Apart from Perth, that is no longer the case. Even after an indifferent season in which his best first-class performance was 3 for 16, Fraser should have been selected ahead of either McCague or Benjamin by virtue of his accuracy, wholehearted commitment and experience. The choice of Gatting was surprising in view of his moderate tour of India two years earlier and the presence in the party of Gooch, another elder statesman. No longer the fleet-footed plunderer of slow bowling, he was quite unable to dominate the spinners and, like Gooch, was frequently undone by the pace and movement of McDermott. Although both men trained and practised harder than most of their younger colleagues, and it was good to see Gatting's tenacity rewarded with a hundred at Adelaide, they proved liabilities in the field. With the accent now on speed and agility in the field and between the wickets, it is extremely unlikely that anyone will again prolong a Test career beyond his mid-thirties.

Very much his own man and by his own admission unhappy with some of the tour selections, Atherton fought on while colleagues fell around him both metaphorically and physically. His defensive technique now approaches the Boycott level and he has abundant powers of concentration. He was admirably self-critical of his own shortcomings as a captain and, if the learning curve appeared stationary at times, it has definitely moved on. Thorpe (444 runs at 49) and Gough (20 wickets at 21 in three Tests) were the undoubted successes. DeFreitas played the innings of his life to pave the way for that astonishing win at Adelaide. Replacements Fraser, Lewis and Ramprakash rekindled their international careers but poor Rhodes was unrecognisable as the star of last summer. Such is the fickle fortune of cricket.

Watched by substantial crowds at every venue, the series did wonders for traditional cricket 'Down Under' and there was not a single dull session in the entire series.

AUSTRALIA v ENGLAND (1st Test)

At Woolloongabba, Brisbane, on 25, 26, 27, 28, 29 November 1994.
Toss: Australia. Result: AUSTRALIA won by 184 runs.
Debuts: None. ‡ (C.White)

AUSTRALIA				
M.J.Slater c Gatting b Gooch	176	(2)	lbw b Gough	45
*M.A.Taylor run out	59	(1)	c Stewart b Tufnell	58
D.C.Boon b Gough	3		b Tufnell	28
M.E.Waugh c Stewart b Gough	140		b Tufnell	15
M.G.Bevan c Hick b Gough	7		b Rhodes b DeFreitas	21
S.K.Warne c Rhodes b Gough	2	(8)	c sub‡ b DeFreitas	0
S.R.Waugh c Hick b DeFreitas	19	(6)	c sub‡ b Tufnell	7
†I.A.Healy c Hick b DeFreitas	7	(7)	not out	45
C.J.McDermott c Gough b McCague	2		c Rhodes b Gough	6
T.B.A.May not out	3		not out	9
G.D.McGrath c Gough b McCague	0			
Extras (B5, LB2, NB1)	8		(B2, LB9, W2, NB1)	14
Total (120.2 overs; 504 minutes)	426		(88 overs; 357 minutes)	248-8d

ENGLAND				
*M.A.Atherton c Healy b McDermott	54		lbw b Warne	23
A.J.Stewart c Healy b McDermott	16		b Warne	33
G.A.Hick c Healy b McDermott	3		c Healy b Warne	80
G.P.Thorpe c and b Warne	28		b Warne	67
G.A.Gooch c Healy b May	20		c Healy b Warne	56
M.W.Gatting lbw b McDermott	10		c Healy b McDermott	13
M.J.McCague b McDermott	1	(10)	lbw b Warne	0
†S.J.Rhodes lbw b McDermott	4	(7)	c Healy b McDermott	2
P.A.J.DeFreitas c Healy b Warne	7	(8)	b Warne	11
D.Gough not out	17	(9)	c M.E.Waugh b Warne	10
P.C.R.Tufnell c Taylor b Warne	0		not out	2
Extras (LB1, NB6)	7		(B9, LB5, NB12)	26
Total (67.2 overs; 271 minutes)	167		(137.2 overs; 523 minutes)	323

ENGLAND	*O*	*M*	*R*	*W*		*O*	*M*	*R*	*W*
DeFreitas	31	8	102	2		22	1	74	2
McCague	19.2	4	96	2					
Gough	32	7	107	4	(2)	23	3	78	2
Tufnell	25	3	72	0	(3)	38	10	79	4
Hick	4	0	22	0		2	1	1	0
Gooch	9	2	20	1	(4)	3	2	5	0
AUSTRALIA									
McDermott	19	3	53	6		23	4	90	2
McGrath	10	2	40	0		19	4	61	0
May	17	3	34	1	(4)	35	16	59	0
Warne	21.2	7	39	3	(3)	50.2	22	71	8
M.E.Waugh						7	1	17	0
Bevan						3	0	11	0

FALL OF WICKETS	*A*	*E*	*A*	*E*
Wkt	*1st*	*1st*	*2nd*	*2nd*
1st	99	22	109	50
2nd	126	35	117	59
3rd	308	82	139	219
4th	326	105	174	220
5th	352	131	183	250
6th	379	133	190	280
7th	407	140	191	309
8th	419	147	201	310
9th	425	151	–	310
10th	426	167	–	323

Umpires: C.J.Mitchley (*South Africa*) (5) and S.G.Randell (17).
Referee: J.R.Reid (*New Zealand*) (11). Test No. 1277/281 (A 543/E 708)

AUSTRALIA v ENGLAND (2nd Test)

At Melbourne Cricket Ground, on 24, 26, 27, 28, 29 December 1994.
Toss: England. Result: AUSTRALIA won by 295 runs.
Debuts: None. ‡ (J.P.Crawley)

AUSTRALIA

M.J.Slater run out	3	(2)	st Rhodes b Tufnell	44
*M.A.Taylor lbw b DeFreitas	9	(1)	lbw b Gough	19
D.C.Boon c Hick b Tufnell	41		lbw b DeFreitas	131
M.E.Waugh c Thorpe b DeFreitas	71		c and b Gough	29
M.G.Bevan c Atherton b Gough	3		c sub‡ b Tufnell	35
S.R.Waugh not out	94		not out	26
†I.A.Healy c Rhodes b Tufnell	17		c Thorpe b Tufnell	17
S.K.Warne c Hick b Gough	6		c DeFreitas b Gough	0
T.B.A.May lbw b Gough	9			
C.J.McDermott b Gough	0	(9)	not out	2
D.W.Fleming c Hick b Malcolm	16			
Extras (LB7, NB3)	10		(B1, LB9, W1, NB6)	17
Total (107.3 overs; 471 minutes)	279		(124 overs; 533 minutes)	320-7d

ENGLAND

*M.A.Atherton lbw b Warne	44	(2)	c Healy b McDermott	25
A.J.Stewart c and b Warne	16	(7)	not out	8
G.A.Hick c Healy b McDermott	23		b Fleming	2
G.P.Thorpe c M.E.Waugh b Warne	51		c Healy b McDermott	9
G.A.Gooch c and b McDermott	15	(1)	c Healy b Fleming	2
M.W.Gatting c S.R.Waugh b Warne	9	(5)	c Taylor b McDermott	25
D.Gough c Healy b McDermott	20	(9)	c Healy b Warne	0
†S.J.Rhodes c M.E.Waugh b Warne	0	(6)	c M.E.Waugh b McDermott	16
P.A.J.DeFreitas c Healy b Warne	14	(8)	lbw b Warne	0
D.E.Malcolm not out	11		c Boon b Warne	0
P.C.R.Tufnell run out (Taylor/Healy)	0		c Healy b McDermott	0
Extras (LB7, NB2)	9		(LB2, NB3)	5
Total (83.4 overs; 340 minutes)	212		(42.5 overs; 184 minutes)	92

ENGLAND	*O*	*M*	*R*	*W*		*O*	*M*	*R*	*W*
Malcolm	28.3	4	78	1		22	3	86	0
DeFreitas	23	4	66	2		26	2	70	1
Gough	26	9	60	4	(4)	25	6	59	3
Tufnell	28	7	59	2	(3)	48	8	90	3
Hick	2	0	9	0		3	2	5	0
AUSTRALIA									
McDermott	24	6	72	3		16.5	5	42	5
Fleming	11	5	30	0		9	1	24	2
M.E.Waugh	3	1	11	0					
Warne	27.4	8	64	6	(3)	13	6	16	3
May	18	5	28	0	(4)	4	1	8	0

FALL OF WICKETS

	A	*E*	*A*	*E*
Wkt	*1st*	*1st*	*2nd*	*2nd*
1st	10	40	61	3
2nd	39	119	81	10
3rd	91	124	157	23
4th	100	140	269	43
5th	171	148	275	81
6th	208	151	316	88
7th	220	185	317	91
8th	242	189	–	91
9th	242	207	–	91
10th	279	212	–	92

Umpires: S.A.Bucknor (*West Indies*) (15) and S.G.Randell (18).
Referee: J.R.Reid (*New Zealand*) (12). Test No. 1278/282 (A 544/E 709)

AUSTRALIA v ENGLAND (3rd Test)

At Sydney Cricket Ground, on 1, 2, 3, 4, 5 January 1995.
Toss: England. Result: MATCH DRAWN.
Debuts: None.

ENGLAND

G.A.Gooch c Healy b Fleming	1		lbw b Fleming	29
*M.A.Atherton b McDermott	88		c Taylor b Fleming	67
G.A.Hick b McDermott	2		not out	98
G.P.Thorpe lbw b McDermott	10		not out	47
J.P.Crawley c M.E.Waugh b Fleming	72			
M.W.Gatting c Healy b McDermott	0			
A.R.C.Fraser c Healy b Fleming	27			
†S.J.Rhodes run out	1			
D.Gough c Fleming b McDermott	51			
D.E.Malcolm b Warne	29			
P.C.R.Tufnell not out	4			
Extras (B8, LB7, NB9)	24		(LB6, W1, NB7)	14
Total (119.2 overs; 478 minutes)	309		(72 overs; 317 minutes)	255-2d

AUSTRALIA

M.J.Slater b Malcolm	11	(2)	c Tufnell b Fraser	103
*M.A.Taylor c and b Gough	49	(1)	b Malcolm	113
D.C.Boon b Gough	3		c Hick b Gough	17
M.E.Waugh c Rhodes b Malcolm	3		lbw b Fraser	25
M.G.Bevan c Thorpe b Fraser	8		c Rhodes b Fraser	7
S.R.Waugh b Gough	1		c Rhodes b Fraser	0
†I.A.Healy c Hick b Gough	10		c Rhodes b Fraser	5
S.K.Warne c Gatting b Fraser	0		not out	36
T.B.A.May c Hick b Gough	0		not out	10
C.J.McDermott not out	21			
D.W.Fleming b Gough	0			
Extras (B6, LB1, NB3)	10		(B12, LB3, W1, NB12)	28
Total (42.5 overs; 211 minutes)	116		(121.4 overs; 514 minutes)	344-7

AUSTRALIA	*O*	*M*	*R*	*W*		*O*	*M*	*R*	*W*
McDermott	30	7	101	5		24	2	76	0
Fleming	26.2	12	52	3		20	3	66	2
Warne	36	10	88	1	(4)	16	2	48	0
May	17	4	35	0	(5)	10	1	55	0
M.E.Waugh	6	1	10	0	(3)	2	1	4	0
Bevan	4	1	8	0					
ENGLAND									
Malcolm	13	4	34	2		21	4	75	1
Gough	18.5	4	49	6		28	4	72	1
Fraser	11	1	26	2		25	3	73	5
Tufnell						35.4	9	61	0
Hick						5	0	21	0
Gooch						7	1	27	0

FALL OF WICKETS

	E	*A*	*E*	*A*
Wkt	*1st*	*1st*	*2nd*	*2nd*
1st	1	12	54	208
2nd	10	15	158	239
3rd	20	18	–	265
4th	194	38	–	282
5th	194	39	–	286
6th	196	57	–	289
7th	197	62	–	292
8th	255	65	–	–
9th	295	116	–	–
10th	309	116	–	–

Umpires: S.A.Bucknor (*West Indies*) (16) and D.B.Hair (10).
Referee: J.R.Reid (*New Zealand*) (13). Test No. 1279/283 (A 545/E 710)

AUSTRALIA v ENGLAND (4th Test)

At Adelaide Oval, on 26, 27, 28, 29, 30 January 1995.
Toss: England. Result: ENGLAND won by 106 runs.
Debuts: Australia – G.A.Blewett, P.E.McIntyre. ‡ (G.D.McGrath)

ENGLAND

G.A.Gooch c M.E.Waugh b Fleming	47		c Healy b McDermott	34
*M.A.Atherton c Boon b Fleming	80		lbw b M.E.Waugh	14
M.W.Gatting c S.R.Waugh b McIntyre	117		b M.E.Waugh	0
G.P.Thorpe c Taylor b Warne	26		c Warne b McDermott	83
J.P.Crawley b Warne	28		c and b M.E.Waugh	71
†S.J.Rhodes c Taylor b McDermott	6		c Fleming b Warne	2
C.C.Lewis c Blewett b McDermott	10		b Fleming	7
P.A.J.DeFreitas c Blewett b McIntyre	21		c Healy b M.E.Waugh	88
A.R.C.Fraser run out (sub‡/McIntyre)	7		c McDermott b M.E.Waugh	5
D.E.Malcolm b McDermott	0		not out	10
P.C.R.Tufnell not out	0		lbw b Warne	0
Extras (B2, LB5, W2, NB2)	11		(B6, LB8)	14
Total (141.3 overs; 559 minutes)	353		(94.5 overs; 382 minutes)	328

AUSTRALIA

M.J.Slater c Atherton b DeFreitas	67	(2)	c Tufnell b Malcolm	5
*M.A.Taylor lbw b Lewis	90	(1)	c Thorpe b Malcolm	13
D.C.Boon c Rhodes b DeFreitas	0		c Rhodes b Fraser	4
M.E.Waugh c Rhodes b Fraser	39		c Gatting b Tufnell	24
S.R.Waugh c Atherton b Lewis	19		b Malcolm	0
G.S.Blewett not out	102		c Rhodes b Lewis	12
†I.A.Healy c Rhodes b Malcolm	74		not out	51
S.K.Warne c Thorpe b Fraser	7		lbw b Lewis	2
D.W.Fleming c Rhodes b Malcolm	0	(10)	lbw b Lewis	24
P.E.McIntyre b Malcolm	0	(11)	lbw b Malcolm	0
C.J.McDermott c Crawley b Fraser	5	(9)	c Rhodes b Lewis	0
Extras (B2, LB7, NB7)	16		(B3, LB5, NB13)	21
Total (121.5 overs; 535 minutes)	419		(61.1 overs; 274 minutes)	156

AUSTRALIA	*O*	*M*	*R*	*W*		*O*	*M*	*R*	*W*
McDermott	41	15	66	3		27	5	96	2
Fleming	25	6	65	2		11	3	37	1
Blewett	16	4	59	0	(6)	4	0	23	0
Warne	31	9	72	2	(3)	30.5	9	82	2
McIntyre	19.3	3	51	2		8	0	36	0
M.E.Waugh	9	1	33	0	(4)	14	4	40	5
ENGLAND									
Malcolm	26	5	78	3		16.1	3	39	4
Fraser	28.5	6	95	3		12	1	37	1
Tufnell	24	5	64	0	(5)	9	3	17	1
DeFreitas	20	3	70	2	(3)	11	3	31	0
Lewis	18	1	81	2	(4)	13	4	24	4
Gooch	5	0	22	0					

FALL OF WICKETS

Wkt	*E 1st*	*A 1st*	*E 2nd*	*A 2nd*
1st	93	128	26	17
2nd	175	130	30	22
3rd	211	202	83	22
4th	286	207	154	23
5th	293	232	169	64
6th	307	396	181	75
7th	334	405	270	83
8th	353	406	317	83
9th	353	414	317	152
10th	353	419	328	156

Umpires: P.D.Parker (2) and S.Venkataraghavan (*India*) (8).
Referee: J.R.Reid (*New Zealand*) (14). Test No. 1280/284 (A 546/E 711)

AUSTRALIA v ENGLAND (5th Test)

At W.A.C.A. Ground, Perth, on 3, 4, 5, 6, 7 February 1995.
Toss: Australia. Result: AUSTRALIA won by 329 runs.
Debuts: None.

AUSTRALIA

M.J.Slater c Lewis b DeFreitas	124	(2)	c Atherton b Fraser	45
*M.A.Taylor c Rhodes b Lewis	9	(1)	b Fraser	52
D.C.Boon c Ramprakash b Lewis	1	(4)	c Rhodes b Malcolm	18
M.E.Waugh c DeFreitas b Lewis	88	(5)	c Rhodes b DeFreitas	1
S.R.Waugh not out	99	(6)	c Ramprakash b Lewis	80
G.S.Blewett c Rhodes b Fraser	20	(7)	c Malcolm b Lewis	115
†I.A.Healy c Lewis b DeFreitas	12	(8)	not out	11
S.K.Warne c Rhodes b DeFreitas	1	(9)	c Lewis b Malcolm	6
J.Angel run out (Malcolm/Rhodes)	11	(3)	run out (Gooch)	0
G.D.McGrath run out (DeFreitas)	0			
C.J.McDermott run out (Lewis/Gooch)	6			
Extras (B14, LB4, W4, NB9)	31		(B1, LB9, NB7)	17
Total (135.5 overs; 590 minutes)	402		(90.3 overs; 404 minutes)	345-8d

ENGLAND

G.A.Gooch lbw b M.E.Waugh	37		c and b McDermott	4
*M.A.Atherton c Healy b McGrath	4		c Healy b McGrath	8
M.W.Gatting b McGrath	0		b McDermott	8
G.P.Thorpe st Healy b Warne	123	(5)	c Taylor b McGrath	0
J.P.Crawley c Warne b M.E.Waugh	0	(6)	c M.E.Waugh b McDermott	0
M.R.Ramprakash b Warne	72	(7)	c S.R.Waugh b M.E.Waugh	42
†S.J.Rhodes b Angel	2	(8)	not out	39
C.C.Lewis c Blewett b McGrath	40	(9)	lbw b McDermott	11
P.A.J.DeFreitas b Angel	0	(10)	c Taylor b McDermott	0
A.R.C.Fraser c Warne b Angel	9	(4)	lbw b McGrath	5
D.E.Malcolm not out	0		b McDermott	0
Extras (B4, LB1, NB3)	8		(LB1, W1, NB4)	6
Total (96.3 overs; 402 minutes)	295		(41 overs; 179 minutes)	123

ENGLAND	*O*	*M*	*R*	*W*		*O*	*M*	*R*	*W*
Malcolm	31	6	93	0		23.3	3	105	2
DeFreitas	29	8	91	3	(4)	22	10	54	1
Fraser	32	11	84	1	(2)	21	3	74	2
Lewis	31.5	8	73	3	(3)	16	1	71	2
Gooch	1	1	0	0					
Ramprakash	11	0	43	0	(5)	8	1	31	0
AUSTRALIA									
Angel	22.3	7	65	3	(3)	3	0	20	0
McGrath	25	6	88	3		13	4	40	3
Blewett	4	1	9	0					
M.E.Waugh	9	2	29	2	(5)	3	0	13	1
Warne	23	8	58	2	(4)	7	3	11	0
McDermott	13	5	41	0	(1)	15	4	38	6

FALL OF WICKETS

Wkt	*A* *1st*	*E* *1st*	*A* *2nd*	*E* *2nd*
1st	47	5	75	4
2nd	55	5	79	17
3rd	238	77	102	26
4th	247	77	115	26
5th	287	235	123	27
6th	320	246	326	27
7th	328	246	333	95
8th	386	247	345	121
9th	388	293	–	123
10th	402	295	–	123

Umpires: K.E.Liebenberg (*South Africa*) (6) and S.G.Randell (19).
Referee: J.R.Reid (*New Zealand*) (15). Test No. 1281/285 (A 547/E 712)

AUSTRALIA v ENGLAND 1994-95

AUSTRALIA – BATTING AND FIELDING

	M	I	NO	HS	Runs	Avge	100	50	Ct/St
G.S.Blewett	2	4	1	115	249	83.00	2	–	3
M.J.Slater	5	10	–	176	623	62.30	3	1	–
S.R.Waugh	5	10	3	99*	345	49.28	–	3	3
M.A.Taylor	5	10	–	113	471	47.10	1	4	7
M.E.Waugh	5	10	–	140	435	43.50	–	2	8
I.A.Healy	5	10	3	74	249	35.57	–	2	23/2
D.C.Boon	5	10	–	131	246	24.60	1	–	2
T.B.A.May	3	5	3	10*	31	15.50	–	–	–
M.G.Bevan	3	6	–	35	81	13.50	–	–	–
D.W.Fleming	3	4	–	24	40	10.00	–	–	2
C.J.McDermott	5	8	2	21*	42	7.00	–	–	3
S.K.Warne	5	10	1	36*	60	6.66	–	–	5
G.D.McGrath	2	2	–	0	0	0.00	–	–	–

Played in one Test: J.Angel 11, 0; P.E.McIntyre 0, 0.

AUSTRALIA – BOWLING

	O	M	R	W	Avge	Best	5wI	10wM
M.E.Waugh	53	11	157	8	19.62	5-40	1	–
S.K.Warne	256.1	84	549	27	20.33	8-71	2	1
C.J.McDermott	232.5	56	675	32	21.09	6-38	4	–
D.W.Fleming	102.2	30	274	10	27.40	3-52	–	–
G.D.McGrath	67	16	229	6	38.16	3-40	–	–

Also bowled: J.Angel 25.3-7-85-3; M.G.Bevan 7-1-19-0; G.S.Blewett 24-5-91-0; P.E.McIntyre 27.3-3-87-2; T.B.A.May 101-30-219-1.

ENGLAND – BATTING AND FIELDING

	M	I	NO	HS	Runs	Avge	100	50	Ct/St
G.P.Thorpe	5	10	1	123	444	49.33	1	3	5
G.A.Hick	3	6	1	98*	208	41.60	–	2	9
M.A.Atherton	5	10	–	88	407	40.70	–	4	4
J.P.Crawley	3	5	–	72	171	34.20	–	2	1
G.A.Gooch	5	10	–	56	245	24.50	–	1	–
D.Gough	3	5	1	51	98	24.50	–	1	4
A.J.Stewart	2	4	1	33	73	24.33	–	–	2
M.W.Gatting	5	9	–	117	182	20.22	1	–	3
P.A.J.DeFreitas	4	8	–	88	141	17.62	–	1	2
C.C.Lewis	2	4	–	40	68	17.00	–	–	3
D.E.Malcolm	4	7	3	29	50	12.50	–	–	1
A.R.C.Fraser	3	5	–	27	53	10.60	–	–	–
S.J.Rhodes	5	9	1	39*	72	9.00	–	–	20/1
P.C.R.Tufnell	4	7	3	4*	6	1.50	–	–	2

Played in one Test: M.J.McCague 1, 0; M.R.Ramprakash 72, 42 (2ct).

ENGLAND – BOWLING

	O	M	R	W	Avge	Best	5wI	10wM
D.Gough	152.5	33	425	20	21.25	6-49	1	–
C.C.Lewis	78.5	14	249	11	22.63	4-24	–	–
A.R.C.Fraser	129.5	25	389	14	27.78	5-73	1	
P.A.J.DeFreitas	184	39	558	13	42.92	3-91	–	–
P.C.R.Tufnell	207.4	45	442	10	44.20	4-79	–	–
D.E.Malcolm	181.1	32	588	13	45.23	4-39		

Also bowled: G.A.Gooch 25-6-74-1; G.A.Hick 16-3-58-0; M.J.McCague 19.2-4-96-2; M.R.Ramprakash 19-1-74-0.

SOUTH AFRICA v NEW ZEALAND (1st Test)

At Wanderers Stadium, Johannesburg, on 25, 26, 27, 28, 29 November 1994.
Toss: New Zealand. Result: NEW ZEALAND won by 137 runs.
Debuts: New Zealand – D.J.Murray.

NEW ZEALAND

B.A.Young c McMillan b Snell	7	(2) c Richardson b De Villiers	18
D.J.Murray c Richardson b De Villiers	25	(1) lbw b De Villiers	0
S.P.Fleming b De Villiers	48	c Richardson b Matthews	15
M.D.Crowe lbw b Snell	83	b De Villiers	0
*K.R.Rutherford c Cronje b Eksteen	68	c McMillan b De Villiers	0
S.K.Thomson b Matthews	84	b Snell	29
†A.C.Parore c McMillan b Matthews	13	c Richardson b Matthews	49
M.N.Hart c Richardson b Matthews	0	b Matthews	34
D.J.Nash c Hudson b Eksteen	18	c Richardson b Matthews	20
S.J.Doull not out	31	not out	14
R.P.de Groen b Snell	26	b Matthews	0
Extras (LB5, W2, NB1)	8	(B9, LB4, W1, NB1)	15
Total	411		194

SOUTH AFRICA

A.C.Hudson c Parore b Nash	10	lbw b Doull	2
G.Kirsten c Crowe b De Groen	9	lbw b Hart	33
B.M.McMillan c Murray b Nash	5	lbw b Doull	42
*W.J.Cronje lbw b De Groen	20	c Parore b De Groen	62
D.J.Cullinan c Parore b Doull	58	c Crowe b Doull	12
J.N.Rhodes lbw b Doull	37	lbw b Doull	0
†D.J.Richardson lbw b Nash	93	c and b Hart	6
R.P.Snell c Crowe b Hart	16	c Doull b Hart	1
C.R.Matthews c Crowe b Hart	4	b Hart	6
C.E.Eksteen c Fleming b Hart	9	b Hart	0
P.S.de Villiers not out	6	not out	1
Extras (B6, LB6)	12	(B17, LB6, W1)	24
Total	279		189

SOUTH AFRICA	O	M	R	W		O	M	R	W
De Villiers	34	8	78	2		23	9	52	4
Snell	33.5	9	112	3		16	5	54	1
Matthews	28	3	98	3		19	9	42	5
McMillan	24	8	56	0	(5)	2	1	1	0
Eksteen	23	10	49	2	(4)	14	5	32	0
Conje	3	0	13	0		1	1	0	0
NEW ZEALAND									
Nash	24	6	81	3		8	2	17	0
Doull	21	6	70	2		15	5	33	4
De Groen	21	2	59	2	(4)	12	3	21	1
Hart	26	7	57	3	(3)	32.4	7	77	5
Thomson						11	6	18	0

FALL OF WICKETS

Wkt	NZ 1st	SA 1st	NZ 2nd	SA 2nd
1st	7	20	0	9
2nd	79	28	32	70
3rd	92	38	33	130
4th	218	73	33	150
5th	249	147	34	150
6th	280	148	103	167
7th	280	173	130	175
8th	354	197	168	180
9th	354	254	190	184
10th	411	279	194	189

Umpires: K.E.Liebenberg (5) and I.D.Robinson (*Zimbabwe*) (9).
Referee: P.J.P.Burge (*Australia*) (11). Test No. 1282/18 (SA 190/NZ 230)

SOUTH AFRICA v NEW ZEALAND (2nd Test)

At Kingsmead, Durban, on 26, 27, 28, 29, 30 December 1994.
Toss: New Zealand. Result: SOUTH AFRICA won by 8 wickets.
Debuts: South Africa – J.B.Commins, S.D.Jack.

NEW ZEALAND

B.A.Young b Jack	2	c Cullinan b McMillan	51
D.J.Murray c Richardson b De Villiers	38	lbw b De Villiers	0
S.P.Fleming c Jack b De Villiers	4	(5) c Richardson b Jack	31
M.D.Crowe c De Villiers b Jack	18	c Richardson b McMillan	10
*K.R.Rutherford c Commins b De Villiers	0	(3) c Commins b McMillan	6
S.A.Thomson c Kirsten b De Villiers	82	b Cronje	35
†A.C.Parore c Kirsten b McMillan	5	run out	1
M.N.Hart c Cronje b McMillan	5	c Richardson b Kirsten	6
S.B.Doull c Richardson b McMillan	0	c Richardson b De Villiers	19
D.K.Morrison not out	24	c McMillan b De Villiers	12
C.Pringle c Kirsten b De Villiers	0	not out	6
Extras (LB4, NB3)	7	(LB11, NB4)	15
Total	185		192

SOUTH AFRICA

A.C.Hudson c Young b Morrison	8	c Parore b Doull	6
G.Kirsten c Parore b Doull	29	not out	66
J.B.Commins c Hart b Doull	30	c Young b Hart	45
D.J.Cullinan lbw b Doull	34	not out	25
*W.J.Cronje c Thomson b Morrison	19		
J.N.Rhodes c Fleming b Hart	1		
B.M.McMillan b Doull	17		
†D.J.Richardson not out	39		
C.R.Matthews c Parore b Morrison	7		
S.D.Jack c Crowe b Morrison	0		
P.S.de Villiers c Fleming b Doull	28		
Extras (LB6, NB8)	14	(LB9, NB2)	11
Total	226	(2 wickets)	153

SOUTH AFRICA	*O*	*M*	*R*	*W*		*O*	*M*	*R*	*W*
De Villiers	24	7	64	5		31.2	10	56	3
Jack	16	7	32	2		15	3	45	1
Matthews	19	11	37	0	(4)	12	3	17	0
McMillan	19	8	40	3	(3)	30	8	53	3
Cronje	4	1	8	0		10	6	10	1
Kirsten						2	2	0	1
NEW ZEALAND									
Morrison	25	4	70	4	(2)	15	1	56	0
Doull	29.4	9	73	5	(1)	15	5	26	1
Pringle	15	5	23	0					
Hart	17	2	54	1	(3)	13.4	2	52	1
Thomson					(4)	2	1	10	0

FALL OF WICKETS

	NZ	*SA*	*NZ*	*SA*
Wkt	*1st*	*1st*	*2nd*	*2nd*
1st	9	13	2	20
2nd	19	61	11	117
3rd	62	110	28	–
4th	65	111	81	–
5th	66	122	144	–
6th	102	141	144	–
7th	114	168	153	–
8th	114	182	153	–
9th	180	182	179	–
10th	185	226	192	–

Umpires: Khizer Hayat (*Pakistan*) (31) and C.J.Mitchley (6).
Referee: P.J.P.Burge (*Australia*) (12). Test No. 1283/19 (SA 191/NZ 231)

SOUTH AFRICA v NEW ZEALAND (3rd Test)

At Newlands, Cape Town, on 2, 3, 4, 5 January 1995.
Toss: New Zealand. Result: SOUTH AFRICA won by seven wickets.
Debuts: South Africa – P.J.R.Steyn.

NEW ZEALAND			
B.A.Young lbw b McMillan	45	c Kirsten b McMillan	51
D.J.Murray c Kirsten b McMillan	5	lbw b De Villiers	3
†A.C.Parore run out	2	c Eksteen b De Villiers	34
M.D.Crowe c Richardson b Jack	18	c Richardson b McMillan	5
*K.R.Rutherford c Kirsten b McMillan	56	lbw b McMillan	26
S.A.Thomson b McMillan	0	run out	16
S.P.Fleming b Jack	78	c Richardson b De Villiers	53
M.N.Hart c Richardson b Jack	24	c Eksteen b Jack	7
S.B.Doull c Cronje b Jack	6	c Rhodes b De Villiers	25
D.K.Morrison not out	0	lbw b De Villiers	1
C.Pringle b De Villiers	30	not out	0
Extras (LB13, NB10)	23	(B5, LB6, W1, NB6)	18
Total	287		239

SOUTH AFRICA			
G.Kirsten b Thomson	64	lbw b Hart	25
P.J.R.Steyn lbw b Thomson	38	c Doull b Thomson	12
J.B.Commins c Rutherford b Hart	27	not out	10
D.J.Cullinan c Young b Thomson	5	hit wicket b Hart	28
*W.J.Cronje c Pringle b Hart	112	not out	14
J.N.Rhodes b Doull	18		
B.M.McMillan lbw b Pringle	18		
†D.J.Richardson c Crowe b Doull	109		
C.E.Eksteen b Hart	22		
S.D.Jack c Murray b Morrison	7		
P.S.de Villiers not out	1		
Extras (B7, LB3, W1, NB8)	19		–
Total	440	(3 wickets)	89

SOUTH AFRICA	*O*	*M*	*R*	*W*		*O*	*M*	*R*	*W*
De Villiers	28.5	7	90	1		28.1	9	61	5
Jack	27	7	68	4		19	7	50	1
McMillan	26	5	65	4		25	9	52	3
Cronje	5	3	8	0		7	3	15	0
Eksteen	26	10	36	0		31	16	46	0
Kirsten	2	0	7	0		1	0	4	0
NEW ZEALAND									
Morrison	34	7	100	1		4	1	5	0
Doull	34.2	12	55	2					
Pringle	28	5	69	1					
Hart	34	8	141	3	(2)	15.2	2	51	2
Thomson	31	7	65	3	(3)	12	3	33	1

FALL OF WICKETS	*NZ*	*SA*	*NZ*	*SA*
Wkt	*1st*	*1st*	*2nd*	*2nd*
1st	17	106	19	37
2nd	19	119	63	37
3rd	61	125	73	69
4th	95	161	115	–
5th	96	225	131	–
6th	179	271	154	–
7th	244	325	173	–
8th	254	410	224	–
9th	254	429	230	–
10th	287	440	239	–

Umpires: K.T.Francis (*Sri Lanka*) (14) and S.B.Lambson (5).
Referee: P.J.P.Burge (*Australia*) (13). Test No. 1284/20 (SA 192/NZ 232)

SOUTH AFRICA v NEW ZEALAND 1994-95

SOUTH AFRICA – BATTING AND FIELDING

	M	I	NO	HS	Runs	Avge	100	50	Ct/St
D.J.Richardson	3	4	1	109	247	82.33	1	1	16
W.J.Cronje	3	5	1	112	227	56.75	1	1	3
G.Kirsten	3	6	1	66*	226	45.20	–	2	6
J.Cummins	2	4	1	45	112	37.33	–	–	2
P.S.de Villiers	3	4	3	28	36	36.00	–	–	1
D.J.Cullinan	3	6	1	58	162	32.40	–	1	1
B.M.McMillan	3	4	–	42	82	20.50	–	–	4
J.N.Rhodes	3	4	–	37	56	14.00	–	–	1
C.E.Eksteen	2	3	–	22	31	10.33	–	–	2
A.C.Hudson	2	4	–	10	26	6.50	–	–	1
C.R.Matthews	2	3	–	7	17	5.66	–	–	1
S.D.Jack	2	2	–	7	7	3.50	–	–	1

Played in one Test: R.P.Snell 16, 1; P.J.R.Steyn 38, 12.

SOUTH AFRICA – BOWLING

	O	M	R	W	Avge	Best	5wI	10wM
C.R.Matthews	78	26	194	16	12.12	5- 42	1	–
P.S.de Villiers	169.2	50	401	20	20.05	5- 61	2	–
B.M.McMillan	126	39	267	13	20.53	4- 65	–	–
S.D.Jack	77	24	195	8	24.37	4- 68	–	–
R.P.Snell	49.5	14	166	4	41.50	3-112	–	–

Also bowled: W.J.Cronje 30-14-54-1; C.E.Eksteen 94-41-163-2; G.Kirsten 5-2-11-1.

NEW ZEALAND – BATTING AND FIELDING

	M	I	NO	HS	Runs	Avge	100	50	Ct/St
S.A.Thomson	3	6	–	84	246	41.00	–	2	1
S.P.Fleming	3	6	–	78	229	38.16	–	2	3
B.A.Young	3	6	–	51	174	29.00	–	2	3
K.R.Rutherford	3	6	–	68	156	26.00	–	2	1
S.B.Doull	3	6	2	31*	95	23.75	–	–	2
M.D.Crowe	3	6	–	83	134	22.33	–	1	6
D.K.Morrison	2	4	2	24*	37	18.50	–	–	–
C.Pringle	2	4	2	30	36	18.00	–	–	1
A.C.Parore	3	6	–	49	104	17.33	–	–	6
M.N.Hart	3	6	–	34	76	12.66	–	–	2
D.J.Murray	3	6	–	38	71	11.83	–	–	2

Played in one Test: R.P.de Groen 26, 0; D.J.Nash 18, 20.

NEW ZEALAND – BOWLING

	O	M	R	W	Avge	Best	5wI	10wM
S.B.Doull	115	37	257	14	18.35	5-73	1	–
M.N.Hart	138.4	28	432	15	28.80	5-77	1	–
S.A.Thomson	56	17	126	4	31.50	3-65	–	–
D.K.Morrison	78	13	231	5	46.20	4-70	–	–

Also bowled: R.P.de Groen 33-5-80-3; D.J.Nash 32-8-98-3; C.Pringle 43-10-92-1.

SOUTH AFRICA v PAKISTAN (Only Test)

At The Wanderers, Johannesburg, on 19, 20, 21, 22, 23 January 1995.
Toss: South Africa. Result: SOUTH AFRICA won by 324 runs.
Debuts: None.

SOUTH AFRICA

G.Kirsten c Aamir b Kabir	62		b Wasim	42
P.J.R.Steyn c Moin b Wasim	1		c Moin b Aamer	17
J.B.Commins b Aqib	13	(6)	run out	0
D.J.Cullinan c Moin b Aqib	0		not out	69
*W.J.Cronje c Asif b Kabir	41	(3)	c Aamir b Aqib	48
J.N.Rhodes c Inzamam b Aamer	72	(5)	c Moin b Wasim	16
B.M.McMillan c Moin b Aqib	113		c Salim b Kabir	33
†D.J.Richardson b Aamer	0		lbw b Aqib	0
C.E.Eksteen c Moin b Wasim	13		not out	2
P.S.de Villiers not out	66			
A.A.Donald c Inzamam b Aamir	15			
Extras (B4, LB18, W6, NB36)	64		(B6, LB5, W15, NB6)	32
Total	460		(7 wickets declared)	259

PAKISTAN

Aamir Sohail c Richardson b De Villiers	23		c McMillan b De Villiers	0
Saeed Anwar c Cullinan b De Villiers	2		c De Villiers b Donald	1
Asif Mujtaba c Richardson b De Villiers	0		c Richardson b McMillan	26
*Salim Malik c Eksteen b Donald	99		lbw b De Villiers	1
Ijaz Ahmed b De Villiers	19	(6)	c Richardson b McMillan	1
Inzamam-ul-Haq b McMillan	19	(5)	c Richardson b De Villiers	95
†Moin Khan c De Villiers b McMillan	9		c Rhodes b Eksteen	0
Wasim Akram b De Villiers	41		c Kirsten b Eksteen	11
Kabir Khan c Richardson b Donald	4		c Eksteen b Donald	10
Aqib Javed not out	0		c Richardson b De Villiers	0
Aamer Nazir b De Villiers	0		not out	1
Extras (LB5, NB9)	14		(B8, LB7, W1, NB3)	19
Total	230			165

PAKISTAN	*O*	*M*	*R*	*W*		*O*	*M*	*R*	*W*
Wasim	36	11	113	2		23	4	53	2
Aqib	29.4	6	102	3		26	2	82	2
Kabir	19.1	4	60	2	(4)	18	0	58	1
Aamer	13.1	1	67	2	(3)	13	1	55	1
Aamir	14.2	2	47	1					
Salim	8	0	49	0					
SOUTH AFRICA									
Donald	17	2	63	2		15	3	53	2
De Villiers	20.5	4	81	6		19.3	11	27	4
McMillan	12	3	46	2		11	1	33	2
Eksteen	7	1	16	0		19	7	34	2
Cronje	9	5	19	0		5	2	3	0

FALL OF WICKETS

Wkt	*SA 1st*	*P 1st*	*SA 2nd*	*P 2nd*
1st	1	20	69	3
2nd	55	20	96	3
3rd	59	44	155	5
4th	138	106	185	98
5th	168	134	185	100
6th	325	158	251	101
7th	325	193	255	124
8th	367	207	–	164
9th	389	230	–	164
10th	460	230	–	165

Umpires: M.J.Kitchen (*England*) (8) and C.J Mitchley (7).
Referee: P.J.P.Burge (*Australia*) (14). Test No. 1285/1 (SA 193/P 217)

THE 1994 FIRST-CLASS SEASON
STATISTICAL HIGHLIGHTS

HIGHEST INNINGS TOTALS

810-4d	Warwickshire v Durham	Birmingham
657-7d	Warwickshire v Glamorgan	Birmingham
625-6d	Durham v Derbyshire	Chesterfield
623-9d	Middlesex v Leicestershire	Leicester
613-8d	South Africans v Sussex	Hove
604-4d	Surrey v Nottinghamshire	Nottingham
603-7d	Hampshire v Surrey	Southampton
597-8d	Nottinghamshire v Warwickshire	Birmingham
591	Worcestershire v Lancashire	Manchester
589†	Lancashire v Derbyshire	Blackpool
570-6d	Surrey v Derbyshire	The Oval
567-8d	England v New Zealand (1st Test)	Nottingham
567	Lancashire v Nottinghamshire	Nottingham
557	Worcestershire v Middlesex	Lord's
556-8d	Durham v Warwickshire	Birmingham
556	Kent v Lancashire	Canterbury
545-8d	Durham v Northamptonshire	Hartlepool
545	Middlesex v Derbyshire	Derby
541-5d	Essex v Kent	Chelmsford
538-6d	Surrey v Durham	Darlington
538	Nottinghamshire v Northamptonshire	Nottingham
536	Warwickshire v Hampshire	Birmingham
533	Glamorgan v Somerset	Swansea
529	Northamptonshire v Derbyshire	Northampton
525-7d	Middlesex v Essex	Uxbridge
521	Lancashire v Somerset	Southport
513-7d	Middlesex v Gloucestershire	Lord's
512	Hampshire v Durham	Portsmouth
511	Middlesex v Durham	Lord's
501	Surrey v Leicestershire	The Oval

† *Highest total after following-on and longest innings (678 min) in County Championship matches.*

HIGHEST FOURTH INNINGS TOTALS

405-6	Essex v Worcestershire (set 405)	Worcester

VICTORY LOSING ONLY TWO WICKETS

Gloucestershire (357-2d, 218-0d) beat Cambridge U (128, 134) Bristol

LOWEST INNINGS TOTALS

73	Oxford University v Durham	Oxford
73	Worcestershire v Yorkshire	Worcester
73†	Derbyshire v Yorkshire	Sheffield
83	Lancashire v Derbyshire	Blackpool
84	Cambridge University v Kent	Cambridge
87	Middlesex v Sussex	Arundel
88	Surrey v Essex	Colchester
90	Leicestershire v Sussex	Leicester
95†	Oxford University v Worcestershire	Worcester
99†	England v South Africa (1st Test)	Lord's

† *One man absent hurt.*

MATCH AVERAGE OF 100 RUNS PER WICKET

113.83	Warwickshire v Durham	Birmingham

County Championship record and second highest in all first-class matches.

MATCH AGGREGATES OF 1400 RUNS

Runs-Wkts		
1570-29	Derbyshire v Durham	Chesterfield
1536-27	Northamptonshire v Middlesex	Northampton
1527-23	Middlesex v Essex	Uxbridge
1480-26	Surrey v Middlesex	The Oval
1412-39	Sussex v Lancashire	Horsham

FIRST TO INDIVIDUAL TARGETS

1000 RUNS	B.C.Lara (in 7 innings)	Warwickshire	June 6
2000 RUNS	B.C.Lara	Warwickshire	September 1
100 WICKETS	–. Highest aggregate: 90 by M.M.Patel (Kent)		

DOUBLE HUNDREDS (24)

M.Azharuddin	205	Derbyshire v Durham	Chesterfield
D.J.Bicknell	235*	Surrey v Nottinghamshire	Nottingham
J.D.Carr	261*	Middlesex v Gloucestershire	Lord's
J.P.Crawley (2)	281*	Lancashire v Somerset	Southport
	250	Lancashire v Nottinghamshire	Nottingham
N.H.Fairbrother	204	Lancashire v Middlesex	Manchester
M.W.Gatting (3)	224*	Middlesex v England A	Lord's
	225	Middlesex v Leicestershire	Leicester
	201*	Middlesex v Northamptonshire	Northampton
G.A.Gooch (3)	236	Essex v Kent	Chelmsford
	210	England v New Zealand (1st Test)	Nottingham
	205	Essex v Worcestershire	Worcester
G.A.Hick	215	Worcestershire v Lancashire	Manchester
G.Kirsten	201*	South Africans v Durham	Chester-le-Street
B.C.Lara	501*	Warwickshire v Durham	Birmingham
		(World record first-class score)	
M.N.Lathwell	206	Somerset v Surrey	Bath
C.C.Lewis	220*	Nottinghamshire v Warwickshire	Birmingham
A.J.Moles	203*	Warwickshire v Surrey	Guildford
J.E.Morris	204	Durham v Warwickshire	Birmingham
		(The first double hundred for Durham)	
M.D.Moxon	274*	Yorkshire v Worcestershire	Worcester
P.V.Simmons	261	Leicestershire v Northamptonshire	Leicester
		(Leicestershire record; on county debut)	
A.W.Smith	202*	Surrey v Oxford University	The Oval
R.G.Twose	277*	Warwickshire v Glamorgan	Birmingham
D.M.Ward	294*	Surrey v Derbyshire	The Oval

HUNDREDS IN FIVE CONSECUTIVE INNINGS

B.C.Lara (Warwicks)	375 WI v England 1993-94, 147 v Glam, 106 and 120* v Leics, 136 v Somerset	St John's/ B'ham/Taunton

He extended this sequence to 6 hundreds in 7 innings and a world record of 7 in 8.

HUNDREDS IN THREE CONSECUTIVE INNINGS

J.D.Carr (Middx)	171* v Somerset, 136 and 106* v Northants	Lord's/N'hampton
G.A.Gooch (Essex)	210 England v NZ, 101 and 205 v Worcs	N'ham/Worcester
D.L.Haynes (Middx)	125 v Worcs, 104 and 103 v Kent	Lord's/Canterbury

HUNDRED IN EACH INNINGS OF A MATCH (5)

J.D.Carr	136	106*	Middlesex v Northamptonshire	Northampton
G.A.Gooch	101	205	Essex v Worcestershire	Worcester
D.L.Haynes	104	103	Middlesex v Kent	Canterbury
B.C.Lara	106	120*	Warwickshire v Leicestershire	Birmingham
T.R.Ward	110	125	Kent v Glamorgan	Abergavenny

MOST RUNS IN A DAY

B.C.Lara	390*	Warwickshire v Durham	Birmingham

World record.

FASTEST AUTHENTIC HUNDRED

K.R.Rutherford	71 balls	New Zealanders v Glamorgan	Swansea

In contrived circumstances, M.G.N.Windows (Gloucestershire) scored 100 off 71 balls against New Zealanders at Bristol.

CARRYING BAT THROUGH COMPLETED INNINGS (4)

C.W.J.Athey	169*	Sussex (319) v Kent	Tunbridge Wells
M.R.Benson	71*	Kent (189) v Hampshire	Canterbury
W.Larkins	158*†	Durham (305) v Gloucestershire	Gateshead
V.P.Terry	141*	Hampshire (305) v Yorkshire	Leeds

† *The first first-class instance for Durham.*

HUNDRED BEFORE LUNCH (5)

		Day		
M.Azharuddin	72*-172*	4	Derbyshire v Durham	Chesterfield
C.L.Hooper	103*	4	Kent v Essex	Chelmsford
B.C.Lara	111*-285	4	Warwickshire v Durham	Birmingham
B.C.Lara	109*	1	Warwickshire v Derbyshire	Chesterfield
M.G.N.Windows	106†	3	Gloucestershire v New Zealanders	Bristol

† *In contrived circumstances.*

MOST RUNS IN OTHER SESSIONS

N.H.Fairbrother	160*	Lancashire v Middlesex	Manchester

(post tea 2nd day)

MOST RUNS IN AN INNINGS FROM SCORING STROKES WORTH FOUR OR MORE

B.C.Lara	308	(10 sixes, 62 fours)	Warwickshire v Durham	Birmingham

World record.

TEN SIXES IN AN INNINGS

C.L.Hooper	183	Kent v Yorkshire	Maidstone
B.C.Lara	501*	Warwickshire v Durham	Birmingham

SLOWEST HUNDRED

J.E.R.Gallian	453 min	Lancashire v Derbyshire	Blackpool

The slowest hundred in County Championship matches.

SLOWEST FIFTY

J.W.Hall	302 min	Sussex v Surrey	The Oval

The slowest fifty in County Championship matches.

FIRST-WICKET PARTNERSHIP OF 100 IN EACH INNINGS

123	171*	D.J.Bicknell/A.J.Stewart	Surrey v Lancashire	Manchester
196	126	D.P.Ostler/R.G.Twose	Warwickshire v Kent	Birmingham

OTHER NOTABLE PARTNERSHIPS

First Wicket

316†	G.A.Gooch/P.J.Prichard	Essex v Kent	Chelmsford

Second Wicket

295	R.G.Twose/B.C.Lara	Warwickshire v Hampshire	Birmingham
263	M.A.Atherton/G.A.Gooch	England v New Zealand (1st Test)	Nottingham

Third Wicket

314	B.C.Lara/T.L.Penney	Warwickshire v Durham	Birmingham
301	G.P.Thorpe/D.M.Ward	Surrey v Derbyshire	The Oval

Fourth Wicket

288	M.W.Gatting/J.D.Carr	Middlesex v England A	Lord's
282*	M.W.Gatting/J.D.Carr	Middlesex v Northamptonshire	Northampton
265	G.A.Hick/T.M.Moody	Worcestershire v Lancashire	Manchester
250	C.M.Gupte/C.J.Hollins	Oxford U v Cambridge U	Lord's

Fifth Wicket

322*†	B.C.Lara/K.J.Piper	Warwickshire v Durham	Birmingham
253*	D.J.Bicknell/A.D.Brown	Surrey v Nottinghamshire	Nottingham

Sixth Wicket

270†	J.D.Carr/P.N.Weekes	Middlesex v Gloucestershire	Lord's
253	P.V.Simmons/P.A.Nixon	Leicestershire v Northants	Leicester

Seventh Wicket

264	J.D.Carr/P.N.Weekes	Middlesex v Somerset	Lord's
235	J.P.Crawley/W.K.Hegg	Lancashire v Nottinghamshire	Nottingham

Eighth Wicket

183	D.A.Leatherdale/ R.K.Illingworth	Worcestershire v Somerset	Taunton

Ninth Wicket

170†	J.C.Adams/K.P.Evans	Nottinghamshire v Somerset	Taunton

Surpassing the oldest surviving county record set in 1869.

Tenth Wicket

122	J.P.Crawley/A.A.Barnett	Lancashire v Somerset	Southport
115	M.Watkinson/P.J.Martin	Lancashire v Sussex	Horsham
102	R.K.Illingworth/P.Mirza	Worcestershire v Kent	Canterbury

* *Unbroken partnership.* † *County record for that wicket.*

EIGHT OR MORE WICKETS IN AN INNINGS (7)

R.L.Johnson	10-45	Middlesex v Derbyshire	Derby
M.J.McCague	9-86	Kent v Derbyshire	Derby
D.E.Malcolm	9-57	England v South Africa (3rd Test)	The Oval
M.M.Patel	8-96	Kent v Lancashire	Canterbury
A.R.K.Pierson	8-42	Leicestershire v Warwickshire	Birmingham
Wasim Akram	8-30	Lancashire v Somerset	Southport
M.Watkinson	8-30	Lancashire v Hampshire	Manchester

TEN OR MORE WICKETS IN A MATCH (29)

C.E.L.Ambrose	(2)	10- 96	Northamptonshire v Derbyshire	Northampton
		10- 88	Northamptonshire v Hampshire	Southampton
I.D.Austin		10- 60	Lancashire v Middlesex	Manchester
J.E.Benjamin		10-132	Surrey v Leicestershire	The Oval
C.A.Connor	(2)	10-126	Hampshire v Northamptonshire	Southampton
		10-132	Hampshire v Kent	Canterbury
A.C.Cummins		10-104	Durham v Northamptonshire	Hartlepool
O.D.Gibson		11-159	Glamorgan v Somerset	Swansea
M.C.Ilott		10-129	Essex v Sussex	Chelmsford
R.L.Johnson		11-110	Middlesex v Derbyshire	Derby
M.J.McCague		15-147	Kent v Derbyshire	Derby
D.E.Malcolm		10-138	England v South Africa (3rd Test)	The Oval
T.A.Munton	(2)	10-132	Warwickshire v Northamptonshire	Northampton
		10-130	Warwickshire v Essex	Birmingham
Mushtaq Ahmed		12-160	Somerset v Worcestershire	Taunton
D.J.Nash		11-169	New Zealand v England (2nd Test)	Lord's

M.M.Patel	(3)	10- 77	Kent v Cambridge University	Cambridge
		10-201	Kent v Lancashire	Canterbury
		10-152	Kent v Durham	Canterbury
F.D.Stephenson	(2)	11- 96	Sussex v Hampshire	Hove
		11- 82	Sussex v Surrey	The Oval
H.R.J.Trump		12-195	Somerset v Sussex	Hove
S.D.Udal		10-163	Hampshire v Surrey	Southampton
C.A.Walsh	(3)	11-143	Gloucestershire v Somerset	Bristol
		12-102	Gloucestershire v Nottinghamshire	Nottingham
		10-160	Gloucestershire v Yorkshire	Cheltenham
Wasim Akram		13-147	Lancashire v Somerset	Southport
M.Watkinson		11- 87	Lancashire v Hampshire	Manchester
R.S.Yeabsley		10-104	Oxford U v Cambridge U	Lord's

HAT-TRICKS (4)

D.G.Cork	Derbyshire v Kent	Derby
P.A.J.DeFreitas	Derbyshire v Hampshire	Southampton
A.Sheriyar	Leicestershire v Durham (2nd inns)	Durham
V.J.Wells	Leicestershire v Durham (1st inns)	Durham

SIX OR MORE WICKET-KEEPING DISMISSALS IN AN INNINGS (5)

R.J.Blakey	5ct, 1st	Yorkshire v Glamorgan	Cardiff
S.A.Marsh (2)	6ct, 1st	Kent v Durham	Canterbury
	6ct	Kent v South Africans	Canterbury
K.J.Piper (2)	7ct	Warwickshire v Essex	Birmingham
	6ct, 1st	Warwickshire v Derbyshire	Chesterfield

NINE OR MORE WICKET-KEEPING DISMISSALS IN A MATCH (4)

W.K.Hegg	10ct	Lancashire v Yorkshire	Leeds
S.A.Marsh	8ct, 1st	Kent v Durham	Canterbury
K.J.Piper (2)	10ct, 1st	Warwickshire v Derbyshire	Chesterfield
	8ct, 1st	Warwickshire v Essex	Birmingham

NO BYES CONCEDED IN TOTAL OF 500 OR MORE (3)

A.C.Parore	New Zealand v England (1st Test) (567-8d)	Nottingham
R.J.Turner	Somerset v Glamorgan (533)	Swansea
C.W.Scott	Durham v Hampshire (512)	Portsmouth

FIVE CATCHES IN AN INNINGS IN THE FIELD

M.C.J.Ball	Gloucestershire v Yorkshire	Cheltenham
R.P.Davis	Warwickshire v Somerset	Taunton
N.V.Knight	Essex v Warwickshire	Birmingham
G.I.Macmillan	Oxford University v Durham	Oxford

EIGHT CATCHES IN A MATCH IN THE FIELD

M.C.J.Ball	Gloucestershire v Yorkshire	Cheltenham

MATCH DOUBLE (100 RUNS AND 10 WICKETS)

M.Watkinson	11, 117; 8-30, 3-57 Lancashire v Hampshire	Manchester

SIXTY EXTRAS IN AN INNINGS

	B	LB	W	NB		
81	11	16	–	54	Middlesex (545) v Derbyshire	Derby
81	21	9	1	50	Lancashire (589) v Derbyshire	Blackpool
81	–	9	7	65	Glamorgan (533) v Somerset	Swansea
81	5	14	4	58	Hampshire (603-7d) v Surrey	Southampton
78	28	22	2	26	Warwickshire (810-4d) v Durham	Birmingham
73	14	35	–	24	Surrey (604-4d) v Nottinghamshire	Nottingham
67	2	8	5	52	Middlesex (525-7d) v Essex	Uxbridge
66	–	4	6	56	Hampshire (512) v Durham	Portsmouth

WARWICKSHIRE'S GOLDEN YEAR

At 3.30pm on 2 September, Warwickshire completed an innings victory against Hampshire to gain their fourth Championship title. They had led the table since the end of July when they ousted Surrey, pace-makers for the first half of the season, and their final margin over second-placed Leicestershire was an emphatic 42 points. Their points tally and results line, apart from the distribution of bonus points, was identical to that of Middlesex, winners of the first purely four-day Britannic Assurance Championship in 1993: 11 wins; one defeat (by Nottinghamshire) and five draws.

The key contribution was made by Brian Charles Lara, whose registration in place of the injured Prabhakar was secured after *Playfair 1994* went to press. His acquisition by Warwickshire's chairman, M.J.K.Smith, then in the Caribbean as England's tour manager, proved especially timely when it was almost immediately followed by the record-breaking 375. Lara's next four first-class innings were all hundreds for Warwickshire. Although this sequence was ended by Richard Johnson, the Middlesex seamer who subsequently became the youngest bowler to take all ten wickets in a first-class innings (subject to the flexibility of birth registrations prevalent on the sub-continent), Lara swiftly made amends with another hundred and then his *magnus opus* against Durham. News of his 501 not out, more than most county sides attain in one innings in a season, was announced in Australia as 'and Brian Lara has just hit half a thousand on his own!'

No batsman since Bradman can have caused the adage 'bowlers win matches' to be so seriously questioned. The key to Warwickshire's success was undoubtedly Lara's rate of scoring, his 2,066 runs coming off just 2,262 balls. Within the four-day format, this allowed their fairly average attack time in which to dismiss the opposition twice. Without Donald, their spearhead, they needed those bonus overs, only two of their wins being gained with a day to spare.

Tim Munton, 81 wickets at 21 and captain for ten matches in Dermot Reeve's absence, played a major role, as did their much-improved 'keeper, Keith Piper, with 66 Championship dismissals and his most prolific season with the bat.

Although Warwickshire's triumph was based on those three outstanding performances, it was essentially a team effort in which every player made a vital contribution. Crucially, in view of the injuries to Reeve and Gladstone Small, they had adequate reserves; particularly impressive was Graeme Welch, whose successful debut in late June was rewarded with an 11-match run which produced 446 runs and 22 wickets.

Warwickshire's intricate staff jigsaw was painstakingly interlocked by Bob Woolmer, their Director of Coaching. He had assessed that most of his team would reach their peak during this particular summer and shrewdly manipulated his charges, spotting and eradicating defects while concentrating on their psychological well-being. Sensibly, he allowed Lara freedom to both rest and satisfy his agents' requirements without incurring petty jealousies among the other players. He was fortunate that England's selectors appeared unimpressed by his players, Munton being especially unlucky. Even more astonishing was the inclusion of only one Warwickshire player, Piper, in the grand total of 36 players who eventually comprised England's two winter touring teams.

BRITANNIC ASSURANCE COUNTY CHAMPIONSHIP 1994 FINAL TABLE

		P	W	L	D	Bonus Bat	Points Bowl	Total Points
1	**WARWICKSHIRE** (16)	17	11	1	5	41	55	272
2	Leicestershire (9)	17	8	7	2	42	60	230
3	Nottinghamshire (7)	17	8	5	4	39	51	218
4	Middlesex (1)	17	7	3	7	43	57	212
5	Northamptonshire (4)	17	8	4	5	28	53	209
6	Essex (11)	17	7	5	5	32	63	207
7	Surrey (6)	17	7	7	3	32	57	201
8	Sussex (10)	17	7	5	5	28	60	200
9	Kent (8)	17	6	7	4	44	58	198
10	Lancashire (13)	17	8	6	3	32	59	194
11	Somerset (5)	17	7	7	3	32	47	191
12	Gloucestershire (17)	17	5	8	4	28	56	172
13	Hampshire (13)	17	4	7	6	32	55	159
13	Yorkshire (12)	17	4	6	7	38	57	159
15	Worcestershire (2)	17	4	6	7	42	52	158
16	Durham (18)	17	4	10	3	32	57	153
17	Derbyshire (15)	17	4	9	4	25	54	143
18	Glamorgan (3)	17	2	8	7	29	50	111

1993 final positions are shown in brackets. Gloucestershire and Hampshire each gained 8 points for batting last in drawn matches where the scores finished level. Lancashire were deducted 25 points for an unsuitable pitch.

SCORING OF POINTS 1994

(a) For a win, 16 points, plus any points scored in the first innings.

(b) In a tie, each side to score eight points, plus any points scored in the first innings.

(c) If the scores are equal in a drawn match, the side batting in the fourth innings to score eight points, plus any points scored in the first innings.

(d) **First Innings Points** (awarded only for performances **in the first 120 overs** of each first innings and retained whatever the result of the match).

(i) A maximum of four batting points to be available as under—

200 to 249 runs — 1 point
250 to 299 runs — 2 points
300 to 349 runs — 3 points
350 runs or over — 4 points

(ii) A maximum of four bowling points to be available as under—

3 to 4 wickets taken — 1 point
5 to 6 wickets taken — 2 points
7 to 8 wickets taken — 3 points
9 to 10 wickets taken — 4 points

(c) If play starts when less than eight hours playing time remains (in which event a one innings match shall be played as provided for in First-Class Playing Condition 20), no first innings points shall be scored. The side winning on the one innings to score 12 points. In a tie, each side to score six points. If the scores are equal in a drawn match, the side batting in the second innings to score six points.

(f) A County which is adjudged to have prepared a pitch unsuitable for First-Class Cricket shall be liable to have 25 points deducted from its aggregate of points under the procedure agreed by the TCCB in December 1988 and revised in December 1993.

(g) The side which has the highest aggregate of points gained at the end of the season shall be the Champion County. Should any sides in the Championship table be equal on points, the side with most wins will have priority.

COUNTY CHAMPIONS

The English County Championship was not officially constituted until December 1889. Prior to that date there was no generally accepted method of awarding the title; although the 'least matches lost' method existed, it was not consistently applied. Rules governing playing qualifications were not agreed until 1873, and the first unofficial points system was not introduced until 1888.

Research has produced a list of champions dating back to 1826, but at least seven different versions exist for the period from 1864 to 1889 (see *The Wisden Book of Cricket Records*). Only from 1890 can any authorised list of county champions commence.

That first official Championship was contested between eight counties: Gloucestershire, Kent, Lancashire, Middlesex, Nottinghamshire, Surrey, Sussex and Yorkshire. The remaining counties were admitted in the following seasons: 1891 – Somerset, 1895 – Derbyshire, Essex, Hampshire, Leicestershire and Warwickshire, 1899 – Worcestershire, 1905 – Northamptonshire, 1921 – Glamorgan, and 1992 – Durham.

The Championship pennant was introduced by the 1951 champions, Warwickshire, and the Lord's Taverners' Trophy was first presented in 1973. The first sponsors, Schweppes (1977 to 1983), were succeeded by BRITANNIC ASSURANCE in 1984.

1890	Surrey	1927	Lancashire	1964	Worcestershire
1891	Surrey	1928	Lancashire	1965	Worcestershire
1892	Surrey	1929	Nottinghamshire	1966	Yorkshire
1893	Yorkshire	1930	Lancashire	1967	Yorkshire
1894	Surrey	1931	Yorkshire	1968	Yorkshire
1895	Surrey	1932	Yorkshire	1969	Glamorgan
1896	Yorkshire	1933	Yorkshire	1970	Kent
1897	Lancashire	1934	Lancashire	1971	Surrey
1898	Yorkshire	1935	Yorkshire	1972	Warwickshire
1899	Surrey	1936	Derbyshire	1973	Hampshire
1900	Yorkshire	1937	Yorkshire	1974	Worcestershire
1901	Yorkshire	1938	Yorkshire	1975	Leicestershire
1902	Yorkshire	1939	Yorkshire	1976	Middlesex
1903	Middlesex	1946	Yorkshire	1977	Kent / Middlesex
1904	Lancashire	1947	Middlesex		
1905	Yorkshire	1948	Glamorgan	1978	Kent
1906	Kent	1949	Middlesex / Yorkshire	1979	Essex
1907	Nottinghamshire			1980	Middlesex
1908	Yorkshire	1950	Lancashire / Surrey	1981	Nottinghamshire
1909	Kent			1982	Middlesex
1910	Kent	1951	Warwickshire	1983	Essex
1911	Warwickshire	1952	Surrey	1984	Essex
1912	Yorkshire	1953	Surrey	1985	Middlesex
1913	Kent	1954	Surrey	1986	Essex
1914	Surrey	1955	Surrey	1987	Nottinghamshire
1919	Yorkshire	1956	Surrey	1988	Worcestershire
1920	Middlesex	1957	Surrey	1989	Worcestershire
1921	Middlesex	1958	Surrey	1990	Middlesex
1922	Yorkshire	1959	Yorkshire	1991	Essex
1923	Yorkshire	1960	Yorkshire	1992	Essex
1924	Yorkshire	1961	Hampshire	1993	Middlesex
1925	Yorkshire	1962	Yorkshire	1994	Warwickshire
1926	Lancashire	1963	Yorkshire		

WORCESTERSHIRE'S UNIQUE SUCCESS

After three forlorn attempts, Worcestershire won their first September final and, having been overwhelmed by the same opposition at the last hurdle of the Benson and Hedges Cup in July, they had the satisfaction of denying Warwickshire a grand slam of all four major titles. It was the first time that the same counties had contested both finals.

This was not a match to rival the previous season's last-ball epic when Warwickshire had managed to muster an improbable 322. The weather saw to that, ending Saturday's play just before lunch when Warwickshire, put in, had clawed their way to 88 for 3, Brian Lara 36 not out. Shepherded by the Trinidadian's 81, the holders eventually managed a creditable 223 for 9 despite having to face a 10.30 start on successive September mornings. In easier conditions, Graeme Hick and Tom Moody cantered to victory by eight wickets with a massive 10.5 overs in hand, their unbroken stand of 198 being a record for the third wicket in these finals.

For the ninth successive time this final had been won by the side batting second. The fact that only three sides have won batting first since 1973, one of those by a solitary run, does suggest that conditions at Lord's in September are not ideal for a 10.30 start. For a later start to be possible, the contest would have to be shortened to at least 55 overs. Alternatively, the competition could be moved to the first half of the season; it does seem illogical to stage the shorter final near the longest day. Emulating overseas limited-overs internationals by having just one interval (between the two innings) would save 30 minutes. Another possibility would be to move this final to The Oval where the pitch provides an ideal surface for one-day cricket.

This has been demonstrated when Worcestershire's semi-final there had produced the world record limited-overs match aggregate of 707 runs, Surrey failing by just seven runs to snatch an incredible victory, their 350 being a world record second innings total in such games. Earlier Moody (180 not out) had registered the competition's highest score against a first-class county and shared a world record limited-overs third-wicket partnership of 309 (unbroken) with his captain, Tim Curtis.

GILLETTE CUP WINNERS

1963	Sussex	1969	Yorkshire	1975	Lancashire
1964	Sussex	1970	Lancashire	1976	Northamptonshire
1965	Yorkshire	1971	Lancashire	1977	Middlesex
1966	Warwickshire	1972	Lancashire	1978	Sussex
1967	Kent	1973	Gloucestershire	1979	Somerset
1968	Warwickshire	1974	Kent	1980	Middlesex

NATWEST TROPHY WINNERS

1981	Derbyshire	1986	Sussex	1991	Hampshire
1982	Surrey	1987	Nottinghamshire	1992	Northamptonshire
1983	Somerset	1988	Middlesex	1993	Warwickshire
1984	Middlesex	1989	Warwickshire	1994	Worcestershire
1985	Essex	1990	Lancashire		

1994 NATWEST TROPHY FINAL

WARWICKSHIRE v WORCESTERSHIRE

At Lord's, London, on 3, 4 September.
Toss: Worcestershire. Result: WORCESTERSHIRE won by 8 wickets.
Match Award: T.M.Moody (Adjudicator: M.J.Procter).

WARWICKSHIRE	**Runs**	**Min**	**Balls**	**6s**	**4s**	**Fall**
A.J.Moles c Rhodes b Newport	8	37	31	–	1	2-17
D.P.Ostler c Lampitt b Newport	4	7	5	–	1	1-8
B.C.Lara c Hick b Haynes	81	175	117	1	7	6-171
P.A.Smith c Haynes b Moody	13	35	30	–	2	3-50
R.G.Twose c Leatherdale b Newport	22	43	42	–	3	4-90
T.L.Penney lbw b Radford	18	44	33	–	2	5-150
*D.A.Reeve c Rhodes b Newport	13	45	34	–	–	7-188
N.M.K.Smith c Illingworth b Lampitt	20	49	36	–	2	8-215
†K.J.Piper not out	16	31	29	–	–	–
G.C.Small run out (Hick/Rhodes)	5	3	4	–	–	9-222
T.A.Munton not out	0	2	1	–	–	–
Extras (B1, LB8, W10, NB4)	23					
Total (60 overs; 240 minutes)	223-9 closed					

WORCESTERSHIRE	**Runs**	**Min**	**Balls**	**6s**	**4s**	**Fall**
*T.S.Curtis b Reeve	11	59	43	–	–	2-29
D.B.D'Oliveira c Lara b Munton	12	54	42	–	1	1-29
G.A.Hick not out	93	138	101	1	12	
T.M.Moody not out	88	134	112	2	10	
G.R.Haynes, D.A.Leatherdale, †S.J.Rhodes, S.R.Lampitt, P.J.Newport, R.K.Illingworth, N.V.Radford did not bat						
Extras (LB6, W11, NB6)	23					
Total (49.1 overs; 194 minutes)	227-2					

WORCESTERSHIRE	*O*	*M*	*R*	*W*	**WARWICKSHIRE**	*O*	*M*	*R*	*W*
Moody	12	4	17	1	Small	12	2	40	0
Newport	12	2	38	4	Munton	12	3	23	1
Radford	12	1	45	1	Reeve	6	1	30	1
Lampitt	11	1	45	1	P.A.Smith	7	1	54	0
Illingworth	6	0	35	0	Twose	5	0	36	0
Haynes	7	0	34	1	N.M.K.Smith	7	0	34	0
					Penney	0.1	0	4	0

Umpires: N.T.Plews and D.R.Shepherd.

THE NATWEST TROPHY 1994

FIRST ROUND 21, 22 June	SECOND ROUND 6, 7 July	QUARTER-FINALS 26, 27 July	SEMI-FINALS 9 August	FINAL 3, 4 September
WORCESTERSHIRE	WORCESTERSHIRE†	WORCESTERSHIRE†	WORCESTERSHIRE	WORCESTERSHIRE (£31,000)
Norfolk†				
NOTTINGHAMSHIRE	Nottinghamshire			
Northumberland†				
NORTHAMPTONSHIRE†	NORTHAMPTONSHIRE	Northamptonshire (£3,875)		
Ireland				
MIDDLESEX	Middlesex†			
Wales MC†				
SURREY†	SURREY†	SURREY	Surrey† (£7,750)	
Staffordshire				
LANCASHIRE†	Lancashire			
Scotland				
GLAMORGAN†	GLAMORGAN†	Glamorgan† (£3,875)		
Lincolnshire				
ESSEX	Essex			
Sussex†				
DERBYSHIRE	DERBYSHIRE	Derbyshire† (£3,875)	Kent (£7,750)	Warwickshire (£15,500)
Gloucestershire†				
DURHAM	Durham†			
Cheshire†				
KENT	KENT	KENT		
Berkshire†				
HAMPSHIRE	Hampshire†			
Cambridgeshire†				
YORKSHIRE	Yorkshire†	Somerset† (£3,875)	WARWICKSHIRE†	
Devon†				
SOMERSET	SOMERSET			
Oxfordshire†				
LEICESTERSHIRE	Leicestershire†	WARWICKSHIRE		
Cumberland†				
WARWICKSHIRE†	WARWICKSHIRE			
Bedfordshire				

† Home team. Winning teams are in capitals. Prize-money shown in brackets.

NATWEST TROPHY
PRINCIPAL RECORDS 1963-94
(Including The Gillette Cup)

Highest Total	413-4	Somerset v Devon	Torquay	1990
Highest Total in a Final	322-5	Warwicks v Sussex	Lord's	1993
Highest Total by a Minor County	305-9	Durham v Glam	Darlington	1991
Highest Total Batting Second	350	Surrey v Worcs	The Oval	1994
Highest Total to Win Batting 2nd	322-5	Warwicks v Sussex	Lord's	1993
Lowest Total	39	Ireland v Sussex	Lord's	1985
Lowest Total in a Final	118	Lancashire v Kent	Lord's	1974
Lowest Total to Win Batting First	98	Worcs v Durham	Chester-le-St	1968

Highest Score	206 A.I.Kallicharran	Warwicks v Oxon	Birmingham	1984
HS (Minor County)	132 G.Robinson	Lincs v Northumb	Jesmond	1971
Hundreds	247 have been scored in GC (93) and NWT (154) matches			
Fastest Hundred	36 balls – G.D.Rose	Somerset v Devon	Torquay	1990
Most Hundreds	7 C.L.Smith	Hampshire		1980-91

Highest Partnership for each Wicket

1st	248	D.M.Smith/C.W.J.Athey	Sussex v Hampshire	Hove	1993
2nd	286	I.S.Anderson/A.Hill	Derbys v Cornwall	Derby	1986
3rd	309*	T.S.Curtis/T.M.Moody	Worcs v Surrey	The Oval	1994
4th	234*	D.Lloyd/C.H.Lloyd	Lancashire v Glos	Manchester	1978
5th	166	M.A.Lynch/G.R.J.Roope	Surrey v Durham	The Oval	1982
6th	123	D.A.Reeve/T.L.Penney	Warwicks v Leics	Leicester	1994
7th	160*	C.J.Richards/I.R.Payne	Surrey v Lincs	Sleaford	1983
8th	83	J.Hartley/D.A.Hale	Oxon v Glos	Oxford	1989
9th	87	M.A.Nash/A.E.Cordle	Glamorgan v Lincs	Swansea	1974
10th	81	S.Turner/R.E.East	Essex v Yorkshire	Leeds	1982

Most Runs		2283 (av 52.96)	G.A.Gooch	Essex	1973-94
Best Bowling	8-21	M.A.Holding	Derbys v Sussex	Hove	1988
	8-31	D.L.Underwood	Kent v Scotland	Edinburgh	1987
Hat-Tricks		J.D.F.Larter	Northants v Sussex	Northampton	1963
		D.A.D.Sydenham	Surrey v Cheshire	Hoylake	1964
		R.N.S.Hobbs	Essex v Middlesex	Lord's	1968
		N.M.McVicker	Warwicks v Lincs	Birmingham	1971
		G.S.Le Roux	Sussex v Ireland	Hove	1985
		M.Jean-Jacques	Derbyshire v Notts	Derby	1987
		J.F.M.O'Brien	Cheshire v Derbys	Chester	1988
Most Wickets		81 (av 14.85)	G.G.Arnold	Surrey	1963-80

Most Wicket-Keeping Dismissals in an Innings

7 (7ct) A.J.Stewart Surrey v Glamorgan Swansea 1994

Most Catches in an Innings

4 – A.S.Brown (Glos 1963), G.Cook (Northants 1972), C.G.Greenidge (Hants 1981), D.C.Jackson (Durham 1984), T.S.Smith (Herts 1984), H.Morris (Glam 1988), C.C.Lewis (Notts 1992).

Most Appearances	61	D.P.Hughes	Lancashire	1969-91
Most Match Awards	9	G.A.Gooch	Essex	1973-93

Most Match Wins 61 – Lancs, Warwicks. **Most Cup/Trophy Wins** 5 – Lancashire.

1994 BENSON AND HEDGES CUP FINAL

WARWICKSHIRE v WORCESTERSHIRE

At Lord's, London, on 9 July.
Toss: Warwickshire. Result: WARWICKSHIRE won by 6 wickets.
Match Award: P.A.Smith.

WORCESTERSHIRE	**Runs**	**Balls**	**6s**	**4s**	**Fall**
*T.S.Curtis c Piper b Small	13	33	–	3	2-28
A.C.H.Seymour b Munton	3	3	–	–	1-10
G.A.Hick lbw b P.A.Smith	27	80	–	3	3-55
T.M.Moody run out	47	84	–	2	8-126
G.R.Haynes c Piper b N.M.K.Smith	22	47	–	1	4-100
D.A.Leatherdale c Ostler b P.A.Smith	4	18	–	–	5-124
†S.J.Rhodes lbw b Twose	0	2	–	–	6-124
S.R.Lampitt c Penney b P.A.Smith	1	7	–	–	7-125
R.K.Illingworth lbw b Reeve	18	26	–	–	9-168
N.V.Radford not out	23	30	–	1	
P.J.Newport not out	1	2	–	–	–
Extras (LB2, W5, NB4)	11				
Total (55 overs; 210 minutes)	170-9 closed				

WARWICKSHIRE	**Runs**	**Balls**	**6s**	**4s**	**Fall**
D.P.Ostler run out	55	77	–	8	1-91
R.G.Twose run out	37	66	–	2	2-98
B.C.Lara c Hick b Newport	8	17	–	–	3-103
P.A.Smith not out	42	42	–	6	–
Asif Din c Rhodes b Moody	15	40	–	1	4-147
*D.A.Reeve not out	9	24	–	2	–
T.L.Penney, †K.J.Piper, N.M.K.Smith, G.C.Small, T.A.Munton did not bat					
Extras (LB1, W5)	6				
Total (44.2 overs; 172 minutes)	172-4				

WARWICKSHIRE	*O*	*M*	*R*	*W*	**WORCESTERSHIRE**	*O*	*M*	*R*	*W*
Small	11	4	26	1	Moody	11	2	31	1
Munton	11	3	29	1	Newport	8	0	29	1
P.A.Smith	11	1	34	3	Lampitt	9.2	1	38	0
Reeve	9	1	38	1	Illingworth	6	0	22	0
N.M.K.Smith	5	0	16	1	Radford	8	0	39	0
Twose	8	1	25	1	Hick	2	0	12	0

Umpires: H.D.Bird and K.E.Palmer.

1994 BENSON AND HEDGES CUP

FIRST ROUND 26 April	SECOND ROUND 10 May	QUARTER-FINALS 24, 25 May	SEMI-FINALS 7, 8 June	FINAL 9 July
WARWICKSHIRE	WARWICKSHIRE			
Northamptonshire		WARWICKSHIRE†		
MIDDLESEX†	Middlesex			
			WARWICKSHIRE	
KENT*	KENT†	Kent (£3,875)		
GLOUCESTERSHIRE*	Gloucestershire			
				WARWICKSHIRE (£31,000)
SURREY†	SURREY†	SURREY		
Somerset				
GLAMORGAN*	Glamorgan			
			Surrey† (£7,750)	
NOTTINGHAMSHIRE†	NOTTINGHAMSHIRE†	Nottinghamshire† (£3,875)		
Minor Counties				
SUSSEX†	Sussex			
Scotland				
ESSEX*	ESSEX†	Essex (£3,875)		
LEICESTERSHIRE†	Leicestershire			
Ireland			Hampshire (£7,750)	
HAMPSHIRE*	HAMPSHIRE†	HAMPSHIRE†		
YORKSHIRE*	Yorkshire			Worcestershire (£15,500)
LANCASHIRE	Lancashire			
Combined Us†		Derbyshire† (£3,875)		
DERBYSHIRE*	DERBYSHIRE†			
			WORCESTERSHIRE†	
DURHAM*	Durham†	WORCESTERSHIRE		
WORCESTERSHIRE*	WORCESTERSHIRE			

† Home team. * Bye. Winning teams are in capitals. Prize-money shown in brackets.

BENSON AND HEDGES CUP PRINCIPAL RECORDS 1972-94

Highest Total	388-7	Essex v Scotland	Chelmsford	1992
Highest Total Batting Second	303-7	Derbys v Somerset	Taunton	1990
Highest Total to Win Batting 2nd	291-5	Warwicks v Lancs	Manchester	1981
Lowest Total	50	Hampshire v Yorks	Leeds	1991
Highest Score	198* G.A.Gooch	Essex v Sussex	Hove	1982
Hundreds	237 have been scored in Benson and Hedges Cup matches			
Fastest Hundred	62 min – M.A.Nash	Glamorgan v Hants	Swansea	1976

Highest Partnership for each Wicket

1st	252	V.P.Terry/C.L.Smith	Hants v Comb Us	Southampton	1990
2nd	285*	C.G.Greenidge/D.R.Turner	Hants v Minor C (S)	Amersham	1973
3rd	269*	P.M.Roebuck/M.D.Crowe	Somerset v Hants	Southampton	1987
4th	184*	D.Lloyd/B.W.Reidy	Lancashire v Derbys	Chesterfield	1980
5th	160	A.J.Lamb/D.J.Capel	Northants v Leics	Northampton	1986
6th	121	P.A.Neale/S.J.Rhodes	Worcs v Yorkshire	Worcester	1988
7th	149*	J.D.Love/C.M.Old	Yorks v Scotland	Bradford	1981
8th	109	R.E.East/N.Smith	Essex v Northants	Chelmsford	1977
9th	83	P.G.Newman/M.A.Holding	Derbyshire v Notts	Nottingham	1985
10th	80*	D.L.Bairstow/M.Johnson	Yorkshire v Derbys	Derby	1981

Best Bowling	7-12 W.W.Daniel	Middx v Minor C (E)	Ipswich	1978
	7-22 J.R.Thomson	Middx v Hampshire	Lord's	1981
	7-32 R.G.D.Willis	Warwicks v Yorks	Birmingham	1981
Hat-Tricks	G.D.McKenzie	Leics v Worcs	Worcester	1972
	K.Higgs	Leics v Surrey	Lord's	1974
	A.A.Jones	Middlesex v Essex	Lord's	1977
	M.J.Procter	Glos v Hampshire	Southampton	1977
	W.Larkins	Northants v Comb Us	Northampton	1980
	E.A.Moseley	Glamorgan v Kent	Cardiff	1981
	G.C.Small	Warwickshire v Leics	Leicester	1984
	N.A.Mallender	Somerset v Comb Us	Taunton	1987
	W.K.M.Benjamin	Leics v Notts	Leicester	1987
	A.R.C.Fraser	Middlesex v Sussex	Lord's	1988

Most Wicket-Keeping Dismissals in an Innings

8 (8ct)	D.J.S.Taylor	Somerset v Comb Us	Taunton	1982

Most Catches in an Innings

5	V.J.Marks	Comb Us v Kent	Oxford	1976

Most Match Awards 21	G.A.Gooch	Essex	1973-94

BENSON AND HEDGES CUP WINNERS

1972	Leicestershire	1980	Northamptonshire	1988	Hampshire
1973	Kent	1981	Somerset	1989	Nottinghamshire
1974	Surrey	1982	Somerset	1990	Lancashire
1975	Leicestershire	1983	Middlesex	1991	Worcestershire
1976	Kent	1984	Lancashire	1992	Hampshire
1977	Gloucestershire	1985	Leicestershire	1993	Derbyshire
1978	Kent	1986	Middlesex	1994	Warwickshire
1979	Essex	1987	Yorkshire		

SUNDAY LEAGUE FINAL TABLE 1994

		P	W	L	T	NR	Pts
1	**WARWICKSHIRE** (10)	17	13	3	–	1	54
2	Worcestershire (16)	17	12	4	–	1	50
3	Kent (2)	17	12	5	–	–	48
4	Lancashire (6)	17	11	5	–	1	46
5	Yorkshire (9)	17	10	6	–	1	42
6	Surrey (3)	17	9	5	–	3	42
7	Glamorgan (1)	17	9	6	1	1	40
8	Derbyshire (11)	17	8	7	–	2	36
9	Durham (7)	17	6	7	1	3	32
10	Leicestershire (14)	17	7	9	–	1	30
11	Nottinghamshire (17)	17	6	8	–	3	30
12	Hampshire (15)	17	7	10	–	–	28
13	Northamptonshire (5)	17	6	9	1	1	28
14	Middlesex (8)	17	6	10	–	1	26
15	Sussex (4)	17	5	11	–	1	22
16	Somerset (18)	17	5	12	–	–	20
17	Essex (12)	17	4	11	1	1	20
18	Gloucestershire (13)	17	4	12	–	1	18

Win = 4 points. Tie/No Result = 2 points. When counties finish with an equal number of points, their places are decided by most wins or, if equal, by higher run-rate.

1993 final positions are shown in brackets.

The Sunday League's sponsors have been John Player & Sons (1969-1986), Refuge Assurance (1987-1991), TCCB (1992) and AXA Equity & Law Insurance (1993-). The competition has been limited to 40 overs per innings, apart from 1993 when it was experimentally extended to 50.

WINNERS

1969 Lancashire
1970 Lancashire
1971 Worcestershire
1972 Kent
1973 Kent
1974 Leicestershire
1975 Hampshire
1976 Kent
1977 Leicestershire
1978 Hampshire
1979 Somerset
1980 Warwickshire
1981 Essex
1982 Sussex
1983 Yorkshire
1984 Essex
1985 Essex
1986 Hampshire
1987 Worcestershire
1988 Worcestershire
1989 Lancashire
1990 Derbyshire
1991 Nottinghamshire
1992 Middlesex
1993 Glamorgan
1994 Warwickshire

SUNDAY LEAGUE PRINCIPAL RECORDS 1969-94

Highest Total		375-4	Surrey v Yorkshire	Scarborough	1994
Highest Total Batting Second		317-6	Surrey v Notts	The Oval	1993
Lowest Total		23	Middlesex v Yorks	Leeds	1974
Highest Score	176	G.A.Gooch	Essex v Glamorgan	Southend	1983
Hundreds	485 have been scored in Sunday League matches				
Fastest Hundred	46 balls	G.D.Rose	Somerset v Glam	Neath	1990

Highest Partnership for each Wicket

1st	239	G.A.Gooch/B.R.Hardie	Essex v Notts	Nottingham	1985
2nd	273	G.A.Gooch/K.S.McEwan	Essex v Notts	Nottingham	1983
3rd	223	S.J.Cook/G.D.Rose	Somerset v Glam	Neath	1990
4th	219	C.G.Greenidge/C.L.Smith	Hampshire v Surrey	Southampton	1987
5th	190	R.J.Blakey/M.J.Foster	Yorkshire v Leics	Leicester	1993
6th	124*	J.J.Whitaker/P.A.Nixon	Leics v Surrey	The Oval	1992
7th	132	K.R.Brown/N.F.Williams	Middx v Somerset	Lord's	1988
8th	110*	C.L.Cairns/B.N.French	Notts v Surrey	The Oval	1993
9th	105	D.G.Moir/R.W.Taylor	Derbyshire v Kent	Derby	1984
10th	57	D.A.Graveney/J.B.Mortimore	Glos v Lancashire	Tewkesbury	1973

Best Bowling	8-26	K.D.Boyce	Essex v Lancashire	Manchester	1971
	7-15	R.A.Hutton	Yorkshire v Worcs	Leeds	1969
	7-39	A.Hodgson	Northants v Somerset	Northampton	1976
	7-41	A.N.Jones	Sussex v Notts	Nottingham	1986

Four Wkts in Four Balls	A.Ward	Derbyshire v Sussex	Derby	1970

Hat-Tricks (24): Derbyshire – A.Ward (1970), C.J.Tunnicliffe (1979); Essex – K.D.Boyce (1971); Glamorgan – M.A.Nash (1975), A.E.Cordle (1979), G.C.Holmes (1987), A.Dale (1993); Gloucestershire – K.M.Curran (1989); Hampshire – J.M.Rice (1975), M.D.Marshall (1981); Kent – R.M.Ellison (1983), M.J.McCague (1992); Leicestershire – G.D.McKenzie (1972); Northamptonshire – A.Hodgson (1976); Nottinghamshire – K.Saxelby (1987), K.P.Evans (1994); Somerset – R.Palmer (1970), I.V.A.Richards (1982); Surrey – M.P.Bicknell (1992); Sussex – A.Buss (1974); Warwickshire – R.G.D.Willis (1973), W.Blenkiron (1974); Worcestershire – R.K.Illingworth (1993); Yorkshire – P.W.Jarvis (1982).

Most Wicket-Keeping Dismissals in an Innings

7 (6ct, 1st)	R.W.Taylor	Derbyshire v Lancs	Manchester	1975

Most Catches in an Innings

5	J.M.Rice	Hants v Warwicks	Southampton	1978

COUNTY CAPS AWARDED IN 1994

Derbyshire	P.A.J.DeFreitas
Durham	M.M.Betts, S.D.Birbeck, S.Lugsden, J.I.Longley, J.E.Morris, M.Saxelby, A.Walker, R.M.S.Weston, P.J.Wilcock
Essex	R.C.Irani, M.S.Kasprowicz, N.V.Knight, J.J.B.Lewis
Glamorgan	O.D.Gibson, D.L.Hemp
Gloucestershire	–
Hampshire	–
Kent	M.M.Patel
Lancashire	G.Chapple, J.P.Crawley, J.E.R.Gallian, P.J.Martin, G.Yates
Leicestershire	P.A.Nixon, P.V.Simmons, V.J.Wells
Middlesex	–
Northamptonshire	M.B.Loye, A.L.Penberthy
Nottinghamshire	C.C.Lewis
Somerset	H.R.J.Trump, R.J.Turner
Surrey	A.D.Brown
Sussex	E.S.H.Giddins
Warwickshire	R.P.Davis, B.C.Lara, T.L.Penney
Worcestershire	G.R.Haynes, D.A.Leatherdale
Yorkshire	

MINOR COUNTIES CHAMPIONSHIP

FINAL TABLE 1994

		P	*W*	*L*	*T*	*D*	*NR*	*Bonus Bat*	*Points Bowl*	*Total Points*
EASTERN DIVISION										
Cambridgeshire	NW	9	4	0	0	5	0	23	21	108
Cumberland	NW	9	3	2	0	4	0	21	24	93
Staffordshire	NW	9	2	1	0	6	0	30	27	89
Suffolk	NW	9	2	1	0	6	0	23	19	82
Norfolk	NW	9	2	0	0	7	0	25	22	79
Lincolnshire		9	2	1	0	6	0	22	22	76
Buckinghamshire		9	1	3	0	4	1	19	22	70
Northumberland		9	2	4	0	3	0	17	14	63
Bedfordshire		9	1	2	0	6	0	18	21	55
Hertfordshire		9	1	6	0	1	1	9	12	42
WESTERN DIVISION										
Devon	NW	9	4	1	0	4	0	16	28	108
Herefordshire	NW	9	4	0	0	5	0	22	14	100
Cheshire	NW	9	3	1	0	4	1	25	21	99
Berkshire	NW	9	3	3	0	3	0	21	25	94
Cornwall	NW	9	3	3	0	3	0	19	24	91
Dorset	NW	9	2	3	0	3	1	14	27	78
Shropshire		9	2	4	0	3	0	17	27	76
Wiltshire		9	1	1	0	7	0	23	19	58
Oxfordshire		9	0	3	0	6	0	16	21	37
Wales		9	0	3	0	6	0	12	21	33

The records of Suffolk and Buckinghamshire each include eight points for drawn matches in which the scores finished level.

NW signifies qualification for 1995 NatWest Trophy.

1994 CHAMPIONSHIP FINAL

CAMBRIDGESHIRE v DEVON

At Worcester on 11, 12 September.
Toss: Devon. Result: MATCH DRAWN (Cambridgeshire 2 points, Devon 3 points – Devon thereby became champions).

CAMBRIDGESHIRE

S.Mohammed c Roebuck b Le Fleming	1	c Folland b Donohue	31
*N.T.Gadsby b Allin	62	not out	60
G.W.Ecclestone c Wyatt b Roebuck	18	lbw b Donohue	32
N.Mohammed c Boase b Roebuck	0		
N.J.Adams b Allin	39	run out	8
D.P.Norman b Allin	4		
†S.L.Williams not out	16	(4) lbw b Roebuck	29
S.Turner not out	6		
T.S.Smith, A.Akhtar, D.F.Ralfs did not bat			
Extras (LB6, W1)	7	(LB5)	5
Total (6 wickets declared)	153	(4 wickets declared)	165

DEVON

N.R.Gaywood c Gadsby b Ralfs	4
J.G.Wyatt run out	39
N.A.Folland c Ecclestone b Smith	18
S.M.Willis not out	29
G.T.J.Townsend lbw b Smith	17
*P.M.Roebuck not out	33
K.Donohue, A.O.F.Le Fleming, †D.K.Boase, M.C.Woodman, A.W.Allin did not bat	
Extras (LB8, NB2)	10
Total (4 wickets declared)	150

DEVON	*O*	*M*	*R*	*W*	*O*	*M*	*R*	*W*
Donohue	12	2	37	0	10	0	48	2
Le Fleming	4	1	6	1	5	1	18	0
Roebuck	15	6	33	2	6	1	26	1
Allin	14.2	1	54	3	5	2	25	0
Woodman	4	0	17	0	11	3	43	0
CAMBRIDGESHIRE								
Turner	14	4	45	0				
Ralfs	7	1	22	1				
Akhtar	10	2	33	0				
Smith	15.3	4	42	2				

FALL OF WICKETS

Wkt	*C 1st*	*D 1st*	*C 2nd*
1st	1	5	51
2nd	36	66	105
3rd	40	74	144
4th	124	99	165
5th	129	–	–
6th	132	–	–
7th	–	–	–
8th	–	–	–
9th	–	–	–
10th	–	–	–

Umpires: P.Adams and R.K.Curtis.

MINOR COUNTIES CHAMPIONS

1895	Norfolk Durham Worcestershire	1927	Staffordshire	1964	Lancashire II		
		1928	Berkshire	1965	Somerset II		
		1929	Oxfordshire	1966	Lincolnshire		
1896	Worcestershire	1930	Durham	1967	Cheshire		
1897	Worcestershire	1931	Leicestershire II	1968	Yorkshire II		
1898	Worcestershire	1932	Buckinghamshire	1969	Buckinghamshire		
1899	Northamptonshire Buckinghamshire	1933	Undecided	1970	Bedfordshire		
		1934	Lancashire II	1971	Yorkshire II		
1900	Glamorgan Durham Northamptonshire	1935	Middlesex II	1972	Bedfordshire		
		1936	Hertfordshire	1973	Shropshire		
		1937	Lancashire II	1974	Oxfordshire		
1901	Durham	1938	Buckinghamshire	1975	Hertfordshire		
1902	Wiltshire	1939	Surrey II	1976	Durham		
1903	Northamptonshire	1946	Suffolk	1977	Suffolk		
1904	Northamptonshire	1947	Yorkshire II	1978	Devon		
1905	Norfolk	1948	Lancashire II	1979	Suffolk		
1906	Staffordshire	1949	Lancashire II	1980	Durham		
1907	Lancashire II	1950	Surrey II	1981	Durham		
1908	Staffordshire	1951	Kent II	1982	Oxfordshire		
1909	Wiltshire	1952	Buckinghamshire	1983	Hertfordshire		
1910	Norfolk	1953	Berkshire	1984	Durham		
1911	Staffordshire	1954	Surrey II	1985	Cheshire		
1912	In abeyance	1955	Surrey II	1986	Cumberland		
1913	Norfolk	1956	Kent II	1987	Buckinghamshire		
1920	Staffordshire	1957	Yorkshire II	1988	Cheshire		
1921	Staffordshire	1958	Yorkshire II	1989	Oxfordshire		
1922	Buckinghamshire	1959	Warwickshire II	1990	Hertfordshire		
1923	Buckinghamshire	1960	Lancashire II	1991	Staffordshire		
1924	Berkshire	1961	Somerset II	1992	Staffordshire		
1925	Buckinghamshire	1962	Warwickshire II	1993	Staffordshire		
1926	Durham	1963	Cambridgeshire	1994	Devon		

MINOR COUNTIES CHAMPIONSHIP RECORDS

Highest Total	621		Surrey II v Devon	The Oval	1928
Lowest Total	14		Cheshire v Staffs	Stoke	1909
Highest Score	282	E.Garnett	Berkshire v Wiltshire	Reading	1908
Most Runs – Season	1212	A.F.Brazier	Surrey II		1949

Record Partnership

2nd	388*	T.H.Clark and A.F.Brazier	Surrey II v Sussex II	The Oval	1949
Best Bowling – Innings	10- 11	S.Turner	Cambs v Cumberland	Penrith	1987
– Match	18-100	N.W.Harding	Kent II v Wiltshire	Swindon	1937
Most Wickets – Season	119	S.F.Barnes	Staffordshire		1906

1994 MINOR COUNTIES CHAMPIONSHIP

LEADING BATTING AVERAGES

(Qualification: 8 completed innings, average 45.00)

		I	*NO*	*HS*	*Runs*	*Avge*
D.J.M.Mercer	Berkshire	17	5	119*	831	69.25
R.J.Evans	Lincolnshire	11	3	115*	553	69.13
J.R.Wileman	Lincolnshire	18	5	142*	863	66.38
A.I.Kallicharran	Herefordshire	16	5	100	725	65.91
M.J.Weston	Herefordshire	12	1	143	643	58.45
N.R.Gaywood	Devon	18	4	139*	814	58.14
T.A.Lester	Oxfordshire	16	6	100*	579	57.90
M.A.Fell	Lincolnshire	15	4	126	620	56.36
G.T.J.Townsend	Devon	15	6	65	500	55.55
C.J.Rogers	Norfolk	17	2	116	775	51.67
S.N.V.Waterton	Oxfordshire	18	3	140*	762	50.80
D.J.Makinson	Cumberland	12	2	102*	507	50.70
S.M.Perrin	Wiltshire	15	2	123*	659	50.69
B.S.Percy	Buckinghamshire	9	1	105	390	48.75
G.E.Loveday	Berkshire	16	2	111	676	48.29
M.J.Roberts	Buckinghamshire	13	1	111*	575	47.92
N.T.Gadsby	Cambridgeshire	20	6	92*	661	47.21
J.A.Waterhouse	Staffordshire	13	4	63	423	47.00
H.V.Patel	Herefordshire	18	2	116	747	46.69
G.D.Reynolds	Dorset	16	4	95*	559	46.58
P.J.Caley	Suffolk	15	6	79	414	46.00

LEADING BOWLING AVERAGES

(Qualification: 20 wickets, average 30.00)

		O	*M*	*R*	*W*	*Avge*
P.M.Roebuck	Devon	286.1	103	554	44	12.59
J.H.Shackleton	Dorset	212.5	81	428	28	15.29
D.M.Carter	Suffolk	109	15	384	24	16.00
G.Miller	Cheshire	181.5	44	518	32	16.19
M.A.Sharp	Cumberland	187.2	39	626	34	18.41
P.J.Lewington	Berkshire	195.4	59	488	26	18.77
R.A.Bunting	Norfolk	234	53	851	44	19.34
A.Willows	Dorset	185	41	547	26	21.04
K.Donohue	Devon	189.3	41	563	26	21.65
J.D.Robinson	Bedfordshire	129	24	525	24	21.88
D.Surridge	Hertfordshire	146.3	27	437	20	21.85
S.G.Plumb	Norfolk	232.1	61	614	28	21.93
S.Turner	Cambridgeshire	207.5	60	594	27	22.00
A.B.Byram	Shropshire	191	33	713	31	23.00
M.J.Marvell	Shropshire	111.2	14	483	21	23.00
S.A.Bradford	Lincolnshire	392	99	1271	55	23.11
A.K.Golding	Suffolk	365.5	71	1160	49	23.67
R.N.Dalton	Bedfordshire	142.3	26	498	21	23.71
M.G.Scothern	Cumberland	225.3	45	788	33	23.88
M.P.Briers	Cornwall	183	22	693	27	25.67
N.A.Fusedale	Berkshire	223.6	58	748	29	25.79
A.R.Clarke	Buckinghamshire	346.5	68	1270	48	26.46
P.G.Newman	Staffordshire	315.3	60	940	35	26.86
P.L.Garlick	Dorset	149.5	36	650	24	27.08
D.J.B.Hartley	Berkshire	231.6	32	944	34	27.76
R.A.Evans	Oxfordshire	315.5	73	823	29	28.38
D.F.Ralfs	Cambridgeshire	256.2	70	687	24	28.63

SECOND XI CHAMPIONSHIP 1994
RAPID CRICKETLINE FINAL TABLE

					Bonus Points		Total
	P	W	L	D	Bat	Bowl	Points
1 SOMERSET (9)	17	10	3	4	44	47	251
2 Yorkshire (3)	17	6	2	9	50	44	190
3 Kent (11)	17	6	2	9	44	49	189
4 Leicestershire (13)	17	5	2	10	54	49	183
5 Northamptonshire (12)	17	3	4	10	53	50	159
6 Gloucestershire (4)	17	4	3	10	43	50	157
7 Durham (14)	17	4	5	8	37	52	149
8 Worcestershire (16)	17	3	3	11	55	46	149
9 Sussex (8)	17	3	1	13	48	49	145
10 Middlesex (1)	17	3	6	8	42	54	144
11 Surrey (6)	17	3	4	10	39	46	133
12 Essex (7)	17	3	5	9	34	50	132
13 Hampshire (10)	17	2	5	10	46	51	129
14 Warwickshire (15)	17	1	2	14	55	52	123
15 Lancashire (2)	17	2	3	12	38	50	120
16 Derbyshire (17)	17	2	4	11	36	48	116
17 Glamorgan (18)	17	2	3	12	41	40	113
18 Nottinghamshire (5)	17	–	5	12	46	45	91

Win = 16 points. 1993 final positions are shown in brackets. Northamptonshire's total includes 8 points from a drawn match that ended with the scores level.

RAPID CRICKETLINE CHAMPIONSHIP PLAYER OF THE SEASON:
D.L.Maddy (Leicestershire) – 1498 runs (av 55.48), 5 hundreds, 21 ct.

SECOND XI CHAMPIONS

1959 Gloucestershire
1960 Northamptonshire
1961 Kent
1962 Worcestershire
1963 Worcestershire
1964 Lancashire
1965 Glamorgan
1966 Surrey
1967 Hampshire
1968 Surrey
1969 Kent
1970 Kent
1971 Hampshire
1972 Nottinghamshire
1973 Essex
1974 Middlesex
1975 Surrey
1976 Kent
1977 Yorkshire
1978 Sussex
1979 Warwickshire
1980 Glamorgan
1981 Hampshire
1982 Worcestershire
1983 Leicestershire
1984 Yorkshire
1985 Nottinghamshire
1986 Lancashire
1987 Kent/Yorkshire
1988 Surrey
1989 Middlesex
1990 Sussex
1991 Yorkshire
1992 Surrey
1993 Middlesex
1994 Somerset

BAIN CLARKSON TROPHY WINNERS

1986 Northamptonshire
1987 Derbyshire
1988 Yorkshire
1989 Middlesex
1990 Lancashire
1991 Nottinghamshire
1992 Surrey
1993 Leicestershire
1994 Yorkshire

THE FIRST-CLASS COUNTIES HONOURS, REGISTER, RECORDS AND 1994 AVERAGES

To the end of the 1994 season
(Including Pakistan's tour of Sri Lanka, July-August 1994)

ABBREVIATIONS

General

*	not out/unbroken partnership	f-c	first-class
b	born	HS	Highest Score
BB	Best innings bowling analysis	LOI	Limited-Overs Internationals
Cap	Awarded 1st XI County Cap	Tests	Official Test Matches
Tours	Overseas tours involving first-class appearances		

Awards

BHC	Benson and Hedges Cup 'Gold' Award
NWT	NatWest Trophy/Gillette Cup 'Man of the Match' Award
Wisden 1994	One of Wisden Cricketers' Almanack's Five Cricketers of 1994
YC 1994	Cricket Writers' Club Young Cricketer of 1994

Competitions		Education	
BHC	Benson and Hedges Cup	BHS	Boys' High School
GC	Gillette Cup	BS	Boys' School
NWT	NatWest Trophy	C	College
SL	Sunday (AXA Equity & Law) League	CE	College of Education
		CFE	College of Further Education
Playing Categories		CHE	College of Higher Education
LB	Bowls right-arm leg-breaks	CS	Comprehensive School
LF	Bowls left-arm fast	GS	Grammar School
LFM	Bowls left-arm fast-medium	HS	High School
LHB	Bats left-handed	IHE	Institute of Higher Education
LM	Bowls left-arm medium pace	LSE	London School of Economics
LMF	Bowls left-arm medium-fast	RGS	Royal Grammar School
OB	Bowls right-arm off-breaks	S	School
RF	Bowls right-arm fast	SFC	Sixth Form College
RFM	Bowls right-arm fast-medium	SM	Secondary Modern School
RHB	Bats right-handed	SS	Secondary School
RM	Bowls right-arm medium pace	TC	Technical College
RMF	Bowls right-arm medium-fast	T(H)S	Technical (High) School
RSM	Bowls right-arm slow-medium	U	University
SLA	Bowls left-arm leg-breaks		
WK	Wicket-keeper		

Teams (see also p 186)

Cav	Cavaliers	NSW	New South Wales
CD	Central Districts	NT	Northern Transvaal
DHR	D.H.Robins' XI	OFS	Orange Free State
DN	Duke of Norfolk's XI	PIA	Pakistan International Airlines
Eng Co	English Counties XI	RW	Rest of the World XI
EP	Eastern Province	SAB	South African Breweries XI
GW	Griqualand West	SAU	South African Universities
Int XI	International XI	WA	Western Australia
IW	International Wanderers	Zim	Zimbabwe (Rhodesia)
ND	Northern Districts		

DERBYSHIRE

Formation of Present Club: 4 November 1870
Colours: Chocolate, Amber and Pale Blue
Badge: Rose and Crown
Championships: (1) 1936
NatWest Trophy/Gillette Cup Winners: (1) 1981
Benson and Hedges Cup Winners: (1) 1993
Sunday League Champions: (1) 1990
Match Awards: NWT 33; BHC 58

Chief Executive: R.G.Taylor
County Cricket Ground, Nottingham Road, Derby DE2 6DA (☎ 01332 383211)
Captain: K.J.Barnett
Scorer: S.W.Tacey
1995 Beneficiary: A.E.Warner.

ADAMS, Christopher John (Repton S), b Whitwell 6 May 1970. 6'0". RHB, OB. Debut 1988. Cap 1992. 1000 runs (1): 1109 (1992). HS 175 v Notts (Nottingham) 1993. BB 4-29 v Lancs (Derby) 1991. Award: BHC 1. **NWT:** HS 106* and BB 1-15 v Berks (Derby) 1992. **BHC:** HS 58 v Middx (Derby) 1993. **SL:** HS 141* v Kent (Chesterfield) 1992. BB 2-15 v Essex (Chelmsford) 1993.

BARNETT, Kim John (Leek HS), b Stoke-on-Trent, Staffs 17 Jul 1960. 6'1". RHB, LB. Debut 1979. Cap 1982. Captain 1983-. Boland 1982-83/1987-88. Staffordshire 1976. Wisden 1988. Benefit 1992. **Tests:** 4 (1988 to 1989); HS 80 v A (Leeds) 1989. LOI: 1 (HS 84). Tours: SA 1989-90 (Eng XI); NZ 1979-80 (DHR); SL 1985-86 (Eng B). 1000 runs (11); most – 1734 (1984). HS 239* v Leics (Leicester) 1988. BB 6-28 v Glam (Chesterfield) 1991. Awards: NWT 3; BHC 10. **NWT:** HS 113* v Glos (Bristol) 1994. BB 6-24 v Cumberland (Kendal) 1984. **BHC:** HS 115 v Glos (Derby) 1987. BB 1-10. **SL:** HS 131* v Essex (Derby) 1984. BB 3-39 v Yorks (Chesterfield) 1979.

BASE, Simon John (Fish Hoek HS, Cape Town), b Maidstone, Kent 2 Jan 1960. 6'2". RHB, RMF. W Province 1981-82/1983-84. Glamorgan 1986-87. Boland 1987-88/1988-89. Border 1989-90 to date. Derbyshire debut 1988. Cap 1990. HS 58 v Yorks (Chesterfield) 1990. 50 wkts (1): 60 (1989). BB 7-60 v Yorks (Chesterfield) 1989. **NWT:** HS 4. BB 2-49 Gm v Sussex (Hove) 1986. **BHC:** HS 15* v Somerset (Taunton) 1990. BB 3-33 v Minor C (Wellington) 1990. **SL:** HS 31 v Kent (Canterbury) 1993. BB 4-14 v Northants (Derby) 1991 and v Glos (Cheltenham) 1993.

CASSAR, Matthew Edward (Sir Joseph Banks HS, Sydney), b Sydney, Australia 16 Oct 1972. 6'0". RHB, RFM. Debut 1994. Qualified for England 1997. HS 66 and BB 3-65 v NZ (Derby) 1994.

CORK, Dominic Gerald (St Joseph's C, Stoke-on-Trent), b Newcastle-under-Lyme, Staffs 7 Aug 1971. 6'2". RHB, RFM. Debut 1990. Cap 1993. Staffordshire 1989-90. LOI: 5 (HS 11; BB 3-49). Tours (Eng A): A 1992-93; SA 1993-94; WI 1991-92. HS 104 v Glos (Cheltenham) 1993. 50 wkts (1): 57 (1991). BB 8-53 (before lunch on his 20th birthday) v Essex (Derby) 1991. Hat-trick 1994. Awards: NWT 2; BHC 2. **NWT:** HS 62 v Kent (Derby) 1994. BB 5-18 v Berks (Derby) 1992. **BHC:** HS 92* v Lancs (Lord's) 1993. BB 4-26 v Durham (Jesmond) 1992. **SL:** HS 66 v Sussex (Eastbourne) 1994. BB 4-44 v Warwks (Chesterfield) 1994.

DeFREITAS, Phillip Anthony Jason (Willesden HS, London), b Scotts Head, Dominica 18 Feb 1966. 6'0". RHB, RFM. UK resident since 1976. Leicestershire 1985-88 (cap 1986). Lancashire 1989-93 (cap 1989). Boland 1993-94. Derbyshire debut/cap 1994. Wisden 1991. MCC YC. **Tests:** 39 (1986-87 to 1994); HS 69 v NZ (Manchester) 1994; BB 7-70 v SL (Lord's) 1991. LOI: 87 (HS 49*; BB 4-35). Tours: A 1986-87, 1990-91; WI 1989-90; NZ 1987-88, 1991-92; P 1987-88; I 1992-93; Z 1988-89 (La). HS 113 Le v Notts (Worksop) 1988. De HS 108 v Leics (Derby) 1994. 50 wkts (7); most – 94 (1986). BB 7-21 La v Middx (Lord's) 1989. De BB 6-39 v Lancs

DeFREITAS – continued:
(Blackpool) 1994. Hat-trick 1994. Awards: NWT 3; BHC 4. **NWT:** HS 69 Le v Lancs (Leicester) 1986. BB 5-13 La v Cumberland (Kendal) 1989. **BHC:** HS 75* La v Hants (Manchester) 1990. BB 5-16 La v Essex (Chelmsford) 1992. **SL:** HS 49* La v Hants (Manchester) 1992. BB 5-26 La v Hants (Southampton) 1993.

GRIFFITH, Frank Alexander (Beaconsfield HS; Wm Morris HS; Haringey Cricket C), b Whipps Cross, Essex 15 Aug 1968. 6'0". RHB, RM. Debut 1988. HS 81 v Glam (Chesterfield) 1992. BB 4-33 v Leics (Ilkeston) 1992. **NWT:** HS 8. BB 1-13. **BHC:** HS 13* and BB 2-48 v Glos (Bristol) 1993. **SL:** HS 31 v Lancs (Manchester) 1994. BB 4-48 v Glam (Derby) 1993.

HARRIS, Andrew James (Hadfield CS; Glossopdale Community C), b Ashton-under-Lyne, Lancs 26 Jun 1973. 6'1". RHB, RM. Debut 1994. HS 10 v Surrey (Oval) 1994. BB 3-40 v Worcs (Derby) 1994. **SL:** HS –. BB 2-49 v Leics (Derby) 1994.

KRIKKEN, Karl Matthew (Rivington & Blackrod HS & SFC), b Bolton, Lancs 9 Apr 1969. Son of B.E. (Lancs and Worcs 1966-69). 5'9". RHB, WK. GW 1988-89. Derbyshire debut 1989. Cap 1992. HS 85* v Glam (Cardiff) 1994. **NWT:** HS 18 v Leics (Derby) 1992. **BHC:** HS 37* v Worcs (Worcester) 1992 and v Lancs (Lord's) 1993. **SL:** HS 44* v Essex (Chelmsford) 1991.

MAHER, Bernard Joseph Michael (Abbotsfield CS; Bishopshalt GS; Loughborough U), b Hillingdon, Middx 11 Feb 1958. 5'10". RHB, WK. Derbyshire debut 1981. Cap 1987. HS 126 v NZ (Derby) 1986. BAC HS 121* v Leics (Derby) 1988. BB 2-69 v Glam (Abergavenny) 1986. **NWT:** HS 44 v Hants (Derby) 1988. **BHC:** HS 50 v Northants (Derby) 1987. **SL:** HS 78 v Lancs (Manchester) 1987.

MALCOLM, Devon Eugene (Richmond C, Sheffield), b Kingston, Jamaica 22 Feb 1963. 6'2". RHB, RF. Debut 1984. Cap 1989. Wisden 1994. **Tests:** 28 (1989 to 1994); HS 18 v WI (Kingston) 1993-94; BB 9-57 v SA (Oval) 1994. LOI: 10 (HS 4; BB 3-40). Tours: A 1990-91; WI 1989-90, 1991-92 (Eng A), 1993-94; I 1992-93; SL 1992-93. HS 51 v Surrey (Derby) 1989. 50 wkts (3); most – 69 (1994). BB 9-57 (Tests). De BB 6-57 v Sussex (Derby) 1993. Award: BHC 1. **NWT:** HS 10* v Leics (Derby) 1992. BB 3-29 v Devon (Exmouth) 1993. **BHC:** HS 15 v Comb Us (Oxford) 1991. BB 5-27 v Middx (Derby) 1988. **SL:** HS 18 v Essex (Chelmsford) 1991. BB 4-21 v Surrey (Derby) 1989 and v Leics (Knypersley) 1990.

O'GORMAN, Timothy Joseph Gerard (St George's C, Weybridge; Durham U), b Woking, Surrey 15 May 1967. Grandson of J.G. (Surrey 1927). 6'2". RHB, OB. Debut 1987. Cap 1992. 1000 runs (2); most – 1116 (1991). HS 148 v Lancs (Manchester) 1991. BB 1-7. Award: NWT 1. **NWT:** HS 89 v Durham (Darlington) 1994. **BHC:** HS 49 v Northants (Derby) 1991 and v Lancs (Lord's) 1993. **SL:** HS 69 v Northants (Northampton) 1992.

RICHARDSON, Alan (Alleyne's HS; Stafford CFE), b Newcastle-under-Lyme, Staffs 6 May 1975. 6'2". RHB, RM. Derbyshire staff 1994 – awaiting f-c debut.

ROLLINS, Adrian Stewart (Little Ilford CS), b Barking, Essex 8 Feb 1972. Brother of R.J. (see ESSEX). 6'5". RHB, WK, occ RM. Debut 1993. HS 97 v Lancs (Blackpool) 1994. **NWT:** HS 6. **BHC:** HS 70 v Lancs (Derby) 1994. **SL:** HS 57 v Notts (Nottingham) 1993.

STEER, Ian **Gary** Samuel (St Edmund Campion S; Sutton Coldfield C; Cheltenham & Gloucester CHE), b Aston, Birmingham 17 Aug 1970. 5'7". RHB, RM. Debut 1993. Warwickshire staff 1990-91. HS 67 v Leics (Leicester) 1993 and Comb Us v NZ (Cambridge) 1994. BB 3-23 v Surrey (Ilkeston) 1993. **BHC:** HS 43 Comb Us v Lancs (Oxford) 1994. **SL:** HS 19 v Leics (Leicester) 1993. BB 1-33.

TAYLOR, Matthew (Rivington & Blackrod HS; Bolton North SFC), b Bolton, Lancs 13 Nov 1973. 6'1". RHB, SLA. Debut 1994. HS 14* v Lancs (Blackpool) 1994. BB 3-25 v NZ (Derby) 1994. BAC BB 2-13 v Glam (Cardiff) 1994.

TWEATS, Timothy Andrew (Endon HS; Stoke-on-Trent SFC), b Stoke-on-Trent, Staffs 18 Apr 1974. 6'3". RHB, RM. Debut 1992. HS 24 v Glam (Cardiff) 1992.

WARNER, Allan Esmond (Tabernacle S, St Kitts), b Birmingham 12 May 1957. 5'7". RHB, RFM. Worcestershire 1982-84. Derbyshire debut 1985. Cap 1987. Benefit 1995. HS 95* v Kent (Canterbury) 1993. BB 5-27 Wo v Glam (Worcester) 1984 and 5-27 (10-120 match) v Glos (Cheltenham) 1993. Award: NWT 1. **NWT:** HS 32 v Kent (Canterbury) 1987. BB 4-39 v Salop (Chesterfield) 1990. **BHC:** HS 35* v Comb Us (Oxford) 1991. BB 4-36 v Notts (Nottingham) 1987. **SL:** HS 68 v Hants (Heanor) 1986. BB 5-39 v Worcs (Knypersley) 1985.

WELLS, Colin Mark (Tideway CS, Newhaven), b Newhaven, Sussex 3 Mar 1960. Elder brother of A.P. (see SUSSEX). 5'11". RHB, RM. Sussex 1979-93 (cap 1982; benefit 1993). Derbyshire debut 1994. Border 1980-81. W Province 1984-85. LOI: 2 (HS 17). 1000 runs (6); most – 1456 (1987). HS 203 Sx v Hants (Hove) 1984. De HS 42 v Kent (Derby) 1994. 50 wkts (2); most – 59 (1984). BB 7-42 Sx v Derbys (Derby) 1991. De BB 4-52 v Middx (Derby) 1994. Awards: BHC 3. **NWT:** HS 76 Sx v Ire (Hove) 1985. BB 3-16 Sx v Scot (Edinburgh) 1991. **BHC:** HS 117 Sx v Glam (Swansea) 1989. BB 4-21 Sx v Middx (Lord's) 1980. **SL:** HS 104* Sx v Warwks (Hove) 1983. BB 4-15 Sx v Worcs (Worcester) 1983.

NEWCOMERS

ALDRED, Paul (Lady Manner's S, Bakewell), b Chellaston 4 Feb 1969. RHB, RM.

CULLINAN, Daryll John (Queens C, Queenstown; Stellenbosch U), b Kimberley, SA 4 Mar 1967. Brother of R.E. (Border and OFS 1984-85 to date). 5'10". RHB, OB. Border 1983-84/1984-85 making debut while at school. WP 1985-86/1990-91. Transvaal 1991-92 to date. At 16yr 304d remains youngest player to score f-c hundred in SA. **Tests** (SA): 8 (1992-93 to 1994); HS 102 v SL (Colombo) 1993-94. LOI (SA): 22 (HS 70*). Tours (SA): E 1994; A 1993-94; SL 1993-94. HS 337* Transvaal v N Transvaal (Jo'burg) 1993-94 (SA f-c record). BB 2-27 Border v Natal B (E London) 1983-84.

OWEN, John Edward (Spondon S, Derby), b Derby 7 Aug 1971. RHB, OB.

DEPARTURES (who made first-class appearances in 1994)

AZHARUDDIN, Mohammed (Nizam C; Osmania U), b Hyderabad, India 8 Feb 1963. 5'11". RHB, RM/LB. Hyderabad 1981-82 to date. Derbyshire 1991 and 1994 (cap 1991). Wisden 1990. **Tests** (I): 62 (1984-85 to 1993-94, 28 as captain); HS 199 v SL (Kanpur) 1986-87. LOI (I): 174 (HS 108*; BB 3-19). Tours (I) (C=captain): E 1986, 1990C; A 1985-86, 1991-92C; SA 1992-93C; WI 1988-89; NZ 1989-90C, 1993-94C; P 1989-90; SL 1985-86, 1993-94C; Z 1983-84 (Young I), 1992-93C. 1000 runs (1+2) inc 2000 (1): 2016 (1991). HS 226 S Zone v C Zone (Jamadoba) 1983-84. De HS 212 v Leics (Leicester) 1991. BB 2-33 Hyderabad v Andhra (Hyderabad) 1987-88. De BB 1-35. **NWT:** HS 74* v Durham (Darlington) 1994. **BHC:** HS 44* v Comb Us (Oxford) 1991. BB 1-17. **SL:** HS 111* v Northants (Northampton) 1994.

BOWLER, P.D. – see SOMERSET.

MORTENSEN, Ole Henrek (Brondbyoster S; Abedore C, Copenhagen), b Vejle, Denmark 29 Jan 1958. 6'3". RHB, RFM. Derbyshire 1983-94 (cap 1986; benefit 1994). Denmark 1975-82. HS 74* v Yorks (Chesterfield) 1987. 50 wkts (2); most – 58 (1991). BB 6-27 v Yorks (Sheffield) 1983. Hat-trick 1987. Awards: NWT 2. **NWT:** HS 11 v Surrey (Derby) 1986. BB 6-14 v Ire (Derby) 1989. **BHC:** HS 5*. BB 3-17 v Leics (Chesterfield) 1986. **SL:** HS 11 v Worcs (Worcester) 1989. BB 4-10 v Leics (Chesterfield) 1985.

SLADDIN, Richard William (Sowerby Bridge HS), b Halifax, Yorks 8 Jan 1969. 6'0". RHB, SLA. Derbyshire 1991-94. HS 51* v Durham (Durham) 1993. BB 6-58 v CU (Cambridge) 1992. BAC BB 5-186 v Essex (Chelmsford) 1991. **SL:** HS 26 v Durham (Durham) 1993. BB 2-26 v Glos (Cheltenham) 1993.

VANDRAU, Matthew James (St Stithian's C, Johannesburg; St John's C, Jo'burg; Witwatersrand U), b Epsom, Surrey 22 Jul 1969. Son of B.M. (Transvaal B 1963). 6'3½". RHB, OB. Transvaal 1990-91 to date. Derbyshire 1993-94. HS 66 and De BB 4-53 v Kent (Derby) 1994. BB 5-42 Transvaal v Border (Jo'burg) 1993-94. **NWT:** HS 27 v Kent (Derby) 1994. BB 2-36 v Durham (Darlington) 1994. **BHC:** HS –. BB 1-46. **SL:** HS 32* v Kent (Canterbury) 1993. BB 3-25 v Leics (Derby) 1994.

DERBYSHIRE 1994

RESULTS SUMMARY

	Place	Won	Lost	Drew	Abandoned
Britannic Assurance Championship	**17th**	4	9	4	
All First-class Matches		5	9	4	
Sunday League	**8th**	8	7		2
NatWest Trophy	Quarter-Finalist				
Benson and Hedges Cup	Quarter-Finalist				

BRITANNIC ASSURANCE CHAMPIONSHIP AVERAGES

BATTING AND FIELDING

Cap		*M*	*I*	*NO*	*HS*	*Runs*	*Avge*	*100*	*50*	*Ct/St*
1991	M.Azharuddin	9	17	1	205	712	44.50	2	1	5
1982	K.J.Barnett	14	23	2	148	841	40.04	1	7	7
1992	C.J.Adams	17	31	3	109*	926	33.07	1	5	16
–	F.A.Griffith	3	5	1	36	123	30.75	–	–	2
1992	T.J.G.O'Gorman	15	27	2	145	729	29.16	2	3	11
1994	P.A.J.DeFreitas	8	13	1	108	338	28.16	1	1	2
–	A.S.Rollins	15	28	2	97	692	26.61	–	6	16
1992	K.M.Krikken	14	26	10	85*	391	24.43	–	2	26/2
–	M.J.Vandrau	12	22	5	66	404	23.76	–	1	8
1989	P.D.Bowler	13	23	–	88	546	23.73	–	2	11
1993	D.G.Cork	12	20	–	94	459	22.95	–	4	15
–	C.M.Wells	11	20	2	42	303	16.83	–	–	4
1990	S.J.Base	7	11	1	33	149	14.90	–	–	6
1987	A.E.Warner	10	15	3	24*	96	8.00	–	–	1
–	M.Taylor	3	4	1	14*	23	7.66	–	–	–
1989	D.E.Malcolm	16	21	9	15*	85	7.08	–	–	1
–	R.W.Sladdin	3	6	–	20	42	7.00	–	–	–

Also played: A.J.Harris (2 matches) 10, 1, 0; O.H.Mortensen (1 match – cap 1986) did not bat; I.G.S.Steer (2 matches) 27 (2 ct).

BOWLING

	O	*M*	*R*	*W*	*Avge*	*Best*	*5wI*	*10wM*
K.J.Barnett	54.2	5	173	13	13.30	5-31	1	–
P.A.J.DeFreitas	273.5	59	812	35	23.20	6-39	3	
D.G.Cork	317.1	52	1070	35	30.57	6-29	2	–
D.E.Malcolm	482.2	83	1793	57	31.45	6-95	2	–
C.M.Wells	153.3	31	469	13	36.07	4-52	–	–
M.J.Vandrau	265.5	59	852	23	37.04	4-53	–	–
S.J.Base	176	26	693	17	40.76	5-92	1	–
A.E.Warner	256	53	817	19	43.00	4-39	–	–

Also bowled: C.J.Adams 30-3-114-3; M.Azharuddin 8-0-46-0; P.D.Bowler 1-0-17-0; F.A.Griffith 67.4-12-210-8; A.J.Harris 32-1-165-5; O.H.Mortensen 7-2-18-1; T.J.G.O'Gorman 0.5-0-8-0; A.S.Rollins 4-0-32-0; R.W.Sladdin 115-20-427-4; I.G.S.Steer 2-0-12-0; M.Taylor 71-18-180-4.

The First-Class Averages (pp 186-200) give the records of Derbyshire players in all first-class county matches (their other opponents being the New Zealanders), with the exception of P.A.J.DeFreitas, D.E.Malcolm and I.G.S.Steer whose full county figures are as above.

DERBYSHIRE RECORDS

FIRST-CLASS CRICKET

Highest Total	For 645		v	Hampshire	Derby	1898
	V 662		by	Yorkshire	Chesterfield	1898
Lowest Total	For 16		v	Notts	Nottingham	1879
	V 23		by	Hampshire	Burton upon T	1958
Highest Innings	For 274	G.A.Davidson	v	Lancashire	Manchester	1896
	V 343*	P.A.Perrin	for	Essex	Chesterfield	1904

Highest Partnership for each Wicket

1st	322	H.Storer/J.Bowden	v	Essex	Derby	1929
2nd	349	C.S.Elliott/J.D.Eggar	v	Notts	Nottingham	1947
3rd	291	P.N.Kirsten/D.S.Steele	v	Somerset	Taunton	1981
4th	328	P.Vaulkhard/D.Smith	v	Notts	Nottingham	1946
5th	302*†	J.E.Morris/D.G.Cork	v	Glos	Cheltenham	1993
6th	212	G.M.Lee/T.S.Worthington	v	Essex	Chesterfield	1932
7th	241*	G.H.Pope/A.E.G.Rhodes	v	Hampshire	Portsmouth	1948
8th	182	A.H.M.Jackson/W.Carter	v	Leics	Leicester	1922
9th	283	A.Warren/J.Chapman	v	Warwicks	Blackwell	1910
10th	132	A.Hill/M.Jean-Jacques	v	Yorkshire	Sheffield	1986

† 346 runs were added for this wicket in two separate partnerships.

Best Bowling	For	10- 40	W.Bestwick	v	Glamorgan	Cardiff	1921
(Innings)	V	10- 45	R.L.Johnson	for	Middlesex	Derby	1994
Best Bowling	For	17-103	W.Mycroft	v	Hampshire	Southampton	1876
(Match)	V	16-101	G.Giffen	for	Australians	Derby	1886

Most Runs – Season	2165	D.B.Carr	(av 48.11)	1959
Most Runs – Career	20516†	D.Smith	(av 31.41)	1927-52
Most 100s – Season	8	P.N.Kirsten		1982
Most 100s – Career	44	K.J.Barnett		1979-94
Most Wkts – Season	168	T.B.Mitchell	(av 19.55)	1935
Most Wkts – Career	1670	H.L.Jackson	(av 17.11)	1947-63

† K.J.Barnett has scored 18863 runs.

LIMITED-OVERS CRICKET

Highest Total	NWT	365-3		v	Cornwall	Derby	1986
	BHC	366-4		v	Comb Us	Oxford	1991
	SL	292-9		v	Worcs	Knypersley	1985
Lowest Total	NWT	79		v	Surrey	The Oval	1967
	BHC	98		v	Worcs	Derby	1994
	SL	61		v	Hampshire	Portsmouth	1990
Highest Innings	NWT	153	A.Hill	v	Cornwall	Derby	1986
	BHC	123	J.E.Morris	v	Somerset	Taunton	1990
	SL	141*	C.J.Adams	v	Kent	Chesterfield	1992
Best Bowling	NWT	8-21	M.A.Holding	v	Sussex	Hove	1988
	BHC	6-33	E.J.Barlow	v	Glos	Bristol	1978
	SL	6- 7	M.Hendrick	v	Notts	Nottingham	1972

DURHAM

Formation of Present Club: 10 May 1882
Colours: Navy blue, yellow and maroon
Badge: Coat of Arms of the County of Durham
Championships: (0) 16th 1994
NatWest Trophy/Gillette Cup Winners: (0) Quarter-Finalist 1992
Benson and Hedges Cup Winners: (0) Second Round 1994
Sunday League Champions: (0) Seventh 1993
Match Awards: NWT 17; BHC 5.

Chief Executive: G.A.Wright
County Ground, Riverside, Chester-le-Street, Co Durham DH3 3QR.
(☎ 0191-387 1717)
Captain: M.A.Roseberry
Scorer: B.Hunt

BAINBRIDGE, Philip (Hanley HS; Stoke-on-Trent SFC; Borough Road CE), b Sneyd Green, Stoke-on-Trent, Staffs 16 Apr 1958. 5'10". RHB, RM. Gloucestershire 1977-90 (cap 1981; benefit 1989). Durham debut/cap 1992. Captain 1994. Wisden 1985. Tours: SL 1986-87 (Gs); Z 1984-85 (EC). 1000 runs (9); most – 1644 (1985). HS 169 Gs v Yorks (Cheltenham) 1988. Du HS 150* v Essex (Chelmsford) 1993. BB 8-53 Gs v Somerset (Bristol) 1986. Du BB 5-53 v Yorks (Leeds) 1993. Awards: NWT 1; BHC 3. **NWT:** HS 89 Gs v Leics (Leicester) 1988. BB 3-49 Gs v Scot (Bristol) 1983. **BHC:** HS 96 Gs v Hants (Southampton) 1988. BB 4-38 v Worcs (Worcester) 1992. **SL:** HS 106* Gs v Somerset (Bristol) 1986. BB 5-22 Gs v Middx (Lord's) 1987.
BETTS, Melvyn Morris (Fyndoune CS, Sacriston), b Sacriston 26 Mar 1975. 5'10". RHB, RMF. Debut 1993. Cap 1994. HS 4. BB 1-19.
BIRBECK, Shaun David (Hetton CS), b Easington 26 Jul 1972. Brother of A. (Durham 1983-90). 5'11". LHB, RM. Debut/cap 1994. HS 6 and BB 2-13 v OU (Oxford) 1994. Awaiting BAC debut. **SL:** HS 9. BB 1-47.
BLENKIRON, Darren Andrew (Bishop Barrington CS, Bishop Auckland), b Solihull, Warwks 4 Feb 1974. Son of W. (Warwks 1964-74, Durham 1975-76). 5'10". LHB, RM. Durham staff/cap 1992. Debut 1994. HS –. **NWT:** HS 56 v Glam (Darlington) 1991. **SL:** HS 39* v Glam (Hartlepool) 1994.
BROWN, Simon John Emmerson (Boldon CS), b Cleadon 29 Jun 1969. 6'3". RHB, LFM. Northamptonshire 1987-90. Durham debut/cap 1992. HS 69 v Leics (Durham) 1994. 50 wkts (2); most – 75 (1994). BB 7-70 v A (Durham) 1993. BAC BB 7-105 v Kent (Canterbury) 1992. Award: NWT 1. **NWT:** HS 7*. BB 5-22 v Cheshire (Bowdon) 1994. **BHC:** HS 4*. BB 2-32 v Minor C (Hartlepool) 1993. **SL:** HS 7. BB 3-26 Nh v Leics (Leicester) 1990.
COX, David Mathew (Greenford HS), b Southall, Middx 2 Mar 1972. 5'10". LHB, SLA. Hertfordshire 1992. MCC YC. Durham staff/cap 1993. Debut 1994. HS 26* and BB 1-92 v SA (Chester-le-St) 1994. BAC HS 0. **SL:** HS –. BB 1-25.
DALEY, James Arthur (Hetton CS), b Sunderland 24 Sep 1973. 5'10". RHB, RM. Debut/cap 1992. MCC YC 1991. HS 159* v Hants (Portsmouth) 1994. **SL:** HS 98* v Kent (Canterbury) 1994.
HUTTON, Stewart (De Brus S, Skelton; Cleveland TC), b Stockton-on-Tees 30 Nov 1969. 6'0". LHB, RSM. Debut/cap 1992. HS 101 v Northants (Hartlepool) 1994. Award: NWT 1. **NWT:** HS 95 v Wilts (Trowbridge) 1993. **BHC:** HS 8. **SL:** HS 70 v Glam (Hartlepool) 1992.
LARKINS, Wayne (Bushmead SS, Eaton Socon), b Roxton, Beds 22 Nov 1953. 5'11". RHB, RM. Northamptonshire 1972-91 (cap 1976; benefit 1986). Durham debut/cap 1992. E Province 1982-83/1983-84. **Tests:** 13 (1979-80 to 1990-91); HS 64 v A (Melbourne) 1990-91. LOI: 25 (HS 124). Tours: A 1979-80, 1990-91; SA 1981-82 (SAB); WI 1989-90; I 1979-80, 1980-81 (Overseas XI). 1000 runs (13);

most – 1863 (1982). HS 252 Nh v Glam (Cardiff) 1983. Du HS 158* v Glos (Gateshead) 1994. BB 5-59 Nh v Worcs (Worcester) 1984. Awards: NWT 2; BHC 7. **NWT:** HS 121* Nh v Essex (Chelmsford) 1987. BB 2-38 Nh v Glos (Bristol) 1985. **BHC:** HS 132 Nh v Warwks (Birmingham) 1982. BB 4-37 Nh v Comb Us (Northampton) 1980. **SL:** HS 172* Nh v Warwks (Luton) 1983. BB 5-32 Nh v Essex (Ilford) 1978.

LONGLEY, Jonathan Ian (Tonbridge S; Durham U), b New Brunswick, New Jersey, USA 12 Apr 1969. 5'7". RHB. Kent 1989-93. Durham debut/cap 1994. Tour: Z 1992-93 (K). HS 110 K v CU (Cambridge) 1992. BAC/Du HS 100* v Derbys (Chesterfield) 1994 – on Du debut. **NWT:** HS 9. **BHC:** HS 57 K v Somerset (Canterbury) 1992. **SL:** HS 88 v Somerset (Taunton) 1994.

LUGSDEN, Steven (St Edmund Campion S, Low Fell), b Gateshead 10 Jul 1976. 6'2". RHB, RFM. Debut 1993 aged 17yr 27d (youngest Durham f-c player). Cap 1994. HS 5* and BB 2-43 v Derbys (Durham) 1993. **SL:** HS –. BB 1-55.

MORRIS, John Edward (Shavington CS; Dane Bank CFE), b Crewe, Cheshire 1 Apr 1964. 5'10". RHB, RM. Derbyshire 1982-93 (cap 1986). GW 1988-89 and 1993-94. Durham debut/cap 1994. **Tests:** 3 (1990); HS 32 v I (Oval) 1990. LOI: 8 (HS 63*). Tour: A 1990-91. 1000 runs (9); most – 1739 (1986). HS 229 De v Glos (Cheltenham) 1993. Du HS 204 v Warwks (Birmingham) 1994. BB 1-6. Du BB 1-37. Awards: NWT 1; BHC 2. **NWT:** HS 94* De v Salop (Chesterfield) 1990. **BHC:** HS 123 De v Somerset (Taunton) 1990. **SL:** HS 134 De v Somerset (Taunton) 1990.

SAXELBY, Mark (Nottingham HS), b Worksop, Notts 4 Jan 1969. 6'3". LHB, RM. Younger brother of K. (Notts 1978-90). Nottinghamshire 1989-93. Durham debut/cap 1994. 1000 runs (1): 1102 (1994). HS 181 v Derbys (Chesterfield) 1994. BB 3-41 Nt v Derbys (Derby) 1991. **NWT:** HS 41 Nt v Bucks (Marlow) 1990. BB 2-42 Nt v Lincs (Nottingham) 1991. **BHC:** HS 32 Nt v Hants (Southampton) 1991. BB 1-36. **SL:** HS 100* Nt v Durham (Chester-le-St) 1993. BB 4-29 Nt v Leics (Leicester) 1991.

SCOTT, Christopher Wilmot (Robert Pattinson CS, N Hykeham), b Thorpe-on-the-Hill, Lincs 23 Jan 1964. 5'8". RHB, WK. Nottinghamshire 1981-91 (cap 1988). Durham debut/cap 1992. HS 108 v Surrey (Darlington) 1994. Held 10 catches for Notts in match v Derbys (Derby) 1988. **NWT:** HS 2. **BHC:** HS 18 Nt v Northants (Northampton) 1988. **SL:** HS 45 v Surrey (Darlington) 1994.

SEARLE, Jason Paul (John Bentley S, Calne; Swindon C), b Bath, Somerset 16 May 1976. 5'9". RHB, OB. Durham staff/cap 1993. Debut 1994. HS 5*.

WALKER, Alan (Shelley HS), b Emley, Yorks 7 Jul 1962. 5'11". LHB, RFM. Northamptonshire 1983-93 (cap 1987). Durham debut/cap 1994. Tour: SA 1991-92 (Nh). HS 41* Nh v Warwks (Birmingham) 1987. Du HS 13 v Somerset (Taunton) 1994. 50 wkts (1): 54 (1988). BB 6-50 Nh v Lancs (Northampton) 1986. Du BB 4-59 v Glam (Hartlepool) 1994. Award: NWT 1. **NWT:** HS 13 v Derbys (Darlington) 1994. BB 4-7 Nh v Ire (Northampton) 1987. **BHC:** HS 15* Nh v Notts (Nottingham) 1987. BB 4-46 Nh v Glos (Northampton) 1985. **SL:** HS 30 Nh v Durham (Northampton) 1993. BB 4-21 Nh v Worcs (Worcester) 1985.

WESTON, Robin Michael Swann (Durham S; Loughborough U), b Durham 7 Jun 1975. Brother of W.P.C. (see WORCESTERSHIRE). 5'10". RHB, LB. Durham staff/cap 1994 – awaiting f-c debut. Minor C debut 1991 when aged 15yr 355d (Durham record).

WILCOCK, Peter James (Balderstone CS; Hopwood Hall C), b Rochdale, Lancs 6 Aug 1974. 6'4". RHB, occ OB. Durham staff/cap 1994 – awaiting f-c debut.

WOOD, John (Crofton HS; Wakefield District C; Leeds Poly), b Wakefield, Yorks 22 Jul 1970. 6'3". RHB, RFM. GW in Nissan Shield 1990-91. Debut/cap 1992. HS 63* v Notts (Chester-le-St) 1993. BB 6-110 v Essex (Stockton) 1994. **NWT:** HS 1. BB 2-22 v Ireland (Dublin) 1992. **BHC:** HS –. BB 1-19. **SL:** HS 28 and BB 2-26 v Worcs (Worcester) 1994.

NEWCOMERS

BOILING, James (Rutlish S, Merton; Durham U), b New Delhi, India 8 Apr 1968. 6'4". RHB, OB. Surrey 1988-94. Tour: A 1992-93 (Eng A). HS 34* Sy v Durham (Darlington) 1994. BB 6-84 (10-203 match) Sy v Glos (Bristol) 1992. Award: BHC 1. **NWT:** HS 24 Sy v Worcs (Oval) 1994. BB 2-22 Sy v Northants (Oval) 1991. **BHC:** HS 9* (twice). BB 3-9 Comb Us v Surrey (Cambridge) 1989. **SL:** HS 23* Sy v Worcs (Worcester) 1993. BB 5-24 Sy v Hants (Basingstoke) 1992.

LIGERTWOOD, David George Coutts (St Peter's C, Adelaide; Adelaide U), b Oxford 16 May 1969. 5'8". RHB, WK. Surrey 1992. Hertfordshire 1990-91. HS 28 Sy v Sussex (Oval) 1992 – on debut. **SL:** HS –.

PRABHAKAR, Manoj (Ghaziabad SS; Delhi C), b Ghaziabad, India 15 Apr 1963. 5'8½". RHB, RM. Delhi 1982-83 to date. **Tests** (I): 33 (1984-85 to 1993-94); HS 95 v NZ (Napier) 1989-90; BB 6-132 v P (Faisalabad) 1989-90. LOI (I): 102 (HS 106; BB 5-35). Tours (I): E 1986, 1990; A 1991-92; SA 1992-93; NZ 1989-90, 1993-94; P 1989-90; SL 1993-94; Z 1983-84 (Young I), 1992-93. HS 229* and BB 6-36 Delhi v Himachal Pradesh (Delhi) 1988-89.

ROSEBERRY, Michael Anthony (Durham S), b Houghton-le-Spring 28 Nov 1966. Elder brother of A. (see GLAMORGAN). 6'1". RHB, RM. Middlesex 1986-94 (cap 1990). Durham captain 1995. Tour: A 1992-93 (Eng A). 1000 runs (4) inc 2000 (1): 2044 (1992). HS 185 M v Leics (Lord's) 1993. BB 1-1. Award: BHC 1. **NWT:** HS 112 and BB 1-22 M v Salop (Telford) 1992. **BHC:** HS 84 M v Minor C (Lord's) 1992. **SL:** HS 119* M v Surrey (Oval) 1994.

DEPARTURES (who made first-class appearances in 1994)

BERRY, Philip John (Saltscar CS; Longlands CFE, Redcar), b Saltburn, Yorks 28 Dec 1966. 6'0". RHB, OB. Yorkshire 1986-90. Durham 1992-94 (cap 1992). HS 76 and BB 7-113 v Middx (Lord's) 1992. **NWT:** HS 9. BB 2-35 v Glam (Cardiff) 1993. **BHC:** HS –. **SL:** HS 6. BB 1-35.

CUMMINS, Anderson Cleophas (Foundation S; Combermere S; Bridgetown U), b Packer's Valley, Barbados 7 May 1966. RHB, RFM. Barbados 1988-89 to date. Durham 1993-94 (cap 1993). **Tests** (WI): 3 (1992-93); HS 14* v P (P-o-S) 1992-93; BB 4-54 v P (St John's) 1992-93. LOI (WI): 45 (HS 41; BB 5-31). Tours (WI): A 1991-92, 1992-93; SL 1993-94. HS 70 v Worcs (Stockton) 1993. 50 wkts (2); most – 56 (1994). BB 6-64 v Somerset (Taunton) 1994. **NWT:** HS 20* v Wilts (Trowbridge) 1993. BB 4-48 v Derbys (Darlington) 1994. **BHC:** HS 21 v Worcs (Stockton) 1994. BB 3-36 v Hants (Stockton) 1993. **SL:** HS 67 v Surrey (Darlington) 1994. BB 4-24 v Hants (Stockton) 1993.

FOWLER, Graeme (Accrington GS; Durham U), b Accrington, Lancs 20 Apr 1957. 5'9½". LHB, RM. Lancashire 1979-92 (cap 1981; benefit 1991). Durham 1993-94 (cap 1993). **Tests:** 21 (1982 to 1984-85); HS 201 v I (Madras) 1984-85. LOI: 26 (HS 81*). Tours: A 1982-83; WI 1982-83 (Int); NZ 1983-84; I/SL 1984-85; P 1983-84; Z 1988-89 (La). 1000 runs (8); most – 1800 (1987). HS 226 La v Kent (Maidstone) 1984. Du HS 138 v Yorks (Leeds) 1993. BB 2-34 La v Warwks (Manchester) 1986. Awards: NWT 2; BHC 3. **NWT:** HS 122 La v Glos (Bristol) 1984. **BHC:** HS 136 La v Sussex (Manchester) 1991. **SL:** HS 124 v Derbys (Durham) 1993.

GRAVENEY, David Anthony (Millfield S), b Bristol 2 Jan 1953. Son of J.K. (Glos 1947-64); nephew of T.W. (Glos, Worcs, Queensland and England 1948/1971-72). 6'4". RHB, SLA. Gloucestershire 1972-90 (cap 1976; captain 1981-88; benefit 1986). Somerset 1991. Durham 1992-94 (cap 1992; captain 1992-93). Tours: SA 1989-90 (Eng XI – manager); SL 1986-87 (Gs – capt). HS 119 Gs v OU (Oxford) 1980. BAC HS 105* Gs v Northants (Bristol) 1981. Du HS 65* v Warwks (Birmingham) 1994. 50 wkts (6); most – 73 (1976). BB 8-85 Gs v Notts (Cheltenham) 1974. Du BB 6-80 v Notts (Nottingham) 1994. Hat-trick 1983. Awards: NWT 2. **NWT:** HS 44 Gs v Surrey (Bristol) 1973. BB 5-11 Gs v Ire (Dublin) 1981. **BHC:** HS 49* Gs v Somerset (Taunton) 1982. BB 3-13 Gs v Scot (Glasgow) 1983. **SL:** HS 56* Gs v Notts (Bristol) 1985. BB 4-22 Gs Hants (Lydney) 1974.

DURHAM 1994

RESULTS SUMMARY

	Place	Won	Lost	Tied	Drew	Abandoned
Britannic Assurance Championship	16th	4	10		3	
All First-class Matches		5	10		4	
Sunday League	9th	6	7	1		3
NatWest Trophy	2nd Round					
Benson and Hedges Cup	2nd Round					

BRITANNIC ASSURANCE CHAMPIONSHIP AVERAGES

BATTING AND FIELDING

Cap		M	I	NO	HS	Runs	Avge	100	50	Ct/St
1994	J.E.Morris	17	31	1	204	1369	45.63	4	5	8
1992	W.Larkins	13	23	2	158*	879	41.85	1	6	10
1994	M.Saxelby	15	29	–	181	1034	35.65	2	4	4
1992	J.A.Daley	8	15	2	159*	454	34.92	1	3	3
1992	S.Hutton	13	23	2	101	627	29.85	1	3	10
1994	J.I.Longley	14	25	2	100*	594	25.82	1	5	7
1993	A.C.Cummins	17	29	2	65	629	23.29	–	3	3
1992	C.W.Scott	17	29	3	108	547	21.03	2	1	53/2
1993	G.Fowler	3	5	–	60	98	19.60	–	1	2
1992	P.Bainbridge	16	28	1	67	523	19.37	–	3	13
1992	D.A.Graveney	12	21	5	65*	306	19.12	–	1	5
1992	S.J.E.Brown	16	23	9	69	234	16.71	–	1	7
1992	J.Wood	13	19	2	51	177	10.41	–	1	3
1994	A.Walker	4	7	2	13	34	6.80	–	–	1
1994	S.Lugsden	4	4	1	2	2	0.66	–	–	–

Also played: P.J.Berry (1 match – cap 1992) 3, 0 (1 ct); D.A.Blenkiron (1 match – cap 1992) did not bat; D.M.Cox (2 matches – cap 1993) 0, 0 (1 ct); J.P.Searle (1 match – cap 1993) 5*, 0*.

BOWLING

	O	M	R	W	Avge	Best	5wI	10wM
S.J.E.Brown	525.1	78	1928	66	29.21	6- 68	5	–
A.C.Cummins	520.3	92	1768	56	31.57	6- 64	4	1
J.Wood	303.4	34	1367	42	32.54	6-110	3	–
D.A.Graveney	447	117	1235	31	39.83	6- 80	1	–
P.Bainbridge	291.5	62	1004	13	77.23	4- 72	–	–

Also bowled: P.J.Berry 15-2-58-0; D.M.Cox 52.5-7-253-0; J.A.Daley 2-0-9-0; W.Larkins 5-0-39-0; S.Lugsden 85.2-11-348-3; J.E.Morris 27.5-3-125-1; J.P.Searle 1-0-7-0; A.Walker 116-23-369-8.

The First-Class Averages (pp 186-200) give the records of Durham players in all first-class county matches (their other opponents being the South Africans and Oxford U), with the exception of:

S.J.E.Brown 18-25-10-69-268-17.86-0-1-8ct. 564.5-87-2044-74-27.62-6/68-6-0.
W.Larkins 15-26-3-158*-960-41.73-1-6-11ct. 5-0-39-0.
J.E.Morris 19-34-1-204-1376-41.69-4-5-8ct. 27.5-3-125-1-125.00-1/37.
C.W.Scott 19-32-3-108-665-22.93-2-3-53ct-3st. Did not bowl.

DURHAM RECORDS

FIRST-CLASS CRICKET

Highest Total	For	625-6d		v	Derbyshire	Chesterfield	1994
	V	810-4d		by	Warwicks	Birmingham	1994
Lowest Total	For	83		v	Lancs	Manchester	1993
	V	73		by	Oxford U	Oxford	1994
Highest Innings	For	204	J.E.Morris	v	Warwicks	Birmingham	1994
	V	501*	B.C.Lara	for	Warwicks	Birmingham	1994

Highest Partnership for each Wicket

1st	222	P.W.G.Parker/J.D.Glendenen	v	Oxford U	Oxford	1992
2nd	206	W.Larkins/D.M.Jones	v	Glamorgan	Cardiff	1992
3rd	205	G.Fowler/S.Hutton	v	Yorkshire	Leeds	1993
4th	201	W.Larkins/J.A.Daley	v	Somerset	Taunton	1992
5th	185	P.W.G.Parker/J.A.Daley	v	Warwicks	Darlington	1993
6th	152	I.T.Botham/A.C.Cummins	v	Worcs	Stockton	1993
7th	106	I.Smith/D.A.Graveney	v	Somerset	Taunton	1992
8th	134	A.C.Cummins/D.A.Graveney	v	Warwicks	Birmingham	1994
9th	88	C.W.Scott/D.A.Graveney	v	Surrey	Darlington	1994
10th	70	D.A.Graveney/S.J.E.Brown	v	Surrey	Durham	1992

Best Bowling	For	7- 70	S.J.E.Brown	v	Australians	Durham	1993
(Innings)	V	7- 37	A.A.Donald	for	Warwicks	Birmingham	1992
Best Bowling	For	10-104	A.C.Cummins	v	Northants	Hartlepool	1994
(Match)	V	10- 87	D.J.Millns	for	Leics	Leicester	1992

Most Runs – Season	1536	W.Larkins	(av 37.46)	1992
Most Runs – Career	3541	W.Larkins	(av 38.91)	1992-94
Most 100s – Season	4	D.M.Jones		1992
	4	W.Larkins		1992
	4	J.E.Morris		1994
Most 100s – Career	8	W.Larkins		1992-94
Most Wkts – Season	74	S.J.E.Brown	(av 27.62)	1994
Most Wkts – Career	179	S.J.E.Brown	(av 32.83)	1992-94

LIMITED-OVERS CRICKET

Highest Total	NWT	320-5		v	Wiltshire	Trowbridge	1993
	BHC	271-6		v	Comb Us	Cambridge	1992
	SL	281-2		v	Derbyshire	Durham	1993
Lowest Total	NWT	82		v	Worcs	Chester-le-St	1968
	BHC	190-8		v	Worcs	Stockton	1994
	SL	105		v	Glamorgan	Colwyn Bay	1993
Highest Innings	NWT	113	W.Larkins	v	Ireland	Dublin	1992
	BHC	110*	W.Larkins	v	Hampshire	Stockton	1993
	SL	131*	W.Larkins	v	Hampshire	Portsmouth	1994
Best Bowling	NWT	7-32	S.P.Davis	v	Lancashire	Chester-le-St	1983
	BHC	4-38	P.Bainbridge	v	Worcs	Worcester	1992
	SL	4-24	A.C.Cummins	v	Hampshire	Stockton	1993

ESSEX

Formation of Present Club: 14 January 1876
Colours: Blue, Gold and Red
Badge: Three Seaxes above Scroll bearing 'Essex'
Championships: (6) 1979, 1983, 1984, 1986, 1991, 1992
NatWest Trophy/Gillette Cup Winners: (1) 1985
Benson and Hedges Cup Winners: (1) 1979
Sunday League Champions: (3) 1981, 1984, 1985
Match Awards: NWT 37; BHC 72

Secretary/General Manager: P.J.Edwards
County Ground, New Writtle Street, Chelmsford CM2 0PG (☎ 01245 252420)
Captain: P.J.Prichard
Scorer: C.F.Driver
1995 Beneficiary: G.A.Gooch (testimonial)

ANDREW, Stephen Jon Walter (Milton Abbey S; Portchester SS), b London 27 Jan 1966. 6'3". RHB, RMF. Hampshire 1984-89. Essex debut 1990. HS 35 v Northants (Chelmsford) 1990. BB 7-47 v Lancs (Manchester) 1993. Awards: BHC 2. **NWT:** HS 1*. BB 2-34 v Scot (Chelmsford) 1990. **BHC:** HS 4*. BB 5-24 H v Essex (Chelmsford) 1987. **SL:** HS 14 v Kent (Maidstone) 1993. BB 4-50 H v Middx (Southampton) 1988.

AYRES, Duncan Wallace (Falmouth CS; Millfield S), b Basildon 8 Oct 1976. 5'11". RHB, RMF. Essex staff 1993 – awaiting f-c debut.

CHILDS, John Henry (Audley Park SM, Torquay), b Plymouth, Devon 15 Aug 1951. 6'0". LHB, SLA. Gloucestershire 1975-84 (cap 1977). Essex debut 1985. Cap 1986. Benefit 1994. Devon 1973-74. Wisden 1986. **Tests:** 2 (1988); HS 2*; BB 1-13. HS 43 v Hants (Chelmsford) 1992. 50 wkts (8); most – 89 (1986). BB 9-56 Gs v Somerset (Bristol) 1981. Ex BB 8-58 v Glos (Colchester) 1986. Awards: BHC 1. **NWT:** HS 14* Gs v Hants (Bristol) 1983. BB 2-15 Gs v Ire (Dublin) 1981. **BHC:** HS 10 Gs v Somerset (Bristol) 1979. BB 3-36 Gs v Glam (Bristol) 1982. **SL:** HS 16* Gs v Warwks (Bristol) 1981. BB 4-15 Gs v Northants (Northampton) 1976.

COUSINS, Darren Mark (Netherhall CS; Impington Village C), b Cambridge 24 Sep 1971. 6'2". RHB, RMF. Cambridgeshire 1990. Debut 1993. HS 11 v Leics (Leicester) 1994. BB 6-35 v CU (Cambridge) 1994. BAC BB 2-78 v Worcs (Worcester) 1994. **NWT:** HS 1*. BB 1-33. **SL:** HS 6. BB 3-18 v Warwks (Birmingham) 1994.

COWAN, Ashley Preston (Framlingham C), b Hitchin, Herts 7 May 1975. 6'4". RHB, RM. Cambridgeshire 1993. Essex staff 1994 – awaiting f-c debut.

GARNHAM, Michael Anthony (Camberwell GS, Melbourne; Scotch C, Perth; Barnstaple GS; N Devon SFC; East Anglia U), b Johannesburg, SA 20 Aug 1960. 5'10". RHB, WK. Gloucestershire 1979. Leicestershire 1980-85 and 1988. Essex debut 1989. Cap 1990. Cambridgeshire 1986-88. HS 123 v Leics (Leicester)1991. Awards: NWT 2; BHC 1. **NWT:** HS 110 Cambs v Warwks (Birmingham) 1988. **BHC:** HS 55 Le v Derbys (Leicester) 1982. **SL:** HS 79* Le v Lancs (Leicester) 1982.

GOOCH, Graham Alan (Norlington Jr HS), b Leytonstone 23 Jul 1953. 6'0". RHB, RM. Debut 1973. Cap 1975. Captain 1986-87, 1989-94. Benefit 1985. Testimonial 1995. W Province 1982-83/1983-84. Wisden 1979. OBE 1991. **Tests:** 113 (1975 to 1994, 34 as captain); HS 333 and record match aggregate of 456 v I (Lord's) 1990; BB 3-39 v P (Manchester) 1992. LOI: 121 (HS 142; BB 3-19). Tours (C=captain): A 1978-79, 1979-80, 1990-91C; SA 1981-82 (SAB); WI 1980-81, 1985-86, 1989-90C; NZ 1991-92C; I 1979-80, 1981-82, 1992-93C; P 1987-88; SL 1981-82. 1000 runs (18+1) inc 2000 (5); most – 2746 (1990). HS 333 (Tests). Ex HS 275 v Kent (Chelmsford) 1988. BB 7-14 v Worcs (Ilford) 1982. Awards: NWT 9 (record); BHC 21 (record). **NWT:** HS 144 v

GOOCH – continued:
Hants (Chelmsford) 1990. BB 3-31 v Warwks (Birmingham) 1986. **BHC:** HS 198* v Sussex (Hove) 1982. BB 3-24 v Sussex (Hove) 1982. **SL:** HS 176 v Glam (Southend) 1983. BB 4-33 v Worcs (Chelmsford) 1984.

HUSSAIN, Nasser (Forest S, Snaresbrook; Durham U), b Madras, India 28 Mar 1968. Brother of M. (Worcs 1985). 5'11". RHB, LB. Debut 1987. Cap 1989. YC 1989. **Tests:** 7 (1989-90 to 1993); HS 71 v A (Nottingham) 1993. LOI: 4 (HS 16). Tours: WI 1989-90, 1991-92 (Eng A), 1993-94; P 1990-91 (Eng A); SL 1990-91 (Eng A). 1000 runs (2); most – 1604 (1993). HS 197 v Surrey (Oval) 1990. BB 1-38. Awards: NWT 1; BHC 1. **NWT:** HS 108 v Cumberland (Chelmsford) 1992. **BHC:** HS 118 Comb Us v Somerset (Taunton) 1989. **SL:** HS 76 v Sussex (Chelmsford) 1994.

ILOTT, Mark Christopher (Francis Combe S, Garston), b Watford, Herts 27 Aug 1970. 6'0½". LHB, LFM. Debut 1988. Cap 1993. Hertfordshire 1987-88. **Tests:** 3 (1993); HS 15 v A (Oval) 1993; BB 3-108 v A (Nottingham) 1993. Tours (Eng A): A 1992-93; SA 1993-94; SL 1990-91. HS 51 v Sussex (Hove) 1993. 50 wkts (3); most – 64 (1992). BB 7-85 v Surrey (Oval) 1993. Award: BHC 1. **NWT:** HS 26 v Glam (Cardiff) 1994. BB 2-23 v Cumberland (Chelmsford) 1992. **BHC:** HS 14 v Worcs (Worcester) 1993. BB 5-21 v Scot (Forfar) 1993. **SL:** HS 24 v Derbys (Derby) 1994. BB 4-15 v Derbys (Derby) 1992.

IRANI, Ronald Charles (Smithills CS, Bolton), b Leigh, Lancs 26 Oct 1971. 6'3". RHB, RM. Lancashire 1990-93. Essex debut/cap 1994. HS 119 v Worcs (Worcester) 1994. BB 4-27 v Kent (Chelmsford) 1994. Award: NWT 1. **NWT:** HS 30 v Glam (Cardiff) 1994. BB 4-49 v Sussex (Hove) 1994. **BHC:** HS –. BB 1-61. **SL:** HS 34 La v Leics (Leicester) 1993. BB 3-22 v Worcs (Worcester) 1994.

KHAN, Gul Abbass (Valentine S, Ilford; Ipswich S; Swansea U), b Gujrat, Pakistan 31 Dec 1973. 5'8". RHB, LB. Essex staff 1993 – awaiting f-c debut.

LEWIS, Jonathan James Benjamin (King Edward VI S, Chelmsford; Roehampton IHE), b Isleworth, Middx 21 May 1970. 5'9½". RHB, RSM. Debut 1990 v Surrey (Oval), scoring 116*. Cap 1994. HS 136* v Notts (Nottingham) 1993. **NWT:** HS 24* v Sussex (Hove) 1994. **SL:** HS 23 v Notts (Ilford) 1994.

PEARSON, Richard Michael (Batley GS; St John's, Cambridge), b Batley, Yorks 27 Jan 1972. 6'3". RHB, OB. Cambridge U 1991-92 (blue 1991-92). Northamptonshire 1992. HS 33* CU v Surrey (Cambridge) 1992. Ex HS 20 v CU (Cambridge) 1994. BAC HS 11 v Glos (Chelmsford) 1994. BB 5-108 CU v Warwks (Cambridge) 1992. BAC BB 2-90 Nh v Warwks (Northampton) 1992. Ex BB 1-39. **NWT:** HS –. BB 1-47. **BHC:** HS 8. BB 2-31 Comb Us v Durham (Cambridge) 1992. **SL:** HS 7. BB 3-33 v Leics (Leicester) 1994.

PRICHARD, Paul John (Brentwood HS), b Billericay 7 Jan 1965. 5'10". RHB, RSM. Debut 1984. Cap 1986. Captain 1995. Tour: A 1992-93 (Eng A). 1000 runs (6); most –1485 (1992). HS 245 v Leics (Chelmsford) 1990. BB 1-28. Awards: BHC 2. **NWT:** HS 94 v Oxon (Chelmsford) 1985. **BHC:** HS 107 v Scot (Glasgow) 1990. **SL:** HS 107 v Notts (Nottingham) 1993.

ROBINSON, Darren David John (Tabor HS, Braintree; Chelmsford CFE), b Braintree 2 Mar 1973. 5'10½". RHB, RMF. Debut 1993. HS 67 v Glos (Bristol) 1993. **SL:** HS 2.

ROLLINS, Robert John (Little Ilford CS), b Plaistow 30 Jan 1974. 5'9". RHB, RM, WK. Brother of A.S. (see DERBYSHIRE). Debut 1992. HS 13 v P (Chelmsford) 1992. BAC HS 7. **SL:** HS 9*.

SUCH, Peter Mark (Harry Carlton CS, Ex Leake, Notts), b Helensburgh, Dunbartonshire 12 Jun 1964. 5'11". RHB, OB. Nottinghamshire 1982-86. Leicestershire 1987-89. Essex debut 1990. Cap 1991. **Tests:** 8 (1993 to 1994); HS 14* and BB 6-67 v A (Manchester) 1993 – on debut. Tours (Eng A): A 1992-93; SA 1993-94. HS 54 v Worcs (Chelmsford) 1993. 50 wkts (2); most – 76 (1993). BB 7-66 v Hants (Southampton) 1994. **NWT:** HS 0*. BB 2-29 v Devon (Exmouth) 1991. **BHC:** HS 4. BB 4-43 v Northants (Northampton) 1992. **SL:** HS 19* v Notts (Ilford) 1994. BB 5-32 v Yorks (Chelmsford) 1993.

WAUGH, Mark Edward (E Hills HS), b Canterbury, Sydney, Australia 2 Jun 1965. Younger twin of S.R. (NSW, Somerset and Australia). 6'1". RHB, RM. NSW 1985-86 to date. Essex 1988-90 (cap 1989) and 1992. Wisden 1990. **Tests** (A): 36 (1990-91 to 1993-94); HS 139* v WI (St John's) 1990-91; BB 4-80 v WI (Bridgetown) 1990-91. LOI (A): 75 (HS 113; BB 5-24). Tours (A): E 1993; SA 1993-94; WI 1990-91; NZ 1992-93; SL 1992-93; Z 1985-86 (Young A), 1987-88 (NSW). 1000 runs (4+3) inc 2000 (1): 2072 (1990). HS 229* NSW v WA (Perth) 1990-91, sharing world record 5th wkt stand of 464* with S.R.Waugh. Ex HS 219* v Lancs (Ilford) 1992. BB 5-37 v Northants (Chelmsford) 1990. Awards: BHC 2. **NWT:** HS 47 v Hants (Chelmsford) 1990. BB 1-51. **BHC:** HS 100 v Northants (Northampton) 1992. BB 3-31 v Scot (Chelmsford) 1992. **SL:** HS 112* v Glam (Neath) 1989. BB 3-26 v Worcs (Worcester) 1992.

NEWCOMERS

DERBYSHIRE, Nicholas Alexander (Ampleforth C; Goldsmith's C, London U), b Ramsbottom, Lancs 11 Sep 1970. 5'11½". RHB, RFM. Lancashire 1994. HS 5. BB 1-48. BAC BB 1-107.

HIBBERT, Andrew James Edward (St Edward's S, Romford), b Harold Wood 17 Dec 1974. RHB.

RICKETTS, Courtney Ian Oswald (St Andrew TC), b Kennington, London, 26 Apr 1965. RHB, SLA. Sussex 1987. HS 29 and BB 2-40 Sx v Worcs (Worcester) 1987. **NWT:** HS –. **BHC:** HS –. BB 1-30. **SL:** HS 9. BB 1-25.

WILLIAMS, Neil FitzGerald (Acland Burghley CS), b Hope Well, St Vincent 2 Jul 1962. 5'11". RHB, RFM. Middlesex 1982-94 (cap 1984; benefit 1994). Windward Is 1982-83 and 1989-90/1991-92. Tasmania 1983-84. MCC YC. **Tests:** 1 (1990); HS 38 and BB 2-148 v I (Oval) 1990. Tour: Z 1984-85 (EC). HS 77 M v Warwks (Birmingham) 1991. 50 wkts (3); most – 63 (1983). BB 8-75 (12-139 match) M v Glos (Lord's) 1992. Award: BHC 1. **NWT:** HS 10 M v Northumb (Jesmond) 1984. BB 4-36 M v Derbys (Derby) 1983. **BHC:** HS 29* M v Surrey (Lord's) 1985. BB 3-16 M v Comb Us (Cambridge) 1982. **SL:** HS 43 M v Somerset (Lord's) 1988. BB 4-39 M v Surrey (Oval) 1988.

DEPARTURES (who made first-class appearances in 1994)

BODEN, D.J.P. – see GLOUCESTERSHIRE.

DIWAN, Muneeb (Sir George Monoux S, Walthamstow), b St Stephen, Canada 20 Mar 1972. 5'9". RHB, RM. Debut 1994. HS 0. **SL:** HS 14 v Notts (Ilford) 1994.

KASPROWICZ, Michael Scott (Brisbane State HS), b South Brisbane, Australia 10 Feb 1972. 6'4". RHB, RF. Queensland 1989-90 to date. Essex 1994 (cap 1994). HS 49 Queensland v WA (Perth) 1989-90. Ex HS 44 v Middx (Uxbridge) 1994. 50 wkts (1+1); most – 60 (1994). BB 7-83 v Somerset (W-s-M) 1994. **NWT:** HS 13. BB 5-60 v Glam (Cardiff) 1994. **BHC:** HS –. BB 2-52 v Leics (Chelmsford) 1994. **SL:** HS 17 v Glos (Chelmsford) 1994. BB 2-38 v Glam (Southend) and v Northants (Chelmsford) 1994.

KNIGHT, N.V. – see WARWICKSHIRE.

SHAHID, N. – see SURREY.

STEPHENSON, J.P. – see HAMPSHIRE.

TOPLEY, Thomas **Donald** (Royal Hospital S, Holbrook, Suffolk), b Canterbury, Kent 25 Feb 1964. Brother of P.A. (Kent 1972-75). 6'3". RHB, RMF. Surrey (v CU) 1985. Essex 1985-94 (cap 1988). GW 1987-88. Norfolk 1984-85. MCC YC. HS 66 v Yorks (Leeds) 1987. 50 wkts (3); most – 77 (1989). BB 7-75 v Derbys (Chesterfield) 1988. Awards: NWT 1; BHC 2. **NWT:** HS 19* v Leics (Leicester) 1992. BB 4-21 v Northumb (Jesmond) 1987. **BHC:** HS 10* v Notts (Chelmsford) 1990. BB 4-22 v Surrey (Chelmsford) 1988. **SL:** HS 38* v Lancs (Manchester) 1991. BB 6-33 v Notts (Colchester) 1988.

ESSEX 1994

RESULTS SUMMARY

	Place	Won	Lost	Tied	Drew	Abandoned
Britannic Assurance Championship	6th	7	5		5	
All First-class Matches		7	5		7	
Sunday League	17th	4	11	1		1
NatWest Trophy	2nd Round					
Benson and Hedges Cup	Quarter-Finalist					

BRITANNIC ASSURANCE CHAMPIONSHIP AVERAGES

BATTING AND FIELDING

Cap		*M*	*I*	*NO*	*HS*	*Runs*	*Avge*	*100*	*50*	*Ct/St*
1975	G.A.Gooch	10	18	2	236	1343	83.93	5	5	10
1994	N.V.Knight	11	19	1	157	786	43.66	3	3	22
1994	R.C.Irani	17	28	6	119	882	40.09	2	7	6
1986	P.J.Prichard	10	16	2	119	560	40.00	3	2	6
1989	N.Hussain	17	29	2	115*	789	29.22	2	3	34
1994	J.J.B.Lewis	14	26	2	109	688	28.66	1	4	9
1990	M.A.Garnham	17	28	4	62	497	20.70	–	4	31/4
–	N.Shahid	9	16	3	91	263	20.23	–	1	13
1989	J.P.Stephenson	14	24	–	144	480	20.00	1	2	4
1986	J.H.Childs	13	16	11	42*	95	19.00	–	–	1
1994	M.S.Kasprowicz	16	23	4	44	298	15.68	–	–	8
1993	M.C.Ilott	12	14	4	30*	138	13.80	–	–	3
1991	P.M.Such	15	19	1	29	125	6.94	–	–	8
–	S.J.W.Andrew	5	7	1	11	29	4.83	–	–	–
–	D.M.Cousins	3	5	–	11	24	4.80	–	–	2

Also batted: M.Diwan (1 match) 0, 0; R.M.Pearson (2 matches) 11, 7, 7 (2 ct); D.D.J.Robinson (1 match) 38 (1 ct).

BOWLING

	O	*M*	*R*	*W*	*Avge*	*Best*	*5wI*	*10wM*
M.C.Ilott	419.3	92	1206	52	23.19	6-24	3	1
P.M.Such	521	139	1397	51	27.39	7-66	5	–
R.C.Irani	225.4	38	757	26	29.11	4-27	–	–
M.S.Kasprowicz	497.3	88	1752	57	30.73	7-83	3	–
J.H.Childs	410.5	101	1139	37	30.78	6-71	2	–
J.P.Stephenson	307	73	977	24	40.70	4-74	–	–

Also bowled: S.J.W.Andrew 123.3-24-374-7; D.M.Cousins 79.4-13-276-6; G.A.Gooch 19.3-9-24-3; N.V.Knight 11.4-0-61-1; J.J.B.Lewis 8-1-32-0; R.M.Pearson 47-10-145-2; N.Shahid 18-2-81-2.

The First-Class Averages (pp 186-200) give the records of Essex players in all first-class county matches (their other opponents being the New Zealanders and Cambridge U), with the exception of:

G.A.Gooch 11-19-2-236-1385-81.47-5-5-11ct. 21.3-10-25-3-8.33-1/0.
M.C.Ilott 13-15-4-30*-149-13.54-0-0-3ct. 447.3-97-1280-53-24.15-6/24-3-1.
P.M.Such 16-20-0-29-149-7.45-0-0-9ct. 538-143-1472-51-28.86-7/66-5-0.

ESSEX RECORDS

FIRST-CLASS CRICKET

Highest Total	For	761-6d		v	Leics	Chelmsford	1990
	V	803-4d		by	Kent	Brentwood	1934
Lowest Total	For	30		v	Yorkshire	Leyton	1901
	V	14		by	Surrey	Chelmsford	1983
Highest Innings	For	343*	P.A.Perrin	v	Derbyshire	Chesterfield	1904
	V	332	W.H.Ashdown	for	Kent	Brentwood	1934

Highest Partnership for each Wicket

1st	316	G.A.Gooch/P.J.Prichard	v	Kent	Chelmsford	1994
2nd	403	G.A.Gooch/P.J.Prichard	v	Leics	Chelmsford	1990
3rd	347*	M.E.Waugh/N.Hussain	v	Lancashire	Ilford	1992
4th	314	Salim Malik/N.Hussain	v	Surrey	The Oval	1991
5th	316	N.Hussain/M.A.Garnham	v	Leics	Leicester	1991
6th	206	J.W.H.T.Douglas/J.O'Connor	v	Glos	Cheltenham	1923
	206	B.R.Knight/R.A.G.Luckin	v	Middlesex	Brentwood	1962
7th	261	J.W.H.T.Douglas/J.Freeman	v	Lancashire	Leyton	1914
8th	263	D.R.Wilcox/R.M.Taylor	v	Warwicks	Southend	1946
9th	251	J.W.H.T.Douglas/S.N.Hare	v	Derbyshire	Leyton	1921
10th	218	F.H.Vigar/T.P.B.Smith	v	Derbyshire	Chesterfield	1947

Best Bowling	For	10- 32	H.Pickett	v	Leics	Leyton	1895
(Innings)	V	10- 40	E.G.Dennett	for	Glos	Bristol	1906
Best Bowling	For	17-119	W.Mead	v	Hampshire	Southampton	1895
(Match)	V	17- 56	C.W.L.Parker	for	Glos	Gloucester	1925

Most Runs – Season	2559	G.A.Gooch	(av 67.34)	1984
Most Runs – Career	29434†	K.W.R.Fletcher	(av 36.88)	1962-88
Most 100s – Season	9	J.O'Connor		1934
	9	D.J.Insole		1955
Most 100s – Career	79	G.A.Gooch		1973-94
Most Wkts – Season	172	T.P.B Smith	(av 27.13)	1947
Most Wkts – Career	1610	T.P.B.Smith	(av 26.68)	1929-51

† G.A.Gooch has scored 26719 runs.

LIMITED-OVERS CRICKET

Highest Total	NWT	386-5		v	Wiltshire	Chelmsford	1988
	BHC	388-7		v	Scotland	Chelmsford	1992
	SL	310-5		v	Glamorgan	Southend	1983
Lowest Total	NWT	100		v	Derbyshire	Brentwood	1965
	BHC	61		v	Lancashire	Chelmsford	1992
	SL	69		v	Derbyshire	Chesterfield	1974
Highest Innings	NWT	144	G.A.Gooch	v	Hampshire	Chelmsford	1990
	BHC	198*	G.A.Gooch	v	Sussex	Hove	1982
	SL	176	G.A.Gooch	v	Glamorgan	Southend	1983
Best Bowling	NWT	5- 8	J.K.Lever	v	Middlesex	Westcliff	1972
	BHC	5-13	J.K.Lever	v	Middlesex	Lord's	1985
	SL	8-26	K.D.Boyce	v	Lancashire	Manchester	1971

GLAMORGAN

Formation of Present Club: 6 July 1888
Colours: Blue and Gold
Badge: Gold Daffodil
Championships: (2) 1948, 1969
NatWest Trophy/Gillette Cup Winners: (0) Finalists 1977
Benson and Hedges Cup Winners: (0) Semi-Finalists 1988
Sunday League Champions: (1) 1993
Match Awards: NWT 33; BHC 42

Secretary: G.R.Stone. **Cricket Secretary:** M.Fatkin
Sophia Gardens, Cardiff, CF1 9XR (☎ 01222 343478)
Captain: H.Morris
Scorer: B.T.Denning
1995 Beneficiary: S.R.Barwick

BARWICK, Stephen Royston (Cwrt Sart CS; Dwr-y-Felin CS), b Neath 6 Sep 1960. 6'2". RHB, RMF. Debut 1981. Cap 1987. Benefit 1995. HS 30 v Hants (Bournemouth) 1988. 50 wkts (2); most – 64 (1989). BB 8-42 v Worcs (Worcester) 1983. Award: BHC 1. **NWT:** HS 6. BB 5-26 v Surrey (Swansea) 1992. **BHC:** HS 18 v Kent (Canterbury) 1984. BB 4-11 v Minor C (Swansea) 1985. **SL:** HS 48* v Worcs (Worcester) 1989. BB 6-28 v Derbys (Derby) 1993.

BUTCHER, Gary Paul (Trinity S; Riddlesdown S; Heath Clark C), b Clapham, London 11 Mar 1975. Son of A.R. (Surrey, Glam and England 1972-92); brother of M.A. (see SURREY). 5'9". RHB, RM. Debut 1994. HS 41 v Leics (Cardiff) 1994. BB 2-36 v OU (Oxford) 1994. **SL:** HS –. BB 2-8 v Somerset (Swansea) 1994.

COTTEY, Phillip Anthony (Bishopston CS, Swansea), b Swansea 2 Jun 1966. 5'4". RHB, OB. Debut 1986. Cap 1992. E Transvaal 1991-92. Tour: Z 1990-91 (Gm). 1000 runs (4); most – 1393 (1994). HS 191 v Somerset (Swansea) 1994. BB 2-42 E Transvaal v W Transvaal (Potchefstroom) 1991-92. Gm BB 1-16. **NWT:** HS 57 v Essex (Cardiff) 1994. BB 1-12. **BHC:** HS 68 v Hants (Southampton) 1989. **SL:** HS 92* v Hants (Ebbw Vale) 1991. BB 2-30 v Sussex (Hove) 1992.

CROFT, Robert Damien Bale (St John Lloyd Catholic CS; W Glam IHE), b Morriston 25 May 1970. 5'10½". RHB, OB. Debut 1989. Cap 1992. Tours (Eng A): SA 1993-94; WI 1991-92; Z 1990-91 (Gm). HS 107 v CU (Cambridge) 1993. BAC HS 91* v Worcs (Abergavenny) 1990. 50 wkts (2); most – 68 (1992). BB 8-66 (14-169 match) v Warwks (Swansea) 1992. **NWT:** HS 50 v Essex (Cardiff) 1994. BB 3-30 v Lincs (Swansea) 1994. **BHC:** HS 30* v Durham (Durham) 1992. BB 3-28 v Comb Us (Cardiff) 1992. **SL:** HS 31* v Yorks (Ebbw Vale) 1992. BB 6-20 v Worcs (Cardiff) 1994.

DALE, Adrian (Chepstow CS; Swansea U), b Germiston, SA 24 Oct 1968 (to UK at 6 mths). 5'11½". RHB, RM. Debut 1989. Cap 1992. Tours: SA 1993-94 (Eng A); Z 1990-91 (Gm). 1000 runs (2); most – 1472 (1993). HS 214* v Middx (Cardiff) 1993. BB 6-18 v Warwks (Cardiff) 1993. Award: NWT 1. **NWT:** HS 110 v Lincs (Swansea) 1994. BB 3-54 v Worcs (Swansea) 1993. **BHC:** HS 53 v Comb Us (Cardiff) 1992. BB 3-24 Comb Us v Surrey (Cambridge) 1989. **SL:** HS 67* v Derbys (Heanor) 1989. BB 6-22 v Durham (Colwyn Bay) 1993.

DALTON, Alistair John (Millfield S), b Bridgend 27 Apr 1973. 5'7". RHB, RM. Wales (MC) 1992-94. Debut 1994. HS 51* v SA (Pontypridd) 1994. BAC HS 44 v Middx (Lord's) 1994.

GIBSON, Ottis Delroy (Ellerslie SS), b Bridgetown, Barbados 16 Mar 1969. 6'2". RHB, RF. Barbados 1990-91 to date. Border 1992-93 to date. Glamorgan debut/cap 1994. HS 85 v NZ (Swansea) 1994. BAC HS 81 v Somerset (Swansea) 1994. 50 wkts (1): 60 (1994). BB 7-78 Barbados v Trinidad (P-of-S) 1991-92. Gm BB 6-64 v Worcs (Cardiff) 1994. Award: NWT 1. **NWT:** HS 44 and BB 3-34 v Essex (Cardiff) 1994. **BHC:** HS 37 and BB 2-50 v Surrey (Oval) 1994. **SL:** HS 33 v Essex (Southend) 1994. BB 2-35 v Sussex (Hove) 1994.

HEMP, David Lloyd (Olchfa CS; Millfield S; W Glamorgan C), b Bermuda 15 Nov 1970. UK resident since 1976. 6'0". LHB, RM. Debut 1991. Cap 1994. Wales (MC) 1992-94. 1000 runs (1): 1452 (1994). HS 136 v Glos (Bristol) 1994. **NWT:** HS 13 v Surrey (Swansea) 1994. **SL:** HS 73 v Middx (Lord's) 1994.

JAMES, Stephen Peter (Monmouth S; Swansea U; Hughes Hall, Cambridge), b Lydney, Glos 7 Sep 1967. 6'0". RHB. Debut 1985. Cap 1992. Cambridge U 1989-90 (blue 1989-90). Mashonaland 1993-94. Tour: Z 1990-91 (Gm). 1000 runs (2); most – 1376 (1992). HS 152* v Lancs (Colwyn Bay) 1992. Awards: NWT 1; BHC 1. **NWT:** HS 123 v Lincs (Swansea) 1994. **BHC:** HS 135 v Comb Us (Cardiff) 1992. **SL:** HS 107 v Sussex (Llanelli) 1993.

LEFEBVRE, Roland Philippe (Montessori Lyceum, Rotterdam; Hague Accademie of Physiotherapy), b Rotterdam, Holland 7 Feb 1963. 6'1". RHB, RMF. Somerset 1990-92 (cap 1991). Glamorgan debut/cap 1993. Holland 1983-90; ICC Trophy 1986 and 1989. Canterbury 1990-91. HS 100 Sm v Worcs (W-s-M) 1991. Gm HS 50 v Worcs (Worcester) 1993. BB 6-53 Canterbury v Auckland (Auckland) 1990-91. BAC BB 5-30 Sm v Glos (Taunton) 1990. Gm BB 4-63 v Kent (Abergavenny) 1994. **NWT:** HS 21* Sm v Warwks (Birmingham) 1991. BB 7-15 Sm v Devon (Torquay) 1990. **BHC:** HS 37 Sm v Middx (Lord's) 1990. BB 3-44 Sm v Surrey (Taunton) 1991. **SL:** HS 36* v Northants (Pentrych) 1993. BB 4-23 v Durham (Hartlepool) 1994.

MAYNARD, Matthew Peter (David Hughes S, Anglesey), b Oldham, Lancs 21 Mar 1966. 5'10½". RHB, RM. Debut 1985 v Yorks (Swansea), scoring 102 out of 117 in 87 min, reaching 100 with 3 sixes off successive balls. Cap 1987. N Districts 1990-91/1991-92. YC 1988. **Tests:** 4 (1988 to 1993-94); HS 35 v WI (Kingston) 1993-94. LOI: 5 (HS 22*). Tours: SA 1989-90 (Eng XI); WI 1993-94. 1000 runs (8); most – 1803 (1991). HS 243 v Hants (Southampton) 1991. BB 3-21 v OU (Oxford) 1987. BAC BB 1-3. Awards: NWT 4; BHC 5. **NWT:** HS 151* v Durham (Darlington) 1991. **BHC:** HS 115 v Comb Us (Cardiff) 1988. **SL:** HS 122* v Leics (Swansea) 1992.

METSON, Colin Peter (Enfield GS; Stanborough S, Welwyn Garden City; Durham U), b Goffs Oak, Herts 2 Jul 1963. 5'5½". RHB, WK. Middlesex 1981-86. Glamorgan debut/cap 1987. HS 96 M v Glos (Uxbridge) 1984. Gm HS 84 v Kent (Maidstone) 1991. **NWT:** HS 21 v Notts (Nottingham) 1992. **BHC:** HS 23 v Kent (Swansea) 1990. **SL:** HS 30* v Hants (Bournemouth) 1990.

MORRIS, Hugh (Blundell's S), b Cardiff 5 Oct 1963. 5'8". LHB, RM.Debut 1981. Cap 1986. Captain 1986-89 and 1993-. Benefit 1994. **Tests:** 3 (1991); HS 44 v WI (Oval) 1991. Tours (Eng A – C=captain): SA 1993-94C; WI 1991-92C; SL 1990-91C. 1000 runs (7) inc 2000 (1): 2276 – inc 10 hundreds – both Gm records (1990). HS 160* v Derbys (Cardiff) 1990. BB 1-6. BAC BB 1-45. Awards: NWT 1; BHC 3. **NWT:** HS 154* v Staffs (Cardiff) 1989. **BHC:** HS 143* v Hants (Southampton) 1989. BB 1-14. **SL:** HS 127* v Surrey (Swansea) 1994.

PARKIN, Owen Thomas (Bournemouth GS, Bath U), b Coventry, Warwks 24 Sep 1972. 6'2". RHB, RFM. Dorset 1992. Debut 1994. HS 2* and BB 2-45 v Middx (Lord's) 1994.

PHELPS, Byron **Stuart** (Glanafan CS; Neath Tertiary C), b Neath 16 Dec 1975. 5'5". RHB, SLA. Debut 1993. Wales (MC) 1993-94. HS 11 and BB 2-70 v Somerset (Swansea) 1994.

REES, Gareth Henry John (Clifton C), b Clifton, Bristol 24 Oct 1974. 6'1". RHB, RSM. Glamorgan staff 1994 – awaiting f-c debut.

ROSEBERRY, Andrew (Durham S), b Sunderland, Co Durham 2 Apr 1971. 6'0". Younger brother of M.A. (see DURHAM). RHB, RM. Leicestershire 1992. Northumberland 1993. HS 94 v CU (Cambridge) 1994. BAC HS 65 v Hants (Southampton) 1994.

SHAW, Adrian David (Neath Tertiary C), b Neath 17 Feb 1972. 5'11". RHB, WK. Wales (MC) 1990-92. Debut 1994. HS 14 v Middx (Lord's) 1994. **SL:** HS –.

THOMAS, Stuart **Darren** (Graig CS, Llanelli; Neath Tertiary C), b Morriston 25 Jan 1975. 6'0". LHB, RFM. Debut v Derbys (Chesterfield) 1992, taking 5-80 when aged 17yr 217d. HS 16* v Hants (Swansea) 1993. BB 5-76 v Worcs (Worcester) 1993. **SL:** HS –. BB 1-34.

WATKIN, Steven Llewellyn (Cymer Afan CS; S Glamorgan CHE), b Maesteg 15 Sep 1964. 6'3". RHB, RMF. Debut 1986. Cap 1989. Wisden 1993. **Tests:** 3 (1991 to 1993); HS 13 and BB 4-65 v A (Oval) 1993. LOI 4 (HS 4; BB 4-49). Tours: WI 1991-92 (Eng A), 1993-94; P 1990-91 (Eng A); Z 1989-90 (Eng A), 1990-91 (Gm). HS 41 v Worcs (Worcester) 1992. 50 wkts (6); most – 94 (1989). BB 8-59 v Warwks (Birmingham) 1988. Award: NWT 1. **NWT:** HS 9. BB 3-18 v Sussex (Cardiff) 1990. **BHC:** HS 15 v Hants (Southampton) 1991. BB 3-28 v Minor C (Trowbridge) 1991. **SL:** 31* v Derbys (Checkley) 1991. BB 5-23 v Warwks (Birmingham) 1990.

WILLIAMS, James Robert Alexander (Clifton C), b Neath 20 Jul 1973. 5'11". RHB, OB. Debut 1993. HS 6.

NEWCOMERS

DAVIES, Andrew Philip (Christ C, Brecon; Trinity C, Carmarthen), b Neath 7 Nov 1976. RHB, RMF. Wales (MC).

JONES, Philip Steffan (Stradey CS; Neath TC), b Llanelli 9 Feb 1974. RHB, RFM. Wales (MC) 1992-94. **BHC:** HS 26* Wales (MC) v Middx (Northop Hall) 1994.

KENDRICK, Neil Michael (Wilson's GS), b Bromley, Kent 11 Nov 1967. 5'11". RHB, SLA. Surrey 1988-94. HS 55 Sy v Middx (Lord's) 1992. 50 wkts (1): 51 (1992). BB 7-115 Sy v Notts (Oval) 1993. **NWT:** HS –. BB 1-51. **BHC:** HS 24 and BB 2-47 Sy v Kent (Canterbury) 1992. **SL:** HS 13* and BB 2-48 Sy v Warwks (Guildford) 1994.

DEPARTURES (who made first-class appearances in 1994)

BASTIEN, Steven (St Bonaventure S, Forest Gate; Haringey Cricket C), b Stepney, London 13 Mar 1963 (of Dominican parents). 6'1". RHB, RMF. Glamorgan 1988-94. Tour: Z 1990-91 (Gm). HS 36* v Warwks (Birmingham) 1988 (his first innings). BB 6-52 (12-105 match) v Essex (Cardiff) 1993. **NWT:** HS 7*. BB 1-42. **BHC:** HS 7. BB 1-29. **SL:** HS 1. BB 2-42 v Kent (Maidstone) 1991.

GLAMORGAN 1994

RESULTS SUMMARY

	Place	Won	Lost	Tied	Drew	Abandoned
Britannic Assurance Championship	18th	2	8		7	
All First-class Matches		2	9		10	
Sunday League	7th	9	6	1		1
NatWest Trophy	Quarter-Finalist					
Benson and Hedges Cup	2nd Round					

BRITANNIC ASSURANCE CHAMPIONSHIP AVERAGES

BATTING AND FIELDING

Cap		*M*	*I*	*NO*	*HS*	*Runs*	*Avge*	*100*	*50*	*Ct/St*
1992	P.A.Cottey	15	25	4	191	1016	48.38	2	3	15
1994	D.L.Hemp	17	30	2	136	1132	40.42	3	6	13
1987	M.P.Maynard	15	26	1	118	863	34.52	1	5	18
1992	S.P.James	12	22	4	116	545	30.27	1	1	12
1986	H.Morris	15	29	2	106	765	28.33	1	5	11
–	A.Roseberry	4	5	1	65	109	27.25	–	1	3
1992	R.D.B.Croft	15	21	2	80	505	26.57	–	2	5
1992	A.Dale	14	23	1	131	504	22.90	1	2	–
1994	O.D.Gibson	17	25	2	81	523	22.73	–	5	7
1987	C.P.Metson	16	20	4	51	315	19.68	–	1	50/7
1993	R.P.Lefebvre	10	11	2	33	176	19.55	–	–	4
–	A.J.Dalton	3	6	–	44	99	16.50	–	–	3
1989	S.L.Watkin	16	19	10	14	79	8.77	–	–	2
–	B.S.Phelps	2	4	1	11	18	6.00	–	–	–
1987	S.R.Barwick	10	16	6	8	35	3.50	–	–	2

Also batted: S.Bastien (2 matches) 1, 0; G.P.Butcher (2 matches) 4, 41 (1 ct); O.T.Parkin (1 match) 2*, 0*; A.D.Shaw (1 match) 1, 14 (2 ct).

BOWLING

	O	*M*	*R*	*W*	*Avge*	*Best*	*5wI*	*10wM*
S.L.Watkin	554.4	122	1563	52	30.05	6-143	2	–
S.R.Barwick	482.5	173	1035	34	30.44	5- 44	1	–
O.D.Gibson	528.5	96	1944	57	34.10	6- 64	4	1
R.P.Lefebvre	307.2	90	777	20	38.85	4- 63	–	–
A.Dale	221	52	781	19	41.10	2- 7	–	–
R.D.B.Croft	528.1	117	1568	32	49.00	5- 80	1	–

Also bowled: S.Bastien 64.3-14-206-4; G.P.Butcher 27-5-94-0; P.A.Cottey 17.4-2-82-1; D.L.Hemp 3-0-24-0; M.P.Maynard 1-0-10-0; O.T.Parkin 28-6-95-2; B.S.Phelps 86-22-241-4.

The First-Class Averages (pp 186-200) give the records of Glamorgan players in all first-class county matches (their other opponents being the New Zealanders, the South Africans, Cambridge U and Oxford U), with the exception of:

R.D.B.Croft 18-24-2-80-569-25.86-0-2-7ct. 689.3-152-2076-40-51.90-5/80-1-0.

A.Dale 17-28-1-131-676-25.03-2-2-3ct. 258-62-906-22-41.18-2/7.

GLAMORGAN RECORDS

FIRST-CLASS CRICKET

Highest Total	For	587-8d		v	Derbyshire	Cardiff	1951
	V	657-7d		by	Warwicks	Birmingham	1994
Lowest Total	For	22		v	Lancashire	Liverpool	1924
	V	33		by	Leics	Ebbw Vale	1965
Highest Innings	For	287*	D.E.Davies	v	Glos	Newport	1939
	V	313*	S.J.Cook	for	Somerset	Cardiff	1990

Highest Partnership for each Wicket

1st	330	A.Jones/R.C.Fredericks	v	Northants	Swansea	1972
2nd	249	S.P.James/H.Morris	v	Oxford U	Oxford	1987
3rd	313	D.E.Davies/W.E.Jones	v	Essex	Brentwood	1948
4th	425*	A.Dale/I.V.A.Richards	v	Middlesex	Cardiff	1993
5th	264	M.Robinson/S.W.Montgomery	v	Hampshire	Bournemouth	1949
6th	230	W.E.Jones/B.L.Muncer	v	Worcs	Worcester	1953
7th	195*	W.Wooller/W.E.Jones	v	Lancashire	Liverpool	1947
8th	202	D.Davies/J.J.Hills	v	Sussex	Eastbourne	1928
9th	203*	J.J.Hills/J.C.Clay	v	Worcs	Swansea	1929
10th	143	T.Davies/S.A.B.Daniels	v	Glos	Swansea	1982

Best Bowling (Innings)	For	10- 51	J.Mercer	v	Worcs	Worcester	1936
	V	10- 18	G.Geary	for	Leics	Pontypridd	1929
Best Bowling (Match)	For	17-212	J.C.Clay	v	Worcs	Swansea	1937
	V	16- 96	G.Geary	for	Leics	Pontypridd	1929

Most Runs – Season	2276	H.Morris	(av 55.51)	1990
Most Runs – Career	34056	A.Jones	(av 33.03)	1957-83
Most 100s – Season	10	H.Morris		1990
Most 100s – Career	52	A.Jones		1957-83
Most Wkts – Season	176	J.C.Clay	(av 17.34)	1937
Most Wkts – Career	2174	D.J.Shepherd	(av 20.95)	1950-72

LIMITED-OVERS CRICKET

Highest Total	NWT	345-2		v	Durham	Darlington	1991
	BHC	302-6		v	Comb Us	Cardiff	1988
	SL	287-8		v	Middlesex	Cardiff	1993
Lowest Total	NWT	76		v	Northants	Northampton	1968
	BHC	68		v	Lancashire	Manchester	1973
	SL	42		v	Derbyshire	Swansea	1979
Highest Innings	NWT	162*	I.V.A.Richards	v	Oxfordshire	Swansea	1993
	BHC	143*	H.Morris	v	Hampshire	Southampton	1989
	SL	130*	J.A.Hopkins	v	Somerset	Bath	1983
Best Bowling	NWT	5-13	R.J.Shastri	v	Scotland	Edinburgh	1988
	BHC	5-17	A.H.Wilkins	v	Worcs	Worcester	1978
	SL	6-20	R.D.B.Croft	v	Worcs	Cardiff	1994

GLOUCESTERSHIRE

Formation of Present Club: 1871
Colours: Blue, Gold, Brown, Silver, Green and Red
Badge: Coat of Arms of the City and County of Bristol
Championships (since 1890): (0) Second 1930, 1931, 1947, 1959, 1969, 1986
NatWest Trophy/Gillette Cup Winners: (1) 1973
Benson and Hedges Cup Winners: (1) 1977
Sunday League Champions: (0) Second 1988
Match Awards: NWT 38; BHC 43

Secretary: P.G.M.August
Phoenix County Ground, Nevil Road, Bristol BS7 9EJ (☎ 0117-924 5216)
Captain: R.C.Russell
Scorer: B.H.Jenkins
1995 Beneficiary: G.G.M.Wiltshire (testimonial)

ALLEYNE, Mark Wayne (Harrison C, Barbados; Cardinal Pole S, London E9; Haringey Cricket C), b Tottenham, London 23 May 1968. 5'10". RHB, RM. Debut 1986. Cap 1990. Tours (Gs): SL 1986-87, 1992-93. 1000 runs (3); most – 1121 (1991). HS 256 v Northants (Northampton) 1990. BB 5-78 v Kent (Cheltenham) 1994. Award: NWT 1. **NWT:** HS 73 v Herts (Bristol) 1993. BB 5-30 v Lincs (Gloucester) 1990. **BHC:** HS 36 v Derbys (Derby) 1987. BB 5-27 v Comb Us (Bristol) 1988. **SL:** HS 134* v Leics (Bristol) 1992. BB 4-35 v Lancs (Manchester) 1992.
AVERIS, James Max Michael (Queen Elizabeth Hospital S, Bristol), b Bristol 28 May 1974. RHB, RFM. Summer contract – awaiting f-c debut. **SL:** HS 2*.
BALL, Martyn Charles John (King Edmund SS; Bath CFE), b Bristol 26 Apr 1970. 5'8". RHB, OB. Debut 1988. Tour (Gs): SL 1992-93. HS 71 v Notts (Bristol) 1993. BB 8-46 (14-169 match) v Somerset (Taunton) 1993. **NWT:** HS 16* v Essex (Cheltenham) 1992. BB 3-42 v Lancs (Gloucester) 1989. **BHC:** HS 20* and BB 2-32 v Kent (Canterbury) 1994. **SL:** HS 28* v Worcs (Worcester) 1994. BB 3-24 v Somerset (Taunton) 1993.
CAWDRON, Michael John (Cheltenham C), b Luton, Beds 7 Oct 1974. 6'2". LHB, RM. Gloucestershire staff 1994 – awaiting f-c debut.
COOPER, Kevin Edwin (Hucknall National SS), b Hucknall, Notts 27 Dec 1957. 6'1". LHB, RFM. Nottinghamshire 1976-92 (cap 1980; benefit 1990). Gloucestershire debut v Board XI (Colombo) 1992-93. Tour: SL 1992-93 (Gs). HS 52 v Lancs (Cheltenham) 1993. 50 wkts (8) inc 100 (1): 101 (1988). BB 8-44 Nt v Middx (Lord's) 1984. Gs BB 5-83 v Yorks (Sheffield) 1993. Awards: NWT 1; BHC 2. **NWT:** HS 11 Nt v Glos (Nottingham) 1982. BB 4-49 Nt v Warwks (Nottingham) 1985. **BHC:** HS 25* Nt v Lancs (Manchester) 1983. BB 4-9 Nt v Yorks (Nottingham) 1989. **SL:** HS 31 Nt v Glos (Nottingham) 1984. BB 4-25 Nt v Hants (Nottingham) 1976.
CUNLIFFE, Robert John (Banbury S; Banbury TC), b Oxford 8 Nov 1973. 5'10". RHB, RM. Debut 1994. Oxfordshire 1991-94. HS 177* v CU (Bristol) 1994. BAC HS 29 v Derbys (Chesterfield) 1994. **SL:** HS 22 v Sussex (Hove) 1993.
DAVIES, Mark (Cwrt Sart CS; Neath Tertiary C), b Neath, Glam 18 Apr 1969. 5'6". RHB, SLA. Glamorgan 1990. Gloucestershire debut 1992. MCC YC. Tour: SL 1992-93 (Gs). HS 54 v Notts (Nottingham) 1994. 50 wkts (1): 56 (1992). BB 5-57 (10-141 match) v Northants (Northampton) 1993. **SL:** HS 14 v Hants (Portsmouth) 1994. BB 2-23 v Middx (Lord's) 1994.
DAWSON, Robert Ian (Millfield S; Newcastle Poly), b Exmouth, Devon 29 Mar 1970. 5'11". RHB, RM. Debut 1992. Devon 1988-91. 1000 runs (1): 1112 (1994). HS 127* v CU (Bristol) 1994. BAC HS 93 v Northants (Bristol) 1994. BB 2-38 v Derbys (Chesterfield) 1994. **NWT:** HS 60 v Devon (Bristol) 1994. BB 1-37. **SL:** HS 45 v Middx (Lord's) 1994.

HANCOCK, Timothy Harold Coulter (St Edward's S, Oxford; Henley C), b Reading, Berks 20 Apr 1972. 5'10". RHB, RM. Debut 1991. Oxfordshire 1990. Tour: SL 1992-93 (Gs). HS 123 v Essex (Chelmsford) 1994. BB 3-10 v Glam (Abergavenny) 1993. **NWT:** HS 45 and BB 2-7 v Herts (Bristol) 1993. **BHC:** HS 23 v Derbys (Bristol) 1993. **SL:** HS 46 v Sussex (Hove) 1993. BB 2-31 v Yorks (Cheltenham) 1994.

HEWSON, Dominic Robert (Cheltenham C), b Cheltenham 3 Oct 1974. 5'8". RHB, occ RM. Gloucestershire staff 1994 – awaiting f-c debut.

HODGSON, Geoffrey **Dean** (Nelson Thomlinson CS, Wigton; Loughborough U), b Carlisle, Cumberland 22 Oct 1966. 6'1". RHB. Debut 1989. Cap 1992. Cumberland 1984-88 (cap 1987 when aged 20 – county record). Warwickshire (SL only) 1987. 1000 runs (4); most – 1320 (1990). HS 166 v Hants (Bristol) 1993. Awards: BHC 2. **NWT:** HS 62 v Yorks (Bristol) 1993. **BHC:** HS 103* v Minor C (Cheltenham) 1992. **SL:** HS 104* v Durham (Bristol) 1993.

PIKE, Vyvian John (Taunton S; Portsmouth Poly), b Taunton, Somerset 13 Aug 1969. 6'2". RHB, LB. Debut 1994. Dorset 1993-94. HS 27 v Derbys (Chesterfield) 1994. BB 6-41 v CU (Bristol) 1994 – on debut. BAC BB 3-109 v Lancs (Manchester) 1994.

RUSSELL, Robert Charles ('Jack') (Archway CS), b Stroud 15 Aug 1963. 5'8½". LHB, WK, occ OB. Debut 1981. Cap 1985. Benefit 1994. Captain 1995. Wisden 1989. **Tests:** 36 (1988 to 1993-94); HS 128* v A (Manchester) 1989. LOI: 26 (HS 50). Tours: A 1990-91, 1992-93 (Eng A); WI 1989-90, 1993-94; NZ 1991-92; P 1987-88; SL 1986-87 (Gs). HS 128* (Tests). Gs HS 120 v Somerset (Bristol) 1990. BB 1-4. Award: BHC 1. **NWT:** HS 42* v Lancs (Gloucester) 1989. **BHC:** HS 51 v Worcs (Worcester) 1991. **SL:** HS 108 v Worcs (Hereford) 1986.

SHEERAZ, Kamran Pasha (Licensed Victuallers' S, Ascot; E Berkshire C, Langley), b Wellington, Shropshire 28 Dec 1973. 6'0". RHB, RMF. Debut 1994. Bedfordshire 1992. HS 1* and BB 2-34 v Northants (Bristol) 1994. **SL:** HS –.

SMITH, Andrew **Michael** (Queen Elizabeth GS, Wakefield; Exeter U), b Dewsbury, Yorks 1 Oct 1967. 5'9". RHB, LM. Debut 1991. HS 51* v Warwks (Bristol) 1992. BB 5-40 v Durham (Gateshead) 1994. **NWT:** HS 8*. BB 3-45 v Somerset (Taunton) 1992. **BHC:** HS 15* Comb Us v Surrey (Oxford) 1990. BB 4-49 Comb Us v Somerset (Oxford) 1988. **SL:** HS 15* v Essex (Cheltenham) 1991. BB 4-38 v Leics (Bristol) 1992.

WILLIAMS, Ricardo Cecil (Ellerslie SS, Barbados; Haringey Cricket C), b Camberwell, London 3 Feb 1968. 5'9". RHB, RM. Debut 1991. HS 44 v Notts (Worksop) 1992. BB 4-28 v CU (Bristol) 1994. BAC BB 3-13 v Kent (Cheltenham) 1994. **SL:** HS 31 v Essex (Chelmsford) 1994. BB 3-33 v Northants (Bristol) 1994.

WILLIAMS, Richard Charles James (Millfield S), b Southmead, Bristol 8 Aug 1969. 5'8". LHB, WK. Debut 1990. Tour: SL 1992-93 (Gs). HS 55* v Derbys (Gloucester) 1991. **SL:** HS 17 v Warwks (Bristol) 1992.

WINDOWS, Matthew Guy Newman (Clifton C; Durham U), b Bristol 5 Apr 1973. Son of A.R. (Glos and CU 1960-68). 5'7". RHB, RSM. Debut 1992. HS 106 v NZ (Bristol) 1994. BAC HS 85 v Lancs (Manchester) 1994. **NWT:** HS 33 v Devon (Bristol) 1994. **BHC:** HS 16* Comb Us v Lancs (Oxford) 1994. **SL:** HS 72 v Somerset (Bristol) 1994.

WRIGHT, Anthony John (Alleyn's GS) b Stevenage, Herts 27 Jun 1962. 6'0". RHB, RM. Gloucestershire debut 1982. Cap 1987. Captain 1990-93. Benefit 1996. Tours (Gs): SL 1986-87, 1992-93 (captain). 1000 runs (5); most – 1596 (1991). HS 184* v Leics (Bristol) 1994. BB 1-16. Awards: NWT 1; BHC 1. **NWT:** HS 107* v Cheshire (Bristol) 1992. **BHC:** HS 97 v Worcs (Bristol) 1990. **SL:** HS 93 v Durham (Stockton) 1992.

NEWCOMERS

BODEN, David Jonathan Peter (Alleynes HS, Stone; Stafford CFE), b Eccleshall, Staffs 26 Nov 1970. 6'3". RHB, RMF. Middlesex 1989. Essex 1992-93. HS 5. BB 4-11 M v OU (Oxford) 1989 – on debut. **SL:** HS 2. BB 2-48 Ex v Durham (Chelmsford) 1993.

LYNCH, Monte Alan (Ryden's S, Walton-on-Thames), b Georgetown, British Guiana 21 May 1958. 5'8". RHB, OB. Surrey 1977-94 (cap 1982; benefit 1991). Guyana 1982-83. LOI: 3 (HS 6). Tours: SA 1983-84 (WI XI); P 1981-82 (Int). 1000 (8); most – 1714 (1985). HS 172* Sy v Kent (Oval) 1989. BB 3-6 Sy v Glam (Swansea) 1981. Awards: NWT 1; BHC 4. **NWT:** HS 129 Sy v Durham (Oval) 1982. BB 2-28 Sy v Glam (Swansea) 1992. **BHC:** HS 112* Sy v Kent (Oval) 1987. **SL:** HS 136 Sy v Yorks (Bradford) 1985. BB 2-2 Sy v Northants (Guildford) 1987 and Sy v Sussex (Hove) 1990.

SRINATH, Javagal, b Mysore, India 31 Aug 1969. 6'3". RHB, RFM. Karnataka 1989-90 to date. **Tests** (I): 12 (1991-92 to 1993-94); HS 21 v A (Brisbane) 1991-92 – on debut; BB 4-33 v SA (Cape Town) 1992-93. LOI (I) 95: (HS 14; BB 5-24). Tours (I): A 1991-92; SA 1992-93; NZ 1993-94; SL 1993-94; Z 1992-93. HS 59 and BB 7-93 Karnataka v Maharashtra (Poona) 1990-91.

SYMONDS, Andrew, b Birmingham 9 Jun 1975. RHB, OB. Emigrated to Australia when 18 months old. Queensland 1993-94 to date. Australian CA. HS 108* Queensland v England XI (Toowoomba) 1994-95. Registration subject to TCCB approval.

WHITBY-COLES, James Graham (Clifton C), b Bath, Somerset 23 Aug 1974. RHB, OB. Summer contract.

DEPARTURES (who made first-class appearances in 1994)

BABINGTON, Andrew Mark (Reigate GS; Borough Road CE), b Middlesex Hospital, London 22 Jul 1963. 6'2". LHB, RFM. Sussex 1986-90. Gloucestershire 1991-94. HS 58 v Sussex (Cheltenham) 1991. BB 8-107 v Kent (Bristol) 1992. Hat-trick 1986. **NWT:** HS 4*. BB 3-8 v Cheshire (Bristol) 1992. **BHC:** HS 27 v Leics (Cheltenham) 1992. BB 4-29 Sx v Surrey (Hove) 1988. **SL:** HS 11 v Essex (Cheltenham) 1991. BB 4-21 v Northants (Moreton) 1992.

BROAD, Brian **Christopher** (Colston's S, Bristol; St Paul's C, Cheltenham), b Knowle, Bristol 29 Sep 1957. 6'4". LHB, RM. Gloucestershire 1979-83 and 1993-94 (cap 1981). Nottinghamshire 1984-92 (cap 1984). OFS 1985-86 (captain). **Tests:** 25 (1984 to 1989); HS 162 v A (Perth) 1986-87. LOI: 34 (HS 106). Tours: A 1986-87, 1987-88; SA 1989-90 (Eng XI); NZ 1987-88; P 1987-88; SL 1992-93 (Gs); Z 1984-85 (EC). 1000 runs (11) inc 2000 (1): 2226 (1990). HS 227* Nt v Kent (Tunbridge W) 1990. Gs HS 145 v Notts (Bristol) 1983. BB 2-14 v WI (Bristol) 1980. Awards: NWT 5; BHC 2. **NWT:** HS 115 Nt v Bucks (Marlow) 1990. **BHC:** HS 122 Nt v Derbys (Derby) 1984. BB 2-73 Nt v Lancs (Nottingham) 1984. **SL:** HS 108 Nt v Glam (Cardiff) 1991. BB 3-46 v Worcs (Bristol) 1982.

HINKS, Simon Graham (St George's S, Gravesend), b Northfleet, Kent 12 Oct 1960. 6'2". LHB, RM. Kent 1982-91 (cap 1985). Gloucestershire 1992-94. Tour: SL 1992-93 (Gs). 1000 runs (3); most – 1588 (1990). HS 234 K v Middx (Canterbury) 1990. Gs HS 88* v Lancs (Manchester) 1992. BB 2-18 K v Notts (Nottingham) 1989. Awards: NWT 1; BHC 1. **NWT:** HS 95 K v Surrey (Canterbury) 1985. **BHC:** HS 85 K v Sussex (Canterbury) 1987. BB 1-15. **SL:** HS 99 K v Glam (Maidstone) 1986. BB 1-3.

WALSH, Courtney Andrew (Excelsior HS), b Kingston, Jamaica 30 Oct 1962. 6'5½". RHB, RF. Jamaica 1981-82 to date (captain 1990-91 to date). Gloucestershire 1984-94 (cap 1985; captain 1993-94). Benefit 1992. Wisden 1986. **Tests** (WI): 65 (1984-85 to 1993-94, 1 as captain); HS 30* v A (Melbourne) 1988-89; BB 6-62 v I (Kingston) 1988-89. LOI (WI): 124 (HS 29*; BB 5-1). Tours (WI): E 1984, 1988, 1991; A 1984-85, 1986-87, 1988-89, 1992-93; NZ 1986-87; I 1987-88; P 1986-87, 1990-91; SL 1993-94; Z 1983-84 (Young WI). HS 66 v Kent (Cheltenham) 1994. 50 wkts (8+1) inc 100 (1): 118 (1986). BB 9-72 v Somerset (Bristol) 1986. Hat-trick 1988-89 (WI). Awards: NWT 2. **NWT:** HS 37 v Herts (Bristol) 1993. BB 6-21 v Kent (Bristol) 1990 and v Cheshire (Bristol) 1992. **BHC:** HS 28 v Comb Us (Bristol) 1989. BB 2-19 v Scot 1985. **SL:** HS 35 v Glam (Cardiff) 1986. BB 4-19 v Kent (Cheltenham) 1987.

continued on p 181

GLOUCESTERSHIRE 1994

RESULTS SUMMARY

	Place	Won	Lost	Drew	Abandoned
Britannic Assurance Championship	12th	5	8	4	
All First-class Matches		6	8	6	1
Sunday League	18th	4	12		1
NatWest Trophy	1st Round				
Benson and Hedges Cup	2nd Round				

BRITANNIC ASSURANCE CHAMPIONSHIP AVERAGES

BATTING AND FIELDING

Cap		M	I	NO	HS	Runs	Avge	100	50	Ct/St
1987	A.J.Wright	17	33	2	184*	1108	35.74	1	6	31
1985	R.C.Russell	17	30	7	85*	807	35.08	–	4	55/1
–	R.I.Dawson	13	25	3	93	743	33.77	–	5	5
–	M.G.N.Windows	9	17	–	85	564	33.17	–	5	10
–	M.Davies	3	6	2	54	122	30.50	–	1	1
–	S.G.Hinks	4	8	–	74	235	29.37	–	2	4
1981	B.C.Broad	9	18	–	128	493	27.38	1	2	9
–	T.H.C.Hancock	17	32	1	123	831	26.80	1	7	9
1990	M.W.Alleyne	17	32	–	109	833	26.03	1	3	16
1992	G.D.Hodgson	8	15	1	113	316	22.57	1	–	3
–	M.C.J.Ball	15	26	2	45	442	18.41	–	–	26
1985	C.A.Walsh	15	24	6	66	274	15.22	–	1	2
–	A.M.Smith	10	12	1	29	146	13.27	–	–	3
–	R.J.Cunliffe	5	10	–	29	130	13.00	–	–	1
–	R.C.Williams	8	13	2	34*	133	12.09	–	–	3
–	V.J.Pike	7	11	3	27	94	11.75	–	–	2
–	K.E.Cooper	11	15	8	18*	77	11.00	–	–	2

Also batted (1 match): K.P.Sheeraz 1*, 0*; R.M.Wight 22, 11.

BOWLING

	O	M	R	W	Avge	Best	5wI	10wM
C.A.Walsh	506	119	1535	89	17.24	7- 42	9	3
M.W.Alleyne	313.3	60	1014	37	27.40	5- 78	1	–
K.E.Cooper	403.2	94	1069	35	30.54	4- 38	–	–
A.M.Smith	243.1	47	809	23	35.17	5- 40	1	–
R.C.Williams	191.5	32	686	19	36.10	3- 13	–	–
V.J.Pike	147.3	28	496	11	45.09	3-109	–	–
M.C.J.Ball	292.3	62	914	19	48.10	5- 69	1	–

Also bowled: M.Davies 72-7-282-5; R.I.Dawson 30-9-73-2; T.H.C.Hancock 36-4-157-2; K.P.Sheeraz 15-2-34-2; R.M.Wight 27-2-139-3.

The First-Class Averages (pp 186-200) give the records of Gloucestershire players in all first-class county matches (their other opponents being the New Zealanders, the South Africans and Cambridge U).

GLOUCESTERSHIRE RECORDS

FIRST-CLASS CRICKET

Highest Total	For	653-6d		v	Glamorgan	Bristol	1928
	V	774-7d		by	Australians	Bristol	1948
Lowest Total	For	17		v	Australians	Cheltenham	1896
	V	12		by	Northants	Gloucester	1907
Highest Innings	For	318*	W.G.Grace	v	Yorkshire	Cheltenham	1876
	V	296	A.O.Jones	for	Notts	Nottingham	1903

Highest Partnership for each Wicket

1st	395	D.M.Young/R.B.Nicholls	v	Oxford U	Oxford	1962
2nd	256	C.T.M.Pugh/T.W.Graveney	v	Derbyshire	Chesterfield	1960
3rd	336	W.R.Hammond/B.H.Lyon	v	Leics	Leicester	1933
4th	321	W.R.Hammond/W.L.Neale	v	Leics	Gloucester	1937
5th	261	W.G.Grace/W.O.Moberley	v	Yorkshire	Cheltenham	1876
6th	320	G.L.Jessop/J.H.Board	v	Sussex	Hove	1903
7th	248	W.G.Grace/E.L.Thomas	v	Sussex	Hove	1896
8th	239	W.R.Hammond/A.E.Wilson	v	Lancashire	Bristol	1938
9th	193	W.G.Grace/S.A.P.Kitcat	v	Sussex	Bristol	1896
10th	131	W.R.Gouldsworthy/J.G.Bessant	v	Somerset	Bristol	1923

Best Bowling	For	10-40	E.G.Dennett	v	Essex	Bristol	1906
(Innings)	V	10-66	A.A.Mailey	for	Australians	Cheltenham	1921
		10-66	K.Smales	for	Notts	Stroud	1956
Best Bowling	For	17-56	C.W.L.Parker	v	Essex	Gloucester	1925
(Match)	V	15-87	A.J.Conway	for	Worcs	Moreton-in-M	1914

Most Runs – Season	2860	W.R.Hammond	(av 69.75)	1933
Most Runs – Career	33664	W.R.Hammond	(av 57.05)	1920-51
Most 100s – Season	13	W.R.Hammond		1938
Most 100s – Career	113	W.R.Hammond		1920-51
Most Wkts – Season	222	T.W.J.Goddard	(av 16.80)	1937
	222	T.W.J.Goddard	(av 16.37)	1947
Most Wkts – Career	3170	C.W.L.Parker	(av 19.43)	1903-35

LIMITED-OVERS CRICKET

Highest Total	NWT	327-7		v	Berkshire	Reading	1966
	BHC	300-4		v	Comb Us	Oxford	1982
	SL	281-2		v	Hampshire	Swindon	1991
Lowest Total	NWT	82		v	Notts	Bristol	1987
	BHC	62		v	Hampshire	Bristol	1975
	SL	49		v	Middlesex	Bristol	1978
Highest Innings	NWT	158	Zaheer Abbas	v	Leics	Leicester	1983
	BHC	154*	M.J.Procter	v	Somerset	Taunton	1972
	SL	134*	M.W.Alleyne	v	Leics	Bristol	1992
Best Bowling	NWT	6-21	C.A.Walsh	v	Kent	Bristol	1990
		6-21	C.A.Walsh	v	Cheshire	Bristol	1992
	BHC	6-13	M.J.Procter	v	Hampshire	Southampton	1977
	SL	6-52	J.N.Shepherd	v	Kent	Bristol	1983

HAMPSHIRE

Formation of Present Club: 12 August 1863
Colours: Blue, Gold and White
Badge: Tudor Rose and Crown
Championships: (2) 1961, 1973
NatWest Trophy/Gillette Cup Winners: (1) 1991
Benson and Hedges Cup Winners: (2) 1988, 1992
Sunday League Champions: (3) 1975, 1978, 1986
Match Awards: NWT 51; BHC 57

Chief Executive: A.F.Baker
County Cricket Ground, Northlands Road, Southampton SO9 2TY
(☎ 01703 333788/9)
Captain: M.C.J.Nicholas
Scorer: V.H Isaacs
1995 Beneficiary: Hampshire CCC

AYMES, Adrian Nigel (Bellemoor SM, Southampton), b Southampton 4 Jun 1964. 6'0". RHB, WK. Debut 1987. Cap 1991. HS 107* v Sussex (Portsmouth) 1993. BB 1-75. **NWT:** HS 34 v Kent (Southampton) 1994. **BHC:** HS 23* v Durham (Stockton) 1993. **SL:** HS 54 v Durham (Portsmouth) 1994.

BOTHAM, Liam James (Rossall S), b Doncaster, Yorks 26 Aug 1977. Son of I.T. (Somerset, Worcs, Durham, Queensland and England 1974-93). 6'0". RHB, RMF. Summer contract – awaiting f-c debut.

BOVILL, James Noel Bruce (Charterhouse; Durham U), b High Wycombe, Bucks 2 Jun 1971. Son of M.E. (Dorset 1957-60). 6'1". RHB, RFM. Debut 1993. Buckinghamshire 1990-92. HS 10 v Glam (Southampton) 1994. BB 5-108 v Leics (Leicester) 1994. **BHC:** HS 14*. BB 2-21 Comb Us v Lancs (Oxford) 1994. **SL:** HS 7*. BB 3-40 v Surrey (Oval) 1993.

CONNOR, Cardigan Adolphus (The Valley SS, Anguilla; Langley C, Berkshire), b The Valley, Anguilla 24 Mar 1961. 5'9". RHB, RFM. Debut 1984. Cap 1988. Buckinghamshire 1979-83. HS 59 v Surrey (Oval) 1993. 50 wkts (4); most – 72 (1994). BB 7-31 v Glos (Portsmouth) 1989. Award: NWT 1. **NWT:** HS 13 v Yorks (Southampton) 1990. BB 4-11 v Cambs (March) 1994. **BHC:** HS 5*. BB 4-19 v Sussex (Hove) 1989. **SL:** HS 25 v Middx (Lord's) 1993. BB 4-11 v Derbys (Portsmouth) 1990.

COWANS, Norman George (Park High SS, Stanmore), b Enfield St Mary, Jamaica 17 Apr 1961. 6'3". RHB, RFM. Middlesex 1980-93 (cap 1984; benefit 1993). Hampshire debut 1994. YC 1982. MCC YC. **Tests:** 19 (1982-83 to 1985); HS 36 v A (Perth) 1982-83; BB 6-77 v A (Melbourne) 1982-83. LOI: 23 (HS 4*; BB 3-44). Tours: A 1982-83; NZ 1983-84; I 1984-85; P 1983-84; SL 1984-85, 1985-86 (Eng B); Z 1980-81 (Mx). HS 66 M v Surrey (Lord's) 1984. H HS 19 v Middx (Southampton) 1994. 50 wkts (6); most – 73 (1984, 1985). BB 6-31 M v Leics (Leicester) 1985. H BB 4-76 v Durham (Portsmouth) 1994. Awards: NWT 1; BHC 1. **NWT:** HS 12* M v Lancs (Lord's) 1984. BB 4-24 M v Yorks (Leeds) 1986. **BHC:** HS 12 M v Derbys (Derby) 1990. BB 4-33 M v Lancs (Lord's) 1983. **SL:** HS 27 M v Notts (Lord's) 1990. BB 6-9 M v Lancs (Lord's) 1991.

FLINT, Darren Peter John (Queen Mary's SFC), b Basingstoke 14 Jun 1970. 6'0". RHB, SLA. Debut 1993. HS 14* v Worcs (Portsmouth) 1993. BB 5-32 v Glos (Bristol) 1993 – on debut.

GARAWAY, Mark (Sandown HS, IoW), b Swindon, Wilts 20 Jul 1973. 5'8". RHB, WK. MCC YC. Hampshire staff 1993 – awaiting f-c debut.

JAMES, Kevan David (Edmonton County HS), b Lambeth, London 18 Mar 1961. 6'0". LHB, LMF. Middlesex 1980-84. Wellington 1982-83. Hampshire debut 1985. Cap 1989. 1000 runs (2); most – 1274 (1991). HS 162 v Glam (Cardiff) 1989. BB 6-22 v A (Southampton) 1985. BAC BB 5-25 v Glos (Southampton) 1988. **NWT:**

HS 42 v Glam (Cardiff) 1989. BB 3-22 v Dorset (Southampton) 1987. **BHC:** HS 45 v Essex (Chelmsford) 1989. BB 3-31 v Middx 1987 and v Glam 1988. **SL:** HS 66 v Glos (Trowbridge) 1989. BB 5-42 v Surrey (Southampton) 1994.

KEECH, Matthew (Northumberland Park S), b Hampstead 21 Oct 1970. 6'0". RHB, RM. Middlesex 1991-93. Hampshire debut 1994. MCC YC. HS 58* M v Notts (Lord's) 1991. H HS 57 v Middx (Southampton) 1994. BB 2-28 M v Glos (Bristol) 1993. **NWT:** HS 3. **BHC:** HS 47 M v Warwks (Lord's) 1991. BB 1-37. **SL:** HS 49* M v Somerset (Taunton) 1991. BB 2-22 M v Northants (Lord's) 1993.

KENDALL, William Salwey (Bradfield C; Keble C, Oxford), b Wimbledon, Surrey 18 Dec 1973. 5'10". RHB, RM. Oxford U debut 1994. Awaiting Hampshire debut. HS 113* OU v Surrey (Oval) 1994.

LANEY, Jason Scott (Pewsey Vale SS; St John's SFC, Marlborough; Leeds U), b Winchester 27 Apr 1973. RHB, OB. Hampshire staff 1993 – awaiting f-c debut. **SL:** HS 12 v Essex (Chelmsford) 1993.

MARU, Rajesh Jamandass (Rook's Heath HS, Harrow; Pinner SFC), b Nairobi, Kenya 28 Oct 1962. 5'6". RHB, SLA. Middlesex 1980-82. Hampshire debut 1984. Cap 1986. Tour: Z 1980-81 (Mx). HS 74 v Glos (Gloucester) 1988. 50 wkts (4); most – 73 (1985). BB 8-41 v Kent (Southampton) 1989. **NWT:** HS 22 v Yorks (Southampton) 1990. BB 3-46 v Leics (Leicester) 1990. **BHC:** HS 9. BB 3-46 v Comb Us (Southampton) 1990. **SL:** HS 33* v Glam (Ebbw Vale) 1991. BB 3-30 v Leics (Leicester) 1988.

MIDDLETON, Tony Charles (Montgomery of Alamein S, and Peter Symonds SFC, Winchester), b Winchester 1 Feb 1964. 5'10½". RHB, SLA. Debut 1984. Cap 1990. Tour: A 1992-93 (Eng A). 1000 runs (2); most – 1780 (1992). HS 221 v Surrey (Southampton) 1992. BB 2-41 v Kent (Canterbury) 1991. Awards: BHC 2. **NWT:** HS 91* v Comb Us (Southampton) 1993. **BHC:** HS 65 v Middx (Southampton) 1992. **SL:** HS 98 v Northants (Bournemouth) 1992.

MORRIS, Robert **Sean** Millner (Stowe S; Durham U), b Great Horwood, Bucks 10 Sep 1968. RHB, OB. 6'0". Debut 1992. HS 174 v Notts (Basingstoke) 1994. **NWT:** HS 34* v Cambs (March) 1994. **SL:** HS 34 v Notts (Basingstoke) 1994.

NICHOLAS, Mark Charles Jefford (Bradfield C), b London 29 Sep 1957. Grandson of F.W.H. (Essex 1912-29). 5'11". RHB, RM. Debut 1978. Cap 1982. Captain 1985-. Benefit 1991. Tours (C=captain): SL 1985-86C (Eng B); Z 1984-85C (EC), 1989-90C (Eng A). 1000 runs (9); most – 1559 (1984). HS 206* v OU (Oxford) 1982. BAC HS 158 v Lancs (Portsmouth) 1984. BB 6-37 v Somerset (Southampton) 1989. Awards: NWT 1; BHC 1. **NWT:** HS 71 v Surrey (Oval) 1989. BB 2-39 v Berks (Southampton) 1985. **BHC:** HS 74 v Glam (Southampton) 1985. BB 4-34 v Minor C (Reading) 1985. **SL:** HS 108 v Glos (Bristol) 1984. BB 4-30 v Glos (Trowbridge) 1989.

SMITH, Robin Arnold (Northlands HS), b Durban, SA 13 Sep 1963. Brother of C.L. (Natal, Glam, Hants and England 1977-78/1992) and grandson of Dr V.L.Shearer (Natal). 5'11". RHB, LB. Natal 1980-81/1984-85. Hampshire debut 1982. Cap 1985. Benefit 1996. Wisden 1989. **Tests:** 53 (1988 to 1994); HS 175 v WI (St John's) 1993-94. LOI: 64 (HS 167* – Eng record). Tours: A 1990-91; WI 1989-90, 1993-94; NZ 1991-92; I/SL 1992-93. 1000 runs (8); most – 1577 (1989). HS 209* v Essex (Southend) 1987. BB 2-11 v Surrey (Southampton) 1985. Awards: NWT 6; BHC 4. **NWT:** HS 125* v Surrey (Oval) 1989. BB 2-13 v Berks (Southampton) 1985. **BHC:** HS 155* v Glam (Southampton) 1989. **SL:** HS 131 v Notts (Nottingham) 1989. BB 1-0.

TERRY, Vivian **Paul** (Millfield S), b Osnabruck, W Germany 14 Jan 1959. 6'0". RHB, RM. Debut 1978. Cap 1983. Benefit 1994. **Tests:** 2 (1984); HS 8. Tour: Z 1984-85 (EC). 1000 runs (10); most – 1469 (1993). HS 190 v SL (Southampton) BAC HS 180 v Derbys (Derby) 1990. Awards: NWT 4; BHC 4. **NWT:** HS 165* v Berks (Southampton) 1985. **BHC:** HS 134 v Comb Us (Southampton) 1990. **SL:** HS 142 v Leics (Southampton) 1986.

THURSFIELD, Martin John (Boldon CS), b South Shields, Co Durham 14 Dec 1971. 6'3". RHB, RM. Middlesex 1990. Hampshire debut 1992. MCC YC. HS 47 v

THURSFIELD – continued:
Glam (Southampton) 1994. BB 6-130 v Middx (Southampton) 1994. **SL:** HS 9. BB 3-31 v Leics (Leicester) 1994.

UDAL, Shaun David (Cove CS), b Farnborough 18 Mar 1969. Grandson of G.F. (Middx 1932 and Leics 1946). 6'2". RHB, OB. Debut 1989. Cap 1992. LOI: 3 (HS 3*; BB 2-39). HS 94 v Glam (Southampton) 1994. 50 wkts (3); most – 74 (1993). BB 8-50 v Sussex (Southampton) 1992. Awards: NWT 1; BHC 1. **NWT:** HS 14 v Kent (Southampton) 1994. BB 3-39 v Kent (Southampton) 1992. **BHC:** HS 9*. BB 4-40 v Middx (Southampton) 1992. **SL:** HS 44 v Lancs (Southampton) 1993. BB 4-51 v Northants (Bournemouth) 1992.

WHITAKER, Paul Robert (Whitcliffe Mount S), b Keighley, Yorks 28 Jun 1973. 5'9". LHB, OB. Debut 1994. Derbyshire staff 1992-93. HS 94 v Leics (Leicester) 1994 – on debut. **SL:** HS 7.

WHITE, Giles William (Millfield S; Loughborough U), b Barnstaple, Devon 23 Mar 1972. 6'0". RHB, LB. Somerset 1991 (one match). Hampshire debut 1994. Devon 1988-94. HS 104 Comb Us v NZ (Cambridge) 1994. H HS 73* v Durham (Portsmouth) 1994. BB 1-30. **NWT:** HS 11 and BB 1-45 Devon v Kent (Canterbury) 1992. **SL:** HS 49* v Surrey (Southampton) 1994.

NEWCOMERS

STEPHENSON, John Patrick (Felsted S; Durham U), b Stebbing, Essex 14 Mar 1965. 6'1". RHB, RM. Essex 1985-94 (cap 1989). Boland 1988-89. **Tests:** 1 (1989); HS 25 v A (Oval) 1989. Tours: WI 1991-92 (Eng A); Z 1989-90 (Eng A). 1000 runs (5); most – 1887 (1990). HS 202* Ex v Somerset (Bath) 1990. BB 6-54 Ex v Notts (Colchester) 1992. Awards: BHC 2. **NWT:** HS 90 Ex v Northants (Chelmsford) 1993. BB 3-78 Ex v Lancs (Chelmsford) 1992. **BHC:** HS 142 Ex v Warwks (Birmingham) 1991. BB 3-22 Ex v Northants (Northampton) 1990. **SL:** HS 109 Ex v Lancs (Colchester) 1990. BB 5-58 Ex v Glos (Chelmsford) 1992.

STREAK, Heath Hilton (Falcon C), b Bulawayo, Rhodesia 16 Mar 1974. Son of D.H. (Rhodesia 1976-77/1978-79). 6'1". RHB, RFM. Debut for Zimbabwe B v Kent (Harare) 1992-93. Matabeland 1993-94. **Tests** (Z): 3 (1993-94); HS 19* v P (Karachi) 1993-94 – on debut; BB 5-56 v P (Rawalpindi) 1993-94. LOI (Z): 7 (HS 11; BB 2-15). Tours (Z): E 1993; P 1993-94. HS 62 Matabeleland Inv XI v Worcs (Bulawayo) 1993-94. BB 5-56 (Tests).

DEPARTURES (who made first-class appearances in 1994)

BENJAMIN, Winston Keithroy Matthew (All Saints S, Antigua), b St John's, Antigua 31 Dec 1964. 6'3". RHB, RFM. Debut (Rest of World XI) 1985. Leicestershire 1986-90 (cap 1989) and 1992. Leeward Is 1985-86 to date. Cheshire 1985. Hampshire 1994. **Tests** (WI): 16 (1987-88 to 1993-94); HS 44 v E (Georgetown) 1993-94; BB 4-46 v SL (Moratuwa) 1993-94. LOI (WI): 75 (HS 31; BB 5-22). Tours (WI): E 1985 (RW), 1988; A 1986-87, 1988-89; I 1987-88; P 1986-87; SL 1993-94. HS 101* Le v Derbys (Leicester) 1990. H HS 54 v Glos (Portsmouth) 1994. 50 wkts (1): 69 (1989). BB 7-54 (inc hat-trick) Le v A (Leicester) 1989. BAC BB 7-83 Le v Lancs (Leicester) 1993. H BB 6-46 v Worcs (Worcester) 1994. Awards: BHC 2. **NWT:** HS 24* Le v Durham (Leicester) 1992. BB 5-32 Le v Derbys (Derby) 1992. **BHC:** HS 45 Le v Middx (Leicester) 1992. BB 5-17 Le v Minor C (Leicester) 1986. **SL:** HS 55 v Glos (Leicester) 1993. BB 4-19 Le v Lancs (Leicester) 1986.

COX, Rupert Michael FIENNES-(Bradfield C), b Guildford, Surrey 20 Aug 1967. 5'9". LHB, OB. Hampshire 1990-94. HS 104* v Worcs (Worcester) 1990 – in second match. **SL:** 23* v Essex (Southampton) 1994.

JEAN-JACQUES, Martin (Aylestone SS, London), b Soufriere, Dominica 2 Jul 1960. 6'0". RHB, RMF. Derbyshire 1986-92. Hampshire 1993-94. Buckinghamshire 1983-85. HS 73 De v Yorks (Sheffield) 1986 (on debut). H HS 22* v Durham (Portsmouth) 1994. BB 8-77 De v Kent (Derby) 1986. H BB 3-44 v Kent (Canterbury) 1994. **NWT:** HS 16 De v Surrey (Derby) 1986. BB 3-23 De v Cambs (Wisbech) 1987. **BHC:** HS 2*. BB 3-22 De v Notts (Nottingham) 1987. **SL:** HS 23 De v Lancs (Derby) 1991. BB 3-36 De v Worcs (Worcester) 1986.

HAMPSHIRE 1994

RESULTS SUMMARY

	Place	Won	Lost	Drew
Britannic Assurance Championship	13th	4	7	6
All First-class Matches		4	7	8
Sunday League	12th	7	10	
NatWest Trophy	2nd Round			
Benson and Hedges Cup	Semi-Finalist			

BRITANNIC ASSURANCE CHAMPIONSHIP AVERAGES

BATTING AND FIELDING

Cap		M	I	NO	HS	Runs	Avge	100	50	Ct/St
1982	M.C.J.Nicholas	17	30	6	145	1115	46.45	3	5	7
1985	R.A.Smith	14	25	–	162	1143	45.72	5	3	3
–	R.S.M.Morris	8	15	2	174	581	44.69	1	3	4
1983	V.P.Terry	17	31	1	164	1056	35.20	4	1	22
1992	S.D.Udal	15	26	3	94	656	28.52	–	4	13
1991	A.N.Aymes	17	28	–	76	635	22.67	–	2	33/4
1990	T.C.Middleton	12	22	3	72	422	22.21	–	1	5
–	G.W.White	9	16	1	73*	324	21.60	–	2	10
1989	K.D.James	11	19	2	53	321	18.88	–	2	2
1986	R.J.Maru	9	15	4	38*	207	18.81	–	–	13
–	W.K.M.Benjamin	9	14	1	54	231	17.76	–	2	4
–	M.Keech	4	7	–	57	113	16.14	–	1	6
–	M.Jean-Jacques	3	5	1	22*	52	13.00	–	–	1
–	J.N.B.Bovill	4	7	5	10	25	12.50	–	–	–
–	M.J.Thursfield	7	10	1	47	103	11.44	–	–	1
1988	C.A.Connor	13	20	1	25	195	10.26	–	–	4
–	N.G.Cowans	12	15	6	19	51	5.66	–	–	3

Also batted (2 matches): R.M.F.Cox 5, 9, 15 (1 ct); D.P.J.Flint 5, 3* (1 ct); P.R.Whitaker 2, 94, 38.

BOWLING

	O	M	R	W	Avge	Best	5wI	10wM
W.K.M.Benjamin	281	97	585	24	24.37	6- 46	2	–
C.A.Connor	541	121	1663	67	24.82	7- 47	2	2
S.D.Udal	625	159	1755	62	28.30	6- 79	6	1
M.J.Thursfield	135	29	454	15	30.26	6-130	1	–
K.D.James	256.1	49	834	22	37.90	4- 78	–	–
N.G.Cowans	349.3	93	986	26	37.92	4- 76	–	–
R.J.Maru	254.1	75	621	15	41.40	3- 61	–	–

Also bowled: J.N.B.Bovill 75.4-14-274-9; D.P.J.Flint 41-10-117-0; M.Jean-Jacques 53.1-4-242-5; M.Keech 9.3-2-39-0; M.C.J.Nicholas 4-2-7-0; P.R.Whitaker 0.1-0-4-0; G.W.White 5-1-13-0.

The First-Class Averages (pp 186-200) give the records of Hampshire players in all first-class county matches (their other opponents being the South Africans and Oxford U), with the exception of R.A.Smith, whose full county figures are as above, and:

J.N.B.Bovill 5-7-5-10-25-12.50-0-0-0ct. 84.4-16-315-9-35.00-5/108-1-0.
G.W.White 10-18-1-73*-362-21.29-0-2-12ct. 5-1-13-0.

HAMPSHIRE RECORDS

FIRST-CLASS CRICKET

Highest Total	For	672-7d		v	Somerset	Taunton	1899
	V	742		by	Surrey	The Oval	1909
Lowest Total	For	15		v	Warwicks	Birmingham	1922
	V	23		by	Yorkshire	Middlesbrough	1965
Highest Innings	For	316	R.H.Moore	v	Warwicks	Bournemouth	1937
	V	302*	P.Holmes	for	Yorkshire	Portsmouth	1920

Highest Partnership for each Wicket

1st	347	V.P.Terry/C.L.Smith	v	Warwicks	Birmingham	1987
2nd	321	G.Brown/E.I.M.Barrett	v	Glos	Southampton	1920
3rd	344	C.P.Mead/G.Brown	v	Yorks	Portsmouth	1927
4th	263	R.E.Marshall/D.A.Livingstone	v	Middlesex	Lord's	1970
5th	235	G.Hill/D.F.Walker	v	Sussex	Portsmouth	1937
6th	411	R.M.Poore/E.G.Wynyard	v	Somerset	Taunton	1899
7th	325	G.Brown/C.H.Abercrombie	v	Essex	Leyton	1913
8th	227	K.D.James/T.M.Tremlett	v	Somerset	Taunton	1985
9th	230	D.A.Livingstone/A.T.Castell	v	Surrey	Southampton	1962
10th	192	H.A.W.Bowell/W.H.Livsey	v	Worcs	Bournemouth	1921

Best Bowling	For	9- 25	R.M.H.Cottam	v	Lancashire	Manchester	1965
(Innings)	V	10- 46	W.Hickton	for	Lancashire	Manchester	1870
Best Bowling	For	16- 88	J.A.Newman	v	Somerset	Weston-s-Mare	1927
(Match)	V	17-119	W.Mead	for	Essex	Southampton	1895

Most Runs – Season	2854	C.P.Mead	(av 79.27)	1928
Most Runs – Career	48892	C.P.Mead	(av 48.84)	1905-36
Most 100s – Season	12	C.P.Mead		1928
Most 100s – Career	138	C.P.Mead		1905-36
Most Wkts – Season	190	A.S.Kennedy	(av 15.61)	1922
Most Wkts – Career	2669	D.Shackleton	(av 18.23)	1948-69

LIMITED-OVERS CRICKET

Highest Total	NWT	371-4		v	Glamorgan	Southampton	1975
	BHC	321-1		v	Minor C (S)	Amersham	1973
	SL	313-2		v	Sussex	Portsmouth	1993
Lowest Total	NWT	98		v	Lancashire	Manchester	1975
	BHC	50		v	Yorkshire	Leeds	1991
	SL	43		v	Essex	Basingstoke	1972
Highest Innings	NWT	177	C.G.Greenidge	v	Glamorgan	Southampton	1975
	BHC	173*	C.G.Greenidge	v	Minor C (S)	Amersham	1973
	SL	172	C.G.Greenidge	v	Surrey	Southampton	1987
Best Bowling	NWT	7-30	P.J.Sainsbury	v	Norfolk	Southampton	1965
	BHC	5-13	S.T.Jefferies	v	Derbyshire	Lord's	1988
	SL	6-20	T.E.Jesty	v	Glamorgan	Cardiff	1975

KENT

Formation of Present Club: 1 March 1859
Substantial Reorganisation: 6 December 1870
Colours: Maroon and White
Badge: White Horse on a Red Ground
Championships: (6) 1906, 1909, 1910, 1913, 1970, 1978
Joint Championship: (1) 1977
NatWest Trophy/Gillette Cup Winners: (2) 1967, 1974
Benson and Hedges Cup Winners: (3) 1973, 1976, 1978
Sunday League Champions: (3) 1972, 1973, 1976
Match Awards: NWT 46; BHC 71

Secretary: S.T.W.Anderson OBE, MC
St Lawrence Ground, Canterbury, CT1 3NZ (☎ 01227 456886)
Captain: M.R.Benson
Scorer: J.C.Foley
1995 Beneficiary: S.A.Marsh

BENSON, Mark Richard (Sutton Valence S), b Shoreham, Sussex 6 Jul 1958. 5'10". LHB, OB. Debut 1980. Cap 1981. Captain 1991-. Benefit 1991. **Tests:** 1 (1986); HS 30 v I (Birmingham) 1986. LOI: 1 (HS 24). 1000 runs (11); most – 1725 (1987). HS 257 v Hants (Southampton) 1991. BB 2-55 v Surrey (Dartford) 1986. Awards: NWT 2; BHC 4. **NWT:** HS 113* v Warwks (Birmingham) 1984. **BHC:** HS 118 v Glam (Swansea) 1990. **SL:** HS 97 v Surrey (Oval) 1982.

COWDREY, Graham Robert (Tonbridge S; Durham U), b Farnborough 27 Jun 1964. Brother of C.S. (Kent, Glam and England 1977-92), son of M.C. (Kent and England 1950-76), grandson of E.A. (Europeans). 5'11". RHB, RM. Debut 1984. Cap 1988. 1000 runs (3); most – 1576 (1990). HS 147 v Glos (Bristol) 1992. BB 1-5. Award: BHC 1. **NWT:** HS 37 v Glos (Bristol) 1990. BB 2-4 v Devon (Canterbury) 1992. **BHC:** HS 70* v Leics (Canterbury) 1991. BB 1-6. **SL:** HS 102* v Leics (Folkestone) 1989. BB 4-15 v Essex (Ilford) 1987.

EALHAM, Mark Alan (Stour Valley SS, Chartham), b Willesborough, Ashford 27 Aug 1969. Son of A.G.E. (Kent 1966-82). 5'9". RHB, RMF. Debut 1989. Cap 1992. Tour: Z 1992-93 (K). HS 85 v Lancs (Lytham) 1993. BB 7-53 v Hants (Canterbury) 1994. Awards: NWT 2. **NWT:** HS 58* v Warwks (Birmingham) 1993. BB 4-10 v Derbys (Derby) 1994. **BHC:** HS 26 v Yorks (Leeds) 1992. BB 4-29 v Somerset (Canterbury) 1992. **SL:** HS 43* v Derbys (Chesterfield) 1992. BB 6-53 v Hants (Basingstoke) 1993.

FLEMING, Matthew Valentine (St Aubyns S, Rottingdean; Eton C), b Macclesfield, Cheshire 12 Dec 1964. 5'11½". RHB, RM. Debut 1989. Cap 1990. Tour: Z 1992-93 (K). HS 116 v WI (Canterbury) 1991. BAC HS 113 v Surrey (Canterbury) 1991. BB 4-31 v Glos (Tunbridge W) 1993. Awards: NWT 1; BHC 4. **NWT:** HS 53 v Devon (Canterbury) 1992. BB 3-34 v Hants (Southampton) 1992. **BHC:** HS 69 v Somerset (Canterbury) 1992. BB 3-52 v Glam (Canterbury) 1993. **SL:** HS 79 v Glos (Cheltenham) 1994. BB 4-36 v Worcs (Canterbury) 1994.

FULTON, David Paul (The Judd S; Kent U), b Lewisham 15 Nov 1971. 6'2". RHB. Debut 1992. HS 109 v CU (Cambridge) 1994. BAC HS 75 v Northants (Canterbury) 1993. **NWT:** HS 18 v Berks (Finchampstead) 1994. **SL:** HS 29 v Lancs (Manchester) 1993.

HEADLEY, Dean Warren (Worcester RGS), b Norton, Stourbridge, Worcs 27 Jan 1970. Son of R.G.A. (Worcs, Jamaica and WI 1958-74); grandson of G.A. (Jamaica and WI 1927-28/1953-54). 6'4". RHB, RFM. Middlesex 1991-92. Kent debut v Zimbabwe B (Harare) 1992-93. Cap 1993. Tour: Z 1992-93 (K). HS 91 M v Leics (Leicester) 1992. K HS 46* v SA (Canterbury) 1994. BB 7-79 v Glos (Tunbridge W) 1993. Award: BHC 1. **NWT:** HS 11* M v Somerset (Taunton) 1991. BB 5-20 M v Salop (Telford) 1992. **BHC:** HS 26 M v Surrey (Lord's) 1991. BB 4-19 M v Sussex (Hove) 1992. **SL:** HS 10* v Glam (Canterbury) 1993. BB 4-23 M v Essex (Lord's) 1992.

IGGLESDEN, Alan Paul (Churchill S, Westerham), b Farnborough 8 Oct 1964. 6'6". RHB, RFM. Debut 1986. Cap 1989. W Province 1987-88. Boland 1992-93. **Tests:** 3 (1989 and 1993-94); HS 3*; BB 2-91 v A (Oval) 1989. LOI: 4 (HS 18; BB 2-12). Tours: WI 1993-94; Z 1989-90 (Eng A), 1992-93 (K). HS 41 v Surrey (Canterbury) 1988. 50 wkts (4); most – 56 (1989). BB 7-28 (12-66 match) Boland v GW (Kimberley) 1992-93. K BB 6-34 v Surrey (Canterbury) 1988. **NWT:** HS 12* v Oxon (Oxford) 1990. BB 4-29 v Cambs (Canterbury) 1991. **BHC:** HS 26* v Worcs (Worcester) 1991. BB 3-24 v Scot (Glasgow) 1991 and v Notts (Nottingham) 1992. **SL:** HS 13* (twice). BB 5-13 v Sussex (Hove) 1989.

LLONG, Nigel James (Ashford North S), b Ashford 11 Feb 1969. 6'0". LHB, OB. Debut 1990. Cap 1993. Tour: Z 1992-93 (K). HS 116* v CU (Cambridge) 1993. BAC HS 108 v Middx (Lord's) 1993. BB 5-63 v CU (Cambridge) 1994. BAC BB 3-70 v Worcs (Tunbridge W) 1992. **NWT:** HS 27* v Middx (Canterbury) 1993. BB 1-11. **BHC:** HS 5. **SL:** HS 64* v Northants (Canterbury) 1993. BB 4-24 v Sussex (Hove) 1993.

McCAGUE, Martin John (Hedland Sr HS; Carine Tafe C), b Larne, N Ireland 24 May 1969. 6'5". RHB, RF. W Australia 1990-91/1991-92. Kent debut 1991. Cap 1992. **Tests:** 2 (1993); HS 11 v A (Leeds) 1993; BB 4-121 v A (Nottingham) 1993. Tour: SA 1993-94 (Eng A). HS 56 v Durham (Canterbury) 1994. 50 wkts (2); most – 57 (1994). BB 9-86 (15-147 match) v Derbys (Derby) 1994. Award: NWT 1. **NWT:** HS 14 v Warwks (Birmingham) 1992. BB 5-26 v Middx (Canterbury) 1993. **BHC:** HS 30 v Derbys (Canterbury) 1992. BB 5-43 v Somerset (Canterbury) 1992. **SL:** HS 22* v Glam (Swansea) 1992. BB 4-19 v Worcs (Canterbury) 1994.

MARSH, Steven Andrew (Walderslade SS; Mid-Kent CFE), b Westminster, London 27 Jan 1961. 5'10". RHB, WK. Debut 1982. Cap 1986. Benefit 1995. Tour: Z 1992-93 (K – captain). HS 125 v Yorks (Canterbury) 1992. BB 2-20 v Warwks (Birmingham) 1990. Set world f-c record by holding eight catches in an innings AND scoring a hundred (v Middx at Lord's) 1991. **NWT:** HS 24* v Middx (Lord's) 1988. **BHC:** HS 71 v Lancs (Manchester) 1991. **SL:** HS 59 v Leics (Canterbury) 1991.

PATEL, Minal Mahesh (Dartford GS; Erith TC), b Bombay, India 7 Jul 1970. 5'9". RHB, SLA. Debut 1989. Cap 1994. HS 43 v Leics (Leicester) 1991. 50 wkts (1): 90 (1994). BB 8-96 v Lancs (Canterbury) 1994. **NWT:** HS –. BB 2-29 v Oxon (Oxford) 1990. **SL:** HS 5. BB 3-50 v Northants (Northampton) 1994.

PENN, Christopher (Dover GS), b Dover 19 Jun 1963. 6'1". LHB, RFM. Debut 1982. Cap 1987. HS 115 v Lancs (Manchester) 1984. 50 wkts (2); most – 81 (1988). BB 7-70 v Middx (Lord's) 1988. **NWT:** HS 20* v Surrey (Oval) 1991. BB 3-30 v Warwks (Canterbury) 1988. **BHC:** HS 24* v Northants (Northampton) 1989. BB 4-34 v Surrey (Canterbury) 1982. **SL:** HS 40 v Sussex (Maidstone) 1982. BB 4-15 v Glos (Maidstone) 1989.

PRESTON, Nicholas William (Meopham SS; Gravesend GS; Exeter U), b Dartford 22 Jan 1972. 6'1". RHB, RFM. Kent staff 1991 – awaiting f-c debut.

SPENCER, Duncan John (Gosnells HS, W Australia), b Nelson, Lancs 5 Apr 1972. 5'8". RHB, RF. Debut 1993. W Australia 1993-94. HS 75 v Z (Canterbury) 1993. BAC HS 13 v Notts (Canterbury) 1994. BB 4-31 v Leics (Leicester) 1994. **SL:** HS 17* v Northants (Canterbury) 1993. BB 2-16 v Essex (Chelmsford) 1994.

TAYLOR, Neil Royston (Cray Valley THS), b Orpington 21 Jul 1959. 6'1". RHB, OB. Debut 1979 v SL (Canterbury), scoring 110 and 11. Cap 1982. Benefit 1992. 1000 runs (10); most – 1979 (1990). HS 204 v Surrey (Canterbury) 1990. BB 2-20 v Somerset (Canterbury) 1985. Awards: BHC 8. **NWT:** HS 85 v Derbys (Canterbury) 1987. BB 3-29 v Dorset (Canterbury) 1989. **BHC:** HS 137 v Surrey (Oval) 1988. **SL:** HS 95 v Hants (Canterbury) 1990.

THOMPSON, Dr **Julian** Barton deCourcy (The Judd S, Tonbridge; Guy's Hospital Medical S, London U), b Cape Town, SA 28 Oct 1968. 6'4". RHB, RFM. Debut 1994. HS 2 and BB 1-89 v Warwks (Birmingham) 1994. **SL:** HS 3*.

WALKER, Matthew Jonathan (King's S, Rochester), b Gravesend 2 Jan 1974. Grandson of Jack (Kent 1949). 5'8". LHB, RM. Debut 1992-93 (Zimbabwe tour). UK debut 1994. Tour: Z 1992-93 (K). HS 107 v Surrey (Oval) 1994. **SL:** HS 69* v Derbys (Derby) 1994.

WARD, Trevor Robert (Hextable CS, nr Swanley), b Farningham 18 Jan 1968. 5'11". RHB, OB. Debut 1986. Cap 1989. Tour: Z 1992-93 (K). 1000 runs (4); most – 1648 (1992). HS 235* v Middx (Canterbury) 1991. BB 2-48 v Worcs (Canterbury) 1990. Awards: NWT 1; BHC 1. **NWT:** HS 120 v Berks (Finchampstead) 1994. BB 1-58. **BHC:** HS 94 v Worcs (Worcester) 1990. **SL:** HS 131 v Notts (Nottingham) 1993. BB 3-20 v Glam (Canterbury) 1989.

WILLIS, Simon Charles (Wilmington GS), b Greenwich, London 19 Mar 1974. 5'8". RHB, OB, WK. Debut 1993. HS 0*. **SL:** HS –.

WREN, Timothy Neil (Harvey GS, Folkestone), b Folkestone 26 Mar 1970. 6'3". RHB, LM. Debut 1990. Tour: Z 1992-93 (K). HS 18* v Worcs (Canterbury) 1994. BB 6-48 v Somerset (Canterbury) 1994. **NWT:** HS 0. **SL:** HS 5*. BB 3-29 v Yorks (Maidstone) 1994.

NEWCOMERS

De SILVA, Pinnaduwage **Aravinda**, b Colombo, Sri Lanka 17 Oct 1965. 5'3½". RHB, OB. Debut (for SL) 1983-84. Nondescripts 1988-89 to date. **Tests** (SL): 43 (1984 to 1994-95, 4 as captain); HS 267 v NZ (Wellington) 1990-91; BB 3-39 v SA (Colombo) 1993-94. LOI (SL): 136 (HS 105; BB 3-58). Tours (SL)(C=captain): E 1984, 1988, 1990C, 1991C; A 1984-85, 1987-88, 1989-90; NZ 1990-91; I 1986-87, 1990-91, 1993-94; P 1985-86, 1991-92C. 1000 runs (0+1): 1308 (1992-93 – SL record). HS 267 (Tests). BB 5-31 Nondescripts v Rio (Colombo) 1992-93.

HERZBERG, Steven, b Carshalton, Surrey 25 May 1967. Emigrated to Australia when aged 9. 6'4". RHB, OB. W Australia 1991-92/1992-93. Tasmania 1993-94. Worcs 2nd XI 1990-91. HS 57* WA v NSW (Sydney) 1992-93. BB 4-66 Tasmania v Victoria (Melbourne) 1993-94. **SL:** HS –.

STANFORD, Edward John (The Downs SS), b Dartford 21 Jan 1971. LHB, SLA.

DEPARTURES (who made first-class appearances in 1994)

HOOPER, Carl Llewellyn (Christchurch SS, Georgetown), b Georgetown, Guyana 15 Dec 1966. 6'1". RHB, OB. Debut (Demerara) 1983-84. Guyana 1984-85 to date. Kent 1992-94 (cap 1992). **Tests** (WI): 40 (1987-88 to 1993-94); HS 178* v P (St John's) 1992-93; BB 5-40 v P (P-o-S) 1992-93. LOI (WI): 115 (HS 113*; BB 4-34). Tours (WI): E 1988, 1991; A 1988-89, 1991-92, 1992-93; NZ 1986-87; I 1987-88; P 1990-91; SL 1993-94; Z 1986-87 (Young WI), 1989-90 (Young WI). 1000 runs (4); most – 1579 (1994). HS 236* v Glam (Canterbury) 1993. BB 5-33 WI v Queensland (Brisbane) 1988-89. K BB 5-52 v Durham (Canterbury) 1994. Awards: NWT 1; BHC 1. **NWT:** HS 136* v Berks (Finchampstead) 1994. BB 2-12 v Middx (Canterbury) 1993. **BHC:** HS 50 v Surrey (Canterbury) 1992. BB 3-28 v Yorks (Leeds) 1992. **SL:** HS 122 v Northants (Northampton) 1994. BB 5-41 v Essex (Maidstone) 1993.

KENT 1994

RESULTS SUMMARY

	Place	Won	Lost	Drew
Britannic Assurance Championship	**9th**	6	7	4
All First-class Matches		8	7	4
Sunday League	**3rd**	12	5	
NatWest Trophy	Semi-Finalist			
Benson and Hedges Cup	Quarter-Finalist			

BRITANNIC ASSURANCE CHAMPIONSHIP AVERAGES

BATTING AND FIELDING

Cap		*M*	*I*	*NO*	*HS*	*Runs*	*Avge*	*100*	*50*	*Ct/St*
1992	C.L.Hooper	16	29	–	183	1579	54.44	5	7	26
1989	T.R.Ward	17	31	1	125	1282	42.73	3	9	25
1982	N.R.Taylor	14	25	3	139	919	41.77	2	4	3
–	M.J.Walker	5	7	–	107	239	34.14	1	–	2
1986	S.A.Marsh	17	29	6	88	732	31.82	–	4	62/4
1981	M.R.Benson	14	26	1	159	699	27.96	1	4	8
1990	M.V.Fleming	15	27	–	73	754	27.92	–	6	3
1992	M.A.Ealham	13	23	1	68*	604	27.45	–	4	7
1988	G.R.Cowdrey	8	14	1	69	315	24.23	–	2	3
–	D.P.Fulton	8	14	–	50	318	22.71	–	1	15
1992	M.J.McCague	9	15	3	56	265	22.08	–	1	4
1993	N.J.Llong	6	10	–	44	188	18.80	–	–	3
1994	M.M.Patel	16	25	2	39	245	10.65	–	–	10
–	D.J.Spencer	4	6	1	13	46	9.20	–	–	1
1993	D.W.Headley	7	11	3	26	71	8.87	–	–	4
1989	A.P.Igglesden	10	15	8	15*	54	7.71	–	–	1
–	T.N.Wren	7	11	4	18*	31	4.42	–	–	2

Also batted (1 match): J.B.D.Thompson 1*, 2.

BOWLING

	O	*M*	*R*	*W*	*Avge*	*Best*	*5wI*	*10wM*
M.J.McCague	300.1	60	953	54	17.64	9- 86	5	1
M.M.Patel	739.2	181	1910	79	24.17	8- 96	4	2
M.A.Ealham	247.4	55	730	27	27.03	7- 53	1	–
T.N.Wren	164.5	30	533	17	31.35	6- 48	1	–
D.W.Headley	257.1	40	908	28	32.42	5-128	1	–
D.J.Spencer	85.5	12	347	10	34.70	4- 31	–	–
C.L.Hooper	414.1	93	1055	29	36.37	5- 52	1	–
A.P.Igglesden	297.1	67	878	21	41.80	5- 38	1	–

Also bowled: G.R.Cowdrey 0.2-0-4-0; M.V.Fleming 230.5-43-737-9; N.J.Llong 10-2-37-0; J.B.D.Thompson 33-6-120-1.

The First-Class Averages (pp 186-200) give the records of Kent players in all first-class county matches (their other opponents being the South Africans and Cambridge U), with the exception of M.J.McCague,whose full county figures are as above.

KENT RECORDS

FIRST-CLASS CRICKET

Highest Total	For	803-4d		v	Essex	Brentwood	1934
	V	676		by	Australians	Canterbury	1921
Lowest Total	For	18		v	Sussex	Gravesend	1867
	V	16		by	Warwicks	Tonbridge	1913
Highest Innings	For	332	W.H.Ashdown	v	Essex	Brentwood	1934
	V	344	W.G.Grace	for	MCC	Canterbury	1876

Highest Partnership for each Wicket

1st	300	N.R.Taylor/M.R.Benson	v	Derbyshire	Canterbury	1991
2nd	366	S.G.Hinks/N.R.Taylor	v	Middlesex	Canterbury	1990
3rd	321*	A.Hearne/J.R.Mason	v	Notts	Nottingham	1899
4th	297	H.T.W.Hardinge/A.P.F.Chapman	v	Hampshire	Southampton	1926
5th	277	F.E.Woolley/L.E.G.Ames	v	New Zealand	Canterbury	1931
6th	284	A.P.F.Chapman/G.B.Legge	v	Lancashire	Maidstone	1927
7th	248	A.P.Day/E.Humphreys	v	Somerset	Taunton	1908
8th	157	A.L.Hilder/A.C.Wright	v	Essex	Gravesend	1924
9th	161	B.R.Edrich/F.Ridgway	v	Sussex	Tunbridge W	1949
10th	235	F.E.Woolley/A.Fielder	v	Worcs	Stourbridge	1909

Best Bowling (Innings)	For	10- 30	C.Blythe	v	Northants	Northampton	1907
	V	10- 48	C.H.G.Bland	for	Sussex	Tonbridge	1899
Best Bowling (Match)	For	17- 48	C.Blythe	v	Northants	Northampton	1907
	V	17-106	T.W.J.Goddard	for	Glos	Bristol	1939
Most Runs – Season		2894	F.E.Woolley		(av 59.06)		1928
Most Runs – Career		47868	F.E.Woolley		(av 41.77)		1906-38
Most 100s – Season		10	F.E.Woolley				1928
		10	F.E.Woolley				1934
Most 100s – Career		122	F.E.Woolley				1906-38
Most Wkts – Season		262	A.P.Freeman		(av 14.74)		1933
Most Wkts – Career		3340	A.P.Freeman		(av 17.64)		1914-36

LIMITED-OVERS CRICKET

Highest Total	NWT	384-6		v	Berkshire	Finchampstead	1994
	BHC	319-8		v	Scotland	Glasgow	1991
	SL	327-6		v	Leics	Canterbury	1993
Lowest Total	NWT	60		v	Somerset	Taunton	1979
	BHC	73		v	Middlesex	Canterbury	1979
	SL	83		v	Middlesex	Lord's	1984
Highest Innings	NWT	136*	C.L.Hooper	v	Berkshire	Finchampstead	1994
	BHC	143	C.J.Tavaré	v	Somerset	Taunton	1985
	SL	142	B.W.Luckhurst	v	Somerset	Weston-s-Mare	1970
Best Bowling	NWT	8-31	D.L.Underwood	v	Scotland	Edinburgh	1987
	BHC	5-21	B.D.Julien	v	Surrey	The Oval	1973
	SL	6- 9	R.A.Woolmer	v	Derbyshire	Chesterfield	1979

LANCASHIRE

Formation of Present Club: 12 January 1864
Colours: Red, Green and Blue
Badge: Red Rose
Championships (since 1890): (7) 1897, 1904, 1926, 1927, 1928, 1930, 1934
Joint Championship: (1) 1950
NatWest Trophy/Gillette Cup Winners: (5) 1970, 1971, 1972, 1975, 1990
Benson and Hedges Cup Winners: (2) 1984, 1990
Sunday League Champions: (3) 1969, 1970, 1989
Match Awards: NWT 55; BHC 59

Chief Executive: J.M.Bower. **Cricket Secretary:** Miss R.B.FitzGibbon
Old Trafford, Manchester M16 0PX (☎ 0161-848 7021)
Captain: M.Watkinson
Scorer: W.Davies
1995 Beneficiary: N.H.Fairbrother

ATHERTON, Michael Andrew (Manchester GS; Downing C, Cambridge), b Failsworth, Manchester 23 Mar 1968. 5'11". RHB, LB. Cambridge U 1987-89 (blue 1987-88-89; captain 1988-89). Lancashire debut 1987. Cap 1989. YC 1990. Wisden 1990. **Tests:** 40 (1989 to 1994, 13 as captain); HS 151 v NZ (Nottingham) 1990; BB 1-60. LOI: 18 (HS 86). Tours (C=captain): A 1990-91; WI 1993-94C; I/SL 1992-93; Z 1989-90 (Eng A). 1000 runs (5); most – 1924 (1990). Scored 1193 in season of f-c debut. HS 199 v Durham (Gateshead) 1992. BB 6-78 v Notts (Nottingham) 1990. Award: NWT 1. **NWT:** HS 109* v Oxon (Oxford) 1992. BB 2-15 v Glos (Manchester) 1990. **BHC:** HS 100 v Derbys (Derby) 1994. BB 4-42 Comb Us v Somerset (Taunton) 1989. **SL:** HS 111 v Essex (Colchester) 1990. BB 3-33 v Notts (Nottingham) 1990.

AUSTIN, Ian David (Haslingden HS), b Haslingden 30 May 1966. 5'10". LHB, RM. Debut 1987. Cap 1990. Tour: Z 1988-89 (La). HS 115* v Derbys (Blackpool) 1992. BB 5-23 (10-60 match) v Middx (Manchester) 1994. **NWT:** HS 57 v Surrey (Oval) 1994. BB 3-36 v Durham (Manchester) 1990. **BHC:** HS 80 v Worcs (Worcester) 1987. BB 4-25 v Surrey (Manchester) 1990. **SL:** HS 48 v Middx (Lord's) 1991. BB 5-56 v Derbys (Derby) 1991.

BARNETT, Alexander Anthony (William Ellis S), b Malaga, Spain, 11 Sep 1970. Great nephew of C.J. (Glos and England 1927-54). 5'11". RHB, SLA. Middlesex 1988-91. Lancashire debut 1992. HS 38 and BB 5-36 v Durham (Manchester) 1993. **NWT:** HS –. BB 2-29 v Northants (Northampton) 1993. **BHC:** HS –. BB 3-43 v Leics (Leicester) 1993. **SL:** HS 11* v Surrey (Oval) 1993. BB 3-15 v Derbys (Derby) 1993.

BROWN, Christopher (Failsworth HS; Tameside TC), b Oldham 16 Aug 1974. 6'2". RHB, OB. Lancashire staff 1994 – awaiting f-c debut.

CHAPPLE, Glen (West Craven HS; Nelson & Colne C), b Skipton, Yorks 23 Jan 1974. 6'1". RHB, RFM. Debut 1992. Cap 1994. HS 109* v Glam (Manchester) 1993 (100 off 27 balls in contrived circumstances). HS (authentic) 37* v Durham (Manchester) 1993. 50 wkts (1): 55 (1994). BB 6-48 v Durham (Stockton) 1994. **NWT:** HS –. BB 1-35. **BHC:** HS –. BB 2-30 v Derbys (Derby) 1994. **SL:** HS 9*. BB 3-29 v Hants (Manchester) 1994.

CRAWLEY, John Paul (Manchester GS; Trinity C, Cambridge), b Maldon, Essex 21 Sep 1971. Brother of M.A. (see NOTTS) and P.M. (CU 1992). 6'1". RHB, RM. Debut 1990. Cap 1994. Cambridge U 1991-93 (blue 1991-92-93; captain 1992-93). YC 1994. **Tests:** 3 (1994); HS 38 v SA (Leeds) 1994. Tour: SA 1993-94 (Eng A). 1000 runs (3); most – 1570 (1994). HS 286 England A v E Province (Port Elizabeth) 1993-94. La HS 281* v Somerset (Southport) 1994. BB 1-90. Award: BHC 1. **NWT:** HS 22 v Scot (Manchester) 1994. **BHC:** HS 73 v Comb Us (Oxford) and v Derbys (Derby) 1994. **SL:** HS 91 v Kent (Canterbury) 1994.

FAIRBROTHER, Neil Harvey (Lymm GS), b Warrington 9 Sep 1963. 5'8". LHB, LM. Debut 1982. Cap 1985. Captain 1992-93. Benefit 1995. **Tests:** 10 (1987 to 1992-93); HS 83 v I (Madras) 1992-93. LOI: 42 (HS 113). Tours: NZ 1987-88, 1991-92; I/SL 1992-93; P 1987-88, 1990-91 (Eng A); SL 1990-91 (Eng A). 1000 runs (9); most – 1740 (1990). HS 366 v Surrey (Oval) 1990 (ground record), including 311 in a day and 100 or more in each session. BB 2-91 v Notts (Manchester) 1987. Awards: NWT 5; BHC 7. **NWT:** HS 93* v Leics (Leicester) 1986. **BHC:** HS 116* v Scot (Manchester) 1988. **SL:** HS 116* v Notts (Nottingham) 1988.

GALLIAN, Jason Edward Riche (Pittwater House S, Sydney; Keble C, Oxford), b Manly, Sydney, Australia 25 Jun 1971. 6'0". RHB, RM. Debut 1990, taking wicket of D.A.Hagan (OU) with his first ball. Cap 1994. Qualified for England 1994. Oxford U 1992-93 (blue 1992-93; captain 1993). Captained Australia YC v England YC 1989-90, scoring 158* in 1st 'Test'. HS 171 v Surrey (Manchester) 1994. BB 4-29 OU v Lancs (Oxford) 1992. La BB 2-27 v Derbys (Blackpool) 1994. **NWT:** HS 1. **BHC:** HS 50 Comb Us v Derbys (Derby) and v Durham (Cambridge) 1992. BB 1-26. **SL:** HS 84 v Essex (Chelmsford) 1994. BB 2-10 v Somerset (Manchester) 1994.

GREEN, Richard James (Bridgewater HS, Cheshire; Mid-Cheshire C), b Warrington 13 Mar 1976. 6'1". RHB, RM. Lancashire staff 1994 – awaiting f-c debut.

HARVEY, Mark Edward (Habergham HS; Loughborough U), b Burnley 26 Jun 1974. 5'9". RHB, RM/LB. Debut 1994. HS 23 v Notts (Nottingham) 1994.

HARVEY, Nicholas Paul (Forest CS, Winnersh), b Ascot, Berks 21 Nov 1973. 5'7". RHB, WK. Berkshire 1993. Lancashire staff 1994 – awaiting f-c debut.

HEGG, Warren Kevin (Unsworth HS, Bury; Stand C, Whitefield), b Whitefield 23 Feb 1968. 5'8". RHB, WK. Debut 1986. Cap 1989. Tours: WI 1986-87 (La); SL 1990-91 (Eng A); Z 1988-89 (La). HS 130 v Northants (Northampton) 1987. Held 11 catches (equalling world f-c match record) v Derbys (Chesterfield) 1989. **NWT:** HS 32 v Surrey (Oval) 1994. **BHC:** HS 31* v Worcs (Lord's) 1990. **SL:** HS 52 v Glam (Colwyn Bay) 1994.

LLOYD, Graham David (Hollins County HS), b Accrington 1 Jul 1969. Son of D. (Lancs and England 1965-83). 5'9". RHB, RM. Debut 1988. Cap 1992. Tour: A 1992-93 (Eng A). 1000 runs (2); most – 1389 (1992). HS 132 v Kent (Manchester) 1992. BB 1-57. **NWT:** HS 39 v Hants (Southampton) 1991. **BHC:** HS 34 v Leics (Leicester) 1993. **SL:** HS 100* v Kent (Maidstone) 1990.

MARTIN, Peter James (Danum S, Doncaster), b Accrington 15 Nov 1968. 6'4". RHB, RFM. Debut 1989. Cap 1994. HS 133 v Durham (Gateshead) 1992. 50 wkts (1): 54 (1994). BB 5-35 v Yorks (Leeds) 1993 (not BAC). BAC BB 5-61 v Northants (Northampton) 1994. **NWT:** HS 16 and BB 3-63 v Surrey (Oval) 1994. **BHC:** HS 10* v Surrey (Oval) 1993. BB 1-35. **SL:** HS 18* v Sussex (Hove) 1992. BB 5-32 v Durham (Stockton) 1994.

SEAL, Peter John (Haslingden HS; Rossendale & Accrington C), b Rawtenstall 16 Apr 1976. 6'0". RHB, RMF. Lancashire staff 1994 – awaiting f-c debut.

SHADFORD, Darren James (Breeze Hill HS; Oldham TC), b Oldham 4 Mar 1975. 6'3". RHB, RMF. Lancashire staff 1994 – awaiting f-c debut. **SL:** HS –.

SPEAK, Nicholas Jason (Parrs Wood HS, Manchester), b Manchester 21 Nov 1966. 6'0". RHB, RM/OB. Debut v Jamaica (Kingston) 1986-87. Cap 1992. Tour: WI 1986-87 (La). 1000 runs (3); most – 1892 (1992). HS 232 v Leics (Leicester) 1992. BB 1-0. **NWT:** HS 60 v Essex (Chelmsford) 1992. **BHC:** HS 82 v Hants (Manchester) 1992. **SL:** HS 102* v Yorks (Leeds) 1992.

TITCHARD, Stephen Paul (Lymm County HS; Priestley C), b Warrington 17 Dec 1967. 6'3". RHB, RM. Debut 1990. HS 135 v Notts (Manchester) 1991. **NWT:** HS 20 v Oxon (Oxford) 1992. **BHC:** HS 82 v Surrey (Oval) 1992. **SL:** HS 96 v Essex (Chelmsford) 1994.

WASIM AKRAM (Islamia C), b Lahore, Pakistan 3 Jun 1966. 6'3". LHB, LF. PACO 1984-85/1985-86. Lahore 1985-86/1986-87. PIA 1987-88 to date. Lancashire debut 1988. Cap 1989. Wisden 1992. **Tests** (P): 55 (1984-85 to 1994-95, 5 as captain); HS 123 v A (Adelaide) 1989-90; BB 7-119 v NZ (Wellington) 1993-94. LOI (P): 174 (HS 86; BB 5-15). Tours (P): E 1987, 1992; A 1988-89, 1989-90, 1991-92, 1992-93; WI 1987-88, 1992-93 (captain); NZ 1984-85, 1992-93, 1993-94; I 1986-87; SL 1984-85 (P U-23), 1985-86, 1994-95. HS 123 (Tests). La HS 122 v Hants (Basingstoke) 1991. 50 wkts (4); most – 82 (1992). BB 8-30 (13-147 match) v Somerset (Southport) 1994. Hat-trick 1988. Award: BHC 1. **NWT:** HS 50 v Surrey (Oval) 1994. BB 4-27 v Lincs (Manchester) 1988. **BHC:** HS 52 v Northants (Northampton) 1989. BB 5-10 v Leics (Leicester) 1993. **SL:** HS 51* v Yorks (Manchester) 1993. BB 5-41 v Northants (Northampton) 1994.

WATKINSON, Michael (Rivington and Blackrod HS, Horwich), b Westhoughton 1 Aug 1961. 6'1". RHB, RMF/OB. Debut 1982. Cap 1987. Captain 1994-. Cheshire 1982. 1000 runs (1): 1016 (1993). HS 155 v Glam (Colwyn Bay) 1994. 50 wkts (6); most – 66 (1992). BB 8-30 (11-87 match) v Hants (Manchester) 1994 – completing match 'double' with 128 runs. Hat-trick 1992. Awards: NWT 2; BHC 2. **NWT:** HS 90 and BB 3-14 v Glos (Manchester) 1990. **BHC:** HS 76 v Northants (Northampton) 1992. BB 5-49 v Yorks (Manchester) 1991. **SL:** HS 83 v Sussex (Manchester) 1991. BB 5-46 v Warwks (Manchester) 1990.

WOOD, Nathan Theo (Wm Hulme's GS), b Thornhill Edge, Yorks 4 Oct 1974. Son of B. (Yorks, Lancs, Derbys and England 1964-83). 5'8". LHB, OB. Lancashire staff 1993 – awaiting f-c debut.

YATES, Gary (Manchester GS), b Ashton-under-Lyne 20 Sep 1967. 6'0". RHB, OB. Debut 1990. Cap 1994. HS 134* v Northants (Manchester) 1993. BB 5-34 v Hants (Manchester) 1994. **NWT:** HS 7* and BB 2-61 v Surrey (Oval) 1994. **BHC:** HS –. BB 2-49 v Derbys (Derby) 1994. **SL:** HS 14 v Notts (Nottingham) 1994. BB 4-34 v Warwks (Birmingham) 1994.

NEWCOMERS

FLINTOFF, Andrew (Ribbleton Hall HS), b Preston 6 Dec 1976. RHB, RM.

KEEDY, Gary (Garforth CS), b Wakefield, Yorks 27 Nov 1974. 6'0". LHB, SLA. Yorkshire 1994 (one match). HS 1.

McKEOWN, Patrick Christopher (Rossall S), b Liverpool 1 Jun 1976. 6'2". RHB.

MARLAND, Lee John (Manchester GS), b Withington 21 Sep 1975. RHB, OB.

THOMPSON, David James (Ernest Bevin S, Wandsworth; Westminster S), b Wandsworth, London 11 Mar 1976. 6'3". RHB, RFM. Surrey 1994 (one match). HS 22 and BB 2-37 Sy v OU (Oval) 1994. Awaiting BAC debut.

DEPARTURES (who made first-class appearances in 1994)

DERBYSHIRE, N.A. – see ESSEX.

FIELDING, Jonathan Mark (Woodhey HS; Bury C), b Bury 13 Mar 1973. 6'1". RHB, SLA. Lancashire 1994. HS 27* and BB 1-15 v CU (Cambridge) 1994. No BAC appearances.

LANCASHIRE 1994

RESULTS SUMMARY

	Place	Won	Lost	Drew	Abandoned
Britannic Assurance Championship	**10th**	8	6	3	
All First-class Matches		8	7	4	
Sunday League	**4th**	11	5		1
NatWest Trophy	2nd Round				
Benson and Hedges Cup	2nd Round				

BRITANNIC ASSURANCE CHAMPIONSHIP AVERAGES

BATTING AND FIELDING

Cap		M	I	NO	HS	Runs	Avge	100	50	Ct/St
1994	J.P.Crawley	14	23	2	281*	1300	61.90	3	4	20
1985	N.H.Fairbrother	11	20	1	204	939	49.42	4	1	13
1992	N.J.Speak	17	30	5	143	1046	41.84	1	7	16
1994	J.E.R.Gallian	10	18	–	171	746	41.44	2	3	6
1987	M.Watkinson	16	26	2	155	831	34.62	2	3	9
1992	G.D.Lloyd	14	23	1	112	653	29.68	1	5	10
–	S.P.Titchard	12	20	–	99	543	27.15	–	3	15
1990	I.D.Austin	10	15	1	50	359	25.64	–	1	5
1989	Wasim Akram	6	10	–	98	244	24.40	–	2	–
1989	M.A.Atherton	9	16	2	51	333	23.78	–	1	10
1989	W.K.Hegg	17	27	4	66	465	20.21	–	2	42/2
1994	G.Yates	12	19	6	54*	219	16.84	–	1	3
1994	G.Chapple	14	20	11	26*	149	16.55	–	–	11
1994	P.J.Martin	17	26	2	57	340	14.16	–	1	4
–	A.A.Barnett	5	4	1	10	13	4.33	–	–	2

Also batted: N.A.Derbyshire (1 match) 5; M.E.Harvey (2 matches) 2, 19, 23 (1 ct).

BOWLING

	O	M	R	W	Avge	Best	5wI	10wM
I.D.Austin	236.5	68	623	33	18.87	5-23	3	1
Wasim Akram	213.2	44	646	27	23.92	8-30	2	1
G.Chapple	421.3	99	1380	52	26.53	6-48	4	–
G.Yates	294.5	65	930	34	27.35	5-34	1	–
M.Watkinson	563.1	162	1639	59	27.77	8-30	1	1
P.J.Martin	566.4	159	1464	51	28.70	5-61	2	–
J.E.R.Gallian	77	9	299	10	29.90	2-27	–	–

Also bowled: A.A.Barnett 124.4-20-440-7; J.P.Crawley 1-0-4-0; N.A.Derbyshire 21-1-107-1; N.H.Fairbrother 1-0-3-0; N.J.Speak 1-0-12-0.

The First-Class Averages (pp 186-200) give the records of Lancashire players in all first-class county matches (their other opponents being Yorkshire in a non-Championship match and Cambridge U), with the exception of:

M.A.Atherton 10-17-2-86-419-27.93-0-2-11ct. 7-2-10-0.

J.P.Crawley 16-27-2-281*-1472-58.88-3-6-20ct. 1-0-4-0.

LANCASHIRE RECORDS

FIRST-CLASS CRICKET

Highest Total	For	863		v	Surrey	The Oval	1990
	V	707-9d		by	Surrey	The Oval	1990
Lowest Total	For	25		v	Derbyshire	Manchester	1871
	V	22		by	Glamorgan	Liverpool	1924
Highest Innings	For	424	A.C.MacLaren	v	Somerset	Taunton	1895
	V	315*	T.W.Hayward	for	Surrey	The Oval	1898

Highest Partnership for each Wicket

1st	368	A.C.MacLaren/R.H.Spooner	v	Glos	Liverpool	1903
2nd	371	F.B.Watson/G.E.Tyldesley	v	Surrey	Manchester	1928
3rd	364	M.A.Atherton/N.H.Fairbrother	v	Surrey	The Oval	1990
4th	324	A.C.MacLaren/J.T.Tyldesley	v	Notts	Nottingham	1904
5th	249	B.Wood/A.Kennedy	v	Warwicks	Birmingham	1975
6th	278	J.Iddon/H.R.W.Butterworth	v	Sussex	Manchester	1932
7th	245	A.H.Hornby/J.Sharp	v	Leics	Manchester	1912
8th	158	J.Lyon/R.M.Ratcliffe	v	Warwicks	Manchester	1979
9th	142	L.O.S.Poidevin/A.Kermode	v	Sussex	Eastbourne	1907
10th	173	J.Briggs/R.Pilling	v	Surrey	Liverpool	1885

Best Bowling	For	10-46	W.Hickton	v	Hampshire	Manchester	1870
(Innings)	V	10-40	G.O.B.Allen	for	Middlesex	Lord's	1929
Best Bowling	For	17-91	H.Dean	v	Yorkshire	Liverpool	1913
(Match)	V	16-65	G.Giffen	for	Australians	Manchester	1886

Most Runs – Season	2633	J.T.Tyldesley	(av 56.02)	1901
Most Runs – Career	34222	G.E.Tyldesley	(av 45.20)	1909-36
Most 100s – Season	11	C.Hallows		1928
Most 100s – Career	90	G.E.Tyldesley		1909-36
Most Wkts – Season	198	E.A.McDonald	(av 18.55)	1925
Most Wkts – Career	1816	J.B.Statham	(av 15.12)	1950-68

LIMITED-OVERS CRICKET

Highest Total	**NWT**	372-5		v	Glos	Manchester	1990
	BHC	330-4		v	Sussex	Manchester	1991
	SL	300-7		v	Leics	Leicester	1993
Lowest Total	**NWT**	59		v	Worcs	Worcester	1963
	BHC	82		v	Yorkshire	Bradford	1972
	SL	71		v	Essex	Chelmsford	1987
Highest Innings	**NWT**	131	A.Kennedy	v	Middlesex	Manchester	1978
	BHC	136	G.Fowler	v	Sussex	Manchester	1991
	SL	134*	C.H.Lloyd	v	Somerset	Manchester	1970
Best Bowling	**NWT**	5-13	P.A.J.DeFreitas	v	Cumberland	Kendal	1989
	BHC	6-10	C.E.H.Croft	v	Scotland	Manchester	1982
	SL	6-29	D.P.Hughes	v	Somerset	Manchester	1977

LEICESTERSHIRE

Formation of Present Club: 25 March 1879
Colours: Dark Green and Scarlet
Badge: Gold Running Fox on Green Ground
Championships: (1) 1975
NatWest Trophy/Gillette Cup Winners: (0) Finalist 1992
Benson and Hedges Cup Winners: (3) 1972, 1975, 1985
Sunday League Champions: (2) 1974, 1977
Match Awards: NWT 35; BHC 58

Chief Executive: A.O.Norman. **Administrative Secretary:** K.P.Hill
County Ground, Grace Road, Leicester LE2 8AD (☎ 0116-283 2128)
Captain: N.E.Briers
Scorer: G.A.York
1995 Beneficiary: T.J.Boon

BOON, Timothy James (Edlington CS, Doncaster), b Doncaster, Yorks 1 Nov 1961. 6'0". RHB, RM. Debut 1980. Cap 1986. Benefit 1995. Tour: Z 1980-81 (Le). 1000 runs (7); most – 1539 (1990). HS 144 v Glos (Leicester) 1984. BB 3-40 v Yorks (Leicester) 1986. Awards: NWT 2; BHC 1. **NWT:** HS 117 v Bucks (Marlow) 1993. **BHC:** HS 103 v Scot (Leicester) 1991. **SL:** HS 135* v Kent (Canterbury) 1993. BB 1-23.

BRIERS, Nigel Edwin (Lutterworth GS; Borough Road CE), b Leicester 15 Jan 1955. 6'0". RHB, RM. Debut 1971 (aged 16yr 103d – youngest Leicestershire player). Cap 1981. Captain 1990-. Benefit 1990. Wisden 1992. Tour: Z 1980-81 (Le). 1000 runs (10); most – 1996 (1990). HS 201* v Warwks (Birmingham) 1983. BB 4-29 v Derbys (Leicester) 1985. Awards: NWT 1; BHC 5. **NWT:** HS 88 v Essex (Leicester) 1992. BB 2-6 v Worcs (Leicester) 1979. **BHC:** HS 102 v Minor C (Stone) 1992. BB 1-26. **SL:** HS 119* v Hants (Bournemouth) 1981. BB 3-29 v Middx (Leicester) 1984.

BRIMSON, Matthew Thomas (Chislehurst & Sidcup GS; Durham U), b Plumstead, London 1 Dec 1970. 6'0". RHB, SLA. Kent staff 1991. Debut 1993. HS 17* v OU (Oxford) 1994. BAC HS 12 v Yorks (Harrogate) 1994. BB 2-66 v Glam (Leicester) 1993. **SL:** HS –. BB 1-28.

DAKIN, Jonathan Michael (King Edward VII S, Johannesburg) b Hitchin, Herts 28 Feb 1973. 6'4". LHB, RM. Debut 1993. HS 18 v Hants (Leicester) 1994. BB 4-45 v CU (Cambridge) 1993 (on debut). **SL:** HS 41 v Sussex (Leicester) 1994. BB 3-32 v Hants (Leicester) 1994.

MACMILLAN, Gregor Innes (Guildford County S; Charterhouse; Southampton U; Keble C, Oxford), b Guildford, Surrey 7 Aug 1969. 6'5". RHB, OB. Oxford U 1993-94 (blue 1993-94; captain 1995). Awaiting Leicestershire f-c debut. HS 69 v CU (Lord's) 1994. BB 3-13 v CU (Lord's) 1993. **BHC:** HS 19 Comb Us v Lancs (Oxford) 1994. BB 1-18. **SL:** HS 48 v Glos (Moreton) 1994.

MADDY, Darren Lee (Wreake Valley C), b Leicester 23 May 1974. 5'9". RHB, RM/OB. Debut 1994. HS 34 v Worcs (Leicester) 1994. **SL:** HS 54 v Glam (Neath) 1994.

MASON, Timothy James (Denstone C), b Leicester 12 Apr 1975. 5'8". RHB, OB. Debut 1994. HS 3. BB 1-22.

MILLNS, David James (Garibaldi CS), b Clipstone, Notts 27 Feb 1965. 6'3". LHB, RF. Nottinghamshire 1988-89. Leicestershire debut 1990. Cap 1991. Tour: A 1992-93 (Eng A). HS 64* v Worcs (Leicester) 1994. 50 wkts (3); most – 76 (1994). BB 9-37 (12-91 match) v Derbys (Derby) 1991. Award: NWT 1. **NWT:** HS 29* v Derbys (Derby) 1992. BB 3-22 v Norfolk (Leicester) 1992. **BHC:** HS 11* v Sussex (Hove) 1991. BB 4-51 v Minor C (Stone) 1992. **SL:** HS 20* v Notts (Leicester) 1991. BB 2-11 v Somerset (Leicester) 1994.

MULLALLY, Alan David (Cannington HS, Perth, Australia; Wembley TC), b Southend-on-Sea, Essex 12 Jul 1969. 6'5". RHB, LFM. W Australia 1987-88/1989-90. Victoria 1990-91. Hampshire (1 match) 1988. Leicestershire debut 1990. Cap 1993. HS 34 WA v Tasmania (Perth) 1989-90. Le HS 29 v Hants (Leicester) 1990. 50 wkts (1): 62 (1993). BB 7-72 (10-170 match) v Glos (Leicester) 1993. **NWT:** HS 19* v Bucks (Marlow) 1993. BB 2-22 v Derbys (Derby) and v Northants (Lord's) 1992. **BHC:** HS 11 v Surrey (Leicester) 1992. BB 2-30 v Ire (Leicester) 1994. **SL:** HS 38 v Kent (Leicester) 1994. BB 3-9 v Essex (Leicester) 1994.

NIXON, Paul Andrew (Ullswater HS, Penrith), b Carlisle, Cumberland 21 Oct 1970. 6'0". LHB, WK. Debut 1989. Cap 1994. Cumberland 1987. MCC YC. 1000 runs (1): 1046 (1994). HS 131 v Hants (Leicester) 1994. **NWT:** HS 32 v Derbys (Derby) 1992. **BHC:** HS 27 v Worcs (Leicester) 1993. **SL:** HS 72 v Notts (Nottingham) 1994.

PARSONS, Gordon James (Woodside County SS, Slough), b Slough, Bucks 17 Oct 1959. Brother-in-law of W.J.Cronje (see below). 6'1". LHB, RMF. Leicestershire 1978-85 (cap 1984) and 1989-. Joint benefit 1994. Warwickshire 1986-88 (cap 1987). Boland 1983-84/1984-85. GW 1985-86/1986-87. OFS 1988-89/1990-91. Buckinghamshire 1977. Tours: NZ 1979-80 (DHR); Z 1980-81 (Le). HS 76 Boland v W Province B (Cape Town) 1984-85. Le HS 70 v Essex (Leicester) 1994. 50 wkts (2); most – 67 (1984). BB 9-72 Boland v Transvaal B (Johannesburg) 1984-85. Le BB 6-11 v OU (Oxford) 1985. BAC BB 6-70 v Surrey (Oval) 1992. Awards: BHC 2. **NWT:** HS 23 v Northants (Northampton) 1984. BB 2-11 v Wilts (Swindon) 1984. **BHC:** HS 63* and BB 4-12 v Scot (Leicester) 1989. **SL:** HS 38* v Lancs (Leicester) 1993. BB 4-19 v Essex (Harlow) 1982.

PIERSON, Adrian Roger Kirshaw (Kent C, Canterbury; Hatfield Poly), b Enfield, Middx 21 Jul 1963. 6'4". RHB, OB. Warwickshire 1985-91. Leicestershire debut 1993. Cambridgeshire 1992. MCC YC. HS 58 v Lancs (Leicester) 1993. BB 8-42 v Warwks (Birmingham) 1994. Award: BHC 1. **NWT:** HS 1*. BB 3-20 Wa v Wilts (Birmingham) 1989. **BHC:** HS 11 Wa v Minor C (Walsall) 1986. BB 3-34 Wa v Lancs (Birmingham) 1988. **SL:** HS 29* v Kent (Leicester) 1994. BB 4-29 v Glos (Moreton) 1994.

ROBINSON, Phillip Edward (Greenhead GS, Keighley), b Keighley, Yorks 3 Aug 1963. 5'9". RHB, LM. Yorkshire 1984-91 (cap 1988). Leicestershire debut 1992. Cumberland 1992. 1000 runs (3); most – 1402 (1990). HS 189 Y v Lancs (Scarborough) 1991. Le HS 86 v Glam (Cardiff) 1994. BB 1-10. Le BB 1-13. Awards: NWT 1; BHC 2. **NWT:** HS 73 v Norfolk (Leicester) 1992. **BHC:** HS 73* Y v Hants (Southampton) 1990. **SL:** HS 104 v Lancs (Manchester) 1992.

SHERIYAR, Alamgir (George Dixon S; Joseph Chamberlain SFC; Oxford Poly), b Birmingham 15 Nov 1973. 6'1". RHB, LF. Debut 1994. HS 16* v SA (Leicester) 1994. BB 4-44, inc hat-trick, and BAC HS 12 v Durham (Durham) 1994 – his second match. **SL:** HS 0*.

SMITH, Benjamin Francis (Kibworth HS), b Corby, Northants 3 Apr 1972. 5'9". RHB, RM. Debut 1990. HS 100* v Durham (Durham) 1992. BB 1-5. Award: NWT 1. **NWT:** HS 63* v Cumb (Netherfield) 1994. **BHC:** HS 43 v Warwks (Leicester) 1993. **SL:** HS 97* v Derbys (Leicester) 1993.

SUTCLIFFE, Iain John (Leeds GS; Queen's C, Oxford), b Leeds, Yorks 20 Dec 1974. 6'2". LHB, occ OB. Oxford U 1994. Awaiting Leicestershire debut. HS 8*. Boxing blue 1993-94.

WELLS, Vincent John (Sir William Nottidge S, Whitstable), b Dartford, Kent 6 Aug 1965. 6'0". RHB, RMF. Kent 1988-91. Leicestershire debut 1992. Cap 1994. HS 167 v Glam (Leicester) 1993. BB 5-43 K v Leics (Leicester) 1990. Le BB 5-50 (inc hat-trick) v Durham (Durham) 1994. Awards: NWT 1; BHC 1. **NWT:** 100* K v Oxon (Oxford) 1990. BB 3-38 v Durham (Leicester) 1992. **BHC:** HS 25 K v Sussex (Canterbury) 1991. BB 4-37 v Worcs (Leicester) 1993. **SL:** HS 101 v Middx (Leicester) 1994. BB 5-10 v Surrey (Oval) 1994.

WHITAKER, John James (Uppingham S), b Skipton, Yorks 5 May 1962. 5'10". RHB, OB. Debut 1983. Cap 1986. Benefit 1993. Wisden 1986. YC 1986. **Tests:** 1 (1986-87); HS 11 v A (Adelaide) 1986-87. LOI: 2 (HS 44*). Tours: A 1986-87; Z 1989-90 (Eng A). 1000 runs (8); most – 1767 (1990). HS 200* v Notts (Leicester) 1986. BB 1-29. Awards: NWT 1; BHC 1. **NWT:** HS 155 v Wilts (Swindon) 1984. **BHC:** HS 100 v Kent (Canterbury) 1991. **SL:** HS 132 v Glam (Swansea) 1984.

NEWCOMERS

BARTLE, Stephen (Blackfoot GS), b Shipley, Yorks 5 Aug 1971. LHB, RFM.

CRONJE, Wessel Johannes (**'Hansie'**) (Grey C, Bloemfontein; OFS U), b Bloemfontein, SA 25 Sep 1969. Son of N.E. (OFS 1960-61/1971-72); brother of F.J.C. (Border 1985-86 to date); brother-in-law of G.J.Parsons (see above). 6'4". RHB, RM. Orange Free State 1987-88 to date (captain 1990-91 to date). **Tests** (SA): 16 (1991-92 to 1994, 1 as captain); HS 135 v I (Pt Eliz) 1992-93; BB 2-17 v I (Cape Town) 1992-93. LOI (SA): 51 (HS 112; BB 5-32). Tours (SA): E 1994; A 1993-94; WI 1991-92; SL 1993-94. 1000 runs (0+1): 1567 (1993-94). HS 251 OFS v A (Bloemfontein) 1993-94. BB 4-47 SA v Kent (Canterbury) 1994.

CROWE, Carl Daniel (Lutterworth GS), b Leicester 25 Nov 1975. RHB, OB.

DITTA, Adil Iqbal (Boynton CS; Acklam SFC, Middlesbrough), b Middlesbrough, Yorks 11 Oct 1974. RHB, RM. **SL:** HS 1*.

DURANT, Cristian Domonic (Oakham S), b Leicester 23 Jan 1977. RHB, WK.

DEPARTURES (who made first-class appearances in 1994)

FOURIE, Brenden Craig (Selbourne HS; Port Elizabeth U), b East London, SA 13 Apr 1970. Brother of S. (Border B 1993-94). 6'1". RHB, RFM. Border 1988-89 to date. Leicestershire 1994 (one match as unregistered player). HS 23* Border v Boland (Stellenbosch) 1990-91. BB 6-74 Border v Transvaal (Jo'burg) 1993-94. Le HS – and BB 3-19 v OU (Oxford) 1994.

HEPWORTH, Peter Nash (Hemsworth HS), b Ackworth, Yorks 4 May 1967. 6'1". RHB, OB. Leicestershire 1988-94. 1000 runs (1): 1119 (1991). HS 129 v Glam (Leicester) 1993. BB 3-30 v Kent (Leicester) 1994. **NWT:** HS –. **BHC:** HS 33 v Sussex (Hove) 1991. BB 4-39 v Scot (Leicester) 1991. **SL:** HS 49 v Northants (Leicester) 1994. BB 5-51 v Worcs (Leicester) 1994.

SIMMONS, Philip Verant (Holy Cross C, Arima), b Arima, Trinidad 18 Apr 1963. 6'3½". RHB, RM. Debut for N Trinidad 1982-83. Trinidad 1982-83 to date (captain 1988-89). Durham 1989-90 (NWT only). Leicestershire 1994 (cap 1994). **Tests** (WI): 19 (1987-88 to 1993-94); HS 110 and BB 2-34 v A (Melbourne) 1992-93. LOI (WI): 83 (HS 122; BB 4-3). Tours (WI): E 1988 (part), 1991, 1992 (RW), 1993 (RW); A 1992-93; I 1987-88; SL 1993-94; Z 1983-84 (Young WI), 1986-87 (Young WI). 1000 runs (1): 1031 (1991). HS 261 v Northants (Leicester) 1994 – on Le debut (county record). BB 5-24 Trinidad v Windward Is (Pointe-à-Pierre) 1990-91. Le BB 4-68 v Hants (Leicester) 1994. Award: BHC 1. **NWT:** HS 33 Du v Middx (Darlington) 1989. BB 3-31 v Cumb (Netherfield) 1994. **BHC:** HS 64 and BB 1-29 v Ire (Leicester) 1994. **SL:** HS 140 v Middx (Leicester) 1994. BB 4-19 v Essex (Leicester) 1994.

STANGER, Ian Michael (Hutcheson's GS, Glasgow; Duncan of Jordanstone Art C, Dundee), b Glasgow, Scotland 5 Oct 1971. 6'0". RHB, RFM. Leicestershire staff 1994 – no f-c appearances. **SL:** HS 6. BB 3-34 v Surrey (Oval) 1994.

LEICESTERSHIRE 1994

RESULTS SUMMARY

	Place	Won	Lost	Drew	Abandoned
Britannic Assurance Championship	2nd	8	7	2	
All First-class Matches		8	7	4	
Sunday League	10th	7	9		1
NatWest Trophy	2nd Round				
Benson and Hedges Cup	2nd Round				

BRITANNIC ASSURANCE CHAMPIONSHIP AVERAGES

BATTING AND FIELDING

Cap		M	I	NO	HS	Runs	Avge	100	50	Ct/St
–	P.E.Robinson	5	7	–	86	305	43.57	–	3	8
1994	P.A.Nixon	17	27	3	131	938	39.08	3	4	54/1
1981	N.E.Briers	17	31	2	154	1042	35.93	2	4	4
1986	J.J.Whitaker	16	28	2	148	871	33.50	2	5	8
1994	V.J.Wells	15	26	3	83	746	32.43	–	5	11
–	B.F.Smith	12	20	3	95	541	31.82	–	3	9
1994	P.V.Simmons	17	30	–	261	953	31.76	1	3	23
1984	G.J.Parsons	16	25	6	70	491	25.84	–	2	17
1986	T.J.Boon	15	26	2	74	578	24.08	–	4	5
–	A.R.K.Pierson	13	17	4	43*	294	22.61	–	–	12
1991	D.J.Millns	17	24	8	64*	301	18.81	–	1	10
–	D.L.Maddy	2	4	–	34	56	14.00	–	–	2
–	P.N.Hepworth	4	8	–	60	83	10.37	–	1	1
1993	A.D.Mullally	13	18	4	23	114	8.14	–	–	5
–	M.T.Brimson	4	8	2	12	28	4.66	–	–	–

Also batted: J.M.Dakin (1 match) 18; T.J.Mason (1 match) 3 (2 ct); A.Sheriyar (2 matches) 12, 0*.

BOWLING

	O	M	R	W	Avge	Best	5wI	10wM
V.J.Wells	285.5	74	1001	41	24.41	5-50	1	–
P.V.Simmons	300.5	81	769	30	25.63	4-68	–	–
D.J.Millns	488	91	1756	68	25.82	6-84	3	–
G.J.Parsons	462.3	131	1208	44	27.45	5-34	1	–
A.R.K.Pierson	444.1	120	1130	34	33.23	8-42	1	–
A.D.Mullally	413.1	110	1174	28	41.92	5-85	1	–

Also bowled: M.T.Brimson 87.4-21-280-4; P.N.Hepworth 72-14-253-9; T.J.Mason 7-0-22-1; A.Sheriyar 54-8-239-8.

The First-Class Averages (pp 186-200) give the records of Leicestershire players in all first-class county matches (their other opponents being the South Africans and Oxford U).

LEICESTERSHIRE RECORDS

FIRST-CLASS CRICKET

Highest Total	For	701-4d		v	Worcs	Worcester	1906
	V	761-6d		by	Essex	Chelmsford	1990
Lowest Total	For	25		v	Kent	Leicester	1912
	V	24		by	Glamorgan	Leicester	1971
		24		by	Oxford U	Oxford	1985
Highest Innings	For	261	P.V.Simmons	v	Northants	Leicester	1994
	V	341	G.H.Hirst	for	Yorkshire	Leicester	1905

Highest Partnership for each Wicket

1st	390	B.Dudleston/J.F.Steele	v	Derbyshire	Leicester	1979
2nd	289*	J.C.Balderstone/D.I.Gower	v	Essex	Leicester	1981
3rd	316*	W.Watson/A.Wharton	v	Somerset	Taunton	1961
4th	290*	P.Willey/T.J.Boon	v	Warwicks	Leicester	1984
5th	233	N.E.Briers/R.W.Tolchard	v	Somerset	Leicester	1979
6th	262	A.T.Sharpe/G.H.S.Fowke	v	Derbyshire	Chesterfield	1911
7th	219*	J.D.R.Benson/P.Whitticase	v	Hampshire	Bournemouth	1991
8th	164	M.R.Hallam/C.T.Spencer	v	Essex	Leicester	1964
9th	160	W.W.Odell/R.T.Crawford	v	Worcs	Leicester	1902
10th	228	R.Illingworth/K.Higgs	v	Northants	Leicester	1977

Best Bowling	For	10- 18	G.Geary	v	Glamorgan	Pontypridd	1929
(Innings)	V	10- 32	H.Pickett	for	Essex	Leyton	1895
Best Bowling	For	16- 96	G.Geary	v	Glamorgan	Pontypridd	1929
(Match)	V	16-102	C.Blythe	for	Kent	Leicester	1909

Most Runs – Season	2446	L.G.Berry	(av 52.04)	1937
Most Runs – Career	30143	L.G.Berry	(av 30.32)	1924-51
Most 100s – Season	7	L.G.Berry		1937
	7	W.Watson		1959
	7	B.F.Davison		1982
Most 100s – Career	45	L.G.Berry		1924-51
Most Wkts – Season	170	J.E.Walsh	(av 18.96)	1948
Most Wkts – Career	2130	W.E.Astill	(av 23.19)	1906-39

LIMITED-OVERS CRICKET

Highest Total	NWT	354-7		v	Wiltshire	Swindon	1984
	BHC	327-4		v	Warwicks	Coventry	1972
	SL	301-7		v	Middlesex	Leicester	1994
Lowest Total	NWT	56		v	Northants	Leicester	1964
	BHC	56		v	Minor C	Wellington	1982
	SL	36		v	Sussex	Leicester	1973
Highest Innings	NWT	156	D.I.Gower	v	Derbyshire	Leicester	1984
	BHC	158*	B.F.Davison	v	Warwicks	Coventry	1972
	SL	152	B.Dudleston	v	Lancashire	Manchester	1975
Best Bowling	NWT	6-20	K.Higgs	v	Staffs	Longton	1975
	BHC	6-35	L.B.Taylor	v	Worcs	Worcester	1982
	SL	6-17	K.Higgs	v	Glamorgan	Leicester	1973

MIDDLESEX

Formation of Present Club: 2 February 1864
Colours: Blue
Badge: Three Seaxes
Championships (since 1890): (10) 1903, 1920, 1921, 1947, 1976, 1980, 1982, 1985, 1990, 1993
Joint Championships: (2) 1949, 1977
NatWest Trophy/Gillette Cup Winners: (4) 1977, 1980, 1984, 1988
Benson and Hedges Cup Winners: (2) 1983, 1986
Sunday League Champions: (1) 1992
Match Awards: NWT 48; BHC 53

Secretary: J.Hardstaff MBE
Lord's Cricket Ground, London NW8 8QN (☎ 0171-289 1300; 0171-286 1310)
Captain: M.W.Gatting
Scorer: M.J.Smith
1995 Beneficiary: J.E.Emburey (testimonial)

BROWN, Keith Robert (Chace S, Enfield), b Edmonton 18 Mar 1963. Brother of G.K. (Middx 1986 and Durham 1992). 5'11". RHB, WK, RSM. Debut 1984. Cap 1990. MCC YC. 1000 runs (2); most – 1505 (1990). HS 200* v Notts (Lord's) 1990. BB 2-7 v Glos (Bristol) 1987. Awards: NWT 2. **NWT:** HS 103* v Surrey (Uxbridge) 1990. **BHC:** HS 56 v Minor C (Lord's) 1990. **SL:** HS 102 v Somerset (Lord's) 1988.

CARR, John Donald (Repton S; Worcester C, Oxford), b St John's Wood 15 Jun 1963. Son of D.B. (Derbys, OU and England 1945-63). 5'11". RHB, RM. Oxford U 1983-85 (blue 1983-84-85). Middlesex 1983-89 (cap 1987) and 1992-. Hertfordshire 1982-84 and 1991. 1000 runs (4); most – 1543 (1994). HS 261* v Glos (Lord's) 1994. BB 6-61 v Glos (Lord's) 1985. **NWT:** HS 83 v Hants (Southampton) 1989. BB 2-19 v Surrey (Oval) 1988. **BHC:** HS 70 v Leics (Leicester) 1992. BB 3-22 Comb Us v Glos (Bristol) 1984. **SL:** HS 104* v Warwks (Lord's) 1992. BB 4-21 v Surrey (Lord's) 1989.

DUTCH, Keith Philip (Nower Hill HS; Weald C), b Harrow 21 Mar 1973. 5'10". RHB, OB. Debut 1993. MCC YC. HS –.

EMBUREY, John Ernest (Peckham Manor SS), b Peckham, London 20 Aug 1952. 6'2". RHB, OB. Debut 1973. Cap 1977. Wisden 1983. W Province 1982-83/1983-84. Benefit 1986. Testimonial 1995. **Tests:** 63 (1978 to 1993, 2 as captain); HS 75 v NZ (Nottingham) 1986; BB 7-78 v A (Sydney) 1986-87. LOI: 61 (HS 34; BB 4-37). Tours: A 1978-79, 1979-80, 1986-87, 1987-88; SA 1981-82 (SAB), 1989-90 (Eng XI); WI 1980-81, 1985-86; NZ 1987-88; I 1979-80, 1981-82, 1992-93; P 1987-88; SL 1977-78 (DHR), 1981-82, 1991-92; Z 1980-81 (Mx). HS 133 v Essex (Chelmsford) 1983. 50 wkts (16) inc 100 (1): 103 (1983). BB 8-40 (12-115 match) v Hants (Lord's) 1993. Awards: NWT 1; BHC 6. **NWT:** HS 36* v Lancs (Manchester) 1978. BB 3-11 v Sussex (Lord's) 1989. **BHC:** HS 50 v Kent (Lord's) 1984. BB 5-37 v Somerset (Taunton) 1991. **SL:** HS 50 v Lancs (Blackpool) 1988. BB 5-23 v Somerset (Taunton) 1991.

FARBRACE, Paul (Geoffrey Chaucer S, Canterbury), b Ash, Kent 7 Jul 1967. 5'10". RHB, WK. Kent 1987-89. Middlesex debut 1990. HS 79 v CU (Cambridge) 1990. BAC HS 75* K v Yorks (Canterbury) 1987. BB 1-64. **NWT:** HS 17 v Berks (Lord's) 1990. **SL:** HS 26* v Lancs (Lord's) 1991.

FELTHAM, Mark Andrew (Tiffin S), b St John's Wood 26 June 1963. 6'2½". RHB, RMF. Surrey 1983-92 (cap 1990). Middlesex debut 1993. MCC YC. HS 101 Sy v Middx (Oval) 1990. M HS 73 v Notts (Lord's) 1993. 50 wkts (1): 56 (1988). BB 6-53 Sy v Leics (Oval) 1990. M BB 5-69 v Derbys (Derby) 1994. Awards: BHC 2. **NWT:** HS 25* v Northants (Uxbridge) 1994. BB 2-23 v Wales MC (Northop Hall) 1994. **BHC:** HS 35 Sy v Kent (Canterbury) 1992. BB 5-28 Sy v Comb Us (Cambridge) 1989. **SL:** HS 75 v Leics (Leicester) 1994. BB 4-35 Sy v Sussex (Guildford) 1986.

FRASER, Angus Robert Charles (Gayton HS, Harrow), b Billinge, Lancs 8 Aug 1965. Brother of A.G.J. (Middx and Essex 1986-92). 6'5". RHB, RFM. Debut 1984. Cap 1988. **Tests:** 21 (1989 to 1994); HS 29 v A (Nottingham) 1989; BB 8-75 v WI (Bridgetown) 1993-94. LOI: 29 (HS 38*; BB 3-22). Tours: A 1990-91; WI 1989-90, 1993-94. HS 92 v Surrey (Oval) 1990. 50 wkts (5); most – 92 (1989). BB 8-75 (Tests). M BB 7-40 v Leics (Lord's) 1993. **NWT:** HS 19 v Durham (Darlington) 1989. BB 4-34 v Yorks (Leeds) 1988. **BHC:** HS 13* v Essex (Lord's) 1988. BB 3-30 v Glos (Lord's) 1992. **SL:** HS 30* v Kent (Canterbury) 1988. BB 4-17 v Hants (Lord's) 1993.

GATTING, Michael William (John Kelly HS), b Kingsbury 6 Jun 1957. 5'10". RHB, RM. Debut 1975. Cap 1977. Captain 1983-. Benefit 1988. YC 1981. Wisden 1983. OBE 1987. **Tests:** 74 (1977-78 to 1993, 23 as captain); HS 207 v I (Madras) 1984-85; BB 1-14. LOI: 92 (HS 115*; BB 3-32). Tours (C=captain): A 1986-87C, 1987-88C; SA 1989-90C (Eng XI); WI 1980-81, 1985-86; NZ 1977-78, 1983-84, 1987-88C; I/SL 1981-82, 1984-85, 1992-93; P 1977-78, 1983-84, 1987-88C; Z 1980-81 (Mx). 1000 runs (16+1) inc 2000 (3); most – 2257 (1984). HS 258 v Somerset (Bath) 1984. BB 5-34 v Glam (Swansea) 1982. Awards: NWT 6; BHC 11. **NWT:** HS 132* v Sussex (Lord's) 1989. BB 2-14 (twice). **BHC:** HS 143* v Sussex (Hove) 1985. BB 4-49 v Sussex (Lord's) 1984. **SL:** HS 124* v Leics (Leicester) 1990. BB 4-30 v Glos (Bristol) 1989.

HARRIS, Gordon Andrew Robert (Merchant Taylors' S, Northwood; Uxbridge TC; Leicester Poly), b Tottenham, London 11 Jan 1964. 6'2½". RHB, RFM. Leicestershire 1986 (one match). Bedfordshire 1988-89. Hertfordshire 1990 to date. Middlesex debut 1994. HS 11 and BB 1-61 v Glam (Lord's) 1994. **SL:** HS –. BB 5-26 v Northants (Northampton) 1994.

HARRISON, Jason Christian (Great Marlow SM; Bucks CHE), b Amersham, Bucks 15 Jan 1972. 6'3". RHB, OB. Debut 1994. Buckinghamshire 1991-93. HS 4. **SL:** HS 2.

JOHNSON, Richard Leonard (Sunbury Manor S; S Pelthorne C), b Chertsey, Surrey 29 Dec 1974. 6'2". RHB, RMF. Debut 1992. HS 50* v CU (Cambridge) 1994. BAC HS 47 v Hants (Southampton) 1994. BB 10-45 v Derbys (Derby) 1994 (first 10-wkt analysis in UK f-c cricket since 1964). **NWT:** HS 12* v Northants (Uxbridge) 1994. BB 1-22. **BHC:** HS 1. BB 1-17. **SL:** HS 18 v Derbys (Lord's) 1993. BB 4-66 v Worcs (Worcester) 1993.

MARC, Kervin (The London Oratory S; Central St Martin C of Art & Design), b Mon Repos, St Lucia 9 Jan 1975. 6'5". RHB, RFM. Debut 1994. MCC YC. HS 9 and BB 2-52 v Lancs (Manchester) 1994.

POOLEY, Jason Calvin (Acton HS), b Hammersmith 8 Aug 1969. 6'0". LHB. Debut 1989. HS 88 v Derbys (Lord's) 1991. **NWT:** HS 33 v Northants (Uxbridge) 1994. **BHC:** HS 8. **SL:** HS 109 v Derbys (Lord's) 1991.

RADFORD, Toby Alexander (St Bartholomew's S, Newbury; Loughborough U), b Caerphilly, Glam 3 Dec 1971. 5'10". RHB, OB. Debut 1994. HS 4. Awaiting BAC debut. **SL:** HS 38 v Worcs (Worcester) 1993.

RAMPRAKASH, Mark Ravin (Gayton HS; Harrow Weald SFC), b Bushey, Herts 5 Sep 1969. 5'9". RHB, RM. Debut 1987. Cap 1990. YC 1991. **Tests:** 14 (1991 to 1993-94); HS 64 v A (Oval) 1993. LOI: 4 (HS 31). Tours: WI 1991-92 (Eng A), 1993-94; NZ 1991-92; P 1990-91 (Eng A); SL 1990-91 (Eng A). 1000 runs (5); most – 1541 (1990). HS 233 v Surrey (Lord's) 1992. BB 1-0. Awards: NWT 1; BHC 2. **NWT:** HS 104 v Surrey (Uxbridge) 1990. BB 2-15 v Ire (Dublin) 1991. **BHC:** HS 119* v Northants (Lord's) 1994. **SL:** HS 147* v Worcs (Lord's) 1990. BB 5-38 v Leics (Lord's) 1993.

SHINE, Kevin James (Maiden Erlegh CS), b Bracknell, Berks 22 Feb 1969. 6'2½". RHB, RFM. Hampshire 1989-93. Middlesex debut 1994. Berkshire 1986. HS 26* H v Middx (Lord's) 1989. M HS 14* v Glam (Lord's) 1994. BB 8-47 (8 wkts in 38 balls inc hat-trick and 4 in 5; 13-105 match) H v Lancs (Manchester) 1992. M BB 4-79 v Eng A (Lord's) 1994. **NWT:** HS –. BB 3-31 v Wales MC (Northop Hall) 1994. **BHC:** HS 0. BB 4-68 H v Surrey (Oval) 1990. **SL:** HS 2*. BB 2-15 H v Northants (Northampton) 1993.

TAYLOR, Charles William (Spendlove S, Charlbury), b Banbury, Oxon 12 Aug 1966. 6'5½". LHB, LMF. Debut 1990. Oxfordshire 1986 and 1990. HS 28* v OU (Oxford) 1993. BAC HS 21 v Kent (Lord's) 1991. BB 5-33 v Yorks (Leeds) 1990. **NWT:** HS –. BB 1-54. **SL:** HS 3*. BB 2-33 v Northants (Lord's) 1993.

TUFNELL, Philip Clive Roderick (Highgate S), b Barnet, Herts 29 Apr 1966. 6'0". RHB, SLA. Debut 1986. Cap 1990. MCC YC. **Tests:** 18 (1990-91 to 1994); HS 22* v I (Madras) 1992-93; BB 7-47 (11-147 match) v NZ (Christchurch) 1991-92. LOI: 18 (HS 5*; BB 3-40). Tours: A 1990-91; WI 1993-94; NZ 1991-92; I/SL 1992-93. HS 37 v Leics (Leicester) and v Yorks (Leeds) 1990. 50 wkts (4); most – 88 (1991). BB 8-29 v Glam (Cardiff) 1993. Award: NWT 1. **NWT:** HS 8. BB 3-29 v Herts (Lord's) 1988. **BHC:** HS 18 v Warwks (Lord's) 1991. BB 3-32 v Northants (Lord's) 1994. **SL:** HS 13* v Glam (Merthyr Tydfil) 1989. BB 5-28 v Leics (Lord's) 1993.

WEEKES, Paul Nicholas (Homerton House SS, Hackney), b Hackney, London 8 Jul 1969. 5'10". LHB, OB. Debut 1990. Cap 1993. MCC YC. HS 117 v Somerset (Lord's) 1994. BB 5-12 v CU (Cambridge) 1994. BAC BB 4-79 v Glam (Lord's) 1994. Award: BHC 1. **NWT:** HS 7. BB 2-36 v Kent (Canterbury) 1993. **BHC:** HS 44* v Glos (Lord's) 1992. BB 3-32 v Warwks (Lord's) 1994. **SL:** HS 66* v Surrey (Lord's) 1993. BB 4-37 v Somerset (Lord's) 1992.

YEABSLEY, Richard Stuart (Haberdashers' Aske's S, Elstree; Keble C, Oxford), b St Albans, Herts 2 Nov 1973. Son of D.I. (Devon 1959-89; Minor Counties 1974-79). 6'4½". RHB, RMF. Oxford U 1993-94 (blue 1993-94). Awaiting Middlesex f-c debut. Devon 1990. Rugby blue. HS 52* OU v Yorks (Oxford) 1994. BB 6-54 (10-104 match) OU v CU (Lord's) 1994. **NWT:** HS 2. **SL:** HS –. BB 5-32 v Essex (Uxbridge) 1994.

NEWCOMERS

FOLLETT, David (Moorlands HS; Stoke-on-Trent TC), b Hanley, Staffs 14 Oct 1968. RHB, RFM.

KHAN, Amer Ali (Muslim Model HS, Lahore; Mao C), b Lahore, Pakistan 5 Nov 1969. RHB, LB.

NASH, David Charles (Sunbury Manor S; Malvern S), b Chertsey, Surrey 19 Jan 1978. RHB, WK.

NASH, Dion Joseph (Dargaville HS; Auckland GS), b Auckland, NZ 20 Nov 1971. 6'1". RHB, RFM. N Districts 1990-91/1991-92. Otago 1992-93 to date. **Tests** (NZ): 6 (1992-93 to 1994); HS 56 and BB 6-76 (11-169 match) v E (Lord's) 1994. LOI (NZ): 10 (HS 40*; BB 3-43). Tours (NZ): E 1994; SL 1992-93; Z 1992-93. HS 56 (Tests). BB 6-30 NZ Academy XI v ND (Rotorua) 1993-94.

RASHID, Umer Bin Abdul (Ealing Green HS; Southbank Poly), b Southampton, Hants 6 Feb 1976. LHB, SLA.

SHAH, Owais Alam (Syon S, Isleworth), b Karachi, Pakistan 22 Oct 1978. RHB.

DEPARTURES (who made first-class appearances in 1994)

HAYNES, Desmond Leo (Barbados Academy; Federal HS), b Holder's Hill, Barbados 15 Feb 1956. 5'11". RHB, RM/LB. Barbados 1976-77 to date (captain 1990-91). Middlesex 1989-94 (cap 1989). Scotland (BHC) 1983. Wisden 1990. **Tests** (WI): 116 (1977-78 to 1993-94, 4 as captain); HS 184 v E (Lord's) 1980; BB 1-2. LOI (WI): 238 (HS 152*). Tours (WI): E 1980, 1984, 1988, 1991; A 1979-80, 1981-82, 1984-85, 1986-87, 1988-89, 1991-92, 1992-93; NZ 1979-80, 1986-87; I 1983-84, 1987-88; P 1980-81, 1986-87, 1990-91 (captain); SL 1993-94; Z 1981-82 (WI B). 1000 runs (3+4) inc 2000 (1): 2346 (1990). HS 255* v Sussex (Lord's) 1990. BB 1-2 (Tests). M BB 1-4. Awards: NWT 1; BHC 3. **NWT:** HS 149* v Lancs (Manchester) 1990. BB 1-41. **BHC:** HS 131 v Sussex (Hove) 1990. BB 1-9. **SL:** HS 142* v Warwks (Birmingham) 1993. BB 1-17.

ROSEBERRY, M.A. – see DURHAM.

WILLIAMS, N.F. – see ESSEX.

MIDDLESEX 1994

RESULTS SUMMARY

	Place	Won	Lost	Drew	Abandoned
Britannic Assurance Championship	4th	7	3	7	
All First-class Matches		8	3	9	
Sunday League	14th	6	10		1
NatWest Trophy	2nd Round				
Benson and Hedges Cup	2nd Round				

BRITANNIC ASSURANCE CHAMPIONSHIP AVERAGES

BATTING AND FIELDING

Cap		M	I	NO	HS	Runs	Avge	100	50	Ct/St
1987	J.D.Carr	17	23	8	261*	1321	88.06	5	5	28
1977	M.W.Gatting	17	25	2	225	1389	60.39	5	5	25
1990	M.R.Ramprakash	17	25	2	135	1261	54.82	4	6	11
1990	M.A.Roseberry	17	27	2	152	1001	40.04	2	6	19
1989	D.L.Haynes	17	27	2	134	973	38.92	5	2	6
1990	K.R.Brown	17	22	8	102*	528	37.71	1	–	48/1
1993	P.N.Weekes	13	16	–	117	552	34.50	1	2	8
1984	N.F.Williams	9	8	3	63	132	26.40	–	1	2
–	K.J.Shine	10	7	5	14*	39	19.50	–	–	4
–	M.A.Feltham	10	13	1	71	230	19.16	–	1	7
–	R.L.Johnson	9	12	2	47	155	15.50	–	–	4
1977	J.E.Emburey	14	17	4	26*	123	9.46	–	–	11
1988	A.R.C.Fraser	9	8	1	16	40	5.71	–	–	1
1990	P.C.R.Tufnell	8	6	1	5	14	2.80	–	–	4

Also batted: G.A.R.Harris (2 matches) 11, 5*; K.Marc (1 match) 9, 8.

BOWLING

	O	M	R	W	Avge	Best	5wI	10wM
A.R.C.Fraser	321	86	802	36	22.27	3-16	–	–
R.L.Johnson	299.4	68	942	36	26.16	10-45	1	1
J.E.Emburey	633	187	1434	52	27.57	6-89	2	–
P.C.R.Tufnell	408.5	107	995	35	28.42	6-35	1	–
M.A.Feltham	321.3	67	989	29	34.10	5-69	1	–
P.N.Weekes	401.3	62	1209	31	39.00	4-79	–	–
N.F.Williams	294	61	1000	24	41.66	6-49	1	–
K.J.Shine	252.3	52	931	20	46.55	3-16	–	–

Also bowled: M.W.Gatting 26-4-97-2; G.A.R.Harris 51-11-215-1; D.L.Haynes 2-2-0-0; K.Marc 29-4-133-3; M.R.Ramprakash 2-0-6-0; M.A.Roseberry 1-0-5-0.

The First-Class Averages (pp 186-200) give the records of Middlesex players in all first-class county matches (their other opponents being England A, the New Zealanders and Cambridge U), with the exception of A.R.C.Fraser and P.C.R.Tufnell whose full county figures are as above.

MIDDLESEX RECORDS

FIRST-CLASS CRICKET

Highest Total	For	642-3d		v	Hampshire	Southampton	1923
	V	665		by	W Indians	Lord's	1939
Lowest Total	For	20		v	MCC	Lord's	1864
	V	31		by	Glos	Bristol	1924
Highest Innings	For	331*	J.D.B.Robertson	v	Worcs	Worcester	1949
	V	316*	J.B.Hobbs	for	Surrey	Lord's	1926

Highest Partnership for each Wicket

1st	367*	G.D.Barlow/W.N.Slack	v	Kent	Lord's	1981
2nd	380	F.A.Tarrant/J.W.Hearne	v	Lancashire	Lord's	1914
3rd	424*	W.J.Edrich/D.C.S.Compton	v	Hampshire	Lord's	1948
4th	325	J.W.Hearne/E.H.Hendren	v	Hampshire	Lord's	1919
5th	338	R.S.Lucas/T.C.O'Brien	v	Sussex	Hove	1895
6th	270	J.D.Carr/P.N.Weekes	v	Glos	Lord's	1994
7th	271*	E.H.Hendren/F.T.Mann	v	Notts	Nottingham	1925
8th	182*	M.H.C.Doll/H.R.Murrell	v	Notts	Lord's	1913
9th	160*	E.H.Hendren/T.J.Durston	v	Essex	Leyton	1927
10th	230	R.W.Nicholls/W.Roche	v	Kent	Lord's	1899

Best Bowling	For	10- 40	G.O.B.Allen	v	Lancashire	Lord's	1929
(Innings)	V	9- 38	R.C.Glasgow†	for	Somerset	Lord's	1924
Best Bowling	For	16-114	G.Burton	v	Yorkshire	Sheffield	1888
(Match)		16-114	J.T.Hearne	v	Lancashire	Manchester	1898
	V	16-109	C.W.L.Parker	for	Glos	Cheltenham	1930

Most Runs – Season	2669	E.H.Hendren	(av 83.41)	1923
Most Runs – Career	40302	E.H.Hendren	(av 48.81)	1907-37
Most 100s – Season	13	D.C.S.Compton		1947
Most 100s – Career	119	E.H.Hendren		1907-37
Most Wkts – Season	158	F.J.Titmus	(av 14.63)	1955
Most Wkts – Career	2361	F.J.Titmus	(av 21.27)	1949-82

LIMITED-OVERS CRICKET

Highest Total	**NWT**	296-4		v	Lancashire	Manchester	1990
	BHC	325-5		v	Leics	Leicester	1992
	SL	290-6		v	Worcs	Lord's	1990
Lowest Total	**NWT**	41		v	Essex	Westcliff	1972
	BHC	73		v	Essex	Lord's	1985
	SL	23		v	Yorkshire	Leeds	1974
Highest Innings	**NWT**	158	G.D.Barlow	v	Lancashire	Lord's	1984
	BHC	143*	M.W.Gatting	v	Sussex	Hove	1985
	SL	147*	M.R.Ramprakash	v	Worcs	Lord's	1990
Best Bowling	**NWT**	6-15	W.W.Daniel	v	Sussex	Hove	1980
	BHC	7-12	W.W.Daniel	v	Minor C	Ipswich	1978
	SL	6- 6	R.W.Hooker	v	Surrey	Lord's	1969

† R.C.Robertson-Glasgow

NORTHAMPTONSHIRE

Formation of Present Club: 31 July 1878
Colours: Maroon
Badge: Tudor Rose
Championships: (0) Second 1912, 1957, 1965, 1976
NatWest Trophy/Gillette Cup Winners: (2) 1976, 1992
Benson and Hedges Cup Winners: (1) 1980
Sunday League Champions: (0) Third 1991
Match Awards: NWT 46; BHC 43

Chief Executive: S.P.Coverdale
County Ground, Wantage Road, Northampton, NN1 4TJ (☎ 01604 32917)
Captain: A.J.Lamb
Scorer: A.C.Kingston
1995 Beneficiary: N.G.B.Cook

BAILEY, Robert John (Biddulph HS), b Biddulph, Staffs 28 Oct 1963. 6'3". RHB, OB. Debut 1982. Cap 1985. Benefit 1993. Staffordshire 1980. YC 1984. **Tests:** 4 (1988 to 1989-90); HS 43 v WI (Oval) 1988. LOI: 4 (HS 43*). Tours: SA 1991-92 (Nh); WI 1989-90. 1000 runs (11); most – 1987 (1990). HS 224* v Glam (Swansea) 1986. BB 5-54 v Notts (Northampton) 1993. Awards: NWT 4; BHC 5. **NWT:** HS 145 v Staffs (Stone) 1991. BB 3-47 v Notts (Northampton) 1990. **BHC:** HS 134 v Glos (Northampton) 1987. BB 1-22. **SL:** HS 125* v Derbys (Derby) 1987. BB 3-23 v Leics (Leicester) 1987.

BOWEN, Mark Nicholas (Sacred Heart, Redcar; St Mary's C; Tees Side Poly), b Redcar, Yorks 6 Dec 1967. 6'2". RHB, RM. Debut v Natal (Durban) 1991-92. Tour: SA 1991-92 (Nh). HS 23* v Durham (Northampton) 1993. BB 4-124 v Kent (Canterbury) 1993. **BHC:** HS 0. BB 1-39. **SL:** HS 27* v Kent (Northampton) 1994. BB 3-35 v Derbys (Derby) 1993.

CAPEL, David John (Roade CS), b Northampton 6 Feb 1963. 5'11". RHB, RMF. Debut 1981. Cap 1986. Benefit 1994. E Province 1985-86/1986-87. **Tests:** 15 (1987 to 1989-90); HS 98 v P (Karachi) 1987-88; BB 3-88 v WI (Bridgetown) 1989-90. LOI: 23 (HS 50*; BB 3-38). Tours: A 1987-88, 1992-93 (Eng A); WI 1989-90; NZ 1987-88; P 1987-88. 1000 runs (3); most – 1311 (1989). HS 134 EP v W Province (Port Elizabeth) 1986-87. Nh HS 126 v Sussex (Hove) 1989. 50 wkts (3); most – 63 (1986). BB 7-46 v Yorks (Northampton) 1987. Awards: NWT 3. **NWT:** HS 101 v Notts (Northampton) 1990. BB 3-21 v Glam (Swansea) 1992. **BHC:** HS 97 v Yorks (Lord's) 1987. BB 4-29 v Warwks (Birmingham) 1986. **SL:** HS 121 v Glam (Northampton) 1990. BB 4-30 v Yorks (Middlesbrough) 1982.

COOK, Nicholas Grant Billson (Lutterworth GS), b Leicester 17 Jun 1956. 6'0". RHB, SLA. Leicestershire 1978-85 (cap 1982). Northamptonshire debut 1986. Cap 1987. Benefit 1995. **Tests:** 15 (1983 to 1989); HS 31 v A (Oval) 1989; BB 6-65 (11-83 match) v P (Karachi) 1983-84. LOI: 3 (HS –; BB 2-18). Tours: NZ 1979-80 (DHR), 1983-84; P 1983-84, 1987-88; SL 1985-86 (Eng B); Z 1980-81 (Le), 1984-85 (EC). HS 75 Le v Somerset (Taunton) 1980. Nh HS 64 v Lancs (Manchester) 1987. 50 wkts (8); most – 90 (1982). BB 7-34 (10-97 match) v Essex (Chelmsford) 1992. **NWT:** HS 13 v Middx (Northampton) 1986. BB 4-24 v Ire (Northampton) 1987. **BHC:** HS 23 Le v Warwks (Leicester) 1984. BB 3-35 v Kent (Northampton) 1989. **SL:** HS 21* v Yorks (Luton) 1994. BB 4-22 v Glam (Pentrych) 1993.

CURRAN, Kevin Malcolm (Marandellas HS), b Rusape, S Rhodesia 7 Sep 1959. Son of K.P. (Rhodesia 1947-48/1953-54). 6'1". RHB, RMF. Zimbabwe 1980-81/1987-88. Natal 1988-89. Gloucestershire 1985-90 (cap 1985). Northamptonshire debut 1991. Cap 1992. Qualified for England 1994. LOI (Z): 11 (HS 73; BB 3-65). Tours (Z): E 1982; SL 1983-84. 1000 runs (5); most – 1353 (1986). HS 144* Gs v Sussex (Bristol) 1990. Nh HS 114 v Yorks (Luton) 1994. 50 wkts (5); most – 67

CURRAN – continued:
(1993). BB 7-47 Natal v Transvaal (Johannesburg) 1988-89 and v Yorks (Harrogate) 1993. Awards: NWT 2; BHC 2. **NWT:** HS 78* v Cambs (Northampton) 1992. BB 4-34 Gs v Northants (Bristol) 1985. **BHC:** HS 57 Gs v Derbys (Derby) 1987. BB 4-41 Gs v Notts (Bristol) 1989. **SL:** HS 92 Gs v Northants (Northampton) 1990. BB 5-15 Gs v Leics (Gloucester) 1988.

DAWOOD, Ismail (Batley GS), b Dewsbury, Yorks 23 Jul 1976. 5'8". RHB, WK. Debut 1994. HS 2*. **SL:** HS 2.

FORDHAM, Alan (Bedford Modern S; Durham U), b Bedford 9 Nov 1964. 6'1". RHB, RM. Debut 1986. Cap 1990. Bedfordshire 1982-85. Tour: SA 1991-92 (Nh). 1000 runs (4); most – 1840 (1991). HS 206* v Yorks (Leeds) 1990. BB 1-25. Awards: NWT 4; BHC 3. **NWT:** HS 132* v Leics (Northampton) 1991. BB 1-3. **BHC:** HS 103 v Scot (Forfar) 1992. **SL:** HS 111 v Durham (Hartlepool) 1994.

HUGHES, John Gareth (Sir Christopher Hatton SS, Wellingborough; Sheffield City Poly), b Wellingborough 3 May 1971. 6'1". RHB, RM. Debut 1990. Tour: SA 1991-92 (Nh). HS 17 and BB 5-69 v Hants (Southampton) 1994. **BHC:** HS –. **SL:** HS 21 v Kent (Canterbury) 1993.

INNES, Kevin John (Weston Favell Upper S), b Wellingborough 24 Sep 1975. 5'10". RHB, RM. 2nd XI debut 1990 (aged 14yr 8m – Northamptonshire record). Debut 1994. HS 0. **BHC:** HS 1. BB 1-25. **SL:** HS 5. BB 1-35.

LAMB, Allan Joseph (Wynberg HS; Abbotts C) b Langebaanweg, Cape Province, SA 20 Jun 1954. 5'8". RHB, RM. W Province 1972-73/1981-82 and 1992-93. OFS 1987-88. Northamptonshire debut/cap 1978. Captain 1989-. Benefit 1988. Testimonial 1996. Wisden 1980. **Tests:** 79 (1982 to 1992, 3 as captain); HS 142 v NZ (Wellington) 1991-92; BB 1-6. LOI: 122 (HS 118). Tours: A 1982-83, 1986-87, 1990-91; WI 1985-86, 1989-90; NZ 1983-84, 1991-92; I/SL 1984-85; P 1983-84. 1000 runs (12) inc 2000 (1): 2049 (1981). HS 294 OFS v E Province (Bloemfontein) 1987-88 – sharing record SA 5th wkt stand of 355 with J.J.Strydom. Nh HS 235 v Yorks (Leeds) 1990. BB 2-29 v Lancs (Lytham) 1991. Awards: NWT 4; BHC 9. **NWT:** HS 129* v Middx (Uxbridge) 1994. BB 1-4. **BHC:** HS 126* v Kent (Canterbury) 1987. BB 1-11. **SL:** HS 132* v Surrey (Guildford) 1985.

LOYE, Malachy Bernhard (Moulton S), b Northampton 27 Sep 1972. 6'2". RHB, OB. Debut 1991. Cap 1994. Tour: SA 1993-94 (Eng A). HS 153* v Kent (Canterbury) 1993. **NWT:** HS 65 v Essex (Chelmsford) 1993. **BHC:** HS 68* v Middx (Lord's) 1994. **SL:** HS 122 v Somerset (Luton) 1993.

MALLENDER, Neil Alan (Beverley GS), b Kirk Sandall, Yorks 13 Aug 1961. 6'0". RHB, RFM. Northamptonshire 1980-86 (cap 1984). Somerset 1987-94 (cap 1987; benefit 1994). Otago 1983-84/1992-93 (captain 1990-91/1992-93). **Tests:** 2 (1992); HS 4; BB 5-50 v P (Leeds) 1992 – on debut. HS 100* Otago v CD (Palmerston N) 1991-92. BAC HS 87* Sm v Sussex (Hove) 1990. Nh HS 71* v OU (Oxford) 1983. 50 wkts (6); most – 56 (1983). BB 7-27 Otago v Auckland (Auckland) 1984-85. Nh BB 7-41 v Derbys (Northampton) 1982. Award: NWT 1. **NWT:** HS 11* (twice). BB 7-37 v Worcs (Northampton) 1984. **BHC:** HS 16* Sm v Hants (Taunton) 1988. BB 5-53 v Leics (Northampton) 1986. **SL:** HS 31* Sm v Durham (Hartlepool) 1993. BB 5-34 v Middx (Tring) 1981.

MONTGOMERIE, Richard Robert (Rugby S; Worcester C, Oxford), b Rugby, Warwks 3 Jul 1971. 5'10½". RHB, OB. Oxford U 1991-94 (blue 1991-92-93-94; captain 1994). Northamptonshire debut 1991. Half blues for rackets and real tennis. 1000 runs (1): 1062 (1994). HS 151 v Derbys (Northampton) 1994. **BHC:** HS 75 Comb Us v Worcs (Oxford) 1992. **SL:** HS 74 v Somerset (Taunton) 1994.

PENBERTHY, Anthony Leonard (Camborne CS), b Troon, Cornwall 1 Sep 1969. 6'1". LHB, RM. Debut 1989. Cap 1994. Cornwall 1987-89. Tour: SA 1991-92 (Nh). HS 101* v CU (Cambridge) 1990. BAC HS 88* v Somerset (Taunton) 1994. BB 5-37 v Glam (Swansea) 1993. Dismissed M.A.Taylor with his first ball in f-c cricket. **NWT:** HS 41* v Essex (Chelmsford) 1993. BB 2-29 v Glam (Swansea) 1992. **BHC:**

HS 24 v Middx (Lord's) 1994. BB 2-22 v Comb Us (Northampton) 1991. **SL:** HS 69* v Glam (Northampton) 1994. BB 5-36 v Glos (Northampton) 1993.

RIPLEY, David (Royds SS, Leeds), b Leeds, Yorks 13 Sep 1966. 5'9". RHB, WK. Debut 1984. Cap 1987. Tour: SA 1991-92 (Nh). HS 134* v Yorks (Scarborough) 1986. BB 2-89 v Essex (Ilford) 1987. Award: BHC 1. **NWT:** HS 27* v Durham (Darlington) 1984. **BHC:** HS 36* v Glos (Bristol) 1991. **SL:** HS 52* v Surrey (Northampton) 1993.

ROBERTS, Andrew Richard (Bishop Stopford CS, Kettering), b Kettering 16 Apr 1971. 5'6". RHB, LB. Debut 1989. Tour: SA 1991-92 (Nh). HS 62 v Notts (Nottingham) 1992. BB 6-72 v Lancs (Lytham) 1991. **NWT:** HS –. BB 1-23. **SL:** HS 20 v Essex (Chelmsford) 1994. BB 3-26 v Hants (Northampton) 1991.

ROBERTS, David James (Mullion CS), b Truro, Cornwall 29 Dec 1976. Cousin of C.K.Bullen (Surrey 1982-91). 5'11". RHB, RSM. Northamptonshire staff 1994 – awaiting f-c debut.

SNAPE, Jeremy Nicholas (Denstone C; Durham U), b Stoke-on-Trent, Staffs 27 Apr 1973. 5'8½". RHB, OB. Debut 1992. HS 43* v SA (Northampton) 1994. BB 2-49 Comb Us v A (Oxford) 1993. Nh BB 1-20. Awaiting BAC debut. Award: BHC 1. **NWT:** HS 5*. **BHC:** HS 52 Comb Us v Hants (Southampton) 1993. BB 3-35 Comb Us v Worcs (Oxford) 1992. **SL:** HS 31* v Leics (Leicester) 1994. BB 3-25 v Essex (Northampton) 1993.

TAYLOR, Jonathan **Paul** (Pingle S, Swadlincote), b Ashby-de-la-Zouch, Leics 8 Aug 1964. 6'2". LHB, LFM. Derbyshire 1984-86. Northamptonshire debut 1991. Cap 1992. Staffordshire 1989-90 (cap 1989). **Tests:** 2 (1992-93 to 1994); HS 17* v I (Calcutta) 1992-93. BB 1-18. LOI: 1 (HS 1). Tours: SA 1993-94 (Eng A – part); I 1992-93. HS 74* v Notts (Northampton) 1992. 50 wkts (2); most – 69 (1993). BB 7-23 v Hants (Bournemouth) 1992. **NWT:** HS 9. BB 3-41 v Glam (Swansea) 1992. **BHC:** HS 6*. BB 3-38 v Lancs (Northampton) 1992. **SL:** HS 24 v Worcs (Northampton) 1993. BB 3-14 De v Glos (Gloucester) 1986.

WALTON, Timothy Charles (Leeds GS; Newcastle upon Tyne Poly), b Low Head, Yorks 8 Nov 1972. 6'0½". RHB, RM. Debut 1994. HS 11 and BB 1-46 v Somerset (Taunton) 1994. **SL:** HS 72 v Glos (Bristol) 1994. BB 2-27 v Leics (Leicester) 1992.

WARREN, Russell John (Kingsthorpe Upper S), b Northampton 10 Sep 1971. 6'1". RHB, OB. Debut 1992. HS 94* v Warwks (Northampton) 1994. Award: NWT 1. **NWT:** HS 100* v Ire (Northampton) 1994. **SL:** HS 71* v Leics (Northampton) 1993.

NEWCOMERS

ATKINS, Craig Stuart, b Melbourne, Australia 29 May 1966. LHB, SLA.

BOSWELL, Scott Antony John (Pocklington S), b Fulford, Yorks 11 Sep 1974. 6'4". RHB, RMF.

BROWN, Jason Fred, b Newcastle-under-Lyme, Staffs 10 Oct 1974. RHB, OB.

FOSTER, Michael James (New C, Pontefract), b Leeds, Yorks 17 Sep 1972. 6'1". RHB, RFM. Yorkshire 1993-94. HS 63* Y v OU (Oxford) 1994. BAC HS 49 Y v Durham (Durham) 1994. BB 3-39 Y v Hants (Southampton) 1993 – on debut. **SL:** HS 118 Y v Leics (Leicester) 1993. BB 2-74 Y v Glos (Cheltenham) 1994.

KUMBLE, Anil (National HS; R.V. Engineering C, Bangalore), b Bangalore, India 17 Oct 1970. 6'1½". RHB, LB. Karnataka 1989-90 to date. **Tests** (I): 17 (1990 to 1993-94); HS 21* v SA (Jo'burg) 1992-93; BB 7-59 (11-128 match) v SL (Lucknow) 1993-94. LOI (I): 46 (HS 24; BB 6-12). Tours (I): E 1990; SA 1992-93; NZ 1993-94; SL 1993-94; Z 1992-93. HS 154* Karnataka v Kerala (Bijapur) 1991-92. BB 7-59 (Tests).

SALES, David John Grimwood (Caterham S), b Carshalton, Surrey 3 Dec 1977. RHB, RM. **SL:** HS 70* (off 56 balls) v Essex (Chelmsford) 1994, when 16yr 289d (youngest to score SL fifty).

STEELE, Mark Vincent (Wellingborough S), b Corby 13 Nov 1976. LHB, RFM.

SWANN, Alec James (Sponne S), b Northampton 26 Oct 1976. RHB, OB.

DEPARTURES – see p 181

NORTHAMPTONSHIRE 1994

RESULTS SUMMARY

	Place	Won	Lost	Tied	Drew	Abandoned
Britannic Assurance Championship	**5th**	8	4		5	
All First-class Matches		8	4		6	1
Sunday League	**13th**	6	9	1		1
NatWest Trophy	Quarter-Finalist					
Benson and Hedges Cup	1st Round					

BRITANNIC ASSURANCE CHAMPIONSHIP AVERAGES

BATTING AND FIELDING

Cap		*M*	*I*	*NO*	*HS*	*Runs*	*Avge*	*100*	*50*	*Ct/St*
1992	K.M.Curran	14	23	4	114	854	44.94	1	7	6
1985	R.J.Bailey	17	31	5	129*	1168	44.92	3	7	11
1990	A.Fordham	11	20	1	158	844	44.42	3	4	7
1978	A.J.Lamb	15	22	1	131	908	43.23	2	5	17
1994	M.B.Loye	13	23	3	132	858	42.90	3	4	7
–	R.R.Montgomerie	8	15	2	151	513	39.46	1	3	8
–	A.R.Roberts	9	12	4	51	261	32.62	–	1	3
–	R.J.Warren	11	19	2	94*	531	31.23	–	5	13
1994	A.L.Penberthy	16	24	4	88*	615	30.75	–	5	7
1990	N.A.Felton	9	17	1	87	421	26.31	–	2	4
1987	D.Ripley	15	23	9	36*	263	18.78	–	–	38/6
1990	C.E.L.Ambrose	14	16	2	78	257	18.35	–	1	16
1992	J.P.Taylor	11	12	6	26	68	11.33	–	–	4
1987	N.G.B.Cook	10	12	1	43*	98	8.90	–	–	3
–	J.G.Hughes	4	6	–	17	47	7.83	–	–	2
–	M.N.Bowen	4	5	–	13	18	3.60	–	–	2

Also batted: D.J.Capel (2 matches – cap 1986) 8, 6, 29 (1 ct); I.Dawood (1 match) 2*; K.J.Innes (1 match) 0, 0; T.C.Walton (2 matches) 5, 11 (2 ct).

BOWLING

	O	*M*	*R*	*W*	*Avge*	*Best*	*5wI*	*10wM*
C.E.L.Ambrose	540	159	1113	77	14.45	7- 44	6	2
J.G.Hughes	137.2	38	428	14	30.57	5- 69	1	–
J.P.Taylor	278.4	45	971	30	32.36	5- 62	1	–
A.L.Penberthy	378.1	78	1325	35	37.85	5- 54	1	–
N.G.B.Cook	252.3	74	652	16	40.75	3- 46	–	–
K.M.Curran	401.5	84	1375	30	45.83	4- 65	–	–
R.J.Bailey	154.1	30	541	11	49.18	5- 59	1	–
A.R.Roberts	242	49	870	17	51.17	3-106	–	–

Also bowled: M.N.Bowen 87.1-14-310-5; D.J.Capel 33-7-89-0; K.J.Innes 10-3-33-0; R.R.Montgomerie 1-0-10-0; T.C.Walton 20-1-98-2.

The First-Class Averages (pp 186-200) give the records of Northamptonshire players in all first-class county matches (their other opponents being the South Africans, their match against Cambridge U being abandoned), with the exception of R.R.Montgomerie, whose full county figures are as above, and:

M.B.Loye 14-25-3-132-908-41.27-3-5-7ct. Did not bowl.
J.N.Snape 1-2-2-43*-54-∞-0-0-0ct. 27-7-91-1-91.00-1/44-0-0.
J.P.Taylor 12-12-6-26-68-11.33-0-0-5ct. 307.4-50-1059-34-31.14-5/62-1-0.

NORTHAMPTONSHIRE RECORDS

FIRST-CLASS CRICKET

Highest Total	For	636-6d		v	Essex	Chelmsford	1990
	V	670-9d		by	Sussex	Hove	1921
Lowest Total	For	12		v	Glos	Gloucester	1907
	V	33		by	Lancashire	Northampton	1977
Highest Innings	For	300	R.Subba Row	v	Surrey	The Oval	1958
	V	333	K.S.Duleepsinhji	for	Sussex	Hove	1930

Highest Partnership for each Wicket

1st	361	N.Oldfield/V.Broderick	v	Scotland	Peterborough	1953
2nd	344	G.Cook/R.J.Boyd-Moss	v	Lancashire	Northampton	1986
3rd	393	A.Fordham/A.J.Lamb	v	Yorkshire	Leeds	1990
4th	370	R.T.Virgin/P.Willey	v	Somerset	Northampton	1976
5th	347	D.Brookes/D.W.Barrick	v	Essex	Northampton	1952
6th	376	R.Subba Row/A.Lightfoot	v	Surrey	The Oval	1958
7th	229	W.W.Timms/F.A.Walden	v	Warwicks	Northampton	1926
8th	164	D.Ripley/N.G.B.Cook	v	Lancashire	Manchester	1987
9th	156	R.Subba Row/S.Starkie	v	Lancashire	Northampton	1955
10th	148	B.W.Bellamy/J.V.Murdin	v	Glamorgan	Northampton	1925

Best Bowling	For	10-127	V.W.C.Jupp	v	Kent	Tunbridge W	1932
(Innings)	V	10- 30	C.Blythe	for	Kent	Northampton	1907
Best Bowling	For	15- 31	G.E.Tribe	v	Yorkshire	Northampton	1958
(Match)	V	17- 48	C.Blythe	for	Kent	Northampton	1907

Most Runs – Season	2198	D.Brookes	(av 51.11)	1952
Most Runs – Career	28980	D.Brookes	(av 36.13)	1934-59
Most 100s – Season	8	R.A.Haywood		1921
Most 100s – Career	67	D.Brookes		1934-59
Most Wkts – Season	175	G.E.Tribe	(av 18.70)	1955
Most Wkts – Career	1097	E.W.Clark	(av 21.31)	1922-47

LIMITED-OVERS CRICKET

Highest Total	NWT	360-2		v	Staffs	Northampton	1990
	BHC	300-9		v	Derbyshire	Derby	1987
	SL	306-2		v	Surrey	Guildford	1985
Lowest Total	NWT	62		v	Leics	Leicester	1974
	BHC	85		v	Sussex	Northampton	1978
	SL	41		v	Middlesex	Northampton	1972
Highest Innings	NWT	145	R.J.Bailey	v	Staffs	Stone	1991
	BHC	134	R.J.Bailey	v	Glos	Northampton	1987
	SL	172*	W.Larkins	v	Warwicks	Luton	1983
Best Bowling	NWT	7-37	N.A.Mallender	v	Worcs	Northampton	1984
	BHC	5-21	Sarfraz Nawaz	v	Middlesex	Lord's	1980
	SL	7-39	A.Hodgson	v	Somerset	Northampton	1976

NOTTINGHAMSHIRE

Formation of Present Club: March/April 1841
Substantial Reorganisation: 11 December 1866
Colours: Green and Gold
Badge: Badge of City of Nottingham
Championships (since 1890): (4) 1907, 1929, 1981, 1987
NatWest Trophy/Gillette Cup Winners: (1) 1987
Benson and Hedges Cup Winners: (1) 1989
Sunday League Champions: (1) 1991
Match Awards: NWT 36; BHC 58

Secretary/General Manager: B.Robson
Trent Bridge, Nottingham NG2 6AG (☎ 0115-982 1525)
Captain: R.T.Robinson
Scorer: G.Stringfellow
1995 Beneficiary: P.Johnson

AFFORD, John Andrew (Spalding GS; Stamford CFE), b Crowland, Lincs 12 May 1964. 6'1½". RHB, SLA. Debut 1984. Cap 1990. Tour: Z 1989-90 (Eng A). HS 22* v Leics (Nottingham) 1989. 50 wkts (4); most – 57 (1991, 1993). BB 6-68 (10-185 match) v Sussex (Nottingham) 1992. Award: BHC 1. **NWT:** HS 2*. BB 3-32 v Herts (Hitchin) 1989. **BHC:** HS 1*. BB 4-38 v Kent (Nottingham) 1989. **SL:** HS 1. BB 3-33 v Northants (Northampton) 1993.

ARCHER, Graeme Francis (Heron Brook Middle S; King Edward VI HS, Stafford), b Carlisle, Cumberland 26 Sep 1970. 6'1". RHB, OB. Debut 1992. Staffordshire 1990. HS 168 v Glam (Worksop) 1994. **NWT:** HS 39 v Cheshire (Warrington) 1993. **BHC:** HS 9. **SL:** HS 49 v Hants (Basingstoke) 1994.

BATES, Richard Terry (Bourne GS; Stamford CFE), b Stamford, Lincs 17 Jun 1972. 6'1". RHB, OB. Lincolnshire 1990-91. Debut 1993. HS 33* v OU (Oxford) 1993. BAC HS 18* v Glos (Bristol) 1993. BB 2-43 v Sussex (Eastbourne) 1993. **SL:** HS 16 v Worcs (Worcester) 1994. BB 3-43 v Derbys (Nottingham) 1993.

CAIRNS, Christopher Lance (Christchurch BHS), b Picton, NZ 13 Jun 1970. Son of B.L. (CD, Otago, ND and NZ 1971-86). 6'2". RHB, RFM. Nottinghamshire 1988-89 and 1992-93 (cap 1993). N Districts 1988-89. Canterbury 1990-91/1992-93. **Tests** (NZ): 10 (1989-90 to 1993-94); HS 78 v A (Perth) 1993-94; BB 6-52 v E (Auckland) 1991-92. LOI (NZ): 22 (HS 70; BB 4-55). Tours (NZ): A 1989-90, 1993-94. HS 110 ND v Auckland (Hamilton) 1988-89. Nt HS 107* v Glos (Worksop) 1992. 50 wkts (2); most – 56 (1992). BB 7-34 (11-100 match) Canterbury v CD (New Plymouth) 1991-92. Nt BB 6-70 v Lancs (Nottingham) 1992 and v Lancs (Manchester) 1993. Awards: NWT 2. **NWT:** HS 77 v Glam (Nottingham) 1992. BB 4-18 v Cheshire (Warrington) 1993. **BHC:** HS 16 v Kent (Nottingham) 1992. BB 2-63 v Somerset (Nottingham) 1993. **SL:** HS 126* v Surrey (Oval) 1993. BB 6-52 v Kent (Nottingham) 1993.

CHAPMAN, Robert James (Farnborough CS; S Notts CFE), b Nottingham 28 Jul 1972. Son of footballer R.O. ('Sammy') (Nottingham Forest, Notts County and Shrewsbury Town). 6'1". RHB, RFM. Debut 1992. HS 25 v Lancs (Nottingham) 1994. BB 2-21 v CU (Cambridge) 1994. BAC BB 1-38. **SL:** HS 2*. BB 2-44 v Lancs (Nottingham) 1994.

DOWMAN, Mathew Peter (St Hugh's CS; Grantham C), b Grantham, Lincs 10 May 1974. 5'10". LHB, RMF. Debut 1994. Scored 267 for England YC v WI YC (Hove) 1993 – record score in youth 'Tests'. HS 38 v Middx (Nottingham) 1994. **SL:** HS 52* v Glam (Nottingham) 1994. BB 1-33.

EVANS, Kevin Paul (Colonel Frank Seely S) b Calverton 10 Sep 1963. Elder brother of R.J. (Notts 1987-90). 6'2". RHB, RMF. Debut 1984. Cap 1990. HS 104 v Surrey (Nottingham) 1992 and v Sussex (Nottingham) 1994. BB 6-67 v Yorks (Nottingham)

1993. **NWT:** HS 21 v Worcs (Worcester) 1994. BB 6-10 v Northumb (Jesmond) 1994. **BHC:** HS 31* v Northants (Northampton) 1988. BB 4-43 v Glam (Cardiff) 1991. **SL:** HS 30 v Kent (Canterbury) 1990 and v Hants (Southampton) 1992. BB 4-26 v Kent (Canterbury) 1994.

FIELD-BUSS, Michael Gwyn (Wanstead HS), b Mtarfa, Malta 23 Sep 1964. 5'10". RHB, OB. Essex 1987. Nottinghamshire debut 1989. HS 34* Ex v Middx (Lord's) 1987. Nt HS 25 v Middx (Lord's) 1991. BB 6-42 v Kent (Nottingham) 1993. **NWT:** HS 5*. BB 4-62 v Worcs (Nottingham) 1992. **BHC:** HS –. **SL:** HS 10* v Hants (Southampton) 1992. BB 3-25 v Worcs (Nottingham) 1993.

FRENCH, Bruce Nicholas (The Meden CS), b Warsop 13 Aug 1959. 5'6". RHB, WK. Debut 1976 (aged 16yr 287d). Cap 1980. Benefit 1991. **Tests:** 16 (1986 to 1987-88); HS 59 v P (Manchester) 1987. LOI: 13 (HS 9*). Tours: A 1986-87, 1987-88; SA 1989-90 (Eng XI); WI 1985-86; NZ 1987-88; I/SL 1984-85; P 1987-88. HS 123 v Durham (Chester-le-St) 1993. BB 1-37. Award: BHC 1. **NWT:** HS 49 v Staffs (Nottingham) 1985. **BHC:** HS 48* v Worcs (Nottingham) 1984. **SL:** HS 37 v Glos (Bristol) 1985.

HINDSON, James Edward (Toot Hill CS, Bingham), b Huddersfield, Yorks 13 Sep 1973. 6'1". RHB, SLA. Debut 1992. HS 11 v Lancs (Nottingham) 1994. BB 5-42 v CU (Nottingham) 1992. BAC BB 5-53 v Glam (Worksop) 1994. **SL:** HS 21 v Middx (Nottingham) 1994. BB 4-19 v Worcs (Worcester) 1994.

JOHNSON, Paul (Grove CS, Balderton), b Newark 24 Apr 1965. 5'7". RHB, RM. Debut 1982. Cap 1986. Benefit 1995. Tour: WI 1991-92 (Eng A). 1000 runs (8); most – 1518 (1990). HS 187 v Lancs (Manchester) 1993. BB 1-9. BAC BB 1-14. Awards: NWT 2; BHC 3. **NWT:** HS 146 v Northumb (Jesmond) 1994. **BHC:** HS 104* v Essex (Chelmsford) 1990. **SL:** HS 167* v Kent (Nottingham) 1993.

LEWIS, Clairmonte **Christopher** (Willesden HS, London), b Georgetown, Guyana 14 Feb 1968. 6'2½". RHB, RFM. Leicestershire 1987-91 (cap 1990). Nottinghamshire debut 1992. Cap 1994. **Tests:** 25 (1990 to 1993-94); HS 117 v I (Madras) 1992-93; BB 6-111 v WI (Birmingham) 1991. LOI: 48 (HS 33; BB 4-30). Tours: A 1990-91 (part); WI 1989-90 (part), 1993-94; NZ 1991-92; I/SL 1992-93. HS 247 v Durham (Chester-le-St) 1993. 50 wkts (2); most – 56 (1990). BB 6-22 Le v OU (Oxford) 1988. BAC BB 6-55 Le v Glam (Cardiff) 1990. Nt BB 6-90 v Surrey (Nottingham) 1992. Award: NWT 1. **NWT:** HS 89 v Northumb (Jesmond) 1994. BB 3-24 v Somerset (Nottingham) 1993. **BHC:** HS 48* v Minor C (Nottingham) 1994. BB 5-46 v Kent (Nottingham) 1992. **SL:** HS 93* Le v Essex (Leicester) 1990. BB 4-13 Le v Essex (Leicester) 1988.

MIKE, Gregory Wentworth (Claremont CS; Basford Hall C), b Nottingham 14 Jul 1966. 6'0". RHB, RMF. Debut 1989. HS 61* v Warwks (Birmingham) 1992. BB 5-44 v Yorks (Middlesbrough) 1994. **NWT:** HS 5*. BB 1-71. **BHC:** HS 29 v Kent (Nottingham) 1989. BB 4-44 v Somerset (Nottingham) 1993. **SL:** HS 51* v Middx (Lord's) 1993. BB 4-41 v Northants (Nottingham) 1994.

NEWELL, Michael (West Bridgford CS), b Blackburn, Lancs 25 Feb 1965. 5'8". RHB, LB. Debut 1984. Cap 1987. 1000 runs (1): 1054 (1987). HS 203* v Derbys (Derby) 1987. BB 2-38 v SL (Nottingham) 1988. BAC BB 1-0. **NWT:** HS 60 v Derbys (Derby) 1987. **BHC:** HS 39 v Somerset (Taunton) 1989. **SL:** HS 109* v Essex (Southend) 1990.

NOON, Wayne Michael (Caistor S), b Grimsby, Lincs 5 Feb 1971. 5'9". RHB, WK. Northamptonshire 1989-93. Nottinghamshire debut 1994. Worcs 2nd XI debut when aged 15yr 199d. Tour: SA 1991-92 (Nh). HS 75 v Northants (Nottingham) 1994. **NWT:** HS 34 v Worcs (Worcester) 1994. **BHC:** HS 9. **SL:** HS 27 v Somerset (Taunton) 1994.

PENNETT, David Barrington (Benton Park GS, Rawdon), b Leeds, Yorks 26 Oct 1969. 6'0". RHB, RMF. Debut 1992. HS 29 v Derbys (Nottingham) 1992. BB 5-36 v Durham (Chester-le-St) 1993. **SL:** HS 12* v Durham (Nottingham) 1992. BB 3-32 v Warwks (Nottingham) 1993.

PICK, Robert Andrew (Alderman Derbyshire CS; High Pavement SFC), b Nottingham 19 Nov 1963. 5'10". LHB, RFM. Debut 1983. Cap 1987. Wellington 1989-90. Tours: WI 1991-92 (Eng A); SL 1990-91 (Eng A). HS 65* v Northants (Nottingham) 1994. 50 wkts (4); most – 67 (1991). BB 7-128 v Leics (Leicester) 1990. Awards: NWT 1; BHC 1. **NWT:** HS 34* v Sussex (Hove) 1983. BB 5-22 v Glos (Bristol) 1987. **BHC:** HS 25* v Hants (Southampton) 1991. BB 4-42 v Northants (Nottingham) 1987. **SL:** HS 24 v Yorks (Hull) 1986 and v Hants (Southampton) 1992. BB 4-32 v Glos (Moreton) 1987.

POLLARD, Paul Raymond (Gedling CS), b Carlton, Nottingham 24 Sep 1968. 5'11". LHB, RM. Debut 1987. Cap 1992. 1000 runs (3); most – 1463 (1993). HS 180 v Derbys (Nottingham) 1993. BB 2-79 v Glos (Bristol) 1993. **NWT:** HS 28 v Worcs (Nottingham) 1992. **BHC:** HS 104 v Surrey (Nottingham) 1994. **SL:** HS 123* v Surrey (Oval) 1989.

ROBINSON, Robert Timothy (Dunstable GS; High Pavement SFC; Sheffield U), b Sutton in Ashfield 21 Nov 1958. 6'0". RHB, RM. Debut 1978. Cap 1983. Captain 1988-. Benefit 1992. Wisden 1985. **Tests:** 29 (1984-85 to 1989); HS 175 v A (Leeds) 1985. LOI: 26 (HS 83). Tours: A 1987-88; SA 1989-90 (Eng XI); NZ 1987-88; WI 1985-86; I/SL 1984-85; P 1987-88. 1000 runs (12) inc 2000 (1): 2032 (1984). HS 220* v Yorks (Nottingham) 1990. BB 1-22. Awards: NWT 4; BHC 7. **NWT:** HS 139 v Worcs (Worcester) 1985. **BHC:** HS 120 v Scot (Glasgow) 1985. **SL:** HS 119* v Lancs (Nottingham) 1994.

WALKER, Lyndsay Nicholas Paton (Cardiff HS, NSW), b Armidale, NSW, Australia 22 Jun 1974. 6'0". RHB. Debut 1994. HS 1.

WILEMAN, Jonathan Ritchie (Stancliffe Hall S, Darley Dale; Malvern C; Salford U), b Sheffield, Yorks 19 Aug 1970. 6'1". RHB, RSM. Nottinghamshire debut 1992, scored 109 v CU (Nottingham) in his only f-c innings for the County. Subsequently appeared for Comb U v A (Oxford) 1993 and Minor C v SA (Torquay) 1994. Awaiting BAC debut. Lincolnshire 1993-94. HS 109 (above).

NEWCOMERS

AFZAAL, Usman (Manvers Pierrepont CS), b Rawalpindi, Pakistan 9 Jun 1977. LHB, SLA.

BANTON, Colin, b Simonstown, SA 15 Sep 1969.

BROADHURST, Mark (Kingstone S, Barnsley) , b Worsborough Common, Barnsley, Yorks 20 Jun 1974. 6'0". RHB, RFM. Yorkshire 1991-94. Tour: SA 1992-93 (Y). Awaiting BAC debut. HS 6. BB 3-61 Y v OU (Oxford) 1991. **SL:** HS –.

DEPARTURES (who made first-class appearances in 1994)

ADAMS, James Clive (Jamaica C, Kingston), b Port Maria, Jamaica 9 Jan 1968. 5'11". LHB, SLA, WK. Jamaica 1984-85 to date. Nottinghamshire 1994. **Tests** (WI): 9 (1991-92 to 1993-94); HS 137 v E (Georgetown) 1993-94; BB 4-43 v SA (Bridgetown) 1991-92 – on debut. LOI (WI): 28 (HS 81*; BB 1-2). Tours (WI): E 1993 (RW); A 1992-93; SL 1993-94; Z 1986-87 (Young WI), 1989-90 (Young WI). HS 144* v Somerset (Taunton) 1994. BB 4-43 (Tests). Nt BB 4-63 v Essex (Ilford) 1994. **NWT:** HS 11 v Worcs (Worcester) 1994. **BHC:** HS 86 v Sussex (Nottingham) 1994. **SL:** HS 93* v Surrey (Nottingham) 1994. BB 2-26 v Glam (Nottingham) 1994.

CRAWLEY, Mark Andrew (Manchester GS; Oriel C, Oxford), b Newton-le-Willows, Lancs 16 Dec 1967. Brother of J.P. (see LANCS) and P.M. (CU 1992). 6'3". RHB, RM. Oxford U 1987-90 (blue 1987-88-89-90; captain 1989). Lancashire 1990. Nottinghamshire 1991-94. 1000 runs (1): 1297 (1992). HS 160* v Derbys (Derby) 1992. BB 6-92 OU v Glam (Oxford) 1990. Nt BB 3-18 v OU (Oxford) 1992. BAC BB 3-21 v Derbys (Derby) 1991. Awards: NWT 1; BHC 1. **NWT:** HS 74* and BB 4-26 v Lincs (Nottingham) 1991 (on debut). **BHC:** HS 58 v Glam (Cardiff) 1991. BB 4-43 v Sussex (Nottingham) 1994. **SL:** HS 94* and BB 3-41 v Leics (Nottingham) 1992.

Continued on p 181

NOTTINGHAMSHIRE 1994

RESULTS SUMMARY

	Place	Won	Lost	Drew	Abandoned
Britannic Assurance Championship	**3rd**	8	5	4	
All First-class Matches		8	6	6	
Sunday League	**11th**	6	8		3
NatWest Trophy	2nd Round				
Benson and Hedges Cup	Quarter-Finalist				

BRITANNIC ASSURANCE CHAMPIONSHIP AVERAGES

BATTING AND FIELDING

Cap		*M*	*I*	*NO*	*HS*	*Runs*	*Avge*	*100*	*50*	*Ct/St*
1994	C.C.Lewis	12	19	4	220*	881	58.73	2	5	18
1983	R.T.Robinson	16	27	1	182	1148	44.15	2	9	6
1986	P.Johnson	15	25	2	132	936	40.69	3	4	4
–	G.F.Archer	14	24	–	168	860	35.83	2	4	16
1992	P.R.Pollard	16	28	1	134	863	31.96	2	4	10
1990	K.P.Evans	15	21	4	104	514	30.23	1	3	11
–	J.C.Adams	17	30	3	144*	781	28.92	2	1	16
–	W.M.Noon	17	28	6	75	583	26.50	–	3	37/5
–	W.A.Dessaur	3	6	–	35	108	18.00	–	–	1
–	G.W.Mike	16	24	3	60*	333	15.85	–	1	1
1987	R.A.Pick	13	18	6	65*	175	14.58	–	1	3
–	M.G.Field-Buss	6	8	4	23	57	14.25	–	–	1
–	M.A.Crawley	6	11	–	45	129	11.72	–	–	6
1990	J.A.Afford	12	15	6	10	34	3.77	–	–	5

Also played: R.T.Bates (1 match) 0, 6; R.J.Chapman (1 match) 25, 2; M.P.Dowman (2 matches) 5, 31, 38; J.E.Hindson (4 matches) 6, 3, 11 (2 ct); D.B.Pennett (1 match) did not bat.

BOWLING

	O	*M*	*R*	*W*	*Avge*	*Best*	*5wI*	*10wM*
C.C.Lewis	345.2	69	1082	46	23.52	5-55	2	–
R.A.Pick	437.2	107	1233	46	26.80	6-62	2	–
G.W.Mike	377.5	88	1303	44	29.61	5-44	1	–
J.C.Adams	335.5	125	699	23	30.39	4-63	–	–
K.P.Evans	394.5	99	1112	36	30.88	4-46	–	–
J.A.Afford	466.3	141	1187	35	33.91	5-48	2	–
M.G.Field-Buss	203.1	59	450	10	45.00	2-50	–	–

Also bowled: R.T.Bates 26-6-74-1; R.J.Chapman 17-1-80-1; M.A.Crawley 62-27-101-1; M.P.Dowman 7-1-22-0; J.E.Hindson 106-27-344-8; D.B.Pennett 3-1-9-0; P.R.Pollard 2-0-20-1; R.T.Robinson 2.1-0-31-1.

The First-Class Averages (pp 186-200) give the records of Nottinghamshire players in all first-class county matches (their other opponents being the South Africans, Cambridge U and Oxford U).

NOTTINGHAMSHIRE RECORDS

FIRST-CLASS CRICKET

Highest Total	For	739-7d		v	Leics	Nottingham	1903
	V	706-4d		by	Surrey	Nottingham	1947
Lowest Total	For	13		v	Yorkshire	Nottingham	1901
	V	16		by	Derbyshire	Nottingham	1879
		16		by	Surrey	The Oval	1880
Highest Innings	For	312*	W.W.Keeton	v	Middlesex	The Oval	1939
	V	345	C.G.Macartney	for	Australians	Nottingham	1921

Highest Partnership for each Wicket

1st	391	A.O.Jones/A.Shrewsbury	v	Glos	Bristol	1899
2nd	398	A.Shrewsbury/W.Gunn	v	Sussex	Nottingham	1890
3rd	369	W.Gunn/J.R.Gunn	v	Leics	Nottingham	1903
4th	361	A.O.Jones/J.R.Gunn	v	Essex	Leyton	1905
5th	266	A.Shrewsbury/W.Gunn	v	Sussex	Hove	1884
6th	303*	F.H.Winrow/P.F.Harvey	v	Derbyshire	Nottingham	1947
7th	301	C.C.Lewis/B.N.French	v	Durham	Chester-le-St	1993
8th	220	G.F.H.Heane/R.Winrow	v	Somerset	Nottingham	1935
9th	170	J.C.Adams/K.P.Evans	v	Somerset	Taunton	1994
10th	152	E.B.Alletson/W.Riley	v	Sussex	Hove	1911

Best Bowling	For	10-66	K.Smales	v	Glos	Stroud	1956
(Innings)	V	10-10	H.Verity	for	Yorkshire	Leeds	1932
Best Bowling	For	17-89	F.C.Matthews	v	Northants	Nottingham	1923
(Match)	V	17-89	W.G.Grace	for	Glos	Cheltenham	1877

Most Runs – Season	2620	W.W.Whysall	(av 53.46)	1929
Most Runs – Career	31592	G.Gunn	(av 35.69)	1902-32
Most 100s – Season	9	W.W.Whysall		1928
	9	M.J.Harris		1971
	9	B.C.Broad		1990
Most 100s – Career	65	J.Hardstaff, jr		1930-55
Most Wkts – Season	181	B.Dooland	(av 14.96)	1954
Most Wkts – Career	1653	T.G.Wass	(av 20.34)	1896-1920

LIMITED-OVERS CRICKET

Highest Total	NWT	344-6		v	Northumb	Jesmond	1994
	BHC	296-6		v	Kent	Nottingham	1989
	SL	329-6		v	Derbyshire	Nottingham	1993
Lowest Total	NWT	123		v	Yorkshire	Scarborough	1969
	BHC	74		v	Leics	Leicester	1987
	SL	66		v	Yorkshire	Bradford	1969
Highest Innings	NWT	149*	D.W.Randall	v	Devon	Torquay	1988
	BHC	130*	C.E.B.Rice	v	Scotland	Glasgow	1982
	SL	167*	P.Johnson	v	Kent	Nottingham	1993
Best Bowling	NWT	6-10	K.P.Evans	v	Northumb	Jesmond	1994
	BHC	6-22	M.K.Bore	v	Leics	Leicester	1980
		6-22	C.E.B.Rice	v	Northants	Northampton	1981
	SL	6-12	R.J.Hadlee	v	Lancashire	Nottingham	1980

SOMERSET

Formation of Present Club: 18 August 1875
Colours: Black, White and Maroon
Badge: Somerset Dragon
Championships: (0) Third 1892, 1958, 1963, 1966, 1981
NatWest Trophy/Gillette Cup Winners: (2) 1979, 1983
Benson and Hedges Cup Winners: (2) 1981, 1982
Sunday League Champions: (1) 1979
Match Awards: NWT 46; BHC 55

Chief Executive: P.W.Anderson
The County Ground, Taunton TA1 1JT (☎ 01823 272946)
Captain: A.N.Hayhurst
Scorer: D.A.Oldam
1995 Beneficiary: Somerset CCC

BIRD, Paul James (Backwell CS), b Bristol 7 May 1971. 6'3". RHB, RFM. Debut 1994. HS 7. **SL:** HS 4. BB 1-18.

CADDICK, Andrew Richard (Papanui HS), b Christchurch, NZ 21 Nov 1968. Son of English emigrants – qualified for England 1992. 6'5". RHB, RFM. Debut 1991. Cap 1992. Represented NZ in 1987-88 Youth World Cup. **Tests:** 8 (1993 to 1993-94); HS 29* v WI (Kingston) 1993-94; BB 6-65 v WI (P-o-S) 1993-94. LOI: 5 (HS 21*; BB 3-39). Tours: A 1992-93 (Eng A); WI 1993-94. HS 58* v Sussex (Hove) 1994. 50 wkts (3); most – 71 (1992). BB 9-32 (12-120 match) v Lancs (Taunton) 1993. Award: NWT 1. **NWT:** HS 8. BB 6-30 v Glos (Taunton) 1992. **BHC:** HS 6*. BB 2-20 v Yorks (Taunton) 1992. **SL:** HS 36* v Durham (Hartlepool) 1993. BB 4-18 v Lancs (Manchester) 1992.

DIMOND, Matthew (Castle S; Richard Huish C), b Taunton 24 Sep 1975. 6'1". RHB, RMF. Debut 1994. HS 25* and BB 4-73 v Yorks (Bradford) 1994. **SL:** HS –.

ECCLESTONE, Simon Charles (Bryanston S; Durham U; Keble C, Oxford), b Great Dunmow, Essex 16 Jul 1971. 6'3". LHB, RM. Oxford U 1994 (blue 1994). Somerset debut 1994. Cambridgeshire 1990-94. HS 80* OU v Notts (Oxford) 1994. Sm HS 24 v Durham (Taunton) 1994. BB 4-66 OU v Surrey (Oval) 1994. **BHC:** HS –. **SL:** HS 66 v Durham (Taunton) 1994. BB 4-31 v Essex (W-s-M) 1994.

HALLETT, Jeremy Charles (Millfield S; Durham U), b Yeovil 18 Oct 1970. 6'2". RHB, RMF. Debut 1990. HS 52 Comb Us v NZ (Cambridge) 1994. Sm HS 15 v Glos (Bristol) 1991. BB 4-59 v Kent (Canterbury) 1994. **BHC:** HS 5*. BB 3-36 Comb Us v Worcs (Cambridge) 1991. **SL:** HS 26 v Sussex (Taunton) 1993. BB 3-41 v Glam (Neath) 1990.

HARDEN, Richard John (King's C, Taunton), b Bridgwater 16 Aug 1965. 5'11". RHB, SLA. Debut 1985. Cap 1989. C Districts 1987-88. 1000 runs (6); most – 1460 (1990). HS 187 v Notts (Taunton) 1992. BB 2-7 CD v Canterbury (Blenheim) 1987-88. Sm BB 2-24 v Hants (Taunton) 1986. Award: NWT 1. **NWT:** HS 108* v Scot (Taunton) 1992. **BHC:** HS 76 v Kent (Canterbury) 1992. **SL:** HS 90* v Surrey (Bath) 1992.

HAYHURST, Andrew Neil (Worsley Wardley HS; Eccles SFC; Leeds Poly), b Davyhulme, Manchester 23 Nov 1962. 5'11". RHB, RM. Lancashire 1985-89. Somerset debut/cap 1990. Captain 1994-. Tours: WI 1986-87 (La); Z 1988-89 (La). 1000 runs (3); most –1559 (1990). HS 172* v Glos (Bath) 1991. BB 4-27 La v Middx (Manchester) 1987. Sm BB 3-27 v Yorks (Middlesbrough) 1992. Awards: NWT 2; BHC 2. **NWT:** HS 91* and BB 5-60 v Warwks (Birmingham) 1991. **BHC:** HS 95 v Notts (Nottingham) 1992. BB 4-50 La v Worcs (Worcester) 1987. **SL:** HS 84 La v Leics (Manchester) 1988. BB 4-37 La v Glam (Pontypridd) 1988 and Sm v Sussex (Hove) 1990.

HOLLOWAY, Piran Christopher Laity (Millfield S; Taunton S; Loughborough U), b Helston, Cornwall 1 Oct 1970. 5'8". LHB, WK. Warwickshire 1988-93. Somerset debut 1994. HS 102* Wa v Worcs (Birmingham) 1992. Sm HS 50 v Northants (Taunton) 1994. **NWT:** HS 16 Wa v Norfolk (Lakenham) 1993. **BHC:** HS 27 Comb Us v Derbys (Oxford) 1991. **SL:** HS 51 Wa v Northants (Northampton) 1992.

KERR, Jason Ian Douglas (Withins HS; Bolton C), b Bolton, Lancs 7 Apr 1974. 6'2". RHB, RMF. Debut 1993. HS 19* and BB 3-47 v Essex (Chelmsford) 1993. **NWT:** HS 0. **SL:** HS 17 v Northants (Luton) 1993. BB 3-34 v Essex (Chelmsford) 1993.

LATHWELL, Mark Nicholas (Braunton S, Devon), b Bletchley, Bucks 26 Dec 1971. 5'8". RHB, RM. Debut 1991. Cap 1992. YC 1993. MCC YC. **Tests:** 2 (1993); HS 33 v A (Nottingham) 1993. Tours (Eng A): A 1992-93; SA 1993-94. 1000 runs (3); most – 1230 (1994). HS 206 v Surrey (Bath) 1994. BB 2-21 v Sussex (Hove) 1994. Awards: NWT 1; BHC 1. **NWT:** HS 103 and BB 1-23 v Salop (Telford) 1993. **BHC:** HS 120 v Surrey (Oval) 1994. **SL:** HS 117 v Notts (Taunton) 1994.

MUSHTAQ AHMED, b Sahiwal, Pakistan 28 Jun 1970. 5'5". RHB, LB. Multan 1986-87/1990-91. United Bank 1986-87 to date. Somerset debut/cap 1993. **Tests (P):** 15 (1989-90 to 1994-95); HS 18 v Z (Karachi) 1993-94; BB 3-32 v E (Lord's) 1992. LOI (P): 79 (HS 17*; BB 3-14). Tours (P): E 1992; A 1989-90, 1991-92, 1992-93; WI 1992-93; NZ 1992-93, 1993-94; SL 1994-95. HS 90 and Sm BB 7-91 (12-175 match) v Sussex (Taunton) 1993. 50 wkts (2+1); most – 85 (1993). BB 9-93 Multan v Peshawar (Sahiwal) 1990-91. Award: NWT 1. **NWT:** HS 35 v Surrey (Taunton) 1993. BB 3-26 v Oxon (Aston Rowant) 1994. **BHC:** HS 7. **SL:** HS 32 v Middx (Bath) 1993. BB 3-17 v Glos (Taunton) 1993.

PARSONS, Keith Alan (The Castle S, Taunton; Richard Huish SFC), b Taunton 2 May 1973. Identical twin brother of K.J. (Somerset staff 1992-94). 6'1". RHB, RM. Debut 1992. HS 63 v Sussex (Taunton) 1993. **NWT:** HS 33 v Notts (Nottingham) 1993. BB 2-47 v Salop (Telford) 1993. **SL:** HS 34 v Sussex (Taunton) 1993. BB 1-19.

ROSE, Graham David (Northumberland Park S, Tottenham), b Tottenham, London 12 Apr 1964. 6'4". RHB, RM. Middlesex 1985-86. Somerset debut 1987. Cap 1988. 1000 runs (1): 1000 (1990). HS 138 v Sussex (Taunton) 1993. 50 wkts (2); most – 57 (1988). BB 6-41 M v Worcs (Worcester) 1985 – on debut. Sm BB 6-47 v Warwks (Bath) 1988. Awards: BHC 2. **NWT:** HS 110 v Devon (Torquay) 1990. BB 3-11 v Salop (Telford) 1993. **BHC:** HS 65 v Hants (Southampton) 1992. BB 4-37 v Sussex (Hove) 1990. **SL:** HS 148 v Glam (Neath) 1990. BB 4-26 v Kent (Taunton) 1993.

TRESCOTHICK, Marcus Edward (Sir Bernard Lovell S), b Keynsham 25 Dec 1975. 6'2". LHB, RM. Debut 1993. Captained E U-19 to WI 1994-95. HS 121 v Surrey (Bath) 1994. Award: NWT 1. **NWT:** HS 116 v Oxon (Aston Rowant) 1994. **SL:** HS 74 v Yorks (Leeds) 1994.

TRUMP, Harvey Russell John (Millfield S), b Taunton 11 Oct 1968. 6'0". RHB, OB. Debut 1988. Cap 1994. HS 48 v Notts (Taunton) 1988 – on debut. 50 wkts (1): 51 (1991). BB 7-52 (inc hat-trick; 14-104 match) v Glos (Gloucester) 1992. **NWT:** HS 4. BB 2-44 v Essex (Taunton) 1989. **BHC:** HS 1. BB 2-23 v Yorks (Taunton) 1992. **SL:** HS 19 v Kent (Taunton) 1991. BB 3-19 v Essex (W-s-M) 1994.

TURNER, Robert Julian (Millfield S; Magdalene C, Cambridge), b Malvern, Worcs 25 Nov 1967. 6'1½". RHB, WK. Brother of S.J. (Somerset 1984-85). Cambridge U 1988-91 (blue 1988-89-90-91; captain 1991). Somerset debut 1991. Cap 1994. HS 104* v NZ (Taunton) 1994. BAC HS 101* v Notts (Taunton) 1992. **NWT:** HS 15 v Warwks (Taunton) 1994. **BHC:** HS 25* Comb Us v Surrey (Oxford) 1990. **SL:** HS 37* v Sussex (Hove) 1994.

Van TROOST, Adrianus Pelrus (Spieringshoek C, Schiedam), b Schiedam, Holland 2 Oct 1972. 6'7". RHB, RF. Debut 1991. Qualified for England 1998. Holland 1990 (opened bowling in ICC Trophy final v Zimbabwe). HS 35 v Lancs (Taunton) 1993. BB 6-48 v Essex (Taunton) 1992. **NWT:** HS 17* v Surrey (Taunton) 1993. BB 5-22 v Oxon (Aston Rowant) 1994. **BHC:** HS 9* and BB 2-38 v Notts (Nottingham) 1993. **SL:** HS 9*. BB 4-23 v Notts (Taunton) 1994.

NEWCOMERS

BATTY, Jeremy David (Bingley GS; Horsforth C), b Bradford, Yorks 15 May 1971. 6'1". RHB, OB. Yorkshire 1989-94. Tours (Y): SA 1991-92, 1992-93. HS 51 Y v SL (Leeds) 1991. BAC HS 50 Y v Notts (Nottingham) 1993. BB 6-48 Y v Notts (Worksop) 1991. **NWT:** HS 4. BB 1-17. **BHC:** HS 2*. BB 1-34. **SL:** HS 13* and BB 4-33 Y v Kent (Scarborough) 1991.

BOWLER, Peter Duncan (Educated at Canberra, Australia), b Plymouth, Devon 30 Jul 1963. 6'1". RHB, OB, occ WK. Leicestershire 1986 – first to score hundred on f-c debut for Leics (100* and 62 v Hants). Tasmania 1986-87. Derbyshire 1988-94 (cap 1989); scored 155* v CU (Cambridge) on debut – only instance of hundreds on debut for two counties. 1000 runs (6) inc 2000 (1): 2044 (1992). HS 241* De v Hants (Portsmouth) 1992. BB 3-41 De v Leics (Leicester) 1991 and De v Yorks (Chesterfield) 1991. Awards: BHC 3. **NWT:** HS 111 De v Berks (Derby) 1992. **BHC:** HS 109 De v Somerset (Taunton) 1990. BB 1-15. **SL:** HS 138* De v Somerset (Derby) 1993. BB 3-31 De v Glos (Cheltenham) 1991.

DEPARTURES (who made first-class appearance in 1994)

CLARKE, Vincent Paul (Sacred Heart C, Perth, Australia; Perth C), b Liverpool, Lancs 11 Nov 1971. 6'3". RHB, RM/LB. Somerset 1994. HS 38 v Glos (Bristol) 1994 – on debut. BB 1-93. **BHC:** HS 22 v Surrey (Oval) 1994. **SL:** HS 26 v Leics (Leicester) 1994. BB 1-15 (twice).

DONELAN, Bradleigh Thomas Peter (Finchley Catholic HS), b Park Royal Hospital, Middx 3 Jan 1968. 6'1". RHB, OB. Sussex 1989-93. Somerset 1994 (one match). MCC YC. HS 68* Sx v Hants (Southampton) 1992. Sm HS 0. BB 6-62 (10-136 match) Sx v Glos (Hove) 1992. Sm BB 1-27. **BHC:** HS 9*. BB 1-41. **SL:** HS 19 Sx v Glos (Hove) 1991 and Sx v Lancs (Manchester) 1993. BB 2-39 Sx v Surrey (Oval) 1992.

FLETCHER, Ian (Millfield S; Loughborough U), b Sawbridgeworth, Herts 31 Aug 1971. 5'11". RHB, RM. Somerset 1991-94. Hertfordshire 1990. HS 65* v Middx (Bath) 1993. **NWT:** (Herts) HS 1. **BHC:** HS 9. **SL:** HS 26 v Derbys (Derby) 1993.

FOLLAND, Nicholas Arthur (Exmouth S; Loughborough U), b Bristol 17 Sep 1963. 6'0½". LHB, RM. Debut for MC v Indians (Trowbridge) 1990 scoring 26 and 82. Somerset 1992-94. Devon 1981-92. England Amateurs 1992. Master at Blundell's S. HS 108* v Sussex (Taunton) 1993. Awards: NWT 1; BHC 1. **NWT:** HS 63 v Notts (Nottingham) 1993. **BHC:** HS 100* Minor C v Notts (Nottingham) 1991. **SL:** HS 107* v Leics (W-s-M) 1993.

MALLENDER, N.A. – see NORTHAMPTONSHIRE.

PAYNE, Andrew (Accrington & Rossendale C), b Rawtenstall, Lancs 20 Oct 1973. 5'10". RHB, RMF. Somerset 1992-94. HS 51* v Glos (Taunton) 1992. BB 2-15 v Worcs (Worcester) 1993. **SL:** HS 55* v Kent (Taunton) 1993. BB 4-37 v Lancs (Manchester) 1994.

SOMERSET 1994

RESULTS SUMMARY

	Place	Won	Lost	Drew
Britannic Assurance Championship	11th	7	7	3
All First-class Matches		7	7	4
Sunday League	16th	5	12	
NatWest Trophy	Quarter-Finalist			
Benson and Hedges Cup	1st Round			

BRITANNIC ASSURANCE CHAMPIONSHIP AVERAGES

BATTING AND FIELDING

Cap		M	I	NO	HS	Runs	Avge	100	50	Ct/St
1990	A.N.Hayhurst	17	29	6	121	1166	50.69	2	9	10
–	M.E.Trescothick	11	20	1	121	924	48.63	2	8	13
1989	R.J.Harden	17	30	5	131*	1055	42.20	2	7	13
1992	M.N.Lathwell	17	31	1	206	1219	40.63	2	9	9
–	N.A.Folland	12	21	1	91	642	32.10	–	4	6
1987	N.A.Mallender	8	12	3	43*	270	30.00	–	–	1
1988	G.D.Rose	15	23	2	121	532	25.33	1	2	15
1994	R.J.Turner	17	26	4	64*	433	19.68	–	2	44/5
–	P.C.L.Holloway	4	6	–	50	114	19.00	–	1	1
1994	H.R.J.Trump	13	20	4	45*	276	17.25	–	–	13
–	I.Fletcher	5	9	1	54*	128	16.00	–	1	3
1993	Mushtaq Ahmed	8	13	3	38	145	14.50	–	–	3
1992	A.R.Caddick	11	17	2	58*	211	14.06	–	1	4
–	V.P.Clarke	2	4	–	38	46	11.50	–	–	–
–	K.A.Parsons	3	5	1	16	38	9.50	–	–	2
–	A.P.van Troost	13	17	5	33	107	8.91	–	–	3
–	S.C.Ecclestone	3	5	–	24	42	8.40	–	–	1
–	J.C.Hallett	3	6	1	10	21	4.20	–	–	–

Also batted: P.J.Bird (2 matches) 0*, 7, 5; M.Dimond (3 matches) 25*, 9 (4 ct); B.T.P.Donelan (1 match) 0; J.I.D.Kerr (1 match) 1, 4 (1 ct); A.Payne (1 match) 34.

BOWLING

	O	M	R	W	Avge	Best	5wI	10wM
A.R.Caddick	347.3	67	1126	49	22.97	6-51	3	–
G.D.Rose	324.1	67	1078	42	25.66	4-40	–	–
Mushtaq Ahmed	377	108	1101	40	27.52	7-94	3	1
H.R.J.Trump	250.4	73	789	26	30.34	6-68	2	1
N.A.Mallender	193.4	51	602	16	37.62	3-23	–	–
A.P.van Troost	326.1	53	1299	34	38.20	4-50	–	–

Also bowled: P.J.Bird 44.5-9-166-0; V.P.Clarke 23-4-105-1; M.Dimond 55.3-8-216-5; B.T.P.Donelan 15-2-59-1; S.C.Ecclestone 17-4-57-0; J.C.Hallett 53.2-15-181-4; A.N.Hayhurst 77.4-23-218-7; J.I.D.Kerr 21-3-91-0; M.N.Lathwell 24-4-87-3; K.A.Parsons 4-0-21-0; A.Payne 12-2-54-0.

The First-Class Averages (pp 186-200) give the records of Somerset players in all first-class county matches (their other opponents being the New Zealanders), with the exception of S.C.Ecclestone and J.C.Hallett, whose full county figures are as above.

SOMERSET RECORDS

FIRST-CLASS CRICKET

Highest Total	For	675-9d		v	Hampshire	Bath	1924
	V	811		by	Surrey	The Oval	1899
Lowest Total	For	25		v	Glos	Bristol	1947
	V	22		by	Glos	Bristol	1920
Highest Innings	For	322	I.V.A.Richards	v	Warwicks	Taunton	1985
	V	424	A.C.MacLaren	for	Lancashire	Taunton	1895

Highest Partnership for each Wicket

1st	346	H.T.Hewett/L.C.H.Palairet	v	Yorkshire	Taunton	1892
2nd	290	J.C.W.MacBryan/M.D.Lyon	v	Derbyshire	Buxton	1924
3rd	319	P.M.Roebuck/M.D.Crowe	v	Leics	Taunton	1984
4th	310	P.W.Denning/I.T.Botham	v	Glos	Taunton	1980
5th	235	J.C.White/C.C.C.Case	v	Glos	Taunton	1927
6th	265	W.E.Alley/K.E.Palmer	v	Northants	Northampton	1961
7th	240	S.M.J.Woods/V.T.Hill	v	Kent	Taunton	1898
8th	172	I.V.A.Richards/I.T.Botham	v	Leics	Leicester	1983
9th	183	C.H.M.Greetham/H.W.Stephenson	v	Leics	Weston-s-Mare	1963
	183	C.J.Tavaré/N.A.Mallender	v	Sussex	Hove	1990
10th	143	J.J.Bridges/A.H.D.Gibbs	v	Essex	Weston-s-Mare	1919

Best Bowling	For	10- 49	E.J.Tyler	v	Surrey	Taunton	1895
(Innings)	V	10- 35	A.Drake	for	Yorkshire	Weston-s-Mare	1914
Best Bowling	For	16- 83	J.C.White	v	Worcs	Bath	1919
(Match)	V	17-137	W.Brearley	for	Lancashire	Manchester	1905

Most Runs – Season	2761	W.E.Alley	(av 58.74)	1961
Most Runs – Career	21142	H.Gimblett	(av 36.96)	1935-54
Most 100s – Season	11	S.J.Cook		1991
Most 100s – Career	49	H.Gimblett		1935-54
Most Wkts – Season	169	A.W.Wellard	(av 19.24)	1938
Most Wkts – Career	2166	J.C.White	(av 18.02)	1909-37

LIMITED-OVERS CRICKET

Highest Total	NWT	413-4		v	Devon	Torquay	1990
	BHC	321-5		v	Sussex	Hove	1990
	SL	360-3		v	Glamorgan	Neath	1990
Lowest Total	NWT	59		v	Middlesex	Lord's	1977
	BHC	98		v	Middlesex	Lord's	1982
	SL	58		v	Essex	Chelmsford	1977
Highest Innings	NWT	162*	C.J.Tavaré	v	Devon	Torquay	1990
	BHC	177	S.J.Cook	v	Sussex	Hove	1990
	SL	175*	I.T.Botham	v	Northants	Wellingborough	1986
Best Bowling	NWT	7-15	R.P.Lefebvre	v	Devon	Torquay	1990
	BHC	5-14	J.Garner	v	Surrey	Lord's	1981
	SL	6-24	I.V.A.Richards	v	Lancashire	Manchester	1983

SURREY

Formation of Present Club: 22 August 1845
Colours: Chocolate
Badge: Prince of Wales' Feathers
Championships (since 1890): (15) 1890, 1891, 1892, 1894, 1895, 1899, 1914, 1952, 1953, 1954, 1955, 1956, 1957, 1958, 1971.
Joint: (1) 1950
NatWest Trophy/Gillette Cup Winners: (1) 1982
Benson and Hedges Cup Winners: (1) 1974
Sunday League Champions: (0) Third 1993
Match Awards: NWT 40; BHC 54

Chief Executive: G.A.Woodman
Kennington Oval, London, SE11 5SS (☎ 0171-582 6660)
Captain: A.J.Stewart
Scorer: K.R.Booth
1995 Beneficiary: Surrey CCC 150th Anniversary (Youth Trust)

BAINBRIDGE, Mark Robert (Teddington S; Richmond upon Thames C), b Isleworth, Middx 11 May 1973. 5'9½". RHB, SLA. Surrey staff 1992 – awaiting f-c debut.

BENJAMIN, Joseph Emmanuel (Cayon HS, St Kitts; Mount Pleasant S, Highgate, Birmingham), b Christ Church, St Kitts 2 Feb 1961. 6'2". RHB, RMF. Warwickshire 1988-91. Surrey debut 1992. Cap 1993. Staffordshire 1986-88. **Tests:** 1 (1994); HS 0 and BB 4-42 v SA (Oval) 1994. HS 42 v Kent (Guildford) 1992. 50 wkts (2); most – 80 (1994). BB 6-19 v Notts (Oval) 1993. Award: NWT 1. **NWT:** HS 25 v Worcs (Oval) 1994. BB 3-26 v Staffs (Oval) 1994. **BHC:** HS 20 Wa v Worcs (Birmingham) 1990. BB 3-52 v Glam (Oval) 1994. **SL:** HS 24 Wa v Lancs (Manchester) 1990. BB 4-44 v Middx (Oval) 1992.

BICKNELL, Darren John (Robert Haining SS; Guildford TC), b Guildford 24 Jun 1967. Elder brother of M.P. 6'4". LHB, LM. Debut 1987. Cap 1990. Tours (Eng A): WI 1991-92; P 1990-91; SL 1990-91; Z 1989-90. 1000 runs (6); most – 1888 (1991). HS 235* v Notts (Nottingham) 1994. BB 2-62 v Northants (Northampton) 1991. Awards: NWT 1; BHC 3. **NWT:** HS 135* v Yorks (Oval) 1989. **BHC:** HS 119 v Hants (Oval) 1990. **SL:** HS 125 v Durham (Durham) 1992.

BICKNELL, Martin Paul (Robert Haining SS), b Guildford 14 Jan 1969. Younger brother of D.J. 6'3". RHB, RFM. Debut 1986. Cap 1989. **Tests:** 2 (1993); HS 14 and BB 3-99 v A (Birmingham) 1993. LOI: 7 (HS 31*; BB 3-55). Tours: A 1990-91; SA 1993-94 (Eng A); Z 1989-90 (Eng A). HS 88 v Hants (Southampton) 1992. 50 wkts (5); most – 71 (1992). BB 9-45 v CU (Oval) 1988. BAC BB 7-52 v Sussex (Oval) 1991. Award: BHC 1. **NWT:** HS 66* v Northants (Oval) 1991. BB 4-35 v Somerset (Taunton) 1993. **BHC:** HS 27* v Lancs (Manchester) 1990. BB 4-49 v Somerset (Oval) 1994. **SL:** HS 20* v Northants (Tring) 1991. BB 5-12 v Northants (Oval) 1994.

BROWN, Alistair Duncan (Caterham S), b Beckenham, Kent 11 Feb 1970. 5'10". RHB, occ LB. Debut 1992. Cap 1994. 1000 runs (2); most – 1382 (1993). HS 175 v Durham (Durham) 1992. **NWT:** HS 52 v Worcs (Oval) 1994. **BHC:** HS 41 v Lancs (Oval) 1992. **SL:** HS 142* v Middx (Oval) 1994.

BUTCHER, Mark Alan (Trinity S; Archbishop Tenison's S, Croydon), b Croydon 23 Aug 1972. Son of A.R. (Surrey, Glamorgan and England 1972-92); brother of G.P. (see GLAMORGAN). 5'11". LHB, RM. Debut 1992. HS 134 v Hants (Southampton) 1994. BB 4-31 v Worcs (Oval) 1994. **NWT:** HS 15 and BB 2-57 v Somerset (Taunton) 1993. **BHC:** HS 5. BB 3-37 v Somerset (Oval) 1994. **SL:** HS 48* v Glam (Oval) 1991 (on 1st XI debut and against team captained by his father). BB 3-23 v Sussex (Oval) 1992.

De la PENA, Jason Michael (Stowe S; Bournside S), b London 16 Sep 1972. 6'4". RHB, RFM. Gloucestershire 1991-93. Surrey staff 1994 – no f-c appearances. HS 7*. BB 4-77 Gs v A (Bristol) 1993. **SL:** HS 0*.

HOLLIOAKE, Adam John (St George's C, Weybridge), b Melbourne, Australia 5 Sep 1971. 5'11". RHB, RMF. Debut 1993, scoring 13 and 123 v Derbys (Ilkeston). Qualified for England 1992. HS 138 v Leics (Oval) 1994. BB 4-48 v Sussex (Oval) 1994. **NWT:** HS 60 v Worcs (Oval) 1994. BB 2-40 v Glam (Swansea) 1994. **BHC:** HS 6. BB 3-48 v Notts (Nottingham) 1994. **SL:** HS 72* v Sussex (Oval) 1994. BB 4-33 v Lancs (Oval) 1993.

KENLOCK, Stratford Garfield (**'Mark'**) (Stockwell Manor S), b Portland, Jamaica 16 Apr 1965. 6'0". LHB, LFM. Debut 1994. HS –. BB 3-104 v Kent (Oval) 1994. **SL:** HS –. BB 4-30 v Yorks (Scarborough) 1994.

KENNIS, Gregor John (Tiffin S), b Yokohama, Japan 9 Mar 1974. 6'1". RHB, OB. MCC YC. Debut 1994. HS 23 v OU (Oval) 1994. Awaiting BAC debut.

KERSEY, Graham James (Bexley & Erith Technical HS), b Plumstead, London 19 May 1971. 5'7". RHB, WK. Kent 1991-92. Surrey debut 1993. HS 39 v Durham (Darlington) 1994. **SL:** HS 50 v Durham (Oval) 1993.

PIGOTT, Anthony Charles Shackleton (Harrow S), b Fulham, London 4 Jun 1958. 6'1". RHB, RFM. Sussex 1978-93 (cap 1982; benefit 1991). Surrey debut 1994. Wellington 1982-83/1983-84. **Tests:** 1 (1983-84); HS 8* and BB 2-75 v NZ (Christchurch) 1983-84. Tours: NZ 1979-80 (DHR), 1983-84 (part). HS 104* Sx v Warwks (Birmingham) 1986. Sy HS 40 v Warwks (Guildford) 1994. 50 wkts (5); most – 74 (1988). BB 7-74 Sx v Northants (Eastbourne) 1982. Sy BB 6-46 v Notts (Nottingham) 1994. Hat-trick 1978 (Sx – his first f-c wkts). **NWT:** HS 53 Sx v Derbys (Hove) 1988. BB 3-4 Sx v Ire (Hove) 1985. **BHC:** HS 49* Sx v Essex (Hove) 1989. BB 3-29 Sx v Leics (Hove) 1991. **SL:** HS 51* Sx v Northants (Hove) 1989. BB 5-24 Sx v Lancs (Manchester) 1986.

SARGEANT, Neil Fredrick (Whitmore HS), b Hammersmith 8 Nov 1965. 5'8". RHB, WK. Debut 1989. HS 49 v Lancs (Manchester) 1991. BB 1-88. **SL:** HS 22 v Glos (Cheltenham) 1990.

SMITH, Andrew William (Sutton Manor HS), b Sutton 30 May 1969. Son of W.A. (Surrey 1961-70). 5'8". RHB, OB. Debut 1993. HS 202* v OU (Oval) 1994. BAC HS 68* v Middx (Oval) 1994. BB 5-103 v Somerset (Bath) 1994. Award: NWT 1. **NWT:** HS –. BB 3-25 v Leics (Leicester) 1993. **BHC:** HS 15* and BB 2-38 v Glam (Oval) 1994. **SL:** HS 58 v Derbys (Ilkeston) 1993. BB 2-28 v Leics (Oval) 1994.

STEWART, Alec James (Tiffin S), b Merton 8 Apr 1963. Son of M.J. (Surrey and England 1954-72). 5'11". RHB, WK. Debut 1981. Cap 1985. Captain 1992-. Benefit 1994. Wisden 1992. **Tests:** 43 (1989-90 to 1994, 2 as captain); HS 190 v P (Birmingham) 1992. LOI: 59 (HS 103). Tours: A 1990-91; WI 1989-90, 1993-94; NZ 1991-92; I 1992-93; SL 1992-93 (captain). 1000 runs (8); most – 1665 (1986). HS 206* v Essex (Oval) 1989. BB 1-7. Held 11 catches (equalling world f-c match record) v Leics (Leicester) 1989. Awards: NWT 2; BHC 4. **NWT:** HS 107* v Middx (Oval) 1988. **BHC:** HS 167* v Somerset (Oval) 1994. **SL:** HS 125 v Lancs (Oval) 1990.

THORPE, Graham Paul (Weydon CS; Farnham C), b Farnham 1 Aug 1969. 5'11". LHB, RM. Debut 1988. Cap 1991. **Tests:** 10 (1993 to 1994); HS 114* v A (Nottingham) 1993 – on debut. LOI: 6 (HS 55). Tours: A 1992-93 (Eng A); WI 1991-92 (Eng A), 1993-94; P 1990-91 (Eng A); SL 1990-91 (Eng A); Z 1989-90 (Eng A). 1000 runs (5); most – 1895 (1992). HS 216 v Somerset (Oval) 1992. BB 4-40 v A (Oval) 1993. BAC BB 2-31 v Essex (Oval) 1989. Award: NWT 1. **NWT:** HS 145* v Lancs (Oval) 1994. **BHC:** HS 103 v Lancs (Oval) 1993. BB 3-35 v Middx (Lord's) 1989. **SL:** HS 115* v Lancs (Manchester) 1991. BB 3-21 v Somerset (Oval) 1991.

WAQAR YOUNIS (Government C, Vehari), b Vehari, Pakistan 16 Nov 1971. 6'0". RHB, RF. Multan 1987-88/1990-91. United Bank 1988-89 to date. Surrey 1990-91 and 1993 (cap 1990). Wisden 1991. **Tests** (P): 31 (1989-90 to 1994-95, 1 as captain); HS 29 v WI (Bridgetown) 1992-93; BB 7-76 v NZ (Faisalabad) 1990-91. LOI (P): 88 (HS 37; BB 6-26). Tours (P): E 1992; A 1989-90; WI 1992-93; NZ 1992-93, 1993-94; SL 1994-95. HS 51 United Bank v PIA (Lahore) 1989-90 Qaid-e-Azam Final. Sy HS 31 v Yorks (Guildford) 1991. 50 wkts (3+3) inc 100 (1): 113 (1991). BB 7-64 United Bank v ADBP (Lahore) 1990-91. Sy BB 7-73 v Warwks (Oval) 1990. Awards: NWT 2. **NWT:** HS 26 v Essex (Oval) 1991. BB 5-40 v Northants (Oval) 1991. **BHC:** HS 5*. BB 3-29 v Somerset (Taunton) 1991. **SL:** HS 39 v Hants (Oval) 1993. BB 5-26 v Kent (Oval) 1990.

WARD, David Mark (Haling Manor HS), b Croydon 10 Feb 1961. 6'1". RHB, OB, occ WK. Debut 1985. Cap 1990. 1000 runs (2) inc 2000 (1): 2072 (1990). HS 294* v Derbys (Oval) 1994. BB 2-66 v Glos (Guildford) 1991. Awards: NWT 1; BHC 1. **NWT:** HS 101* v Glam (Swansea) 1992. **BHC:** HS 73 v Notts (Nottingham) 1994. **SL:** HS 102* v Hants (Southampton) 1990.

NEWCOMERS

NOWELL, Richard William (Trinty S, Croydon), b Croydon 29 Dec 1975. LHB, SLA.

RATCLIFFE, Jason David (Sharman's Cross SS; Solihull SFC), b Solihull, Warwks 19 Jun 1969. Son of D.P. (Warwks 1957-68). 6'4". RHB, RM. Warwickshire 1988-94. Tours (Wa): SA 1991-92, 1992-93; Z 1993-94. HS 127* Wa v CU (Cambridge) 1989. BAC HS 101 Wa v Sussex (Birmingham) 1993. BB 1-4. BAC BB 1-6. Awards: NWT 2. **NWT:** HS 105 Wa v Yorks (Leeds) 1993. **BHC:** HS 29 Wa v Surrey (Oval) 1991. **SL:** HS 37 Wa v Somerset (Birmingham) 1989. BB 2-11 Wa v Glam (Neath) 1993.

SHAHID, Nadeem (Ipswich S), b Karachi, Pakistan 23 Apr 1969. 6'0". RHB, LB. Essex 1989-94. Suffolk 1988. 1000 runs (1): 1003 (1990). HS 132 Ex v Kent (Chelmsford) 1992. BB Ex 3-91 v Surrey (Oval) 1990. **NWT:** HS 85* Ex v Glam (Cardiff) 1994. BB 1-0. **BHC:** HS 42 Ex v Hants (Chelmsford) 1991. **SL:** HS 64 Ex v Sussex (Hove) 1993.

SLIPPER, Oliver Michael (St Edward's S, Oxford), b Slough, Bucks 10 Mar 1976. RHB, RM.

TUDOR, Alex Jeremy (St Mark's S, Hammersmith; City of Westminster C), b London 23 Oct 1977. RHB, RFM.

DEPARTURES (who made first-class appearances in 1994)

BOILING, J. – see DURHAM.

CUFFY, Cameron Eustace (St Martins SS), b South Rivers, St Vincent, WI 8 Feb 1970. 6'7". RHB, RF. Windward Is 1990-91 to date. Surrey 1994. HS 14* Windward Is v Leeward Is (Castries) 1992-93. Sy HS 10 v Durham (Darlington) 1994. BB 6-81 Windward Is v Jamaica (Kingston) 1993-94. Sy BB 4-70 v Lancs (Manchester) 1994 (Sy debut). **NWT:** HS 2*. BB 4-43 v Lancs (Oval) 1994. **BHC:** HS –. **SL:** HS –.

KENDRICK, N.M. – see GLAMORGAN.

LYNCH, M.A. – see GLOUCESTERSHIRE.

MURPHY, Anthony John (Xaverian C; Swansea U), b Manchester 6 Aug 1962. 6'0". RHB, RMF. Lancashire 1985-88. Surrey 1989-94. Cheshire 1984-85. Tour: WI 1986-87 (La). HS 38 v Glos (Oval) 1989. 50 wkts (1): 65 (1989). BB 6-97 v Derbys (Derby) 1989. Award: NWT 1. **NWT:** HS 1*. BB 6-26 v Glam (Swansea) 1994. **BHC:** HS 5*. BB 2-23 v Middx (Lord's) 1991. **SL:** HS 9*. BB 4-22 v Glos (Oval) 1989.

THOMPSON, D.J. – see LANCASHIRE.

SURREY 1994

RESULTS SUMMARY

	Place	Won	Lost	Drew	Abandoned
Britannic Assurance Championship	**7th**	7	7	3	
All First-class Matches		7	7	4	
Sunday League	**6th**	9	5		3
NatWest Trophy	Semi-Finalist				
Benson and Hedges Cup	Semi-Finalist				

BRITANNIC ASSURANCE CHAMPIONSHIP AVERAGES

BATTING AND FIELDING

Cap		*M*	*I*	*NO*	*HS*	*Runs*	*Avge*	*100*	*50*	*Ct/St*
1990	D.J.Bicknell	17	28	3	235*	1261	50.44	3	6	4
1991	G.P.Thorpe	14	21	3	190	897	49.83	2	4	9
1994	A.D.Brown	17	24	2	172	1049	47.68	2	6	16
1990	D.M.Ward	16	22	1	294*	921	43.85	1	5	10
1985	A.J.Stewart	10	14	2	142	514	42.83	2	2	15/1
1982	M.A.Lynch	3	6	1	60	208	41.60		1	6
–	M.A.Butcher	11	17	2	134	574	38.26	1	3	19
–	A.J.Hollioake	17	23	3	138	722	36.10	3	3	12
–	J.Boiling	5	4	2	34*	65	32.50	–	–	5
–	A.W.Smith	13	19	3	68*	291	18.18	–	1	3
–	A.C.S.Pigott	8	11	–	40	160	14.54	–	–	1
–	N.M.Kendrick	6	9	2	25	94	13.42	–	–	5
1989	M.P.Bicknell	8	10	2	38	99	12.37	–	–	5
–	G.J.Kersey	6	9	2	39	86	12.28	–	–	16/2
–	N.F.Sargeant	8	11	2	27	91	10.11	–	–	18
1993	J.E.Benjamin	15	16	1	33*	148	9.86	–	–	5
–	C.E.Cuffy	12	15	8	10	42	6.00	–	–	1

Also played (1 match): S.G.Kenlock did not bat (1 ct).

BOWLING

	O	*M*	*R*	*W*	*Avge*	*Best*	*5wI*	*10wM*
J.E.Benjamin	563.2	127	1578	76	20.76	6- 27	5	1
A.C.S.Pigott	268.3	73	737	29	25.41	6- 46	1	–
C.E.Cuffy	389.3	106	1082	36	30.05	4- 70	–	–
M.P.Bicknell	280.4	67	865	27	32.03	5- 44	1	–
A.J.Hollioake	264.1	44	958	26	36.84	4- 48	–	–
M.A.Butcher	195.4	46	637	15	42.46	4- 31	–	–
A.W.Smith	362	66	1283	25	51.32	5-103	1	–

Also bowled: D.J.Bicknell 1-0-1-0; J.Boiling 78-24-171-4; A.D.Brown 15-1-47-0; N.M.Kendrick 153.3-30-500-7; S.G.Kenlock 28-6-104-3; M.A.Lynch 10-2-35-0; A.J.Stewart 2-0-10-0; G.P.Thorpe 5-0-23-0.

The First-Class Averages (pp 186-200) give the records of Surrey players in all first-class county matches (their other opponents being Oxford U), with the exception of J.E.Benjamin, D.J.Bicknell, M.P.Bicknell, A.J.Stewart and G.P.Thorpe whose full county figures are as above.

SURREY RECORDS

FIRST-CLASS CRICKET

Highest Total	For	811		v	Somerset	The Oval	1899
	V	863		by	Lancashire	The Oval	1990
Lowest Total	For	14		v	Essex	Chelmsford	1983
	V	16		by	MCC	Lord's	1872
Highest Innings	For	357*	R.Abel	v	Somerset	The Oval	1899
	V	366	N.H.Fairbrother	for	Lancashire	The Oval	1990

Highest Partnership for each Wicket

1st	428	J.B.Hobbs/A.Sandham	v	Oxford U	The Oval	1926
2nd	371	J.B.Hobbs/E.G.Hayes	v	Hampshire	The Oval	1909
3rd	413	D.J.Bicknell/D.M.Ward	v	Kent	Canterbury	1990
4th	448	R.Abel/T.W.Hayward	v	Yorkshire	The Oval	1899
5th	308	J.N.Crawford/F.C.Holland	v	Somerset	The Oval	1908
6th	298	A.Sandham/H.S.Harrison	v	Sussex	The Oval	1913
7th	262	C.J.Richards/K.T.Medlycott	v	Kent	The Oval	1987
8th	205	I.A.Greig/M.P.Bicknell	v	Lancashire	The Oval	1990
9th	168	E.R.T.Holmes/E.W.J.Brooks	v	Hampshire	The Oval	1936
10th	173	A.Ducat/A.Sandham	v	Essex	Leyton	1921

Best Bowling	For	10-43	T.Rushby	v	Somerset	Taunton	1921
(Innings)	V	10-28	W.P.Howell	for	Australians	The Oval	1899
Best Bowling	For	16-83	G.A.R.Lock	v	Kent	Blackheath	1956
(Match)	V	15-57	W.P.Howell	for	Australians	The Oval	1899

Most Runs – Season	3246	T.W.Hayward	(av 72.13)	1906
Most Runs – Career	43554	J.B.Hobbs	(av 49.72)	1905-34
Most 100s – Season	13	T.W.Hayward		1906
	13	J.B.Hobbs		1925
Most 100s – Career	144	J.B.Hobbs		1905-34
Most Wkts – Season	252	T.Richardson	(av 13.94)	1895
Most Wkts – Career	1755	T.Richardson	(av 17.87)	1892-1904

LIMITED-OVERS CRICKET

Highest Total	NWT	350		v	Worcs	The Oval	1994
	BHC	331-5		v	Hampshire	The Oval	1990
	SL	375-4		v	Yorkshire	Scarborough	1994
Lowest Total	NWT	74		v	Kent	The Oval	1967
	BHC	89		v	Notts	Nottingham	1984
	SL	64		v	Worcs	Worcester	1978
Highest Innings	NWT	146	G.S.Clinton	v	Kent	Canterbury	1985
	BHC	121*	G.S.Clinton	v	Kent	The Oval	1988
	SL	142*	A.D.Brown	v	Middlesex	The Oval	1994
Best Bowling	NWT	7-33	R.D.Jackman	v	Yorkshire	Harrogate	1970
	BHC	5-21	P.H.L.Wilson	v	Comb Us	The Oval	1979
	SL	6-25	Intikhab Alam	v	Derbyshire	The Oval	1974

SUSSEX

Formation of Present Club: 1 March 1839
Substantial Reorganisation: August 1857
Colours: Dark Blue, Light Blue and Gold
Badge: County Arms of Six Martlets
Championships: (0) Second 1902, 1903, 1932, 1933, 1934, 1953, 1981
NatWest Trophy/Gillette Cup Winners: (4) 1963, 1964, 1978, 1986
Benson and Hedges Cup Winners: (0) Semi-Finalists 1982
Sunday League Champions: (1) 1982
Match Awards: NWT 49; BHC 49

Secretary: N.Bett
County Ground, Eaton Road, Hove BN3 3AN (☎ 01273 732161)
Captain: A.P.Wells
Scorer: L.V.Chandler
1995 Beneficiary: Sussex CCC Benefit Trust

ATHEY, Charles **William** Jeffrey (Stainsby SS; Acklam Hall HS), b Middlesbrough, Yorks 27 Sep 1957. 5'9½". RHB, RM. Yorkshire 1976-83 (cap 1980). Gloucestershire 1984-92 (cap 1985; captain 1989; benefit 1990). Sussex debut/cap 1993. **Tests:** 23 (1980 to 1988); HS 123 v P (Lord's) 1987. LOI: 31 (HS 142*). Tours: A 1986-87, 1987-88; SA 1989-90 (Eng A); WI 1980-81; NZ 1979-80 (DHR), 1987-88; P 1987-88; SL 1985-86 (Eng B). 1000 runs (12); most – 1812 (1984). HS 184 Eng B v Sri Lanka (Galle) 1985-86. BAC HS 181 Gs v Sussex (Cheltenham) 1992. Sx HS 169* v Kent (Tunbridge W) 1994. BB 3-3 Gs v Hants (Bristol) 1985. Sx BB 2-40 v Notts (Eastbourne) 1993. Awards: NWT 4; BHC 5. **NWT:** HS 115 Y v Kent (Leeds) 1980. BB 1-18. **BHC:** HS 95 Gs v Northants (Northampton) 1987. BB 4-48 Gs v Comb Us (Bristol) 1984. **SL:** HS 121* Gs v Worcs (Moreton) 1985. BB 5-35 Y v Derbys (Chesterfield) 1981.

GIDDINS, Edward Simon Hunter (Eastbourne C), b Eastbourne 20 Jul 1971. 6'4½". RHB, RMF. Debut 1991. Cap 1994. MCC YC. HS 24 v Essex (Chelmsford) 1994. 50 wkts (1): 60 (1994). BB 5-32 v Derbys (Eastbourne) 1992. **NWT:** HS 13 v Essex (Hove) 1994. BB 2-21 v Northants (Northampton) 1993. **BHC:** HS 0. BB 2-42 v Glam (Cardiff) 1993. **SL:** HS 9*. BB 4-23 v Kent (Tunbridge W) 1994.

GREENFIELD, Keith (Falmer HS), b Brighton 6 Dec 1968. 6'0". RHB, RM. Debut 1987. HS 127* v CU (Hove) 1991. BB 2-40 and BAC HS 107 v Essex (Hove) 1993. Award: NWT 1. **NWT:** HS 96* v Wales (Hove) 1993. BB 2-35 v Glam (Hove) 1993. **BHC:** HS 62 v Leics (Leicester) 1992. BB 1-35. **SL:** HS 79 v Glam (Hove) 1992. BB 3-44 v Worcs (Hove) 1993.

HALL, James William (Chichester HS), b Chichester 30 Mar 1968. 6'3". RHB, OB. Debut 1990. Cap 1992. 1000 runs (2); most – 1140 (1990 – debut season). HS 140* v Lancs (Hove) 1992. Award: BHC 1. **NWT:** HS 47 v Bucks (Beaconsfield) 1992. **BHC:** HS 81 v Surrey (Hove) 1992. **SL:** HS 77 v Notts (Nottingham) 1992.

HEMMINGS, Edward Ernest (Campion S), b Leamington Spa, Warwks 20 Feb 1949. 5'10". RHB, OB. Warwickshire 1966-78 (cap 1974). Nottinghamshire 1979-92 (cap 1980; benefit 1987). Sussex debut/cap 1993. **Tests:** 16 (1982 to 1990-91); HS 95 v A (Sydney) 1982-83; BB 6-58 v NZ (Birmingham) 1990. LOI: 33 (HS 8*; BB 4-52). Tours: A 1982-83, 1987-88, 1990-91; SA 1974-75 (DHR); WI 1982-83 (Int), 1989-90; NZ 1987-88; P 1981-82 (Int), 1987-88. HS 127* Nt v Yorks (Worksop) 1982. Sx HS 17* v Middx (Lord's) 1993. 50 wkts (15); most – 94 (1984). BB 10-175 Int XI v WI XI (Kingston) 1982-83. BAC BB 7-23 Nt v Lancs (Nottingham) 1983.

HEMMINGS – continued:
Sx BB 7-31 (12-58 match) v Leics (Horsham) 1993. 2 hat-tricks: 1977 (Wa), 1984 (Nt). Awards: NWT 1; BHC 1. **NWT:** HS 31* Nt v Staffs (Nottingham) 1985. BB 3-27 Nt v Warwks (Nottingham) 1985. **BHC:** HS 61* Wa v Leics (Birmingham) 1974. BB 4-47 Nt v Glos (Bristol) 1989. **SL:** HS 44* Wa v Kent (Birmingham) 1971. BB 5-22 Wa v Notts (Birmingham) 1974.

HUMPHRIES, Shaun (The Weald, Billingshurst; Kingston C, London), b Horsham 11 Jan 1973. 5'9". RHB, WK. Debut 1993. HS –. Awaiting BAC debut.

JARVIS, Paul William (Bydales CS, Marske), b Redcar, Yorks 29 Jun 1965. 5'10". RHB, RFM. Yorkshire 1981-93 (cap 1986); youngest Yorkshire debutant at 16yr 75d). Sussex debut 1994. **Tests:** 9 (1987-88 to 1992-93); HS 29* and BB 4-107 v WI (Lord's) 1988. LOI: 16 (HS 16*; BB 5-35). Tours: SA 1989-90 (Eng XI); WI 1986-87 (Y); NZ 1987-88; I/SL 1992-93; P 1987-88. HS 80 Y v Northants (Scarborough) 1992. Sx HS 70* v SA (Hove) 1994. 50 wkts (4); most – 81 (1987). BB 7-55 Y v Surrey (Leeds) 1986. Sx BB 7-58 v Somerset (Hove) 1994. Hat-trick 1985 (Y). **NWT:** HS 16 Y v Somerset (Leeds) 1985. BB 4-41 Y v Leics (Leeds) 1987. **BHC:** HS 42 Y v Lancs (Leeds) 1990. BB 4-34 Y v Warwks (Birmingham) 1992. **SL:** HS 38* Y v Glam (Middlesbrough) 1993. BB 6-27 Y v Somerset (Taunton) 1989.

LAW, Danny Richard (Steyning GS), b Lambeth, London 15 Jul 1975. 6'5". RHB, RFM. Debut 1993. HS 11 v Glos (Hove) 1993. BB 2-38 v Worcs (Hove) 1993.

LENHAM, Neil John (Brighton C), b Worthing 17 Dec 1965. Son of L.J. (Sussex 1956-70). 5'11". RHB, RM. Debut 1984. Cap 1990. 1000 runs (3); most – 1663 (1990). HS 222* v Kent (Hove) 1992. BB 4-13 v Durham (Durham) 1993. Awards: NWT 1; BHC 1. **NWT:** HS 82* v Essex (Hove) 1994. BB 2-12 v Ire (Downpatrick) 1990. **BHC:** HS 82 v Somerset (Hove) 1986. BB 1-3. **SL:** HS 86 v Kent (Hove) 1991. BB 5-28 v Durham (Durham) 1993.

LEWRY, Jason David (Durrington HS, Worthing), b Worthing 2 Apr 1971. 6'2". LHB, LMF. Debut 1994. HS 6*. BB 4-40 v Middx (Arundel) 1994. **SL:** HS 1*. BB 2-43 v Middx (Arundel) 1994.

MOORES, Peter (King Edward VI S, Macclesfield), b Macclesfield, Cheshire 18 Dec 1962. 6'0". RHB, WK. Worcestershire 1983-84. Sussex debut 1985. Cap 1989. OFS 1988-89. HS 116 v Somerset (Hove) 1989. **NWT:** HS 26 v Scot (Edinburgh) 1991. **BHC:** HS 76 v Middx (Hove) 1990. **SL:** HS 57 v Hants (Hove) 1992.

NEWELL, Keith (Ifield Community C), b Crawley 25 Mar 1972. Brother of M. (see NEWCOMERS). 6'0". RHB, RM. Sussex staff 1993 – awaiting f-c debut. **SL:** HS 10 v Yorks (Hove) 1994.

NORTH, John Andrew (Chichester HS), b Slindon 19 Nov 1970. 5'9". RHB, RM. Debut 1990. HS 114 v Essex (Hove) 1993. BB 4-47 v SL (Hove) 1991. BAC BB 3-32 v Worcs (Hove) 1993. **NWT:** HS 20 v Wales (Hove) 1993. **BHC:** HS 22 v Scot (Hove) 1991. BB 3-24 v Leics (Leicester) 1992. **SL:** HS 56 v Durham (Horsham) 1992. BB 3-29 v Kent (Hove) 1991.

PEIRCE, Michael **Toby** Edward (Ardingly C; Durham U), b Maidenhead, Berks 14 Jun 1973. 5'10". LHB, SLA. Combined Us 1994. Sussex staff 1993 – awaiting county f-c debut. HS 24 Comb Us v NZ (Cambridge) 1994. **SL:** HS 6.

PHILLIPS, Nicholas Charles (Wm Parker S, Hastings), b Pembury, Kent 10 May 1974. 5'10½". RHB, OB. Debut 1993. HS 37* v SA (Hove) 1994. BB 3-39 v CU (Hove) 1993. Awaiting BAC debut. **SL:** HS 11* v Worcs (Worcester) 1994. BB 2-19 v Somerset (Hove) 1994.

REMY, Carlos Charles (St Aloyous C; Haringey Cricket C), b Castries, St Lucia 24 Jul 1968. 5'9". RHB, RM. Debut 1989. HS 60 v Northants (Northampton) 1994. BB 4-63 v CU (Hove) 1990. BAC BB 3-27 v Lancs (Hove) 1992. **NWT:** HS 1. **SL:** HS 19 v Essex (Hove) 1993. BB 4-31 v Lancs (Hove) 1992.

SALISBURY, Ian David Kenneth (Moulton CS), b Northampton 21 Jan 1970. 5'11". RHB, LB. Debut 1989. Cap 1991. MCC YC. YC 1992. Wisden 1992. **Tests:** 7 (1992 to 1994); HS 50 v P (Manchester) 1992; BB 4-163 v WI (Georgetown) 1993-94. LOI: 4 (HS 5; BB 3-41). Tours: WI 1991-92 (Eng A), 1993-94; I 1992-93; P 1990-91 (Eng A); SL 1990-91 (Eng A). HS 68 v Derbys (Hove) 1990. 50 wkts (2); most – 87 (1992). BB 7-54 (12-138 match) v Yorks (Hove) 1992. Award: BHC 1. **NWT:** HS 14* v Essex (Hove) 1991. BB 3-28 v Bucks (Beaconsfield) 1992. **BHC:** HS 17* and BB 3-40 v Kent (Canterbury) 1991. **SL:** HS 27* v Glos (Cheltenham) 1992. BB 5-30 v Leics (Leicester) 1992.

SMITH, David Mark (Battersea GS), b Balham, London 9 Jan 1956. 6'4". LHB, RM. Surrey 1973-83 and 1987-88 (cap 1980). Worcestershire 1984-86 (cap 1984). Sussex debut/cap 1989. Testimonial 1994. 2nd XI captain 1995. **Tests:** 2 (1985-86); HS 47 v WI (P-of-S) 1985-86. LOI: 2 (HS 10*). Tour: WI 1985-86. 1000 runs (7); most – 1305 (1989). HS 213 v Essex (Southend) 1992. BB 3-40 Sy v Sussex (Oval) 1976. Sx BB –. Awards: NWT 4; BHC 5. **NWT:** HS 124 v Warwks (Lord's) 1993. BB 3-39 Sy v Derbys (Ilkeston) 1976. **BHC:** HS 126 Wo v Warwks (Worcester) 1985. BB 4-29 Sy v Kent (Oval) 1980. **SL:** HS 87* Sy v Hants (Oval) 1980. BB 2-21 Sy v Worcs (Byfleet) 1973.

SPEIGHT, Martin Peter (Hurstpierpoint C; Durham U), b Walsall, Staffs 24 Oct 1967. 5'9". RHB, WK. Debut 1986. Cap 1991. Wellington 1989-90 to date. 1000 runs (3); most – 1375 (1990). HS 184 v Notts (Eastbourne) 1993. BB 1-2. Award: BHC 1. **NWT:** HS 50 v Warwks (Lord's) 1993. **BHC:** HS 83 Comb Us v Glos (Bristol) 1988. **SL:** HS 126 v Somerset (Taunton) 1993.

STEPHENSON, Franklyn Dacosta (Samuel Jackson Prescod Poly), b St James, Barbados 8 Apr 1959. 6'3½". RHB, RFM. Barbados 1981-82 and 1989-90. Tasmania 1981-82. Gloucestershire 1982-83. Nottinghamshire 1988-91 (cap 1988). OFS 1991-92 to date. Sussex debut/cap 1992. Staffordshire 1980. Wisden 1988. Tours (WI XI): SA 1982-83, 1983-84. 1000 runs (1): 1018 (1988). HS 165 Barbados v Leeward Is (Basseterre) 1981-82. Sx HS 133 v Somerset (Hove) 1992. 50 wkts (5) inc 100 (1): 125 (1988). BB 8-47 (15-106 match) Nt v Essex (Nottingham) 1989. Sx BB 7-29 (11-107 match) v Worcs (Worcester) 1992. Scored 111 and 117 and took 11-222 Nt v Yorks (Nottingham) 1988. Double 1988. Awards: NWT 1; BHC 3. **NWT:** HS 40 v Warwks (Birmingham) 1992. BB 3-8 v Bucks (Beaconsfield) 1992. **BHC:** HS 98* Nt v Worcs (Nottingham) 1990. BB 5-30 Nt v Yorks (Nottingham) 1991. **SL:** HS 103 v Surrey (Hove) 1993. BB 5-23 v Essex (Hove) 1993.

WELLS, Alan Peter (Tideway CS, Newhaven), b Newhaven 2 Oct 1961. Younger brother of C.M. (see DERBYSHIRE). 6'0". RHB, RM. Debut 1981. Cap 1986. Captain 1992-. Benefit 1996. Border 1981-82. Tours: SA 1989-90 (Eng XI), 1993-94 (Eng A). 1000 runs (8); most – 1784 (1991). HS 253* v Yorks (Middlesbrough) 1991. BB 3-67 v Worcs (Worcester) 1987. Awards: NWT 2. **NWT:** HS 119 v Bucks (Beaconsfield) 1992. **BHC:** HS 74 v Middx (Hove) 1990. BB 1-17. **SL:** HS 127 v Hants (Portsmouth) 1993. BB 1-0.

NEWCOMERS

BATES, Justin J. (Hurstpierpoint C), b Farnborough, Kent 9 Apr 1976. RHB, OB.

EDWARDS Alexander David (Imberhorne CS, E Grinstead; Loughborough U), b Cuckfield 2 Aug 1975. 6'0". RHB, RFM. **SL:** HS –.

KIRTLEY, Robert **James** (Clifton C), b Eastbourne 10 Jan 1975. RHB, RFM.

NEWELL, Mark (Ifield Community C), b Crawley 19 Dec 1973. Brother of K. (see above). RHB, OB.

SUSSEX 1994

RESULTS SUMMARY

	Place	Won	Lost	Drew	Abandoned
Britannic Assurance Championship	**8th**	7	5	5	
All First-class Matches		7	5	6	
Sunday League	**15th**	5	11		1
NatWest Trophy	1st Round				
Benson and Hedges Cup	2nd Round				

BRITANNIC ASSURANCE CHAMPIONSHIP AVERAGES

BATTING AND FIELDING

Cap		M	I	NO	HS	Runs	Avge	100	50	Ct/St
1991	M.P.Speight	16	28	–	126	950	33.92	1	4	19
1993	C.W.J.Athey	17	32	1	169*	964	31.09	2	3	14
1986	A.P.Wells	17	32	3	84	889	30.65	–	7	15
1990	N.J.Lenham	13	25	1	102	729	30.37	1	4	2
1989	D.M.Smith	7	14	3	74	326	29.63	–	3	6
1992	J.W.Hall	13	25	–	85	729	29.16	–	7	9
1992	F.D.Stephenson	17	28	1	107	752	27.85	1	5	9
1989	P.Moores	17	30	2	70*	733	26.17	–	4	60
–	C.C.Remy	5	9	1	60	168	21.00	–	2	2
1991	I.D.K.Salisbury	15	23	5	49	325	18.05	–	–	19
–	P.W.Jarvis	16	25	4	44	258	12.28	–	–	3
1993	E.E.Hemmings	14	24	12	14*	88	7.33	–	–	5
–	J.D.Lewry	3	6	4	6*	14	7.00	–	–	–
1994	E.S.H.Giddins	16	22	4	24	83	4.61	–	–	2

Also batted (1 match): K Greenfield 35*, 26*.

BOWLING

	O	M	R	W	Avge	Best	5wI	10wM
F.D.Stephenson	480.5	108	1345	67	20.07	6-50	6	2
E.S.H.Giddins	424.4	88	1357	60	22.61	5-38	3	–
I.D.K.Salisbury	430	137	1215	47	25.85	6-55	3	–
E.E.Hemmings	422	140	959	33	29.06	7-66	2	–
P.W.Jarvis	462.2	85	1648	49	33.63	7-58	1	–

Also bowled: C.W.J.Athey 18-1-78-1; K Greenfield 16-1-76-0; N.J.Lenham 9-0-24-0; J.D.Lewry 65-13-209-6; C.C.Remy 41-6-152-3; A.P.Wells 7-2-27-0.

The First-Class Averages (pp 186-200) give the records of Sussex players in all first-class county matches (their other opponents being the South Africans), with the exception of I.D.K.Salisbury, whose full county figures are as above, and:
A.P.Wells 18-34-4-84-893-29.76-0-7-15ct. 14-2-75-1-75.00-1/48.

SUSSEX RECORDS

FIRST-CLASS CRICKET

Highest Total	For	705-8d		v	Surrey	Hastings	1902
	V	726		by	Notts	Nottingham	1895
Lowest Total	For	19		v	Surrey	Godalming	1830
		19		v	Notts	Hove	1873
	V	18		by	Kent	Gravesend	1867
Highest Innings	For	333	K.S.Duleepsinhji	v	Northants	Hove	1930
	V	322	E.Paynter	for	Lancashire	Hove	1937

Highest Partnership for each Wicket

1st	490	E.H.Bowley/J.G.Langridge	v	Middlesex	Hove	1933
2nd	385	E.H.Bowley/M.W.Tate	v	Northants	Hove	1921
3rd	298	K.S.Ranjitsinhji/E.H.Killick	v	Lancashire	Hove	1901
4th	326*	J.Langridge/G.Cox	v	Yorkshire	Leeds	1949
5th	297	J.H.Parks/H.W.Parks	v	Hampshire	Portsmouth	1937
6th	255	K.S.Duleepsinhji/M.W.Tate	v	Northants	Hove	1930
7th	344	K.S.Ranjitsinhji/W.Newham	v	Essex	Leyton	1902
8th	229*	C.L.A.Smith/G.Brann	v	Kent	Hove	1902
9th	178	H.W.Parks/A.F.Wensley	v	Derbyshire	Horsham	1930
10th	156	G.R.Cox/H.R.Butt	v	Cambridge U	Cambridge	1908

Best Bowling	For	10- 48	C.H.G.Bland	v	Kent	Tonbridge	1899
(Innings)	V	9- 11	A.P.Freeman	for	Kent	Hove	1922
Best Bowling	For	17-106	G.R.Cox	v	Warwicks	Horsham	1926
(Match)	V	17- 67	A.P.Freeman	for	Kent	Hove	1922

Most Runs – Season	2850	J.G.Langridge	(av 64.77)	1949
Most Runs – Career	34152	J.G.Langridge	(av 37.69)	1928-55
Most 100s – Season	12	J.G.Langridge		1949
Most 100s – Career	76	J.G.Langridge		1928-55
Most Wkts – Season	198	M.W.Tate	(av 13.47)	1925
Most Wkts – Career	2211	M.W.Tate	(av 17.41)	1912-37

LIMITED-OVERS CRICKET

Highest Total	NWT	327-6		v	Bucks	Beaconsfield	1992
	BHC	305-6		v	Kent	Hove	1982
	SL	312-8		v	Hampshire	Portsmouth	1993
Lowest Total	NWT	49		v	Derbyshire	Chesterfield	1969
	BHC	61		v	Middlesex	Hove	1978
	SL	61		v	Derbyshire	Derby	1978
Highest Innings	NWT	141*	G.D.Mendis	v	Warwicks	Hove	1980
	BHC	117	R.D.V.Knight	v	Surrey	The Oval	1977
		117	C.M.Wells	v	Glamorgan	Swansea	1989
	SL	129	A.W.Greig	v	Yorkshire	Scarborough	1976
Best Bowling	NWT	6- 9	A.I.C.Dodemaide	v	Ireland	Downpatrick	1990
	BHC	5- 8	Imran Khan	v	Northants	Northampton	1978
	SL	7-41	A.N.Jones	v	Notts	Nottingham	1986

WARWICKSHIRE

Formation of Present Club: 8 April 1882
Substantial Reorganisation: 19 January 1884
Colours: Dark Blue, Gold and Silver
Badge: Bear and Ragged Staff
Championships: (4) 1911, 1951, 1972, 1994
NatWest Trophy/Gillette Cup Winners: (4) 1966, 1968, 1989, 1993
Benson and Hedges Cup Winners: (1) 1994
Sunday League Champions: (2) 1980, 1994
Match Awards: NWT 53; BHC 47

General Secretary: D.L.Amiss
County Ground, Edgbaston, Birmingham, B5 7QU (☎ 0121-446 4422)
Captain: D.A.Reeve
Scorer: A.E.Davis
1995 Beneficiary: P.A.Smith

ALTREE, Darren Anthony, b Rugby 30 Sep 1974. RHB, LFM. Warwickshire staff 1994 – awaiting f-c debut.

ASIF DIN, Mohamed (Ladywood CS, Birmingham), b Kampala, Uganda 21 Sep 1960. 5'9½". RHB, LB. Debut 1981. Cap 1987. Benefit 1994. MCC YC. Tours (Wa): SA 1991-92, 1992-93; Z 1993-94. 1000 runs (2); most – 1425 (1988). HS 217 v Mashonaland XI (Harare) 1993-94. UK HS 158* v CU (Cambridge) 1988. BAC HS 140 v Leics (Leicester) 1991. BB 5-61 v Boland (Brackenfell) 1992-93. BAC BB 5-100 v Glam (Birmingham) 1982. Awards: NWT 3; BHC 1. **NWT:** HS 104 v Sussex (Lord's) 1993. BB 5-40 v Herts (St Albans) 1990. **BHC:** HS 137 v Somerset (Birmingham) 1991. BB 1-26. **SL:** HS 132* v Hants (Southampton) 1993. BB 1-11.

BELL, Michael Anthony Vincent (Bishop Milner CS; Dudley TC), b Birmingham 19 Dec 1966. 6'2". RHB, LMF. Debut 1992. MCC YC. Tour (Wa): Z 1993-94. HS 22* and BB 7-48 v Glos (Birmingham) 1993. **BHC:** HS –. BB 2-34 v Middx (Lord's) 1994. **SL:** HS 6*. BB 5-19 v Leics (Birmingham) 1994.

BROWN, Douglas Robert (Alloa Academy; W London IHE), b Stirling, Scotland 29 Oct 1969. 6'2". RHB, RFM. Scotland 1989. Warwickshire debut 1991-92 (SA tour). Tour: SA 1991-92 (Wa). HS 54 v Surrey (Guildford) 1994. BB 4-25 v Essex (Birmingham) 1994. **BHC:** HS 24 Scot v Notts (Glasgow) 1990. BB 3-50 Scot v Northants (Northampton) 1990. **SL:** HS 14 v Middx (Lord's) 1992. BB 3-21 v Hants (Birmingham) 1992.

BURNS, Michael (Walney CS), b Barrow-in-Furness, Lancs 6 Jun 1969. 6'0". RHB, WK, occ RM. Cumberland 1988-90. Debut 1992. HS 78 v CU (Cambridge) 1992. BAC HS 22 v Sussex (Birmingham) 1993. **BHC:** HS 22 v Leics (Leicester) 1993. **SL:** HS 37 v Derbys (Birmingham) 1994.

DAVIS, Richard Peter (King Ethelbert's S, Birchington; Thanet TC), b Westbrook, Margate, Kent 18 Mar 1966. 6'3". RHB, SLA. Kent 1986-93 (cap 1990). Warwickshire debut 1993-94 (Zimbabwe tour). Cap 1994. Tours: Z 1992-93 (K) 1993-94 (Wa). HS 67 K v Hants (Southampton) 1989. Wa HS 35* v Glam (Birmingham) 1994. 50 wkts (2); most – 74 (1992). BB 7-64 K v Durham (Gateshead) 1992. K BB 6-94 v Yorks (Scarborough) 1994. Award: BHC 1. **NWT:** HS 22 K v Warwks (Birmingham) 1992. BB 3-19 K v Bucks (Canterbury) 1988. **BHC:** HS 18* K v Glam (Canterbury) 1993. BB 2-33 K v Sussex (Hove) 1988. **SL:** HS 40* K v Northants (Canterbury) 1991. BB 5-52 K v Somerset (Bath) 1989.

DONALD, Allan Anthony (Grey College HS), b Bloemfontein, SA 20 Oct 1966. 6'2". RHB, RF. OFS 1985-86 to date. Warwickshire 1987-93 (cap 1989). Wisden 1991. **Tests** (SA): 17 (1991-92 to 1994); HS 27 v E (Leeds) 1994; BB 7-84 (12-139 match) v I (Pt Eliz) 1992-93. LOI (SA): 46 (HS 7*; BB 5-29). Tours (SA): E 1994; A 1993-94; WI 1991-92; SL 1993-94. HS 46* OFS v W Province (Cape Town) 1990-91. Wa HS 41 v Notts (Birmingham) 1992. 50 wkts (3+1); most – 86 (1989). BB 8-37 OFS v Transvaal (Johannesburg) 1986-87. Wa BB 7-37 v Durham (Birmingham) 1992. Awards: NWT 3. **NWT:** HS 14* v Northants (Birmingham) 1992. BB 5-12 v Wilts (Birmingham) 1989. **BHC:** HS 23* v Leics (Leicester) 1989. BB 4-28 v Scot (Perth) 1987. **SL:** HS 18* v Middx (Lord's) 1988. BB 4-23 v Surrey (Oval) 1992.

FROST, Tony, b Stoke-on-Trent, Staffs 17 Nov 1975. RHB, WK. Warwickshire staff 1994 – awaiting f-c debut.

GILES, Ashley Fraser (George Abbot S, Guildford), b Chertsey, Surrey 19 Mar 1973. 6'3". RHB, SLA. Debut 1993. HS 23 v Kent (Canterbury) 1993. BB 1-27.

KHAN, Wasim Gulzar (Small Heath CS; Josiah Mason SFC, Erdington), b Birmingham 26 Feb 1971. 6'1". LHB, LB. Warwickshire staff 1991 – awaiting f-c debut. **SL:** HS 7.

MOLES, Andrew James (Finham Park CS; Butts CHE), b Solihull 12 Feb 1961. 5'10". RHB, RM. Debut 1986. Cap 1987. GW 1986-87/1988-89. Tours (Wa): SA 1991-92, 1992-93. 1000 runs (6); most – 1854 (1990). HS 230* GW v N Transvaal B (Verwoerdburg) 1988-89. Wa HS 224* v Glam (Swansea) 1990. BB 3-21 v OU (Oxford) 1987. BAC BB 3-50 v Essex (Chelmsford) 1987. Awards: NWT 2; BHC 1. **NWT:** HS 127 v Bucks (Birmingham) 1987. **BHC:** HS 72 v Scot (Perth) 1987. BB 1-11. **SL:** HS 96* v Glam (Birmingham) 1992. BB 2-24 v Worcs (Worcester) 1987.

MUNTON, Timothy Alan (Sarson HS; King Edward VII Upper S), b Melton Mowbray, Leics 30 Jul 1965. 6'5". RHB, RMF. Debut 1985. Cap 1989. Wisden 1994. **Tests:** 2 (1992); HS 25* v P (Manchester) 1992; BB 2-22 v P (Leeds) 1992. Tours: SA 1992-93 (Wa); WI 1991-92 (Eng A); P 1990-91 (Eng A); SL 1990-91 (Eng A); Z 1993-94 (Wa). HS 47 v Kent (Birmingham) 1992 and v Mashonaland Inv XI (Harare) 1993-94. 50 wkts (5); most – 81 (1994). BB 8-89 (11-128 match) v Middx (Birmingham) 1991. Award: BHC 1. **NWT:** HS 5. BB 3-36 v Kent (Canterbury) 1989. **BHC:** HS 13 v Leics (Leicester) 1989. BB 4-35 v Surrey (Oval) 1991. **SL:** HS 15* v Yorks (Scarborough) 1994. BB 5-23 v Glos (Moreton) 1990.

OSTLER, Dominic Piers (Princethorpe C; Solihull TC), b Solihull 15 Jul 1970. 6'3". RHB, RM. Debut 1990. Cap 1991. Tour: SA 1992-93 (Wa). 1000 runs (4); most – 1284 (1991). HS 192 v Surrey (Guildford) 1992. Awards: NWT 2. **NWT:** HS 104 and BB 1-4 v Norfolk (Lakenham) 1993. **BHC:** HS 65* v Somerset (Taunton) 1992. **SL:** HS 84* v Sussex (Hove) 1994.

PENNEY, Trevor Lionel (Prince Edward S, Salisbury), b Salisbury, Rhodesia 12 Jun 1968. 6'0". RHB, RM. Qualified for England 1992. Debut for Boland 1991-92. Warwickshire debut 1991-92 (SA tour). UK debut v CU (Cambridge) 1992, scoring 102*. Cap 1994. Mashonaland 1993-94. Tours (Wa): SA 1991-92, 1992-93; Z 1993-94. HS 151 v Middx (Lord's) 1992. BB 3-18 Mashonaland v Mashonaland U-24 (Harare) 1993-94. Award: NWT 1. **NWT:** HS 65* v Leics (Leicester) 1994. BB 1-8. **BHC:** HS 39 v Middx (Lord's) 1994. **SL:** HS 83* v Kent (Canterbury) 1993.

PIPER, Keith John (Haringey Cricket C), b Leicester 18 Dec 1969. 5'6". RHB, WK. Debut 1989. Cap 1992. Tours (Wa): SA 1991-92, 1992-93; Z 1993-94. HS 116* v Durham (Birmingham) 1994. BB 1-57. **NWT:** HS 16* v Worcs (Lord's) 1994. **BHC:** HS 11* v Surrey (Oval) 1991. **SL:** HS 30 v Lancs (Manchester) 1990.

POWELL, Michael James (Lawrence Sheriff S, Rugby), b Bolton, Lancs 5 Apr 1975. 5'11". RHB, RM. Warwickshire staff 1994 – awaiting f-c debut.

REEVE, Dermot Alexander (King George V S, Kowloon), b Kowloon, Hong Kong 2 Apr 1963. 6'0". RHB, RMF. Sussex 1983-87 (cap 1986). Warwickshire debut 1988. Cap 1989. Captain 1993-. Benefit 1996. Hong Kong 1982 (ICC Trophy). MCC YC. **Tests:** 3 (1991-92); HS 59 v NZ (Christchurch) 1991-92 (on debut); BB 1-4. LOI: 25 (HS 33*; BB 3-20). Tours (C=captain): SA 1992-93C (Wa); NZ 1991-92; I 1992-93; Z 1993-94C (Wa). 1000 runs (2); most – 1412 (1990). HS 202* v

REEVE – continued:
Northants (Northampton) 1990. 50 wkts (2); most – 55 (1984). BB 7-37 Sx v Lancs (Lytham) 1987. Wa BB 6-73 v Kent (Tunbridge W) 1991. Awards: NWT 4; BHC 2. **NWT:** HS 81* v Sussex (Lord's) 1993. BB 4-20 Sx v Lancs (Lord's) 1986. **BHC:** HS 80 v Essex (Birmingham) 1991. BB 4-42 Sx v Kent (Canterbury) 1987. **SL:** HS 100 v Lancs (Birmingham) 1991. BB 5-23 v Essex (Birmingham) 1988.

SMALL, Gladstone Cleophas (Moseley S; Hall Green TC), b St George, Barbados 18 Oct 1961. 5'11". RHB, RFM. Debut 1979-80 (DHR XI in NZ). Warwickshire debut 1980. Cap 1982. Benefit 1992. S Australia 1985-86. **Tests:** 17 (1986 to 1990); HS 59 v A (Oval) 1989; BB 5-48 v A (Melbourne) 1986-87. LOI: 53 (HS 18*; BB 4-31). Tours: A 1986-87, 1990-91; SA 1992-93 (Wa); WI 1989-90; NZ 1979-80 (DHR); P 1981-82 (Int); Z 1993-94 (Wa). HS 70 v Lancs (Manchester) 1988. 50 wkts (6); most – 80 (1988). BB 7-15 v Notts (Birmingham) 1988. Award: NWT 1. **NWT:** HS 33 v Surrey (Lord's) 1982. BB 3-22 v Glam (Cardiff) 1982. **BHC:** HS 22 v Kent (Canterbury) 1990. BB 4-22 v Glam (Birmingham) 1990. **SL:** HS 40* v Essex (Ilford) 1984. BB 5-29 v Surrey (Birmingham) 1980.

SMITH, Neil Michael Knight (Warwick S), b Birmingham 27 Jul 1967. Son of M.J.K. (Leics, Warwks and England 1951-75). 6'0". RHB, OB. Debut 1987. Cap 1993. MCC YC. Tours (Wa): SA 1991-92; Z 1993-94. HS 161 v Yorks (Leeds) 1989. BB 7-42 v Lancs (Birmingham) 1994. Awards: NWT 1; BHC 1. **NWT:** HS 52 v Yorks (Leeds) 1990. BB 5-17 v Norfolk (Lakenham) 1993. **BHC:** HS 32 v Somerset (Taunton) 1992. BB 3-29 v Middx (Lord's) 1994. **SL:** HS 56 v Derbys (Chesterfield) 1994. BB 5-26 v Lancs (Manchester) 1993.

SMITH, Paul Andrew (Heaton GS), b Jesmond, Northumb 15 Apr 1964. Son of K.D. sr (Leics 1950-51) and brother of K.D. jr (Warwks 1973-85). 6'2". RHB, RFM. Debut 1982. Cap 1986. Benefit 1995. MCC YC. Tour: SA 1991-92 (Wa). 1000 runs (2); most – 1508 (1986). HS 140 v Worcs (Worcester) 1989. BB 6-91 v Derbys (Birmingham) 1992. 2 hat-tricks: 1989, 1990. Awards: BHC 3. **NWT:** HS 79 v Durham (Birmingham) 1986. BB 4-37 v Yorks (Leeds) 1993. **BHC:** HS 74 v Northants (Birmingham) 1989. BB 3-28 v Middx (Lord's) 1991. **SL:** HS 93* v Middx (Birmingham) 1989. BB 5-36 v Worcs (Birmingham) 1993.

TWOSE, Roger Graham (King's C, Taunton), b Torquay, Devon 17 Apr 1968. Nephew of R.W.Tolchard (Leics and England 1965-83). 6'0". LHB, RM. Debut 1989. Cap 1992. N Districts 1989-90. C Districts 1991-92 to date (captain 1993-94). Devon 1988-89. MCC YC. Tours (Wa): SA 1991-92, 1992-93; Z 1993-94. 1000 runs (2); most – 1412 (1992). HS 277* v Glam (Birmingham) 1994. BB 6-28 v Surrey (Guildford) 1994. Awards: NWT 2. **NWT:** HS 110 v Beds (Birmingham) 1994. BB 3-39 v Sussex (Birmingham) 1992. **BHC:** HS 62 v Yorks (Birmingham) 1992. BB 1-33. **SL:** HS 100 v Leics (Birmingham) 1992. BB 3-31 v Durham (Darlington) 1993.

WELCH, Graeme (Hetton CS), b Durham 21 Mar 1972. 5'11½". RHB, RM. Debut 1994. HS 84* v Notts (Birmingham) 1994. BB 4-74 v Yorks (Scarborough) 1994. **NWT:** HS 0*. **SL:** HS 26 v Surrey (Guildford) and v Yorks (Scarborough) 1994. BB 2-30 v Sussex (Hove) 1994.

NEWCOMERS

KNIGHT, Nicholas Verity (Felsted S; Forest Court C, Loughborough U), b Watford, Herts 28 Nov 1969. 6'0". LHB. Essex 1991-94 (cap 1994). HS 157 Ex v Sussex (Chelmsford) 1994. BB 1-61. **NWT:** HS 81* Ex v Cumberland (Chelmsford) 1992. **BHC:** HS 36 Ex v Glos (Bristol) 1991. **SL:** HS 61* Ex v Worcs (Worcester) 1994. BB 1-14.

SINGH, Anurag (King Edward's, Birmingham), b Kanpur, India 9 Sep 1975. RHB, OB.

VESTERGAARD, Søren, b Copenhagen, Denmark 1 Mar 1972. RHB, RMF. Represented Denmark in 1994 ICC Trophy.

DEPARTURES – see p 181

WARWICKSHIRE 1994

RESULTS SUMMARY

	Place	Won	Lost	Drew	Abandoned
Britannic Assurance Championship	1st	11	1	5	
All First-class Matches		11	1	6	
Sunday League	1st	13	3	1	
NatWest Trophy	Finalist				
Benson and Hedges Cup	Winners				

BRITANNIC ASSURANCE CHAMPIONSHIP AVERAGES

BATTING AND FIELDING

Cap		M	I	NO	HS	Runs	Avge	100	50	Ct/St
1994	B.C.Lara	15	25	2	501*	2066	89.82	9	3	11
1992	R.G.Twose	17	30	5	277*	1395	55.80	3	6	8
1987	A.J.Moles	11	20	3	203*	863	50.76	1	5	5
1991	D.P.Ostler	17	28	2	186	1012	38.92	1	6	14
1994	T.L.Penney	15	23	3	111	774	38.70	1	1	14
–	G.Welch	11	15	3	84*	446	37.16	–	4	5
1987	Asif Din	3	4	1	42*	107	35.66	–	–	1
–	D.R.Brown	3	6	2	54	113	28.25	–	1	–
1993	N.M.K.Smith	17	21	4	65	435	25.58	–	2	3
1992	K.J.Piper	17	24	4	116*	454	22.70	1	1	61/5
1986	P.A.Smith	11	16	2	65	313	22.35	–	1	2
–	J.D.Ratcliffe	2	4	–	69	80	20.00	–	1	1
1994	R.P.Davis	11	9	2	35*	131	18.71	–	–	15
1989	D.A.Reeve	8	9	1	33	109	13.62	–	–	18
1989	T.A.Munton	17	17	7	36	106	10.60	–	–	4
1982	G.C.Small	11	10	1	23	78	8.66	–	–	2

Also batted (1 match): M.A.V.Bell 4* (1 ct).

BOWLING

	O	M	R	W	Avge	Best	5wI	10wM
T.A.Munton	693.4	177	1745	81	21.54	7-52	6	2
G.C.Small	339	79	946	36	26.27	5-46	1	–
R.P.Davis	337	99	984	31	31.74	6-94	2	–
P.A.Smith	182	40	594	18	33.00	3-24	–	–
N.M.K.Smith	581	141	1690	49	34.48	7-42	4	–
R.G.Twose	185.5	38	535	15	35.66	6-28	1	–
G.Welch	263	63	949	22	43.13	4-74	–	–

Also bowled: Asif Din 2-0-9-0; M.A.V.Bell 31-5-108-3; D.R.Brown 35-5-118-5; B.C.Lara 21-1-112-0; D.P.Ostler 1.1-0-13-0; D.A.Reeve 138-44-299-8.

The First-Class Averages (pp 186-200) give the records of Warwickshire players in all first-class county matches (their other opponents being Oxford U).

WARWICKSHIRE RECORDS

FIRST-CLASS CRICKET

Highest Total	For	810-4d		v	Durham	Birmingham	1994
	V	887		by	Yorkshire	Birmingham	1896
Lowest Total	For	16		v	Kent	Tonbridge	1913
	V	15		by	Hampshire	Birmingham	1922
Highest Innings	For	501*	B.C.Lara	v	Durham	Birmingham	1994
	V	322	I.V.A.Richards	for	Somerset	Taunton	1985

Highest Partnership for each Wicket

1st	377*	N.F.Horner/K.Ibadulla	v	Surrey	The Oval	1960
2nd	465*	J.A.Jameson/R.B.Kanhai	v	Glos	Birmingham	1974
3rd	327	S.P.Kinneir/W.G.Quaife	v	Lancashire	Birmingham	1901
4th	470	A.I.Kallicharran/G.W.Humpage	v	Lancashire	Southport	1982
5th	322*	B.C.Lara/K.J.Piper	v	Durham	Birmingham	1994
6th	220	H.E.Dollery/J.Buckingham	v	Derbyshire	Derby	1938
7th	250	H.E.Dollery/J.S.Ord	v	Kent	Maidstone	1953
8th	228	A.J.W.Croom/R.E.S.Wyatt	v	Worcs	Dudley	1925
9th	154	G.W.Stephens/A.J.W.Croom	v	Derbyshire	Birmingham	1925
10th	128	F.R.Santall/W.Sanders	v	Yorkshire	Birmingham	1930

Best Bowling (Innings)	For	10-41	J.D.Bannister	v	Comb Servs	Birmingham	1959
	V	10-36	H.Verity	for	Yorkshire	Leeds	1931
Best Bowling (Match)	For	15-76	S.Hargreave	v	Surrey	The Oval	1903
	V	17-92	A.P.Freeman	for	Kent	Folkestone	1932

Most Runs – Season	2417	M.J.K.Smith	(av 60.42)	1959
Most Runs – Career	35146	D.L.Amiss	(av 41.64)	1960-87
Most 100s – Season	9	A.I.Kallicharran		1984
	9	B.C.Lara		1994
Most 100s – Career	78	D.L.Amiss		1960-87
Most Wkts – Season	180	W.E.Hollies	(av 15.13)	1946
Most Wkts – Career	2201	W.E.Hollies	(av 20.45)	1932-57

LIMITED-OVERS CRICKET

Highest Total	NWT	392-5		v	Oxfordshire	Birmingham	1984
	BHC	308-4		v	Scotland	Birmingham	1988
	SL	301-6		v	Essex	Colchester	1982
Lowest Total	NWT	109		v	Kent	Canterbury	1971
	BHC	96		v	Leics	Leicester	1972
	SL	65		v	Kent	Maidstone	1979
Highest Innings	NWT	206	A.I.Kallicharran	v	Oxfordshire	Birmingham	1984
	BHC	137*	T.A.Lloyd	v	Lancashire	Birmingham	1985
	SL	132*	Asif Din	v	Hampshire	Southampton	1993
Best Bowling	NWT	6-32	K.Ibadulla	v	Hampshire	Birmingham	1965
		6-32	A.I.Kallicharran	v	Oxfordshire	Birmingham	1984
	BHC	7-32	R.G.D.Willis	v	Yorkshire	Birmingham	1981
	SL	6-20	N.Gifford	v	Northants	Birmingham	1985

WORCESTERSHIRE

Formation of Present Club: 11 March 1865
Colours: Dark Green and Black
Badge: Shield Argent a Fess between three Pears Sable
Championships: (5) 1964, 1965, 1974, 1988, 1989
NatWest Trophy/Gillette Cup Winners: (1) 1994
Benson and Hedges Cup Winners: (1) 1991
Sunday League Champions: (3) 1971, 1987, 1988
Match Awards: NWT 42; BHC 58

Secretary: Revd M.D.Vockins
County Ground, New Road, Worcester, WR2 4QQ (☎ 01905 422694)
Captain: T.S.Curtis
Scorer: J.W.Sewter
1995 Beneficiary: N.V.Radford

BRINKLEY, James Edward (Marist C, Canberra; Trinity C, Perth), b Helensburgh, Scotland 13 Mar 1974. 6'3". RHB, RFM. Debut 1993-94 (Zimbabwe tour). UK debut 1994. Tour: Z 1993-94 (Wo). HS 10* v Matabeleland Inv XI (Bulawayo) 1993-94 – on debut. BAC HS 5. BB 6-98 v Surrey (Oval) 1994 on UK debut.

BROOKE, Matthew Peter (Bruntcliffe HS, Morley), b Morley, Yorks 14 Apr 1972. 6'2". RHB, RMF. Worcestershire staff 1994 – awaiting f-c debut.

CHURCH, Matthew John (St George's C, Weybridge), b Guildford, Surrey 26 Jul 1972. 6'2". RHB, RM. Debut 1994. MCC YC. HS 38 v Yorks (Worcester) 1994. **SL:** HS 18 v Notts (Worcester) 1994.

CURTIS, Timothy Stephen (Worcester RGS; Durham U; Magdalene C, Cambridge), b Chislehurst, Kent 15 Jan 1960. 5'11". RHB, LB. Debut 1979. Cap 1984. Captain 1992-. Benefit 1994. Cambridge U 1983 (blue). **Tests:** 5 (1988 to 1989), HS 41 v A (Birmingham) 1989. Tours (Wo): Z 1990-91, 1993-94 (captain). 1000 runs (10); most – 1829 (1992). HS 248 v Somerset (Worcester) 1991. BB 2-17 v OU (Oxford) 1991. BAC BB 2-72 v Warwks (Worcester) 1987 and v Derbys (Worcester) 1992. Awards: NWT 6; BHC 2. **NWT:** HS 136* v Surrey (Oval) 1994. BB 1-6. **BHC:** HS 97 v Warwks (Birmingham) 1990. **SL:** HS 124 v Somerset (Taunton) 1990.

EDWARDS, Timothy (Mounts Bay S), b Penzance, Cornwall 24 Jun 1974. 5'3". RHB, WK. Debut 1993. Somerset staff 1991-92 (YTS trainee). HS 47 v OU (Worcester) 1994. BAC HS 30* v Yorks (Worcester) 1994. **SL:** HS 16* v Yorks (Worcester) 1994.

EYERS, Christopher John (Worcester RGS, Staffordshire U), b Aylesbury, Bucks 28 Mar 1972. 6'1". RHB, RM. Worcestershire staff 1993 – awaiting f-c debut.

HAYNES, Gavin Richard (High Park S; King Edward VI S, Stourbridge), b Stourbridge 29 Sep 1969. 5'10". RHB, RM. Debut 1991. Cap 1994. Tour: Z 1993-94 (Wo). 1000 runs (1): 1021 (1994). HS 158 v Kent (Worcester) 1993. BB 3-19 v Hants (Worcester) 1994. Awards: NWT 1; BHC 1. **NWT:** HS 98 and BB 1-9 v Norfolk (Lakenham) 1994. **BHC:** HS 65 v Hants (Worcester) 1994. BB 2-22 v Glam (Cardiff) 1992. **SL:** HS 83 v Hants (Worcester) 1994. BB 2-21 v Warwks (Birmingham) 1993.

HICK, Graeme Ashley (Prince Edward HS, Salisbury), b Salisbury, Rhodesia 23 May 1966. 6'3". RHB, OB. Zimbabwe 1983-84/1985-86. Worcestershire debut 1984. Cap 1986. N Districts 1987-88/1988-89. Queensland 1990-91. Wisden 1986. **Tests:** 29 (1991 to 1994); HS 178 v I (Bombay) 1992-93; BB 4-126 v NZ (Wellington) 1991-92. LOI: 40 (HS 105*; BB 2-7). Tours: E 1985 (Z); WI 1993-94; NZ 1991-92; I 1992-93; SL 1983-84 (Z), 1992-93; Z 1990-91 (Wo). 1000 runs (10+1) inc 2000 (3); most – 2713 (1988); youngest to score 2000 (1986). 1019 runs before June 1988. HS 405* (Worcs record and then second highest in UK f-c matches) v Somerset (Taunton) 1988. BB 5-37 v Glos (Worcester) 1990. Awards: NWT 4; BHC 8. **NWT:** HS 172* v Devon (Worcester) 1987. BB 4-54 v Hants (Worcester)

HICK – continued:
1988 and v Surrey (Oval) 1994. **BHC:** HS 109 v Comb Us (Worcester) 1989. BB 3-36 v Warwks (Birmingham) 1990. **SL:** HS 120* v Essex (Chelmsford) 1993. BB 4-42 v Sussex (Worcester) 1988.

ILLINGWORTH, Richard Keith (Salts GS), b Bradford, Yorks 23 Aug 1963. 5'11". RHB, SLA. Debut 1982. Cap 1986. Natal 1988-89. **Tests:** 2 (1991); HS 13 (twice) and BB 3-110 (including wicket of P.V.Simmons with first ball) v WI (Nottingham) 1991 – on debut. LOI: 18 (HS 14; BB 3-33). Tours: NZ 1991-92; P 1990-91 (Eng A); SL 1990-91 (Eng A); Z 1989-90 (Eng A), 1990-91 (Wo), 1993-94 (Wo). HS 120* v Warwks (Worcester) 1987. 50 wkts (4); most – 75 (1990). BB 7-50 v OU (Oxford) 1985. BAC BB 6-28 v Glos (Gloucester) 1993. **NWT:** HS 22 v Northants (Northampton) 1984. BB 4-20 v Devon (Worcester) 1987. **BHC:** HS 36* v Kent (Worcester) 1990. BB 4-36 v Yorks (Bradford) 1985. **SL:** HS 31 v Yorks (Worcester) 1994. BB 5-24 v Somerset (Worcester) 1983.

LAMPITT, Stuart Richard (Kingswinford S; Dudley TC), b Wolverhampton, Staffs 29 Jul 1966. 5'11". RHB, RMF. Debut 1985. Cap 1989. Tours (Wo): Z 1990-91, 1993-94. HS 122 v Middx (Lord's) 1994. 50 wkts (3); most – 64 (1994). BB 5-32 v Kent (Worcester) 1989. Awards: NWT 1; BHC 3. **NWT:** HS 17 v Glam (Swansea) 1993. BB 5-22 v Suffolk (Bury St E) 1990. **BHC:** HS 41 v Glam (Worcester) 1990. BB 6-26 v Derbys (Derby) 1994. **SL:** HS 41* v Leics (Worcester) 1993. BB 5-67 v Middx (Lord's) 1990.

LEATHERDALE, David Anthony (Pudsey Grangefield S), b Bradford, Yorks 26 Nov 1967. 5'10½". RHB, RM. Debut 1988. Cap 1994. Tour: Z 1993-94 (Wo). HS 157 v Somerset (Worcester) 1991. BB 2-11 v CU (Cambridge) 1994. BAC BB 1-12. **NWT:** HS 43 v Hants (Worcester) 1988. BB 3-14 v Norfolk (Lakenham) 1994. **BHC:** HS 30 v Hants (Worcester) 1994. **SL:** HS 62* v Kent (Folkestone) 1988. BB 2-15 v Warwks (Birmingham) 1994.

MIRZA, Parvaz (Small Heath S), b Birmingham 17 Dec 1970. 5'11". RHB, RM. Debut 1994. Herefordshire 1992. HS 40 v Kent (Canterbury) 1994. BB 4-29 v OU (Worcester) 1994 – on debut. BAC BB 3-48 v Kent (Canterbury) 1994. **SL:** HS 0. BB 2-41 v Surrey (Oval) 1994.

MOODY, Thomas Masson (Guildford GS, WA), b Adelaide, Australia 2 Oct 1965. 6'6½". RHB, RM. W Australia 1985-86 to date. Warwickshire 1990 (cap 1990). Worcestershire 1991-92 (cap 1991) and 1994. **Tests** (A): 8 (1989-90 to 1992-93); HS 106 v SL (Brisbane) 1989-90; BB 1-17. LOI (A): 34 (HS 89; BB 3-56). Tours (A): E 1989; I 1989-90 (WA); SL 1992-93. 1000 runs (3+1); most – 1887 (1991). HS 210 v Warwks (Worcester) 1991. BB 7-43 (10-109 match) WA v Victoria (Perth) 1990-91. Wo/BAC BB 4-24 v Derbys (Derby) 1994. Awards: NWT 2; BHC 5. **NWT:** HS 180* v Surrey (Oval) 1994. BB 2-33 v Norfolk (Lakenham) 1994. **BHC:** HS 110* v Derbys (Worcester) 1991. BB 4-59 v Somerset (Worcester) 1992. **SL:** HS 160 v Kent (Worcester) 1991 (on Wo 1st XI debut). BB 3-18 v Somerset (Taunton) 1994.

NEWPORT, Philip John (High Wycombe RGS; Portsmouth Poly), b High Wycombe, Bucks 11 Oct 1962. 6'3". RHB, RFM. Debut 1982. Cap 1986. Boland 1987-88. N Transvaal 1992-93. Buckinghamshire 1981-82. **Tests:** 3 (1988 to 1990-91); HS 40* v A (Perth) 1990-91; BB 4-87 v SL (Lord's) 1988 (on debut). Tours: A 1990-91 (part); P 1990-91 (Eng A); SL 1990-91 (Eng A); Z 1993-94 (Wo). HS 98 v NZ (Worcester) 1990. BAC HS 96 v Essex (Worcester) 1990. 50 wkts (7); most – 93 (1988). BB 8-52 v Middx (Lord's) 1988. Award: BHC 1. **NWT:** HS 25 v Northants (Northampton) 1984. BB 4-30 v Northants (Worcester) 1994. **BHC:** HS 28 v Kent (Worcester) 1990. BB 5-22 v Warwks (Birmingham) 1987. **SL:** HS 26* v Leics (Leicester) 1987 and v Surrey (Worcester) 1993. BB 4-18 v Glam (Worcester) 1989.

RADFORD, Neal Victor (Athlone BHS, Johannesburg), b Luanshya, N Rhodesia 7 Jun 1957. Brother of W.R. (OFS). 5'11". RHB, RFM. Transvaal 1978-79/1988-89. Lancashire 1980-84. Worcestershire debut/cap 1985. Benefit 1995. Wisden 1985. **Tests:** 3 (1986 to 1987-88); HS 12* v NZ (Lord's) 1986; BB 2-131 v I (Birmingham) 1986. LOI: 6 (HS 0*; BB 1-32). Tours: NZ 1987-88; Z 1990-91 (Wo), 1993-94 (Wo). HS 76*

La v Derbys (Blackpool) 1981. Wo HS 73* v Notts (Nottingham) 1992. 50 wkts (6) inc 100 (2); most – 109 (1987). BB 9-70 v Somerset (Worcester) 1986. Award: NWT 1. **NWT:** HS 37 v Essex (Chelmsford) 1987. BB 7-19 v Beds (Bedford) 1991. **BHC:** HS 40 v Glam (Worcester) 1990. BB 4-25 v Northants (Northampton) 1988. **SL:** HS 70 v Durham (Stockton) 1993. BB 5-32 v Warwks (Worcester) 1987.

RHODES, Steven John (Lapage Middle S; Carlton-Bolling S, Bradford), b Bradford, Yorks 17 Jun 1964. Son of W.E. (Notts 1961-64). 5'7". RHB, WK. Yorkshire 1981-84. Worcestershire debut 1985. Cap 1986. Wisden 1994. **Tests:** 6 (1994); HS 65* v SA (Leeds) 1994. LOI: 6 (HS 56). Tours: SA 1993-94 (Eng A); WI 1991-92 (Eng A); SL 1985-86 (Eng B), 1990-91 (Eng A); Z 1989-90 (Eng A), 1990-91 (Wo), 1993-94 (Wo). HS 116* v Warwks (Worcester) 1992. Awards: NWT 1; BHC 1. **NWT:** HS 61 v Derbys (Worcester) 1989. **BHC:** HS 51* v Warwks (Birmingham) 1987. **SL:** HS 48* v Kent (Worcester) 1989.

SOLANKI, Vikram Singh (Regis S, Wolverhampton), b Udaipur, India 1 Apr 1976. 6'0". RHB, OB. Worcestershire staff 1993 – awaiting f-c debut. **SL:** HS 22 v Middx (Worcester) 1993.

SPIRING, Karl Ruben (Monmouth S), b Southport, Lancs 13 Nov 1974. 5'11". RHB, OB. Debut 1994. HS 56 v OU (Worcester) 1994 – on debut (also scored 52). Awaiting BAC debut. **SL:** HS 7.

TOLLEY, Christopher Mark (King Edward VI C, Stourbridge; Loughborough U), b Kidderminster 30 Dec 1967. 5'9". RHB, LMF. Debut 1989. Cap 1993. Tours (Wo): Z 1990-91, 1993-94. HS 84 v Derbys (Derby) 1994. BB 5-55 v Kent (Worcester) 1993. Award: BHC 1. **NWT:** HS 12* v Glam (Swansea) 1993. BB 3-25 v Derbys (Worcester) 1993. **BHC:** HS 77 Comb Us v Lancs (Cambridge) 1990. BB 1-12. **SL:** HS 5*. BB 4-50 v Hants (Portsmouth) 1993.

WESTON, William **Philip** Christopher (Durham S), b Durham 16 Jun 1973. Son of M.P. (Durham; England RFU); brother of R.M.S. (see DURHAM). 6'3". LHB, LM. Debut 1991. Tour: Z 1993-94 (Wo). HS 113 v OU (Worcester) 1993. BAC HS 109 v Derbys (Kidderminster) 1993. BB 2-39 v P (Worcester) 1992. BAC BB –. **NWT:** HS 31 v Scot (Edinburgh) 1993. **BHC:** HS 32* v Essex (Worcester) 1993. **SL:** HS 26 v Lancs (Worcester) 1993.

WYLIE, Alex (Bromsgrove S; Warwick C of Ag), b Tamworth, Staffs 20 Feb 1973. 6'2½". LHB, RF. Debut 1993. HS 0. BB 1-50.

NEWCOMERS

ELLIS, Scott William Kenneth (Shrewsbury S), b Newcastle-under-Lyme, Staffs 3 Oct 1975. RHB, RMF.

WARDLE, Craig Richard (Bolton Catholic SFC), b Bury, Lancs 3 Oct 1975. RHB, SLA.

DEPARTURES (who made first-class appearances in 1994)

D'OLIVEIRA, Damian Basil (Blessed Edward Oldcorne SS), b Cape Town, SA 19 Oct 1960. Son of B.L. (Worcs and England 1964-80). 5'9". RHB, OB. Worcestershire 1982-94 (cap 1985; joint benefit 1993). MCC YC. Tours: Z 1984-85 (EC), 1990-91 (Wo), 1993-94. 1000 runs (4); most – 1263 (1990). HS 237 v OU (Oxford) 1991. BAC HS 155 v Lancs (Manchester) 1990. BB 4-68 v OU (Worcester) 1994. BAC BB 3-36 v Essex (Chelmsford) 1993. Awards: NWT 2; BHC 2. **NWT:** HS 99 v Oxon (Worcester) 1986. BB 2-17 v Suffolk (Bury St E) 1990. **BHC:** HS 66 v Yorks (Leeds) 1986. BB 3-12 v Scot (Glasgow) 1986. **SL:** HS 103 v Surrey (Worcester) 1985. BB 3-23 v Derbys (Derby) 1983. Appointed 2nd XI captain and assistant coach 1995.

SEYMOUR, Adam Charles Hylton (Millfield S), b Royston, Cambs 7 Dec 1967. 6'2". LHB, RM. Essex 1988-91. Worcestershire 1992-94. Tour: Z 1993-94 (Wo). HS 157 Ex v Glam (Cardiff) 1991. Wo HS 133 v OU (Oxford) 1992 – on Wo debut. **NWT:** HS 25 and BB 1-5 v Norfolk (Lakenham) 1994. **BHC:** HS 23 v Comb Us (Oxford) 1992. **SL:** HS 57 v Sussex (Worcester) 1994.

WORCESTERSHIRE 1994

RESULTS SUMMARY

	Place	Won	Lost	Drew	Abandoned
Britannic Assurance Championship	**15th**	4	6	7	
All First-class Matches		5	6	9	
Sunday League	**2nd**	12	4		1
NatWest Trophy	**Winners**				
Benson and Hedges Cup	**Finalist**				

BRITANNIC ASSURANCE CHAMPIONSHIP AVERAGES

BATTING AND FIELDING

Cap		*M*	*I*	*NO*	*HS*	*Runs*	*Avge*	*100*	*50*	*Ct/St*
1986	G.A.Hick	10	17	–	215	996	58.58	4	2	10
1986	S.J.Rhodes	10	16	6	76*	525	52.50	–	4	27/6
1991	T.M.Moody	16	25	2	159	1049	45.60	3	5	18
1994	D.A.Leatherdale	15	23	2	139	800	38.09	1	3	17
1984	T.S.Curtis	16	28	1	180	903	33.44	3	1	7
–	W.P.C.Weston	15	24	1	94	728	31.65	–	6	5
1994	G.R.Haynes	17	28	1	141	827	30.62	1	3	10
1989	S.R.Lampitt	15	23	3	122	586	29.30	1	2	11
1993	C.M.Tolley	5	8	1	84	161	23.00	–	1	1
–	T.Edwards	7	9	6	30*	64	21.33	–	–	15
1986	R.K.Illingworth	17	23	4	59*	384	20.21	–	2	8
1986	P.J.Newport	15	21	5	41	313	19.56	–	–	3
–	P.Mirza	2	4	1	40	47	15.66	–	–	1
–	M.J.Church	3	5	–	38	65	13.00	–	–	1
1985	N.V.Radford	14	20	4	25	161	10.06	–	–	4
–	J.E.Brinkley	7	9	2	5	16	2.28	–	–	3

Also batted: D.B.D'Oliveira (1 match – cap 1985) 19, 48; A.C.H.Seymour (2 matches) 7, 27, 31.

BOWLING

	O	*M*	*R*	*W*	*Avge*	*Best*	*5wI*	*10wM*
S.R.Lampitt	498	124	1442	60	24.03	5-33	2	–
R.K.Illingworth	611	184	1401	48	29.18	4-51	–	–
P.J.Newport	480.2	96	1538	51	30.15	4-50	–	–
N.V.Radford	427.1	97	1323	35	37.80	5-93	1	–
T.M.Moody	183	46	533	14	38.07	4-24	–	–
J.E.Brinkley	187	32	637	10	63.70	6-98	1	–

Also bowled: M.J.Church 1-0-4-0; T.S.Curtis 8-1-43-0; D.B.D'Oliveira 23-2-85-2; G.R.Haynes 104.3-23-305-7; G.A.Hick 101.2-24-314-7; D.A.Leatherdale 80.1-12-278-2; P.Mirza 48-13-162-4; C.M.Tolley 118-23-413-7; W.P.C.Weston 13-4-47-0.

The First-Class Averages (pp 186-200) give the records of Worcestershire players in all first-class county matches (their other opponents being the New Zealanders, Cambridge U and Oxford U), with the exception of:

G.A.Hick 11-19-0-215-1101-57.94-4-3-11ct. 107.2-24-343-8-42.87-3/64.

S.J.Rhodes 11-18-7-100*-628-57.09-1-4-29ct-6st. Did not bowl.

WORCESTERSHIRE RECORDS

FIRST-CLASS CRICKET

Highest Total	For	633		v Warwicks	Worcester	1906
	V	701-4d		by Leics	Worcester	1906
Lowest Total	For	24		v Yorkshire	Huddersfield	1903
	V	30		by Hampshire	Worcester	1903
Highest Innings	For	405*	G.A.Hick	v Somerset	Taunton	1988
	V	331*	J.D.B.Robertson	for Middlesex	Worcester	1949

Highest Partnership for each Wicket

1st	309	F.L.Bowley/H.K.Foster	v	Derbyshire	Derby	1901
2nd	287*	T.S.Curtis/G.A.Hick	v	Glamorgan	Neath	1986
3rd	314	M.J.Horton/T.W.Graveney	v	Somerset	Worcester	1962
4th	281	J.A.Ormrod/Younis Ahmed	v	Notts	Nottingham	1979
5th	393	E.G.Arnold/W.B.Burns	v	Warwicks	Birmingham	1909
6th	265	G.A.Hick/S.J.Rhodes	v	Somerset	Taunton	1988
7th	205	G.A.Hick/P.J.Newport	v	Yorkshire	Worcester	1988
8th	184	S.J.Rhodes/S.R.Lampitt	v	Derbyshire	Kidderminster	1991
9th	181	J.A.Cuffe/R.D.Burrows	v	Glos	Worcester	1907
10th	119	W.B.Burns/G.A.Wilson	v	Somerset	Worcester	1906

Best Bowling	For	9- 23	C.F.Root	v Lancashire	Worcester	1931
(Innings)	V	10- 51	J.Mercer	for Glamorgan	Worcester	1936
Best Bowling	For	15- 87	A.J.Conway	v Glos	Moreton-in-M	1914
(Match)	V	17-212	J.C.Clay	for Glamorgan	Swansea	1937

Most Runs – Season	2654	H.H.I.Gibbons	(av 52.03)	1934
Most Runs – Career	33490	D.Kenyon	(av 33.19)	1946-67
Most 100s – Season	10	G.M.Turner		1970
	10	G.A.Hick		1988
Most 100s – Career	72	G.M.Turner		1967-82
Most Wkts – Season	207	C.F.Root	(av 17.52)	1925
Most Wkts – Career	2143	R.T.D.Perks	(av 23.73)	1930-55

LIMITED-OVERS CRICKET

Highest Total	NWT	404-3		v Devon	Worcester	1987
	BHC	314-5		v Lancashire	Manchester	1980
	SL	307-4		v Derbyshire	Worcester	1975
Lowest Total	NWT	98		v Durham	Chester-le-St	1968
	BHC	81		v Leics	Worcester	1983
	SL	86		v Yorkshire	Leeds	1969
Highest Innings	NWT	180*	T.M.Moody	v Surrey	The Oval	1994
	BHC	143*	G.M.Turner	v Warwicks	Birmingham	1976
	SL	160	T.M.Moody	v Kent	Worcester	1991
Best Bowling	NWT	7-19	N.V.Radford	v Beds	Bedford	1991
	BHC	6- 8	N.Gifford	v Minor C (S)	High Wycombe	1979
	SL	6-26	A.P.Pridgeon	v Surrey	Worcester	1978

YORKSHIRE

Formation of Present Club: 8 January 1863
Substantial Reorganisation: 10 December 1891
Colours: Dark Blue, Light Blue and Gold
Badge: White Rose
Championships (since 1890): (29) 1893, 1896, 1898, 1900, 1901, 1902, 1905, 1908, 1912, 1919, 1922, 1923, 1924, 1925, 1931, 1932, 1933, 1935, 1937, 1938, 1939, 1946, 1959, 1960, 1962, 1963, 1966, 1967, 1968. Joint: (1) 1949
NatWest Trophy/Gillette Cup Winners: (2) 1965, 1969
Benson and Hedges Cup Winners: (1) 1987
Sunday League Champions: (1) 1983
Match Awards: NWT 26; BHC 55

Chief Executive: C.D.Hassell. **Secretary:** D.Ryder
Headingley Cricket Ground, Leeds, LS6 3BU (☎ 0113-278 7394)
Captain: M.D.Moxon
Scorer: J.T.Potter
1995 Beneficiary: A.A.Metcalfe

BLAKEY, Richard John (Rastrick GS), b Huddersfield 15 Jan 1967. 5'9". RHB, WK. Debut 1985. Cap 1987. YC 1987. **Tests:** 2 (1992-93); HS 6. LOI: 3 (HS 25). Tours: SA 1991-92 (Y); WI 1986-87 (Y); I 1992-93; P 1990-91 (Eng A); SL 1990-91 (Eng A); Z 1989-90 (Eng A). 1000 runs (5); most – 1361 (1987). HS 221 Eng A v Z (Bulawayo) 1989-90. Y HS 204* v Glos (Leeds) 1987. BB 1-68. Awards: BHC 2. **NWT:** HS 75 v Warwks (Leeds) 1993. **BHC:** HS 79 v Surrey (Oval) 1990. **SL:** HS 130* v Kent (Scarborough) 1991.

BYAS, David (Scarborough C), b Kilham 26 Aug 1963. 6'4". LHB, RM. Debut 1986. Cap 1991. Tours (Y): SA 1991-92, 1992-93. 1000 runs (3); most – 1557 (1991). HS 156 v Essex (Chelmsford) 1993. BB 3-55 v Derbys (Chesterfield) 1990. **NWT:** HS 71 v Somerset (Leeds) 1994. BB 1-23. **BHC:** HS 92 v Hants (Leeds) 1991. BB 2-38 v Somerset (Leeds) 1989. **SL:** HS 106* v Derbys (Chesterfield) 1993. BB 3-19 v Notts (Leeds) 1989.

CHAPMAN, Colin Anthony (Beckfoot GS, Bingley; Bradford & Ilkley Art C), b Bradford 8 Jun 1971. 5'8½". RHB, WK. Debut 1990. Tour: SA 1992-93 (Y). HS 20 v Middx (Uxbridge) 1990. **SL:** HS 36* v Middx (Scarborough) 1990.

GOUGH, Darren (Priory CS, Lundwood), b Barnsley 18 Sep 1970. 5'11". RHB, RFM. Debut 1989. Cap 1993. **Tests:** 4 (1994); HS 65 v NZ (Manchester) 1994 – on debut; BB 4-46 v SA (Lord's) 1994. LOI: 3 (HS –; BB 2-36). Tours: SA 1991-92 (Y), 1992-93 (Y), 1993-94 (Eng A). HS 72 v Northants (Northampton) 1991. 50 wkts (2); most – 62 (1994). BB 7-42 (10-96 match) v Somerset (Taunton) 1993. **NWT:** HS 16 and BB 3-31 v Warwks (Leeds) 1993. **BHC:** HS 7*. BB 2-29 v Somerset (Taunton) and v Kent (Leeds) 1992. **SL:** HS 72* v Leics (Leicester) 1991. BB 5-13 v Sussex (Hove) 1994.

GRAYSON, Adrian **Paul** (Bedale CS), b Ripon 31 Mar 1971. 6'1". RHB, SLA. Debut 1990. Tour: SA 1991-92 (Y). 1000 runs (1): 1046 (1994). HS 100 v Worcs (Worcester) 1994. BB 2-43 v Hants (Leeds) 1994. **NWT:** HS 29 v Devon (Exmouth) 1994. BB 1-25. **BHC:** HS 22* and BB 1-30 v Hants (Southampton) 1994. **SL:** HS 55 v Kent (Maidstone) 1994. BB 4-25 v Glam (Cardiff) 1994.

HAMILTON, Gavin Mark (Hurstmere SS, Kent), b Broxburn, Scotland 16 Sep 1974. 6'1". RHB, RFM. Scotland 1993-94. Yorkshire debut 1994. HS 48 v Kent (Maidstone) 1994. BB 5-65 Scot v Ire (Eglinton) 1993. Y BB 2-76 v Kent (Maidstone) 1994. **SL:** HS 16* v Kent (Maidstone) 1994. BB 2-27 v Warwks (Scarborough) 1994.

HARTLEY, Peter John (Greenhead GS; Bradford C), b Keighley 18 Apr 1960. 6'0". RHB, RMF. Warwickshire 1982. Yorkshire debut 1985. Cap 1987. Tours (Y): SA 1991-92; WI 1986-87. HS 127* v Lancs (Manchester) 1988. 50 wkts (4); most – 61 (1994). BB 8-111 v Sussex (Hove) 1992. Awards: NWT 1; BHC 1. **NWT:** HS 52 and BB 5-46 v Hants (Southampton) 1990. **BHC:** HS 29* v Notts (Nottingham) 1986. BB 5-43 v Scot (Leeds) 1986. **SL:** HS 51 v Northants (Tring) 1990. BB 5-36 v Sussex (Scarborough) 1993.

KELLETT, Simon Andrew (Whitcliffe Mount S), b Mirfield 16 Oct 1967. 6'2". RHB. Debut 1989. Cap 1992. Wellington 1991-92. Tours (Y): SA 1991-92, 1992-93. 1000 runs (2); most – 1326 (1992). HS 125* v Derbys (Chesterfield) 1991. **NWT:** HS 38 v Northumb (Leeds) 1992. **BHC:** HS 45 v Surrey (Oval) 1990. **SL:** HS 118* v Derbys (Leeds) 1992.

KETTLEBOROUGH, Richard Allan (Worksop C), b Sheffield 15 Mar 1973. 6'0". LHB, RM. Debut 1994. HS 25 v Northants (Luton) 1994 – on debut. **SL:** HS 28 v Somerset (Leeds) 1994. BB 1-17.

McGRATH, Anthony (Yorkshire Martyrs Collegiate S), b Bradford 6 Oct 1975. 6'2". RHB, OB. Yorkshire staff 1994 – awaiting f-c debut.

METCALFE, Ashley Anthony (Bradford GS; University C, London), b Horsforth 25 Dec 1963. 5'8". RHB, OB. Debut 1983 v Notts (Bradford), scoring 122. Cap 1986. Benefit 1995. YC 1986. OFS 1988-89. Tours (Y): SA 1991-92, 1992-93; WI 1986-87. 1000 runs (6) inc 2000 (1): 2047 (1990). HS 216* v Middx (Leeds) 1988. BB 2-18 v Warwks (Scarborough) 1987. Awards: NWT 2; BHC 5. **NWT:** HS 127* v Warwks (Leeds) 1990. BB 2-44 v Wilts (Trowbridge) 1987. **BHC:** HS 114 v Lancs (Manchester) 1991. **SL:** HS 116 v Middx (Lord's) 1991.

MILBURN, Stuart Mark (Upper Nidderdale HS), b Harrogate 29 Sep 1972. 6'1". RHB, RMF. Debut 1992. HS 5. BB 2-74 v Worcs (Worcester) 1994.

MOXON, Martyn Douglas (Holgate GS, Barnsley), b Barnsley 4 May 1960. 6'0". RHB, RM. Debut 1981 v Essex (Leeds), scoring 5 and 116. Cap 1984. Captain 1990-. Benefit 1993. GW 1982-83/1983-84. Wisden 1992. **Tests:** 10 (1986 to 1989); HS 99 v NZ (Auckland) 1987-88. LOI: 8 (HS 70). Tours (C=captain): A 1987-88, 1992-93C (Eng A); SA 1992-93C (Y); WI 1986-87 (Y); NZ 1987-88; I 1984-85; SL 1984-85, 1985-86 (Eng B). 1000 runs (10); most – 1669 (1991). HS 274* v Worcs (Worcester) 1994. BB 3-24 v Hants (Southampton) 1989. Awards: NWT 4; BHC 7. **NWT:** HS 107* v Warwks (Leeds) 1990. BB 2-19 v Norfolk (Leeds) 1990. **BHC:** HS 141* v Glam (Cardiff) 1991. BB 5-31 v Warwks (Leeds) 1991. **SL:** HS 129* v Surrey (Oval) 1991. BB 3-29 v Sussex (Hove) 1990.

PARKER, Bradley (Bingley GS), b Mirfield 23 Jun 1970. 5'11". RHB, RM. Debut 1992. HS 127 v Surrey (Scarborough) 1994. **SL:** HS 36 v Sussex (Hove) 1994.

ROBINSON, Mark Andrew (Hull GS), b Hull 23 Nov 1966. 6'3". RHB, RFM. Northamptonshire 1987-90 (cap 1990). Canterbury 1988-89. Yorkshire debut 1991. Cap 1992. Tours (Y): SA 1991-92, 1992-93. Failed to score in 12 successive f-c innings 1990 – world record. HS 19* Nh v Essex (Chelmsford) 1988. Y HS 16* v Essex (Chelmsford) 1993. 50 wkts (1): 50 (1992). BB 9-37 (12-124 match) v Northants (Harrogate) 1993. Award: BHC 1. **NWT:** HS 3*. BB 4-32 Nh v Somerset (Taunton) 1989. **BHC:** HS 3*. BB 3-20 Nh v Scot (Glasgow) 1989. **SL:** HS 6*. BB 4-23 v Northants (Leeds) 1993.

SILVERWOOD, Christopher Eric Wilfred (Garforth CS), b Pontefract 5 Mar 1975. 6'1". RHB, RFM. Debut 1993. HS 26 v Essex (Leeds) 1994. BB 4-67 v Durham (Durham) 1994. **NWT:** HS 8*. BB 1-38. **BHC:** HS 2. BB 1-19. **SL:** HS 9. BB 3-29 v Worcs (Worcester) 1994.

STEMP, Richard David (Brittania HS, Rowley Regis), b Erdington, Birmingham 11 Dec 1967. 6'0". RHB, SLA. Worcestershire 1990-92. Yorkshire debut 1993. Tour: SA 1992-93 (Y). HS 37 v Essex (Chelmsford) 1993. BB 6-37 v Durham (Durham) 1994. **NWT:** HS 1*. BB 1-31. **BHC:** HS –. **SL:** HS 23* v Warwks (Birmingham) 1993. BB 3-18 Wo v Derbys (Worcester) 1991.

VAUGHAN, Michael Paul (Silverdale CS, Sheffield), b Manchester, Lancs 29 Oct 1974. 6'2". RHB, OB. Debut 1993. 1000 runs (1): 1066 (1994). HS 117 v Northants (Luton) 1994. BB 4-39 v OU (Oxford) 1994. BAC BB 2-62 v Glos (Cheltenham) 1994. **NWT:** HS 10 v Somerset (Leeds) 1994. **BHC:** HS 0. **SL:** HS 12 v Glos (Cheltenham) 1994.

WHARF, Alexander George (Buttershaw Upper S), b Bradford 4 Jun 1975. 6'5". RHB, RMF. Debut 1994. HS 46 and BB 1-78 v Warwks (Scarborough) 1994 – on debut. **SL:** HS – and BB 3-39 v Warwks (Scarborough) 1994.

WHITE, Craig (Flora Hill HS, Bendigo, Australia; Bendigo HS), b Morley Hall 16 Dec 1969. 6'0". RHB, RFM. Debut 1990. Cap 1993. **Tests:** 4 (1994); HS 51 v NZ (Lord's) 1994; BB 3-18 v NZ (Manchester) 1994. Victoria 1990-91. Tours (Y): SA 1991-92, 1992-93. HS 146 v Durham (Leeds) 1993. BB 5-40 v Essex (Leeds) 1994. **NWT:** HS 65* v Devon (Exmouth) 1994. BB 2-41 v Warwks (Leeds) 1993. **BHC:** HS 26 v Notts (Leeds) 1992. BB 2-30 v Northants (Leeds) 1993. **SL:** HS 63 v Surrey (Scarborough) 1992. BB 3-25 v Hants (Leeds) 1994.

NEWCOMERS

BEVAN, Michael Gwyl, b Belconnen, ACT, Australia 8 May 1970. LHB, SLA. S Australia 1989-90. NSW 1990-91 to date. LOI (A): 3 (HS 39*). Tour: Z 1991-92 (Aus B). 1000 runs (0+1): 1312 (1993-94). HS 203* NSW v WA (Sydney) 1993-94. BB 3-6 NSW v Wellington (Sydney) 1990-91.

MORRIS, Alexander Corfield (Holgate S, Barnsley), b Barnsley 4 Oct 1976. LHB, RM. Made 2nd XI debut when 16y 332d.

SCHOFIELD, Christopher John (Kingstone S, Barnsley), b Barnsley 21 Mar 1976. RHB.

DEPARTURES (who made first-class appearances in 1994)

BATTY, J.D. – see SOMERSET.

BROADHURST, M. – see NOTTINGHAMSHIRE.

FOSTER, M.J. – see NORTHAMPTONSHIRE.

KEEDY, G. – see LANCASHIRE.

RICHARDSON, Richard Benjamin (**'Richie'**), b Five Islands, Antigua 12 Jan 1962. RHB, RM. Leeward Is 1981-82 to date (captain 1993-94). Yorkshire 1993-94 (cap 1993). **Tests** (WI): 76 (1983-84 to 1993-94, 14 as captain); HS 194 v I (Georgetown) 1988-89. LOI (WI): 202 (HS 122; BB 1-4). Tours (WI)(C=captain): E 1984, 1988, 1990 (RW), 1991; A 1984-85, 1986-87, 1988-89, 1992-93C; NZ 1986-87; I 1983-84, 1987-88; P 1986-87, 1990-91; SL 1993-94C. 1000 runs (1+2); most – 1403 (1991). HS 194 (Tests). Y HS 112 v Warwks (Birmingham) 1993. BB 5-40 Leeward Is v E (St John's) 1985-86 (his first f-c wkts). Y BB 1-5. **NWT:** HS 90 v Glos (Bristol) 1993. **BHC:** HS 52 v Northants (Leeds) 1993. **SL:** HS 103 v Notts (Nottingham) 1993.

WEEKES, Lesroy Charlesworth (Montserrat SS), b Montserrat, WI 19 Jul 1971. 6'2". RHB, RFM. Leeward Is 1993-94. Yorkshire 1994 (one match as unregistered player). HS 46 and BB 4-54 Leeward Is v Guyana (Blairmont, Berbice) 1993-94. Y HS – and BB 2-43 v NZ (Leeds) 1994.

YORKSHIRE 1994

RESULTS SUMMARY

	Place	Won	Lost	Drew	Abandoned
Britannic Assurance Championship	**13th**	4	6	7	
All First-class Matches		7	6	7	
Sunday League	**5th**	10	6		1
NatWest Trophy	2nd Round				
Benson and Hedges Cup	2nd Round				

BRITANNIC ASSURANCE CHAMPIONSHIP AVERAGES

BATTING AND FIELDING

Cap		M	I	NO	HS	Runs	Avge	100	50	Ct/St
–	J.D.Batty	3	6	5	26*	78	78.00	–	–	3
1984	M.D.Moxon	15	27	3	274*	1224	51.00	3	6	6
1993	C.White	7	11	2	108*	449	49.88	1	3	4
1987	R.J.Blakey	17	31	7	94*	1044	43.50	–	10	54/3
–	A.P.Grayson	16	27	3	100	955	39.79	1	7	16
–	B.Parker	9	16	2	127	520	37.14	1	4	6
–	M.P.Vaughan	13	25	–	117	858	34.32	2	3	3
1991	D.Byas	17	31	–	104	1050	33.87	2	7	21
1993	R.B.Richardson	8	15	–	76	488	32.53	–	4	8
1992	S.A.Kellett	8	14	–	50	258	18.42	–	1	11
–	G.M.Hamilton	3	4	–	48	70	17.50	–	–	2
1987	P.J.Hartley	14	22	3	61	330	17.36	–	1	2
–	M.J.Foster	2	4	–	49	66	16.50	–	–	3
1993	D.Gough	8	13	1	54	166	13.83	–	1	1
–	C.E.W.Silverwood	8	14	3	26	125	11.36	–	–	1
–	R.D.Stemp	17	26	2	28	235	9.79	–	–	7
1986	A.A.Metcalfe	2	4	–	12	15	3.75	–	–	1
1992	M.A.Robinson	16	21	7	7	48	3.42	–	–	5

Also played (1 match): G.Keedy 1; R.A.Kettleborough 24*, 25; S.M.Milburn did not bat; A.G.Wharf 0, 46.

BOWLING

	O	M	R	W	Avge	Best	5wI	10wM
D.Gough	270.1	63	847	40	21.17	6-66	2	–
C.White	120.1	25	405	17	23.82	5-40	1	–
P.J.Hartley	505.1	103	1558	57	27.33	5-89	1	–
R.D.Stemp	546.5	201	1269	41	30.95	6-37	2	–
C.E.W.Silverwood	231	42	831	26	31.96	4-67	–	–
M.A.Robinson	530	149	1443	43	33.55	5-48	1	–

Also bowled: J.D.Batty 77.4-18-259-6; D.Byas 16-4-52-2; M.J.Foster 15-5-41-1; A.P.Grayson 85.3-28-194-6; G.M.Hamilton 67.2-13-270-4; R.A.Kettleborough 6-2-18-0; S.M.Milburn 24.2-4-77-3; M.P.Vaughan 165.3-40-514-7; A.G.Wharf 23-4-78-1.

The First-Class Averages (pp 186-200) give the records of Yorkshire players in all first-class county matches (their other opponents being Lancashire in a non-Championship match, the New Zealanders and Oxford U), with the exception of G.M.Hamilton, whose full county figures are as above, and:

D.Gough 9-14-1-54-209-16.07-0-1-1ct. 309-72-960-45-21.33-6/66-3-0.

C.White 9-14-2-108*-532-44.33-1-4-5ct. 157.1-36-503-25-20.12-5/40-2-0.

YORKSHIRE RECORDS

FIRST-CLASS CRICKET

Highest Total	For 887		v	Warwicks	Birmingham	1896
	V 630		by	Somerset	Leeds	1901
Lowest Total	For 23		v	Hampshire	Middlesbrough	1965
	V 13		by	Notts	Nottingham	1901
Highest Innings	For 341	G.H.Hirst	v	Leics	Leicester	1905
	V 318*	W.G.Grace	for	Glos	Cheltenham	1876

Highest Partnerships for each Wicket

1st	555	P.Holmes/H.Sutcliffe	v	Essex	Leyton	1932
2nd	346	W.Barber/M.Leyland	v	Middlesex	Sheffield	1932
3rd	323*	H.Sutcliffe/M.Leyland	v	Glamorgan	Huddersfield	1928
4th	312	D.Denton/G.H.Hirst	v	Hampshire	Southampton	1914
5th	340	E.Wainwright/G.H.Hirst	v	Surrey	The Oval	1899
6th	276	M.Leyland/E.Robinson	v	Glamorgan	Swansea	1926
7th	254	W.Rhodes/D.C.F.Burton	v	Hampshire	Dewsbury	1919
8th	292	R.Peel/Lord Hawke	v	Warwicks	Birmingham	1896
9th	192	G.H.Hirst/S.Haigh	v	Surrey	Bradford	1898
10th	149	G.Boycott/G.B.Stevenson	v	Warwicks	Birmingham	1982

Best Bowling	For 10-10	H.Verity	v	Notts	Leeds	1932
(Innings)	V 10-37	C.V.Grimmett	for	Australians	Sheffield	1930
Best Bowling	For 17-91	H.Verity	v	Essex	Leyton	1933
(Match)	V 17-91	H.Dean	for	Lancashire	Liverpool	1913

Most Runs – Season	2883	H.Sutcliffe	(av 80.08)	1932
Most Runs – Career	38561	H.Sutcliffe	(av 50.20)	1919-45
Most 100s – Season	12	H.Sutcliffe		1932
Most 100s – Career	112	H.Sutcliffe		1919-45
Most Wkts – Season	240	W.Rhodes	(av 12.72)	1900
Most Wkts – Career	3608	W.Rhodes	(av 16.00)	1898-1930

LIMITED-OVERS CRICKET

Highest Total	NWT	317-4		v	Surrey	Lord's	1965
	BHC	317-5		v	Scotland	Leeds	1986
	SL	318-7		v	Leics	Leicester	1993
Lowest Total	NWT	76		v	Surrey	Harrogate	1970
	BHC	111		v	Notts	Nottingham	1989
	SL	74		v	Warwicks	Birmingham	1972
Highest Innings	NWT	146	G.Boycott	v	Surrey	Lord's	1965
	BHC	142	G.Boycott	v	Worcs	Worcester	1980
	SL	130*	R.J.Blakey	v	Kent	Scarborough	1991
Best Bowling	NWT	6-15	F.S.Trueman	v	Somerset	Taunton	1965
	BHC	6-27	A.G.Nicholson	v	Minor C (N)	Middlesbrough	1972
	SL	7-15	R.A.Hutton	v	Worcs	Leeds	1969

GLOUCESTERSHIRE – DEPARTURES (continued from p 113)

WIGHT, Robert Marcus (KCS, Wimbledon; Exeter U; Trinity Hall, Cambridge), b Kensington, London 12 Sep 1969. Distant cousin of P.B. (British Guiana, Somerset and Canterbury 1950/51-1965). 6'2". RHB, OB. Debut/blue Cambridge U 1992. Gloucestershire 1993-94. HS 62* CU v OU (Lord's) 1992. Gs HS 54 v Leics (Leicester) 1993. BB 3-65 CU v Kent (Cambridge) 1992. Gs BB 3-71 v Yorks (Sheffield) 1993. Hockey for Devon 1989-91; CU hockey blue 1991-92 (captain 1992). **NWT:** HS 18 v Herts (Bristol) 1993. BB 1-24. **SL:** HS 11* v Middx (Moreton) 1993. BB 2-28 v Glam (Bristol) 1994.

NORTHAMPTONSHIRE – DEPARTURES (continued from p 143)

AMBROSE, Curtly Elconn Lynwall (All Saints Village SS), b Swetes Village, Antigua 21 Sep 1963. Cousin of R.M.Otto (Leeward Is 1979-80/1990-91). 6'7". LHB, RF. Leeward Is 1985-86 to date. Northamptonshire 1989-94 (cap 1990). Wisden 1991. **Tests** (WI): 48 (1987-88 to 1993-94); HS 53 v A (P-of-S) 1990-91; BB 8-45 v E (Bridgetown) 1989-90. LOI (WI): 104 (HS 26*; BB 5-17). Tours (WI): E 1988, 1991; A 1988-89, 1992-93; P 1990-91; SL 1993-94. HS 78 v Somerset (Taunton) 1994. 50 wkts (5+1); most – 77 (1994). BB 8-45 (Tests). Nh BB 7-44 v Hants (Southampton) 1994. Award: NWT 1. **NWT:** HS 48 v Lancs (Lord's) 1990. BB 4-7 v Yorks (Northampton) 1992. **BHC:** HS 17* v Kent (Northampton) 1989. BB 4-31 v Essex (Northampton) 1992. **SL:** HS 37 v Notts (Nottingham) 1994. BB 4-20 v Lancs and v Kent (Northampton) 1994.

FELTON, Nigel Alfred (Millfield S; Loughborough U), b Guildford, Surrey 24 Oct 1960. 5'8". LHB, OB. Somerset 1982-88 (cap 1986). Northamptonshire 1989-94 (cap 1990). Tour: SA 1991-92 (Nh). 1000 runs (5); most – 1538 (1990). HS 173* Sm v Kent (Taunton) 1983. Nh HS 122 v Glam (Northampton) 1990. BB 1-48. Awards: NWT 2; BHC 2. **NWT:** HS 87 Sm v Kent (Taunton) 1984. **BHC:** HS 82 v Lancs (Northampton) 1992. **SL:** HS 96 Sm v Essex (Chelmsford) 1986.

NOTTINGHAMSHIRE – DEPARTURES (continued from p 148)

DESSAUR, Wayne Anthony (Loughborough GS), b Nottingham 4 Feb 1971. 6'0". RHB, RM. Nottinghamshire 1992-94. HS 148 v CU (Nottingham) 1992. BAC HS 104 v Derbys (Nottingham) 1993. **SL:** HS 13* v Somerset (Bath) 1992.

PIPES, David John (Lilley & Stone S, Newark), b Lincoln 26 Apr 1977. 6'2". RHB, RM. Nottinghamshire 1994 (one match). HS 11* v OU (Oxford) 1994. No BAC appearance.

SYLVESTER, Steven Antony (Wellesbourne SM; Buckinghamshire C; Goldsmiths' C, London U), b Chalfont St Giles, Bucks 26 Sep 1968. 5'11". RHB, LFM. Middlesex 1991-92. Nottinghamshire 1994 (one match). Buckinghamshire 1991-92. HS 6*. BB 2-34 M v CU (Cambridge) 1992. BAC BB 2-35 M v Lancs (Lord's) 1992. Nt BB 1-38. **BHC:** HS 0. BB 1-31. **SL:** HS 1*.

WARWICKSHIRE – DEPARTURES (continued from p 168)

LARA, Brian Charles, b Santa Cruz, Trinidad 2 May 1969. 5'8". LHB, LB. Trinidad 1987-88 to date. Warwickshire 1994 (cap 1994). Wisden 1994. **Tests** (WI): 16 (1990-91 to 1993-94); HS 375 (world Test record) v E (St John's) 1993-94. LOI (WI): 68 (HS 153; BB 2-5). Tours (WI): E 1991; A 1991-92, 1992-93; P 1990-91; SL 1993-94; Z 1989-90 (Young WI). 1000 runs (1+1) inc 2000 (1): 2066 off 2262 balls (1994). HS 501* (world f-c record) v Durham (Birmingham) 1994. Scored 6 hundreds in his first 7 innings for Warwks (147, 106, 120*, 136, 26, 140, 501*). BB 1-22. **NWT:** HS 81 v Worcs (Lord's) 1994. **BHC:** HS 70 v Surrey (Oval) 1994. **SL:** HS 75 v Notts (Birmingham) 1994. Returns in 1996.

RATCLIFFE, J.D. – see SURREY.

CAMBRIDGE v OXFORD
(149th UNIVERSITY MATCH)

At Lord's, London, on 29, 30 June, 1 July.
Toss: Oxford. Result: MATCH DRAWN.

OXFORD UNIVERSITY

*R.R.Montgomerie lbw b Whittall	33
G.I.Macmillan c Whittall b Hodgson	69
C.M.Gupte run out	122
S.C.Ecclestone c Whittall b Haste	13
C.J.Hollins c Hodgson b Haste	131
H.S.Malik c Cake b Pitcher	13
R.S.Yeabsley run out	1
N.F.C.Martin lbw b Pitcher	7
†C.J.Townsend not out	18
P.W.Trimby c Stanley b Pitcher	4
A.W.Maclay not out	6
Extras (B3, LB27, W6)	36
Total (9 wickets declared)	453

CAMBRIDGE UNIVERSITY

G.W.Jones c Martin b Yeabsley	21	lbw b Yeabsley	2
R.D.Mann c Hollins b Yeabsley	31	c Hollins b Yeabsley	7
J.Ratledge c Macmillan b Yeabsley	0	lbw b Yeabsley	0
R.Q.Cake c Macmillan b Maclay	27	c Gupte b Hollins	27
J.P.Carroll lbw b Trimby	2	b Ecclestone	5
J.S.Hodgson c Townsend b Yeabsley	29	b Yeabsley	54
D.E.Stanley lbw b Maclay	0	b Macmillan	9
*A.R.Whittall c Hollins b Maclay	40	not out	91
N.J.Haste c Macmillan b Yeabsley	10	c Trimby b Ecclestone	22
C.M.Pitcher c Macmillan b Yeabsley	43	not out	0
†F.J.Cooke not out	34		
Extras (LB8, NB8)	16	(B7, LB10, W1, NB8)	26
Total	253	(8 wickets)	243

CAMBRIDGE	*O*	*M*	*R*	*W*		*O*	*M*	*R*	*W*
Pitcher	20	2	95	3					
Haste	23	2	96	2					
Whittall	33	6	123	1					
Hodgson	32	7	85	1					
Ratledge	6	0	24	0					
OXFORD									
Ecclestone	4	0	23	0	(4)	18	6	31	2
Yeabsley	22.5	7	54	6	(1)	21	7	50	4
Trimby	30	5	91	1	(5)	13	3	37	0
Maclay	13	2	30	3	(2)	11	2	22	0
Hollins	8	1	34	0	(3)	24	5	64	1
Macmillan	5	2	9	0		10	4	22	1
Malik	1	0	4	0					

FALL OF WICKETS

Wkt	*OU 1st*	*CU 1st*	*CU 2nd*
1st	104	44	14
2nd	118	44	14
3rd	148	69	21
4th	398	80	27
5th	399	94	83
6th	405	94	105
7th	418	140	170
8th	420	171	229
9th	436	186	–
10th	–	253	–

Umpires: J.W.Holder and B.Leadbeater.

UNIVERSITY MATCH RESULTS

Played: 149. Wins: Cambridge 55; Oxford 47. Drawn: 47. Abandoned: 1.
This, the oldest surviving first-class fixture, dates from 1827 and, wartime interruptions apart, has been played annually since 1838. With the exception of five matches played in the area of Oxford (1829, 1843, 1846, 1848 and 1850), all the fixtures have been played at Lord's.

1827	Drawn
1829	Oxford
1836	Oxford
1838	Oxford
1839	Cambridge
1840	Cambridge
1841	Cambridge
1842	Cambridge
1843	Cambridge
1844	Drawn
1845	Cambridge
1846	Oxford
1847	Cambridge
1848	Oxford
1849	Cambridge
1850	Oxford
1851	Cambridge
1852	Oxford
1853	Oxford
1854	Oxford
1855	Oxford
1856	Cambridge
1857	Oxford
1858	Oxford
1859	Cambridge
1860	Cambridge
1861	Cambridge
1862	Cambridge
1863	Oxford
1864	Oxford
1865	Oxford
1866	Oxford
1867	Cambridge
1868	Cambridge
1869	Cambridge
1870	Cambridge
1871	Oxford
1872	Cambridge
1873	Oxford
1874	Oxford
1875	Oxford
1876	Cambridge
1877	Oxford
1878	Cambridge
1879	Cambridge
1880	Cambridge
1881	Oxford
1882	Cambridge
1883	Cambridge
1884	Oxford
1885	Cambridge
1886	Oxford
1887	Oxford
1888	Drawn
1889	Cambridge
1890	Cambridge
1891	Cambridge
1892	Oxford
1893	Cambridge
1894	Oxford
1895	Cambridge
1896	Oxford
1897	Cambridge
1898	Oxford
1899	Drawn
1900	Drawn
1901	Drawn
1902	Cambridge
1903	Oxford
1904	Drawn
1905	Cambridge
1906	Cambridge
1907	Cambridge
1908	Oxford
1909	Drawn
1910	Oxford
1911	Oxford
1912	Cambridge
1913	Cambridge
1914	Oxford
1919	Oxford
1920	Drawn
1921	Cambridge
1922	Cambridge
1923	Oxford
1924	Cambridge
1925	Drawn
1926	Cambridge
1927	Cambridge
1928	Drawn
1929	Drawn
1930	Cambridge
1931	Oxford
1932	Drawn
1933	Drawn
1934	Drawn
1935	Cambridge
1936	Cambridge
1937	Oxford
1938	Drawn
1939	Oxford
1946	Oxford
1947	Drawn
1948	Oxford
1949	Cambridge
1950	Drawn
1951	Oxford
1952	Drawn
1953	Cambridge
1954	Drawn
1955	Drawn
1956	Drawn
1957	Cambridge
1958	Cambridge
1959	Oxford
1960	Drawn
1961	Drawn
1962	Drawn
1963	Drawn
1964	Drawn
1965	Drawn
1966	Oxford
1967	Drawn
1968	Drawn
1969	Drawn
1970	Drawn
1971	Drawn
1972	Cambridge
1973	Drawn
1974	Drawn
1975	Drawn
1976	Oxford
1977	Drawn
1978	Drawn
1979	Cambridge
1980	Drawn
1981	Drawn
1982	Cambridge
1983	Drawn
1984	Oxford
1985	Drawn
1986	Cambridge
1987	Drawn
1988	Abandoned
1989	Drawn
1990	Drawn
1991	Drawn
1992	Cambridge
1993	Oxford
1994	Drawn

CAMBRIDGE UNIVERSITY

BASHFORTH, Michael Charles (Queen's C, Taunton; Robinson C), b Manly, Sydney, Australia 17 May 1972. 5'11". RHB, RM. Debut 1994. HS 9*.

CAKE, Russell Quentin (KCS, Wimbledon; St John's C), b Chertsey, Surrey 16 May 1973. 5'7". RHB. Debut 1993; blue 1993-94. HS 108 Comb Us v A (Oxford) 1993. CU HS 107 v Glam (Cambridge) 1994. Hockey blue.

CARROLL, John Paul (Rendcomb C, Cirencester; Homerton C), b Bebington, Cheshire 14 Jul 1972. 6'2". RHB, RM. Debut 1992; blue 1992-93-94. HS 92 v Kent (Cambridge) 1992.

COOKE, Fraser James (W Bridgford S; Millfield S; Fitzwilliam C), b Hall Green, Birmingham 2 Apr 1972. 5'9". RHB, WK. Debut/blue 1994. HS 34* v OU (Lord's) 1994.

HALL, Michael Anthony Thor (Winchester C; Gonville & Caius C), b Windsor, Berks 7 Aug 1970. 6'1". LHB, SLA. Debut 1994. HS 4.

HASTE, Nicholas John (Wellingborough S; Pembroke C), b Northampton 13 Nov 1972. 6'0". RHB, RM. Debut 1993; blue 1993-94. HS 36 v OU (Lord's) 1993. BB 4-69 v Glam (Cambridge) 1994.

HODGSON, James Simon (Wellington C; Durham U; Hughes Hall), b Guildford, Surrey 30 Apr 1969. Great nephew of N.A.Knox (Surrey & England 1904-10). 5'10". RHB, OB. Debut/blue 1994. HS 54 v OU (Lord's) 1994. BB 4-14 v Essex (Cambridge) 1994.

JONES, Garri Wyn (King's S, Chester; Gonville & Caius C), b Birmingham 1 May 1970. Brother of R.O. (Glamorgan staff 1993-94). 5'7". LHB, OB. Debut 1991; blue 1992-93-94. HS 74 v Essex (Cambridge) 1994.

MANN, Robin David (Wellingborough S; St John's C), b Middlesbrough, Yorks 31 Oct 1973. 5'11". RHB. Debut/blue 1994. HS 53 v Worcs (Cambridge) 1994.

PITCHER, Christopher Michael (St Edward's S, Oxford; Selwyn C), b Croydon, Surrey 26 Aug 1973. 6'2". RHB, RM. Debut 1992; blue 1992-93-94. HS 43 v OU (Lord's) 1994. BB 4-37 v Kent (Cambridge) 1994.

RATLEDGE, John (Bolton S; St John's C), b Preston, Lancs 8 Aug 1974. 5'8". RHB, RM. Debut/blue 1994. HS 79 v Lancs (Cambridge) 1994.

STANLEY, Donald Eric (Abingdon S; Gonville & Caius C), b Bromley, Kent 8 Mar 1972. 6'2". RHB. Debut/blue 1994. HS 48 v Glam (Cambridge) 1994.

WHITTALL, Andrew Richard (Falcon C, Zimbabwe; Trinity C), b Mutare, Zimbabwe 28 Mar 1973. Cousin of G.J. (Zimbabwe). 6'3". RHB, OB. Debut 1993; blue 1993-94; captain 1994-95. HS 91* v OU (Lord's) 1994. BB 3-79 v Sussex (Hove) 1993.

OXFORD UNIVERSITY

ECCLESTONE, Simon Charles – see SOMERSET.

GUPTE, Chinmay Madhukar (John Lyon S, Harrow; Pembroke C), b Poona, India 5 Jul 1972. Son of M.S. (Maharashtra). 5'7". RHB, SLA. Debut 1991; blue 1991-93-94. HS 122 v CU (Lord's) 1994. BB 2-41 v Notts (Oxford) 1991.

HOLLINS, Christopher Jonathan (Tonbridge S; Durham U; Keble C), b Bromley, Kent 20 Mar 1971. Son of John (England soccer international). 5'7". RHB, OB. Debut/blue 1994. HS 131 v CU (Lord's) 1994. BB 4-64 v Notts (Oxford) 1994. Soccer blue.

KENDALL, William Salwey – see HAMPSHIRE.

MACLAY, Alasdair Worsfold (Horris Hill S; Winchester C; St Edmund Hall), b Salisbury, Wilts 15 Oct 1973. 6'3". RHB, RMF. Debut 1993; blue 1994. HS 6*. BB 3-30 v CU (Lord's) 1994.

MACMILLAN, Gregor Innes (captain 1995) – see LEICESTERSHIRE.

MALIK, Hasnain Siddiq (KCS, Wimbledon; Keble C), b Sargodha, Pakistan 21 Apr 1973. 5'11". LHB, OB. Debut 1992; blue 1994. HS 64* v Hants (Oxford) 1993. BB 3-10 v Hants (Oxford) 1994.

MARTIN, Neil Frederick Clay (King Edward's S, Birmingham; Durham U; Birmingham U; Keble C), b Birmingham 19 Oct 1969. 6'3". RHB, RM. Debut/blue 1994. HS 26 v Hants (Oxford) 1994. BB 2-84 v Surrey (Oval) 1994. Rugby blue.

MONTGOMERIE, Richard Robert (captain 1994) – see NORTHAMPTONSHIRE.

RIDLEY, Andrew Claude (St Aloysius C, Sydney; Sydney U; Exeter C), b Sydney, Australia 2 Aug 1968. 5'11". LHB, RM. Debut 1994. HS 36* v Glam (Oxford) 1994.

SUTCLIFFE, Iain John – see LEICESTERSHIRE.

TOWNSEND, Christopher James (Dean Close S; Brasenose C), b Wokingham, Berks 1 Dec 1972. 6'0". RHB, WK. Grandson of W.D.Wickson (Surrey President 1992). Debut 1992; blue 1992-94. HS 22 v Yorks (Oxford) 1994.

TRIMBY, Patrick William (Shrewsbury S; Worcester C), b Shrewsbury, Shrops 31 Jan 1972. 6'1½". LHB, LB. Debut 1993; blue 1993-94. Shropshire 1992. HS 11 v Worcs (Worcester) 1994. BB 5-84 v Durham (Oxford) 1994.

YEABSLEY, Richard Stuart – see MIDDLESEX.

YOUNG CRICKETER OF THE YEAR

This annual award, made by The Cricket Writers' Club (founded in 1946), is currently restricted to players qualified for England and under the age of 23 on 1 April. In 1986 their ballot resulted in a dead heat. Only six of their selections (marked †) have failed to win an England cap.

1950	R.Tattersall	1973	M.Hendrick
1951	P.B.H.May	1974	P.H.Edmonds
1952	F.S.Trueman	1975	A.Kennedy†
1953	M.C.Cowdrey	1976	G.Miller
1954	P.J.Loader	1977	I.T.Botham
1955	K.F.Barrington	1978	D.I.Gower
1956	B.Taylor†	1979	P.W.G.Parker
1957	M.J.Stewart	1980	G.R.Dilley
1958	A.C.D.Ingleby-Mackenzie†	1981	M.W.Gatting
1959	G.Pullar	1982	N.G.Cowans
1960	D.A.Allen	1983	N.A.Foster
1961	P.H.Parfitt	1984	R.J.Bailey
1962	P.J.Sharpe	1985	D.V.Lawrence
1963	G.Boycott	1986	A.A.Metcalfe†
1964	J.M.Brearley	1986	J.J.Whitaker
1965	A.P.E.Knott	1987	R.J.Blakey
1966	D.L.Underwood	1988	M.P.Maynard
1967	A.W.Greig	1989	N.Hussain
1968	R.M.H.Cottam	1990	M.A.Atherton
1969	A.Ward	1991	M.R.Ramprakash
1970	C.M.Old	1992	I.D.K.Salisbury
1971	J.Whitehouse†	1993	M.N.Lathwell
1972	D.R.Owen-Thomas†	1994	J.P.Crawley

1994 FIRST-CLASS AVERAGES

These averages involve the 462 cricketers who played in the 201 first-class matches staged in the British Isles during the 1994 season.

'Cap' denotes the season in which the player was awarded a 1st XI cap by the county he represented in 1994. Durham do not award caps on merit; each player receives his cap on joining the staff.

Team abbreviations: CU – Cambridge University; De – Derbyshire; Du – Durham; E – England; EA – England A; Ex – Essex; Gm – Glamorgan; Gs – Gloucestershire; H – Hampshire; Ire – Ireland; K – Kent; La – Lancashire; Le – Leicestershire; M – Middlesex; MC – Minor Counties; Nh – Northamptonshire; Nt – Nottinghamshire; NZ – New Zealand(ers); OU – Oxford University; SA – South Africa(ns); Sc – Scotland; Sm – Somerset; Sy – Surrey; Sx – Sussex; Us – Combined Universities; W – President's (World) XI; Wa – Warwickshire; Wo – Worcestershire; Y – Yorkshire.

† Left-handed batsman.

BATTING AND FIELDING

	Cap	*M*	*I*	*NO*	*HS*	*Runs*	*Avge*	*100*	*50*	*Ct/St*
Adams, C.J.(De)	1992	18	32	3	109*	969	33.41	1	5	16
†Adams, J.C.(Nt)	—	18	32	5	144*	950	35.18	3	2	17
Afford, J.A.(Nt)	1990	15	17	6	10	36	3.27	–	–	5
Alleyne, M.W.(Gs)	1990	20	37	1	109	1184	32.88	2	6	16
†Ambrose, C.E.L.(Nh)	1990	14	16	2	78	257	18.35	–	1	16
Andrew, S.J.W.(Ex)	—	6	8	1	11	37	5.28	–	–	–
Archer, G.F.(Nt)	—	16	26	–	168	878	33.76	2	4	17
†Arnold, K.A.(MC)	—	1	1	1	0*	0	–	–	–	–
†Arthurton, K.L.T.(W)	—	1	1	–	60	60	60.00	–	1	–
Asif Din (Wa)	1987	3	4	1	42*	107	35.66	–	–	1
Atherton, M.A.(La/E)	1989	16	27	2	111	899	35.96	2	4	14
Athey, C.W.J.(Sx)	1993	18	34	1	169*	1022	30.96	2	3	14
†Austin, I.D.(La)	1990	11	16	1	50	386	25.73	–	1	5
Aymes, A.N.(H)	1991	19	32	3	76	697	24.03	–	2	36/4
Azharuddin, M.(De)	1991	9	17	1	205	712	44.50	2	1	5
†Babington, A.M.(Gs)	—	1	–	–	–	–	–	–	–	–
Bailey, R.J.(Nh)	1985	18	33	5	129*	1214	43.35	3	7	12
Bainbridge, P.(Du)	1992	18	31	1	68	660	22.00	–	5	13
Ball, M.C.J.(Gs)	—	17	28	3	45	468	18.72	–	–	31
Baptiste, E.A.E.(W)	—	1	1	1	20*	20	–	–	–	–
Barnett, A.A.(La)	—	6	5	1	10	14	3.50	–	–	3
Barnett, K.J.(De)	1982	15	24	2	148	847	38.50	1	7	7
Barwick, S.R.(Gm)	1987	12	16	6	8	35	3.50	–	–	3
Base, S.J.(De)	1990	8	12	1	33	160	14.54	–	–	6
Bashforth, M.C.(CU)	—	3	5	3	9*	13	6.50	–	–	1
Bastien, S.(Gm)	—	5	3	–	6	7	2.33	–	–	2
Bates, R.T.(Nt)	—	2	4	1	8	15	5.00	–	–	1
Batty, J.D.(Y)	—	3	6	5	26*	78	78.00	–	–	3
Batty, J.N.(Us)	—	1	2	–	6	9	4.50	–	–	1
Bell, M.A.V.(Wa)	—	1	1	1	4*	4	–	–	–	1
Benjamin, J.E.(Sy/E)	1993	16	17	1	33*	148	9.25	–	–	5
Benjamin, K.C.G.(W)	—	1	–	–	–	–	–	–	–	–
Benjamin, W.K.M.(H)	—	9	14	1	54	231	17.76	–	2	4
†Benson, M.R.(K)	1981	16	28	1	159	737	27.29	1	4	10
Berry, P.J.(Du)	1992	1	2	–	3	3	1.50	–	–	1
†Bicknell, D.J.(Sy/EA)	1990	18	30	4	235*	1354	52.07	3	7	4

	Cap	M	I	NO	HS	Runs	Avge	100	50	Ct/St
Bicknell, M.P.(Sy/EA)	1989	9	11	2	41	140	15.55	–	–	5
†Birbeck, S.D.(Du)	1994	1	1	–	6	6	6.00	–	–	1
Bird, P.J.(Sm)	—	2	3	1	7	12	6.00	–	–	–
Blakey, R.J.(Y)	1987	20	36	9	94*	1236	45.77	–	11	65/4
†Blenkiron, D.A.(Du)	1992	1	–	–	–	–	–	–	–	–
Boiling, J.(Sy)	—	6	6	2	34*	75	18.75	–	–	7
Boon, T.J.(Le)	1986	16	28	2	74	606	23.30	–	4	5
Bovill, J.N.B.(H/Us)	—	6	9	5	10	35	8.75	–	–	1
Bowen, M.N.(Nh)	—	5	5	–	13	18	3.60	–	–	2
Bowler, P.D.(De)	1989	13	23	–	88	546	23.73	–	2	11
Briers, N.E.(Le)	1981	19	35	3	154	1216	38.00	2	5	5
Brimson, M.T.(Le)	—	5	9	3	17*	45	7.50	–	–	–
Brinkley, J.E.(Wo)	—	10	10	2	5	16	2.00	–	–	3
†Broad, B.C.(Gs)	1981	10	20	–	128	496	24.80	1	2	9
Broadhurst, M.(Y)	—	1	1	–	6	6	6.00	–	–	–
Brown, A.D.(Sy)	1994	17	24	2	172	1049	47.68	2	6	16
Brown, D.R.(Wa)	—	3	6	2	54	113	28.25	–	1	–
Brown, K.R.(M)	1990	20	25	9	102*	639	39.93	1	1	55/1
Brown, S.J.E.(Du/W)	1992	19	25	10	69	268	17.86	–	1	9
Bullen, C.K.(MC)	—	1	1	–	2	2	2.00	–	–	1
Burns, M.(Wa)	—	1	1	1	36*	36	–	–	–	–
Butcher, G.P.(Gm)	—	3	3	–	41	50	16.66	–	–	2
†Butcher, M.A.(Sy)	—	12	19	2	134	613	36.05	1	3	21
†Byas, D.(Y)	1991	20	36	1	104	1297	37.05	2	9	23
Caddick, A.R.(Sm)	1992	12	18	2	58*	219	13.68	–	1	5
Cake, R.Q.(CU/Us)	—	10	18	1	107	647	38.05	1	3	4
Capel, D.J.(Nh)	1986	2	3	–	29	43	14.33	–	–	1
Carr, J.D.(M)	1987	20	27	10	261*	1543	90.76	6	7	31
Carroll, J.P.(CU)	—	9	15	2	90	246	18.92	–	1	2
Cassar, M.E.(De)	—	1	1	–	66	66	66.00	–	1	–
Chapman, R.J.(Nt)	—	3	4	–	25	36	9.00	–	–	1
Chapple, G.(La)	1994	15	21	11	26*	150	15.00	–	–	11
†Childs, J.H.(Ex)	1986	15	17	12	42*	96	19.20	–	–	1
Church, M.J.(Wo)	—	3	5	–	38	65	13.00	–	–	1
Clarke, V.P.(Sm)	—	2	4	–	38	46	11.50	–	–	–
Cockbain, I.(MC)	—	1	2	1	14	27	27.00	–	–	–
Connor, C.A.(H)	1988	15	22	3	25	215	11.31	–	–	4
Cook, N.G.B.(Nh)	1987	11	12	1	43*	98	8.90	–	–	3
Cooke, F.J.(CU)	—	9	10	4	34*	80	13.33	–	–	9/1
Cooke, G.(Ire)	—	1	–	–	–	–	–	–	–	–
†Cooper, K.E.(Gs)	—	12	16	9	18*	84	12.00	–	–	2
Cork, D.G.(De)	1993	13	21	–	94	507	24.14	–	4	15
Cottey, P.A.(Gm)	1992	19	33	6	191	1393	51.59	3	6	16
Cousins, D.M.(Ex)	—	4	5	–	11	24	4.80	–	–	2
Cowans, N.G.(H)	—	12	15	6	19	51	5.66	–	–	3
Cowdrey, G.R.(K)	1988	10	16	1	114	470	31.33	1	2	4
†Cox, D.M.(Du)	1993	3	4	1	26*	32	10.66	–	–	1
†Cox, R.M.F.(H)	—	4	7	1	46	114	19.00	–	–	3
Crawley, J.P.(La/E/EA)	1994	20	34	3	281*	1570	50.64	3	6	25
Crawley, M.A.(Nt)	—	8	14	1	45	172	13.23	–	–	7
Croft, R.D.B.(Gm/EA)	1992	19	25	2	80	600	26.08	–	2	7
Cronje, W.J.(SA)	—	13	20	1	108	661	34.78	1	3	11
Crowe, M.D.(NZ)	—	9	16	2	142	654	46.71	3	3	6
Cuffy, C.E.(Sy)	—	12	15	8	10	42	6.00	–	–	1
Cullinan, D.J.(SA)	—	9	14	3	94	428	38.90	–	4	5
Cummins, A.C.(Du)	1993	17	29	2	65	629	23.29	–	3	3

	Cap	M	I	NO	HS	Runs	Avge	100	50	Ct/St
Cunliffe, R.J.(Gs)	—	7	13	1	177*	354	29.50	1	–	5
Curran, K.M.(Nh)	1992	15	25	5	114	973	48.65	1	8	7
Curtis, T.S.(Wo)	1984	18	32	1	180	960	30.96	3	1	7
†Dakin, J.M.(Le)	—	2	3	–	18	29	9.66	–	–	–
Dale, A.(Gm/EA)	1992	18	29	1	131	711	25.39	2	2	3
Daley, J.A.(Du)	1992	10	18	2	159*	513	32.06	1	3	3
Dalton, A.J.(Gm)	—	6	10	2	51*	188	23.50	–	1	5
Davies, M.(Gs)	—	4	8	2	54	173	28.83	–	1	1
Davis, H.T.(NZ)	—	7	7	4	3*	9	3.00	–	–	2
Davis, R.P.(Wa)	1994	12	9	2	35*	131	18.71	–	–	15
Dawood, I.(Nh)	—	1	1	1	2*	2	–	–	–	–
Dawson, R.I.(Gs)	—	16	30	4	127*	1112	42.76	1	7	7
Dean, S.J.(MC)	—	1	2	–	39	73	36.50	–	–	1
DeFreitas, P.A.J.(De/E)	1994	14	21	2	108	545	28.68	1	3	5
Derbyshire, N.A.(La)	—	2	1	–	5	5	5.00	–	–	–
Dessaur, W.A.(Nt)	—	5	9	1	35	154	19.25	–	–	2
De Villiers, P.S.(SA)	—	8	5	1	14	43	10.75	–	–	2
Dimond, M.(Sm)	—	3	2	1	25*	34	34.00	–	–	4
Diwan, M.(Ex)	—	1	2	–	0	0	0.00	–	–	–
Doak, N.G.(Ire)	—	1	2	1	27*	31	31.00	–	–	1
D'Oliveira, D.B.(Wo)	1985	3	5	–	61	156	31.20	–	1	1
Donald, A.A.(SA)	—	8	6	3	27	68	22.66	–	–	4
Donelan, B.T.P.(Sm)	—	1	1	–	0	0	0.00	–	–	–
†Douglas, M.W.(NZ)	—	1	2	–	24	28	14.00	–	–	–
†Dowman, M.P.(Nt)	—	3	5	–	38	111	22.20	–	–	–
Ealham, M.A.(K)	1992	15	26	2	68*	638	26.58	–	4	8
†Ecclestone, S.C.(Sm/OU)	—	13	19	4	80*	334	22.26	–	1	3
Edwards, T.(Wo)	—	9	11	7	47	116	29.00	–	–	20
Emburey, J.E.(M)	1977	15	19	5	78*	203	14.50	–	1	11
Evans, K.P.(Nt)	1990	16	21	4	104	514	30.23	1	3	12
Evans, R.J.(MC)	—	1	2	–	59	89	44.50	–	1	1
†Fairbrother, N.H.(La)	1985	12	22	2	204	1002	50.10	4	1	16
Feltham, M.A.(M)	—	13	16	1	71	256	17.06	–	1	7
†Felton, N.A.(Nh)	1990	10	19	1	87	445	24.72	–	2	5
Field-Buss, M.G.(Nt)	—	8	9	4	23	72	14.40	–	–	1
Fielding, J.M.(La)	—	1	1	1	27*	27	–	–	–	–
Fleming, M.V.(K)	1990	16	29	1	73	810	28.92	–	6	3
†Fleming, S.P.(NZ)	—	9	16	1	151	591	39.40	2	1	5
Fletcher, I.(Sm)	—	6	10	1	54*	179	19.88	–	2	3
Flint, D.P.J.(H)	—	3	2	1	5	8	8.00	–	–	1
†Folland, N.A.(Sm)	—	13	22	1	91	671	31.95	–	4	6
Fordham, A.(Nh)	1990	11	20	1	158	844	44.42	3	4	7
Foster, M.J.(Y)	—	4	6	1	63*	159	31.80	–	1	5
Fourie, B.C.(Le)	—	1	–	–	–	–	–	–	–	–
†Fowler, G.(Du)	1993	4	7	–	68	227	32.42	–	3	2
Fraser, A.R.C.(M/E)	1988	14	15	1	16	80	5.71	–	–	3
French, B.N.(Nt)	1980	1	–	–	–	–	–	–	–	2
Fulton, D.P.(K)	—	10	16	–	109	433	27.06	1	1	17
Gallian, J.E.R.(La)	1994	12	20	–	171	874	43.70	2	5	6
Garnham, M.A.(Ex)	1990	18	30	5	62	542	21.68	–	4	33/5
Gatting, M.W.(M)	1977	19	27	3	225	1671	69.62	6	6	28
Gibson, O.D.(Gm)	1994	20	31	4	85	710	26.29	–	7	7
Giddins, E.S.H.(Sx)	1994	17	22	4	24	83	4.61	–	–	2
Gooch, G.A.(Ex/E)	1975	17	29	2	236	1747	64.70	6	5	15
Gough, D.(Y/E)	1993	13	19	3	65	355	22.18	–	2	1
Govan, J.W.(Sc)	—	1	–	–	–	–	–	–	–	–

	Cap	M	I	NO	HS	Runs	Avge	100	50	Ct/St
Graham, P.C.(MC)	—	1	1	–	0	0	0.00	–	–	2
Graham, S.(Ire)	—	1	1	1	2*	2	–	–	–	–
Graveney, D.A.(Du)	1992	13	22	6	65*	317	19.81	–	1	5
Grayson, A.P.(Y)	—	19	31	4	100	1046	38.74	1	7	19
†Greatbatch, M.J.(NZ)	—	9	18	3	84	528	35.20	–	3	4
Greenfield, K.(Sx)	—	1	2	2	35*	61	–	–	–	–
Griffith, F.A.(De)	—	3	5	1	36	123	30.75	–	–	2
Gupte, C.M.(OU)	—	10	17	2	122	541	36.06	2	1	7
Hall, J.W.(Sx)	1992	14	27	–	85	789	29.22	–	7	9
†Hall, M.A.T.(CU)	—	2	2	–	4	5	2.50	–	–	–
Hallett, J.C.(Sm/Us)	—	4	8	1	52	79	11.28	–	1	1
Hamilton, G.M.(Y/Sc)	—	4	4	–	48	70	17.50	–	–	2
Hancock, T.H.C.(Gs)	—	20	37	1	123	920	25.55	1	7	10
Harden, R.J.(Sm)	1989	18	31	5	131*	1061	40.80	2	7	13
Harper, R.A.(W)	—	1	1	–	18	18	18.00	–	–	–
Harris, A.J.(De)	—	2	3	–	10	11	3.66	–	–	–
Harris, G.A.R.(M)	—	2	2	1	11	16	16.00	–	–	–
Harrison, G.D.(Ire)	—	1	2	1	105*	148	148.00	1	–	–
Harrison, J.C.(M)	—	1	2	–	4	4	2.00	–	–	2
†Hart, M.N.(NZ)	—	9	11	3	36	146	18.25	–	–	5
Hartland, B.R.(NZ)	—	8	16	–	65	337	21.06	–	2	6
Hartley, P.J.(Y)	1987	16	23	3	61	343	17.15	–	1	3
Harvey, M.E.(La)	—	2	3	–	23	44	14.66	–	–	1
Haste, N.J.(CU)	—	9	12	2	22	112	11.20	–	–	2
Hayhurst, A.N.(Sm)	1990	18	30	6	121	1250	52.08	2	10	10
Haynes, D.L.(M)	1989	17	27	2	134	973	38.92	5	2	6
Haynes, G.R.(Wo)	1994	20	32	2	141	1021	34.03	2	4	12
Headley, D.W.(K)	1993	9	13	5	46*	134	16.75	–	–	5
Hegg, W.K.(La)	1989	19	30	4	66	518	19.92	–	2	46/3
Hemmings, E.E.(Sx)	1993	14	24	12	14*	88	7.33	–	–	5
†Hemp, D.L.(Gm)	1994	21	38	4	136	1452	42.70	4	8	16
Hepworth, P.N.(Le)	—	5	10	–	60	113	11.30	–	1	1
Hick, G.A.(Wo/E)	1986	17	29	1	215	1538	54.92	5	5	22
Hindson, J.E.(Nt)	—	4	3	–	11	20	6.66	–	–	2
†Hinks, S.G.(Gs)	—	5	10	–	74	242	24.20	–	2	4
Hodgson, G.D.(Gs)	1992	9	16	1	113	367	24.46	1	1	3
Hodgson, J.S.(CU)	—	9	15	1	54	256	18.28	–	1	8
Hoey, C.J.(Ire)	—	1	–	–	–	–	–	–	–	–
Hollins, C.J.(OU)	—	8	10	2	131	415	51.87	1	2	6
Hollioake, A.J.(Sy)	—	17	23	3	138	722	36.10	3	3	12
†Holloway, P.C.L.(Sm)	—	4	6	–	50	114	19.00	–	1	1
Hooper, C.L.(K)	1992	16	29	–	183	1579	54.44	5	7	26
Hudson, A.C.(SA)	—	12	19	1	116	382	21.22	1	1	8
Hughes, J.G.(Nh)	—	4	6	–	17	47	7.83	–	–	2
Humphries, M.I.(MC)	—	1	1	–	0	0	0.00	–	–	3
Hussain, N.(Ex)	1989	19	31	2	115*	922	31.79	2	5	34
†Hutton, S.(Du)	1992	14	24	2	101	662	30.09	1	3	10
Igglesden, A.P.(K)	1989	11	16	8	15*	61	7.62	–	–	2
Illingworth, R.K.(Wo)	1986	20	25	6	59*	438	23.05	–	3	8
†Ilott, M.C.(Ex/EA)	1993	14	16	5	45*	194	17.63	–	–	3
Innes, K.J.(Nh)	—	1	2	–	0	0	0.00	–	–	–
Irani, R.C.(Ex)	1994	18	29	6	119	965	41.95	2	8	6
†James, K.D.(H)	1989	13	22	2	53	417	20.85	–	2	2
James, S.P.(Gm)	1992	16	28	5	150	877	38.13	3	1	18
Jarvis, P.W.(Sx)	—	17	27	6	70*	347	16.52	–	1	4
Jean-Jacques, M.(H)	—	3	5	1	22*	52	13.00	–	–	1

	Cap	M	I	NO	HS	Runs	Avge	100	50	Ct/St
Johnson, P.(Nt)	1986	17	29	2	132	1170	43.33	4	5	6
Johnson, R.L.(M)	—	11	13	3	50*	205	20.50	–	1	5
†Jones, G.W.(CU)	—	8	13	–	74	220	16.92	–	1	–
Kasprowicz, M.S.(Ex)	1994	17	24	4	44	326	16.30	–	–	9
Keech, M.(H)	—	5	9	–	57	141	15.66	–	1	6
†Keedy, G.(Y)	—	1	1	–	1	1	1.00	–	–	–
Kellett, S.A.(Y)	1992	9	16	–	50	266	16.62	–	1	11
Kendall, W.S.(OU)	—	9	10	3	113*	253	36.14	1	–	8
Kendrick, N.M.(Sy)	—	7	11	2	25	112	12.44	–	–	6
†Kenlock, S.G.(Sy)	—	2	–	–	–	–	–	–	–	1
Kennis, G.J.(Sy)	—	1	2	–	23	41	20.50	–	–	2
Kerr, J.I.D.(Sm)	—	1	2	–	4	5	2.50	–	–	1
Kersey, G.J.(Sy)	—	7	11	2	39	127	14.11	–	–	16/2
†Kettleborough, R.A.(Y)	—	1	2	1	25	49	49.00	–	–	–
†Kirsten, G.(SA)	—	11	19	3	201*	751	46.93	2	5	5
Kirsten, P.N.(SA)	—	10	16	5	130	549	49.90	2	1	5
†Knight, N.V.(Ex)	1994	12	21	1	157	944	47.20	4	3	22
Krikken, K.M.(De)	1992	15	27	10	85*	426	25.05	–	2	26/2
Lamb, A.J.(Nh)	1978	15	22	1	131	908	43.23	2	5	17
Lampitt, S.R.(Wo)	1989	17	26	5	122	624	29.71	1	2	12
†Lara, B.C.(Wa)	1994	15	25	2	501*	2066	89.82	9	3	11
Larkins, W.(Du/W)	1992	16	27	3	158*	976	40.66	1	6	11
Larsen, G.R.(NZ)	—	8	12	4	40*	168	21.00	–	–	4
Lathwell, M.N.(Sm)	1992	18	32	1	206	1230	39.67	2	9	10
Leatherdale, D.A.(Wo)	1994	17	25	3	139	987	44.86	2	3	17
Lefebvre, R.P.(Gm)	1993	12	14	3	33	240	21.81	–	–	5
Lenham, N.J.(Sx)	1990	14	27	1	102	809	31.11	1	5	2
Lewis, C.C.(Nt)	1994	12	19	4	220*	881	58.73	2	5	18
Lewis, D.A.(Ire)	—	1	2	1	113*	152	152.00	1	–	–
Lewis, J.J.B.(Ex)	1994	16	29	3	109	751	28.88	1	4	9
†Lewry, J.D.(Sx)	—	4	6	4	6*	14	7.00	–	–	–
Liebenberg, G.F.J.(SA)	—	7	11	1	64*	226	22.60	–	2	9/3
†Llong, N.J.(K)	1993	7	11	–	44	209	19.00	–	–	3
Lloyd, G.D.(La)	1992	16	27	3	112	684	28.50	1	5	11
Longley, J.I.(Du)	1994	14	25	2	100*	594	25.82	1	5	7
Loye, M.B.(Nh/EA)	1994	15	26	3	132	914	39.73	3	5	7
Lugsden, S.(Du)	1994	5	5	2	2	2	0.66	–	–	–
Lynch, M.A.(Sy)	1982	4	7	1	60	238	39.66	–	1	6
McCague, M.J.(K/EA)	1992	10	16	3	56	285	21.92	–	1	5
McGurk, G.B.J.(Sc)	—	1	2	1	34	45	45.00	–	–	–
Maclay, A.W.(OU)	—	9	8	4	6*	16	4.00	–	–	–
McMillan, B.M.(SA)	—	9	11	3	132	467	58.37	1	3	10
Macmillan, G.I.(OU)	—	10	17	3	69	395	28.21	–	3	20
Maddy, D.L.(Le)	—	3	6	–	34	80	13.33	–	–	3
Malcolm, D.E.(De/E)	1989	18	22	9	15*	89	6.84	–	–	2
†Malik, H.S.(OU)	—	5	7	1	53*	110	18.33	–	1	3
Mallender, N.A.(Sm)	1987	8	12	3	43*	270	30.00	–	–	1
Mann, R.D.(CU)	—	9	16	–	53	248	15.50	–	1	2
Marc, K.(M)	—	1	2	–	9	17	8.50	–	–	–
Marsh, S.A.(K)	1986	19	31	6	88	807	32.28	–	5	69/5
Marshall, M.D.(W)	—	1	–	–	–	–	–	–	–	–
Martin, N.F.C.(OU)	—	10	10	1	26	74	8.22	–	–	5
Martin, P.J.(La)	1994	18	27	3	57	383	15.95	–	1	4
Maru, R.J.(H)	1986	9	15	4	38*	207	18.81	–	–	13
Mason, T.J.(Le)	—	1	1	–	3	3	3.00	–	–	2
Matthews, C.R.(SA)	—	9	6	2	62*	143	35.75	–	1	2

	Cap	M	I	NO	HS	Runs	Avge	100	50	Ct/St
Maynard, M.P.(Gm)	1987	16	28	1	118	975	36.11	2	5	18/1
Metcalfe, A.A.(Y)	1986	2	4	–	12	15	3.75	–	–	1
Metson, C.P.(Gm)	1987	18	22	4	51	398	22.11	–	1	54/7
Middleton, T.C.(H)	1990	13	23	3	102	524	26.20	1	1	8
Mike, G.W.(Nt)	—	17	26	3	60*	365	15.86	–	1	1
Milburn, S.M.(Y)	—	1	–	–	–	–	–	–	–	–
Millar, R.B.(Ire)	—	1	–	–	–	–	–	–	–	2
†Millns, D.J.(Le)	1991	19	27	10	64*	348	20.47	–	1	12
Mirza, P.(Wo)	—	3	5	1	40	47	11.75	–	–	1
Moles, A.J.(Wa)	1987	11	20	3	203*	863	50.76	1	5	5
Montgomerie, R.R.(Nh/OU/Us)	—	19	34	3	151	1062	34.25	2	8	12
Moody, T.M.(Wo)	1991	18	28	3	159	1160	46.40	3	6	20
Moore, E.R.(Ire)	—	1	–	–	–	–	–	–	–	–
Moores, P.(Sx)	1989	18	32	2	70*	766	25.53	–	4	61/1
†Morris, H.(Gm)	1986	16	31	2	106	885	30.51	1	6	13
Morris, J.E.(Du/W)	1994	20	35	1	204	1433	42.14	4	6	8
Morris, R.S.M.(H)	—	9	17	3	174	686	49.00	2	3	4
Morrison, D.K.(NZ)	—	2	3	2	10*	10	10.00	–	–	1
Mortensen, O.H.(De)	1986	2	–	–	–	–	–	–	–	–
Moxon, M.D.(Y)	1984	17	30	4	274*	1458	56.07	4	6	8
Mullally, A.D.(Le)	1993	14	19	4	23	114	7.60	–	–	6
Munton, T.A.(Wa)	1989	18	17	7	36	106	10.60	–	–	4
Murphy, A.J.(Sy)	—	1	1	1	10*	10	–	–	–	–
Mushtaq Ahmed (Sm)	1993	9	14	3	38	168	15.27	–	–	4
Myles, S.D.(MC)	—	1	1	1	59*	59	–	–	1	3
Nash, D.J.(NZ)	—	8	11	6	56	177	35.40	–	1	5
Newman, P.G.(MC)	—	1	1	–	8	8	8.00	–	–	–
Newport, P.J.(Wo)	1986	17	24	5	41	345	18.15	–	–	3
Nicholas, M.C.J.(H)	1982	19	32	6	145	1182	45.46	3	5	7
†Nixon, P.A.(Le)	1994	19	30	3	131	1046	38.74	3	4	60/2
Noon, W.M.(Nt)	—	18	30	6	75	617	25.70	–	3	38/5
O'Gorman, T.J.G.(De)	1992	16	28	2	145	872	33.53	3	3	12
Orr, D.A.(Sc)	—	1	–	–	–	–	–	–	–	1
Ostler, D.P.(Wa)	1991	18	29	2	186	1161	43.00	2	6	14
Owens, M.B.(NZ)	—	6	8	2	4	8	1.33	–	–	2
Parker, B.(Y)	1992	10	18	2	127	578	36.12	1	4	6
Parkin, O.T.(Gm)	—	2	2	2	2*	2	–	–	–	–
Parore, A.C.(NZ)	—	11	18	4	71	399	28.50	–	2	21
†Parsons, G.J.(Le)	1984	16	25	6	70	491	25.84	–	2	17
Parsons, K.A.(Sm)	—	3	5	1	16	38	9.50	–	–	2
Patel, M.M.(K)	1994	18	27	2	39	256	10.24	–	–	12
Patterson, B.M.W.(Sc)	—	1	2	–	114	136	68.00	1	–	1
Payne, A.(Sm)	—	1	1	–	34	34	34.00	–	–	–
Pearson, R.M.(Ex)	—	3	4	–	20	45	11.25	–	–	2
†Peirce, M.T.E.(Us)	—	1	2	–	24	24	12.00	–	–	1
†Penberthy, A.L.(Nh)	1994	17	25	5	88*	658	32.90	–	5	9
†Penn, C.(K)	1987	1	1	–	0	0	0.00	–	–	–
Pennett, D.B.(Nt)	—	1	–	–	–	–	–	–	–	–
Penney, T.L.(Wa)	1994	16	24	3	111	798	38.00	1	1	14
Phelps, B.S.(Gm)	—	2	4	1	11	18	6.00	–	–	–
Philip, I.L.(Sc)	—	1	2	–	22	32	16.00	–	–	2
Phillips, N.C.(Sx)	—	1	2	1	37*	37	37.00	–	–	1
†Pick, R.A.(Nt)	1987	16	22	7	65*	227	15.13	–	1	4
Pierson, A.R.K.(Le)	—	15	20	5	43*	334	22.26	–	–	15
Pigott, A.C.S.(Sy)	—	8	11	–	40	160	14.54	–	–	1
Pike, V.J.(Gs)	—	9	12	4	27	114	14.25	–	–	2

	Cap	M	I	NO	HS	Runs	Avge	100	50	Ct/St
Piper, K.J.(Wa)	1992	17	24	4	116*	454	22.70	1	1	61/5
Pipes, D.J.(Nt)	—	1	2	1	11*	12	12.00	–	–	–
Pitcher, C.M.(CU/Us)	—	10	14	4	43	116	11.60	–	–	4
Pocock, B.A.(NZ)	—	7	14	2	103*	374	31.16	1	2	8
†Pollard, P.R.(Nt)	1992	18	31	1	134	905	30.16	2	4	11
†Pooley, J.C.(M)	—	3	4	–	40	77	19.25	–	–	2
Prichard, P.J.(Ex)	1986	11	17	2	119	569	37.93	3	2	6
Pringle, C.(NZ)	—	8	8	–	24	88	11.00	–	–	2
Radford, N.V.(Wo)	1985	15	20	4	25	161	10.06	–	–	6
Radford, T.A.(M)	—	1	1	–	4	4	4.00	–	–	1
Ramprakash, M.R.(M)	1990	18	26	2	135	1270	52.91	4	6	13
Ratcliffe, J.D.(Wa)	—	3	5	–	69	87	17.40	–	1	1
Ratledge, J.(CU)	—	9	16	–	79	227	14.18	–	1	1
Rea, M.P.(Ire)	—	1	2	–	49	76	38.00	–	–	–
Reeve, D.A.(Wa)	1989	9	10	1	33	116	12.88	–	–	18
Remy, C.C.(Sx)	—	6	11	1	60	194	19.40	–	2	3
Rhodes, J.N.(SA)	—	12	16	3	77	477	36.69	–	3	8
Rhodes, S.J.(Wo/E/EA)	1986	18	27	11	100*	896	56.00	1	5	59/8
Richardson, D.J.(SA)	—	10	12	3	88	286	31.77	–	2	23/1
Richardson, M.S.(Sc)	—	1	–	–	–	–	–	–	–	–
Richardson, R.B.(Y)	1993	9	16	–	76	551	34.43	–	5	9
†Ridley, A.C.(OU)	—	3	4	1	36*	65	21.66	–	–	–
Ripley, D.(Nh)	1987	16	23	9	36*	263	18.78	–	–	40/6
Roberts, A.R.(Nh)	—	9	12	4	51	261	32.62	–	1	3
Roberts, S.J.(NZ)	—	2	4	–	24	32	8.00	–	–	–
Robinson, D.D.J.(Ex)	—	1	1	–	38	38	38.00	–	–	1
Robinson, M.A.(Y)	1992	19	23	8	9	58	3.86	–	–	5
Robinson, P.E.(Le)	—	5	7	–	86	305	43.57	–	3	8
Robinson, R.T.(Nt)	1983	19	31	1	182	1276	42.53	2	10	7
Rollins, A.S.(De)	—	16	29	2	97	708	26.22	–	6	18
Rollins, R.J.(Ex)	—	1	1	–	9	9	9.00	–	–	1
Rose, G.D.(Sm)	1988	16	24	2	121	548	24.90	1	2	16
Roseberry, A.(Gm)	—	6	8	1	94	249	35.57	–	2	3
Roseberry, M.A.(M)	1990	20	32	2	152	1097	36.56	2	6	21
†Russell, R.C.(Gs)	1985	19	34	8	85*	901	34.65	–	4	58/1
Rutherford, K.R.(NZ)	—	9	17	1	129	603	37.68	2	2	1
Salisbury, I.D.K.(Sx/E)	1991	16	25	6	49	331	17.42	–	–	19
†Salmond, G.(Sc)	—	1	1	1	28*	28	–	–	–	–
Sargeant, N.F.(Sy)	—	9	13	2	46	166	15.09	–	–	18
†Saxelby, M.(Du)	1994	17	32	–	181	1102	34.43	2	4	4
Scott, C.W.(Du/W)	1992	20	33	3	108	670	22.33	2	3	56/2
Scriven, T.J.A.(MC)	—	1	1	–	8	8	8.00	–	–	–
Searle, J.P.(Du)	1993	1	2	2	5*	5	–	–	–	–
†Seymour, A.C.H.(Wo)	—	3	5	–	87	179	35.80	–	1	–
Shahid, N.(Ex)	—	10	18	4	91	326	23.28	–	1	13
Shaw, A.D.(Gm)	—	3	3	1	14	18	9.00	–	–	6
†Shaw, T.G.(SA)	—	9	5	3	66	82	41.00	–	1	4
Sheeraz, K.P.(Gs)	—	1	2	2	1*	1	–	–	–	–
Sheridan, K.L.P.(Sc)	—	1	–	–	–	–	–	–	–	–
Sheriyar, A.(Le)	—	4	3	2	16*	28	28.00	–	–	–
Shine, K.J.(M)	—	13	8	5	14*	39	13.00	–	–	4
Silverwood, C.E.W.(Y)	—	9	15	3	26	127	10.58	–	–	2
Simmons, P.V.(Le)	1994	17	30	–	261	953	31.76	1	3	23
Sladdin, R.W.(De)	—	3	6	–	20	42	7.00	–	–	–
Sleep, P.R.(W)	—	1	1	1	79*	79	–	–	1	–
Small, G.C.(Wa)	1982	11	10	1	23	78	8.66	–	–	2

	Cap	M	I	NO	HS	Runs	Avge	100	50	Ct/St
Smith, A.M.(Gs)	—	12	14	2	29	162	13.50	–	–	3
Smith, A.W.(Sy)	—	14	21	5	202*	524	32.75	1	1	3
Smith, B.F.(Le)	—	14	23	3	95	628	31.40	–	4	10
†Smith, D.M.(Sx)	1989	7	14	3	74	326	29.63	–	3	6
Smith, N.M.K.(Wa)	1993	18	21	4	65	435	25.58	–	2	3
Smith, P.A.(Wa)	1986	12	17	3	65	363	25.92	–	2	2
Smith, R.A.(H/E)	1985	17	29	–	162	1263	43.55	5	4	6
†Smyth, S.G.(Ire)	—	1	1	–	70	70	70.00	–	1	–
Snape, J.N.(Nh/Us)	—	2	4	2	43*	76	38.00	–	–	3
Snell, R.P.(SA)	—	8	8	3	94	143	28.60	–	1	–
Speak, N.J.(La)	1992	19	34	6	143	1304	46.57	3	7	16
Speight, M.P.(Sx)	1991	17	29	–	126	991	34.17	1	4	20
Spencer, D.J.(K)	—	4	6	1	13	46	9.20	–	–	1
Spiring, K.R.(Wo)	—	1	2	–	56	108	54.00	–	2	2
Stanley, D.E.(CU)	—	5	8	2	48	91	15.16	–	–	2
Steer, I.G.S.(De/Us)	—	3	3	1	67	142	71.00	–	1	4
Stemp, R.D.(Y)	—	20	28	2	28	263	10.11	–	–	9
Stephenson, F.D.(Sx)	1992	17	28	1	107	752	27.85	1	5	9
Stephenson, J.P.(Ex)	1989	16	27	1	144	535	20.57	1	2	9
Stewart, A.J.(Sy/E)	1985	16	23	3	142	936	46.80	3	4	20/1
Storie, A.C.(Sc)	—	1	2	2	102*	166	–	1	1	–
Such, P.M.(Ex/E/EA)	1991	20	23	2	29	167	7.95	–	–	9
†Sutcliffe, I.J.(OU)	—	5	4	1	8*	18	6.00	–	–	2
Sylvester, S.A.(Nt)	—	1	1	1	6*	6	–	–	–	–
Symcox, P.L.(SA)	—	7	5	3	39*	104	52.00	–	–	2
†Taylor, C.W.(M)	—	3	1	–	0	0	0.00	–	–	1
†Taylor, J.P.(Nh/E)	1992	13	14	7	26	68	9.71	–	–	5
Taylor, M.(De)	—	4	5	2	14*	25	8.33	–	–	–
Taylor, N.R.(K)	1982	16	27	3	139	1049	43.70	3	4	4
Terry, V.P.(H)	1983	19	34	1	164	1286	38.96	5	2	25
†Thomas, S.D.(Gm)	—	1	1	1	15*	15	–	–	–	–
Thompson, D.J.(Sy)	—	1	2	–	22	39	19.50	–	–	–
Thompson, J.B.D.(K)	—	1	2	1	2	3	3.00	–	–	–
Thomson, S.A.(NZ)	—	10	19	7	69	408	34.00	–	4	5
†Thorpe, G.P.(Sy/E)	1991	16	25	4	190	1136	54.09	2	7	11
Thursfield, M.J.(H)	—	9	12	1	47	106	9.63	–	–	1
Titchard, S.P.(La)	—	13	21	–	99	549	26.14	–	3	16
Tolley, C.M.(Wo)	1993	7	11	3	84	180	22.50	–	1	3
Topley, T.D.(Ex)	1988	1	1	–	2	2	2.00	–	–	–
Townsend, C.J.(OU)	—	10	9	3	22	61	10.16	–	–	13/4
†Trescothick, M.E.(Sm)	—	11	20	1	121	924	48.63	2	8	13
†Trimby, P.W.(OU/Us)	—	6	6	2	11	23	5.75	–	–	3
Trump, H.R.J.(Sm)	1994	14	20	4	45*	276	17.25	–	–	14
Tufnell, P.C.R.(M/E)	1990	9	6	1	5	14	2.80	–	–	5
Turner, R.J.(Sm)	1994	18	27	5	104*	537	24.40	1	2	46/6
†Twose, R.G.(Wa)	1992	18	31	5	277*	1411	54.26	3	6	8
Udal, S.D.(H)	1992	17	30	4	94	684	26.30	–	4	16
Vandrau, M.J.(De)	—	13	23	5	66	435	24.16	–	1	9
Van Troost, A.P.(Sm)	—	14	18	6	33	108	9.00	–	–	3
Vaughan, M.P.(Y)	—	16	30	1	117	1066	36.75	3	3	8
†Walker, A.(Du)	1994	4	7	2	13	34	6.80	–	–	1
Walker, L.N.P.(Nt)	—	1	2	–	1	1	0.50	–	–	–
†Walker, M.J.(K)	—	5	7	–	107	239	34.14	1	–	2
Walsh, C.A.(Gs)	1985	15	24	6	66	274	15.22	–	1	2
Walton, T.C.(Nh)	—	2	2	–	11	16	8.00	–	–	2
Ward, D.M.(Sy)	1990	16	22	1	294*	921	43.85	1	5	10

	Cap	M	I	NO	HS	Runs	Avge	100	50	Ct/St
Ward, T.R.(K)	1989	19	33	1	125	1368	42.75	3	10	29
Warke, S.J.S.(Ire)	—	1	2	–	60	73	36.50	–	1	–
Warner, A.E.(De)	1987	10	15	3	24*	96	8.00	–	–	1
Warren, R.J.(Nh)	—	12	21	2	94*	566	29.78	–	5	14
†Wasim Akram (La)	1989	6	10	–	98	244	24.40	–	2	–
Watkin, S.L.(Gm)	1989	18	21	11	14	92	9.20	–	–	2
Watkinson, M.(La)	1987	18	28	2	155	889	34.19	2	3	10
Weekes, L.C.(Y)	—	1	–	–	–	–	–	–	–	1
Weekes, P.N.(M)	1983	16	21	2	117	648	34.10	1	2	10
Welch, G.(Wa)	—	12	15	3	84*	446	37.16	–	4	5
Wells, A.P.(Sx/EA)	1986	19	35	4	84	909	29.32	–	7	15
Wells, C.M.(De)	—	11	20	2	42	303	16.83	–	–	4
Wells, V.J.(Le)	1994	16	28	4	87*	871	36.29	–	6	13
†Wessels, K.C.(SA)	—	12	18	2	105	679	42.43	1	4	17
†Weston, W.P.C.(Wo)	—	17	28	1	94	818	30.29	–	6	6
Wharf, A.G.(Y)	—	1	2	–	46	46	23.00	–	–	–
Whitaker, J.J.(Le)	1986	18	32	2	148	958	31.93	2	6	9
†Whitaker, P.R.(H)	—	2	3	–	94	134	44.66	–	1	–
White, C.(Y/E)	1993	13	20	2	108*	663	36.83	1	5	8
White, G.W.(H/Us)	—	11	20	1	104	467	24.57	1	2	13
Whittall, A.R.(CU)	—	9	11	2	91*	193	21.44	–	1	3
Wight, R.M.(Gs)	—	2	3	1	22	53	26.50	–	–	–
Wileman, J.R.(MC)	—	1	2	1	42*	50	50.00	–	–	3
Williams, N.F.(M)	1984	10	9	4	63	134	26.80	–	1	2
Williams, R.C.(Gs)	—	10	14	2	38	171	14.25	–	–	4
†Williams, R.C.J.(Gs)	—	1	–	–	–	–	–	–	–	4/1
Williamson, J.G.(Sc)	—	1	–	–	–	–	–	–	–	–
Windows, M.G.N.(Gs/Us)	—	11	21	–	106	730	34.76	1	5	11
Wood, J.(Du)	1992	15	22	3	51	194	10.21	–	1	3
Wren, T.N.(K)	—	7	11	4	18*	31	4.42	–	–	2
Wright, A.J.(Gs)	1987	19	36	3	184*	1202	36.42	1	7	32
Yates, G.(La)	1994	13	20	7	54*	272	20.92	–	2	3
Yeabsley, R.S.(OU)	—	6	3	1	52*	53	26.50	–	1	5
Young, B.A.(NZ/W)	—	10	18	–	122	688	38.22	1	5	11

BOWLING

See BATTING and FIELDING section for details of caps and teams.

	Cat	O	M	R	W	Avge	Best	5wI	10wM
Adams, C.J.	OB	30	3	114	3	38.00	2- 16	–	–
Adams, J.C.	SLA	340.5	125	720	23	31.30	4- 63	–	–
Afford, J.A.	SLA	541.3	164	1376	40	34.40	5- 48	2	–
Alleyne, M.W.	RM	351.3	68	1103	41	26.90	5- 78	1	–
Ambrose, C.E.L.	RF	540	159	1113	77	14.45	7- 44	6	2
Andrew, S.J.W.	RMF	150.3	33	425	9	47.22	2- 28	–	–
Arnold, K.A.	RFM	40	10	93	4	23.25	2- 29	–	–
Asif Din	LB	2	0	9	0	–	–	–	–
Atherton, M.A.	LB	7	2	10	0	–	–	–	–
Athey, C.W.J.	RM	18	1	78	1	78.00	1- 1	–	–
Austin, I.D.	RM	251.5	72	662	33	20.06	5- 23	3	1
Azharuddin, M.	RM	8	0	46	0	–	–	–	–
Babington, A.M.	RFM	23.5	7	42	1	42.00	1- 27	–	–
Bailey, R.J.	OB	166.1	33	568	11	51.63	5- 59	1	–
Bainbridge, P.	RM	315.4	67	1082	14	77.28	4- 72	–	–
Ball, M.C.J.	OB	325.3	78	955	21	45.47	5- 69	1	–
Baptiste, E.A.E.	RFM	2	0	15	0	–	–	–	–

	Cat	O	M	R	W	Avge	Best	5wI	10wM
Barnett, A.A.	SLA	191.4	39	627	10	62.70	2- 35	–	–
Barnett, K.J.	LB	54.2	5	173	13	13.30	5- 31	1	–
Barwick, S.R.	RMF	549.5	208	1131	36	31.41	5- 44	1	–
Base, S.J.	RMF	199	30	782	23	34.00	5- 92	1	–
Bashforth, M.C.	RM	28	9	108	0	–	–	–	–
Bastien, S.	RMF	138.3	40	384	8	48.00	2- 47	–	–
Bates, R.T.	OB	47	8	147	2	73.50	1- 52	–	–
Batty, J.D.	OB	77.4	18	259	6	43.16	2- 57	–	–
Bell, M.A.V.	LMF	31	5	108	3	36.00	3- 89	–	–
Benjamin, J.E.	RMF	591.2	130	1658	80	20.72	6- 27	5	1
Benjamin, K.C.G.	RFM	15	4	53	0	–	–	–	–
Benjamin, W.K.M.	RFM	281	97	585	24	24.37	6- 46	2	–
Berry, P.J.	OB	15	2	58	0	–	–	–	–
Bicknell, D.J.	LM	1	0	1	0	–	–	–	–
Bicknell, M.P.	RFM	319.4	75	977	29	33.68	5- 44	1	–
Birbeck, S.D.	RM	7	2	13	2	6.50	2- 13	–	–
Bird, P.J.	RFM	44.5	9	166	0	–	–	–	–
Boiling, J.	OB	107	33	237	6	39.50	2- 38	–	–
Bovill, J.N.B.	RFM	119.4	23	421	14	30.07	5-108	1	–
Bowen, M.N.	RM	113.1	21	395	6	65.83	2- 90	–	–
Bowler, P.D.	OB	1	0	17	0	–	–	–	–
Brimson, M.T.	SLA	121.1	31	347	5	69.40	1- 25	–	–
Brinkley, J.E.	RFM	233	40	779	18	43.27	6- 98	1	–
Broadhurst, M.	RFM	11	0	52	1	52.00	1- 45	–	–
Brown, A.D.	LB	15	1	47	0	–	–	–	–
Brown, D.R.	RFM	35	5	118	5	23.60	4- 25	–	–
Brown, S.J.E.	LFM	578.5	88	2108	75	28.10	6- 68	6	–
Bullen, C.K.	OB	12.4	2	72	2	36.00	2- 42	–	–
Butcher, G.P.	RM	37	5	148	2	74.00	2- 36	–	–
Butcher, M.A.	RM	206.4	50	670	16	41.87	4- 31	–	–
Byas, D.	RM	16	4	52	2	26.00	1- 16	–	–
Caddick, A.R.	RFM	372.3	71	1186	51	23.25	6- 51	3	–
Capel, D.J.	RMF	33	7	89	0	–	–	–	–
Carroll, J.P.	RM	6	1	22	0	–	–	–	–
Cassar, M.E.	RFM	24.2	3	94	3	31.33	3- 65	–	–
Chapman, R.J.	RFM	48.4	10	187	4	46.75	2- 21	–	–
Chapple, G.	RFM	458.4	110	1474	55	26.80	6- 48	4	–
Childs, J.H.	SLA	464.3	117	1254	39	32.15	6- 71	2	–
Church, M.J.	RM	1	0	4	0	–	–	–	–
Clarke, V.P.	RM/LB	23	4	105	1	105.00	1- 93	–	–
Connor, C.A.	RFM	574.4	131	1764	72	24.50	7- 47	2	2
Cook, N.G.B.	SLA	283.3	85	715	17	42.05	3- 46	–	–
Cooke, G.	RMF	23	6	65	2	32.50	1- 26	–	–
Cooper, K.E.	RFM	418.2	98	1095	38	28.81	4- 38	–	–
Cork, D.G.	RFM	329.1	53	1112	37	30.05	6- 29	2	–
Cottey, P.A.	OB	24.4	3	106	2	53.00	1- 16	–	–
Cousins, D.M.	RMF	112	21	337	13	25.92	6- 35	1	–
Cowans, N.G.	RFM	349.3	93	986	26	37.92	4- 76	–	–
Cowdrey, G.R.	RM	0.2	0	4	0	–	–	–	–
Cox, D.M.	SLA	74.5	11	345	1	345.00	1- 92	–	–
Crawley, J.P.	RM	1	0	4	0	–	–	–	–
Crawley, M.A.	RM	77	33	132	1	132.00	1- 48	–	–
Croft, R.D.B.	OB	715.3	154	2166	41	52.82	5- 80	1	–
Cronje, W.J.	RM	159.5	45	395	13	30.38	4- 47	–	–
Crowe, M.D.	RM	12	0	81	2	40.50	2- 81	–	–
Cuffy, C.E.	RF	389.3	106	1082	36	30.05	4- 70	–	–

	Cat	O	M	R	W	Avge	Best	5wI	10wM
Cummins, A.C.	RFM	520.3	92	1768	56	31.57	6- 64	4	1
Curran, K.M.	RMF	423.5	86	1463	31	47.19	4- 65	–	–
Curtis, T.S.	LB	8	1	43	0	–	–	–	–
Dakin, J.M.	RM	11	1	36	1	36.00	1- 36	–	–
Dale, A.	RM	277	65	975	23	42.39	2- 7	–	–
Daley, J.A.	RM	2	0	9	0	–	–	–	–
Davies, M.	SLA	104.3	14	370	6	61.66	3- 53	–	–
Davis, H.T.	RF	131.4	9	719	9	79.88	3-127	–	–
Davis, R.P.	SLA	341	102	986	31	31.80	6- 94	2	–
Dawson, R.I.	RM	30	9	73	2	36.50	2- 38	–	–
DeFreitas, P.A.J.	RFM	530.5	108	1621	65	24.93	6- 39	4	–
Derbyshire, N.A.	RFM	44	5	168	2	84.00	1- 48	–	–
De Villiers, P.S.	RFM	277.3	59	922	38	24.26	6- 67	2	–
Dimond, M.	RMF	55.3	8	216	5	43.20	4- 73	–	–
D'Oliveira, D.B.	OB	74	22	176	7	25.14	4- 68	–	–
Donald, A.A.	RF	212.2	42	775	25	31.00	5- 58	2	–
Donelan, B.T.P.	OB	15	2	59	1	59.00	1- 27	–	–
Dowman, M.P.	RM	12	2	45	0	–	–	–	–
Ealham, M.A.	RMF	265.4	62	762	27	28.22	7- 53	1	–
Ecclestone, S.C.	RMF	298.3	70	825	22	37.50	4- 66	–	–
Emburey, J.E.	OB	674	204	1514	59	25.66	6- 89	2	–
Evans, K.P.	RMF	413.5	105	1143	38	30.07	4- 46	–	–
Fairbrother, N.H.	LM	1	0	3	0	–	–	–	–
Feltham, M.A.	RMF	382.3	83	1140	34	33.52	5- 69	1	–
Field-Buss, M.G.	OB	245.1	71	540	12	45.00	2- 23	–	–
Fielding, J.M.	SLA	19.4	6	53	2	26.50	1- 15	–	–
Fleming, M.V.	RM	239.5	48	746	9	82.88	2- 36	–	–
Flint, D.P.J.	SLA	49	13	129	1	129.00	1- 12	–	–
Foster, M.J.	RFM	37.5	12	100	3	33.33	2- 4	–	–
Fourie, B.C.	RMF	28	2	73	4	18.25	3- 19	–	–
Fraser, A.R.C.	RFM	532.5	142	1343	50	26.86	3- 16	–	–
Fulton, D.P.	SLA	0.1	0	0	0	–	–	–	–
Gallian, J.E.R.	RM	95	10	368	10	36.80	2- 27	–	–
Gatting, M.W.	RM	26	4	97	2	48.50	1- 10	–	–
Gibson, O.D.	RF	579.5	100	2171	60	36.18	6- 64	4	1
Giddins, E.S.H.	RMF	450.4	89	1463	60	24.38	5- 38	3	–
Gooch, G.A.	RM	31.3	11	60	3	20.00	1- 0	–	–
Gough, D.	RFM	479.2	100	1526	62	24.61	6- 66	3	–
Govan, J.W.	OB	33	6	137	1	137.00	1- 57	–	–
Graham, P.C.	RM	29.3	5	83	4	20.75	2- 39	–	–
Graham, S.	RM	19	3	43	1	43.00	1- 8	–	–
Graveney, D.A.	SLA	456	121	1247	31	40.22	6- 80	1	–
Grayson, A.P.	SLA	103.3	34	236	8	29.50	2- 43	–	–
Greenfield, K.	RM	16	1	76	0	–	–	–	–
Griffith, F.A.	RM	67.4	12	210	8	26.25	3- 32	–	–
Gupte, C.M.	SLA	1	0	16	0	–	–	–	–
Hall, M.A.T.	LM/SLA	2	0	2	0	–	–	–	–
Hallett, J.C.	RMF	84.2	24	270	8	33.75	4- 59	–	–
Hamilton, G.M.	RMF	100.2	20	364	5	72.80	2- 76	–	–
Hancock, T.H.C.	RM	47	7	207	3	69.00	2- 16	–	–
Harper, R.A.	OB	16	1	58	1	58.00	1- 58	–	–
Harris, A.J.	RM	32	1	165	5	33.00	3- 40	–	–
Harris, G.A.R.	RFM	51	11	215	1	215.00	1- 61	–	–
Harrison, G.D.	OB	27	4	84	0	–	–	–	–
Hart, M.N.	SLA	335.3	104	850	18	47.22	4-106	–	–
Hartley, P.J.	RMF	562.1	116	1701	61	27.88	5- 89	1	–

	Cat	O	M	R	W	Avge	Best	5wI	10wM
Haste, N.J.	RM	233	39	910	13	70.00	4- 69	–	–
Hayhurst, A.N.	RM	87.4	24	265	9	29.44	2- 5	–	–
Haynes, D.L.	RM/LB	2	2	0	0	–	–	–	–
Haynes, G.R.	RM	108.3	23	319	7	45.57	3- 19	–	–
Headley, D.W.	RFM	295.3	48	989	36	27.47	5- 60	2	–
Hemmings, E.E.	OB	422	140	959	33	29.06	7- 66	2	–
Hemp, D.L.	RM	8	0	41	0	–	–	–	–
Hepworth, P.N.	OB	72	14	253	9	28.11	3- 30	–	–
Hick, G.A.	OB	173.2	55	462	11	42.00	3- 64	–	–
Hindson, J.E.	SLA	106	27	344	8	43.00	5- 53	1	–
Hodgson, J.S.	OB	272.3	85	732	15	48.80	4- 14	–	–
Hoey, C.J.	LB	24	2	79	0	–	–	–	–
Hollins, C.J.	OB	236.3	32	890	19	46.84	4- 64	–	–
Hollioake, A.J.	RMF	264.1	44	958	26	36.84	4- 48	–	–
Hooper, C.L.	OB	414.1	93	1055	29	36.37	5- 52	1	–
Hughes, J.G.	RM	137.2	38	428	14	30.57	5- 69	1	–
Hussain, N.	LB	1	0	1	0	–	–	–	–
Igglesden, A.P.	RFM	316.1	75	929	24	38.70	5- 38	1	–
Illingworth, R.K.	SLA	679.1	211	1499	49	30.59	4- 51	–	–
Ilott, M.C.	LFM	497.5	115	1391	59	23.57	6- 24	3	1
Innes, K.J.	RM	10	3	33	0	–	–	–	–
Irani, R.C.	RM	249.4	42	834	28	29.78	4- 27	–	–
James, K.D.	LMF	280.1	56	900	26	34.61	4- 78	–	–
Jarvis, P.W.	RFM	496.2	89	1773	51	34.76	7- 58	1	–
Jean-Jacques, M.	RMF	53.1	4	242	5	48.40	3- 44	–	–
Johnson, R.L.	RMF	350.4	85	1059	40	26.47	10- 45	1	1
Kasprowicz, M.S.	RF	527.3	91	1869	60	31.15	7- 83	3	–
Keech, M.	RM	9.3	2	39	0	–	–	–	–
Kendrick, N.M.	SLA	185.3	36	606	9	67.33	3-159	–	–
Kenlock, S.G.	LMF	53	11	186	3	62.00	3-104	–	–
Kerr, J.I.D.	RMF	21	3	91	0	–	–	–	–
Kettleborough, R A	RM	6	2	18	0	–	–	–	–
Kirsten, G.	OB	22.5	5	97	0	–	–	–	–
Kirsten, P.N.	OB	18	4	76	2	38.00	1- 23	–	–
Knight, N.V.	RM	11.4	0	61	1	61.00	1- 61	–	–
Lampitt, S.R.	RMF	512.5	127	1484	64	23.18	5- 33	2	–
Lara, B.C.	LB	21	1	112	0	–	–	–	–
Larkins, W.	RM	5	0	39	0	–	–	–	–
Larsen, G.R.	RM	226.4	73	494	21	23.52	5- 24	1	–
Lathwell, M.N.	RM	29	4	119	3	39.66	2- 21	–	–
Leatherdale, D A	RM	108.1	22	339	5	67.80	2- 11	–	–
Lefebvre, R.P.	RMF	365.2	108	896	25	35.84	4- 63	–	–
Lenham, N.J.	RM	9	0	24	0	–	–	–	–
Lewis, C.C.	RFM	345.2	69	1082	46	23.52	5- 55	2	–
Lewis, D.A.	RM	6	1	27	1	27.00	1- 27	–	–
Lewis, J.J.B.	RSM	8	1	32	0	–	–	–	–
Lewry, J.D.	LMF	96	20	315	7	45.00	4- 40	–	–
Llong, N.J.	OB	41.3	11	113	6	18.83	5- 63	1	–
Lugsden, S.	RFM	106.2	16	412	3	137.33	1- 15	–	–
Lynch, M.A.	OB	10	2	35	0	–	–	–	–
McCague, M.J.	RF	341.1	67	1084	57	19.01	9- 86	5	1
Maclay, A.W.	RMF	204.4	35	669	9	74.33	3- 30	–	–
McMillan, B.M.	RFM	222.4	49	662	19	34.84	4- 47	–	–
Macmillan, G.I.	OB	94	17	324	7	46.28	1- 15	–	–
Malcolm, D.E.	RF	551.3	97	2015	69	29.20	9- 57	3	1
Malik, H.S.	OB	68	14	241	7	34 42	3- 10	–	–

	Cat	O	M	R	W	Avge	Best	5wI	10wM
Mallender, N.A.	RFM	193.4	51	602	16	37.62	3- 23	–	–
Marc, K.	RFM	29	4	133	3	44.33	2- 52	–	–
Marshall, M.D.	RF	16	2	60	3	20.00	3- 60	–	–
Martin, N.F.C.	RM	144.4	27	480	7	68.57	2- 84	–	–
Martin, P.J.	RFM	614.4	173	1580	54	29.25	5- 61	2	–
Maru, R.J.	SLA	254.1	75	621	15	41.40	3- 61	–	–
Mason, T.J.	OB	7	0	22	1	22.00	1- 22	–	–
Matthews, C.R.	RFM	263.3	71	749	17	44.05	3- 25	–	–
Maynard, M.P.	RM	1	0	10	0	–	–	–	–
Mike, G.W.	RMF	406.1	92	1422	45	31.60	5- 44	1	–
Milburn, S.M.	RMF	24.2	4	77	3	25.66	2- 74	–	–
Millns, D.J.	RF	532	99	1901	76	25.01	6- 44	4	–
Mirza, P.	RM	61.4	14	193	9	21.44	4- 29	–	–
Montgomerie, R.R.	OB	4	0	28	0	–	–	–	–
Moody, T.M.	RM	195	48	572	15	38.13	4- 24	–	–
Moore, E.R.	LFM	34.1	6	115	0	–	–	–	–
Morris, J.E.	RM	27.5	3	125	1	125.00	1- 37	–	–
Morrison, D.K.	RFM	36	6	117	4	29.25	2- 40	–	–
Mortensen, O.H.	RFM	23	5	48	2	24.00	1- 18	–	–
Mullally, A.D.	LFM	448.1	121	1255	33	38.03	5- 85	1	–
Munton, T.A.	RMF	699.4	181	1748	81	21.58	7- 52	6	2
Murphy, A.J.	RMF	22	8	50	2	25.00	2- 42	–	–
Mushtaq Ahmed	LB	404	114	1196	45	26.57	7- 94	4	1
Myles, S.D.	RM	1	0	2	0	–	–	–	–
Nash, D.J.	RFM	228.4	51	775	25	31.00	6- 76	2	1
Newman, P.G.	RFM	36	9	108	3	36.00	2- 57	–	–
Newport, P.J.	RFM	516.2	103	1654	53	31.20	4- 50	–	–
Nicholas, M.C.J.	RM	4	2	7	0	–	–	–	–
O'Gorman, T.J.G.	OB	0.5	0	8	0	–	–	–	–
Ostler, D.P.	RM	1.1	0	13	0	–	–	–	–
Owens, M.B.	RFM	127	31	424	17	24.94	5- 74	1	–
Parkin, O.T.	RFM	54	9	170	4	42.50	2- 45	–	–
Parore, A.C.	(WK)	5	0	55	0	–	–	–	–
Parsons, G.J.	RMF	462.3	131	1208	44	27.45	5- 34	1	–
Parsons, K.A.	RM	4	0	21	0	–	–	–	–
Patel, M.M.	SLA	811.2	202	2058	90	22.86	8- 96	6	3
Payne, A.	RMF	12	2	54	0	–	–	–	–
Pearson, R.M.	OB	74	17	226	4	56.50	1- 39	–	–
Penberthy, A.L.	RM	400.1	83	1374	37	37.13	5- 54	1	–
Penn, C.	RFM	13	4	51	1	51.00	1- 51	–	–
Pennett, D.B.	RMF	3	1	9	0	–	–	–	–
Phelps, B.S.	SLA	86	22	241	4	60.25	2- 70	–	–
Philip, I.L.	SLA	5	0	47	0	–	–	–	–
Phillips, N.C.	OB	36	5	127	2	63.50	2-127	–	–
Pick, R.A.	RFM	507.2	122	1413	54	26.16	6- 62	2	–
Pierson, A.R.K.	OB	500.4	131	1267	37	34.24	8- 42	1	–
Pigott, A.C.S.	RFM	268.3	73	737	29	25.41	6- 46	1	–
Pike, V.J.	LB	199	51	578	20	28.90	6- 41	1	–
Pipes, D.J.	RM	8	3	19	0	–	–	–	–
Pitcher, C.M.	RM	258.5	56	902	20	45.10	4- 37	–	–
Pollard, P.R.	RM	2	0	20	1	20.00	1- 20	–	–
Prichard, P.J.	RSM	1	0	11	0	–	–	–	–
Pringle, C.	RFM	258	74	739	18	41.05	5- 58	1	–
Radford, N.V.	RFM	459.1	106	1408	39	36.10	5- 93	1	–
Ramprakash, M.R.	RM	2	0	6	0	–	–	–	–
Ratledge, J.	RM	16	0	66	0	–	–	–	–

	Cat	O	M	R	W	Avge	Best	5wI	10wM
Reeve, D.A.	RMF	144	48	308	10	30.80	2- 9	–	–
Remy, C.C.	RM	61	6	241	5	48.20	2- 67	–	–
Rhodes, J.N.	RM	1	0	10	0	–	–	–	–
Richardson, M.S.	RM	24	3	94	2	47.00	2- 41	–	–
Roberts, A.R.	LB	242	49	870	17	51.17	3-106	–	–
Roberts, S.J.	RFM	47.2	7	163	8	20.37	4- 60	–	–
Robinson, M.A.	RFM	619	171	1658	45	36.84	5- 48	1	–
Robinson, R.T.	RM	2.1	0	31	1	31.00	1- 31	–	–
Rollins, A.S.	RM	4	0	32	0	–	–	–	–
Rose, G.D.	RM	344.1	69	1136	44	25.81	4- 40	–	–
Roseberry, M.A.	RM	1	0	5	0	–	–	–	–
Salisbury, I.D.K.	LB	474	143	1336	48	27.83	6- 55	3	–
Scriven, T.J.A.	SLA	11	2	54	3	18.00	3- 43	–	–
Searle, J.P.	OB	1	0	7	0	–	–	–	–
Shahid, N.	LB	30	6	106	3	35.33	2- 20	–	–
Shaw, T.G.	SLA	312.4	90	828	21	39.42	4- 29	–	–
Sheeraz, K.P.	RMF	15	2	34	2	17.00	2- 34	–	–
Sheridan, K.L.P.	SLA	49	19	96	2	48.00	1- 34	–	–
Sheriyar, A.	LF	98	14	400	11	36.36	4- 44	–	–
Shine, K.J.	RFM	332.4	76	1156	29	39.86	4- 79	–	–
Silverwood, C.E.W.	RFM	249	46	883	27	32.70	4- 67	–	–
Simmons, P.V.	RM	300.5	81	769	30	25.63	4- 68	–	–
Sladdin, R.W.	SLA	115	20	427	4	106.75	2-155	–	–
Sleep, P.R.	LB	2	0	9	0	–	–	–	–
Small, G.C.	RFM	339	79	946	36	26.27	5- 46	1	–
Smith, A.M.	LM	298.3	59	1004	32	31.37	5- 40	1	–
Smith, A.W.	OB	374	67	1340	28	47.85	5-103	1	–
Smith, N.M.K.	OB	582	141	1693	49	34.55	7- 42	4	–
Smith, P.A.	RFM	182	40	594	18	33.00	3- 24	–	–
Smyth, S.G.		1	0	14	0	–	–	–	–
Snape, J.N.	OB	63	20	210	4	52.50	2- 80	–	–
Snell, R.P.	RFM	200.1	38	666	18	37.00	3- 38	–	–
Speak, N.J.	RM/OB	1	0	12	0	–	–	–	–
Spencer, D.J.	RF	85.5	12	347	10	34.70	4- 31	–	–
Steer, I.G.S.	RM	2	0	12	0	–	–	–	–
Stemp, R.D.	SLA	669.1	252	1493	49	30.46	6- 37	2	–
Stephenson, F.D.	RFM	480.5	108	1345	67	20.07	6- 50	6	2
Stephenson, J.P.	RM	332	75	1066	26	41.00	4- 74	–	–
Stewart, A.J.	RM	2	0	10	0	–	–	–	–
Storie, A.C.	RM	12	2	31	1	31.00	1- 22	–	–
Such, P.M.	OB	670	183	1757	57	30.82	7- 66	5	–
Sylvester, S.A.	LFM	22	3	57	1	57.00	1- 38	–	–
Symcox, P.L.	OB	280.5	86	761	28	27.17	5- 29	2	–
Taylor, C.W.	LMF	79	22	217	7	31.00	2- 19	–	–
Taylor, J.P.	LFM	333.4	56	1141	36	31.69	5- 62	1	–
Taylor, M.	SLA	82.1	24	205	7	29.28	3- 25	–	–
Thomas, S.D.	RFM	30	3	108	3	36.00	2- 80	–	–
Thompson, D.J.	RMF	27	4	123	3	41.00	2- 37	–	–
Thompson, J.B.D.	RMF	33	6	120	1	120.00	1- 89	–	–
Thomson, S.A.	OB	247	61	633	8	79.12	2- 50	–	–
Thorpe, G.P.	RM	5	0	23	0	–	–	–	–
Thursfield, M.J.	RM	163	39	524	17	30.82	6-130	1	–
Tolley, C.M.	LMF	148	36	486	8	60.75	3- 52	–	–
Topley, T.D.	RMF	16	3	47	1	47.00	1- 22	–	–
Trimby, P.W.	LB	243.3	48	718	26	27.61	5- 84	1	–
Trump, H.R.J.	OB	268.4	76	873	26	33.57	6- 68	2	1

	Cat	O	M	R	W	Avge	Best	5wI	10wM
Tufnell, P.C.R.	SLA	463.5	128	1107	39	28.38	6- 35	1	–
Twose, R.G.	RM	190.5	41	544	15	36.26	6- 28	1	–
Udal, S.D.	OB	678	174	1872	69	27.13	6- 79	7	1
Vandrau, M.J.	OB	290.5	63	965	26	37.11	4- 53	–	–
Van Troost, A.P.	RF	346.1	58	1330	35	38.00	4- 50	–	–
Vaughan, M.P.	OB	228.3	53	678	14	48.42	4- 39	–	–
Walker, A.	RFM	116	23	369	8	46.12	4- 59	–	–
Walsh, C.A.	RF	506	119	1535	89	17.24	7- 42	9	3
Walton, T.C.	RM	20	1	98	2	49.00	1- 46	–	–
Warke, S.J.S.		5	1	13	0	–	–	–	–
Warner, A.E.	RFM	256	53	817	19	43.00	4- 39	–	–
Wasim Akram	LF	213.2	44	646	27	23.92	8- 30	2	1
Watkin, S.L.	RMF	613.4	140	1708	55	31.05	6-143	2	–
Watkinson, M.	RMF	631.1	173	1823	63	28.93	8- 30	1	1
Weekes, L.C.	RFM	24.2	2	135	4	33.75	2- 43	–	–
Weekes, P.N.	OB	484.2	91	1383	41	33.73	5- 12	1	–
Welch, G.	RM	267	63	970	22	44.09	4- 74	–	–
Wells, A.P.	RM	14	2	75	1	75.00	1- 48	–	–
Wells, C.M.	RM	153.3	31	469	13	36.07	4- 52	–	–
Wells, V.J.	RMF	301.5	78	1053	42	25.07	5- 50	1	–
Wessels, K.C.	RM	2	0	7	0	–	–	–	–
Weston, W.P.C.	LM	21	7	84	0	–	–	–	–
Wharf, A.G.	RMF	23	4	78	1	78.00	1- 78	–	–
Whitaker, P.R.	OB	0.1	0	4	0	–	–	–	–
White, C.	RFM	235.2	53	761	33	23.06	5- 40	2	–
White, G.W.	LB	5	1	13	0	–	–	–	–
Whittall, A.R.	OB	295.3	59	1060	11	96.36	2- 34	–	–
Wight, R.M.	OB	55	9	230	5	46.00	3- 76	–	–
Williams, N.F.	RFM	326	71	1088	26	41.84	6- 49	1	–
Williams, R.C.	RM	245.5	46	856	26	32.92	4- 28	–	–
Williamson, J.G.	RM	27	5	77	0	–	–	–	–
Wood, J.	RFM	345.4	38	1501	45	33.35	6-110	3	–
Wren, T.N.	LM	164.5	30	533	17	31.35	6- 48	1	–
Yates, G.	OB	320.5	70	1013	37	27.37	5- 34	1	–
Yeabsley, R.S.	RMF	174.5	26	567	21	27.00	6- 54	1	1
Young, B.A.	(WK)	8	0	76	1	76.00	1- 76	–	–

FIRST-CLASS CAREER RECORDS

Compiled by Philip Bailey

The following career records are for all players who appeared in first-class cricket during the 1994 season, and are complete to the end of that season. Some players who did not appear in 1994 but may do so in 1995 are also included. The tour of Sri Lanka by Pakistan in August and September 1994 is included.

BATTING AND FIELDING

'1000' denotes instances of scoring 1000 runs in a season. Where these have been achieved outside the UK, they are shown after a plus sign.

	M	*I*	*NO*	*HS*	*Runs*	*Avge*	*100*	*1000*	*Ct/St*
Adams, C.J.	105	165	16	175	4826	32.38	10	1	103
Adams, J.C.	82	136	22	144*	4461	39.13	10	–	81
Afford, J.A.	144	133	55	22*	294	3.76	–	–	47
Alleyne, M.W.	163	267	28	256	7286	30.48	10	3	130/2
Ambrose, C.E.L.	157	199	45	78	2301	14.94	–	–	51
Andrew, S.J.W.	117	91	36	35	404	7.34	–	–	24
Archer, G.F.	29	48	5	168	1561	36.30	3	–	28
Arnold, K.A.	3	1	1	0*	0	–	–	–	3
Arthurton, K.L.T.	78	125	16	157*	4829	44.30	14	–	41
Asif Din	210	341	45	217	9058	30.60	9	2	114
Atherton, M.A.	170	292	30	199	11644	44.44	34	5	145
Athey, C.W.J.	422	703	68	184	22751	35.82	49	12	399/2
Austin, I.D.	64	85	18	115*	1666	24.86	2	–	12
Aymes, A.N.	88	124	31	107*	2808	30.19	1	–	191/18
Azharuddin, M.	165	247	27	226	11617	52.80	40	1+2	156
Babington, A.M.	95	101	40	58	515	8.44	–	–	32
Bailey, R.J.	269	453	70	224*	16221	42.35	34	11	193
Bainbridge, P.	311	517	72	169	15086	33.90	24	9	138
Ball, M.C.J.	54	82	12	71	991	14.15	–	–	67
Baptiste, E.A.E.	196	273	34	136*	6882	28.79	3	–	94
Barnett, A.A.	50	48	20	38	263	9.39	–	–	14
Barnett, K.J.	364	581	54	239*	20565	39.02	44	11	229
Barwick, S.R.	197	189	71	30	819	6.94	–	–	43
Base, S.J.	131	167	34	58	1508	11.33	–	–	60
Bashforth, M.C.	3	5	3	9*	13	6.50	–	–	1
Bastien, S.	54	41	18	36*	182	7.91	–	–	7
Bates, R.T.	7	9	4	33*	85	17.00	–	–	3
Batty, J.D.	64	67	20	51	703	14.95	–	–	25
Batty, J.N.	1	2	–	6	9	4.50	–	–	1
Bell, M.A.V.	14	20	9	22*	79	7.18	–	–	5
Benjamin, J.E.	76	83	24	42	617	10.45	–	–	20
Benjamin, K.C.G.	52	61	18	52*	590	13.72	–	–	7
Benjamin, W.K.M.	161	200	36	101*	3640	22.19	1	–	87
Benson, M.R.	279	470	34	257	17685	40.56	46	11	136
Berry, P.J.	26	38	13	76	516	20.64	–	–	10
Betts, M.M.	1	2	1	4	4	4.00	–	–	–
Bevan, M.G.	54	91	16	203*	4041	53.88	15	0+1	28
Bicknell, D.J.	159	278	28	235*	10136	40.54	24	6	60
Bicknell, M.P.	141	165	45	88	2128	17.73	–	–	52
Birbeck, S.D.	1	1	–	6	6	6.00	–	–	1
Bird, P.J.	2	3	1	7	12	6.00	–	–	–

	M	*I*	*NO*	*HS*	*Runs*	*Avge*	*100*	*1000*	*Ct/St*
Blakey, R.J.	199	327	47	221	9407	33.59	9	5	361/34
Blenkiron, D.A.	1	–	–	–	–	–	–	–	–
Boden, D.J.P.	4	3	–	5	10	3.33	–	–	2
Boiling, J.	45	56	23	34*	435	13.18	–	–	38
Boon, T.J.	242	407	42	144	11644	31.90	14	7	119
Bovill, J.N.B.	7	11	7	10	38	9.50	–	–	1
Bowen, M.N.	13	14	4	23*	116	11.60	–	–	3
Bowler, P.D.	158	275	25	241*	9925	39.70	20	6	106/1
Briers, N.E.	366	601	59	201*	17680	32.61	28	10	151
Brimson, M.T.	7	10	3	17*	45	6.42	–	–	–
Brinkley, J.E.	11	11	3	10*	26	3.25	–	–	3
Broad, B.C.	340	613	38	227*	21892	38.07	50	11	189
Broadhurst, M.	5	3	–	6	7	2.33	–	–	–
Brown, A.D.	47	74	6	175	3171	46.63	8	2	40
Brown, D.R.	6	9	4	54	167	33.40	–	–	2
Brown, K.R.	174	261	51	200*	7423	35.34	11	2	273/18
Brown, S.J.E.	70	87	34	69	687	12.96	–	–	23
Bullen, C.K.	31	36	7	65	665	22.93	–	–	31
Burns, M.	9	14	1	78	217	16.69	–	–	16/2
Butcher, G.P.	3	3	–	41	50	16.66	–	–	2
Butcher, M.A.	20	32	6	134	883	33.96	1	–	25
Byas, D.	139	232	22	156	6886	32.79	11	3	146
Caddick, A.R.	58	74	13	58*	919	15.06	–	–	21
Cairns, C.L.	87	123	16	110	3415	31.91	3	–	39
Cake, R.Q.	21	37	7	108	1119	37.30	2	–	9
Capel, D.J.	272	411	61	134	10322	29.49	12	3	129
Carr, J.D.	175	274	44	261*	9014	39.19	20	4	193
Carroll, J.P.	22	36	3	92	490	14.84	–	–	4
Cassar, M.E.	1	1	–	66	66	66.00	–	–	–
Chapman, C.A.	4	7	1	20	72	12.00	–	–	5/2
Chapman, R.J.	4	4	–	25	36	9.00	–	–	1
Chapple, G.	25	36	19	109*	425	25.00	1	–	11
Childs, J.H.	358	326	159	43	1576	9.43	–	–	109
Church, M.J.	3	5	–	38	65	13.00	–	–	1
Clarke, V.P.	2	4	–	38	46	11.50	–	–	–
Cockbain, I.	47	80	10	98	1483	21.18	–	–	22
Connor, C.A.	185	162	42	59	1304	10.86	–	–	54
Cook, N.G.B.	356	365	96	75	3137	11.66	–	–	197
Cooke, F.J.	9	10	4	34*	80	13.33	–	–	9/1
Cooke, G.	1	–	–	–	–	–	–	–	–
Cooper, K.E.	300	324	82	52	2443	10.09	–	–	92
Cork, D.G.	78	108	14	104	2195	23.35	1	–	51
Cottam, A.C.	6	8	1	31	43	6.14	–	–	1
Cottey, P.A.	126	203	33	191	6014	35.37	10	4	76
Cousins, D.M.	5	7	1	11	24	4.00	–	–	2
Cowans, N.G.	239	248	68	66	1605	8.91	–	–	63
Cowdrey, G.R.	146	230	28	147	6957	34.44	13	3	77
Cox, D.M.	3	4	1	26*	32	10.66	–	–	1
Cox, R.M.F.	19	29	4	104*	605	24.20	1	–	12
Crawley, J.P.	80	133	13	286	5950	49.58	11	3	66
Crawley, M.A.	80	126	22	160*	3378	32.48	8	1	67
Croft, R.D.B.	117	163	37	107	3289	26.10	1	–	50
Cronje, W.J.	74	132	11	251	4689	38.75	13	0+1	50
Crowe, M.D.	235	393	58	299	18710	55.85	67	2+5	212
Cuffy, C.E.	31	41	18	14*	108	4.69	–	–	4
Cullinan, D.J.	95	167	24	337*	5568	38.93	11	–	89

	M	I	NO	HS	Runs	Avge	100	1000	Ct/St
Cummins, A.C.	55	82	10	70	1397	19.40	–	–	13
Cunliffe, R.J.	7	13	1	177*	354	29.50	1	–	5
Curran, K.M.	241	368	62	144*	11026	36.03	19	5	131
Curtis, T.S.	288	490	59	248	17910	41.55	35	10	162
Dakin, J.M.	3	4	–	18	34	8.50	–	–	–
Dale, A.	98	161	16	214*	4888	33.71	9	2	39
Daley, J.A.	25	44	3	159*	1266	30.87	1	–	12
Dalton, A.J.	6	10	2	51*	188	23.50	–	–	5
Davies, M.	39	57	18	54	555	14.23	–	–	19
Davis, H.T.	27	30	17	30*	141	10.84	–	–	10
Davis, R.P.	138	164	41	67	1930	15.69	–	–	123
Dawood, I.	1	1	1	2*	2	–	–	–	–
Dawson, R.I.	31	55	5	127*	1550	31.00	1	1	21
Dean, S.J.	1	2	–	39	73	36.50	–	–	1
DeFreitas, P.A.J.	212	291	30	113	5826	22.32	6	–	66
De la Pena, J.M.	4	4	2	7*	8	4.00	–	–	–
Derbyshire, N.A.	2	1	–	5	5	5.00	–	–	–
De Silva, P.A.	119	177	19	267	7610	48.16	19	0+1	71
Dessaur, W.A.	14	22	1	148	643	30.61	2	–	5
De Villiers, P.S.	79	106	29	50	1213	15.75	–	–	36
Dimond, M.	3	2	1	25*	34	34.00	–	–	4
Diwan, M.	1	2	–	0	0	0.00	–	–	–
Doak, N.G.	2	4	1	27*	58	19.33	–	–	3
D'Oliveira, D.B.	232	362	22	237	9445	27.77	10	4	203
Donald, A.A.	192	221	89	46*	1508	11.42	–	–	76
Donelan, B.T.P.	53	66	21	68*	1105	24.55	–	–	14
Douglas, M.W.	59	108	13	144	3080	32.42	5	–	55
Dowman, M.P.	3	5	–	38	111	22.20	–	–	–
Dutch, K.P.	1	–	–	–	–	–	–	–	2
Ealham, M.A.	53	83	13	85	1988	28.40	–	–	18
Ecclestone, S.C.	13	19	4	80*	334	22.26	–	–	3
Edwards, T.	10	11	7	47	116	29.00	–	–	21
Emburey, J.E.	482	608	125	133	11395	23.59	7	–	434
Evans, K.P.	115	158	38	104	3119	25.99	3	–	90
Evans, R.J.	7	11	3	59	201	25.12	–	–	5
Fairbrother, N.H.	257	408	62	366	14317	41.37	31	9	169
Farbrace, P.	38	48	11	79	694	18.75	–	–	86/12
Feltham, M.A.	143	177	43	101	3070	22.91	1	–	59
Felton, N.A.	211	361	21	173*	10242	30.12	15	5	122
Field-Buss, M.G.	36	41	14	34*	307	11.37	–	–	12
Fielding, J.M.	1	1	1	27*	27	–	–	–	–
Fleming, M.V.	103	167	20	116	4597	31.27	5	–	44
Fleming, S.P.	33	52	5	151	1737	36.95	5	–	35
Fletcher, I.	14	22	3	65*	460	24.21	–	–	4
Flint, D.P.J.	13	15	6	14*	55	6.11	–	–	8
Folland, N.A.	32	56	5	108*	1755	34.41	2	–	20
Fordham, A.	131	231	18	206*	8655	40.63	20	4	84
Foster, M.J.	5	7	1	63*	165	27.50	–	–	6
Fourie, B.C.	30	41	13	23*	318	11.35	–	–	5
Fowler, G.	292	495	27	226	16663	35.60	36	8	152/5
Fraser, A.R.C.	157	173	40	92	1502	11.29	–	–	31
French, B.N.	358	468	91	123	7141	18.94	2	–	814/100
Fulton, D.P.	18	31	1	109	798	26.60	1	–	30
Gallian, J.E.R.	33	55	4	171	2061	40.41	5	–	17
Garnham, M.A.	206	280	55	123	6192	27.52	5	–	428/41
Gatting, M.W.	474	740	116	258	31785	50.93	82	16+1	423

	M	I	NO	HS	Runs	Avge	100	1000	Ct/St
Gibson, O.D.	46	68	11	85	1241	21.77	–	–	15
Giddins, E.S.H.	45	50	19	24	124	4.00	–	–	9
Giles, A.F.	2	4	1	23	53	17.66	–	–	0
Gooch, G.A.	525	888	72	333	40174	49.23	112	18+1	510
Gough, D.	76	98	23	72	1228	16.37	–	–	13
Govan, J.W.	12	14	1	50	137	10.53	–	–	6
Graham, P.C.	1	1	–	0	0	0.00	–	–	2
Graham, S.	2	3	1	35	64	32.00	–	–	–
Graveney, D.A.	457	580	178	119	7107	17.67	2	–	241
Grayson, A.P.	43	66	9	100	1723	30.22	1	1	32
Greatbatch, M.J.	134	237	28	202*	7541	36.08	14	–	110
Greenfield, K.	34	56	10	127*	1409	30.63	4	–	32
Griffith, F.A.	34	50	5	81	847	18.82	–	–	18
Gupte, C.M.	32	48	7	122	1174	28.63	2	–	13
Habib, A.	1	2	1	12	19	19.00	–	–	–
Hall, J.W.	78	140	10	140*	4130	31.76	5	2	36
Hall, M.A.T.	2	2	–	4	5	2.50	–	–	–
Hallett, J.C.	16	15	3	52	120	10.00	–	–	6
Hamilton, G.M.	5	5	–	48	70	14.00	–	–	2
Hancock, T.H.C.	52	94	6	123	2177	24.73	2	–	31
Harden, R.J.	191	308	49	187	10096	38.98	20	6	145
Harper, R.A.	188	244	41	234	6811	33.55	8	–	243
Harris, A.J.	2	3	–	10	11	3.66	–	–	–
Harris, G.A.R.	3	4	2	11	22	11.00	–	–	–
Harrison, G.D.	11	18	2	105*	593	37.06	1	–	2
Harrison, J.C.	1	2	–	4	4	2.00	–	–	2
Hart, M.N.	48	62	9	83	985	18.58	–	–	48
Hartland, B.R.	67	123	8	129	3019	26.25	4	–	43
Hartley, P.J.	154	184	45	127*	3022	21.74	2	–	49
Harvey, M.E.	2	3	–	23	44	14.66	–	–	1
Haste, N.J.	19	21	3	36	188	10.44	–	–	7
Hayhurst, A.N.	138	221	28	172*	6770	35.07	13	3	48
Haynes, D.L.	351	596	69	255*	24219	45.95	59	3+4	184/1
Haynes, G.R.	44	65	6	158	1893	32.08	3	1	21
Headley, D.W.	53	62	16	91	887	19.28	–	–	24
Hegg, W.K.	167	243	47	130	4782	24.39	2	–	379/47
Hemmings, E.E.	511	671	162	127*	9463	18.59	1	–	211
Hemp, D.L.	44	76	9	136	2298	34.29	4	1	28
Hepworth, P.N.	59	98	8	129	2113	23.47	3	1	31
Herzberg, S.	9	9	3	57*	126	21.00	–	–	3
Hick, G.A.	276	450	46	405*	23124	57.23	77	10+1	331
Hindson, J.E.	7	4	–	11	21	5.25	–	–	2
Hinks, S.G.	182	319	19	234	8715	29.05	11	3	114
Hodgson, G.D.	94	162	10	166	5151	33.88	8	4	42
Hodgson, J.S.	9	15	1	54	256	18.28	–	–	8
Hoey, C.J.	4	4	1	8	21	7.00	–	–	1
Hollins, C.J.	8	10	2	131	415	51.87	1	–	6
Hollioake, A.J.	22	32	3	138	1074	37.03	4	–	16
Holloway, P.C.L.	18	27	7	102*	618	30.90	1	–	32/1
Hooper, C.L.	167	259	28	236*	10448	45.22	25	4	181
Hudson, A.C.	90	166	9	184*	5449	34.70	10	0+1	84
Hughes, J.G.	10	15	–	17	58	3.86	–	–	3
Humphries, M.I.	1	1	–	0	0	0.00	–	–	3
Humphries, S.	1	–	–	–	–	–	–	–	2
Hussain, N.	141	213	31	197	7833	43.04	20	2	174
Hutton, S.	32	56	2	101	1537	28.46	1	–	21

	M	*I*	*NO*	*HS*	*Runs*	*Avge*	*100*	*1000*	*Ct/St*
Igglesden, A.P.	138	149	55	41	800	8.51	–	–	36
Illingworth, R.K.	283	314	84	120*	4941	21.48	3	–	122
Ilott, M.C.	82	88	24	51	883	13.79	–	–	23
Innes, K.J.	1	2	–	0	0	0.00	–	–	–
Irani, R.C.	27	40	7	119	1108	33.57	2	–	11
James, K.D.	170	248	42	162	6490	31.50	8	2	54
James, S.P.	113	196	17	152*	5869	32.78	14	2	89
Jarvis, P.W.	173	210	58	80	2474	16.27	–	–	43
Jean-Jacques, M.	60	74	17	73	681	11.94	–	–	15
Johnson, P.	248	409	40	187	13736	37.22	31	8	157/1
Johnson, R.L.	13	16	3	50*	214	16.46	–	–	6
Jones, G.W.	27	46	2	74	729	16.56	–	–	2
Kasprowicz, M.S.	46	64	8	49	810	14.46	–	–	19
Keech, M.	25	43	4	58*	725	18.58	–	–	15
Keedy, G.	1	1	–	1	1	1.00	–	–	–
Kellett, S.A.	81	138	9	125*	4006	31.05	2	2	72
Kendall, W.S.	9	10	3	113*	253	36.14	1	–	8
Kendrick, N.M.	55	72	19	55	862	16.26	–	–	47
Kenlock, S.G.	2	–	–	–	–	–	–	–	1
Kennis, G.J.	1	2	–	23	41	20.50	–	–	2
Kerr, J.I.D.	8	13	3	19*	72	7.20	–	–	4
Kersey, G.J.	23	34	6	39	468	16.71	–	–	64/6
Kettleborough, R.A.	1	2	1	25	49	49.00	–	–	–
Kirsten, G.	73	131	14	201*	5131	43.85	12	–	55
Kirsten, P.N.	300	521	57	271	20920	45.08	53	5+1	181
Knight, N.V.	46	74	8	157	2454	37.18	7	–	59
Krikken, K.M.	102	149	30	85*	2329	19.57	–	–	223/19
Kumble, A.	53	62	14	154*	1377	28.68	3	–	24
Lamb, A.J.	450	744	104	294	31131	48.64	86	12	353
Lampitt, S.R.	124	153	30	122	2761	22.44	1	–	74
Lara, B.C.	80	130	4	501*	7320	58.09	22	1+1	102
Larkins, W.	469	819	54	252	26405	34.51	57	13	295
Larsen, G.R.	83	127	29	161	2895	29.54	1	–	55
Lathwell, M.N.	67	119	4	206	4025	35.00	7	3	52
Law, D.R.	3	2	–	11	11	5.50	–	–	–
Leatherdale, D.A.	78	118	11	157	3297	30.81	5	–	73
Lefebvre, R.P.	74	86	16	100	1439	20.55	1	–	36
Lenham, N.J.	154	267	23	222*	8075	33.09	16	3	58
Lewis, C.C.	132	196	25	247	5343	31.24	7	–	103
Lewis, D.A.	7	13	3	122*	541	54.10	2	–	2
Lewis, J.J.B.	45	76	12	136*	2422	37.84	4	–	29
Lewry, J.D.	4	6	4	6*	14	7.00	–	–	–
Liebenberg, G.F.J.	43	79	6	142	2117	29.00	4	–	35/3
Ligertwood, D.C.G.	4	7	–	28	63	9.00	–	–	7/1
Llong, N.J.	35	52	8	116*	1435	32.61	2	–	25
Lloyd, G.D.	99	163	19	132	5397	37.47	10	2	67
Longley, J.I.	24	42	2	110	955	23.87	2	–	15
Loye, M.B.	52	81	9	153*	2507	34.81	5	–	39
Lugsden, S.	6	6	3	5*	7	2.33	–	–	–
Lynch, M.A.	319	518	60	172*	16281	35.54	34	8	323
McCague, M.J.	59	73	16	56	771	13.52	–	–	33
McGurk, G.B.J.	2	3	1	63	108	54.00	–	–	3
Maclay, A.W.	10	9	5	6*	16	4.00	–	–	–
McMillan, B.M.	94	150	25	136	4743	37.94	7	–	94
Macmillan, G.I.	19	31	4	69	731	27.07	–	–	25
Maddy, D.L.	3	6	–	34	80	13.33	–	–	3

	M	I	NO	HS	Runs	Avge	100	1000	Ct/St
Maher, B.J.M.	133	205	36	126	3689	21.82	4	–	289/14
Malcolm, D.E.	168	191	58	51	1035	7.78	–	–	28
Malik, H.S.	15	21	4	64*	348	20.47	–	–	9
Mallender, N.A.	334	382	119	100*	4557	17.32	1	–	107
Mann, R.D.	9	16	–	53	248	15.50	–	–	2
Marc, K.	1	2	–	9	17	8.50	–	–	–
Marsh, S.A.	211	300	53	125	7009	28.37	7	–	497/40
Marshall, M.D.	393	499	68	120*	10620	24.64	7	–	139
Martin, N.F.C.	10	10	1	26	74	8.22	–	–	5
Martin, P.J.	84	94	27	133	1423	21.23	1	–	21
Maru, R.J.	210	205	50	74	2560	16.51	–	–	225
Mason, T.J.	1	1	–	3	3	3.00	–	–	2
Matthews, C.R.	68	75	22	105	1063	20.05	1	–	32
Maynard, M.P.	227	372	39	243	13818	41.49	30	8	204/3
Metcalfe, A.A.	190	329	19	216*	10692	34.49	24	6	69
Metson, C.P.	204	265	58	96	3737	18.05	–	–	491/41
Middleton, T.C.	107	183	16	221	5705	34.16	13	2	78
Mike, G.W.	35	52	8	61*	851	19.34	–	–	10
Milburn, S.M.	3	2	1	5	7	7.00	–	–	–
Millar, R.B.	1	–	–	–	–	–	–	–	2
Millns, D.J.	92	108	42	64*	1006	15.24	–	–	48
Mirza, P.	3	5	1	40	47	11.75	–	–	1
Moles, A.J.	195	351	37	230*	12964	41.28	25	6	124
Montgomerie, R.R.	45	76	9	151	2310	34.47	4	1	29
Moody, T.M.	175	288	22	210	12128	45.59	37	3+1	154
Moore, E.R.	2	–	–	–	–	–	–	–	–
Moores, P.	173	247	31	116	5282	24.45	4	–	370/40
Morris, H.	259	447	43	160*	15192	37.60	37	7	163
Morris, J.E.	260	431	28	229	16004	39.71	39	9	109
Morris, R.S.M.	22	40	4	174	1267	35.19	2	–	25
Morrison, D.K.	113	119	40	46*	773	9.78	–	–	41
Mortensen, O.H.	157	173	94	74*	709	8.97	–	–	47
Moxon, M.D.	276	472	36	274*	18301	41.97	38	10	203
Mullally, A.D.	88	94	25	34	560	8.11	–	–	23
Munton, T.A.	180	181	70	47	1096	9.87	–	–	63
Murphy, A.J.	84	86	39	38	323	6.87	–	–	17
Mushtaq Ahmed	94	114	15	90	1321	13.34	–	–	55
Myles, S.D.	7	11	2	59*	189	21.00	–	–	4
Nash, D.J.	30	46	13	56	676	20.48	–	–	17
Newell, M.	102	178	26	203*	4636	30.50	6	1	93/1
Newman, P.G.	135	171	33	115	2160	15.66	1	–	36
Newport, P.J.	233	270	79	98	4798	25.12	–	–	69
Nicholas, M.C.J.	358	587	86	206*	17052	34.03	32	9	210
Nixon, P.A.	83	117	28	131	2628	29.52	5	1	211/17
Noon, W.M.	30	46	8	75	767	20.18	–	–	61/8
North, J.A.	23	31	6	114	513	20.52	1	–	4
O'Gorman, T.J.G.	101	169	21	148	4611	31.15	9	2	66
Orr, D.A.	3	2	1	23*	37	37.00	–	–	3/3
Ostler, D.P.	93	160	14	192	5288	36.21	7	4	85
Owens, M.B.	26	30	16	8*	45	3.21	–	–	9
Parker, B.	11	20	2	127	615	34.16	1	–	7
Parkin, O.T.	2	2	2	2*	2	–	–	–	–
Parore, A.C.	63	90	15	155*	2468	32.90	4	–	137/13
Parsons, G.J.	294	389	90	76	5825	19.48	–	–	106
Parsons, K.A.	9	16	2	63	173	12.35	–	–	5
Patel, M.M.	40	54	12	43	453	10.78	–	–	20

	M	I	NO	HS	Runs	Avge	100	1000	Ct/St
Patterson, B.M.W.	7	12	–	114	641	53.41	3	–	9
Payne, A.	4	4	2	51*	124	62.00	–	–	2
Pearson, R.M.	34	39	7	33*	305	9.53	–	–	11
Peirce, M.T.E.	1	2	–	24	24	12.00	–	–	1
Penberthy, A.L.	65	95	14	101*	1727	21.32	1	–	39
Penn, C.	128	146	36	115	2048	18.61	1	–	56
Pennett, D.B.	20	15	3	29	80	6.66	–	–	3
Penney, T.L.	59	93	21	151	2904	40.33	6	–	33
Phelps, B.S.	3	4	1	11	18	6.00	–	–	–
Philip, I.L.	9	15	1	145	636	45.42	3	–	9
Phillips, N.C.	2	2	1	37*	37	37.00	–	–	1
Pick, R.A.	167	169	50	65*	1766	14.84	–	–	40
Pierson, A.R.K.	90	107	40	58	999	14.91	–	–	35
Pigott, A.C.S.	254	306	65	104*	4765	19.77	1	–	120
Pike, V.J.	9	12	4	27	114	14.25	–	–	2
Piper, K.J.	93	126	20	116*	2114	19.94	2	–	236/15
Pipes, D.J.	1	2	1	11*	12	12.00	–	–	–
Pitcher, C.M.	25	30	9	43	239	11.38	–	–	9
Pocock, B.A.	44	80	10	139*	2036	29.08	5	–	25
Pollard, P.R.	118	206	11	180	6424	32.94	11	3	112
Pooley, J.C.	22	37	2	88	794	22.68	–	–	12
Prabhakar, M.	118	156	28	229*	5609	43.82	15	–	49
Prichard, P.J.	226	363	43	245	11546	36.08	23	6	146
Pringle, C.	50	59	11	45*	600	12.50	–	–	13
Radford, N.V.	286	287	71	76*	3407	15.77	–	–	130
Radford, T.A.	1	1	–	4	4	4.00	–	–	1
Ramprakash, M.R.	160	257	37	233	8937	40.62	19	5	83
Ratcliffe, J.D.	78	144	8	127*	3863	28.40	3	–	47
Ratledge, J.	9	16	–	79	227	14.18	–	–	1
Rea, M.P.	8	16	1	115	500	33.33	1	–	2
Reeve, D.A.	219	291	72	202*	7431	33.93	5	2	172
Remy, C.C.	20	27	3	60	475	19.79	–	–	7
Rhodes, J.N.	66	108	12	135*	3544	36.91	5	–	42
Rhodes, S.J.	259	344	105	116*	7988	33.42	7	–	642/83
Richardson, D.J.	156	244	36	134	5340	22.08	3	–	438/32
Richardson, M.S.	2	–	–	–	–	–	–	–	1
Richardson, R.B.	191	318	25	194	12280	41.91	32	1+2	178
Ridley, A.C.	3	4	1	36*	65	21.66	–	–	–
Ripley, D.	212	276	72	134*	4929	24.16	6	–	464/65
Roberts, A.R.	54	73	18	62	1011	18.38	–	–	22
Roberts, S.J.	52	47	12	55	367	10.48	–	–	13
Robinson, D.D.J.	3	5	–	67	150	30.00	–	–	3
Robinson, M.A.	137	141	60	19*	237	2.92	–	–	27
Robinson, P.E.	156	255	34	189	7518	34.01	7	3	125
Robinson, R.T.	349	605	76	220*	22637	42.79	51	12	219
Rollins, A.S.	23	42	6	97	1100	30.55	–	–	23/1
Rollins, R.J.	5	7	1	13	42	7.00	–	–	6/3
Rose, G.D.	155	212	40	138	5139	29.87	6	1	83
Roseberry, A.	7	10	1	94	263	29.22	–	–	3
Roseberry, M.A.	159	265	32	185	8693	37.30	18	4	118
Russell, R.C.	301	436	98	128*	9469	28.01	4	–	701/94
Rutherford, K.R.	164	288	25	317	10433	39.66	24	–	124
Salisbury, I.D.K.	120	145	41	68	1801	17.31	–	–	89
Salmond, G.	4	6	1	118	352	70.40	1	–	2
Sargeant, N.F.	50	65	11	49	778	14.40	–	–	109/16
Saxelby, M.	53	90	7	181	2642	31.83	2	1	13

	M	I	NO	HS	Runs	Avge	100	1000	Ct/St
Scott, C.W.	115	153	29	108	2709	21.84	2	–	245/17
Scriven, T.J.A.	4	3	–	8	19	6.33	–	–	–
Searle, J.P.	1	2	2	5*	5	–	–	–	–
Seymour, A.C.H.	36	62	5	157	1699	29.80	2	–	17
Shahid, N.	66	99	16	132	2562	30.86	2	1	64
Shaw, A.D.	3	3	1	14	18	9.00	–	–	6
Shaw, T.G.	113	156	39	105	2581	22.05	1	–	92
Sheeraz, K.P.	1	2	2	1*	1	–	–	–	–
Sheridan, K.L.P.	2	–	–	–	–	–	–	–	–
Sheriyar, A.	4	3	2	16*	28	28.00	–	–	–
Shine, K.J.	67	55	26	26*	297	10.24	–	–	11
Silverwood, C.E.W.	10	16	3	26	127	9.76	–	–	3
Simmons, P.V.	122	215	8	261	7030	33.96	13	1	124
Sims, R.J.	4	3	–	28	31	10.33	–	–	2
Sladdin, R.W.	33	42	9	51*	372	11.27	–	–	14
Sleep, P.R.	175	285	50	182	8201	34.89	15	–	104/1
Small, G.C.	298	381	87	70	4269	14.52	–	–	92
Smith, A.M.	45	52	10	51*	478	11.38	–	–	7
Smith, A.W.	28	44	7	202*	1084	29.29	1	–	10
Smith, B.F.	57	86	12	100*	2025	27.36	1	–	25
Smith, D.M.	319	513	91	213	15265	36.17	28	7	204
Smith, N.M.K.	77	109	16	161	2299	24.72	1	–	20
Smith, P.A.	215	343	41	140	7993	26.46	4	2	58
Smith, R.A.	279	475	73	209*	17813	44.31	45	8	174
Smyth, S.G.	2	3	1	70	91	45.50	–	–	–
Snape, J.N.	4	6	2	43*	94	23.50	–	–	4
Snell, R.P.	62	78	14	94	1104	17.25	–	–	16
Speak, N.J.	93	161	15	232	5869	40.19	10	3	61
Speight, M.P.	112	185	13	184	6300	36.62	12	3	91
Spencer, D.J.	14	16	2	75	200	14.28	–	–	9
Spiring, K.R.	1	2	–	56	108	54.00	–	–	2
Stanley, D.E.	5	8	2	48	91	15.16	–	–	2
Stanworth, J.	44	40	11	50*	266	9.17	–	–	63/10
Steer, I.G.S.	7	10	3	67	299	42.71	–	–	4
Stemp, R.D.	59	68	20	37	652	13.58	–	–	25
Stephenson, F.D.	187	289	32	165	7243	28.18	9	1	81
Stephenson, J.P.	188	324	32	202*	10230	35.03	18	5	113
Stewart, A.J.	269	444	50	206*	15524	39.40	30	8	342/13
Storie, A.C.	55	90	16	106	1720	23.24	2	–	36
Streak, H.H.	11	17	4	62	204	15.69	–	–	4
Such, P.M.	181	166	51	54	753	6.54	–	–	70
Sutcliffe, I.J.	5	4	1	8*	18	6.00	–	–	2
Sylvester, S.A.	6	3	2	6*	6	6.00	–	–	2
Symcox, P.L.	71	113	9	107	2604	25.03	1	–	42
Taylor, C.W.	32	25	9	28*	175	10.93	–	–	6
Taylor, J.P.	80	79	34	74*	455	10.11	–	–	28
Taylor, M.	4	5	2	14*	25	8.33	–	–	–
Taylor, N.R.	296	503	66	204	17350	39.70	41	10	151
Terry, V.P.	265	446	41	190	15036	37.12	36	10	290
Thomas, S.D.	11	15	7	16*	86	10.75	–	–	3
Thompson, D.J.	1	2	–	22	39	19.50	–	–	–
Thompson, J.B.D.	1	2	1	2	3	3.00	–	–	–
Thomson, S.A.	74	124	35	167	3654	41.05	6	–	33
Thorpe, G.P.	141	232	33	216	8414	42.28	15	5	99
Thursfield, M.J.	14	16	3	47	142	10.92	–	–	1
Titchard, S.P.	43	75	4	135	2129	29.98	1	–	33

	M	I	NO	HS	Runs	Avge	100	1000	Ct/St
Tolley, C.M.	60	69	21	84	1043	21.72	–	–	26
Topley, T.D.	120	138	29	66	1693	15.53	–	–	70
Townsend, C.J.	16	14	5	22	69	7.66	–	–	23/4
Trescothick, M.E.	14	26	1	121	938	37.52	2	–	17
Trimby, P.W.	12	8	4	11	26	6.50	–	–	5
Trump, H.R.J.	88	97	30	48	784	11.70	–	–	61
Tufnell, P.C.R.	152	150	60	37	908	10.08	–	–	65
Turner, R.J.	65	101	20	104*	1977	24.40	2	–	103/21
Tweats, T.A.	1	1	–	24	24	24.00	–	–	1
Twose, R.G.	101	172	21	277*	5528	36.60	8	2	57
Udal, S.D.	68	93	18	94	1672	22.29	–	–	30
Van Troost, A.P.	43	45	18	35	258	9.55	–	–	9
Vandrau, M.J.	33	54	8	66	943	20.50	–	–	18
Vaughan, M.P.	18	34	1	117	1184	35.87	3	1	8
Walker, A.	101	98	47	41*	698	13.68	–	–	39
Walker, L.N.P.	1	2	–	1	1	0.50	–	–	–
Walker, M.J.	6	9	1	107	278	34.75	1	–	3
Walsh, C.A.	300	378	87	66	3664	12.59	–	–	77
Walton, T.C.	2	2	–	11	16	8.00	–	–	2
Waqar Younis	114	122	34	51	1139	12.94	–	–	30
Ward, D.M.	150	236	33	294*	7931	39.06	16	2	116/3
Ward, T.R.	132	225	15	235*	8039	38.28	18	4	115
Warke, S.J.S.	13	24	2	144*	966	43.90	2	–	8
Warner, A.E.	185	250	44	95*	3498	16.98	–	–	44
Warren, R.J.	19	30	4	94*	649	24.96	–	–	17
Wasim Akram	158	211	25	123	4060	21.82	4	–	52
Watkin, S.L.	157	170	53	41	1058	9.04	–	–	33
Watkinson, M.	237	350	42	155	8097	26.28	7	1	118
Waugh, M.E.	188	296	43	229*	14346	56.70	48	4+3	221
Weekes, L.C.	4	5	1	46	70	17.50	–	–	3
Weekes, P.N.	46	61	11	117	1659	33.18	1	–	35
Welch, G.	12	15	3	84*	446	37.16	–	–	5
Wells, A.P.	279	462	73	253*	15415	39.62	34	8	175
Wells, C.M.	290	461	72	203	12704	32.65	21	6	91
Wells, V.J.	62	99	13	167	2481	28.84	1	–	37
Wessels, K.C.	274	469	41	254	21318	49.80	55	2+5	232
Weston, W.P.C.	48	79	9	113	2236	31.94	2	–	17
Wharf, A.G.	1	2	–	46	46	23.00	–	–	–
Whitaker, J.J.	261	417	46	200*	13886	37.42	27	8	159
Whitaker, P.R.	2	3	–	94	134	44.66	–	–	–
White, C.	65	95	18	146	2617	33.98	2	–	42
White, G.W.	12	21	1	104	509	25.45	1	–	13
Whittall, A.R.	19	20	4	91*	273	17.06	–	–	5
Wight, R.M.	19	31	5	62*	593	22.80	–	–	11
Wileman, J.R.	3	5	2	109	217	72.33	1	–	6
Williams, J.R.A.	1	2	–	6	6	3.00	–	–	–
Williams, N.F.	222	253	51	77	3909	19.35	–	–	59
Williams, R.C.	22	34	6	44	393	14.03	–	–	5
Williams, R.C.J.	25	27	8	55*	284	14.94	–	–	58/13
Williamson, J.G.	1	–	–	–	–	–	–	–	–
Willis, S.C.	1	1	1	0*	0	–	–	–	2
Windows, M.G.N.	14	26	–	106	939	36.11	1	–	13
Wood, J.	32	45	7	63*	524	13.78	–	–	6
Wren, T.N.	15	17	6	18*	55	5.00	–	–	7
Wright, A.J.	236	411	31	184*	10863	28.58	13	5	183
Wylie, A.	1	1	–	0	0	0.00	–	–	–

	M	I	NO	HS	Runs	Avge	100	1000	Ct/St
Yates, G.	45	60	28	134*	1119	34.96	3	–	16
Yeabsley, R.S.	16	16	5	52*	191	17.36	–	–	10
Young, B.A.	105	173	36	138*	4725	34.48	5	–	218/11

BOWLING

'50wS' denotes instances of taking 50 or more wickets in a season. Where these have been achieved outside the UK, they are shown after a plus sign.

	Runs	Wkts	Avge	Best	5wI	10wM	50wS
Adams, C.J.	981	18	54.50	4- 29	–	–	–
Adams, J.C.	1655	45	36.77	4- 43	–	–	–
Afford, J.A.	12935	393	32.91	6- 68	14	2	4
Alleyne, M.W.	4315	129	33.44	5- 78	1	–	–
Ambrose, C.E.L.	13278	651	20.39	8- 45	32	7	5+1
Andrew, S.J.W.	9708	297	32.68	7- 47	7	–	–
Archer, G.F.	72	0	–	–	–	–	–
Arnold, K.A.	314	10	31.40	5- 57	1	–	–
Arthurton, K.L.T.	444	15	29.60	3- 14	–	–	–
Asif Din	4393	79	55.60	5- 61	2	–	–
Atherton, M.A.	4684	107	43.77	6- 78	3	–	–
Athey, C.W.J.	2617	48	54.52	3- 3	–	–	–
Austin, I.D.	3714	112	33.16	5- 23	4	1	–
Aymes, A.N.	75	1	75.00	1- 75	–	–	–
Azharuddin, M.	593	7	84.71	2- 33	–	–	–
Babington, A.M.	7587	208	36.47	8-107	3	–	–
Bailey, R.J.	3541	84	42.15	5- 54	2	–	–
Bainbridge, P.	12657	341	37.11	8- 53	10	–	–
Ball, M.C.J.	3946	111	35.54	8- 46	5	1	–
Baptiste, E.A.E.	14446	580	24.90	8- 76	26	3	1
Barnett, A.A.	5191	113	45.93	5- 36	5	–	–
Barnett, K.J.	5575	152	36.67	6- 28	3	–	–
Barwick, S.R.	15078	435	34.66	8- 42	10	1	2
Base, S.J.	11159	386	28.90	7- 60	16	1	1
Bashforth, M.C.	108	0	–	–	–	–	–
Bastien, S.	4672	123	37.98	6- 52	7	1	–
Bates, R.T.	425	8	53.12	2- 43	–	–	–
Batty, J.D.	5286	140	37.75	6- 48	3	–	–
Bell, M.A.V.	1068	39	27.38	7- 48	3	–	–
Benjamin, J.E.	7241	253	28.62	6- 19	13	1	2
Benjamin, K.C.G.	4237	169	25.07	7- 51	6	–	–
Benjamin, W.K.M.	11687	459	25.46	7- 54	23	2	1
Benson, M.R.	493	5	98.60	2- 55	–	–	–
Berry, P.J.	1756	39	45.02	7-113	1	1	–
Betts, M.M.	19	1	19.00	1- 19	–	–	–
Bevan, M.G.	762	9	84.66	3- 6	–	–	–
Bicknell, D.J.	287	3	95.66	2- 62	–	–	–
Bicknell, M.P.	12620	479	26.34	9- 45	20	2	5
Birbeck, S.D.	13	2	6.50	2- 13	–	–	–
Bird, P.J.	166	0	–	–	–	–	–
Blakey, R.J.	68	1	68.00	1- 68	–	–	–
Boden, D.J.P.	284	7	40.57	4- 11	–	–	–
Boiling, J.	3424	83	41.25	6- 84	2	1	–
Boon, T.J.	563	11	51.18	3- 40	–	–	–
Bovill, J.N.B.	469	17	27.58	5-108	1	–	–
Bowen, M.N.	1196	30	39.86	4-124	–	–	–

	Runs	Wkts	Avge	Best	5wI	10wM	50wS
Bowler, P.D.	1511	20	75.55	3- 41	–	–	–
Briers, N.E.	988	32	30.87	4- 29	–	–	–
Brimson, M.T.	413	7	59.00	2- 66	–	–	–
Brinkley, J.E.	858	24	35.75	6- 98	1	–	–
Broad, B.C.	1037	16	64.81	2- 14	–	–	–
Broadhurst, M.	231	7	33.00	3- 61	–	–	–
Brown, A.D.	131	0	–	–	–	–	–
Brown, D.R.	322	13	24.76	4- 25	–	–	–
Brown, K.R.	162	5	32.40	2- 7	–	–	–
Brown, S.J.E.	6756	205	32.95	7- 70	12	–	2
Bullen, C.K.	1150	40	28.75	6-119	1	–	–
Burns, M.	8	0	–	–	–	–	–
Butcher, G.P.	148	2	74.00	2- 36	–	–	–
Butcher, M.A.	1221	32	38.15	4- 31	–	–	–
Byas, D.	682	12	56.83	3- 55	–	–	–
Caddick, A.R.	5922	220	26.91	9- 32	13	4	3
Cairns, C.L.	7975	273	29.21	7- 34	10	2	2
Capel, D.J.	14940	457	32.69	7- 46	12	–	3
Carr, J.D.	2939	68	43.22	6- 61	3	–	–
Carroll, J.P.	22	0	–	–	–	–	–
Cassar, M.E.	94	3	31.33	3- 65	–	–	–
Chapman, R.J.	264	6	44.00	2- 21	–	–	–
Chapple, G.	2109	71	29.70	6- 48	4	–	1
Childs, J.H.	28078	941	29.83	9- 56	50	8	8
Church, M.J.	4	0	–	–	–	–	–
Clarke, V.P.	105	1	105.00	1- 93	–	–	–
Connor, C.A.	15893	493	32.23	7- 31	12	3	4
Cook, N.G.B.	25507	879	29.01	7- 34	31	4	8
Cooke, G.	65	2	32.50	1- 26	–	–	–
Cooper, K.E.	21700	799	27.15	8- 44	26	1	8
Cork, D.G.	5846	209	27.97	8- 53	5	1	1
Cottam, A.C.	280	6	46.66	1- 1	–	–	–
Cottey, P.A.	532	8	66.50	2- 42	–	–	–
Cousins, D.M.	446	14	31.85	6- 35	1	–	–
Cowans, N.G.	16461	662	24.86	6- 31	23	1	6
Cowdrey, G.R.	753	11	68.45	1- 5	–	–	–
Cox, D.M.	345	1	345.00	1- 92	–	–	–
Cox, R.M.F.	1	0	–	–	–	–	–
Crawley, J.P.	108	1	108.00	1- 90	–	–	–
Crawley, M.A.	2985	64	46.64	6- 92	1	–	–
Croft, R.D.B.	10797	259	41.68	8- 66	10	1	2
Cronje, W.J.	1117	30	37.90	4- 47	–	–	–
Crowe, M.D.	3939	119	33.10	5- 18	4	–	–
Cuffy, C.E.	2398	88	27.25	6- 81	3	–	–
Cullinan, D.J.	70	3	23.33	2- 27	–	–	–
Cummins, A.C.	5294	175	30.25	6- 64	7	1	2
Curran, K.M.	13345	507	26.32	7- 47	15	4	5
Curtis, T.S.	722	11	65.63	2- 17	–	–	–
Dakin, J.M.	120	5	24.00	4- 45	–	–	–
Dale, A.	4093	109	37.55	6- 18	1	–	–
Daley, J.A.	9	0	–	–	–	–	–
Davies, M.	3590	104	34.51	5- 57	3	1	1
Davis, H.T.	2572	79	32.55	5- 37	2	–	–
Davis, R.P.	12260	353	34.73	7- 64	15	2	2
Dawson, R.I.	75	2	37.50	2- 38	–	–	–
DeFreitas, P.A.J.	19162	687	27.89	7- 21	36	3	7

	Runs	Wkts	Avge	Best	5wI	10wM	50wS
De la Pena, J.M.	294	7	42.00	4- 77	–	–	–
Derbyshire, N.A.	168	2	84.00	1- 48	–	–	–
De Silva, P.A.	1404	50	28.08	5- 31	3	–	–
Dessaur, W.A.	94	0	–	–	–	–	–
De Villiers, P.S.	7282	301	24.19	6- 43	15	1	–
Dimond, M.	216	5	43.20	4- 73	–	–	–
Doak, N.G.	0	0	–	–	–	–	–
D'Oliveira, D.B.	2111	50	42.22	4- 68	–	–	–
Donald, A.A.	16510	679	24.31	8- 37	37	5	3+1
Donelan, B.T.P.	4627	106	43.65	6- 62	4	1	–
Douglas, M.W.	120	4	30.00	2- 29	–	–	–
Dowman, M.P.	45	0	–	–	–	–	–
Dutch, K.P.	18	0	–	–	–	–	–
Ealham, M.A.	3550	117	30.34	7- 53	5	–	–
Ecclestone, S.C.	825	22	37.50	4- 66	–	–	–
Emburey, J.E.	38956	1503	25.91	8- 40	67	10	16
Evans, K.P.	8208	245	33.50	6- 67	4	–	–
Evans, R.A.	97	3	32.33	3- 40	–	–	–
Fairbrother, N.H.	426	5	85.20	2- 91	–	–	–
Farbrace, P.	64	1	64.00	1- 64	–	–	–
Feltham, M.A.	11311	355	31.86	6- 53	7	–	1
Felton, N.A.	345	2	172.50	1- 48	–	–	–
Field-Buss, M.G.	2292	62	36.96	6- 42	1	–	–
Fielding, J.M.	53	2	26.50	1- 15	–	–	–
Fleming, M.V.	4661	112	41.61	4- 31	–	–	–
Fleming, S.P.	110	0	–	–	–	–	–
Flint, D.P.J.	1195	32	37.34	5- 32	1	–	–
Fordham, A.	238	3	79.33	1- 25	–	–	–
Foster, M.J.	150	6	25.00	3- 39	–	–	–
Fourie, B.C.	2729	99	27.56	6- 74	3	–	–
Fowler, G.	366	10	36.60	2- 34	–	–	–
Fraser, A.R.C.	12646	486	26.02	8- 75	19	2	5
French, B.N.	70	1	70.00	1- 37	–	–	–
Fulton, D.P.	0	0	–	–	–	–	–
Gallian, J.E.R.	1646	40	41.15	4- 29	–	–	–
Garnham, M.A.	39	0	–	–	–	–	–
Gatting, M.W.	4592	156	29.43	5- 34	2	–	–
Gibson, O.D.	4756	161	29.54	7- 78	8	2	1
Giddins, E.S.H.	3996	122	32.75	5- 32	5	–	1
Giles, A.F.	128	3	42.66	1- 27	–	–	–
Gooch, G.A.	8206	236	34.77	7- 14	3	–	–
Gough, D.	6803	223	30.50	7- 42	8	1	2
Govan, J.W.	1079	41	26.31	6- 70	2	–	–
Graham, P.C.	83	4	20.75	2- 39	–	–	–
Graham, S.	43	1	43.00	1- 8	–	–	–
Graveney, D.A.	29867	981	30.44	8- 85	40	7	6
Grayson, A.P.	766	11	69.63	2- 43	–	–	–
Greatbatch, M.J.	65	0	–	–	–	–	–
Greenfield, K.	345	5	69.00	2- 40	–	–	–
Griffith, F.A.	1820	55	33.09	4- 33	–	–	–
Gupte, C.M.	276	4	69.00	2- 41	–	–	–
Hall, J.W.	14	0	–	–	–	–	–
Hall, M.A.T.	2	0	–	–	–	–	–
Hallett, J.C.	1256	29	43.31	4- 59	–	–	–
Hamilton, G.M.	464	10	46.40	5- 65	1	–	–
Hancock, T.H.C.	479	13	36.84	3- 10	–	–	–

	Runs	Wkts	Avge	Best	5wI	10wM	50wS
Harden, R.J.	952	19	50.10	2- 7	–	–	–
Harper, R.A.	13737	513	26.77	6- 24	24	3	2
Harris, A.J.	165	5	33.00	3- 40	–	–	–
Harris, G.A.R.	249	1	249.00	1- 61	–	–	–
Harrison, G.D.	609	23	26.47	9-113	2	–	–
Hart, M.N.	3526	109	32.34	5- 37	4	–	–
Hartley, P.J.	13591	416	32.67	8-111	14	–	4
Haste, N.J.	1625	23	70.65	4- 69	–	–	–
Hayhurst, A.N.	4351	98	44.39	4- 27	–	–	–
Haynes, D.L.	268	8	33.50	1- 2	–	–	–
Haynes, G.R.	803	14	57.35	3- 19	–	–	–
Headley, D.W.	4723	138	34.22	7- 79	6	–	–
Hegg, W.K.	7	0	–	–	–	–	–
Hemmings, E.E.	43961	1500	29.30	10-175	70	15	15
Hemp, D.L.	41	0	–	–	–	–	–
Hepworth, P.N.	1269	30	42.30	3- 30	–	–	–
Herzberg, S.	1131	28	40.39	4- 66	–	–	–
Hick, G.A.	7265	176	41.27	5- 37	4	1	–
Hindson, J.E.	532	17	31.29	5- 42	2	–	–
Hinks, S.G.	383	8	47.87	2- 18	–	–	–
Hodgson, G.D.	65	0	–	–	–	–	–
Hodgson, J.S.	732	15	48.80	4- 14	–	–	–
Hoey, C.J.	334	9	37.11	3- 38	–	–	–
Hollins, C.J.	890	19	46.84	4- 64	–	–	–
Hollioake, A.J.	1263	31	40.74	4- 48	–	–	–
Hooper, C.L.	9841	285	34.52	5- 33	9	–	–
Hudson, A.C.	4	0	–	–	–	–	–
Hughes, J.G.	878	21	41.50	5- 69	1	–	–
Hussain, N.	307	2	153.50	1- 38	–	–	–
Hutton, S.	5	0	–	–	–	–	–
Igglesden, A.P.	12185	462	26.37	7- 28	22	4	4
Illingworth, R.K.	19833	641	30.94	7- 50	22	5	4
Ilott, M.C.	8045	274	29.36	7- 85	12	1	3
Innes, K.J.	33	0	–	–	–	–	–
Irani, R.C.	1132	33	34.30	4- 27	–	–	–
James, K.D.	9070	281	32.27	6- 22	7	–	–
James, S.P.	3	0	–	–	–	–	–
Jarvis, P.W.	15384	546	28.17	7- 55	19	3	4
Jean-Jacques, M.	4514	124	36.40	8- 77	2	1	–
Johnson, P.	510	5	102.00	1- 9	–	–	–
Johnson, R.L.	1188	42	28.28	10- 45	1	1	–
Kasprowicz, M.S.	4674	141	33.14	7- 83	7	–	1+1
Keech, M.	188	5	37.60	2- 28	–	–	–
Kellett, S.A.	19	0	–	–	–	–	–
Kendrick, N.M.	4825	133	36.27	7-115	6	1	1
Kenlock, S.G.	186	3	62.00	3-104	–	–	–
Kerr, J.I.D.	496	15	33.06	3- 47	–	–	–
Kettleborough, R.A.	18	0	–	–	–	–	–
Kirsten, G.	525	15	35.00	6- 68	1	–	–
Kirsten, P.N.	4649	117	39.73	6- 48	2	–	–
Knight, N.V.	93	1	93.00	1- 61	–	–	–
Krikken, K.M.	40	0	–	–	–	–	–
Kumble, A.	5576	225	24.78	7- 59	14	3	–
Lamb, A.J.	199	8	24.87	2- 29	–	–	–
Lampitt, S.R.	8355	286	29.21	5- 32	10	–	3
Lara, B.C.	215	1	215.00	1- 22	–	–	–

	Runs	Wkts	Avge	Best	5wI	10wM	50wS
Larkins, W.	1915	42	45.59	5- 59	1	–	–
Larsen, G.R.	3449	111	31.07	6- 64	3	–	–
Lathwell, M.N.	515	9	57.22	2- 21	–	–	–
Law, D.R.	216	5	43.20	2- 38	–	–	–
Leatherdale, D.A.	398	6	66.33	2- 11	–	–	–
Lefebvre, R.P.	5220	143	36.50	6- 53	2	–	–
Lenham, N.J.	1674	38	44.05	4- 13	–	–	–
Lewis, C.C.	11550	392	29.46	6- 22	15	3	2
Lewis, D.A.	276	5	55.20	2- 39	–	–	–
Lewis, J.J.B.	32	0	–	–	–	–	–
Lewry, J.D.	315	7	45.00	4- 40	–	–	–
Liebenberg, G.F.J.	10	1	10.00	1- 10	–	–	–
Llong, N.J.	537	17	31.58	5- 63	1	–	–
Lloyd, G.D.	186	1	186.00	1- 57	–	–	–
Loye, M.B.	1	0	–	–	–	–	–
Lugsden, S.	497	5	99.40	2- 43	–	–	–
Lynch, M.A.	1395	26	53.65	3- 6	–	–	–
McCague, M.J.	5403	204	26.48	9- 86	14	2	2
Maclay, A.W.	720	10	72.00	3- 30	–	–	–
McMillan, B.M.	6239	230	27.12	5- 35	4	–	–
Macmillan, G.I.	535	14	38.21	3- 13	–	–	–
Maher, B.J.M.	234	4	58.50	2- 69	–	–	–
Malcolm, D.E.	16613	528	31.46	9- 57	16	2	3
Malik, H.S.	743	14	53.07	3- 10	–	–	–
Mallender, N.A.	24022	916	26.22	7- 27	36	5	6
Marc, K.	133	3	44.33	2- 52	–	–	–
Marsh, S.A.	227	2	113.50	2- 20	–	–	–
Marshall, M.D.	30579	1602	19.08	8- 71	85	13	8+5
Martin, N.F.C.	480	7	68.57	2- 84	–	–	–
Martin, P.J.	6582	188	35.01	5- 35	3	–	1
Maru, R.J.	16278	495	32.88	8- 41	15	1	4
Mason, T.J.	22	1	22.00	1- 22	–	–	–
Matthews, C.R.	4581	191	23.98	6- 22	6	–	–
Maynard, M.P.	686	6	114.33	3- 21	–	–	–
Metcalfe, A.A.	316	4	79.00	2- 18	–	–	–
Metson, C.P.	0	0	–	–	–	–	–
Middleton, T.C.	241	5	48.20	2- 41	–	–	–
Mike, G.W.	2814	76	37.02	5- 44	2	–	–
Milburn, S.M.	227	4	56.75	2- 74	–	–	–
Millns, D.J.	7977	297	26.85	9- 37	17	2	3
Mirza, P.	193	9	21.44	4- 29	–	–	–
Moles, A.J.	1860	40	46.50	3- 21	–	–	–
Montgomerie, R.R.	65	0	–	–	–	–	–
Moody, T.M.	3858	117	32.97	7- 43	1	1	–
Moore, E.R.	168	1	168.00	1- 34	–	–	–
Moores, P.	16	0	–	–	–	–	–
Morris, H.	380	2	190.00	1- 6	–	–	–
Morris, J.E.	902	7	128.85	1- 6	–	–	–
Morris, R.S.M.	1	0	–	–	–	–	–
Morrison, D.K.	10622	337	31.51	7- 82	14	–	–
Mortensen, O.H.	10364	434	23.88	6- 27	16	1	2
Moxon, M.D.	1481	28	52.89	3- 24	–	–	–
Mullally, A.D.	7462	214	34.86	7- 72	4	1	1
Munton, T.A.	13417	502	26.72	8- 89	22	5	5
Murphy, A.J.	7934	208	38.14	6- 97	6	–	1
Mushtaq Ahmed	9432	382	24.69	9- 93	25	6	2+1

	Runs	Wkts	Avge	Best	5wI	10wM	50wS
Myles, S.D.	95	0	–	–	–	–	–
Nash, D.J.	1986	74	26.83	6- 30	5	1	–
Newell, M.	282	7	40.28	2- 38	–	–	–
Newman, P.G.	9844	315	31.25	8- 29	6	–	2
Newport, P.J.	19377	703	27.56	8- 52	29	3	7
Nicholas, M.C.J.	3219	72	44.70	6- 37	2	–	–
North, J.A.	1577	44	35.84	4- 47	–	–	–
O'Gorman, T.J.G.	215	3	71.66	1- 7	–	–	–
Ostler, D.P.	122	0	–	–	–	–	–
Owens, M.B.	1802	71	25.38	5- 74	1	–	–
Parkin, O.T.	170	4	42.50	2- 45	–	–	–
Parore, A.C.	55	0	–	–	–	–	–
Parsons, G.J.	20755	695	29.86	9- 72	19	1	2
Parsons, K.A.	35	0	–	–	–	–	–
Patel, M.M.	3919	141	27.79	8- 96	10	5	1
Payne, A.	187	5	37.40	2- 15	–	–	–
Pearson, R.M.	3615	60	60.25	5-108	1	–	–
Penberthy, A.L.	3805	105	36.25	5- 37	2	–	–
Penn, C.	9840	296	33.24	7- 70	12	–	2
Pennett, D.B.	1510	43	35.11	5- 36	1	–	–
Penney, T.L.	183	6	30.50	3- 18	–	–	–
Phelps, B.S.	363	5	72.60	2- 70	–	–	–
Philip, I.L.	47	0	–	–	–	–	–
Phillips, N.C.	230	5	46.00	3- 39	–	–	–
Pick, R.A.	14004	431	32.49	7-128	14	3	4
Pierson, A.R.K.	6391	166	38.50	8- 42	8	–	–
Pigott, A.C.S.	20164	650	31.02	7- 74	24	1	5
Pike, V.J.	578	20	28.90	6- 41	1	–	–
Piper, K.J.	57	1	57.00	1- 57	–	–	–
Pipes, D.J.	19	0	–	–	–	–	–
Pitcher, C.M.	2053	37	55.48	4- 37	–	–	–
Pocock, B.A.	35	0	–	–	–	–	–
Pollard, P.R.	268	4	67.00	2- 79	–	–	–
Pooley, J.C.	11	0	–	–	–	–	–
Prabhakar, M.	8763	301	29.11	6- 36	9	1	–
Prichard, P.J.	497	2	248.50	1- 28	–	–	–
Pringle, C.	4635	154	30.09	7- 52	6	2	–
Radford, N.V.	25927	972	26.67	9- 70	47	7	6
Ramprakash, M.R.	678	8	84.75	1- 0	–	–	–
Ratcliffe, J.D.	235	4	58.75	1- 4	–	–	–
Ratledge, J.	66	0	–	–	–	–	–
Reeve, D.A.	11354	409	27.76	7- 37	6	–	2
Remy, C.C.	937	19	49.31	4- 63	–	–	–
Rhodes, J.N.	49	1	49.00	1- 13	–	–	–
Rhodes, S.J.	30	0	–	–	–	–	–
Richardson, M.S.	158	4	39.50	2- 41	–	–	–
Richardson, R.B.	235	6	39.16	5- 40	1	–	–
Ripley, D.	103	2	51.50	2- 89	–	–	–
Roberts, A.R.	4257	97	43.88	6- 72	1	–	–
Roberts, S.J.	4798	166	28.90	5- 59	5	–	–
Robinson, M.A.	10684	323	33.07	9- 37	7	2	1
Robinson, P.E.	329	3	109.66	1- 10	–	–	–
Robinson, R.T.	285	4	71.25	1- 22	–	–	–
Rollins, A.S.	32	0	–	–	–	–	–
Rose, G.D.	10566	351	30.10	6- 41	7	–	2
Roseberry, M.A.	387	4	96.75	1- 1	–	–	–

	Runs	Wkts	Avge	Best	5wI	10wM	50wS
Russell, R.C.	53	1	53.00	1- 4	–	–	–
Rutherford, K.R.	1000	22	45.45	5- 72	1	–	–
Salisbury, I.D.K.	12335	338	36.49	7- 54	14	2	2
Sargeant, N.F.	88	1	88.00	1- 88	–	–	–
Saxelby, M.	765	9	85.00	3- 41	–	–	–
Scott, C.W.	10	0	–	–	–	–	–
Scriven, T.J.A.	446	10	44.60	3- 43	–	–	–
Searle, J.P.	7	0	–	–	–	–	–
Seymour, A.C.H.	27	0	–	–	–	–	–
Shahid, N.	1081	27	40.03	3- 91	–	–	–
Shaw, T.G.	9803	354	27.69	7- 79	12	2	–
Sheeraz, K.P.	34	2	17.00	2- 34	–	–	–
Sheridan, K.L.P.	200	3	66.66	1- 34	–	–	–
Sheriyar, A.	400	11	36.36	4- 44	–	–	–
Shine, K.J.	5712	148	38.59	8- 47	7	1	–
Silverwood, C.E.W.	958	28	34.21	4- 67	–	–	–
Simmons, P.V.	2720	78	34.87	5- 24	1	–	–
Sladdin, R.W.	3805	93	40.91	6- 58	2	–	–
Sleep, P.R.	14299	363	39.39	8-133	9	–	–
Small, G.C.	23153	811	28.54	7- 15	28	2	6
Smith, A.M.	3494	97	36.02	5- 40	1	–	–
Smith, A.W.	1727	33	52.33	5-103	1	–	–
Smith, B.F.	121	1	121.00	1- 5	–	–	–
Smith, D.M.	1574	30	52.46	3- 40	–	–	–
Smith, N.M.K.	6138	154	39.85	7- 42	8	–	–
Smith, P.A.	9867	275	35.88	6- 91	7	–	–
Smith, R.A.	693	12	57.75	2- 11	–	–	–
Smyth, S.G.	21	0	–	–	–	–	–
Snape, J.N.	385	7	55.00	2- 49	–	–	–
Snell, R.P.	5351	191	28.01	6- 33	6	1	–
Speak, N.J.	104	2	52.00	1- 0	–	–	–
Speight, M.P.	32	2	16.00	1- 2	–	–	–
Spencer, D.J.	1257	34	36.97	4- 31	–	–	–
Steer, I.G.S.	46	3	15.33	3- 23	–	–	–
Stemp, R.D.	4408	138	31.94	6- 37	7	1	–
Stephenson, F.D.	16673	693	24.05	8- 47	39	10	5
Stephenson, J.P.	4877	145	33.63	6- 54	4	–	–
Stewart, A.J.	375	3	125.00	1- 7	–	–	–
Storie, A.C.	230	3	76.66	1- 17	–	–	–
Streak, H.H.	765	20	38.25	5- 56	1	–	–
Such, P.M.	13833	459	30.13	7- 66	21	3	2
Sylvester, S.A.	377	5	75.40	2- 34	–	–	–
Symcox, P.L.	4436	141	31.46	7- 93	4	–	–
Taylor, C.W.	2395	68	35.22	5- 33	1	–	–
Taylor, J.P.	6831	222	30.77	7- 23	8	1	2
Taylor, M.	205	7	29.28	3- 25	–	–	–
Taylor, N.R.	891	16	55.68	2- 20	–	–	–
Terry, V.P.	58	0	–	–	–	–	–
Thomas, S.D.	1068	41	26.04	5- 76	3	–	–
Thompson, D.J.	123	3	41.00	2- 37	–	–	–
Thompson, J.B.D.	120	1	120.00	1- 89	–	–	–
Thomson, S.A.	3741	94	39.79	5- 49	1	–	–
Thorpe, G.P.	1043	20	52.15	4- 40	–	–	–
Thursfield, M.J.	832	26	32.00	6-130	1	–	–
Tolley, C.M.	3440	96	35.83	5- 55	1	–	–
Topley, T.D.	10147	367	27.64	7- 75	15	2	3

	Runs	Wkts	Avge	Best	5wI	10wM	50wS
Trimby, P.W.	1187	38	31.23	5- 84	1	–	–
Trump, H.R.J.	7500	199	37.68	7- 52	8	2	1
Tufnell, P.C.R.	15911	504	31.56	8- 29	23	2	4
Turner, R.J.	26	0	–	–	–	–	–
Twose, R.G.	3324	101	32.91	6- 28	2	–	–
Udal, S.D.	7154	225	31.79	8- 50	14	3	3
Van Troost, A.P.	3399	93	36.54	6- 48	3	–	–
Vandrau, M.J.	2401	68	35.30	5- 42	2	–	–
Vaughan, M.P.	720	15	48.00	4- 39	–	–	–
Walker, A.	7318	232	31.54	6- 50	2	–	1
Walsh, C.A.	27152	1213	22.38	9- 72	70	14	8+1
Walton, T.C.	98	2	49.00	1- 46	–	–	–
Waqar Younis	10983	547	20.07	7- 64	50	12	3+3
Ward, D.M.	113	2	56.50	2- 66	–	–	–
Ward, T.R.	537	6	89.50	2- 48	–	–	–
Warke, S.J.S.	13	0	–	–	–	–	–
Warner, A.E.	12308	386	31.88	5- 27	5	1	–
Wasim Akram	13731	635	21.62	8- 30	50	11	4
Watkin, S.L.	15573	526	29.60	8- 59	20	3	6
Watkinson, M.	19259	574	33.55	8- 30	23	2	6
Waugh, M.E.	4970	130	38.23	5- 37	1	–	–
Weekes, L.C.	381	14	27.21	4- 54	–	–	–
Weekes, P.N.	2581	67	38.52	5- 12	1	–	–
Welch, G.	970	22	44.09	4- 74	–	–	–
Wells, A.P.	765	10	76.50	3- 67	–	–	–
Wells, C.M.	13982	409	34.18	7- 42	7	–	2
Wells, V.J.	2923	111	26.33	5- 43	2	–	–
Wessels, K.C.	556	12	46.33	2- 25	–	–	–
Weston, W.P.C.	389	4	97.25	2- 39	–	–	–
Wharf, A.G.	78	1	78.00	1- 78	–	–	–
Whitaker, J.J.	268	2	134.00	1- 29	–	–	–
Whitaker, P.R.	4	0	–	–	–	–	–
White, C.	1771	63	28.11	5- 40	3	–	–
White, G.W.	43	1	43.00	1- 30	–	–	–
Whittall, A.R.	2029	30	67.63	3- 79	–	–	–
Wight, R.M.	1456	33	44.12	3- 65	–	–	–
Williams, N.F.	17360	580	29.93	8- 75	18	2	3
Williams, R.C.	1599	38	42.07	4- 28	–	–	–
Williamson, J.G.	77	0	–	–	–	–	–
Windows, M.G.N.	3	0	–	–	–	–	–
Wood, J.	2770	78	35.51	6-110	4	–	–
Wren, T.N.	1200	32	37.50	6- 48	1	–	–
Wright, A.J.	68	1	68.00	1- 16	–	–	–
Wylie, A.	73	1	73.00	1- 50	–	–	–
Yates, G.	4039	92	43.90	5- 34	2	–	–
Yeabsley, R.S.	1329	41	32.41	6- 54	1	1	–
Young, B.A.	76	1	76.00	1- 76	–	–	–

LEADING CURRENT PLAYERS

Leading first-class career averages (and fielding aggregates) of players currently registered for county cricket (to the end of the 1994 season).

BATTING
(Qualification: 100 innings)

	Runs	*Avge*
G.A.Hick	23124	57.23
M.E.Waugh	14346	56.70
M.W.Gatting	31785	50.93
J.P.Crawley	5950	49.58
G.A.Gooch	40174	49.23
A.J.Lamb	31131	48.64
P.A.de Silva	7466	48.48
T.M.Moody	12128	45.59
M.A.Atherton	11644	44.44
R.A.Smith	17813	44.31
M.Prabhakar	5609	43.82
N.Hussain	7833	43.04
R.T.Robinson	22637	42.79
R.J.Bailey	16221	42.35
G.P.Thorpe	8414	42.28
M.D.Moxon	18301	41.97
T.S.Curtis	17910	41.55
M.P.Maynard	13818	41.49
N.H.Fairbrother	14317	41.37
A.J.Moles	12964	41.28
A.Fordham	8655	40.63
M.R.Ramprakash	8937	40.62
M.R.Benson	17685	40.56
D.J.Bicknell	10136	40.54
N.J.Speak	5869	40.19
J.E.Morris	16004	39.71
N.R.Taylor	17350	39.70
P.D.Bowler	9925	39.70
A.P.Wells	15415	39.62
A.J.Stewart	15524	39.40
J.D.Carr	9014	39.19
D.M.Ward	7931	39.06
K.J.Barnett	20565	39.02
R.J.Harden	10096	38.98
D.J.Cullinan	5568	38.93
W.J.Cronje	4689	38.75
T.R.Ward	8039	38.28

BOWLING
(Qualification: 100 wickets)

	Wkts	*Avge*
Waqar Younis	533	20.00
Wasim Akram	616	21.87
F.D.Stephenson	693	24.05
A.A.Donald	679	24.31
Mushtaq Ahmed	373	24.57
A.Kumble	225	24.78
N.G.Cowans	662	24.86
J.E.Emburey	1503	25.91
A.R.C.Fraser	486	26.02
N.A.Mallender	916	26.22
K.M.Curran	507	26.32
V.J.Wells	111	26.33
M.P.Bicknell	479	26.34
A.P.Igglesden	462	26.37
M.J.McCague	204	26.48
N.V.Radford	972	26.67
T.A.Munton	502	26.72
D.J.Millns	297	26.85
A.R.Caddick	220	26.91
K.E.Cooper	799	27.15
P.J.Newport	703	27.56
D.A.Reeve	409	27.76
M.M.Patel	141	27.79
P.A.J.DeFreitas	687	27.89
D.G.Cork	209	27.97
P.W.Jarvis	546	28.17
G.C.Small	811	28.54
J.E.Benjamin	253	28.62
S.J.Base	386	28.90
N.G.B.Cook	879	29.01
M.Prabhakar	301	29.11
C.L.Cairns	273	29.212
S.R.Lampitt	286	29.213
E.E.Hemmings	1500	29.30
M.C.Ilott	274	29.36
M.W.Gatting	156	29.43
C.C.Lewis	392	29.46

WICKET-KEEPING

	Total	*Ct*	*St*
B.N.French	914	814	100
R.C.Russell	795	701	94
S.J.Rhodes	725	642	83
S.A.Marsh	537	497	40
C.P.Metson	532	491	41
D.Ripley	529	464	65
M.A.Garnham	469	428	41
W.K.Hegg	426	379	47

FIELDING

	Ct
G.A.Gooch	510
J.E.Emburey	434
M.W.Gatting	423
C.W.J.Athey	399
A.J.Lamb	353
G.A.Hick	331
M.A.Lynch	323
W.Larkins	295

TEST CAREER RECORDS

These records are complete to 1 February 1995 and include the final Ashes Test which began on that date. They cover all Tests whose full scores appear in this edition (Nos 1242 to 1285 inclusive). Except for the England figures, which include all players registered for county cricket in 1995, these records are restricted to those who have played Test cricket since 17 August 1993. Full career records for all Tests prior to that date are published in *The Wisden Book of Test Cricket (Fourth Edition)*.

ENGLAND

BATTING AND FIELDING

	M	*I*	*NO*	*HS*	*Runs*	*Avge*	*100*	*50*	*Ct/St*
M.A.Atherton	45	84	1	151	3324	40.04	7	23	34
C.W.J.Athey	23	41	1	123	919	22.97	1	4	13
R.J.Bailey	4	8	–	43	119	14.87	–	–	–
K.J.Barnett	4	7	–	80	207	29.57	–	2	1
J.E.Benjamin	1	1	–	0	0	0.00	–	–	–
M.R.Benson	1	2	–	30	51	25.50	–	–	–
M.P.Bicknell	2	4	–	14	26	6.50	–	–	–
R.J.Blakey	2	4	–	6	7	1.75	–	–	2
A.R.Caddick	8	14	2	29*	170	14.16	–	–	4
D.J.Capel	15	25	1	98	374	15.58	–	2	6
J.H.Childs	2	4	4	2*	2	–	–	–	1
N.G.B.Cook	15	25	4	31	179	8.52	–	–	5
N.G.Cowans	19	29	7	36	175	7.95	–	–	9
J.P.Crawley	6	10	–	72	230	23.00	–	2	5
T.S.Curtis	5	9	–	41	140	15.55	–	–	3
P.A.J.DeFreitas	43	66	5	88	910	14.91	–	4	14
J.E.Emburey	63	95	20	75	1705	22.73	–	10	33
N.H.Fairbrother	10	15	1	83	219	15.64	–	1	4
A.R.C.Fraser	24	34	4	29	233	7.76	–	–	6
B.N.French	16	21	4	59	308	18.11	–	1	38/1
M.W.Gatting	79	138	14	207	4409	35.55	10	21	59
G.A.Gooch	118	215	6	333	8900	42.58	20	46	103
D.Gough	7	10	3	65	244	34.85	–	2	4
E.E.Hemmings	16	21	4	95	383	22.52	–	2	5
G.A.Hick	32	56	2	178	1933	35.79	2	11	50
N.Hussain	7	13	2	71	284	25.81	–	1	3
A.P.Igglesden	3	5	3	3*	6	3.00	–	–	1
R.K.Illingworth	2	4	2	13	31	15.50	–	–	1
M.C.Ilott	3	5	1	15	28	7.00	–	–	–
P.W.Jarvis	9	15	2	29*	132	10.15	–	–	2
A.J.Lamb	79	139	10	142	4656	36.09	14	18	75
W.Larkins	13	25	1	64	493	20.54	–	3	8
M.N.Lathwell	2	4	–	33	78	19.50	–	–	–
C.C.Lewis	27	44	2	117	1009	24.02	1	4	23
M.J.McCague	3	5	–	11	21	4.20	–	–	1
D.E.Malcolm	32	47	16	29	208	6.70	–	–	5
N.A.Mallender	2	3	–	4	8	2.66	–	–	–
M.P.Maynard	4	8	–	35	87	10.87	–	–	3
H.Morris	3	6	–	44	115	19.16	–	–	3
J.E.Morris	3	5	2	32	71	23.66	–	–	3

ENGLAND – BATTING AND FIELDING (continued)

	M	I	NO	HS	Runs	Avge	100	50	Ct/St
M.D.Moxon	10	17	1	99	455	28.43	–	3	10
T.A.Munton	2	2	1	25*	25	25.00	–	–	–
P.J.Newport	3	5	1	40*	110	27.50	–	–	1
A.C.S.Pigott	1	2	1	8*	12	12.00	–	–	–
N.V.Radford	3	4	1	12*	21	7.00	–	–	–
M.R.Ramprakash	15	26	1	72	498	19.92	–	2	11
D.A.Reeve	3	5	–	59	124	24.80	–	1	1
S.J.Rhodes	11	17	5	65*	294	24.50	–	1	46/3
R.T.Robinson	29	49	5	175	1601	36.38	4	6	8
R.C.Russell	36	58	11	128*	1255	26.70	1	4	90/8
I.D.K.Salisbury	7	13	1	50	205	17.08	–	1	3
G.C.Small	17	24	7	59	263	15.47	–	1	9
D.M.Smith	2	4	–	47	80	20.00	–	–	–
R.A.Smith	53	97	14	175	3677	44.30	9	24	35
J.P.Stephenson	1	2	–	25	36	18.00	–	–	–
A.J.Stewart	45	82	6	190	3055	40.19	7	15	55/4
P.M.Such	8	11	4	14*	65	9.28	–	–	2
J.P.Taylor	2	4	2	17*	34	17.00	–	–	–
V.P.Terry	2	3	–	8	16	5.33	–	–	2
G.P.Thorpe	15	29	3	123	1152	44.30	2	9	19
P.C.R.Tufnell	22	32	17	22*	62	4.13	–	–	10
S.L.Watkin	3	5	–	13	25	5.00	–	–	1
J.J.Whitaker	1	1	–	11	11	11.00	–	–	1
N.F.Williams	1	1	–	38	38	38.00	–	–	–
C.White	4	6	–	51	131	21.83	–	1	3

ENGLAND

BOWLING

	O	R	W	Avge	Best	5wI	10wM
M.A.Atherton	61	282	1	282.00	1- 60	–	–
K.J.Barnett	6	32	0	–	–	–	–
J.E.Benjamin	28	80	4	20.00	4- 42	–	–
M.P.Bicknell	87	263	4	65.75	3- 99	–	–
A.R.Caddick	323.2	1033	23	44.91	6- 65	2	–
D.J.Capel	333.2	1064	21	50.66	3- 88	–	–
J.H.Childs	86	183	3	61.00	1- 13	–	–
N.G.B.Cook	695.4	1689	52	32.48	6- 65	4	1
N.G.Cowans	575.2	2003	51	39.27	6- 77	2	–
T.S.Curtis	3	7	0	–	–	–	–
P.A.J.DeFreitas	1612.4	4585	138	33.22	7- 70	4	–
J.E.Emburey	2535.1	5564	147	37.85	7- 78	6	–
N.H.Fairbrother	2	9	0	–	–	–	–
A.R.C.Fraser	1074	2759	99	27.86	8- 75	7	–
M.W.Gatting	125.2	317	4	79.25	1- 14	–	–
G.A.Gooch	442.3	1069	23	46.47	3- 39	–	–
D.Gough	323.1	991	37	26.78	6- 49	1	–
E.E.Hemmings	739.3	1825	43	42.44	6- 58	1	–
G.A.Hick	399.5	973	19	51.21	4-126	–	–
A.P.Igglesden	92.3	329	6	54.83	2- 91	–	–
R.K.Illingworth	56.4	213	4	53.25	3-110	–	–
M.C.Ilott	129	412	8	51.50	3-108	–	–
P.W.Jarvis	318.4	965	21	45.95	4-107	–	–

ENGLAND - BOWLING (continued)

	O	R	W	Avge	Best	5wI	10wM
A.J.Lamb	5	23	1	23.00	1- 6	–	–
C.C.Lewis	939.2	2870	77	37.27	6-111	2	–
M.J.McCague	98.5	390	6	65.00	4-121	–	–
D.E.Malcolm	1212.5	4026	111	36.27	9- 57	5	2
N.A.Mallender	74.5	215	10	21.50	5- 50	1	–
M.D.Moxon	8	30	0	–	–	–	–
T.A.Munton	67.3	200	4	50.00	2- 22	–	–
P.J.Newport	111.3	417	10	41.70	4- 87	–	–
A.C.S.Pigott	17	75	2	37.50	2- 75	–	–
N.V.Radford	113	351	4	87.75	2-131	–	–
M.R.Ramprakash	40.1	130	0	–	–	–	–
D.A.Reeve	24.5	60	2	30.00	1- 4	–	–
R.T.Robinson	1	0	0	–	–	–	–
I.D.K.Salisbury	234.1	933	16	58.31	4-163	–	–
G.C.Small	654.3	1871	55	34.01	5- 48	2	–
R.A.Smith	4	6	0	–	–	–	–
A.J.Stewart	3.2	13	0	–	–	–	–
P.M.Such	362.5	805	22	36.59	6- 67	1	–
J.P.Taylor	48	156	3	52.00	1- 18	–	–
G.P.Thorpe	8	15	0	–	–	–	–
P.C.R.Tufnell	1063	2671	68	39.27	7- 47	4	1
S.L.Watkin	89	305	11	27.72	4- 65	–	–
N.F.Williams	41	148	2	74.00	2-148	–	–
C.White	78.1	258	8	32.25	3- 18	–	–

AUSTRALIA

BATTING AND FIELDING

	M	I	NO	HS	Runs	Avge	100	50	Ct/St
J.Angel	4	7	1	11	35	5.83	–	–	1
M.G.Bevan	6	10	–	91	324	32.40	–	3	5
G.S.Blewett	2	4	1	115	249	83.00	2	–	3
D.C.Boon	97	175	20	200	6959	44.89	20	30	90
A.R.Border	156	265	44	205	11174	50.56	27	63	156
P.A.Emery	1	1	1	8*	8	–	–	–	5/1
D.W.Fleming	4	4	–	24	40	10.00	–	–	2
M.L.Hayden	1	2	–	15	20	10.00	–	–	1
I.A.Healy	69	103	13	113*	2429	26.98	2	15	222/16
M.G.Hughes	53	70	8	72*	1032	16.64	–	2	23
J.L.Langer	6	9	–	69	241	26.77	–	3	2
C.J.McDermott	65	84	12	42*	897	12.45	–	–	15
G.D.McGrath	9	10	2	9	15	1.87	–	–	–
P.E.McIntyre	1	2	–	0	0	0.00	–	–	–
D.R.Martyn	7	12	1	74	317	28.81	–	3	1
T.B.A.May	24	28	12	42*	225	14.06	–	–	6
P.R.Reiffel	12	13	3	51	227	22.70	–	1	5
M.J.Slater	23	40	1	176	2024	51.89	6	8	4
M.A.Taylor	62	112	7	219	4852	46.20	13	29	83
S.K.Warne	34	48	8	74*	569	14.22	–	1	23
M.E.Waugh	44	71	4	140	2832	42.26	7	17	59
S.R.Waugh	72	111	21	177*	4011	44.56	7	24	53

AUSTRALIA

BOWLING

	O	R	W	Avge	Best	5wI	10wM
J.Angel	124.4	463	10	46.30	3-54	–	–
M.G.Bevan	15	67	1	67.00	1-21	–	–
G.S.Blewett	24	91	0	–	–	–	–
D.C.Boon	6	14	0	–	–	–	–
A.R.Border	668.1	1525	39	39.10	7-46	2	1
D.W.Fleming	150.2	435	17	25.58	4-75	–	–
M.G.Hughes	2047.3	6017	212	28.38	8-87	7	1
C.J.McDermott	2564.1	7697	270	28.50	8-97	13	2
G.D.McGrath	359.2	958	25	38.32	4-92	–	–
P.E.McIntyre	27.3	87	2	43.50	2-51	–	–
D.R.Martyn	1	0	0	–	–	–	–
T.B.A.May	1096.1	2606	75	34.74	5- 9	3	–
P.R.Reiffel	396.4	1050	31	33.87	6-71	2	–
M.J.Slater	1.1	4	1	4.00	1- 4	–	–
M.A.Taylor	7	26	1	26.00	1-11	–	–
S.K.Warne	1768.4	3833	161	23.80	8-71	9	2
M.E.Waugh	400	1124	33	34.06	5-40	1	–
S.R.Waugh	960.1	2574	67	38.41	5-28	3	–

SOUTH AFRICA

BATTING AND FIELDING

	M	I	NO	HS	Runs	Avge	100	50	Ct/St
J.B.Commins	3	6	1	45	125	25.00	–	–	2
W.J.Cronje	20	36	4	135	1200	37.50	4	3	9
D.J.Cullinan	12	22	2	102	669	33.45	1	4	4
P.S.de Villiers	13	18	5	66*	218	16.76	–	1	7
A.A.Donald	18	24	13	27	128	11.63	–	–	5
C.E.Eksteen	4	7	2	22	51	10.20	–	–	4
A.C.Hudson	18	33	1	163	1116	34.87	2	9	13
S.D.Jack	2	2	–	7	7	3.50	–	–	1
G.Kirsten	13	24	1	72	856	37.21	–	6	14
P.N.Kirsten	12	22	2	104	626	31.30	1	4	8
B.M.McMillan	17	27	3	113	879	36.62	1	6	21
C.R.Matthews	13	19	5	62*	288	20.57	–	1	–
J.N.Rhodes	20	33	5	101*	1009	36.03	1	6	11
D.J.Richardson	21	32	2	109	799	26.63	1	5	86/–
R.P.Snell	5	8	1	48	95	13.57	–	–	1
P.J.R.Steyn	2	4	–	38	68	17.00	–	–	–
P.L.Symcox	5	6	–	50	160	26.66	–	1	–
K.C.Wessels	16	29	2	118	1027	38.03	2	6	12
K.C.Wessels (A/SA)	40	71	3	179	2788	41.00	6	15	30

SOUTH AFRICA

BOWLING

	O	R	W	Avge	Best	5wI	10wM
W.J.Cronje	236.1	427	6	71.16	2-17	–	–
P.S.de Villiers	614.1	1613	64	25.20	6-43	4	2
A.A.Donald	698.5	2094	79	26.50	7-84	4	1
C.E.Eksteen	143	291	4	72.75	2-34	–	–
S.D.Jack	77	195	8	24.37	4-68	–	–
G.Kirsten	48.1	133	2	66.50	1- 0	–	–
P.N.Kirsten	9	30	0	–	–	–	–
B.M.McMillan	577.2	1476	51	28.94	4-65	–	–
C.R.Matthews	504.3	1142	41	27.85	5-42	2	–
J.N.Rhodes	2	5	0	–	–	–	–
R.P.Snell	170.5	538	19	28.31	4-74	–	–
P.L.Symcox	142.5	383	8	47.87	3-75	–	–
K.C.Wessels (A/SA)	15	42	0	–	–	–	–

WEST INDIES

BATTING AND FIELDING

	M	I	NO	HS	Runs	Avge	100	50	Ct/St
J.C.Adams	12	19	6	174*	1132	87.07	3	6	15
C.E.L.Ambrose	48	70	13	53	680	11.92	–	1	10
K.L.T.Arthurton	23	37	5	157*	1078	33.68	2	6	14
K.C.G.Benjamin	10	14	2	43*	83	6.91	–	–	–
W.K.M.Benjamin	16	19	1	44	276	15.33	–	–	8
S.Chanderpaul	5	8	2	77	303	50.50	–	4	4
C.E.Cuffy	2	3	1	1	1	0.50	–	–	1
A.C.Cummins	5	6	1	50	98	19.60	–	1	1
R.Dhanraj	1	2	–	4	5	2.50	–	–	–
R.A.Harper	25	32	3	74	535	18.44	–	3	36
D.L.Haynes	116	202	25	184	7487	42.29	18	39	65
C.L.Hooper	43	73	6	178*	2094	31.25	4	10	47
B.C.Lara	19	32	–	375	1826	57.06	3	10	30
J.R.Murray	15	19	2	85	416	24.47	–	2	53/2
R.B.Richardson	76	130	11	194	5445	45.75	15	25	82
P.V.Simmons	22	41	2	110	919	23.56	1	3	21
C.A.Walsh	68	92	28	30*	578	9.03	–	–	9
S.C.Williams	4	7	1	49	138	23.00	–	–	6

WEST INDIES

BOWLING

	O	R	W	Avge	Best	5wI	10wM
J.C.Adams	120.4	391	9	43.44	4-43	–	–
C.E.L.Ambrose	1968.1	4616	219	21.07	8-45	11	3
K.L.T.Arthurton	32	77	0	–	–	–	–
K.C.G.Benjamin	371.3	1218	43	28.32	6-66	2	–
W.K.M.Benjamin	480.2	1251	51	24.52	4-46	–	–
S.Chanderpaul	85	272	2	136.00	1-63	–	–
C.E.Cuffy	52.4	190	5	38.00	3-80	–	–
A.C.Cummins	103	342	8	42.75	4-54	–	–
R.Dhanraj	25	93	2	46.50	1-46	–	–
R.A.Harper	602.3	1291	46	28.06	6-57	1	–
D.L.Haynes	3	8	1	8.00	1- 2	–	–
C.L.Hooper	875	2330	45	51.77	5-40	2	–
B.C.Lara	2	4	0	–	–	–	–
R.B.Richardson	11	18	0	–	–	–	–
P.V.Simmons	66	158	2	79.00	2-34	–	–
C.A.Walsh	2340.2	6185	239	25.87	6-62	7	1

NEW ZEALAND

BATTING AND FIELDING

	M	I	NO	HS	Runs	Avge	100	50	Ct/St
T.E.Blain	11	20	3	78	456	26.82	–	2	19/2
C.L.Cairns	10	17	–	78	349	20.52	–	2	6
M.D.Crowe	73	126	11	299	5364	46.64	17	18	69
H.T.Davis	1	2	2	0*	0	–	–	–	–
R.P.de Groen	5	10	4	26	45	7.50	–	–	–
S.B.Doull	9	16	2	31*	210	15.00	–	–	7
S.P.Fleming	7	14	–	92	507	36.21	–	4	6
M.J.Greatbatch	34	61	5	146*	1858	33.17	3	9	25
C.Z.Harris	5	10	1	56	116	12.88	–	1	2
M.N.Hart	9	16	3	36	237	18.23	–	–	5
B.R.Hartland	9	18	–	52	303	16.83	–	1	5
A.H.Jones	37	70	7	186	2898	46.00	7	11	25
G.R.Larsen	1	2	–	8	10	5.00	–	–	2
D.K.Morrison	37	55	18	42	297	8.02	–	–	13
D.J.Murray	3	6	–	38	71	11.83	–	–	2
D.J.Nash	7	11	5	56	166	27.66	–	1	6
M.B.Owens	8	12	6	8*	16	2.66	–	–	3
A.C.Parore	15	27	2	71	512	20.48	–	2	40/2
D.N.Patel	25	47	6	99	848	20.68	–	3	8
B.A.Pocock	6	12	–	34	135	11.25	–	–	1
C.Pringle	13	20	4	30	171	10.68	–	–	3
K.R.Rutherford	51	91	7	107*	2275	27.08	3	17	30
M.L.Su'a	11	15	4	44	131	11.90	–	–	6
S.A.Thomson	14	28	4	120*	889	37.04	1	5	7
W.Watson	15	18	6	11	60	5.00	–	–	4
B.A.Young	11	22	–	120	749	34.04	1	6	18

NEW ZEALAND

BOWLING

	O	R	W	Avge	Best	5wI	10wM
C.L.Cairns	332.3	1207	28	43.10	6- 52	2	–
M.D.Crowe	229.3	676	14	48.28	2- 25	–	–
H.T.Davis	21	93	1	93.00	1- 93	–	–
R.P.de Groen	176.4	505	11	45.90	3- 40	–	–
S.B.Doull	276	830	30	27.66	5- 66	2	–
M.J.Greatbatch	1	0	0	–	–	–	–
C.Z.Harris	22	103	0	–	–	–	–
M.N.Hart	378.3	995	26	38.26	5- 77	1	–
A.H.Jones	41.4	144	1	144.00	1- 40	–	–
G.R.Larsen	44.4	116	2	58.00	2-116	–	–
D.K.Morrison	1333.2	4412	125	35.29	7- 89	8	–
D.J.Nash	248	749	24	31.20	6- 76	2	1
M.B.Owens	179	585	17	34.41	4- 99	–	–
D.N.Patel	675	2030	45	45.11	6- 50	3	–
B.A.Pocock	2	10	0	–	–	–	–
C.Pringle	460.3	1283	27	47.51	7- 52	1	1
K.R.Rutherford	42.4	161	1	161.00	1- 38	–	–
M.L.Su'a	383	1058	32	33.06	5- 73	2	–
S.A.Thomson	275.4	785	17	46.17	3- 63	–	–
W.Watson	581	1387	40	34.67	6- 78	1	–

INDIA

BATTING AND FIELDING

	M	I	NO	HS	Runs	Avge	100	50	Ct/St
M.Azharuddin	65	94	4	199	4198	46.64	14	14	68
R.K.Chauhan	13	10	3	15*	64	9.14	–	–	8
V.G.Kambli	14	19	1	227	1029	57.16	4	3	6
Kapil Dev	131	184	15	163	5248	31.05	8	27	64
A.R.Kapoor	1	2	–	15	16	8.00	–	–	1
A.Kumble	20	21	4	52*	249	14.64	–	1	9
S.V.Manjrekar	33	53	5	218	1855	38.64	4	8	21
N.R.Mongia	7	11	1	80	342	34.20	–	1	16/2
M.Prabhakar	36	54	8	120	1490	32.39	1	9	19
S.L.V.Raju	21	27	9	31	228	12.66	–	–	5
N.S.Sidhu	34	52	2	124	2013	40.26	6	10	8
J.Srinath	15	21	11	60	227	22.70	–	2	7
S.R.Tendulkar	35	51	5	179	2425	52.71	8	12	28
Correction of 1994 *Playfair*:									
Maninder Singh	35	38	12	15	99	3.80	–	–	9

INDIA

BOWLING

	O	R	W	Avge	Best	5wI	10wM
M.Azharuddin	1.1	12	0	–	–	–	–
R.K.Chauhan	522.5	1151	33	34.87	3- 8	–	–
Kapil Dev	4623.2	12867	434	29.64	9- 83	23	2
A.R.Kapoor	37	122	1	122.00	1- 90	–	–
A.Kumble	1094.3	2510	99	25.35	7- 59	5	1
S.V.Manjrekar	2.5	15	0	–	–	–	–
M.Prabhakar	1226.5	3533	94	37.58	6-132	3	–
S.L.V.Raju	1027	2273	81	28.06	6- 12	5	1
N.S.Sidhu	1	9	0	–	–	–	–
J.Srinath	587	1549	41	37.78	4- 33	–	–
S.R.Tendulkar	72	191	4	47.75	2- 10	–	–

PAKISTAN

BATTING AND FIELDING

	M	I	NO	HS	Runs	Avge	100	50	Ct/St
Aamer Malik	14	19	3	117	656	35.31	2	1	15
Aamir Nazir	3	6	3	6*	8	2.66	–	–	–
Aamir Sohail	20	37	1	205	1330	36.94	2	9	20
Akram Raza	8	10	1	32	132	14.66	–	–	8
Aqib Javed	16	16	4	10	33	2.75	–	–	1
Ashfaq Ahmed	1	2	1	1*	1	1.00	–	–	–
Asif Mujtaba	20	33	3	65*	756	25.20	–	7	17
Ata-ur-Rehman	9	9	3	19	48	8.00	–	–	2
Atif Rauf	1	2	–	16	25	12.50	–	–	–
Basit Ali	13	22	1	103	757	36.04	1	5	4
Ijaz Ahmed	21	29	–	122	817	28.17	2	3	17
Inzamam-ul-Haq	20	34	7	135*	1174	43.48	3	6	20
Javed Miandad	124	189	21	280*	8832	52.57	23	43	93/1
Kabir Khan	2	2	–	10	14	7.00	–	–	–
Mohsin Kamal	9	11	7	13*	37	9.25	–	–	4
Moin Khan	13	19	3	115*	309	19.31	1	–	34/2
Mushtaq Ahmed	18	26	6	27	163	8.15	–	–	5
Rashid Latif	13	18	3	68*	459	30.60	–	3	39/4
Saeed Anwar	10	18	–	169	839	46.61	2	5	4
Salim Malik	81	119	19	237	4697	46.97	13	24	53
Shoaib Mohammad	42	63	7	203*	2622	46.82	7	12	21
Tausif Ahmed	34	38	20	33*	318	17.66	–	–	9
Waqar Younis	33	41	6	29	312	8.91	–	–	4
Wasim Akram	58	77	11	123	1350	20.45	1	4	20
Zahid Fazal	8	14	–	78	264	18.85	–	1	5

PAKISTAN

BOWLING

	O	R	W	Avge	Best	5wI	10wM
Aamer Malik	26	89	1	89.00	1- 0	–	–
Aamir Nazir	79.1	325	6	54.16	2- 67	–	–
Aamir Sohail	77.2	256	6	42.66	2- 67	–	–
Akram Raza	220.2	620	13	47.69	3- 46	–	–
Aqib Javed	435.4	1310	30	43.66	4-100	–	–
Ashfaq Ahmed	23	53	2	26.50	2- 31	–	–
Asif Mujtaba	37	122	2	61.00	1- 0	–	–
Ata-ur-Rehman	212	720	21	34.28	3- 28	–	–
Basit Ali	1	6	0	–	–	–	–
Ijaz Ahmed	9	18	1	18.00	1- 9	–	–
Javed Miandad	245	682	17	40.11	3- 74	–	–
Kabir Khan	47.1	157	4	39.25	2- 60	–	–
Mohsin Kamal	224.4	822	24	34.25	4-116	–	–
Mushtaq Ahmed	556.2	1605	44	36.47	4-121	–	–
Rashid Latif	2	11	0	–	–	–	–
Saeed Anwar	3	4	0	–	–	–	–
Salim Malik	61.2	204	5	40.80	1- 3	–	–
Shoaib Mohammad	47	130	5	26.00	2- 8	–	–
Tausif Ahmed	1296.2	2950	93	31.72	6- 45	3	–
Waqar Younis	1142.5	3640	190	19.15	7- 76	19	4
Wasim Akram	2210.3	5744	248	23.16	7-119	17	3

SRI LANKA

BATTING AND FIELDING

	M	I	NO	HS	Runs	Avge	100	50	Ct/St
S.D.Anurasiri	17	21	4	24	88	5.17	–	–	3
M.S.Atapattu	3	6	–	1	1	0.16	–	–	–
P.B.Dassanayake	11	17	2	36	196	13.06	–	–	19/5
P.A.de Silva	46	79	4	267	2872	38.29	7	12	21
H.D.P.K.Dharmasena	6	10	–	54	139	13.90	–	1	2
A.P.Gurusinha	31	52	7	137	1787	39.71	5	6	22
S.T.Jayasuriya	16	25	5	81	611	30.55	–	4	17
R.S.Kalpage	8	14	1	63	265	20.38	–	2	6
D.K.Liyanage	8	8	–	23	66	8.25	–	–	–
R.S.Mahanama	32	53	–	153	1687	31.83	3	9	19
M.Muralitharan	16	18	11	20*	128	18.28	–	–	6
K.R.Pushpakumara	3	4	1	8	20	6.66	–	–	–
A.Ranatunga	54	90	5	135*	2961	34.83	4	18	22
S.Ranatunga	4	7	1	118	282	47.00	2	–	–
D.P.Samaraweera	5	10	–	42	134	13.40	–	–	4
H.P.Tillekeratne	28	45	7	116	1413	37.18	1	9	62/–
W.P.U.C.J.Vaas	4	5	1	16*	37	9.25	–	–	–
K.P.J.Warnaweera	10	12	3	20	39	4.33	–	–	–
G.P.Wickremasinghe	15	22	4	22	151	8.38	–	–	7

SRI LANKA

BOWLING

	O	R	W	Avge	Best	5wI	10wM
S.D.Anurasiri	616.1	1442	37	38.97	4- 71	–	–
P.A.de Silva	130	413	11	37.54	3- 39	–	–
H.D.P.K.Dharmasena	276.2	637	17	37.47	6- 99	1	–
A.P.Gurusinha	201.4	593	18	32.94	2- 7	–	–
S.T.Jayasuriya	95	345	4	86.25	2- 46	–	–
R.S.Kalpage	152.5	405	6	67.50	2- 27	–	–
D.K.Liyanage	211.5	622	17	36.58	4- 56	–	–
R.S.Mahanama	6	30	0	–	–	–	–
M.Muralitharan	700.5	1846	56	32.96	5-101	3	–
K.R.Pushpakumara	81.4	329	12	27.41	7-116	1	–
A.Ranatunga	360.2	942	14	67.28	2- 17	–	–
H.P.Tillekeratne	3	6	0	–	–	–	–
W.P.U.C.J.Vaas	147.3	315	10	31.50	4- 74	–	–
K.P.J.Warnaweera	388.5	1021	32	31.90	4- 25	–	–
G.P.Wickremasinghe	457	1479	29	51.00	5- 73	1	–

ZIMBABWE

BATTING AND FIELDING

	M	I	NO	HS	Runs	Avge	100	50	Ct/St
D.H.Brain	6	9	1	28	80	10.00	–	–	–
E.A.Brandes	6	10	1	18	60	6.66	–	–	3
G.K.Bruk-Jackson	2	4	–	31	39	9.75	–	–	–
A.D.R.Campbell	10	16	1	99	639	42.60	–	6	5
M.H.Dekker	6	8	1	68*	197	28.14	–	2	8
A.Flower	10	15	3	115	585	48.75	1	6	19/2
G.W.Flower	10	16	–	96	390	24.37	–	2	1
D.L.Houghton	10	15	1	266	829	59.21	3	2	7
W.R.James	4	4	–	33	61	15.25	–	–	16/–
M.P.Jarvis	5	3	1	2*	4	2.00	–	–	2
S.G.Peall	4	6	2	30	60	15.00	–	–	1
J.A.Rennie	3	4	1	19*	24	8.00	–	–	–
P.A.Strang	1	1	–	6	6	6.00	–	–	–
H.H.Streak	6	8	1	20	49	7.00	–	–	2
G.J.Whittall	6	8	1	61*	143	20.42	–	1	3

BOWLING

	O	R	W	Avge	Best	5wI	10wM
D.H.Brain	213	578	22	26.27	5-42	1	–
E.A.Brandes	210.4	598	17	35.17	3-45	–	–
A.D.R.Campbell	3	4	0	–	–	–	–
M.H.Dekker	6	5	0	–	–	–	–
A.Flower	0.1	0	0	–	–	–	–
G.W.Flower	61	173	2	86.50	1- 8	–	–
D.L.Houghton	0.5	0	0	–	–	–	–
M.P.Jarvis	212.1	393	11	35.72	3-30	–	–
S.G.Peall	148	303	4	75.75	2-89	–	–
J.A.Rennie	109.4	256	3	85.33	2-22	–	–
P.A.Strang	25	65	3	21.66	3-65	–	–
H.H.Streak	245.4	588	21	28.00	5-56	1	–
G.J.Whittall	139	300	8	37.50	4-70	–	–

LIMITED-OVERS INTERNATIONALS CAREER RECORDS

These records are complete to 1 February 1995. Except for the England figures, which include all players registered for county cricket in 1995, these records are restricted to those who have appeared in limited-overs internationals since 24 July 1993.

ENGLAND

BATTING AND FIELDING

	M	*I*	*NO*	*HS*	*Runs*	*Avge*	*100*	*50*	*Ct/St*
M.A.Atherton	22	22	2	86	841	42.05	–	7	5
C.W.J.Athey	31	30	3	142*	848	31.40	2	4	1
R.J.Bailey	4	4	2	43*	137	68.50	–	–	1
K.J.Barnett	1	1	–	84	84	84.00	–	1	–
J.E.Benjamin	2	1	–	0	0	0.00	–	–	–
M.R.Benson	1	1	–	24	24	24.00	–	–	–
M.P.Bicknell	7	6	2	31*	96	24.00	–	–	2
R.J.Blakey	3	2	–	25	25	12.50	–	–	2/1
A.R.Caddick	5	3	3	21*	24	–	–	–	1
D.J.Capel	23	19	2	50*	327	19.23	–	1	6
N.G.B.Cook	3	–	–	–	–	–	–	–	2
D.G.Cork	5	1	–	11	11	11.00	–	–	–
N.G.Cowans	23	8	3	4*	13	2.60	–	–	5
J.P.Crawley	3	3	–	18	34	11.33	–	–	–
P.A.J.DeFreitas	91	59	23	49*	551	15.30	–	–	25
J.E.Emburey	61	45	10	34	501	14.31	–	–	19
N.H.Fairbrother	44	42	9	113	1268	38.42	1	9	19
A.R.C.Fraser	31	13	5	38*	76	9.50	–	–	1
B.N.French	13	8	3	9*	34	6.80	–	–	13/3
M.W.Gatting	92	88	17	115*	2095	29.50	1	9	22
G.A.Gooch	125	122	6	142	4290	36.98	8	23	45
D.Gough	7	4	1	45	59	19.66	–	–	1
E.E.Hemmings	33	12	6	8*	30	5.00	–	–	5
G.A.Hick	44	43	6	105*	1473	39.81	1	12	25
N.Hussain	4	4	1	16	43	14.33	–	–	2
A.P.Igglesden	4	3	1	18	20	10.00	–	–	1
R.K.Illingworth	18	7	2	14	61	12.20	–	–	8
P.W.Jarvis	16	8	2	16*	31	5.16	–	–	1
A.J.Lamb	122	118	16	118	4010	39.31	4	26	31
W.Larkins	25	24	–	124	591	24.62	1	–	8
C.C.Lewis	48	36	11	33	315	12.60	–	–	20
M.A.Lynch	3	3	–	6	8	2.66	–	–	1
D.E.Malcolm	10	5	2	4	9	3.00	–	–	1
M.P.Maynard	5	5	1	22*	59	14.75	–	–	1
J.E.Morris	8	8	1	63*	167	23.85	–	1	2
M.D.Moxon	8	8	–	70	174	21.75	–	1	5
N.V.Radford	6	3	2	0*	0	0.00	–	–	2
M.R.Ramprakash	4	4	2	31	47	23.50	–	–	3
D.A.Reeve	25	17	9	33*	241	30.12	–	–	11
S.J.Rhodes	9	8	2	56	107	17.83	–	1	9/2
R.T.Robinson	26	26	–	83	597	22.96	–	3	6
R.C.Russell	26	19	6	50	261	20.07	–	1	26/5

ENGLAND – BATTING AND FIELDING (continued)

	M	I	NO	HS	Runs	Avge	100	50	Ct/St
I.D.K.Salisbury	4	2	1	5	7	7.00	–	–	1
G.C.Small	53	24	9	18*	98	6.53	–	–	7
D.M.Smith	2	2	1	10*	15	15.00	–	–	–
R.A.Smith	64	63	8	167*	2218	40.32	4	13	23
A.J.Stewart	61	56	4	103	1567	30.13	1	10	47/4
J.P.Taylor	1	1	–	1	1	1.00	–	–	–
G.P.Thorpe	10	10	–	89	292	29.20	–	2	5
P.C.R.Tufnell	19	10	9	5*	15	15.00	–	–	3
S.D.Udal	7	5	3	11*	30	15.00	–	–	1
S.L.Watkin	4	2	–	4	4	2.00	–	–	–
C.M.Wells	2	2	–	17	22	11.00	–	–	–
J.J.Whitaker	2	2	1	44*	48	48.00	–	–	1
C.White	1	1	–	0	0	0.00	–	–	–

BOWLING

	Overs	Runs	Wkts	Avge	Best	4w
C.W.J.Athey	1	10	0	–	–	–
R.J.Bailey	6	25	0	–	–	–
J.E.Benjamin	12	47	1	47.00	1-22	–
M.P.Bicknell	68.5	347	13	26.69	3-55	–
A.R.Caddick	53	258	6	43.00	3-39	–
D.J.Capel	173	805	17	47.35	3-38	–
N.G.B.Cook	24	95	5	19.00	2-18	–
D.G.Cork	53	213	5	42.60	3-49	–
N.G.Cowans	213.4	913	23	39.69	3-44	–
P.A.J.DeFreitas	848.1	3284	104	31.57	4-35	1
J.E.Emburey	570.5	2346	76	30.86	4-37	2
N.H.Fairbrother	1	9	0	–	–	–
A.R.C.Fraser	291.4	1069	35	30.54	4-22	1
M.W.Gatting	65.2	336	10	33.60	3-32	–
G.A.Gooch	344.2	1516	36	42.11	3-19	–
D.Gough	60.4	227	12	18.91	5-44	1
E.E.Hemmings	292	1294	37	34.97	4-52	1
G.A.Hick	95	460	13	35.38	3-41	–
A.P.Igglesden	28	122	2	61.00	2-12	–
R.K.Illingworth	182.1	760	24	31.66	3-33	–
P.W.Jarvis	146.3	672	24	28.00	5-35	2
A.J.Lamb	1	3	0	–	–	–
W.Larkins	2.3	22	0	–	–	–
C.C.Lewis	391.4	1735	61	28.44	4-30	3
D.E.Malcolm	87.4	404	16	25.25	3-40	–
N.V.Radford	58	230	2	115.00	1-32	–
D.A.Reeve	161.3	686	18	38.11	3-20	–
I.D.K.Salisbury	31	177	5	35.40	3-41	–
G.C.Small	465.3	1942	58	33.48	4-31	1
J.P.Taylor	3	20	0	–	–	–
P.C.R.Tufnell	160	676	15	45.06	3-40	–
S.D.Udal	68	243	8	30.37	2-37	–
S.L.Watkin	36.5	193	7	27.57	4-49	1
C.White	5	22	0	–	–	–

AUSTRALIA

BATTING AND FIELDING

	M	I	NO	HS	Runs	Avge	100	50	Ct/St
J.Angel	2	1	–	0	0	0.00	–	–	–
M.G.Bevan	15	13	5	53*	432	54.00	–	1	6
D.C.Boon	173	169	14	122	5693	36.72	5	36	42
A.R.Border	273	252	39	127*	6524	30.62	3	39	127
P.A.Emery	1	1	1	11*	11	–	–	–	3/–
D.W.Fleming	13	4	3	5*	9	9.00	–	–	3
M.L.Hayden	13	12	1	67	286	26.00	–	2	4
I.A.Healy	120	81	26	56	1196	21.74	–	2	143/24
M.G.Hughes	33	17	8	20	100	11.11	–	–	6
D.M.Jones	164	161	25	145	6068	44.61	7	46	54
J.L.Langer	6	5	2	36	125	41.66	–	–	1/1
S.G.Law	4	4	1	110	134	44.66	1	–	1
C.J.McDermott	126	76	17	37	420	7.11	–	–	26
G.D.McGrath	28	10	4	10	24	4.00	–	–	2
D.R.Martyn	11	10	1	51*	166	18.44	–	1	6
T.B.A.May	41	11	7	15	36	9.00	–	–	1
P.R.Reiffel	40	25	13	58	238	19.83	–	1	14
G.R.Robertson	4	3	2	5*	7	7.00	–	–	–
M.A.Slater	22	22	–	73	528	24.00	–	4	4
M.A.Taylor	70	67	1	94	2094	31.72	–	19	34
S.K.Warne	35	18	3	55	205	13.66	–	1	11
M.E.Waugh	88	84	8	121*	2583	33.98	4	17	35
S.R.Waugh	176	156	38	86	3607	30.56	–	18	61
T.J.Zoehrer	22	15	3	50	130	10.83	–	1	21/2

AUSTRALIA

BOWLING

	Overs	Runs	Wkts	Avge	Best	4w
J.Angel	17	66	2	33.00	1-29	–
M.G.Bevan	2	17	0	–	–	–
D.C.Boon	6.4	52	0	–	–	–
A.R.Border	443.3	2071	73	28.36	3-20	–
D.W.Fleming	119.5	490	19	25.78	4-39	2
M.G.Hughes	273.1	1115	38	29.34	4-44	1
D.M.Jones	17.4	81	3	27.00	2-34	–
S.G.Law	34	136	3	45.33	2-52	–
C.J.McDermott	1144.4	4625	184	25.13	5-44	5
G.D.McGrath	251.5	902	42	21.47	5-52	4
T.B.A.May	367.2	1560	33	47.27	3-51	–
P.R.Reiffel	352.5	1282	48	26.70	4-13	2
G.R.Robertson	24	127	0	–	–	–
M.A.Slater	1	11	0	–	–	–
S.K.Warne	323.2	1209	63	19.19	4-19	5
M.E.Waugh	255.5	1244	46	27.04	5-24	2
S.R.Waugh	1199.3	5292	159	33.28	4-33	2

SOUTH AFRICA

BATTING AND FIELDING

	M	*I*	*NO*	*HS*	*Runs*	*Avge*	*100*	*50*	*Ct/St*
D.J.Callaghan	24	21	6	169*	438	29.20	1	–	4
S.J.Cook	4	4	–	35	67	16.75	–	–	1
W.J.Cronje	65	62	11	112	1916	37.56	2	10	24
D.N.Crookes	3	3	–	20	30	10.00	–	–	–
D.J.Cullinan	35	34	3	70*	782	25.22	–	4	11
P.S.de Villiers	54	22	12	15	83	8.30	–	–	11
A.A.Donald	47	15	8	7*	29	4.14	–	–	5
C.E.Eksteen	5	1	1	0*	0	0.00	–	–	1
A.C.Hudson	52	51	–	108	1442	28.27	1	11	7
S.D.Jack	2	2	–	6	7	3.50	–	–	3
G.Kirsten	24	24	2	112*	751	34.13	1	4	6
P.N.Kirsten	40	40	6	97	1293	38.02	–	9	11
A.P.Kuiper	22	20	5	63*	414	27.60	–	1	3
B.M.McMillan	41	26	10	48*	326	20.37	–	–	24
C.R.Matthews	36	16	6	26	97	9.70	–	–	4
M.W.Pringle	17	8	3	13*	48	9.60	–	–	2
J.N.Rhodes	65	62	9	66	1542	29.09	–	5	24
D.J.Richardson	66	45	17	53	591	21.10	–	1	81/12
M.J.R.Rindel	7	7	2	106*	201	40.20	1	–	4
D.B.Rundle	2	2	–	6	6	3.00	–	–	3
T.G.Shaw	9	6	4	17*	26	13.00	–	–	2
E.O.Simons	20	15	3	24	203	16.91	–	–	5
R.P.Snell	39	25	8	51	243	14.29	–	1	7
E.L.R.Stewart	5	5	1	23*	57	14.25	–	–	3/–
P.L.Symcox	14	12	2	12	61	6.10	–	–	2
K.C.Wessels	55	54	4	90	1627	32.54	–	12	30
K.C.Wessels (A/SA)	109	105	7	107	3367	34.35	1	26	49

SOUTH AFRICA

BOWLING

	Overs	*Runs*	*Wkts*	*Avge*	*Best*	*4w*
D.J.Callaghan	67	316	10	31.60	3-32	–
W.J.Cronje	356.1	1502	39	38.51	5-32	1
D.N.Crookes	10	48	0	–	–	–
P.S.de Villiers	479.1	1636	55	29.74	4-27	1
A.A.Donald	417.2	1639	65	25.21	5-29	2
C.E.Eksteen	35	163	2	81.50	1-26	–
S.D.Jack	18	86	3	28.66	2-41	–
G.Kirsten	1	8	0	–	–	–
P.N.Kirsten	30.3	152	6	25.33	3-31	–

SOUTH AFRICA – BOWLING (continued)

	Overs	Runs	Wkts	Avge	Best	4w
A.P.Kuiper	98	518	18	28.77	3-33	–
B.M.McMillan	330.5	1484	37	40.10	4-32	1
C.R.Matthews	327.5	1290	55	23.45	4-10	3
M.W.Pringle	145	604	22	27.45	4-11	1
M.J.R.Rindel	19	89	3	29.66	2-15	–
D.B.Rundle	16	95	5	19.00	4-42	1
T.G.Shaw	84	298	9	33.11	2-19	–
E.O.Simons	178	730	32	22.81	4-42	1
R.P.Snell	327.3	1484	41	36.19	5-40	3
P.L.Symcox	101	394	11	35.81	3-20	–
K.C.Wessels	2	11	0	–	–	–
K.C.Wessels (A/SA)	124.5	666	18	37.00	2-16	–

WEST INDIES

BATTING AND FIELDING

	M	I	NO	HS	Runs	Avge	100	50	Ct/St
J.C.Adams	39	26	10	81*	497	31.06	–	4	21/4
C.E.L.Ambrose	107	54	25	26*	379	13.06	–	–	31
K.L.T.Arthurton	74	64	13	84	1506	29.52	–	9	19
K.C.G.Benjamin	23	11	7	17	54	13.50	–	–	4
W.K.M.Benjamin	77	48	12	31	250	6.94	–	–	14
B.St A.Browne	4	3	2	8*	8	8.00	–	–	–
S.L.Campbell	5	5	–	36	63	12.60	–	–	1
S.Chanderpaul	6	4	–	22	49	12.25	–	–	1
C.E.Cuffy	9	5	3	16*	19	9.50	–	–	2
A.C.Cummins	58	37	9	44*	429	15.32	–	–	10
R.Dhanraj	6	2	1	8	8	8.00	–	–	1
R.A.Harper	81	52	15	45*	555	15.00	–	–	38
D.L.Haynes	238	237	28	152*	8648	41.37	17	57	58
R.I.C.Holder	15	11	1	50	221	22.10	–	1	5
C.L.Hooper	125	110	26	113*	2690	32.02	2	14	62
B.C.Lara	80	80	7	153	3057	41.87	4	23	45
J.R.Murray	29	13	4	30*	99	11.00	–	–	29/4
R.B.Richardson	202	195	27	122	5641	33.57	5	41	70
P.V.Simmons	93	91	6	122	2577	30.31	4	15	32
C.A.Walsh	135	47	18	30	240	8.27	–	–	18
S.C.Williams	13	13	2	73*	452	41.09	–	3	2

WEST INDIES

BOWLING

	Overs	Runs	Wkts	Avge	Best	4w
J.C.Adams	13	59	2	29.50	1- 2	–
C.E.L.Ambrose	952.5	3326	152	21.88	5-17	8
K.L.T.Arthurton	78.5	381	18	21.16	3-31	–
K.C.G.Benjamin	192.1	799	31	25.77	3-34	–
W.K.M.Benjamin	672.3	2754	90	30.60	5-22	1
B.St A.Browne	30	156	2	78.00	2-50	–
S.Chanderpaul	10	67	0	–	–	–
C.E.Cuffy	73.1	283	6	47.16	2-19	–
A.C.Cummins	480.2	2023	72	28.09	5-31	3
R.Dhanraj	44	170	10	17.00	4-26	1
R.A.Harper	652	2595	73	35.54	4-40	1
D.L.Haynes	5	24	0	–	–	–
C.L.Hooper	840.4	3618	117	30.92	4-34	1
B.C.Lara	4	22	2	11.00	2 -5	–
R.B.Richardson	9.4	46	1	46.00	1- 4	–
P.V.Simmons	333.5	1387	42	33.02	4- 3	1
C.A.Walsh	1190.4	4540	148	30.67	5- 1	6

NEW ZEALAND

BATTING AND FIELDING

	M	I	NO	HS	Runs	Avge	100	50	Ct/St
N.J.Astle	3	3	–	25	45	15.00	–	–	–
T.E.Blain	38	38	11	49*	442	16.37	–	–	37/1
C.L.Cairns	22	19	4	70	360	24.00	–	1	12
M.D.Crowe	138	136	18	105*	4510	38.22	3	33	65
H.T.Davis	2	–	–	–	–	–	–	–	1
R.P.de Groen	12	8	3	7*	12	2.40	–	–	2
M.W.Douglas	4	4	–	30	45	11.25	–	–	1
S.B.Doull	8	7	4	19*	61	20.33	–	–	–
S.P.Fleming	18	17	1	90	348	21.75	–	2	5
L.K.Germon	1	–	–	–	–	–	–	–	1/–
M.J.Greatbatch	67	67	5	111	1748	28.19	2	10	25
C.Z.Harris	57	49	14	68*	822	23.48	–	3	13
M.N.Hart	10	6	–	16	49	8.16	–	–	7
B.A.Hartland	16	16	1	68*	311	20.73	–	2	5
R.L.Hayes	1	1	–	13	13	13.00	–	–	–
A.H.Jones	87	87	9	93	2784	35.69	–	25	23
G.R.Larsen	58	34	15	37	364	19.15	–	–	8
R.T.Latham	33	33	4	60	583	20.10	–	1	11
D.K.Morrison	70	29	12	20*	132	7.76	–	–	17
D.J.Murray	1	1	–	3	3	3.00	–	–	–
D.J.Nash	15	11	3	40*	94	11.75	–	–	4
A.C.Parore	30	26	4	108	834	37.90	1	5	27/6
D.N.Patel	47	36	3	40	371	11.24	–	–	12
M.W.Priest	12	10	2	24	95	11.87	–	–	2
C.Pringle	58	38	19	34*	184	9.68	–	–	5
K.R.Rutherford	114	108	9	108	2875	29.04	2	16	35
M.L.Su'a	10	7	2	12*	24	4.80	–	–	1
S.A.Thomson	36	34	5	83	755	26.03	–	5	8
J.T.C.Vaughan	6	6	1	33	90	18.00	–	–	–
W.Watson	61	24	13	21	86	7.81	–	–	9
B.A.Young	39	38	4	74	914	26.88	–	3	16/–

NEW ZEALAND

BOWLING

	Overs	Runs	Wkts	Avge	Best	4w
N.J.Astle	13.4	87	1	87.00	1-46	–
C.L.Cairns	159	736	22	33.45	4-55	1
M.D.Crowe	216	954	29	32.89	2- 9	–
H.T.Davis	6	51	0	–	–	–
R.P.de Groen	91.3	477	8	59.62	2-34	–
S.B.Doull	68.4	405	6	67.50	2-42	–
S.P.Fleming	0.5	5	0	–	–	–
M.J.Greatbatch	1	5	0	–	–	–
C.Z.Harris	402.2	1863	53	35.15	3-15	–
M.N.Hart	81.2	314	11	28.54	5-22	1
R.L.Hayes	7	31	0	–	–	–
A.H.Jones	51	216	4	54.00	2-42	–
G.R.Larsen	520.1	1914	42	45.57	4-24	1
R.T.Latham	75	386	11	35.09	5-32	1
D.K.Morrison	562.3	2546	87	29.26	4-33	1
D.J.Nash	110	546	12	45.50	3-43	–
D.N.Patel	311.5	1288	29	44.41	3-22	–
M.W.Priest	84.3	418	4	104.50	2-27	–
C.Pringle	499.1	2189	95	23.04	5-45	3
K.R.Rutherford	64.5	323	10	32.30	2-39	–
M.L.Su'a	64.1	297	8	37.12	4-59	1
S.A.Thomson	228.3	1010	25	40.40	3-14	–
J.T.C.Vaughan	27	113	0	–	–	–
W.Watson	541.5	2247	74	30.36	4-27	1

INDIA

BATTING AND FIELDING

	M	I	NO	HS	Runs	Avge	100	50	Ct/St
P.K.Amre	37	30	5	84*	513	20.52	–	2	12
S.A.Ankola	14	8	4	7*	14	3.50	–	–	1
M.Azharuddin	187	174	34	108*	5114	36.52	3	28	75
A.C.Bedade	12	10	3	52	159	22.71	–	1	4
Bhupinder Singh	2	1	–	6	6	6.00	–	–	–
R.K.Chauhan	20	8	3	26*	73	14.60	–	–	5
A.D.Jadeja	33	31	1	104	996	33.20	1	6	11
V.G.Kambli	52	49	13	100*	1522	42.27	1	10	7
Kapil Dev	224	198	39	175*	3783	23.79	1	14	71
A.Kumble	59	25	10	24	148	9.86	–	–	20
Maninder Singh	59	18	14	8*	49	12.25	–	–	18
N.R.Mongia	22	11	6	40*	104	20.80	–	–	29/9
M.Prabhakar	113	82	18	106	1519	23.73	2	7	25
B.K.V.Prasad	11	1	–	–	–	–	–	–	4
S.L.V.Raju	40	11	5	8	29	4.83	–	–	7
W.V.Raman	26	26	1	114	588	23.52	1	3	1
A.K.Sharma	31	27	6	59*	424	20.19	–	3	6
C.Sharma	65	35	16	101*	456	24.00	1	–	6
R.J.Shastri	150	128	21	109	3108	29.04	4	18	40
N.S.Sidhu	83	80	6	134*	3119	42.14	5	23	14
J.Srinath	70	28	12	14	100	6.25	–	–	8
S.R.Tendulkar	89	86	9	115	2756	35.79	3	21	24
V.Yadav	19	12	2	34*	118	11.80	–	–	12/7

INDIA

BOWLING

	Overs	Runs	Wkts	Avge	Best	4w
P.K.Amre	0.2	4	0	–	–	–
S.A.Ankola	89.3	386	11	35.09	3-33	–
M.Azharuddin	90	468	12	39.00	3-19	–
Bhupinder Singh	17	78	3	26.00	3-34	–
R.K.Chauhan	168	714	21	34.00	3-29	–
A.D.Jadeja	87	432	8	54.00	2-16	–
V.G.Kambli	0.4	7	1	7.00	1- 7	–
Kapil Dev	1867	6946	253	27.45	5-43	4
A.Kumble	540.1	2187	69	31.69	6-12	3
Maninder Singh	522.1	2067	66	31.31	4-22	1
M.Prabhakar	930	3872	141	27.46	5-35	5
B.K.V.Prasad	83.2	383	8	47.87	3-36	–
S.L.V.Raju	344.5	1431	44	32.52	4-46	2
W.V.Raman	21	145	2	72.50	1-23	–
A.K.Sharma	190	875	15	58.33	3-41	–
C.Sharma	472.3	2336	67	34.86	3-22	–
R.J.Shastri	1102.1	4650	129	36.04	5-15	3
N.S.Sidhu	0.3	2	0	–	–	–
J.Srinath	594.3	2529	101	25.03	5-24	2
S.R.Tendulkar	329.1	1501	30	50.03	4-34	1

PAKISTAN

BATTING AND FIELDING

	M	I	NO	HS	Runs	Avge	100	50	Ct/St
Aamer Hanif	1	1	1	17*	17	–	–	–	–
Aamer Malik	24	23	1	90	556	25.27	–	5	13
Aamir Nazir	6	1	1	1*	1	–	–	–	–
Aamir Sohail	70	70	1	134	2269	32.88	3	14	20
Abdul Qadir	104	68	26	41*	641	15.26	–	–	21
Akram Raza	47	24	14	33*	191	19.10	–	–	19
Aqib Javed	105	28	17	17	79	7.18	–	–	12
Ashfaq Ahmed	3	–	–	–	–	–	–	–	–
Asif Mujtaba	60	49	14	113*	1029	29.40	1	6	16
Ata-ur-Rehman	23	8	4	11*	21	5.25	–	–	–
Basit Ali	38	34	6	127*	1057	37.75	1	8	7
Ijaz Ahmed	115	101	17	124*	2235	26.60	4	9	36
Inzamam-ul-Haq	81	79	11	137*	2630	38.67	3	19	21
Irfan Bhatti	1	–	–	–	–	–	–	–	1
Javed Miandad	228	215	40	119*	7327	41.86	8	50	68/2
Kabir Khan	2	–	–	–	–	–	–	–	–
Manzoor Elahi	51	43	12	50*	707	22.80	–	1	20
Moin Khan	29	17	6	23	168	15.27	–	–	29/8
Mushtaq Ahmed	82	41	16	17*	203	8.12	–	–	18
Rashid Latif	65	44	13	39	477	15.38	–	–	61/18
Saeed Anwar	75	74	5	131	2359	34.18	7	7	19
Salim Malik	207	187	27	102	5246	32.78	5	33	64
Waqar Younis	104	46	16	37	312	10.40	–	–	10
Wasim Akram	183	139	26	86	1591	14.07	–	1	33
Zahid Fazal	19	18	3	98*	348	23.20	–	2	2

PAKISTAN

BOWLING

	Overs	Runs	Wkts	Avge	Best	4w
Aamer Hanif	3.4	27	1	27.00	1-27	–
Aamer Malik	20	86	3	28.66	2-35	–
Aamir Nazir	47.3	224	7	32.00	3-43	–
Aamir Sohail	367.4	1609	42	38.30	3-43	–
Abdul Qadir	850	3453	132	26.15	5-44	6
Akram Raza	413.3	1539	37	41.59	3-18	–
Aqib Javed	879.4	3582	113	31.69	7-37	2
Ashfaq Ahmed	17	84	0	–	–	–
Asif Mujtaba	121	631	7	90.14	2-38	–
Ata-ur-Rehman	195.5	888	17	52.23	3-32	–
Basit Ali	5	21	1	21.00	1-17	–
Ijaz Ahmed	63	272	3	90.66	2-31	–
Inzamam-ul-Haq	5.4	42	2	21.00	1- 4	–
Irfan Bhatti	8	22	2	11.00	2-22	–
Javed Miandad	72.4	297	7	42.42	2-22	–
Kabir Khan	19.2	66	3	22.00	2-32	–
Manzoor Elahi	262.5	1149	25	45.96	3-22	–
Mushtaq Ahmed	682.3	3014	92	32.76	3-14	–
Saeed Anwar	23	121	2	60.50	1-15	–
Salim Malik	345	1702	52	32.73	5-35	1
Waqar Younis	871.5	3802	176	21.60	6-26	15
Wasim Akram	1577.3	5982	263	22.74	5-15	15

SRI LANKA

BATTING AND FIELDING

	M	I	NO	HS	Runs	Avge	100	50	Ct/St
S.D.Anurasiri	45	18	12	11	62	10.33	–	–	10
U.D.U.Chandana	5	3	–	26	46	15.33	–	–	3
P.B.Dassanayake	15	10	2	20*	85	10.62	–	–	9/4
A.M.de Silva	4	2	–	8	12	6.00	–	–	4/2
P.A.de Silva	149	145	14	107*	4226	32.25	3	31	41
H.P.D.K.Dharmasena	8	4	3	23*	46	46.00	–	–	1
U.N.K.Fernando	2	2	2	20*	22	–	–	–	–/–
A.A.W.Gunawardene	1	1	–	2	2	2.00	–	–	–
A.P.Gurusinha	103	101	5	117*	2627	27.36	1	15	36
U.C.Hathurusinghe	26	25	1	66	589	24.54	–	4	4
S.T.Jayasuriya	73	67	2	140	1161	17.86	1	6	25

SRI LANKA – BATTING AND FIELDING (continued)

	M	*I*	*NO*	*HS*	*Runs*	*Avge*	*100*	*50*	*Ct/St*
R.S.Kalpage	61	50	24	51	643	24.73	–	1	21
R.S.Kaluwitharana	19	17	3	31	144	10.28	–	–	4/6
D.K.Liyanage	9	6	1	16	56	11.20	–	–	1
R.S.Mahanama	115	112	12	119*	2969	29.69	3	19	66
M.Muralitharan	19	6	4	4*	6	3.00	–	–	7
K.R.Pushpakumara	10	2	2	14*	17	–	–	–	2
C.P.H.Ramanayake	59	34	14	26	210	10.50	–	–	11
A.Ranatunga	157	150	28	101*	4366	35.78	1	30	34
S.Ranatunga	8	8	–	70	222	27.75	–	2	1
R.J.Ratnayake	70	55	18	33*	612	16.54	–	–	11
M.A.R.Samarasekera	39	39	2	76	844	22.81	–	4	5
D.P.Samaraweera	5	4	–	49	91	22.75	–	–	3
H.P.Tillekeratne	97	83	19	104	1757	27.45	1	6	51/5
W.P.U.C.J.Vaas	22	8	5	33	47	15.66	–	–	2
A.P.Weerakkody	1	1	–	2	2	2.00	–	–	–
A.H.Wickramaratne	3	2	–	3	4	2.00	–	–	–
G.P.Wickremasinghe	61	22	8	21*	105	7.50	–	–	11

SRI LANKA

BOWLING

	Overs	*Runs*	*Wkts*	*Avge*	*Best*	*4w*
S.D.Anurasiri	350	1463	32	45.71	3-40	–
U.C.U.Chandana	3	21	0	–	–	–
P.A.de Silva	317.2	1577	34	46.38	3-58	–
H.P.D.K.Dharmasena	56.5	255	8	31.87	4-37	1
A.P.Gurusinha	244.1	1261	26	48.50	2-25	–
U.C.Hathurusinghe	92	395	9	43.88	4-57	1
S.T.Jayasuriya	335.3	1637	51	32.09	6-29	3
R.S.Kalpage	493.3	2123	58	36.60	4-36	1
D.K.Liyanage	62	282	7	40.28	3-49	–
R.S.Mahanama	0.2	7	0	–	–	–
M.Muralitharan	159	656	17	38.58	2- 6	–
K.R.Pushpakumara	79.2	373	9	41.44	3-25	–
C.P.H.Ramanayake	454.2	1934	64	30.21	4-17	1
A.Ranatunga	707	3390	70	48.42	4-14	1
R.J.Ratnayake	595.5	2712	76	35.68	5-32	2
M.A.M.Samarasekera	56.2	291	0	–	–	–
H.P.Tillekeratne	17.5	66	3	22.00	1- 3	–
W.P.U.C.J.Vaas	174	672	26	25.84	4-20	1
A.P.Weerakkody	6	41	0	–	–	–
G.P.Wickremasinghe	442.2	1893	48	39.43	3-28	–

ZIMBABWE

BATTING AND FIELDING

	M	*I*	*NO*	*HS*	*Runs*	*Avge*	*100*	*50*	*Ct/St*
D.H.Brain	22	17	3	27	105	7.50	–	–	5
E.A.Brandes	24	18	3	55	182	12.13	–	1	6
G.K.Bruk-Jackson	1	1	–	12	12	12.00	–	–	–
I.P.Butchart	20	16	2	54	252	18.00	–	1	4
A.D.R.Campbell	23	21	1	131*	423	21.15	1	1	4
M.H.Dekker	19	18	1	79	339	19.94	–	2	5
A.Flower	31	30	2	115*	921	32.89	1	6	20/4
G.W.Flower	21	19	1	84*	505	28.05	–	5	13
D.L.Houghton	42	40	–	142	1107	27.67	1	9	21/2
W.R.James	10	8	1	29	101	14.42	–	–	6/–
G.C.Martin	5	4	–	16	31	7.75	–	–	–
S.G.Peall	13	11	1	21	81	8.10	–	–	–
J.A.Rennie	9	6	5	20*	47	47.00	–	–	3
A.H.Shah	26	26	2	60*	390	16.25	–	1	6
P.A.Strang	4	4	2	21*	54	27.00	–	–	1
H.H.Streak	14	11	4	18*	80	11.42	–	–	2
A.C.Waller	22	21	3	83*	488	27.11	–	2	8
G.J.Whittall	12	12	2	53	216	21.60	–	1	2

ZIMBABWE

BOWLING

	Overs	*Runs*	*Wkts*	*Avge*	*Best*	*4w*
D.H.Brain	176.5	821	21	39.09	3-51	–
E.A.Brandes	205.5	1016	29	35.03	4-21	1
I.P.Butchart	117	640	12	53.33	3-57	–
A.D.R.Campbell	11	44	0	–	–	–
M.H.Dekker	50.5	241	9	26.77	2-16	–
A.Flower	1	9	0	–	–	–
G.W.Flower	76.3	411	12	34.25	3-15	–
D.L.Houghton	2	19	1	19.00	1-19	–
G.C.Martin	22	95	2	47.50	1-15	–
S.G.Peall	106	467	5	93.40	3-54	–
J.A.Rennie	63.4	352	4	88.00	2-42	–
A.H.Shah	177.3	794	18	44.11	3-33	–
P.A.Strang	39	153	4	38.25	2-30	–
H.H.Streak	118.1	525	17	30.88	4-44	1
G.J.Whittall	45.3	244	8	30.50	3-58	–

FIRST-CLASS CRICKET RECORDS

To the end of the 1994 season
(Including Pakistan's tour of Sri Lanka, July-August 1994)

TEAM RECORDS

HIGHEST INNINGS TOTALS

1107	Victoria v New South Wales	Melbourne	1926-27
1059	Victoria v Tasmania	Melbourne	1922-23
951-7d	Sind v Baluchistan	Karachi	1973-74
944-6d	Hyderabad v Andhra	Secunderabad	1993-94
918	New South Wales v South Australia	Sydney	1900-01
912-8d	Holkar v Mysore	Indore	1945-46
910-6d	Railways v Dera Ismail Khan	Lahore	1964-65
903-7d	England v Australia	The Oval	1938
887	Yorkshire v Warwickshire	Birmingham	1896
863	Lancashire v Surrey	The Oval	1990
860-6d	Tamil Nadu v Goa	Panjim	1988-89

There have been 28 instances of a team scoring 800 runs or more in an innings, the most recent being 810-4d by Warwickshire v Durham at Birmingham in 1994. Tamil Nadu's total of 860-6d was boosted to 912 by 52 penalty runs.

HIGHEST SECOND INNINGS TOTAL

770	New South Wales v South Australia	Adelaide	1920-21

HIGHEST FOURTH INNINGS TOTAL

654-5	England v South Africa	Durban	1938-39

HIGHEST MATCH AGGREGATE

2376	Maharashtra v Bombay	Poona	1948-49

RECORD MARGIN OF VICTORY

Innings and 851 runs:	Railways v Dera Ismail Khan	Lahore	1964-65

MOST RUNS IN A DAY

721	Australians v Essex	Southend	1948

MOST HUNDREDS IN AN INNINGS

6	Holkar v Mysore	Indore	1945-46

LOWEST INNINGS TOTALS

12	†Oxford University v MCC and Ground	Oxford	1877
12	Northamptonshire v Gloucestershire	Gloucester	1907
13	Auckland v Canterbury	Auckland	1877-78
13	Nottinghamshire v Yorkshire	Nottingham	1901
14	Surrey v Essex	Chelmsford	1983
15	MCC v Surrey	Lord's	1839
15	†Victoria v MCC	Melbourne	1903-04
15	†Northamptonshire v Yorkshire	Northampton	1908
15	Hampshire v Warwickshire	Birmingham	1922

†*Batted one man short*

There have been 26 instances of a team being dismissed for under 20, the most recent being by Surrey in 1983 (above).

LOWEST MATCH AGGREGATE BY ONE TEAM

34 (16 and 18)	Border v Natal	East London	1959-60

LOWEST COMPLETED MATCH AGGREGATE BY BOTH TEAMS

105	MCC v Australians	Lord's	1878

FEWEST RUNS IN AN UNINTERRUPTED DAY'S PLAY

95	Australia (80) v Pakistan (15-2)	Karachi	1956-57

TIED MATCHES

Before 1948 a match was considered to be tied if the scores were level after the fourth innings, even if the side batting last had wickets in hand when play ended. Law 22 was amended in 1948 and since then a match has been tied only when the scores are level after the fourth innings has been completed. There have been 53 tied first-class matches, five of which would not have qualified under the current law. The most recent is:

Worcestershire (203/325-8d) v Nottinghamshire (233/295)	Nottingham	1993

BATTING RECORDS

HIGHEST INDIVIDUAL INNINGS

501*	B.C.Lara	Warwickshire v Durham	Birmingham	1994
499	Hanif Mohammad	Karachi v Bahawalpur	Karachi	1958-59
452*	D.G.Bradman	New South Wales v Queensland	Sydney	1929-30
443*	B.B.Nimbalkar	Maharashtra v Kathiawar	Poona	1948-49
437	W.H.Ponsford	Victoria v Queensland	Melbourne	1927-28
429	W.H.Ponsford	Victoria v Tasmania	Melbourne	1922-23
428	Aftab Baloch	Sind v Baluchistan	Karachi	1973-74
424	A.C.MacLaren	Lancashire v Somerset	Taunton	1895
405*	G.A.Hick	Worcestershire v Somerset	Taunton	1988
385	B.Sutcliffe	Otago v Canterbury	Christchurch	1952-53
383	C.W.Gregory	New South Wales v Queensland	Brisbane	1906-07
377	S.V.Manjrekar	Bombay v Hyderabad	Bombay	1990-91
375	B.C.Lara	West Indies v England	St John's	1993-94
369	D.G.Bradman	South Australia v Tasmania	Adelaide	1935-36
366	N.H.Fairbrother	Lancashire v Surrey	The Oval	1990
366	M.V.Sridhar	Hyderabad v Andhra	Secunderabad	1993-94
365*	C.Hill	South Australia v NSW	Adelaide	1900-01
365*	G.St A.Sobers	West Indies v Pakistan	Kingston	1957-58
364	L.Hutton	England v Australia	The Oval	1938
359*	V.M.Merchant	Bombay v Maharashtra	Bombay	1943-44
359	R.B.Simpson	New South Wales v Queensland	Brisbane	1963-64
357*	R.Abel	Surrey v Somerset	The Oval	1899
357	D.G.Bradman	South Australia v Victoria	Melbourne	1935-36
356	B.A.Richards	South Australia v W Australia	Perth	1970-71
355*	G.R.Marsh	W Australia v S Australia	Perth	1989-90
355	B.Sutcliffe	Otago v Auckland	Dunedin	1949-50
352	W.H.Ponsford	Victoria v New South Wales	Melbourne	1926-27
350	Rashid Israr	Habib Bank v National Bank	Lahore	1976-77

There have been 111 triple hundreds in first-class cricket, W.V.Raman (313) and Arjan Kripal Singh (302*) for Tamil Nadu v Goa at Panjim in 1988-89 providing the only instance of two batsmen scoring 300 in the same innings.

MOST HUNDREDS IN SUCCESSIVE INNINGS

6	C.B.Fry	Sussex and Rest of England	1901
6	D.G.Bradman	South Australia and D.G.Bradman's XI	1938-39
6	M.J.Procter	Rhodesia	1970-71

TWO DOUBLE HUNDREDS IN A MATCH

244	202*	A.E.Fagg	Kent v Essex	Colchester	1938

TRIPLE HUNDRED AND HUNDRED IN A MATCH

333	123	G.A.Gooch	England v India	Lord's	1990

DOUBLE HUNDRED AND HUNDRED IN A MATCH MOST TIMES

4	Zaheer Abbas	Gloucestershire	1976-81

TWO HUNDREDS IN A MATCH MOST TIMES

8	Zaheer Abbas	Gloucestershire and PIA	1976-82
7	W.R.Hammond	Gloucestershire, England and MCC	1927-45

MOST HUNDREDS IN A SEASON

18	D.C.S.Compton	1947	16	J.B.Hobbs	1925

MOST HUNDREDS IN A CAREER

	Total		*100th Hundred*	
	Hundreds	*Inns*	*Season*	*Inns*
J.B.Hobbs	197	1315	1923	821
E.H.Hendren	170	1300	1928-29	740
W.R.Hammond	167	1005	1935	679
C.P.Mead	153	1340	1927	892
G.Boycott	151	1014	1977	645
H.Sutcliffe	149	1088	1932	700
F.E.Woolley	145	1532	1929	1031
L.Hutton	129	814	1951	619
W.G Grace	126	1493	1895	1113
D.C.S.Compton	123	839	1952	552
T.W.Graveney	122	1223	1964	940
D.G.Bradman	117	338	1947-48	295
I.V.A.Richards	114	796	1988-89	658
G.A.Gooch	112	888	1992-93	820
Zaheer Abbas	108	768	1982-83	658
A.Sandham	107	1000	1935	871
M.C.Cowdrey	107	1130	1973	1035
T.W.Hayward	104	1138	1913	1076
J.H.Edrich	103	979	1977	945
G.M.Turner	103	792	1982	779
E.Tyldesley	102	961	1934	919
L.E.G.Ames	102	951	1950	915
D.L.Amiss	102	1139	1986	1081

Most 400s:	2 – W.H.Ponsford
Most 300s or more:	6 – D.G.Bradman
Most 200s or more:	37 – D.G.Bradman; 36 – W.R.Hammond

MOST RUNS IN A MONTH

1294 (avge 92.42)	L.Hutton	Yorkshire	June 1949

MOST RUNS IN A SEASON

Runs			*I*	*NO*	*HS*	*Avge*	*100*	*Season*
3816	D.C.S.Compton	Middlesex	50	8	246	90.85	18	1947
3539	W.J.Edrich	Middlesex	52	8	267*	80.43	12	1947
3518	T.W.Hayward	Surrey	61	8	219	66.37	13	1906

The feat of scoring 3000 runs in a season has been achieved on 28 occasions, the most recent instance being by W.E.Alley (3019) in 1961. The highest aggregate in a season since 1969, when the number of County Championship matches was substantially reduced, is 2755 by S.J.Cook in 1991.

1000 RUNS IN A SEASON MOST TIMES

28	W.G.Grace (Gloucestershire), F.E.Woolley (Kent)

HIGHEST BATTING AVERAGE IN A SEASON
(Qualification: 12 innings)

Avge			*I*	*NO*	*HS*	*Runs*	*100*	*Season*
115.66	D.G.Bradman	Australians	26	5	278	2429	13	1938
102.53	G.Boycott	Yorkshire	20	5	175*	1538	6	1979
102.00	W.A.Johnston	Australians	17	16	28*	102	–	1953
101.70	G.A.Gooch	Essex	30	3	333	2746	12	1990
100.12	G.Boycott	Yorkshire	30	5	233	2503	13	1971

FASTEST HUNDRED AGAINST AUTHENTIC BOWLING

35 min	P.G.H.Fender	Surrey v Northamptonshire	Northampton	1920

FASTEST DOUBLE HUNDRED

113 min	R.J.Shastri	Bombay v Baroda	Bombay	1984-85

FASTEST TRIPLE HUNDRED

181 min	D.C.S.Compton	MCC v NE Transvaal	Benoni	1948-49

MOST SIXES IN AN INNINGS

15	J.R.Reid	Wellington v N Districts	Wellington	1962-63
14	Shakti Singh	Himachal Pradesh v Haryana	Dharmsala	1990-91
13	Majid Khan	Pakistanis v Glamorgan	Swansea	1967
13	C.G.Greenidge	D.H.Robins' XI v Pakistanis	Eastbourne	1974
13	C.G.Greenidge	Hampshire v Sussex	Southampton	1975
13	G.W.Humpage	Warwickshire v Lancashire	Southport	1982
13	R.J.Shastri	Bombay v Baroda	Bombay	1984-85

MOST SIXES IN A MATCH

17	W.J.Stewart	Warwickshire v Lancashire	Blackpool	1959

MOST SIXES IN A SEASON

80	I.T.Botham	Somerset and England	1985

MOST BOUNDARIES IN AN INNINGS

72	B.C.Lara	Warwickshire v Durham	Birmingham	1994

MOST RUNS OFF ONE OVER

36	G.St A.Sobers	Nottinghamshire v Glamorgan	Swansea	1968
36	R.J.Shastri	Bombay v Baroda	Bombay	1984-85

Both batsmen hit all six balls of an over (bowled by M.A.Nash and Tilak Raj respectively) for six.

MOST RUNS IN A DAY

390*	B.C.Lara	Warwickshire v Durham	Birmingham	1994

There have been 19 instances of a batsman scoring 300 or more runs in a day.

HIGHEST PARTNERSHIPS

First Wicket

561	Waheed Mirza/Mansoor Akhtar	Karachi W v Quetta	Karachi	1976-77
555	P.Holmes/H.Sutcliffe	Yorkshire v Essex	Leyton	1932
554	J.T.Brown/J.Tunnicliffe	Yorkshire v Derbys	Chesterfield	1898

Second Wicket

475	Zahir Alam/L.S.Rajput	Assam v Tripura	Gauhati	1991-92
465*	J.A.Jameson/R.B.Kanhai	Warwickshire v Glos	Birmingham	1974
455	K.V.Bhandarkar/B.B.Nimbalkar	Maha'tra v Kathiawar	Poona	1948-49

Third Wicket

467	A.H.Jones/M.D.Crowe	N Zealand v Sri Lanka	Wellington	1990-91
456	Khalid Irtiza/Aslam Ali	United Bank v Multan	Karachi	1975-76
451	Mudassar Nazar/Javed Miandad	Pakistan v India	Hyderabad	1982-83
445	P.E.Whitelaw/W.N.Carson	Auckland v Otago	Dunedin	1936-37
434	J.B.Stollmeyer/G.E.Gomez	Trinidad v Br Guiana	Port-of-Spain	1946-47
424*	W.J.Edrich/D.C.S.Compton	Middlesex v Somerset	Lord's	1948

Fourth Wicket

577	V.S.Hazare/Gul Mahomed	Baroda v Holkar	Baroda	1946-47
574*	C.L.Walcott/F.M.M.Worrell	Barbados v Trinidad	Port-of-Spain	1945-46
502*	F.M.M.Worrell/J.D.C.Goddard	Barbados v Trinidad	Bridgetown	1943-44
470	A.I.Kallicharran/G.W.Humpage	Warwickshire v Lancs	Southport	1982

Fifth Wicket

464*†	M.E.Waugh/S.R.Waugh	NSW v W Australia	Perth	1990-91
405	S.G.Barnes/D.G.Bradman	Australia v England	Sydney	1946-47
397	W.Bardsley/C.Kelleway	NSW v S Australia	Sydney	1920-21
393	E.G.Arnold/W.B.Burns	Worcs v Warwickshire	Birmingham	1909

† Includes 20 runs credited under ACB playing conditions for 10 no-balls which, under the Laws of cricket, would have produced 7 runs.

Sixth Wicket

487*	G.A.Headley/C.C.Passailaigue	Jamaica v Tennyson's	Kingston	1931-32
428	W.W.Armstrong/M.A.Noble	Australians v Sussex	Hove	1902
411	R.M.Poore/E.G.Wynyard	Hampshire v Somerset	Taunton	1899

Seventh Wicket

347	D.St E.Atkinson/C.C.Depeiza	W Indies v Australia	Bridgetown	1954-55
344	K.S.Ranjitsinhji/W.Newham	Sussex v Essex	Leyton	1902
340	K.J.Key/H.Philipson	Oxford U v Middlesex	Chiswick Park	1887

Eighth Wicket

433	V.T.Trumper/A.Sims	Australians v C'bury	Christchurch	1913-14
292	R.Peel/Lord Hawke	Yorkshire v Warwicks	Birmingham	1896
270	V.T.Trumper/E.P.Barbour	NSW v Victoria	Sydney	1912-13

Ninth Wicket

283	J.Chapman/A.Warren	Derbys v Warwicks	Blackwell	1910
251	J.W.H.T.Douglas/S.N.Hare	Essex v Derbyshire	Leyton	1921
245	V.S.Hazare/N.D.Nagarwalla	Maharashtra v Baroda	Poona	1939-40

Tenth Wicket

307	A.F.Kippax/J.E.H.Hooker	NSW v Victoria	Melbourne	1928-29
249	C.T.Sarwate/S.N.Banerjee	Indians v Surrey	The Oval	1946
235	F.E.Woolley/A.Fielder	Kent v Worcs	Stourbridge	1909

MOST RUNS IN A CAREER

	Career	I	NO	HS	Runs	Avge	100
J.B.Hobbs	1905-34	1315	106	316*	**61237**	50.65	197
F.E.Woolley	1906-38	1532	85	305*	**58969**	40.75	145
E.H.Hendren	1907-38	1300	166	301*	**57611**	50.80	170
C.P.Mead	1905-36	1340	185	280*	**55061**	47.67	153
W.G.Grace	1865-1908	1493	105	344	**54896**	39.55	126
W.R.Hammond	1920-51	1005	104	336*	**50551**	56.10	167
H.Sutcliffe	1919-45	1088	123	313	**50138**	51.95	149
G.Boycott	1962-86	1014	162	261*	**48426**	56.83	151
T.W.Graveney	1948-71/72	1223	159	258	**47793**	44.91	122
T.W.Hayward	1893-1914	1138	96	315*	**43551**	41.79	104
D.L.Amiss	1960-87	1139	126	262*	**43423**	42.86	102
M.C.Cowdrey	1950-76	1130	134	307	**42719**	42.89	107
A.Sandham	1911-37/38	1000	79	325	**41284**	44.82	107
G.A.Gooch	1973-94	888	72	333	**40174**	49.23	112
L.Hutton	1934-60	814	91	364	**40140**	55.51	129
M.J.K.Smith	1951-75	1091	139	204	**39832**	41.84	69
W.Rhodes	1898-1930	1528	237	267*	**39802**	30.83	58
J.H.Edrich	1956-78	979	104	310*	**39790**	45.47	103
R.E.S.Wyatt	1923-57	1141	157	232	**39405**	40.04	85
D.C.S.Compton	1936-64	839	88	300	**38942**	51.85	123
G.E.Tyldesley	1909-36	961	106	256*	**38874**	45.46	102
J.T.Tyldesley	1895-1923	994	62	295*	**37897**	40.60	86
K.W.R.Fletcher	1962-88	1167	170	228*	**37665**	37.77	63
C.G.Greenidge	1970-92	889	75	273*	**37354**	45.88	92
J.W.Hearne	1909-36	1025	116	285*	**37252**	40.98	96
L.E.G.Ames	1926-51	951	95	295	**37248**	43.51	102
D.Kenyon	1946-67	1159	59	259	**37002**	33.63	74
W.J.Edrich	1934-58	964	92	267*	**36965**	42.39	86
J.M.Parks	1949-76	1227	172	205*	**36673**	34.76	51
D.Denton	1894-1920	1163	70	221	**36479**	33.37	69
G.H.Hirst	1891-1929	1215	151	341	**36323**	34.13	60
I.V.A.Richards	1971/72-93	796	62	322	**36212**	49.33	114
A.Jones	1957-83	1168	72	204*	**36049**	32.89	56
W.G.Quaife	1894-1928	1203	185	255*	**36012**	35.37	72
R.E.Marshall	1945/46-72	1053	59	228*	**35725**	35.94	68
G.Gunn	1902-32	1061	82	220	**35208**	35.96	62

BOWLING RECORDS

ALL TEN WICKETS IN AN INNINGS

This feat has been achieved on 74 occasions at first-class level.
Three Times: A.P.Freeman (1929, 1930, 1931)
Twice: V.E.Walker (1859, 1865); H.Verity (1931, 1932); J.C.Laker (1956)

Instances since 1945:

W.E.Hollies	Warwickshire v Notts	Birmingham	1946
J.M.Sims	East v West	Kingston on Thames	1948
J.K.R.Graveney	Gloucestershire v Derbyshire	Chesterfield	1949
T.E.Bailey	Essex v Lancashire	Clacton	1949
R.Berry	Lancashire v Worcestershire	Blackpool	1953
S.P.Gupte	President's XI v Combined XI	Bombay	1954-55
J.C.Laker	Surrey v Australians	The Oval	1956
K.Smales	Nottinghamshire v Glos	Stroud	1956
G.A.R.Lock	Surrey v Kent	Blackheath	1956
J.C.Laker	England v Australia	Manchester	1956

P.M.Chatterjee	Bengal v Assam	Jorhat	1956-57
J.D.Bannister	Warwicks v Combined Services	Birmingham	1959
A.J.G.Pearson	Cambridge U v Leicestershire	Loughborough	1961
N.I.Thomson	Sussex v Warwickshire	Worthing	1964
P.J.Allan	Queensland v Victoria	Melbourne	1965-66
I.J.Brayshaw	Western Australia v Victoria	Perth	1967-68
Shahid Mahmood	Karachi Whites v Khairpur	Karachi	1969-70
E.E.Hemmings	International XI v W Indians	Kingston	1982-83
P.Sunderam	Rajasthan v Vidarbha	Jodhpur	1985-86
S.T.Jefferies	Western Province v OFS	Cape Town	1987-88
Imran Adil	Bahawalpur v Faisalabad	Faisalabad	1989-90
G.P.Wickremasinghe	Sinhalese SC v Kalutara	Colombo	1991-92
R.L.Johnson	Middlesex v Derbyshire	Derby	1994

MOST WICKETS IN A MATCH

19	J.C.Laker	England v Australia	Manchester	1956

MOST WICKETS IN A SEASON

Wkts		*Season*	*Matches*	*Overs*	*Mdns*	*Runs*	*Avge*
304	A.P.Freeman	1928	37	1976.1	423	5489	18.05
298	A.P.Freeman	1933	33	2039	651	4549	15.26

The feat of taking 250 wickets in a season has been achieved on 12 occasions, the last instance being by A.P.Freeman in 1933. 200 or more wickets in a season have been taken on 59 occasions, the last being by G.A.R.Lock (212 wickets, average 12.02) in 1957.

The highest aggregates of wickets taken in a season since the reduction of County Championship matches in 1969 are as follows:

Wkts		*Season*	*Matches*	*Overs*	*Mdns*	*Runs*	*Avge*
134	M.D.Marshall	1982	22	822	225	2108	15.73
131	L.R.Gibbs	1971	23	1024.1	295	2475	18.89
125	F.D.Stephenson	1988	22	819.1	196	2289	18.31
121	R.D.Jackman	1980	23	746.2	220	1864	15.40

Since 1969 there have been 46 instances of bowlers taking 100 wickets in a season.

MOST HAT-TRICKS IN A CAREER

7	D.V.P.Wright
6	T.W.J.Goddard, C.W.L.Parker
5	S.Haigh, V.W.C.Jupp, A.E.G.Rhodes, F.A.Tarrant

MOST WICKETS IN A CAREER

	Career	*Runs*	Wkts	*Avge*	*100w*
W.Rhodes	1898-1930	69993	4187	16.71	23
A.P.Freeman	1914-36	69577	3776	18.42	17
C.W.L.Parker	1903-35	63817	3278	19.46	16
J.T.Hearne	1888-1923	54352	3061	17.75	15
T.W.J.Goddard	1922-52	59116	2979	19.84	16
W.G.Grace	1865-1908	51545	2876	17.92	10
A.S.Kennedy	1907-36	61034	2874	21.23	15
D.Shackleton	1948-69	53303	2857	18.65	20
G.A.R.Lock	1946-70/71	54709	2844	19.23	14
F.J.Titmus	1949-82	63313	2830	22.37	16
M.W.Tate	1912-37	50571	2784	18.16	13+1
G.H.Hirst	1891-1929	51282	2739	18.72	15
C.Blythe	1899-1914	42136	2506	16.81	14
D.L.Underwood	1963-87	49993	2465	20.28	10

	Career	Runs	Wkts	Avge	100w
W.E.Astill	1906-39	57783	**2431**	23.76	9
J.C.White	1909-37	43759	**2356**	18.57	14
W.E.Hollies	1932-57	48656	**2323**	20.94	14
F.S.Trueman	1949-69	42154	**2304**	18.29	12
J.B.Statham	1950-68	36999	**2260**	16.37	13
R.T.D.Perks	1930-55	53770	**2233**	24.07	16
J.Briggs	1879-1900	35431	**2221**	15.95	12
D.J.Shepherd	1950-72	47302	**2218**	21.32	12
E.G.Dennett	1903-26	42571	**2147**	19.82	12
T.Richardson	1892-1905	38794	**2104**	18.43	10
T.E.Bailey	1945-67	48170	**2082**	23.13	9
R.Illingworth	1951-83	42023	**2072**	20.28	10
F.E.Woolley	1906-38	41066	**2068**	19.85	8
N.Gifford	1960-88	48731	**2068**	23.56	4
G.Geary	1912-38	41339	**2063**	20.03	11
D.V.P.Wright	1932-57	49307	**2056**	23.98	10
J.A.Newman	1906-30	51111	**2032**	25.15	9
A.Shaw	1864-97	24579	**2027†**	12.12	9
S.Haigh	1895-1913	32091	**2012**	15.94	11

† *Excluding one wicket for which no analysis is available.*

ALL-ROUND RECORDS

THE 'DOUBLE'

3000 runs and 100 wickets: J.H.Parks (1937)
2000 runs and 200 wickets: G.H.Hirst (1906)
2000 runs and 100 wickets: F.E.Woolley (4), J.W.Hearne (3), W.G.Grace (2), G.H.Hirst (2), W.Rhodes (2), T.E.Bailey, D.E.Davies, G.L.Jessop, V.W.C.Jupp, James Langridge, F.A.Tarrant, C.L.Townsend, L.F.Townsend
1000 runs and 200 wickets: M.W.Tate (3), A.E.Trott (2), A.S.Kennedy

Most Doubles: W.Rhodes (16), G.H.Hirst (14), V.W.C.Jupp (10)

Double in Debut Season: D.B.Close (1949) – aged 18, he is the youngest to achieve this feat

The feat of scoring 1000 runs and taking 100 wickets in a season has been achieved on 305 occasions, R.J.Hadlee (1984) and F.D.Stephenson (1988) being the only players to complete the 'double' since the reduction of County Championship matches in 1969.

WICKET-KEEPING RECORDS

MOST DISMISSALS IN AN INNINGS

9 (8ct, 1st)	Tahir Rashid	Habib Bank v PACO	Gujranwala	1992-93
8 (8ct)	A.T.W.Grout	Queensland v W Australia	Brisbane	1959-60
8 (8ct)	D.E.East	Essex v Somerset	Taunton	1985
8 (8ct)	S.A.Marsh	Kent v Middlesex	Lord's	1991
8 (6ct, 2st)	T.J.Zoehrer	Australians v Surrey	The Oval	1993

MOST DISMISSALS IN A MATCH

12 (8ct, 4st)	E.Pooley	Surrey v Sussex	The Oval	1868
12 (9ct, 3st)	D.Tallon	Queensland v NSW	Sydney	1938-39
12 (9ct, 3st)	H.B.Taber	NSW v South Australia	Adelaide	1968-69

MOST CATCHES IN A MATCH

11	A.Long	Surrey v Sussex	Hove	1964
11	R.W.Marsh	W Australia v Victoria	Perth	1975-76
11	D.L.Bairstow	Yorkshire v Derbyshire	Scarborough	1982
11	W.K.Hegg	Lancashire v Derbyshire	Chesterfield	1989
11	A.J.Stewart	Surrey v Leicestershire	Leicester	1989
11	T.J.Nielsen	S Australia v W Australia	Perth	1990-91

MOST DISMISSALS IN A SEASON

128 (79ct, 49st)	L.E.G.Ames	1929

MOST DISMISSALS IN A CAREER

	Career	**Dismissals**	*Ct*	*St*
R.W.Taylor	1960-88	**1649**	1473	176
J.T.Murray	1952-75	**1527**	1270	257
H.Strudwick	1902-27	**1497**	1242	255
A.P.E.Knott	1964-85	**1344**	1211	133
F.H.Huish	1895-1914	**1310**	933	377
B.Taylor	1949-73	**1294**	1083	211
D.Hunter	1889-1909	**1253**	906	347
H.R.Butt	1890-1912	**1228**	953	275
J.H.Board	1891-1914/15	**1207**	852	355
H.Elliott	1920-47	**1206**	904	302
J.M.Parks	1949-76	**1181**	1088	93
R.Booth	1951-70	**1126**	948	178
L.E.G.Ames	1926-51	**1121**	703	418
D.L.Bairstow	1970-90	**1099**	961	138
G.Duckworth	1923-47	**1096**	753	343
H.W.Stephenson	1948-64	**1082**	748	334
J.G.Binks	1955-75	**1071**	895	176
T.G.Evans	1939-69	**1066**	816	250
A.Long	1960-80	**1046**	922	124
G.O.Dawkes	1937-61	**1043**	895	148
R.W.Tolchard	1965-83	**1037**	912	125
W.L.Cornford	1921-47	**1017**	675	342

FIELDING RECORDS

MOST CATCHES IN AN INNINGS

7	M.J.Stewart	Surrey v Northamptonshire	Northampton	1957
7	A.S.Brown	Gloucestershire v Nottinghamshire	Nottingham	1966

MOST CATCHES IN A MATCH

10	W.R.Hammond	Gloucestershire v Surrey	Cheltenham	1928

MOST CATCHES IN A SEASON

78	W.R.Hammond	1928	77	M.J.Stewart	1957

MOST CATCHES IN A CAREER

1018	F.E.Woolley	1906-38	784	J.G.Langridge	1928-55
887	W.G.Grace	1865-1908	764	W.Rhodes	1898-1930
830	G.A.R.Lock	1946-70/71	758	C.A.Milton	1948-74
819	W.R.Hammond	1920-51	754	E.H.Hendren	1907-38
813	D.B.Close	1949-86			

TEST CRICKET RECORDS

To the end of the 1994 season
(Including Pakistan's tour of Sri Lanka, July-August 1994)

TEAM RECORDS

HIGHEST INNINGS TOTALS

903-7d	England v Australia	The Oval	1938
849	England v West Indies	Kingston	1929-30
790-3d	West Indies v Pakistan	Kingston	1957-58
758-8d	Australia v West Indies	Kingston	1954-55
729-6d	Australia v England	Lord's	1930
708	Pakistan v England	The Oval	1987
701	Australia v England	The Oval	1934
699-5	Pakistan v India	Lahore	1989-90
695	Australia v England	The Oval	1930
687-8d	West Indies v England	The Oval	1976
681-8d	West Indies v England	Port-of-Spain	1953-54
676-7	India v Sri Lanka	Kanpur	1986-87
674-6	Pakistan v India	Faisalabad	1984-85
674	Australia v India	Adelaide	1947-48
671-4	New Zealand v Sri Lanka	Wellington	1990-91
668	Australia v West Indies	Bridgetown	1954-55
659-8d	Australia v England	Sydney	1946-47
658-8d	England v Australia	Nottingham	1938
657-8d	Pakistan v West Indies	Bridgetown	1957-58
656-8d	Australia v England	Manchester	1964
654-5	England v South Africa	Durban	1938-39
653-4d	England v India	Lord's	1990
653-4d	Australia v England	Leeds	1993
652-7d	England v India	Madras	1984-85
652-8d	West Indies v England	Lord's	1973
652	Pakistan v India	Faisalabad	1982-83
650-6d	Australia v West Indies	Bridgetown	1964-65
The highest innings for other countries are:			
622-9d	South Africa v Australia	Durban	1969-70
547-8d	Sri Lanka v Australia	Colombo (SSC)	1992-93
456	Zimbabwe v India	Harare	1992-93

LOWEST INNINGS TOTALS

26	New Zealand v England	Auckland	1954-55
30	South Africa v England	Port Elizabeth	1895-96
30	South Africa v England	Birmingham	1924
35	South Africa v England	Cape Town	1898-99
36	Australia v England	Birmingham	1902
36	South Africa v Australia	Melbourne	1931-32
42	Australia v England	Sydney	1887-88
42	New Zealand v Australia	Wellington	1945-46
42	India v England	Lord's	1974
43	South Africa v England	Cape Town	1888-89
44	Australia v England	The Oval	1896
45	England v Australia	Sydney	1886-87
45	South Africa v Australia	Melbourne	1931-32
46	England v West Indies	Port-of-Spain	1993-94
47	South Africa v England	Cape Town	1888-89
47	New Zealand v England	Lord's	1958

The lowest innings for other countries are:

53	West Indies v Pakistan	Faisalabad	1986-87
62	Pakistan v Australia	Perth	1981-82
71	Sri Lanka v Pakistan	Kandy	1994-95
134	Zimbabwe v Pakistan	Karachi	1993-94

BATTING RECORDS

HIGHEST INDIVIDUAL INNINGS

375	B.C.Lara	WI v E	St John's	1993-94
365*	G.St A.Sobers	WI v P	Kingston	1957-58
364	L.Hutton	E v A	The Oval	1938
337	Hanif Mohammad	P v WI	Bridgetown	1957-58
336*	W.R.Hammond	E v NZ	Auckland	1932-33
334	D.G.Bradman	A v E	Leeds	1930
333	G.A.Gooch	E v I	Lord's	1990
325	A.Sandham	E v WI	Kingston	1929-30
311	R.B.Simpson	A v E	Manchester	1964
310*	J.H.Edrich	E v NZ	Leeds	1965
307	R.M.Cowper	A v E	Melbourne	1965-66
304	D.G.Bradman	A v E	Leeds	1934
302	L.G.Rowe	WI v E	Bridgetown	1973-74
299*	D.G.Bradman	A v SA	Adelaide	1931-32
299	M.D.Crowe	NZ v SL	Wellington	1990-91
291	I.V.A.Richards	WI v E	The Oval	1976
287	R.E.Foster	E v A	Sydney	1903-04
285*	P.B.H.May	E v WI	Birmingham	1957
280*	Javed Miandad	P v I	Hyderabad	1982-83
278	D.C.S.Compton	E v P	Nottingham	1954
277	B.C.Lara	WI v A	Sydney	1992-93
274	R.G.Pollock	SA v A	Durban	1969-70
274	Zaheer Abbas	P v E	Birmingham	1971
271	Javed Miandad	P v NZ	Auckland	1988-89
270*	G.A.Headley	WI v E	Kingston	1934-35
270	D.G.Bradman	A v E	Melbourne	1936-37
268	G.N.Yallop	A v P	Melbourne	1983-84
267	P.A.de Silva	SL v NZ	Wellington	1990-91
266	W.H.Ponsford	A v E	The Oval	1934
262*	D.L.Amiss	E v WI	Kingston	1973-74
261	F.M.M.Worrell	WI v E	Nottingham	1950
260	C.C.Hunte	WI v P	Kingston	1957-58
260	Javed Miandad	P v E	The Oval	1987
259	G.M.Turner	NZ v WI	Georgetown	1971-72
258	T.W.Graveney	E v WI	Nottingham	1957
258	S.M.Nurse	WI v NZ	Christchurch	1968-69
256	R.B.Kanhai	WI v I	Calcutta	1958-59
256	K.F.Barrington	E v A	Manchester	1964
255*	D.J.McGlew	SA v NZ	Wellington	1952-53
254	D.G.Bradman	A v E	Lord's	1930
251	W.R.Hammond	E v A	Sydney	1928-29
250	K.D.Walters	A v NZ	Christchurch	1976-77
250	S.F.A.F.Bacchus	WI v I	Kanpur	1978-79

The highest individual innings for other countries are:

236*	S.M.Gavaskar	I v WI	Madras	1983-84
121	D.L.Houghton	Z v I	Harare	1992-93

MOST RUNS IN A SERIES

Runs			Series	M	I	NO	HS	Avge	100	50
974	D.G.Bradman	A v E	1930	5	7	–	334	139.14	4	–
905	W.R.Hammond	E v A	1928-29	5	9	1	251	113.12	4	–
839	M.A.Taylor	A v E	1989	6	11	1	219	83.90	2	5
834	R.N.Harvey	A v SA	1952-53	5	9	–	205	92.66	4	3
829	I.V.A.Richards	WI v E	1976	4	7	–	291	118.42	3	2
827	C.L.Walcott	WI v A	1954-55	5	10	–	155	82.70	5	2
824	G.St A.Sobers	WI v P	1957-58	5	8	2	365*	137.33	3	3
810	D.G.Bradman	A v E	1936-37	5	9	–	270	90.00	3	1
806	D.G.Bradman	A v SA	1931-32	5	5	1	299*	201.50	4	–
798	B.C.Lara	WI v E	1993-94	5	8	–	375	99.75	2	2
779	E.de C.Weekes	WI v I	1948-49	5	7	–	194	111.28	4	2
774	S.M.Gavaskar	I v WI	1970-71	4	8	3	220	154.80	4	3
761	Mudassar Nazar	P v I	1982-83	6	8	2	231	126.83	4	1
758	D.G.Bradman	A v E	1934	5	8	–	304	94.75	2	1
753	D.C.S.Compton	E v SA	1947	5	8	–	208	94.12	4	2
752	G.A.Gooch	E v I	1990	3	6	–	333	125.33	3	2

HIGHEST PARTNERSHIP FOR EACH WICKET

1st	413	V.Mankad/Pankaj Roy	I v NZ	Madras	1955-56
2nd	451	W.H.Ponsford/D.G.Bradman	A v E	The Oval	1934
3rd	467	A.H.Jones/M.D.Crowe	NZ v SL	Wellington	1990-91
4th	411	P.B.H.May/M.C.Cowdrey	E v WI	Birmingham	1957
5th	405	S.G.Barnes/D.G.Bradman	A v E	Sydney	1946-47
6th	346	J.H.W.Fingleton/D.G.Bradman	A v E	Melbourne	1936-37
7th	347	D.St E.Atkinson/C.C.Depeiza	WI v A	Bridgetown	1954-55
8th	246	L.E.G.Ames/G.O.B.Allen	E v NZ	Lord's	1931
9th	190	Asif Iqbal/Intikhab Alam	P v E	The Oval	1967
10th	151	B.F.Hastings/R.O.Collinge	NZ v P	Auckland	1972-73

WICKET PARTNERSHIPS OF OVER 300

467	3rd	A.H.Jones/M.D.Crowe	NZ v SL	Wellington	1990-91
451	2nd	W.H.Ponsford/D.G.Bradman	A v E	The Oval	1934
451	3rd	Mudassar Nazar/Javed Miandad	P v I	Hyderabad	1982-83
446	2nd	C.C.Hunte/G.St A.Sobers	WI v P	Kingston	1957-58
413	1st	V.Mankad/Pankaj Roy	I v NZ	Madras	1955-56
411	4th	P.B.H.May/M.C.Cowdrey	E v WI	Birmingham	1957
405	5th	S.G.Barnes/D.G.Bradman	A v E	Sydney	1946-47
399	4th	G.St A.Sobers/F.M.M.Worrell	WI v E	Bridgetown	1959-60
397	3rd	Qasim Omar/Javed Miandad	P v SL	Faisalabad	1985-86
388	4th	W.H.Ponsford/D.G.Bradman	A v E	Leeds	1934
387	1st	G.M.Turner/T.W.Jarvis	NZ v WI	Georgetown	1971-72
382	2nd	L.Hutton/M.Leyland	E v A	The Oval	1938
382	1st	W.M.Lawry/R.B.Simpson	A v WI	Bridgetown	1964-65
370	3rd	W.J.Edrich/D.C.S.Compton	E v SA	Lord's	1947
369	2nd	J.H.Edrich/K.F.Barrington	E v NZ	Leeds	1965
359	1st	L.Hutton/C.Washbrook	E v SA	Jo'burg	1948-49
351	2nd	G.A.Gooch/D.I.Gower	E v A	The Oval	1985
350	4th	Mushtaq Mohammad/Asif Iqbal	P v NZ	Dunedin	1972-73

347	7th	D.St E.Atkinson/C.C.Depeiza	WI v A	Bridgetown	1954-55
346	6th	J.H.W.Fingleton/D.G.Bradman	A v E	Melbourne	1936-37
344*	2nd	S.M.Gavaskar/D.B.Vengsarkar	I v WI	Calcutta	1978-79
341	3rd	E.J.Barlow/R.G.Pollock	SA v A	Adelaide	1963-64
338	3rd	E.de C.Weekes/F.M.M.Worrell	WI v E	Port-of-Spain	1953-54
336	4th	W.M.Lawry/K.D.Walters	A v WI	Sydney	1968-69
332	5th	A.R.Border/S.R.Waugh	A v E	Leeds	1993
331	2nd	R.T.Robinson/D.I.Gower	E v A	Birmingham	1985
329	1st	G.R.Marsh/M.A.Taylor	A v E	Nottingham	1989
323	1st	J.B.Hobbs/W.Rhodes	E v A	Melbourne	1911-12
322	4th	Javed Miandad/Salim Malik	P v E	Birmingham	1992
319	3rd	A.Melville/A.D.Nourse	SA v E	Nottingham	1947
316†	3rd	G.R.Viswanath/Yashpal Sharma	I v E	Madras	1981-82
308	7th	Waqar Hassan/Imtiaz Ahmed	P v NZ	Lahore	1955-56
308	3rd	R.B.Richardson/I.V.A.Richards	WI v A	St John's	1983-84
308	3rd	G.A.Gooch/A.J.Lamb	E v I	Lord's	1990
303	3rd	I.V.A.Richards/A.I.Kallicharran	WI v E	Nottingham	1976
303	3rd	M.A.Atherton/R.A.Smith	E v WI	St John's	1993-94
301	2nd	A.R.Morris/D.G.Bradman	A v E	Leeds	1948

† *415 runs were added for this wicket in two separate partnerships.*

4000 RUNS IN TESTS

Runs			*M*	*I*	*NO*	*HS*	*Avge*	*100*	*50*
11174	A.R.Border	A	156	265	44	205	50.56	27	63
10122	S.M.Gavaskar	I	125	214	16	236*	51.12	34	45
8832	Javed Miandad	P	124	189	21	280*	52.57	23	43
8655	G.A.Gooch	E	113	205	6	333	43.49	20	45
8540	I.V.A.Richards	WI	121	182	12	291	50.23	24	45
8231	D.I.Gower	E	117	204	18	215	44.25	18	39
8114	G.Boycott	E	108	193	23	246*	47.72	22	42
8032	G.St A.Sobers	WI	93	160	21	365*	57.78	26	30
7624	M.C.Cowdrey	E	114	188	15	182	44.06	22	38
7558	C.G.Greenidge	WI	108	185	16	226	44.72	19	34
7515	C.H.Lloyd	WI	110	175	14	242*	46.67	19	39
7487	D.L.Haynes	WI	116	202	25	184	42.49	18	39
7249	W.R.Hammond	E	85	140	16	336*	58.45	22	24
7110	G.S.Chappell	A	87	151	19	247*	53.86	24	31
6996	D.G.Bradman	A	52	80	10	334	99.94	29	13
6971	L.Hutton	E	79	138	15	364	56.67	19	33
6868	D.B.Vengsarkar	I	116	185	22	166	42.13	17	35
6806	K.F.Barrington	E	82	131	15	256	58.67	20	35
6564	D.C.Boon	A	89	160	18	200	46.22	18	30
6227	R.B.Kanhai	WI	79	137	6	256	47.53	15	28
6149	R.N.Harvey	A	79	137	10	205	48.41	21	24
6080	G.R.Viswanath	I	91	155	10	222	41.93	14	35
5807	D.C.S.Compton	E	78	131	15	278	50.06	17	28
5445	R.B.Richardson	WI	76	130	11	194	45.75	15	25
5410	J.B.Hobbs	E	61	102	7	211	56.94	15	28
5357	K.D.Walters	A	74	125	14	250	48.26	15	33
5345	I.M.Chappell	A	75	136	10	196	42.42	14	26
5334	J.G.Wright	NZ	82	148	7	185	37.82	12	23
5248	Kapil Dev	I	131	184	15	163	31.05	8	27
5234	W.M.Lawry	A	67	123	12	210	47.15	13	27
5230	M.D.Crowe	NZ	70	120	11	299	47.98	17	17
5200	I.T.Botham	E	102	161	6	208	33.54	14	22
5138	J.H.Edrich	E	77	127	9	310*	43.54	12	24
5062	Zaheer Abbas	P	78	124	11	274	44.79	12	20

Runs			*M*	*I*	*NO*	*HS*	*Avge*	*100*	*50*
4882	T.W.Graveney	E	79	123	13	258	44.38	11	20
4869	R.B.Simpson	A	62	111	7	311	46.81	10	27
4737	I.R.Redpath	A	66	120	11	171	43.45	8	31
4656	A.J.Lamb	E	79	139	10	142	36.09	14	18
4555	H.Sutcliffe	E	54	84	9	194	60.73	16	23
4537	P.B.H.May	E	66	106	9	285*	46.77	13	22
4502	E.R.Dexter	E	62	102	8	205	47.89	9	27
4455	E.de C.Weekes	WI	48	81	5	207	58.61	15	19
4415	K.J.Hughes	A	70	124	6	213	37.41	9	22
4399	A.I.Kallicharran	WI	66	109	10	187	44.43	12	21
4389	A.P.E.Knott	E	95	149	15	135	32.75	5	30
4378	M.Amarnath	I	69	113	10	138	42.50	11	24
4334	R.C.Fredericks	WI	59	109	7	169	42.49	8	26
4275	M.A.Taylor	A	54	97	6	219	46.97	12	24
4227	M.W.Gatting	E	74	129	14	207	36.75	9	21
4114	Mudassar Nazar	P	76	116	8	231	38.09	10	17
4040	Salim Malik	P	77	111	19	165	43.91	11	22
4020	M.Azharuddin	I	62	88	3	199	47.29	14	13
The highest aggregates for other countries are:									
3471	B.Mitchell	SA	42	80	9	189*	48.88	8	21
2804	A.Ranatunga	SL	51	86	4	135*	34.19	4	17
499	A.Flower	Z	7	12	3	115	55.44	1	5

MOST HUNDREDS

					Opponents								
			200s	*Inns*	*E*	*A*	*SA*	*WI*	*NZ*	*I*	*P*	*SL*	*Z*
34	S.M.Gavaskar	I	4	214	4	8	–	13	2	–	5	2	–
29	D.G.Bradman	A	12	80	19	–	4	2	–	4	–	–	–
27	A.R.Border	A	2	265	8	–	–	3	5	4	6	1	–
26	G.St A.Sobers	WI	2	160	10	4	–	–	1	8	3	–	–
24	G.S.Chappell	A	4	151	9	–	–	5	3	1	6	–	–
24	I.V.A.Richards	WI	3	182	8	5	–	–	1	8	2	–	–
23	Javed Miandad	P	6	189	2	6	–	2	7	5	–	1	–
22	G.Boycott	E	1	193	–	7	1	5	2	4	3	–	–
22	M.C.Cowdrey	E	–	188	–	5	3	6	2	3	3	–	–
22	W.R.Hammond	E	7	140	–	9	6	1	4	2	–	–	–
21	R.N.Harvey	A	2	137	6	–	8	3	–	4	–	–	–
20	K.F.Barrington	E	1	131	–	5	2	3	3	3	4	–	–
20	G.A.Gooch	E	2	205	–	4	–	5	4	5	1	1	–

The most hundreds for countries not included above is: South Africa – 9 in 62 innings by A.D.Nourse; New Zealand – 17 in 120 innings by M.D.Crowe; Sri Lanka – 7 in 74 innings by P.A.de Silva; Zimbabwe – 1 in 12 innings by A.Flower and D.L.Houghton.

The most double hundreds by batsmen not qualifying for the above list is four by Zaheer Abbas (12 hundreds for Pakistan) and three by R.B.Simpson (12 hundreds for Australia).

BOWLING RECORDS

MOST WICKETS IN AN INNINGS

10- 53	J.C.Laker	E v A	Manchester	1956
9- 28	G.A.Lohmann	E v SA	Johannesburg	1895-96
9- 37	J.C.Laker	E v A	Manchester	1956
9- 52	R.J.Hadlee	NZ v A	Brisbane	1985-86
9- 56	Abdul Qadir	P v E	Lahore	1987-88
9- 57	D.E.Malcolm	E v SA	The Oval	1994
9- 69	J.M.Patel	I v A	Kanpur	1959-60
9- 83	Kapil Dev	I v WI	Ahmedabad	1983-84
9- 86	Sarfraz Nawaz	P v A	Melbourne	1978-79
9- 95	J.M.Noreiga	WI v I	Port-of-Spain	1970-71
9-102	S.P.Gupte	I v WI	Kanpur	1958-59
9-103	S.F.Barnes	E v SA	Johannesburg	1913-14
9-113	H.J.Tayfield	SA v E	Johannesburg	1956-57
9-121	A.A.Mailey	A v E	Melbourne	1920-21
The best innings analyses for other countries are:				
8- 83	J.R.Ratnayeke	SL v P	Sialkot	1985-86
5- 42	D.H.Brain	Z v P	Lahore	1993-94

MOST WICKETS IN A TEST

19- 90	J.C.Laker	E v A	Manchester	1956
17-159	S.F.Barnes	E v SA	Johannesburg	1913-14
16-136†	N.D.Hirwani	I v WI	Madras	1987-88
16-137†	R.A.L.Massie	A v E	Lord's	1972
15- 28	J.Briggs	E v SA	Cape Town	1888-89
15- 45	G.A.Lohmann	E v SA	Port Elizabeth	1895-96
15- 99	C.Blythe	E v SA	Leeds	1907
15-104	H.Verity	E v A	Lord's	1934
15-123	R.J.Hadlee	NZ v A	Brisbane	1985-86
15-124	W.Rhodes	E v A	Melbourne	1903-04

† *On debut.*

MOST WICKETS IN A SERIES

Wkts			*Series*	*M*	*Balls*	*Runs*	*Avge*	*5 wI*	*10 wM*
49	S.F.Barnes	E v SA	1913-14	4	1356	536	10.93	7	3
46	J.C.Laker	E v A	1956	5	1703	442	9.60	4	2
44	C.V.Grimmett	A v SA	1935-36	5	2077	642	14.59	5	3
42	T.M.Alderman	A v E	1981	6	1950	893	21.26	4	–
41	R.M.Hogg	A v E	1978-79	6	1740	527	12.85	5	2
41	T.M.Alderman	A v E	1989	6	1616	712	17.36	6	1
40	Imran Khan	P v I	1982-83	6	1339	558	13.95	4	2
39	A.V.Bedser	E v A	1953	5	1591	682	17.48	5	1
39	D.K.Lillee	A v E	1981	6	1870	870	22.30	2	1
38	M.W.Tate	E v A	1924-25	5	2528	881	23.18	5	1
37	W.J.Whitty	A v SA	1910-11	5	1395	632	17.08	2	–
37	H.J.Tayfield	SA v E	1956-57	5	2280	636	17.18	4	1
36	A.E.E.Vogler	SA v E	1909-10	5	1349	783	21.75	4	1
36	A.A.Mailey	A v E	1920-21	5	1465	946	26.27	4	2
35	G.A.Lohmann	E v SA	1895-96	3	520	203	5.80	4	2
35	B.S.Chandrasekhar	I v E	1972-73	5	1747	662	18.91	4	–
35	M.D.Marshall	WI v E	1988	5	1219	443	12.65	3	1

200 WICKETS IN TESTS

Wkts			M	Balls	Runs	Avge	5 wI	10 wM
434	Kapil Dev	I	131	27740	12867	29.64	23	2
431	R.J.Hadlee	NZ	86	21918	9611	22.29	36	9
383	I.T.Botham	E	102	21815	10878	28.40	27	4
376	M.D.Marshall	WI	81	17584	7876	20.94	22	4
362	Imran Khan	P	88	19458	8258	22.81	23	6
355	D.K.Lillee	A	70	18467	8493	23.92	23	7
325	R.G.D.Willis	E	90	17357	8190	25.20	16	–
309	L.R.Gibbs	WI	79	27115	8989	29.09	18	2
307	F.S.Trueman	E	67	15178	6625	21.57	17	3
297	D.L.Underwood	E	86	21862	7674	25.83	17	6
266	B.S.Bedi	I	67	21364	7637	28.71	14	1
259	J.Garner	WI	58	13169	5433	20.97	7	–
252	J.B.Statham	E	70	16056	6261	24.84	9	1
249	M.A.Holding	WI	60	12680	5898	23.68	13	2
248	R.Benaud	A	63	19108	6704	27.03	16	1
246	G.D.McKenzie	A	60	17681	7328	29.78	16	3
242	B.S.Chandrasekhar	I	58	15963	7199	29.74	16	2
236	A.V.Bedser	E	51	15918	5876	24.89	15	5
236	Abdul Qadir	P	67	17126	7742	32.80	15	5
235	G.St A.Sobers	WI	93	21599	7999	34.03	6	–
235	Wasim Akram	P	55	12484	5378	22.88	16	3
231	C.J.McDermott	A	58	13400	6694	28.97	9	2
228	R.R.Lindwall	A	61	13650	5251	23.03	12	–
222	C.A.Walsh	WI	65	13197	5824	26.23	6	1
219	C.E.L.Ambrose	WI	48	11809	4616	21.07	11	3
216	C.V.Grimmett	A	37	14513	5231	24.21	21	7
212	M.G.Hughes	A	53	12285	6017	28.38	7	1
202	A.M.E.Roberts	WI	47	11136	5174	25.61	11	2
202	J.A.Snow	E	49	12021	5387	26.66	8	1
200	J.R.Thomson	A	51	10535	5601	28.00	8	–
The highest aggregates for other countries are:								
170	H.J.Tayfield	SA	37	13568	4405	25.91	14	2
73	R.J.Ratnayake	SL	23	4961	2563	35.10	5	–
18	D.H.Brain	Z	4	978	431	23.94	1	–

HAT-TRICKS

F.R.Spofforth	Australia v England	Melbourne	1878-79
W.Bates	England v Australia	Melbourne	1882-83
J.Briggs	England v Australia	Sydney	1891-92
G.A.Lohmann	England v South Africa	Port Elizabeth	1895-96
J.T.Hearne	England v Australia	Leeds	1899
H.Trumble	Australia v England	Melbourne	1901-02
H.Trumble	Australia v England	Melbourne	1903-04
T.J.Matthews (2)*	Australia v South Africa	Manchester	1912
M.J.C.Allom†	England v New Zealand	Christchurch	1929-30
T.W.J.Goddard	England v South Africa	Johannesburg	1938-39
P.J.Loader	England v West Indies	Leeds	1957
L.F.Kline	Australia v South Africa	Cape Town	1957-58
W.W.Hall	West Indies v Pakistan	Lahore	1958-59
G.M.Griffin	South Africa v England	Lord's	1960
L.R.Gibbs	West Indies v Australia	Adelaide	1960-61
P.J.Petherick	New Zealand v Pakistan	Lahore	1976-77
C.A.Walsh‡	West Indies v Australia	Brisbane	1988-89
M.G.Hughes‡	Australia v West Indies	Perth	1988-89

** Hat-trick in each innings. † Four wickets in five balls. ‡ Involving both innings.*

WICKET-KEEPING RECORDS

MOST DISMISSALS IN AN INNINGS

7	Wasim Bari	Pakistan v New Zealand	Auckland	1978-79
7	R.W.Taylor	England v India	Bombay	1979-80
7	I.D.S.Smith	New Zealand v Sri Lanka	Hamilton	1990-91
6	A.T.W.Grout	Australia v South Africa	Johannesburg	1957-58
6	D.T.Lindsay	South Africa v Australia	Johannesburg	1966-67
6	J.T.Murray	England v India	Lord's	1967
6†	S.M.H.Kirmani	India v New Zealand	Christchurch	1975-76
6	R.W.Marsh	Australia v England	Brisbane	1982-83
6	S.A.R.Silva	Sri Lanka v India	Colombo (SSC)	1985-86
6	R.C.Russell	England v Australia	Melbourne	1990-91

†*Including one stumping.*

MOST STUMPINGS IN AN INNINGS

5	K.S.More	India v West Indies	Madras	1987-88

MOST DISMISSALS IN A TEST

10	R.W.Taylor	England v India	Bombay	1979-80
9†	G.R.A.Langley	Australia v England	Lord's	1956
9	D.A.Murray	West Indies v Australia	Melbourne	1981-82
9	R.W.Marsh	Australia v England	Brisbane	1982-83
9	S.A.R.Silva	Sri Lanka v India	Colombo (SSC)	1985-86
9†	S.A.R.Silva	Sri Lanka v India	Colombo (PSS)	1985-86
9	D.J.Richardson	South Africa v India	Port Elizabeth	1992-93
9	Rashid Latif	Pakistan v New Zealand	Auckland	1993-94

† *Including one stumping.*

MOST DISMISSALS IN A SERIES

28	R.W.Marsh	Australia v England	1982-83
26 (inc 3st)	J.H.B.Waite	South Africa v New Zealand	1961-62
26	R.W.Marsh	Australia v West Indies (6 Tests)	1975-76
26 (inc 5st)	I.A.Healy	Australia v England (6 Tests)	1993
24 (inc 2st)	D.L.Murray	West Indies v England	1963
24	D.T.Lindsay	South Africa v Australia	1966-67
24 (inc 3st)	A.P.E.Knott	England v Australia (6 Tests)	1970-71
24	I.A.Healy	Australia v England	1990-91

100 DISMISSALS IN TESTS

Total			*Tests*	*Ct*	*St*
355	R.W.Marsh	Australia	96	343	12
272†	P.J.L.Dujon	West Indies	81	267	5
269	A.P.E.Knott	England	95	250	19
228	Wasim Bari	Pakistan	81	201	27
219	T.G.Evans	England	91	173	46
205	I.A.Healy	Australia	62	191	14
198	S.M.H.Kirmani	India	88	160	38
189	D.L.Murray	West Indies	62	181	8
187	A.T.W.Grout	Australia	51	163	24
176	I.D.S.Smith	New Zealand	63	168	8
174	R.W.Taylor	England	57	167	7
141	J.H.B.Waite	South Africa	50	124	17
130	K.S.More	India	49	110	20
130	W.A.S.Oldfield	Australia	54	78	52
114†	J.M.Parks	England	46	103	11
104	Salim Yousuf	Pakistan	32	91	13

The most dismissals for other countries are Sri Lanka 34 (S.A.R.Silva 33ct, 1st in 9 Tests) and Zimbabwe 16 (A.Flower 14ct, 2st in 7 Tests).

† *Including two catches taken in the field.*

FIELDING RECORDS

MOST CATCHES IN AN INNINGS

5	V.Y.Richardson	Australia v South Africa	Durban	1935-36
5	Yajurvindra Singh	India v England	Bangalore	1976-77
5	M.Azharuddin	India v Pakistan	Karachi	1989-90
5	K.Srikkanth	India v Australia	Perth	1991-92

MOST CATCHES IN A TEST

7	G.S.Chappell	Australia v England	Perth	1974-75
7	Yajurvindra Singh	India v England	Bangalore	1976-77
7	H.P.Tillekeratne	Sri Lanka v New Zealand	Colombo (SSC)	1992-93

MOST CATCHES IN A SERIES

15	J.M.Gregory	Australia v England	1920-21

100 CATCHES IN TESTS

Total			*Tests*
156	A.R.Border	Australia	156
122	G.S.Chappell	Australia	87
122	I.V.A.Richards	West Indies	121
120	I.T.Botham	England	102
120	M.C.Cowdrey	England	114
110	R.B.Simpson	Australia	62
110	W.R.Hammond	England	85
109	G.St A.Sobers	West Indies	93
108	S.M.Gavaskar	India	125
105	I.M.Chappell	Australia	75
103	G.A.Gooch	England	113

MOST TEST APPEARANCES FOR EACH COUNTRY

			Opponents								
			E	*A*	*SA*	*WI*	*NZ*	*I*	*P*	*SL*	*Z*
England	117	D.I.Gower	–	42	–	19	13	24	17	2	–
Australia	156	A.R.Border	47	–	6	31	23	20	22	7	–
South Africa	50	J.H.B.Waite	21	14	–	–	15	–	–	–	–
West Indies	121	I.V.A.Richards	36	34	–	–	7	28	16	–	–
New Zealand	86	R.J.Hadlee	21	23	–	10	–	14	12	6	–
India	131	Kapil Dev	27	20	4	25	10	–	29	14	2
Pakistan	124	Javed Miandad	22	25	–	16	18	28	–	12	3
Sri Lanka	51	A.Ranatunga	4	7	3	1	9	14	13	–	–

The most appearances for Zimbabwe is 7 by A.D.R.Campbell, A.Flower, G.W.Flower and D.L.Houghton.

MOST CONSECUTIVE TEST APPEARANCES

153	A.R.Border	Australia	March 1979 to March 1994
106	S.M.Gavaskar	India	January 1975 to February 1987

MOST MATCHES BETWEEN APPEARANCES

104	Younis Ahmed	Pakistan	November 1969 to February 1987
103	D.Shackleton	England	November 1951 to June 1963

The longest interval between appearances is 22 years 222 days (March 1970 to October 1992) by A.J.Traicos of South Africa and Zimbabwe.

MOST TESTS AS CAPTAIN

93	A.R.Border	Australia	December 1984 to March 1994

MOST UMPIRING APPEARANCES

59	H.D.Bird	July 1973 to July 1994

SUMMARY OF ALL TEST MATCHES

To 27 September 1994
(Including Sri Lanka v Pakistan 1994-95)

	Opponents	*Tests*	*Won by* *E*	*A*	*SA*	*WI*	*NZ*	*I*	*P*	*SL*	*Z*	*Tied*	*Drawn*
England	Australia	280	89	108	–	–	–	–	–	–	–	–	83
	South Africa	105	47	–	19	–	–	–	–	–	–	–	39
	West Indies	109	25	–	–	46	–	–	–	–	–	–	38
	New Zealand	75	34	–	–	–	4	–	–	–	–	–	37
	India	81	31	–	–	–	–	14	–	–	–	–	36
	Pakistan	52	14	–	–	–	–	–	7	–	–	–	31
	Sri Lanka	5	3	–	–	–	–	–	–	1	–	–	1
Australia	South Africa	59	–	31	13	–	–	–	–	–	–	–	15
	West Indies	77	–	30	–	26	–	–	–	–	–	1	20
	New Zealand	32	–	13	–	–	7	–	–	–	–	–	12
	India	50	–	24	–	–	–	8	–	–	–	1	17
	Pakistan	34	–	12	–	–	–	–	9	–	–	–	13
	Sri Lanka	7	–	4	–	–	–	–	–	0	–	–	3
South Africa	West Indies	1	–	–	0	1	–	–	–	–	–	–	–
	New Zealand	17	–	–	9	–	2	–	–	–	–	–	6
	India	4	–	–	1	–	–	0	–	–	–	–	3
	Sri Lanka	3	–	–	1	–	–	–	–	0	–	–	2
West Indies	New Zealand	24	–	–	–	8	4	–	–	–	–	–	12
	India	62	–	–	–	26	–	6	–	–	–	–	30
	Pakistan	31	–	–	–	12	–	–	7	–	–	–	12
	Sri Lanka	1	–	–	–	0	–	–	–	0	–	–	1
New Zealand	India	32	–	–	–	–	6	12	–	–	–	–	14
	Pakistan	36	–	–	–	–	4	–	16	–	–	–	16
	Sri Lanka	11	–	–	–	–	4	–	–	1	–	–	6
	Zimbabwe	2	–	–	–	–	1	–	–	–	0	–	1
India	Pakistan	44	–	–	–	–	–	4	7	–	–	–	33
	Sri Lanka	14	–	–	–	–	–	7	–	1	–	–	6
	Zimbabwe	2	–	–	–	–	–	1	–	–	0	–	1
Pakistan	Sri Lanka	14	–	–	–	–	–	–	8	1	–	–	5
	Zimbabwe	3	–	–	–	–	–	–	2	–	0	–	1
		1267	243	222	43	119	32	52	56	4	0	2	494

	Tests	*Won*	*Lost*	*Drawn*	*Tied*	*Toss Won*
England	707	243	199	265	–	348
Australia	539	222	152	163	2	271
South Africa	189	43	81	65	–	91
West Indies	305	119	72	113	1	158
New Zealand	229	32	93	104	–	116
India	289	52	96	140	1	144
Pakistan	214	56	47	111	–	108
Sri Lanka	55	4	27	24	–	28
Zimbabwe	7	0	4	3	–	3

LIMITED-OVERS INTERNATIONALS RESULTS SUMMARY

1970-71 to 1994 (including Sri Lanka v Pakistan August 1994)

	Opponents	*Matches*	*Won by* *E*	*A*	*SA*	*WI*	*NZ*	*I*	*P*	*SL*	*Z*	*B*	*C*	*EA*	*UAE*	*Tied*	*NR*
England	Australia	55	25	28	–	–	–	–	–	–	–	–	–	–	–	1	1
	South Africa	4	4	–	0	–	–	–	–	–	–	–	–	–	–	–	–
	West Indies	48	20	–	–	26	–	–	–	–	–	–	–	–	–	–	2
	New Zealand	41	21	–	–	–	17	–	–	–	–	–	–	–	–	–	3
	India	29	16	–	–	–	–	13	–	–	–	–	–	–	–	–	–
	Pakistan	36	23	–	–	–	–	–	12	–	–	–	–	–	–	–	1
	Sri Lanka	11	8	–	–	–	–	–	–	3	–	–	–	–	–	–	–
	Zimbabwe	1	0	–	–	–	–	–	–	–	1	–	–	–	–	–	–
	Canada	1	1	–	–	–	–	–	–	–	–	–	0	–	–	–	–
	East Africa	1	1	–	–	–	–	–	–	–	–	–	–	0	–	–	–
Australia	South Africa	16	–	8	8	–	–	–	–	–	–	–	–	–	–	–	–
	West Indies	69	–	26	–	41	–	–	–	–	–	–	–	–	–	1	1
	New Zealand	60	–	41	–	–	17	–	–	–	–	–	–	–	–	–	2
	India	41	–	24	–	–	–	14	–	–	–	–	–	–	–	–	3
	Pakistan	38	–	18	–	–	–	–	17	–	–	–	–	–	–	1	2
	Sri Lanka	25	–	18	–	–	–	–	–	5	–	–	–	–	–	–	2
	Zimbabwe	5	–	4	–	–	–	–	–	–	1	–	–	–	–	–	–
	Bangladesh	1	–	1	–	–	–	–	–	–	–	0	–	–	–	–	–
	Canada	1	–	1	–	–	–	–	–	–	–	–	0	–	–	–	–
S Africa	West Indies	8	–	–	4	4	–	–	–	–	–	–	–	–	–	–	–
	New Zealand	4	–	–	1	–	3	–	–	–	–	–	–	–	–	–	–
	India	13	–	–	7	–	–	6	–	–	–	–	–	–	–	–	–
	Pakistan	4	–	–	1	–	–	–	3	–	–	–	–	–	–	–	–
	Sri Lanka	5	–	–	2	–	–	–	–	2	–	–	–	–	–	–	1
	Zimbabwe	2	–	–	1	–	–	–	–	–	0	–	–	–	–	–	1
W Indies	New Zealand	14	–	–	–	11	2	–	–	–	–	–	–	–	–	–	1
	India	42	–	–	–	30	–	11	–	–	–	–	–	–	–	1	–
	Pakistan	73	–	–	–	50	–	–	21	–	–	–	–	–	–	2	–
	Sri Lanka	19	–	–	–	16	–	–	–	2	–	–	–	–	–	–	1
	Zimbabwe	4	–	–	–	4	–	–	–	–	0	–	–	–	–	–	–
N Zealand	India	33	–	–	–	–	15	18	–	–	–	–	–	–	–	–	–
	Pakistan	34	–	–	–	–	14	–	18	–	–	–	–	–	–	1	1
	Sri Lanka	27	–	–	–	–	20	–	–	6	–	–	–	–	–	–	1
	Zimbabwe	5	–	–	–	–	5	–	–	–	0	–	–	–	–	–	–
	Bangladesh	1	–	–	–	–	1	–	–	–	–	0	–	–	–	–	–
	East Africa	1	–	–	–	–	1	–	–	–	–	–	–	0	–	–	–
India	Pakistan	40	–	–	–	–	–	12	26	–	–	–	–	–	–	–	2
	Sri Lanka	33	–	–	–	–	–	21	–	10	–	–	–	–	–	–	2
	Zimbabwe	10	–	–	–	–	–	9	–	–	0	–	–	–	–	1	2
	Bangladesh	2	–	–	–	–	–	2	–	–	–	0	–	–	–	–	–
	East Africa	1	–	–	–	–	–	1	–	–	–	–	–	0	–	–	–
	U A Emirates	1	–	–	–	–	–	1	–	–	–	–	–	–	0	–	–
Pakistan	Sri Lanka	45	–	–	–	–	–	–	36	8	–	–	–	–	–	–	1
	Zimbabwe	6	–	–	–	–	–	–	6	–	0	–	–	–	–	–	–
	Bangladesh	2	–	–	–	–	–	–	2	–	–	0	–	–	–	–	–
	Canada	1	–	–	–	–	–	–	1	–	–	–	0	–	–	–	–
	U A Emirates	1	–	–	–	–	–	–	1	–	–	–	–	–	0	–	–
Sri Lanka	Zimbabwe	3	–	–	–	–	–	–	–	3	0	–	–	–	–	–	–
	Bangladesh	3	–	–	–	–	–	–	–	3	–	0	–	–	–	–	–
		920	119	169	24	182	95	108	143	42	2	0	0	0	0	8	28

LEAGUE TABLE OF L-O INTERNATIONALS

	Matches	Won	Lost	Tied	No Result	% Won (exc NR)
West Indies	277	182	86	4	5	66.91
Australia	311	169	128	3	11	56.33
England	227	119	100	1	7	54.09
Pakistan	280	143	126	4	7	52.38
India	245	108	128	2	7	45.37
New Zealand	220	95	116	1	8	44.81
South Africa	56	24	30	–	2	44.44
Sri Lanka	171	42	121	–	8	25.76
Zimbabwe	36	2	32	1	1	5.71
Bangladesh	9	–	9	–	–	–
Canada	3	–	3	–	–	–
East Africa	3	–	3	–	–	–
United Arab Emirates	2	–	2	–	–	–

RECORDS

To the end of the 1994 season
(Including Pakistan's tour of Sri Lanka, July-August 1994)

TEAM RECORDS

HIGHEST TOTALS BY EACH COUNTRY

363-7	(55 overs)	ENGLAND v Pakistan	Nottingham	1992
360-4	(50 overs)	WEST INDIES v Sri Lanka	Karachi	1987-88
338-4	(50 overs)	NEW ZEALAND v Bangladesh	Sharjah	1989-90
338-5	(60 overs)	PAKISTAN v Sri Lanka	Swansea	1983
332-3	(50 overs)	AUSTRALIA v Sri Lanka	Sharjah	1989-90
313-7	(49.2 overs)	SRI LANKA v Zimbabwe	New Plymouth	1991-92
312-4	(50 overs)	ZIMBABWE v Sri Lanka	New Plymouth	1991-92
299-4	(40 overs)	INDIA v Sri Lanka	Bombay	1986-87
288-2	(46.4 overs)	SOUTH AFRICA v India	Delhi	1991-92

HIGHEST TOTAL BATTING SECOND

WINNING:	313-7	(49.2 overs)	Sri Lanka v Zimbabwe	New Plymouth	1991-92
LOSING:	289-7	(40 overs)	Sri Lanka v India	Bombay	1986-87

HIGHEST MATCH AGGREGATE

626-14	(120 overs)	Pakistan v Sri Lanka	Swansea	1983

LOWEST TOTALS BY EACH COUNTRY†

43	(19.5 overs)	PAKISTAN v West Indies	Cape Town	1992-93
45	(40.3 overs)	CANADA v England	Manchester	1979
55	(28.3 overs)	SRI LANKA v West Indies	Sharjah	1986-87
63	(25.5 overs)	INDIA v Australia	Sydney	1980-81
64	(35.5 overs)	NEW ZEALAND v Pakistan	Sharjah	1985-86
69	(28 overs)	SOUTH AFRICA v Australia	Sydney	1993-94
70	(25.2 overs)	AUSTRALIA v England	Birmingham	1977
70	(26.3 overs)	AUSTRALIA v New Zealand	Adelaide	1985-86
87	(29.3 overs)	WEST INDIES v Australia	Sydney	1992-93
93	(36.2 overs)	ENGLAND v Australia	Leeds	1975
99	(36.3 overs)	ZIMBABWE v West Indies	Hyderabad (Ind)	1993-94

† *Excluding instances when the number of overs was reduced after play began.*

LOWEST MATCH AGGREGATE

91-12	(54.2 overs)	England v Canada	Manchester	1979

LARGEST MARGINS OF VICTORY

232 runs	Australia beat Sri Lanka	Adelaide	1984-85
206 runs	New Zealand beat Australia	Adelaide	1985-86
202 runs	England beat India	Lord's	1975
10 wickets	Nine instances		

TIED MATCHES

Australia	222-9	West Indies	222-5	Melbourne	1983-84
England	226-5	Australia	226-8	Nottingham	1989
West Indies	186-5	Pakistan	186-9	Lahore	1991-92
India	126	West Indies	126	Perth	1991-92
Australia	228-7	Pakistan	228-9	Hobart	1992-93
Pakistan	244-6	West Indies	244-5	Georgetown	1992-93
India	248-5	Zimbabwe	248	Indore	1993-94
Pakistan	161-9	New Zealand	161	Auckland	1993-94

BATTING RECORDS

HIGHEST INDIVIDUAL SCORE FOR EACH COUNTRY

189*	I.V.A.Richards	WEST INDIES v England	Manchester	1984
175*	Kapil Dev	INDIA v Zimbabwe	Tunbridge Wells	1983
171*	G.M.Turner	NEW ZEALAND v East Africa	Birmingham	1975
167*	R.A.Smith	ENGLAND v Australia	Birmingham	1993
145	D.M.Jones	AUSTRALIA v England	Brisbane	1990-91
142	D.L.Houghton	ZIMBABWE v New Zealand	Hyderabad	1987-88
137*	Inzamam-ul-Haq	PAKISTAN v New Zealand	Sharjah	1993-94
121	R.L.Dias	SRI LANKA v India	Bangalore	1982-83
112*	G.Kirsten	SOUTH AFRICA v Australia	Melbourne	1993-94

HIGHEST PARTNERSHIP FOR EACH WICKET

1st	212	G.R.Marsh/D.C.Boon	A v I	Jaipur	1986-87
2nd	263	Aamir Sohail/Inzamam-ul-Haq	P v NZ	Sharjah	1993-94
3rd	224*	D.M.Jones/A.R.Border	A v SL	Adelaide	1984-85
4th	173	D.M.Jones/S.R.Waugh	A v P	Perth	1986-87
5th	152	I.V.A.Richards/C.H.Lloyd	WI v SL	Brisbane	1984-85
6th	154	R.B.Richardson/P.J.L.Dujon	WI v P	Sharjah	1991-92
7th	115	P.J.L.Dujon/M.D.Marshall	WI v P	Gujranwala	1986-87
8th	119	P.R.Reiffel/S.K.Warne	A v SA	Port Elizabeth	1993-94
9th	126*	Kapil Dev/S.M.H.Kirmani	I v Z	Tunbridge Wells	1983
10th	106*	I.V.A.Richards/M.A.Holding	WI v E	Manchester	1984

4000 RUNS

		M	*I*	*NO*	*HS*	**Runs**	*Avge*	*100*	*50*
D.L.Haynes	WI	238	237	28	152*	**8648**	41.37	17	57
Javed Miandad	P	228	215	40	119*	**7327**	41.86	8	50
I.V.A.Richards	WI	187	167	24	189*	**6721**	47.00	11	45
A.R.Border	A	273	252	39	127*	**6524**	30.62	3	39
D.M.Jones	A	164	161	25	145	**6068**	44.61	7	46
R.B.Richardson	WI	202	195	27	122	**5641**	33.57	5	41
D.C.Boon	A	162	158	11	122	**5243**	35.66	5	33
C.G.Greenidge	WI	128	127	13	133*	**5134**	45.03	11	31
Ramiz Raja	P	159	158	11	119*	**4915**	33.43	8	29
Salim Malik	P	191	172	23	102	**4755**	31.91	5	28
M.Azharuddin	I	174	161	31	108*	**4661**	35.85	3	26
M.D.Crowe	NZ	134	133	18	105*	**4412**	38.36	3	32
G.R.Marsh	A	117	115	6	126*	**4357**	39.97	9	22
G.A.Gooch	E	121	118	6	142	**4229**	37.75	8	23
K.Srikkanth	I	146	145	4	123	**4092**	29.02	4	27
A.J.Lamb	E	122	118	16	118	**4010**	39.31	4	26

The leading aggregates for other countries are:

		M	*I*	*NO*	*HS*	**Runs**	*Avge*	*100*	*50*
A.Ranatunga	SL	144	137	25	98	**3805**	33.97	–	26
K.C.Wessels	SA	49	48	4	90	**1484**	33.72	–	11
D.L.Houghton	Z	36	34	–	142	**1010**	29.70	1	8

BOWLING RECORDS

BEST ANALYSIS FOR EACH COUNTRY

7-37	Aqib Javed	PAKISTAN v India	Sharjah	1991-92
7-51	W.W.Davis	WEST INDIES v Australia	Leeds	1983
6-12	A.Kumble	INDIA v West Indies	Calcutta	1993-94
6-14	G.J.Gilmour	AUSTRALIA v England	Leeds	1975
6-29	S.T.Jayasuriya	SRI LANKA v England	Moratuwa	1992-93
5-20	V.J.Marks	ENGLAND v New Zealand	Wellington	1983-84
5-23	R.O.Collinge	NEW ZEALAND v India	Christchurch	1975-76
5-29	A.A.Donald	SOUTH AFRICA v India	Calcutta	1991-92
4-21	E.A.Brandes	ZIMBABWE v England	Albury	1991-92

HAT-TRICKS

Jalaluddin	Pakistan v Australia	Hyderabad	1982-83
B.A.Reid	Australia v New Zealand	Sydney	1985-86
C.Sharma	India v New Zealand	Nagpur	1987-88
Wasim Akram	Pakistan v West Indies	Sharjah	1989-90
Wasim Akram	Pakistan v Australia	Sharjah	1989-90
Kapil Dev	India v Sri Lanka	Calcutta	1990-91
Aqib Javed	Pakistan v India	Sharjah	1991-92
D.K.Morrison	New Zealand v India	Napier	1993-94

100 WICKETS

		M	*Balls*	*Runs*	**Wkts**	*Avge*	*Best*	*4w*
Wasim Akram	P	174	8937	5628	**254**	22.15	5-15	15
Kapil Dev	I	220	11082	6833	**251**	27.22	5-43	4
Imran Khan	P	175	7461	4845	**182**	26.62	6-14	4
C.J.McDermott	A	116	6301	4258	**170**	25.04	5-44	5
R.J.Hadlee	NZ	115	6182	3407	**158**	21.56	5-25	6
M.D.Marshall	WI	136	7175	4233	**157**	26.96	4-18	6
S.R.Waugh	A	167	6831	5067	**152**	33.33	4-33	2
C.E.L.Ambrose	WI	104	5579	3248	**151**	21.50	5-17	8
Waqar Younis	P	88	4327	3081	**149**	20.67	6-26	12
J.Garner	WI	98	5330	2752	**146**	18.84	5-31	5
I.T.Botham	E	116	6271	4139	**145**	28.54	4-31	3
M.A.Holding	WI	102	5473	3034	**142**	21.36	5-26	6
E.J.Chatfield	NZ	114	6065	3621	**140**	25.86	5-34	4
C.A.Walsh	WI	124	6622	4239	**134**	31.63	5- 1	6
Abdul Qadir	P	104	5100	3453	**132**	26.15	5-44	6
M.Prabhakar	I	102	5056	3457	**129**	26.79	5-35	5
R.J.Shastri	I	150	6613	4650	**129**	36.04	5-15	3
I.V.A.Richards	WI	187	5644	4228	**118**	35.83	6-41	3
M.C.Snedden	NZ	93	4519	3235	**114**	28.37	4-34	1
Mudassar Nazar	P	122	4855	3431	**111**	30.90	5-28	2
C.L.Hooper	WI	115	4642	3300	**110**	30.00	4-34	1
S.P.O'Donnell	A	87	4350	3102	**108**	28.72	5-13	6
D.K.Lillee	A	63	3593	2145	**103**	20.82	5-34	6
P.A.J.DeFreitas	E	87	4861	3154	**100**	31.54	4-35	1

The leading aggregates for other countries are:

J.R.Ratnayeke	SL	78	3573	2865	**85**	33.70	4-23	1
A.A.Donald	SA	46	2456	1614	**62**	26.03	5-29	1
E.A.Brandes	Z	23	1175	987	**28**	35.25	4-21	1

WICKET-KEEPING RECORDS

MOST DISMISSALS IN AN INNINGS

5	R.W.Marsh	Australia v England	Leeds	1981
5	R.G.de Alwis	Sri Lanka v Australia	Colombo (PSS)	1982-83
5	S.M.H.Kirmani	India v Zimbabwe	Leicester	1983
5†	S.Viswanath	India v England	Sydney	1984-85
5†	K.S.More	India v New Zealand	Sharjah	1987-88
5	H.P.Tillekeratne	Sri Lanka v Pakistan	Sharjah	1990-91
5†	N.R.Mongia	India v New Zealand	Auckland	1993-94

† *Including 2 stumpings.*

MOST DISMISSALS IN A CAREER

		M	*Ct*	*St*	**Dis**
P.J.L.Dujon	WI	169	183	21	**204**
I.A.Healy	A	109	127	19	**146**
R.W.Marsh	A	92	120	4	**124**
Salim Yousuf	P	86	81	22	**103**

FIELDING RECORDS

MOST CATCHES IN AN INNINGS

5	J.N.Rhodes	South Africa v West Indies	Bombay	1993-94

MOST CATCHES IN A CAREER

127 A.R.Border (A) in 273 matches. 101 I.V.A.Richards (WI) in 187 matches.

ALL-ROUND RECORDS

1000 RUNS AND 100 WICKETS

		M	*R*	*W*
I.T.Botham	England	116	2113	145
R.J.Hadlee	New Zealand	115	1749	158
C.L.Hooper	West Indies	115	2177	110
Imran Khan	Pakistan	175	3709	182
Kapil Dev	India	220	3766	251
Mudassar Nazar	Pakistan	122	2624	111
S.P.O'Donnell	Australia	87	1242	108
M.Prabhakar	India	102	1253	129
I.V.A.Richards	West Indies	187	6721	118
R.J.Shastri	India	150	3108	129
Wasim Akram	Pakistan	174	1490	254
S.R.Waugh	Australia	167	3401	152

1000 RUNS AND 100 DISMISSALS

		M	*R*	*Dis*
P.J.L.Dujon	West Indies	169	1945	204
R.W.Marsh	Australia	92	1225	124

MOST APPEARANCES FOR EACH COUNTRY

Australia	273	A.R.Border	Sri Lanka	144	A.Ranatunga
West Indies	238	D.L.Haynes	England	122	A.J.Lamb
Pakistan	228	Javed Miandad	South Africa	52	D.J.Richardson
India	220	Kapil Dev	Zimbabwe	36	D.L.Houghton
New Zealand	149	J.G.Wright			

ENGLAND v WEST INDIES

1928 to 1993-94

	Captains					
Season	*England*	*West Indies*	*P*	*E*	*WI*	*D*
1928	A.P.F.Chapman	R.K.Nunes	3	3	–	–
1929-30	Hon.F.S.G.Calthorpe	E.L.G.Hoad[1]	4	1	1	2
1933	D.R.Jardine[2]	G.C.Grant	3	2	–	1
1934-35	R.E.S.Wyatt	G.C.Grant	4	1	2	1
1939	W.R.Hammond	R.S.Grant	3	1	–	2
1947-48	G.O.B.Allen[3]	J.D.C.Goddard[4]	4	–	2	2
1950	N.W.D.Yardley[5]	J.D.C.Goddard	4	1	3	–
1953-54	L.Hutton	J.B.Stollmeyer	5	2	2	1
1957	P.B.H.May	J.D.C.Goddard	5	3	–	2
1959-60	P.B.H.May[6]	F.C.M.Alexander	5	1	–	4
1963	E.R.Dexter	F.M.M.Worrell	5	1	3	1
1966	M.C.Cowdrey[7]	G.St A.Sobers	5	1	3	1
1967-68	M.C.Cowdrey	G.St A.Sobers	5	1	–	4
1969	R.Illingworth	G.St A.Sobers	3	2	–	1
1973	R.Illingworth	R.B.Kanhai	3	–	2	1
1973-74	M.H.Denness	R.B.Kanhai	5	1	1	3
1976	A.W.Greig	C.H.Lloyd	5	–	3	2
1980	I.T.Botham	C.H.Lloyd[8]	5	–	1	4
1980-81	I.T.Botham	C.H.Lloyd	4	–	2	2
1984	D.I.Gower	C.H.Lloyd	5	–	5	–
1985-86	D.I.Gower	I.V.A.Richards	5	–	5	–
1988	J.E.Emburey[9]	I.V.A.Richards	5	–	4	1
1989-90	G.A.Gooch[10]	I.V.A.Richards[11]	4	1	2	1
1991	G.A.Gooch	I.V.A.Richards	5	2	2	1
1993-94	M.A.Atherton	R.B.Richardson[12]	5	1	3	1
	Lord's		14	4	4	6
	Manchester		11	3	5	3
	The Oval		13	5	6	2
	Nottingham		7	–	4	3
	Birmingham		5	1	2	2
	Leeds		9	3	5	1
	Bridgetown		11	2	4	5
	Port-of-Spain		15	4	6	5
	Georgetown		8	1	3	4
	Kingston		12	2	5	5
	St John's		4	–	2	2
	In England		59	16	26	17
	In West Indies		50	9	20	21
	Totals		109	25	46	38

The following deputised for the official captain:
[1]N.Betancourt (2nd), M.P.Fernandes (3rd), R.K.Nunes (4th). [2]R.E.S.Wyatt (3rd). [3]R.Cranston (1st). [4]G.A.Headley (1st), G.E.Gomez (2nd). [5]F.R.Brown (4th). [6]M.C.Cowdrey (4th and 5th). [7]M.J.K.Smith (1st), D.B.Close (5th). [8]I.V.A.Richards (5th). [9]M.W.Gatting (1st), C.S.Cowdrey (4th), G.A.Gooch (5th). [10]A.J.Lamb (4th and 5th). [11]D.L.Haynes (3rd). [12]C.A.Walsh (5th).

HIGHEST INNINGS TOTALS

England	in England	619-6d	Nottingham	1957
	in West Indies	849	Kingston	1929-30
West Indies	in England	687-8d	The Oval	1976
	in West Indies	681-8d	Port-of-Spain	1953-54

LOWEST INNINGS TOTALS

England	in England	71	Manchester	1976
	in West Indies	46	Port-of-Spain	1993-94
West Indies	in England	86	The Oval	1957
	in West Indies	102	Bridgetown	1934-35

HIGHEST MATCH AGGREGATE

1815 for 34 wickets	Kingston	1929-30

LOWEST MATCH AGGREGATE

309 for 29 wickets	Bridgetown	1934-35

HIGHEST INDIVIDUAL INNINGS

England	in England	285*	P.B.H.May	Birmingham	1957
		258	T.W.Graveney	Nottingham	1957
		203	D.L.Amiss	The Oval	1976
		202*	L.Hutton	The Oval	1950
	in West Indies	325	A.Sandham	Kingston	1929-30
		262*	D.L.Amiss	Kingston	1973-74
		205*	E.H.Hendren	Port-of-Spain	1929-30
		205	L.Hutton	Kingston	1953-54
West Indies	in England	291	I.V.A.Richards	The Oval	1976
		261	F.M.M.Worrell	Nottingham	1950
		232	I.V.A.Richards	Nottingham	1976
		223	C.G.Greenidge	Manchester	1984
		214*	C.G.Greenidge	Lord's	1984
		209*	B.F.Butcher	Nottingham	1966
	in West Indies	375	B.C.Lara	St John's	1993-94
		302	L.G.Rowe	Bridgetown	1973-74
		270*	G.A.Headley	Kingston	1934-35
		226	G.St A.Sobers	Bridgetown	1959-60
		223	G.A.Headley	Kingston	1929-30
		220	C.L.Walcott	Bridgetown	1953-54
		209	C.A.Roach	Georgetown	1929-30
		206	E.de C.Weekes	Port-of-Spain	1953-54

196 hundreds have been scored in this series: England 93, West Indies 103.

HUNDRED IN EACH INNINGS

England	118	143	A.J.Stewart	Bridgetown	1993-94
West Indies	114	112	G.A.Headley	Georgetown	1929-30
	106	107	G.A.Headley	Lord's	1939
	134	101	C.G.Greenidge	Manchester	1976

CARRIED BAT THROUGH INNINGS

England	202*	(344)	L.Hutton	The Oval	1950
	154*	(252)	G.A.Gooch	Leeds	1991
West Indies	191*	(372)	F.M.M.Worrell	Nottingham	1957
	75*	(176)	D.L.Haynes	The Oval	1991

HIGHEST AGGREGATE OF RUNS IN A SERIES

England	in England	489 (av 97.80)	P.B.H.May	1957
	in West Indies	693 (av 115.50)	E.H.Hendren	1929-30
West Indies	in England	829 (av 118.42)	I.V.A.Richards	1976
	in West Indies	798 (av 99.75)	B.C.Lara	1993-94

RECORD WICKET PARTNERSHIPS – ENGLAND

1st	212	C.Washbrook (102), R.T.Simpson (94)	Nottingham	1950
2nd	266	P.E.Richardson (126), T.W.Graveney (258)	Nottingham	1957
3rd	303	M.A.Atherton (135), R.A.Smith (175)	St John's	1993-94
4th	411	P.B.H.May (285*), M.C.Cowdrey (154)	Birmingham	1957
5th	150	A.J.Stewart (143), G.P.Thorpe (84)	Bridgetown	1993-94
6th	163	A.W.Greig (148), A.P.E.Knott (87)	Bridgetown	1973-74
7th	197	M.J.K.Smith (96), J.M.Parks (101*)	Port-of-Spain	1959-60
8th	217	T.W.Graveney (165), J.T.Murray (112)	The Oval	1966
9th	109	G.A.R.Lock (89), P.I.Pocock (13)	Georgetown	1967-68
10th	128	K.Higgs (63), J.A.Snow (59*)	The Oval	1966

RECORD WICKET PARTNERSHIPS – WEST INDIES

1st	298	C.G.Greenidge (149), D.L.Haynes (167)	St John's	1989-90
2nd	287*	C.G.Greenidge (214*), H.A.Gomes (92*)	Lord's	1984
3rd	338	E.de C.Weekes (206), F.M.M.Worrell (167)	Port-of-Spain	1953-54
4th	399	G.St A.Sobers (226), F.M.M.Worrell (187*)	Bridgetown	1959-60
5th	265	S.M.Nurse (137), G.St A.Sobers (174)	Leeds	1966
6th	274*	G.St A.Sobers (163*), D.A.J.Holford (105*)	Lord's	1966
7th	155*†	G.St A.Sobers (150*), B.D.Julien (121)	Lord's	1973
8th	99	C.A.McWatt (54), J.K.Holt (48*)	Georgetown	1953-54
9th	150	E.A.E.Baptiste (87*), M.A.Holding (69)	Birmingham	1984
10th	67*	M.A.Holding (58*), C.E.H.Croft (17*)	St John's	1980-81

† 231 runs were added for this wicket; G.St A.Sobers retired ill and was succeeded by K.D.Boyce after 155 had been scored.

HAT-TRICK

England	P.J.Loader	Leeds	1957

BEST INNINGS BOWLING ANALYSIS

England	in England	8-103	I.T.Botham	Lord's	1984
	in West Indies	8- 75	A.R.C.Fraser	Bridgetown	1993-94
West Indies	in England	8- 92	M.A.Holding	The Oval	1976
	in West Indies	8- 45	C.E.L.Ambrose	Bridgetown	1989-90

BEST MATCH BOWLING ANALYSIS

England	in England	12-119	F.S.Trueman	Birmingham	1963
	in West Indies	13-156	A.W.Greig	Port-of-Spain	1973-74
West Indies	in England	14-149	M.A.Holding	The Oval	1976
	in West Indies	11- 84	C.E.L.Ambrose	Port-of-Spain	1993-94

HIGHEST AGGREGATE OF WICKETS IN A SERIES

England	in England	34 (av 17.47)	F.S.Trueman	1963
	in West Indies	27 (av 18.66)	J.A.Snow	1967-68
West Indies	in England	35 (av 12.65)	M.D.Marshall	1988
	in West Indies	27 (av 16.14)	J.Garner	1985-86
		27 (av 17.65)	M.D.Marshall	1985-86

FIRST-CLASS UMPIRES 1995

BALDERSTONE, John Christopher (Paddock Council S, Huddersfield), b Longwood, Huddersfield, Yorks 16 Nov 1940. RHB, SLA. Yorkshire 1961-69. Leicestershire 1971-86 (cap 1973; testimonial 1984). **Tests:** 2 (1976); HS 35 v WI (Leeds) 1976; BB 1-80. Tour: Z 1980-81 (Le). 1000 runs (11); most – 1482 (1982). HS 181* Le v Glos (Leicester) 1984. BB 6-25 Le v Hants (Southampton) 1978. Hat-trick 1976 (Le). F-c career: 390 matches; 19034 runs @ 34.11, 32 hundreds; 310 wickets @ 26.32; 210 ct. Soccer for Huddersfield Town, Carlisle United, Doncaster Rovers and Queen of the South. Appointed 1988. Umpired 1 LOI (1994).

BIRD, Harold Dennis ('Dickie') (Raley SM, Barnsley), b Barnsley, Yorks 19 Apr 1933. RHB, RM. Yorkshire 1956-59. Leicestershire 1960-64 (cap 1960). MBE 1986. 1000 runs (1): 1028 (1960). HS 181* Y v Glam (Bradford) 1959. F-c career: 93 matches; 3314 runs @ 20.71, 2 hundreds. Appointed 1970. Umpired 59 Tests (world record – 1973 to 1994), including 3 in Zimbabwe 1992-93, 3 in West Indies 1992-93, and 2 in New Zealand 1993-94. Officiated in 68 LOI (1973 to 1994), including 1975, 1979, 1983 and 1987-88 World Cup finals, 1985-86 Asia Cup and 7 Sharjah tournaments. **Appointed to International Panel 1994.**

BOND, John David ('Jack') (Bolton S), b Kearsley, Lancs 6 May 1932. RHB, LB. Lancashire 1955-72 (cap 1955; captain 1968-72; coach 1973; manager 1980-86; benefit 1970). Nottinghamshire 1974 (captain/coach 1974). 1000 runs (2); most – 2125 (1963). HS 157 La v Hants (Manchester) 1962. Test selector 1974. F-c career: 362 matches; 12125 runs @ 25.90, 14 hundreds; 222 ct. Appointed 1988.

BURGESS, Graham Iefvion (Millfield S), b Glastonbury, Somerset 5 May 1943. RHB, RM. Somerset 1966-79 (cap 1968; testimonial 1977). HS 129 v Glos (Taunton) 1973. BB 7-43 (13-75 match) v OU (Oxford) 1975. F-c career: 252 matches; 7129 runs @ 18.90, 2 hundreds; 474 wickets @ 28.57. Appointed 1991.

CONSTANT, David John, b Bradford-on-Avon, Wilts 9 Nov 1941. LHB, SLA. Kent 1961-63. Leicestershire 1965-68. HS 80 Le v Glos (Bristol) 1966. F-c career: 61 matches; 1517 runs @ 19.20; 1 wicket @ 36.00. Appointed 1969. Umpired 36 Tests (1971 to 1988) and 29 LOI (1972 to 1990). Represented Gloucestershire at bowls 1984-86.

DUDLESTON, Barry (Stockport S), b Bebington, Cheshire 16 Jul 1945. RHB, SLA. Leicestershire 1966-80 (cap 1969; benefit 1980). Gloucestershire 1981-83. Rhodesia 1976-80. 1000 runs (8); most – 1374 (1970). HS 202 Le v Derbys (Leicester) 1979. BB 4-6 Le v Surrey (Leicester) 1972. F-c career: 295 matches; 14747 runs @ 32.48, 32 hundreds; 47 wickets @ 29.04. Appointed 1984. Umpired 2 Tests (1991 to 1992) and 1 LOI (1992).

HAMPSHIRE, John Harry (Oakwood THS, Rotherham), b Thurnscoe, Yorks 10 Feb 1941. RHB, LB. Son of J. (Yorks 1937); brother of A.W. (Yorks 1975). Yorkshire 1961-81 (cap 1963; benefit 1976; captain 1979-80). Derbyshire 1982-84 (cap 1982). Tasmania 1967-69, 1977-79. **Tests:** 8 (1969 to 1975); 403 runs @ 26.86, HS 107 v WI (Lord's) 1969 on debut (only England player to score hundred at Lord's on debut in Tests). Tours: A 1970-71; SA 1972-73 (DHR), 1974-75 (DHR); WI 1964-65 (Cav); NZ 1970-71; P 1967-68 (Cwlth XI); SL 1969-70; Z 1980-81 (Le XI). 1000 runs (15); most – 1596 (1978). HS 183* Y v Sussex (Hove) 1971. BB 7-52 Y v Glam (Cardiff) 1963. F-c career: 577 matches; 28059 runs @ 34.55, 43 hundreds; 30 wickets @ 54.56; 445 ct. Appointed 1985. Umpired 11 Tests (1989 to 1993), including 4 in Pakistan 1989-90, and 5 LOI (1989 to 1992).

HARRIS, John Henry, b Taunton, Somerset 13 Feb 1936. LHB, RFM. Somerset 1952-59. Suffolk 1960-62. Devon 1975. HS 41 v Worcs (Taunton) 1957. BB 3-29 v Worcs (Bristol) 1959. F-c career: 15 matches; 154 runs @ 11.00; 19 wickets @ 32.57. Appointed 1983.

HOLDER, John Wakefield (Combermere S, Barbados), b St George, Barbados 19 Mar 1945. RHB, RFM. Hampshire 1968-72. Hat-trick 1972. HS 33 v Sussex (Hove) 1971. BB 7-79 v Glos (Gloucester) 1972. F-c career: 47 matches; 374 runs @ 10.68;

HOLDER, JOHN – continued:
139 wickets @ 24.56. Appointed 1983. Umpired 10 Tests (1988 to 1991), including 4 in Pakistan 1989-90, and 13 LOI (1988 to 1993-94) including 1989-90 Nehru Cup and 1993-94 Sharjah Champions Trophy.

HOLDER, Vanburn Alonza (Richmond SM, Barbados), b Bridgetown, Barbados 8 Oct 1945. RHB, RFM. Barbados 1966-78. Worcestershire 1968-80 (cap 1970; benefit 1979). Shropshire 1981. **Tests** (WI): 40 (1969 to 1978-79); HS 42 v NZ (P-o-S) 1971-72; BB 6-28 v A (P-o-S) 1977-78. LOI: 12. Tours (WI): E 1969, 1973, 1976; A 1975-76; I 1974-75, 1978-79; P 1973-74 (RW), 1974-75; SL 1974-75, 1978-79. HS 122 Barbados v Trinidad (Bridgetown) 1973-74. BB 7-40 Wo v Glam (Cardiff) 1974. F-c career: 311 matches; 3559 runs @ 13.03, 1 hundred; 947 wickets @ 24.48. Appointed 1992.

JESTY, Trevor Edward (Privet County SS, Gosport), b Gosport, Hants 2 Jun 1948. RHB, RM. Hampshire 1966-84 (cap 1971; benefit 1982). Surrey 1985-87 (cap 1985; captain 1985). Lancashire 1988-91 (cap 1989). Border 1973-74. GW 1974-76, 1980-81. Canterbury 1979-80. Wisden 1982. LOI: 10. Tours: WI 1982-83 (Int); Z 1988-89 (La). 1000 runs (10); most – 1645 (1982). HS 248 H v CU (Cambridge) 1984. Scored 122* La v OU (Oxford) 1991 in his final f-c innings. 50 wkts (2); most – 52 (1981). BB 7-75 H v Worcs (Southampton) 1976. F-c career: 490 matches; 21916 runs @ 32.71, 35 hundreds; 585 wickets @ 27.47. Appointed 1994.

JONES, Allan Arthur (St John's C, Horsham), b Horley, Surrey 9 Dec 1947. RHB, RFM. Sussex 1966-69. Somerset 1970-75 (cap 1972). Northern Transvaal 1972-73. Middlesex 1976-79 (cap 1976). Orange Free State 1976-77. Glamorgan 1980-81. HS 33 M v Kent (Canterbury) 1978. BB 9-51 Sm v Sussex (Hove) 1972. F-c career: 214 matches; 799 runs @ 5.39; 549 wickets @ 28.07. Appointed 1985.

JULIAN, Raymond (Wigston SM), b Cosby, Leics 23 Aug 1936. RHB, WK. Leicestershire 1953-71 (cap 1961). HS 51 v Worcs (Worcester) 1962. F-c career: 192 matches; 2581 runs @ 9.73; 421 dismissals (382 ct, 39 st). Appointed 1972.

KITCHEN, Mervyn John (Backwell SM, Nailsea), b Nailsea, Somerset 1 Aug 1940. LHB, RM. Somerset 1960-79 (cap 1966; testimonial 1973). Tour: Rhodesia 1972-73 (Int W). 1000 runs (7); most – 1730 (1968). HS 189 v Pakistanis (Taunton) 1967. BB 1-4. F-c career: 354 matches; 15230 runs @ 26.25, 17 hundreds; 2 wickets @ 54.50. Appointed 1982. Umpired 7 Tests (1990 to 1993) and 11 LOI (1983 to 1994). **Appointed to International Panel 1995.**

LEADBEATER, Barrie (Harehills SS), b Harehills, Leeds, Yorks 14 Aug 1943. RHB, RM. Yorkshire 1966-79 (cap 1969; joint benefit with G.A.Cope 1980). Tour: WI 1969-70 (DN). HS 140* v Hants (Portsmouth) 1976. F-c career: 147 matches; 5373 runs @ 25.34, 1 hundred; 1 wicket 5.00. Appointed 1981. Umpired 4 LOI (1983).

LYONS, Kevin James (Lady Mary's HS), b Cardiff, Glam 18 Dec 1946. RHB, RM. Glamorgan 1967-77. Tour: WI 1969-70 (Glam). HS 92 v CU (Cambridge) 1972. F-c career: 62 matches; 1673 runs @ 19.68; 2 wickets @ 126.00. F-c umpire 1985-91. Worcestershire CCC coach 1992-93. Re-appointed 1994.

MEYER, Barrie John (Boscombe SS), b Bournemouth, Hants 21 Aug 1932. RHB, WK. Gloucestershire 1957-71 (cap 1958; benefit 1971). HS 63 v Indians (Cheltenham) 1959, v OU (Bristol) 1962, and v Sussex (Bristol) 1964. F-c career: 406 matches; 5367 runs @ 14.16; 826 dismissals (707 ct, 119 st). Soccer for Bristol Rovers, Plymouth Argyle, Newport County and Bristol City. Appointed 1973. Umpired 26 Tests (1978 to 1993) and 23 LOI (1977 to 1993), including 1979 and 1983 World Cup finals.

PALMER, Kenneth Ernest (Southbroom SM, Devizes), b Winchester, Hants 22 Apr 1937. RHB, RFM. Brother of R. (below) and father of G.V. (Somerset 1982-88). Somerset 1955-69 (cap 1958; testimonial 1968). Tours: WI 1963-64 (Cav); P 1963-64 (Cwlth XI). **Tests:** 1 (1964-65; while coaching in South Africa): 10 runs; 1 wicket. 1000 runs (1): 1036 (1961). 100 wickets (4); most – 139 (1963). HS 125* v Northants (Northampton) 1961. BB 9-57 v Notts (Nottingham) 1963. F-c career: 314 matches; 7761 runs @ 20.64, 2 hundreds; 866 wickets @ 21.34. Appointed 1972. Umpired 22 Tests (1978 to 1994) and 19 LOI (1977 to 1994). **International Panel 1994.**

PALMER, Roy (Southbroom SM, Devizes), b Devizes, Wilts 12 Jul 1942. RHB, RFM. Brother of K.E. (above). Somerset 1965-70. HS 84 v Leics (Taunton) 1967. BB 6-45 v Middx (Lord's) 1967. F-c career: 74 matches; 1037 runs @ 13.29; 172 wickets @ 31.62. Appointed 1980. Umpired 2 Tests (1992 to 1993) and 7 LOI (1983 to 1994).

PLEWS, Nigel Trevor (Mundella GS, Nottingham), b Nottingham 5 Sep 1934. Former policeman (Fraud Squad). No first-class appearances. Appointed 1982. Umpired 7 Tests (1988 to 1994) and 5 LOI (1986 to 1994). **Appointed to International Panel 1994.**

SHARP, George (Elwick Road SS, Hartlepool), b West Hartlepool, Co Durham 12 Mar 1950. RHB, WK, occ LM. Northamptonshire 1968-85 (cap 1973; benefit 1982). HS 98 v Yorks (Northampton) 1983. BB 1-47. F-c career: 306 matches; 6254 runs @ 19.85; 1 wicket @ 70.00; 655 dismissals (565 ct, 90 st). Appointed 1992.

SHEPHERD, David Robert (Barnstaple GS; St Luke's C, Exeter), b Bideford, Devon 27 Dec 1940. RHB, RM. Gloucestershire 1965-79 (cap 1969; joint benefit with J.Davey 1978). Scored 108 on debut (v OU). Devon 1959-64. 1000 runs (2); most – 1079 (1970). HS 153 v Middx (Bristol) 1968. F-c career: 282 matches; 10672 runs @ 24.47, 12 hundreds; 2 wickets @ 53.00. Appointed 1981. Umpired 23 Tests (1985 to 1994), including 4 in South Africa 1992-93, 1993-94. Officiated in 56 LOI (1983 to 1993-94), including 1987-88 and 1991-92 World Cups, 1985-86 Asia Cup and 5 Sharjah tournaments. **Appointed to International Panel 1994.**

WHITE, Robert Arthur (Chiswick GS), b Fulham, London 6 Oct 1936. LHB, OB. Middlesex 1958-65 (cap 1963). Nottinghamshire 1966-80 (cap 1966; benefit 1974). 1000 runs (1): 1355 (1963). HS 116* Nt v Surrey (Oval) 1967. BB 7-41 Nt v Derbys (Ilkeston) 1971. F-c career: 413 matches; 12452 runs @ 23.18, 5 hundreds; 693 wickets @ 30.50. Appointed 1983.

WHITEHEAD, Alan Geoffrey Thomas, b Butleigh, Somerset 28 Oct 1940. LHB, SLA. Somerset 1957-61. HS 15 v Hants (Southampton) 1959 and v Leics (Leicester) 1960. BB 6-74 v Sussex (Eastbourne) 1959. F-c career: 38 matches; 137 runs @ 5.70; 67 wickets @ 34.41. Appointed 1970. Umpired 5 Tests (1982 to 1987) and 12 LOI (1979 to 1987).

WIGHT, Peter Bernard (St Stanislaus C), b Georgetown, British Guiana 25 Jun 1930. RHB, OB. Brother of G.L. (West Indies 1949-53), H.A. and N. (all British Guiana). British Guiana 1950-51. Somerset 1953-65 (cap 1954; benefit 1963). Canterbury 1963-64. 1000 runs (10); most – 2375 (1960). HS 222* v Kent (Taunton) 1959. BB 6-29 v Derbys (Chesterfield) 1957. F-c career: 333 matches; 17773 runs @ 33.09, 28 hundreds; 68 wickets @ 33.26. Appointed 1966.

WILLEY, Peter (Seaham SS), b Sedgefield, Co Durham 6 Dec 1949. RHB, OB. Northamptonshire 1966-83 (cap 1971; benefit 1981). Leicestershire 1984-91 (cap 1984; captain 1987). E Province 1982-85. Northumberland 1992. Tests: 26 (1976 to 1986); 1184 runs @ 26.90, HS 102* v WI (St John's) 1980-81; 7 wkts 65.14, BB 2-73 v WI (Lord's) 1980. LOI: 26. Tours: A 1979-80; SA 1972-73 (DHR), 1981-82 (SAB); WI 1980-81, 1985-86; I 1979-80; SL 1977-78 (DHR). 1000 runs (10); most – 1783 (1982). HS 227 Nh v Somerset (Northampton) 1976. 50 wkts (3); most – 52 (1979). BB 7-37 Nh v OU (Oxford) 1975. F-c career: 559 matches; 24361 runs @ 30.56, 44 hundreds; 756 wickets @ 30.95. Appointed 1993.

RESERVE FIRST-CLASS LIST: P.ADAMS, A.CLARKSON, M.J.HARRIS, M.K.REED, J.F.STEELE.

INTERNATIONAL PANEL: H.D.Bird, M.J.Kitchen, N.T.Plews, D.R.Shepherd (England); D.B.Hair, S.G.Randell (Australia); V.K.Ramaswamy, S.Venkataraghavan (India): B.L.Aldridge, R.S.Dunne (New Zealand); Khizer Hayat, Mahboob Shah (Pakistan); K.E.Liebenberg, S.B.Lambson (South Africa); B.C.Cooray, K.T.Francis (Sri Lanka); S.U.Bucknor, L.H.Barker (West Indies); K.Kanjee, I.D.Robinson (Zimbabwe).

STANDBY/THIRD UMPIRES FOR TEST MATCHES: J.C.Balderstone, J.H.Hampshire, J.W.Holder, G.Sharp, A.G.T.Whitehead, P.Willey.

TEXACO TROPHY PANEL: Four Test umpires plus J.H.Hampshire and R.Palmer.

See page 90 for key to abbreviations.

PRINCIPAL FIXTURES 1995

** Includes Sunday play*

Thursday 13 April

Fenner's: Cambridge U v Yorks
The Parks: Oxford U v Durham

Tuesday 18 April

Tetley Bitter Shield
Edgbaston: Britannic Assurance Champions (Warwicks) v England 'A' (Four days)
Other Matches
Fenner's: Cambridge U v Lancs
The Parks: Oxford U v Glam
Taunton: Second XI Champions (Somerset) v England Under-19 (Four days)

Friday 21 April

The Parks: Combined Us v Northants (One day)

Sunday 23 April

Benson and Hedges Cup
Derby: Derbys v Northants
Stockton: Durham v Leics
Chelmsford: Essex v Glam
Bristol: Glos v Combined Us
Lord's: Middx v Hants
Leek: Minor Cos v Lancs
Trent Bridge: Notts v Warwicks
Taunton: Somerset v Sussex
The Oval: Surrey v Ireland
Worcester: Worcs v Scotland

Tuesday 25 April

Benson and Hedges Cup
Chelmsford: Essex v Middx
Cardiff: Glam v Combined Us
Southampton: Hants v Glos
Canterbury: Kent v Surrey
Old Trafford: Lancs v Leics
Leek: Minor Cos v Notts
Glasgow (Titwood): Scotland v Derbys
Hove: Sussex v Ireland
Edgbaston: Warwicks v Durham
Headingley: Yorks v Worcs

Thursday 27 April

Britannic Assurance Championship
*Derby: Derbys v Sussex
*Stockton: Durham v Hants
*Chelmsford: Essex v Leics
*Canterbury: Kent v Northants
*Taunton: Somerset v Glam
*The Oval: Surrey v Glos
*Edgbaston: Warwicks v Middx
Other Matches
Fenner's: Cambridge U v Notts
The Parks: Oxford U v Worcs
Headingley: Yorks v Lancs (Four days)

Sunday 30 April

Headingley: Yorks v Lancs (One day)

Tuesday 2 May

Benson and Hedges Cup
Fenner's: Combined Us v Essex
Stockton: Durham v Notts
Bristol: Glos v Middx
Southampton: Hants v Glam
Canterbury: Kent v Somerset
Leicester: Leics v Minor Cos
Northampton: Northants v Worcs
Glasgow (Hamilton Crescent): Scotland v Yorks
The Oval: Surrey v Sussex
Edgbaston: Warwicks v Lancs

Thursday 4 May

Britannic Assurance Championship
Chelmsford: Essex v Worcs
Cardiff: Glam v Northants
Old Trafford: Lancs v Durham
Leicester: Leics v Yorks
Lord's: Middx v Hants
Trent Bridge: Notts v Derbys
Taunton: Somerset v Glos
Hove: Sussex v Kent
Edgbaston: Warwicks v Surrey

Sunday 7 May

AXA Equity & Law League
Chelmsford: Essex v Worcs
Cardiff: Glam v Northants
Old Trafford: Lancs v Durham
Leicester: Leics v Yorks
Lord's: Middx v Hants
Trent Bridge: Notts v Derbys
Taunton: Somerset v Glos
Hove: Sussex v Kent
Edgbaston: Warwicks v Surrey

Tuesday 9 May

Benson and Hedges Cup
The Parks: Combined Us v Hants
Chelmsford: Essex v Glos
Cardiff: Glam v Middx
Comber (North Down CC): Ireland v Kent
Old Trafford: Lancs v Notts
Leicester: Leics v Warwicks
Jesmond: Minor Cos v Durham
Taunton: Somerset v Surrey
Worcester: Worcs v Derbys
Headingley: Yorks v Northants

Thursday 11 May

Britannic Assurance Championship
Chesterfield: Derbys v Yorks
Swansea: Glam v Sussex
Bristol: Glos v Notts
Canterbury: Kent v Leics
Old Trafford: Lancs v Warwicks
Northampton: Northants v Somerset
The Oval: Surrey v Durham
Worcester: Worcs v Middx
Other Matches
Fenner's: Cambridge U v Essex
The Parks: Oxford U v Hants

Saturday 13 May

Tourist Match
Arundel: Lavinia, Duchess of Norfolk's XI v West Indians (One day)

Sunday 14 May

AXA Equity & Law League
Chesterfield: Derbys v Yorks
Swansea: Glam v Sussex
Bristol: Glos v Notts
Canterbury: Kent v Leics
Old Trafford: Lancs v Warwicks
Northampton: Northants v Somerset
The Oval: Surrey v Durham
Worcester: Worcs v Middx
Tourist Match
Southampton: Hants v West Indians (One day)
Other Match
Fenner's: Cambridge U v Oxford U (One day)

Tuesday 16 May

Benson and Hedges Cup
Chesterfield: Derbys v Yorks
Swansea: Glam v Glos
Southampton: Hants v Essex
Eglinton: Ireland v Somerset
Old Trafford: Lancs v Durham
Lord's: Middx v Combined Us
Northampton: Northants v Scotland
Trent Bridge: Notts v Leics
Hove: Sussex v Kent
Edgbaston: Warwicks v Minor Cos
Tetley Bitter Challenge
Worcester: Worcs v West Indians

Thursday 18 May

Britannic Assurance Championship
Chester-le-Street (Riverside): Durham v Warwicks
Southampton: Hants v Kent
Leicester: Leics v Derbys
Lord's: Middx v Lancs
Northampton: Northants v Surrey
Hove: Sussex v Essex
Bradford: Yorks v Glam
Other Match
The Parks: Oxford U v Notts

Friday 19 May

Tetley Bitter Challenge
*Taunton: Somerset v West Indians

Sunday 21 May

AXA Equity & Law League
Chester-le-Street (Riverside): Durham v Warwicks
Southampton: Hants v Kent
Leicester: Leics v Derbys
Lord's: Middx v Lancs
Northampton: Northants v Surrey
Hove: Sussex v Essex
Headingley: Yorks v Glam

Wednesday 24 May

TEXACO TROPHY
Trent Bridge: ENGLAND v WEST INDIES
(First Limited-over International)
Britannic Assurance Championship
Tunbridge Wells: Kent v Glam

Thursday 25 May

Britannic Assurance Championship
Chelmsford: Essex v Middx
Gloucester: Glos v Worcs
Portsmouth: Hants v Sussex
Liverpool: Lancs v Notts
Leicester: Leics v Durham
Edgbaston: Warwicks v Somerset
Sheffield: Yorks v Northants
Other Match
The Parks: Oxford U v Derbys

Friday 26 May

TEXACO TROPHY
The Oval: ENGLAND v WEST INDIES
(Second Limited-over International)

Sunday 28 May

TEXACO TROPHY
Lord's: ENGLAND v WEST INDIES
(Third Limited-over International)
AXA Equity & Law League
Chelmsford: Essex v Middx
Gloucester: Glos v Worcs
Portsmouth: Hants v Sussex
Tunbridge Wells: Kent v Glam
Old Trafford: Lancs v Notts
Leicester: Leics v Durham
Edgbaston: Warwicks v Somerset
Sheffield: Yorks v Northants

Tuesday 30 May

Benson and Hedges Cup
Quarter-Finals
Tetley Bitter Challenge
†Leicester or Old Trafford: Leics or Lancs v West Indians
†Warwicks to play West Indians if both Leics and Lancs involved in B&H Quarter-Finals

Thursday 1 June

Britannic Assurance Championship
Chester-le-Street (Riverside): Durham v Kent
Cardiff: Glam v Hants
Lord's: Middx v Derbys
Trent Bridge: Notts v Essex
Taunton: Somerset v Yorks
Hove: Sussex v Glos
Worcester: Worcs v Surrey

Friday 2 June

#The Parks: Oxford U v Leics
#Rest day on Sunday 4 June

Saturday 3 June

Tetley Bitter Challenge
*Northampton: Northants v West Indians

Sunday 4 June

AXA Equity & Law League
Chester-le-Street (Riverside): Durham v Kent
Cardiff: Glam v Hants
Lord's: Middx v Derbys
Trent Bridge: Notts v Essex
Taunton: Somerset v Yorks
Hove: Sussex v Glos
Worcester: Worcs v Surrey

Wednesday 7 June

Britannic Assurance Championship
Basingstoke: Hants v Leics

Thursday 8 June

FIRST CORNHILL INSURANCE TEST MATCH
***Headingley: ENGLAND v WEST INDIES**
Britannic Assurance Championship
Derby: Derbys v Northants
Chelmsford: Essex v Durham
Canterbury: Kent v Glos
Old Trafford: Lancs v Glam
Trent Bridge: Notts v Worcs
The Oval: Surrey v Somerset
Edgbaston: Warwicks v Sussex

Friday 9 June

*Fenner's: Cambridge U v Middx

Sunday 11 June

AXA Equity & Law League
Derby: Derbys v Northants
Chelmsford: Essex v Durham
Basingstoke: Hants v Leics
Canterbury: Kent v Glos
Old Trafford: Lancs v Glam
Trent Bridge: Notts v Worcs
The Oval: Surrey v Somerset
Edgbaston: Warwicks v Sussex

Tuesday 13 June

Benson and Hedges Cup
Semi-Finals

Thursday 15 June

Britannic Assurance Championship
Derby: Derbys v Somerset
Colwyn Bay: Glam v Middx
Bristol: Glos v Hants
Leicester: Leics v Notts
Luton: Northants v Essex
Horsham: Sussex v Surrey
Worcester: Worcs v Lancs
Headingley: Yorks v Kent
Tourist Match
Edinburgh: Scotland v West Indians (One day)

Friday 16 June

*Fenner's: Cambridge U v Warwicks

Saturday 17 June

Tetley Bitter Challenge
*Chester-le-Street (Riverside): Durham v West Indians

Sunday 18 June

AXA Equity & Law League
Derby: Derbys v Somerset
Colwyn Bay: Glam v Middx
Bristol: Glos v Hants
Leicester: Leics v Notts
Luton: Northants v Essex
Horsham: Sussex v Surrey
Worcester: Worcs v Lancs
Headingley: Yorks v Kent

Tuesday 20 June

The Parks: Oxford U v Middx

Thursday 22 June

SECOND CORNHILL INSURANCE TEST MATCH
***Lord's: ENGLAND v WEST INDIES**
Britannic Assurance Championship
Chester-le-Street (Riverside): Durham v Derbys
Southampton: Hants v Worcs
Old Trafford: Lancs v Essex
Northampton: Northants v Leics
Trent Bridge: Notts v Kent
Bath: Somerset v Sussex
The Oval: Surrey v Glam
Edgbaston: Warwicks v Yorks

Friday 23 June

*Bristol: Glos v Oxford U

Sunday 25 June

AXA Equity & Law League
Chester-le-Street (Riverside): Durham v Derbys
Southampton: Hants v Worcs
Old Trafford: Lancs v Essex
Northampton: Northants v Leics
Trent Bridge: Notts v Kent
Bath: Somerset v Sussex
The Oval: Surrey v Glam
Edgbaston: Warwicks v Yorks

Tuesday 27 June

NatWest Trophy
First Round
March: Cambs v Derbys
Chester (Boughton Hall): Cheshire v Essex
St Austell: Cornwall v Middx
Chester-le-Street (Riverside): Durham v Herefords
Cardiff: Glam v Dorset
Bristol: Glos v Suffolk
Old Trafford: Lancs v Norfolk
Leicester: Leics v Hants
Northampton: Northants v Holland
Trent Bridge: Notts v Scotland
Stone: Staffs v Kent
The Oval: Surrey v Berks
Hove: Sussex v Devon
Edgbaston: Warwicks v Somerset

Worcester: Worcs v Cumberland
Headingley: Yorks v Ireland

Wednesday 28 June

Tourist Match
The Parks: Combined Us v West Indians (Three days)

Thursday 29 June

Britannic Assurance Championship
Derby: Derbys v Hants
Ilford: Essex v Warwicks
Swansea: Glam v Durham
Lord's: Middx v Surrey
Trent Bridge: Notts v Somerset
Worcester: Worcs v Leics
Middlesbrough: Yorks v Glos

Saturday 1 July

Tetley Bitter Challenge
*Hove: Sussex v West Indians
Other Matches
Canterbury: England Under-19 v South Africa Under-19 (First Youth Limited-over International)
*Folkestone: Kent v Cambridge U

Sunday 2 July

AXA Equity & Law League
Derby: Derbys v Hants
Ilford: Essex v Warwicks
Swansea: Glam v Durham
Lord's: Middx v Surrey
Trent Bridge: Notts v Somerset
Worcester: Worcs v Leics
Middlesbrough: Yorks v Glos

Monday 3 July

Tourist Match
England Amateur XI v Australia 'A' (One day)

Tuesday 4 July

Chelmsford: England Under-19 v South Africa Under-19 (Second Youth Limited-over International)

Wednesday 5 July

Britannic Assurance Championship
Maidstone: Kent v Derbys

Tourist Match
Taunton: Somerset v Australia 'A' (Three days)
Other Match
Lord's: Oxford U v Cambridge U (Varsity Match) (Three days)

Thursday 6 July

THIRD CORNHILL INSURANCE TEST MATCH
†Edgbaston: ENGLAND v WEST INDIES
†Rest day on Sunday 9 July
Britannic Assurance Championship
Darlington: Durham v Worcs
Bristol: Glos v Middx
Southampton: Hants v Yorks
Old Trafford: Lancs v Northants
Leicester: Leics v Warwicks
The Oval: Surrey v Essex
Arundel: Sussex v Notts

Saturday 8 July

Tourist Match
*Neath: Glam v Australia 'A' (Three days)

Sunday 9 July

AXA Equity & Law League
Darlington: Durham v Worcs
Bristol: Glos v Middx
Southampton: Hants v Yorks
Maidstone: Kent v Derbys
Old Trafford: Lancs v Northants
Leicester: Leics v Warwicks
The Oval: Surrey v Essex
Arundel: Sussex v Notts

Wednesday 12 July

NatWest Trophy
Second Round
Chester (Boughton Hall) or Chelmsford: Cheshire or Essex v Yorks or Ireland
Chester-le-Street (Riverside) or Brockhampton: Durham or Herefords v Glos or Suffolk
Old Trafford or Lakenham: Lancs or Norfolk v Worcs or Cumberland
Leicester or Southampton: Leics or Hants v Glam or Dorset
Trent Bridge or Forfar (Strathmore

CC): Notts or Scotland v Northants or Holland
The Oval or Reading: Surrey or Berks v Cornwall or Middx
Hove or Torquay: Sussex or Devon v Cambs or Derbys
Edgbaston or Taunton: Warwicks or Somerset v Staffs or Kent
Tourist Match
Reading: Minor Cos v Australia 'A' (One day)

Thursday 13 July

Tourist Match
Reading: Minor Cos v West Indians (One day)

Saturday 15 July

#Lord's: *Benson and Hedges Cup Final*
Tourist Match
Dublin (Castle Ave): Ireland v West Indians (One day)
#Reserve days Sunday 16 and Monday 17 July

Sunday 16 July

†*AXA Equity & Law League*
Derby: Derbys v Sussex
Chester-le-Street (Riverside): Durham v Hants
Chelmsford: Essex v Leics
Canterbury: Kent v Northants
Taunton: Somerset v Glam
The Oval: Surrey v Glos
Edgbaston: Warwicks v Middx
†Matches involving B&H Cup Finalists to be played on Tuesday 18 July

Monday 17 July

Harrogate: Costcutter Cup (Three days)

Tuesday 18 July

Tourist Match
Headingley: Yorks v Australia 'A' (One day)

Wednesday 19 July

Tetley Bitter Challenge
Canterbury: Kent v West Indians
Tourist Match
Chesterfield: Derbys v Australia 'A' (Three days)

Thursday 20 July

Britannic Assurance Championship
Southend: Essex v Somerset
Cardiff: Glam v Warwicks
Cheltenham: Glos v Lancs
Northampton: Northants v Hants
Guildford: Surrey v Notts
Hove: Sussex v Leics
Harrogate: Yorks v Durham
Other Match
Taunton (TBC): England Under-19 v South Africa Under-19 (First Youth Test Match) (Four days)

Saturday 22 July

Tetley Bitter Challenge
*Lord's: Middx v West Indians
Tourist Match
*Worcester: Worcs v Australia 'A' (Three days)

Sunday 23 July

AXA Equity & Law League
Southend: Essex v Somerset
Cardiff: Glam v Warwicks
Cheltenham: Glos v Lancs
Northampton: Northants v Hants
Guildford: Surrey v Notts
Hove: Sussex v Leics
Headingley: Yorks v Durham

Wednesday 26 July

Tourist Match
Cheltenham: Glos v Australia 'A' (One day)

Thursday 27 July

FOURTH CORNHILL INSURANCE TEST MATCH
***Old Trafford: ENGLAND v WEST INDIES**
Britannic Assurance Championship
Derby: Derbys v Glam
Cheltenham: Glos v Essex
Leicester: Leics v Surrey
Lord's: Middx v Sussex
Trent Bridge: Notts v Yorks
Taunton: Somerset v Lancs

Edgbaston: Warwicks v Northants
Worcester: Worcs v Kent

Friday 28 July

Tourist Match
*Southampton: Hants v Australia 'A' (Four days)

Sunday 30 July

AXA Equity & Law League
Derby: Derbys v Glam
Cheltenham: Glos v Essex
Leicester: Leics v Surrey
Lord's: Middx v Sussex
Cleethorpes: Notts v Yorks
Taunton: Somerset v Lancs
Edgbaston: Warwicks v Northants
Worcester: Worcs v Kent

Tuesday 1 August

NatWest Trophy
Quarter-Finals

Wednesday 2 August

Tetley Bitter Challenge
†Derby or Edgbaston: Derbys or Warwicks v West Indians
†Somerset to play West Indians if both Derbys and Warwicks involved in NWT Quarter-Finals

Thursday 3 August

Britannic Assurance Championship
Colchester: Essex v Hants
Canterbury: Kent v Surrey
Lytham: Lancs v Sussex
Lord's: Middx v Notts
Northampton: Northants v Durham
Scarborough: Yorks v Worcs
Tourist Match
*Leicester: Leics v Australia 'A' (Four days)
Other Match
Worcester: England Under-19 v South Africa Under-19 (Second Youth Test Match) (Four days)

Saturday 5 August

Tetley Bitter Challenge
*Bristol: Glos v West Indians

Sunday 6 August

AXA Equity & Law League
Colchester: Essex v Hants
Canterbury: Kent v Surrey
Old Trafford: Lancs v Sussex
Lord's: Middx v Notts
Northampton: Northants v Durham
Scarborough: Yorks v Worcs

Tuesday 8 August

Tourist Match
The Oval: Surrey v Australia 'A' (One day)

Thursday 10 August

FIFTH CORNHILL INSURANCE TEST MATCH
***Trent Bridge: ENGLAND v WEST INDIES**
Britannic Assurance Championship
Chester-le-Street (Riverside): Durham v Middx
Swansea: Glam v Essex
Southampton: Hants v Warwicks
Leicester: Leics v Lancs
Northampton: Northants v Glos
Taunton: Somerset v Kent
The Oval: Surrey v Yorks
Kidderminster: Worcs v Derbys
Other Match
*Headingley: England Under-19 v South Africa Under-19 (Third Youth Test Match) (Four days)

Friday 11 August

Tourist Match
*Hove: Sussex v Australia 'A' (Four days)

Saturday 12 August

*Dublin (Rathmines): Ireland v Scotland (Three days)

Sunday 13 August

AXA Equity & Law League
Chester-le-Street (Riverside): Durham v Middx
Pontypridd: Glam v Essex
Southampton: Hants v Warwicks
Leicester: Leics v Lancs
Northampton: Northants v Glos

Taunton: Somerset v Kent
The Oval: Surrey v Yorks
Worcester: Worcs v Derbys

Tuesday 15 August

NatWest Trophy
Semi-Finals

Wednesday 16 August

Tetley Bitter Challenge
†Pontypridd or Southampton: Glam or Hants v West Indians
†Leics to play West Indians if both Glam and Hants involved in NWT Semi-Finals

Thursday 17 August

Britannic Assurance Championship
Chester-le-Street (Riverside): Durham v Somerset
Bristol: Glos v Derbys
Old Trafford: Lancs v Yorks
Lord's: Middx v Kent
Trent Bridge: Notts v Warwicks
Eastbourne: Sussex v Worcs
Tourist Match
*Edgbaston: TCCB XI v Australia 'A' (Four days)

Thursday 17 or Friday 18 August

Bain Hogg Trophy
Semi-Finals

Saturday 19 August

Tetley Bitter Challenge
*Chelmsford: Essex v West Indians

Sunday 20 August

AXA Equity & Law League
Chester-le-Street (Riverside): Durham v Somerset
Bristol: Glos v Derbys
Old Trafford: Lancs v Yorks
Lord's: Middx v Kent
Trent Bridge: Notts v Warwicks
Eastbourne: Sussex v Worcs

Wednesday 23 August

Britannic Assurance Championship
Abergavenny: Glam v Glos

Thursday 24 August

SIXTH CORNHILL INSURANCE TEST MATCH
***The Oval: ENGLAND v WEST INDIES**
Britannic Assurance Championship
Derby: Derbys v Surrey
Hartlepool: Durham v Sussex
Portsmouth: Hants v Lancs
Canterbury: Kent v Essex
Northampton: Northants v Notts
Weston-super-Mare: Somerset v Leics
Edgbaston: Warwicks v Worcs
Headingley: Yorks v Middx

Sunday 27 August

AXA Equity & Law League
Derby: Derbys v Surrey
Hartlepool: Durham v Sussex
Ebbw Vale: Glam v Glos
Portsmouth: Hants v Lancs
Canterbury: Kent v Essex
Northampton: Northants v Notts
Weston-super-Mare: Somerset v Leics
Worcester: Worcs v Warwicks
Headingley: Yorks v Middx

Tuesday 29 August

Britannic Assurance Championship
Chelmsford: Essex v Derbys
Leicester: Leics v Glam
Uxbridge: Middx v Northants
Trent Bridge: Notts v Hants
The Oval: Surrey v Lancs
Edgbaston: Warwicks v Glos
Worcester: Worcs v Somerset

Wednesday 30 August

Scarborough: Yorks v West Indians (Tesco International) (Three days)

Saturday 2 September

#Lord's: *NatWest Trophy Final*
Other Match
Scarborough: Yorks v Durham (Northern Electric Trophy) (One day)
#Reserve days Sunday 3 and Monday 4 September

Sunday 3 September

†*AXA Equity & Law League*
Chelmsford: Essex v Derbys
Leicester: Leics v Glam
Uxbridge: Middx v Northants
Trent Bridge: Notts v Hants
The Oval: Surrey v Lancs
Edgbaston: Warwicks v Glos
Worcester: Worcs v Somerset
Other Match
Scarborough: President's XI v West Indians
(McCain Challenge) (One day)
†Matches involving NWT Finalists to be played on Tuesday 5 September

Monday 4 September

Bain Hogg Trophy Final (One day)
Scarborough: Tetley Bitter Festival Trophy (Three days)

Wednesday 6 September

The Oval: Surrey v New South Wales (Three days)

Thursday 7 September

Britannic Assurance Championship
Cardiff: Glam v Notts
Bristol: Glos v Durham
Southampton: Hants v Somerset
Old Trafford: Lancs v Kent
Uxbridge: Middx v Leics
Northampton: Northants v Worcs
Edgbaston: Warwicks v Derbys
Scarborough: Yorks v Sussex

Sunday 10 September

AXA Equity & Law League
Cardiff: Glam v Notts
Bristol: Glos v Durham
Southampton: Hants v Somerset
Old Trafford: Lancs v Kent
Uxbridge: Middx v Leics
Northampton: Northants v Worcs
Edgbaston: Warwicks v Derbys
Scarborough: Yorks v Sussex
Other Match
The Oval: Surrey v New South Wales (One day)

Thursday 14 September

Britannic Assurance Championship
Derby: Derbys v Lancs
Chester-le-Street (Riverside): Durham v Notts
Chelmsford: Essex v Yorks
Canterbury: Kent v Warwicks
Leicester: Leics v Glos
Taunton: Somerset v Middx
The Oval: Surrey v Hants
Hove: Sussex v Northants
Worcester: Worcs v Glam

Sunday 17 September

AXA Equity & Law League
Derby: Derbys v Lancs
Chester-le-Street (Riverside): Durham v Notts
Chelmsford: Essex v Yorks
Canterbury: Kent v Warwicks
Leicester: Leics v Glos
Taunton: Somerset v Middx
The Oval: Surrey v Hants
Hove: Sussex v Northants
Worcester: Worcs v Glam

SECOND XI FIXTURES 1995

Abbreviations: (SEC) Second Eleven Championship (Three days)
(BH) Bain Hogg Trophy (One day)

APRIL

Mon 17	(SEC)	Leicester	Leics v Glos
Tue 18	(SEC)	Derby	Derbys v Lancs
	(SEC)	Uxbridge	Middx v Glam
		Taunton	Somerset v England Under-19 (Four days)
Fri 21	(BH)	Derby	Derbys v Lancs
Sun 23	(SEC)	Taunton (King's College)	Somerset v Sussex
Mon 24	(SEC)	Ramsbottom	Lancs v Northants
	(SEC)	Leicester	Leics v Kent
	(SEC)	Kidderminster	Worcs v Warwicks

MAY

Mon 1	(SEC)	Chester-le-Street CC	Durham v Glam
	(SEC)	Chelmsford	Essex v Derbys
	(SEC)	Oakham	Leics v Yorks
	(SEC)	North Perrott	Somerset v Glos
	(SEC)	Cheam	Surrey v Middx
	(SEC)	Hove	Sussex v Lancs
	(SEC)	Knowle & Dorridge	Warwicks v Northants
Thu 4	(BH)	The Oval	Surrey v Essex
Fri 5	(BH)	Southampton	Hants v Somerset
	(BH)	Canterbury	Kent v MCC YCs
	(BH)	Worcester	Worcs v Glos
Mon 8	(SEC)	Derby	Derbys v Durham
	(SEC)	Ammanford	Glam v Kent
	(SEC)	Bristol	Glos v Northants
	(SEC)	Uxbridge	Middx v Lancs
	(SEC)	The Oval	Surrey v Essex
	(SEC)	Bingley	Yorks v Warwicks
		Horsham	Sussex v England Under-19 (Three days)
Wed 10	(SEC)	Trent Bridge	Notts v Somerset
Thu 11	(BH)	Derby	Derbys v Durham
	(BH)	Leicester	Leics v Middx
Fri 12	(BH)	Hove	Sussex v Kent
Mon 15	(SEC)	Chelmsford	Essex v Sussex
	(SEC)	Cheltenham (Dowty Arle Court)	Glos v Surrey
	(SEC)	Finchampstead	Hants v Notts
	(SEC)	Uxbridge	Middx v Leics
	(SEC)	Taunton	Somerset v Glam
	(SEC)	Coventry & N Warwicks	Warwicks v Durham
	(SEC)	Harrogate	Yorks v Derbys
Thu 18	(BH)	Chelmsford	Essex v Sussex
	(BH)	Uxbridge	Middx v Leics
	(BH)	Headingley	Yorks v Derbys
Fri 19	(BH)	Canterbury	Kent v Surrey
	(BH)	Old Trafford	Lancs v Derbys
	(BH)	Edgbaston	Warwicks v Northants

Mon 22	(SEC)	Felling	Durham v Surrey
	(SEC)	Swansea	Glam v Yorks
	(SEC)	Bristol	Glos v Essex
	(SEC)	Canterbury	Kent v Sussex
	(SEC)	Harrow	Middx v Northants
	(SEC)	Taunton	Somerset v Lancs
	(SEC)	Solihull CC	Warwicks v Hants
	(SEC)	Worcester	Worcs v Leics
Thu 25	(BH)	Canterbury	Kent v Sussex
	(BH)	Walsall	Minor Cos v Leics
	(BH)	Taunton	Somerset v Hants
Fri 26	(BH)	Durham City CC	Durham v Lancs
	(BH)	Walsall	Minor Cos v Warwicks
	(BH)	Worcester	Worcs v Hants
	(BH)	Castleford	Yorks v Notts
Mon 29	(SEC)	Derby	Derbys v Sussex
	(SEC)	Shildon CC	Durham v Glos
	(SEC)	Pontardulais	Glam v Worcs
	(SEC)	Maidstone	Kent v Somerset
	(SEC)	Barwell	Leics v Notts
	(SEC)	Oundle School	Northants v Yorks
Tue 30	(SEC)	Bournemouth Sports Club	Hants v Essex
JUNE			
Thu 1	(BH)	Chesterfield	Derbys v Yorks
Fri 2	(BH)	Chelmsford	Essex v Kent
	(BH)	Bristol	Glos v Glam
	(BH)	Old Trafford	Lancs v Yorks
	(BH)	Slough	MCC YCs v Sussex
	(BH)	Uxbridge	Middx v Northants
Mon 5	(SEC)	Southend	Essex v Middx
	(SEC)	Bristol	Glos v Notts
	(SEC)	Southampton	Hants v Kent
	(SEC)	Old Trafford	Lancs v Durham
	(SEC)	Old Northamptonians	Northants v Somerset
	(SEC)	Middleton Sports Club	Sussex v Warwicks
	(SEC)	Old Hill	Worcs v Derbys
Thu 8	(BH)	Lancaster	Lancs v Durham
	(BH)	Southgate	MCC YCs v Surrey
	(BH)	Taunton	Somerset v Worcs
Fri 9	(BH)	Panteg	Glam v Worcs
	(BH)	Slough	MCC YCs v Essex
	(BH)	Southgate	Middx v Minor Cos
	(BH)	Northampton	Northants v Warwicks
	(BH)	Worksop College	Notts v Durham
Mon 12	(SEC)	Rocester (Abbotsholme School)	Derbys v Middx
	(SEC)	Darlington CC	Durham v Hants
	(SEC)	Melton Mowbray	Leics v Glam
	(SEC)	Oundle School	Northants v Worcs
	(SEC)	Collingham	Notts v Kent
	(SEC)	Oxted	Surrey v Warwicks
	(SEC)	York CC	Yorks v Lancs
Thu 15	(BH)	Bishop Auckland	Durham v Derbys
	(BH)	Haywards Heath	Sussex v MCC YCs
	(BH)	Bradford (Park Ave)	Yorks v Lancs
Fri 16	(BH)	Wickford	Essex v Surrey

	(BH)	Old Trafford	Lancs v Notts
Mon 19	(SEC)	Chelmsford	Essex v Durham
	(SEC)	Swansea	Glam v Glos
	(SEC)	Sittingbourne (Gore Court)	Kent v Warwicks
	(SEC)	Hinckley	Leics v Northants
	(SEC)	Worksop CC	Notts v Lancs
	(SEC)	Cheam	Surrey v Yorks
	(SEC)	Hove	Sussex v Hants
	(SEC)	Kidderminster	Worcs v Somerset
Thu 22	(BH)	Leicester	Leics v Northants
	(BH)	Farnsfield	Notts v Lancs
	(BH)	Hove	Sussex v Essex
Fri 23	(BH)	Stratford-upon-Avon	Warwicks v Minor Cos
	(BH)	Bromsgrove School	Worcs v Glam
Mon 26	(SEC)	Rocester (Abbotsholme School)	Derbys v Leics
	(SEC)	South Shields CC	Durham v Notts
	(SEC)	Ilford	Essex v Warwicks
	(SEC)	Ashford	Kent v Worcs
	(SEC)	Preston	Lancs v Glam
	(SEC)	Southgate	Middx v Sussex
	(SEC)	Cheam	Surrey v Somerset
		Bradford (Park Ave)	Yorks v England Under-19 (Three days)
Tue 27	(BH)	Southampton	Hants v Glos
Wed 28	(SEC)	Southampton	Hants v Glos
Thu 29	(BH)	Philadelphia CC	Durham v Notts
	(BH)	Marlow	Minor Cos v Middx
Fri 30	(BH)	Leicester	Leics v Warwicks
	(BH)	Slough	MCC YCs v Kent
	(BH)	Old Northamptonians	Northants v Minor Cos
	(BH)	Glastonbury	Somerset v Glam

JULY

Mon 3	(SEC)	Chester-le-Street (Riverside)	Durham v Kent
	(SEC)	Pontymister	Glam v Notts
	(SEC)	Bristol	Glos v Yorks
	(SEC)	Portsmouth	Hants v Worcs
	(SEC)	Rossall School (Fleetwood)	Lancs v Leics
	(SEC)	Northampton	Northants v Essex
	(SEC)	Studley CC	Warwicks v Middx
Tue 4	(SEC)	Derby	Derbys v Somerset
	(SEC)	Hove	Sussex v Surrey
Thu 6	(BH)	Bournemouth Sports Club	Hants v Worcs
	(BH)	Aston Unity CC	Warwicks v Middx
Fri 7	(BH)	Chelmsford	Essex v MCC YCs
	(BH)	Tring	Northants v Middx
	(BH)	Caythorpe CC	Notts v Derbys
	(BH)	Hove	Sussex v Surrey
Mon 10	(SEC)	Usk	Glam v Hants
	(SEC)	Canterbury	Kent v Essex
	(SEC)	Kibworth	Leics v Surrey
	(SEC)	Harrow	Middx v Glos
	(SEC)	Northampton	Northants v Notts
	(SEC)	Horsham	Sussex v Durham
	(SEC)	Worcester	Worcs v Lancs
Tue 11	(SEC)	Elland	Yorks v Somerset

Thu 13	(BH)	Swansea	Glam v Hants
	(BH)	Canterbury	Kent v Essex
	(BH)	Northampton	Northants v Leics
Fri 14	(BH)	Bristol	Glos v Somerset
	(BH)	Harrow	Middx v Warwicks
Mon 17	(SEC)	Old Trafford	Lancs v Hants
	(SEC)	Wellingborough School	Northants v Kent
	(SEC)	Trent Bridge	Notts v Yorks
	(SEC)	Taunton	Somerset v Leics
	(SEC)	The Oval	Surrey v Derbys
	(SEC)	Nuneaton (Griff & Coton)	Warwicks v Glam
	(SEC)	Worcester	Worcs v Middx
Thu 20	(BH)	Bristol	Glos v Hants
	(BH)	Barwell	Leics v Minor Cos
	(BH)	Welbeck CC	Notts v Yorks
	(BH)	Halesowen	Worcs v Somerset
Fri 21	(BH)	Belper	Derbys v Notts
	(BH)	Southampton	Hants v Glam
	(BH)	Sleaford	Minor Cos v Northants
	(BH)	Weston-super-Mare	Somerset v Glos
	(BH)	The Oval	Surrey v Sussex
Mon 24	(SEC)	Chelmsford	Essex v Lancs
	(SEC)	Southgate	Middx v Hants
	(SEC)	Bedford School	Northants v Derbys
	(SEC)	Southwell CC	Notts v Sussex
	(SEC)	The Oval	Surrey v Kent
	(SEC)	Moseley CC	Warwicks v Leics
	(SEC)	Marske-by-Sea	Yorks v Durham
Wed 26	(BH)	Bridgend	Glam v Glos
Thu 27	(BH)	Bristol	Glos v Worcs
	(BH)	The Oval	Surrey v Kent
	(BH)	Old Edwardians CC	Warwicks v Leics
	(BH)	Marske-by-Sea	Yorks v Durham
Fri 28	(BH)	Boldon CC	Durham v Yorks
	(BH)	Swansea	Glam v Somerset
	(BH)	The Oval	Surrey v MCC YCs
Mon 31	(SEC)	Maidstone	Kent v Derbys
	(SEC)	Crosby (Northern)	Lancs v Glos
	(SEC)	Lensbury CC	Middx v Durham
	(SEC)	Nottingham High School	Notts v Essex
	(SEC)	Clevedon	Somerset v Hants
	(SEC)	Bradford (Park Ave)	Yorks v Worcs

AUGUST

Mon 7	(SEC)	Derby	Derbys v Glam
	(SEC)	Bournemouth Sports Club	Hants v Northants
	(SEC)	Old Trafford	Lancs v Kent
	(SEC)	Worksop College	Notts v Surrey
	(SEC)	Taunton	Somerset v Warwicks
	(SEC)	Hove	Sussex v Glos
	(SEC)	Worcester	Worcs v Essex
Mon 14	(SEC)	Chesterfield	Derbys v Hants
	(SEC)	Seaton Carew	Durham v Northants
	(SEC)	Colchester	Essex v Glam
	(SEC)	Gloucester (King's School)	Glos v Kent
Mon 14	(SEC)	Oxted	Surrey v Worcs
	(SEC)	Middleton	Sussex v Leics

	(SEC)	Walmley CC	Warwicks v Notts
	(SEC)	Sheffield (Abbeydale Park)	Yorks v Middx
Thu 17/ Fri 18	(BH)		Bain Hogg Trophy Semi-Finals
Mon 21	(SEC)	Cardiff	Glam v Northants
	(SEC)	Gloucester (Tuffley Park)	Glos v Derbys
	(SEC)	Southampton	Hants v Surrey
	(SEC)	Uxbridge (RAF Vine Lane)	Middx v Notts
	(SEC)	Taunton	Somerset v Durham
	(SEC)	Solihull CC	Warwicks v Lancs
	(SEC)	Worcester	Worcs v Sussex
	(SEC)	Todmorden	Yorks v Essex
Thu 24			TCCB 2nd XI Regional Challenge Semi-Finals (Four days)
		Leicester	Central v The North
		Chelmsford	South East v South West
Mon 28	(SEC)	Chester-le-Street (Riverside)	Durham v Leics
	(SEC)	Bristol	Glos v Worcs
	(SEC)	Folkestone	Kent v Middx
Tue 29	(SEC)	Derby	Derbys v Warwicks
	(SEC)	Coggeshall	Essex v Somerset
	(SEC)	Southampton	Hants v Yorks
	(SEC)	Northampton	Northants v Surrey
	(SEC)	Hove	Sussex v Glam
SEPTEMBER			
Mon 4	(BH)		Bain Hogg Trophy Final (Reserve day Tuesday 5th)
Wed 6	(SEC)	Chelmsford	Essex v Leics
	(SEC)	Pontypridd	Glam v Surrey
	(SEC)	Eltham (British Gas plc)	Kent v Yorks
	(SEC)	Trent Bridge	Notts v Derbys
	(SEC)	Hove	Sussex v Northants
	(SEC)	Stratford-upon-Avon	Warwicks v Glos
	(SEC)	Worcester	Worcs v Durham
Mon 11	(SEC)	Hinckley	Leics v Hants
	(SEC)	Trent Bridge	Notts v Worcs
	(SEC)	Taunton	Somerset v Middx
	(SEC)	Headingley	Yorks v Sussex
Tue 12	(SEC)	Old Trafford	Lancs v Surrey
Thu 14		Edgbaston	TCCB Second XI Regional Challenge Final (Four days)

MINOR COUNTIES FIXTURES 1995

APRIL		*Benson & Hedges Cup*
Sun 23	Leek	Minor Counties v Lancashire
Tue 25	Leek	Minor Counties v Nottinghamshire
		Friendly Match
Sun 30	Arundel	Lavinia, Duchess of Norfolk's XI v Minor Counties
MAY		*Benson & Hedges Cup*
Tue 2	Leicester	Leicestershire v Minor Counties
Tue 9	Jesmond	Minor Counties v Durham

Tue 16	Edgbaston	Warwickshire v Minor Counties
		MCC Trophy, Preliminary Round
Sun 21	Shrewsbury	Shropshire v Dorset
	Falmouth	Cornwall v Devon
	Warrington	Cheshire v Staffordshire
	Aylesbury	Buckinghamshire v Bedfordshire
		Bain Hogg Trophy
Thu 25	Walsall	Minor Counties v Leicestershire 2nd XI
Fri 26	Walsall	Minor Counties v Warwickshire 2nd XI
		Championship
Sun 28	Kidmore End	(W) Berkshire v Shropshire
	Sleaford	(E) Lincolnshire v Hertfordshire
	Colwyn Bay	(W) Wales v Herefordshire
	Swindon	(W) Wiltshire v Devon
Tue 30	Thame CC	(W) Oxfordshire v Shropshire
	Mildenhall	(E) Suffolk v Hertfordshire
JUNE		*Friendly Match*
Thu 1	(tba)	NAYC v Minor Counties
		Championship
Sun 4	Exmouth	(W) Devon v Cornwall
	Hitchin	(E) Hertfordshire v Norfolk
	Jesmond	(E) Northumberland v Lincolnshire
	Challow & Childrey	(W) Oxfordshire v Wiltshire
	Pontardulais	(W) Wales v Cheshire
Tue 6	High Wycombe	(E) Buckinghamshire v Staffordshire
	Wisbech	(E) Cambridgeshire v Norfolk
	Leominster (Dales)	(W) Herefordshire v Cheshire
		Bain Hogg Trophy
Fri 9	Southgate	Middlesex 2nd XI v Minor Counties
		MCC Trophy, First Round
Sun 11	Wrekin College or Sherborne School	Shropshire or Dorset v Cornwall or Devon
	Warrington or Walsall	Cheshire or Staffordshire v Buckinghamshire or Bedfordshire
	Thame CC	Oxfordshire v Berkshire
	Trowbridge	Wiltshire v Cambridgeshire
	Northop Hall	Wales v Cumberland
	Shenley Park	Hertfordshire v Lincolnshire
	Brockhampton	Herefordshire v Norfolk
	Framlingham College	Suffolk v Northumberland
		Championship
Mon 12	Shifnal	(W) Shropshire v Cornwall
Wed 14	Toft	(W) Cheshire v Cornwall
	Leek	(E) Staffordshire v Cambridgeshire
Sun 18	Bedford Town	(E) Bedfordshire v Suffolk
	Millom	(E) Cumberland v Lincolnshire
	Colwall CC	(W) Herefordshire v Berkshire
	Radlett	(E) Hertfordshire v Northumberland
	Pressed Steel	(W) Oxfordshire v Dorset
	Marchwiel	(W) Wales v Wiltshire
Tue 20	Beaconsfield	(E) Buckinghamshire v Northumberland
Wed 21	Ransome's	(E) Suffolk v Cambridgeshire
		Bain Hogg Trophy
Fri 23	Stratford upon Avon	Warwickshire 2nd XI v Minor Counties
		Championship
Sun 25	Cleethorpes	(E) Lincolnshire v Buckinghamshire

Tue 27		*NatWest Trophy, First Round*
		Bain Hogg Trophy
Thu 29	Marlow	Minor Counties v Middlesex 2nd XI
Fri 30	Old Northamptonians	Northants 2nd XI v Minor Counties
JULY		
Sun 2		*MCC Trophy, Quarter-Finals*
		Championship
Tue 4	Wolverhampton	(E) Staffordshire v Northumberland
Wed 5	Slough	(E) Buckinghamshire v Cambridgeshire
	Weymouth	(W) Dorset v Herefordshire
Sun 9	Falkland CC	(W) Berkshire v Dorset
	Marlow	(E) Buckinghamshire v Cumberland
	Bourne	(E) Lincolnshire v Norfolk
	Wellington	(W) Shropshire v Devon
	Pontypridd	(W) Wales v Oxfordshire
	Marlborough CC	(W) Wiltshire v Herefordshire
Tue 11	Bowdon	(W) Cheshire v Devon
	St Albans	(E) Hertfordshire v Cumberland
		Tourist Matches
Wed 12	Reading	Minor Counties v Australia 'A'
Thu 13	Reading	Minor Counties v West Indians
		Championship
Sun 16	Netherfield	(E) Cumberland v Cambridgeshire
	Dean Park	(W) Dorset v Wales
	Brockhampton	(W) Herefordshire v Oxfordshire
	Jesmond	(E) Northumberland v Bedfordshire
	Shrewsbury	(W) Shropshire v Cheshire
Mon 17	Shenley Park	(E) Hertfordshire v Staffordshire
Tue 18	Barrow	(E) Cumberland v Bedfordshire
	Jesmond	(E) Northumberland v Cambridgeshire
		Bain Hogg Trophy
Thu 20	Barwell CC	Leicestershire 2nd XI v Minor Counties
Fri 21	Sleaford	Minor Counties v Northants 2nd XI
Sun 23		*MCC Trophy, Semi-Finals*
		Championship
Mon 24	Truro	*(W) Cornwall v Berkshire
Tue 25	Lakenham	(E) Norfolk v Cumberland
	Longton	(E) Staffordshire v Lincolnshire
Wed 26	Sidmouth	(W) Devon v Berkshire
Thu 27	Lakenham	(E) Norfolk v Bedfordshire
	Ipswich School	(E) Suffolk v Cumberland
Sun 30	Camborne	(W) Cornwall v Wales
	Sherborne School	(W) Dorset v Devon
	Christ Church	(W) Oxfordshire v Cheshire
	Trowbridge	(W) Wiltshire v Shropshire
Mon 31	Lakenham	(E) Norfolk v Buckinghamshire
	Copdock CC	(E) Suffolk v Staffordshire
AUGUST		
Tue 1	Finchampstead	(W) Berkshire v Cheshire
	Hereford City	(W) Herefordshire v Shropshire
Wed 2	March	(E) Cambridgeshire v Lincolnshire
	Lakenham	(E) Norfolk v Staffordshire
	Bury St Edmunds	(E) Suffolk v Buckinghamshire
Sun 6	Dunstable	(E) Bedfordshire v Buckinghamshire
	Usk	(W) Wales v Berkshire
	Westbury	(W) Wiltshire v Cornwall

Tue 8	Wardown Park	(E) Bedfordshire v Staffordshire
	Dorchester	(W) Dorset v Cornwall
Thu 10	March	(E) Cambridgeshire v Hertfordshire
Sun 13	Reading	(W) Berkshire v Wiltshire
	Oxton	(W) Cheshire v Dorset
	St Austell	(W) Cornwall v Oxfordshire
	Hertford	(E) Hertfordshire v Bedfordshire
	Lincoln Lindum	(E) Lincolnshire v Suffolk
	Jesmond	(E) Northumberland v Norfolk
Mon 14	Brewood	(E) Staffordshire v Cumberland
Tue 15	Plymouth	(W) Devon v Oxfordshire
	Jesmond	(E) Northumberland v Suffolk
	Bridgnorth	(W) Shropshire v Dorset
Sun 20	Southill Park	(E) Bedfordshire v Lincolnshire
	New Brighton	(W) Cheshire v Wiltshire
	Carlisle	(E) Cumberland v Northumberland
	Torquay	(W) Devon v Herefordshire
	Oswestry	(W) Shropshire v Wales
Tue 22	Falmouth	*(W) Cornwall v Herefordshire
Wed 23	Lord's	*MCC Trophy Final*
		Championship
Sun 27	Amersham	(E) Buckinghamshire v Hertfordshire
	Bovey Tracey	(W) Devon v Wales
	Dean Park	(W) Dorset v Wiltshire
	N Runcton	(E) Norfolk v Suffolk
	Banbury CC	(W) Oxfordshire v Berkshire
Wed 30	Saffron Walden	(E) Cambridgeshire v Bedfordshire
SEPTEMBER		
Sun 10	Worcester	*Championship Final (2 days)*

*These matches could be affected by progress in MCC Trophy.

ICC TOURS PROGRAMME

(Full Member Countries)

1995-96

Aug/Sep	Sri Lanka to Pakistan*
Oct/Dec	New Zealand to India
Oct/Jan	England to South Africa
Nov/Dec	Pakistan to Australia*
Nov/Jan	West Indies to Australia
Dec/Jan	Sri Lanka to Australia
Jan	Zimbabwe to New Zealand
Feb/Mar	World Cup in India/Pakistan/ Sri Lanka
Mar/May	New Zealand to West Indies*

1996

May/Jul	India to England
Jun/Sep	Pakistan to England

1996-97

Aug	Australia to Sri Lanka*
Sep/Oct	Australia to India*
Nov/Dec	England to Sri Lanka
Nov/Dec	New Zealand to India
Nov/Feb	West Indies to Australia
Dec/Jan	Pakistan to Australia
Jan/Mar	England to New Zealand
Feb/Mar	Australia to New Zealand
Feb/Apr	India to West Indies

1997

May/Aug	Australia to England

1997-98

Aug/Sep	New Zealand to Sri Lanka*
Oct/Dec	South Africa to Pakistan
Oct/Dec	West Indies to Pakistan
Nov/Jan	New Zealand to Australia*
	South Africa to Australia
	England to West Indies

1998	South Africa to England
1998-99	England to Australia
1999	New Zealand to England
	World Cup in England
1999-2000	India to Australia
2000	West Indies to England

* Unconfirmed

FIELDING CHART

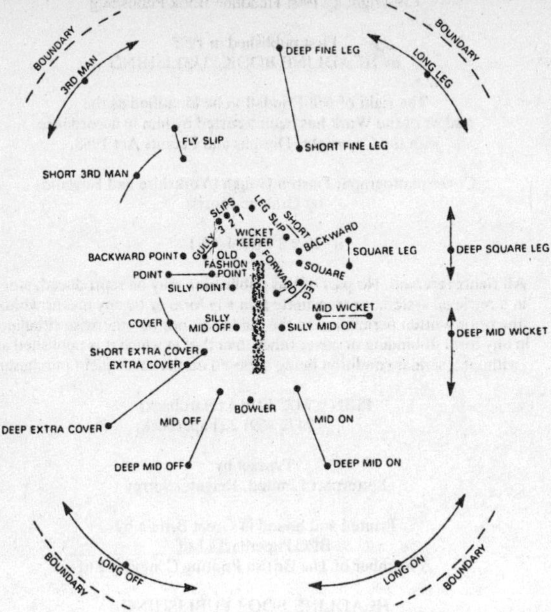

First published in 1995
by HEADLINE BOOK PUBLISHING

Cover photograph: Darren Gough (Yorkshire and England)
by Graham Morris

10 9 8 7 6 5 4 3 2 1

ISBN 0 7472 1210 4 (Hardback)
0 7472 4691 2 (Paperback)

Typeset by
Letterpart Limited, Reigate, Surrey

Printed and bound in Great Britain by
BPC Paperbacks Ltd
A member of The British Printing Company Ltd

HEADLINE BOOK PUBLISHING
A division of Hodder Headline PLC
338 Euston Road
London NW1 3BH